The Illusion Series

Side A, The B Side, and EP

D. Kelly

D. Kelly

The Acceptance Series –
Breaking Kate – Book One
Catching Kate – Book 1.5
Releasing Kate- Book Two
Loving Kate – Book Three
Christmas with the Houstons – Book Four

Stand Alone Novels
Chasing Cassidy
Sharing Rylee
The Evolution of Us
The Last Resort Motel – Room 13

The Illusion Series
Just an Illusion – Side A
Just an Illusion – The B Side
Just an Illusion – EP
Just an Illusion - Unplugged
Just an Illusion – Encore (coming October 24th 2018)
Interlude – Jordan's Book (coming January 29th 2019)
(Untitled) Darren's Book (coming April 2019)
(Untitled) Eli's Book (coming July 2019)
http://www.dkellyauthor.com/all-books

Table of Contents

Just an Illusion – Side A
D. Kelly

D. Kelly

Just an Illusion – Side A

dedication

For Mandy,
You are the only person in the world I could imagine dedicating this
book to.
I love you always.

D. Kelly

"Any man's life, told truly, is a novel..."
—Ernest Hemingway

Amelia

Present Day – Two Years After The Tour

Stories are meant to be told. I firmly believe that, or I wouldn't have pursued a career in writing. And yet, some stories should *never* be told for a variety of reasons. My story—*OUR* story—is on the cusp of both of those beliefs. When I first met them, it was quickly decided I would write their story. And their story is a *great* story, one I want to tell with *all* my heart and soul. One their fans truly deserve after all this time. The only problem is, in order to tell their story, I have to tell mine, too, since they've become so intricately entwined. I'm not sure I'm ready to share *my* story yet. My heart may not survive if I do.

As I release an exhausted sigh, I pause momentarily and deeply inhale the scent of the Pacific Ocean. The beautiful sunset's reflection shines on the waves, looking like a million shimmering suns. The silence in the house is all encompassing and allows me to take a few moments to appreciate life. It's funny how so many things can change over the course of a few years. How one person's life can go from private to public in the blink of an eye. How easily we transition beyond our humble beginnings, instead winding up in the lap of luxury. How fate *always* seems to find a way to intervene.

When I started this journey, I lived in a small, one-bedroom apartment in Encino, California. And now, I'm living most people's dream. My home—well, technically it's *their* home—is a beautiful beachfront house with every amenity I could have ever dreamed of. But at the end of the day, it's just a house, and a house isn't a home until you make it one. Even though it's been over two years since I officially moved in, making this house my home is still a feat I haven't quite yet mastered. If I accept this house, I have to accept the realities that come with it—realities I'm not ready to acknowledge. *Realities I should have long ago accepted.*

His ultimatum tonight threw me into a tailspin. He knows he's making me relive the best and worst days of my life. It's not his fault;

they're his, too, and he's waited long enough. He genuinely wants to make this a home for us, but he's worried my heart may not completely be his.

Is it?

I love him. I've always loved him, but being *in* love with someone is different than loving them. The only way to figure it out for sure is to write *THE* story—his, mine, theirs, and ours.

I turn away from the window, fire up my laptop, and uncork a bottle of my favorite Pinot Grigio, filling the largest wine glass I own. It's cool, and the alcohol warms me going down. If I'm going to do this, I need something to soothe me. Especially when I have to read his notes and pull all of Belle's articles. I need those most of all for this story to be truly complete.

It's just a story, Amelia, you write them all the time. It doesn't have to be published; you're just purging it from your system and getting it on paper. But if anyone ever got their hands on it ... If they find out you finally wrote it, there's no coming back.

Closing my eyes, I wage the internal battle with myself. He gave me a deadline; I have seventy-two hours to answer his proposal. Three days. I'm not quite sure if three days is long enough for my heart to catch up with my mind. It doesn't matter; he's serious this time.

The boys left and went camping, giving me time to do this, to gather myself. He was hesitant to leave me alone, knowing how hard it will be for me. Eventually, I convinced him I'd be fine. I'm not so sure now, but it doesn't matter. It's time to put on my big girl panties and give him an answer. Which leaves me only one thing left to do.

It's time to write our story.

Belle's First BAD Announcement

Three Years Ago

Slammers!

It's your girl Belle here, and I've got some freaking amazing news to share with you! This girl and her best friend Mel are heading out for a night with BAD. That's right, you heard me—Bastards and Dangerous are in town, and I've got a feeling I'm going to have a super scoop for you all tomorrow. Keep your fingers crossed these backstage passes will shed some light on the super-secret info BAD has been teasing us all with for weeks!

Don't forget, live today like there's no tomorrow!

Xs and Os,

Belle

The Day It All Began

"Amelia! Are you really wearing *that* to the BAD concert?"

Bastards and Dangerous, otherwise known as BAD, are all of the above from what I hear. I'm not a fan. I've got eclectic tastes in music, but they're just a little too loud for me. Since I'm not a fan, I don't feel the need to wear the overly obvious *I'm a groupie* BAD shirt Belle brought over for me. Instead, I'm wearing my best curve-hugging jeans, my favorite black Converse, and a dark blue V-neck sweater. The concert is at The Greek, an outdoor venue. Our nights have been hovering at fifty degrees all week, which is unusually cold for Southern California, especially for late August. Global warming at its finest, but I'm not going to freeze so I can fit in with the crowd.

"Yes, Belle, this is exactly what I'm wearing. Don't like it? I'll happily bow out and you can give my ticket to someone else," I answer with a smug smile.

"No, it's fine. You can come like that. I only hope they're not offended when they meet you and you're not supporting them," she says while crossing her arms and giving me her best pouty face.

"I don't know why you think we're even going to meet them. They're *the* biggest band out there right now. Besides, I highly doubt they'll care if one person out of the millions they've met isn't branded in something they make a commission off of."

She rolls her eyes at me. "I've already told you it's inevitable. Thanks to my kickass job as music editor at *Slammed Magazine*, we've got great press seats. *And* they sent VIP backstage passes so I can interview them."

I laugh, I can't help it. "Belle, I love you, but their manager said '*if* they have time' you can interview them. You know as well as I do bands don't stick around the venue any longer than necessary. By the time we get backstage, they'll be long gone."

"Nope." She pauses to slick on her lip gloss before finishing her thought. "That's how it *usually* works, but not tonight. Something big is coming down the pipeline, they're getting ready to announce something. *Everyone* is talking about it. *Slammed* is the biggest entertainment magazine on the market and they *want* us there. They've *never* had someone hand deliver backstage passes to us before. That's why I took them instead of giving them to some rookie reporter. And that's why I want *you* there, too. Since you're an author, you can help me craft an amazing story."

"One book, Belle. I've got one book out. Using the word author is reaching a bit." She has way too much faith in me.

"Amelia Greyson! Stop belittling yourself. You may only have one book out, but I know you have at least ten more on your computer you don't think are good enough to publish. Your *one* book has been number one on the New York Times bestseller list for the last three weeks! That's huge! It's author status at its finest. You need to be proud of your accomplishment, I know I am. I tell everyone I can about my best friend the author."

Belle is beaming, her smile is as wide as I've ever seen it, and I know she's right. It is huge for me; it's a dream come true. But it could also be a fluke, so I'm not planning on moving out of my cozy one-bedroom apartment anytime soon.

"Alright, we're wasting time being sentimental. Let's get out of here and go meet your BAD boys."

She giggles. "I'm hoping I can get one of them to be bad with me tonight!" We both burst into laughter and head down to the limo; at least *Slammed* sends their staff out to events in style.

Once we're settled in our seats at the venue, Belle is bouncing around like an excited teenager, but then again, so is almost everyone else here. Thankfully, we're in the press section, so it's not teeming with overly excited fans. The people in this section at least pretend to tone it down a bit ... that is, until the show starts.

The opening act was good, but for the life of me, I can't remember what they said their name was. I'll have to ask Belle later. She's having a blast, just like everyone else. I'm trying to act excited for her sake, but it's hard to feign excitement for a band you don't really like.

When the music begins to blare and the lights start flashing at seizure-inducing speeds, the band runs onto the stage one by one.

How in the world can they even see with all those strobe lights?

"How the fuck are you doing tonight, Los Angeles?"

The crowd's response is deafening. Another band member picks up a mic. "I don't think you heard Noah when he asked you how the fuck are you doing tonight, Los Angeles?"

The crowd screams even louder, and I'm wishing I would have brought some earplugs to help take down the decibels a bit. I forgot how loud rock concerts are. *Or maybe I just selectively blocked it from my memory.*

Another guy walks out from the side of the stage; he's cute in a tatted up rock star kind of way. "Alright, we're about to kick this bitch off, but before we do and you all are too drunk and hyped up to remember, Sawyer has some news we want to share with you."

One of the four takes his spot on the drums, the other guys are assembling themselves with guitars, and Sawyer—I'm assuming—takes the mic. He looks a lot like the cute one who came out first, just a little more sinful. I think Belle mentioned there were brothers in the band. I can't say for sure from here, but I think he even has dimples. Witnessing their sex appeal up close and personal reminds me of Belle's earlier wish, and I have to admit I agree with her. I wouldn't be opposed to being bad with them for a night. Even if their music isn't for me.

"Los Angeles, are you ready to rock?"

More deafening screams. I think a girl in the front row just passed out. Good God, it isn't all that, and neither are they. They're just men. Sexy as sin, granted, but still just men, and self-proclaimed bastards at that.

"First, I want to say thank you all for coming out to see us tonight. There aren't any other California shows on our tour schedule since we're winding up our current tour. However, we have some really big news to announce and needed to stop off to give *Slammed Magazine* an exclusive interview."

My eyes lock on Belle's; hers are as wide as saucers. She had no clue the extent of their generosity when they gave *Slammed* tickets and passes. They must have really wanted to keep this a secret if *Slammed* didn't even get a heads up, only an "if they have time" statement. It's why the passes were hand delivered. They're smart; they knew the hottest entertainment magazine on the planet wouldn't flake on them.

"So we figured two birds, one stone. We play for you in our awesome home state and then do the interview before heading back out on the road. Of course, it goes without saying we strongly encourage you to pick up *Slammed Magazine* in two weeks to read about our exciting news. Or at the very least, go to Slammedinc.com and check out the entertainment updates."

The crowd explodes into thunderous cheers and applause as the band kicks off the show. Belle has mellowed somewhat, and I know she's wondering how she's going to pull this off in just a few short days. I'll definitely have to help her now. *Slammed just* went to print with next week's issue, and it'll be out in a few days. She's got a small window of time to write and perfect this article before the following week's issue goes to print. It's kind of presumptuous of them to announce when the article will be out, but then again, any magazine worth their readers would do whatever they have to in order to scoop this story. Even if it means putting out a special edition, which is what is likely going to happen.

Whatever her worries are, Belle's over them in a flash, and she bounces back up to dance and scream the night away. Of course, I'm not a total downer, so I join her dance party and we celebrate her happiness. Even though I'm not a fan of the band, I'm a huge fan of Belle, and this article is going to launch her career even farther. I'm so proud of her.

The band leaves the stage for a quick break, and before they come back onstage for their encore, Belle and I make our way down to the backstage entrance. We're not the only ones with this idea, but we *are* the only ones with the passes granting us access to BAD. Thankfully, there are a few bodyguards posted who are able to guide us through the crowd of crazy bitches. I seriously thought one was going to fight me just to get my pass. Little does she know, I've been there and done that. I can take down a crazy bitch in a hot second if necessary. *I left that all behind me for a reason.* Hardcore fans are crazy; they're constantly throwing their underwear and yelling out crazed delusions of having rock star babies. Or even worse, trying to act out that fantasy by drugging them and tampering with condoms. These women, and even some men, have no shame. Don't they realize these men are just people? I don't know how celebrities do it.

People don't realize all you give up to live out your dreams—the demons you take on, the heavy toll it takes on your life. How can anyone get used to that? How could you ever trust anyone enough to forge a new friendship or fall in love? I'd always question if they truly wanted me or what I have to give them.

We're ushered down a long corridor, our footsteps echoing behind us. Up ahead of us, the band is huddled together getting ready to go back onstage for their encore. From the looks of it, besides the normal crew and staff, we are literally the only people back here with passes.

Interesting ...

We're greeted by a large man with a security all-access badge about halfway between the entrance and where the band is standing. I wouldn't ever want to wind up on this guy's bad side. He's intimidating. "We have to go past the band to get to the green room

15

where they'll meet with you later. Please, don't make me get rough with you two. If you have fangirl shit to get out of your system, do it in the green room. Don't say anything to them as we pass, and don't freak out or try to grope them. You're here in a professional capacity, and I hope you'll continue to act that way."

Belle and I exchange knowing glances, and I know she's thinking exactly what I am. This guy is a dick. But he's doing his job, and I'm sure it's a difficult one. Belle is a fan, but she's a professional first. As for me, I don't fangirl over *anyone*, let alone a band I don't even like.

As we pass the band, their PA is giving them a two-minute countdown. One of the guys looks up at us as we walk by with an interested look on his face. He's cute, and from the smirk on his face, he knows it. I still feel his eyes on me as we walk by; however, when I cock my head to the side, I find it's the one with the dimples who is staring at my ass. These jeans were *so* worth the price I paid for them.

Mr. Gruff and Serious deposits us in the green room and lets us know we can help ourselves to anything. Then he informs us he'll be right outside the door as he closes it behind him.

"Amelia! Pinch me! Can you believe this? BAD gave one, and *only* one, exclusive interview, and it's mine! Oh my God! This is going to skyrocket my career as long as I don't screw it up." Her excitement makes me laugh. She has nothing to worry about; her work is amazing.

"Belle, you've got this. Get your squealing out now, take some deep breaths, and get ready for the story of your life. I'm so proud of you, and I'm right here to help take notes, too."

"Thanks, Mel, I knew I could count on you." After giving me a quick hug, she does indeed get her squealing out of her system while watching the band on the very large TV mounted on the wall.

I can't stop thinking about Dimples watching me as we passed by. The thought brings heat between my legs, even if I shouldn't let it. He's not relationship material, and I'm not supermodel gorgeous. Besides, all these men have a reputation for one-night stands and unemotional flings. Those are two things I can't do, *not anymore*. When I'm sleeping with someone, it's because I'm invested in them emotionally. Which is probably why I haven't had sex with a man in over a year.

Don't believe everything you hear, Amelia. You know better than most how things are blown out of proportion in this industry.

After the encore, the sounds of the thunderous applause echo all the way into the green room. Even the walls are shaking from it.

Belle's nerves are starting to kick in because she's simultaneously tapping her foot and picking at her nails, both of which are nervous habits of hers. "Belle, you need to breathe. They're just people. You've interviewed tons of musicians before and I've never seen you this nervous."

"I know, Mel, but this is *BAD*, and they're the holy grail of interviews. I can't help but be nervous, and of course their excessive good looks only make it worse." I can't argue with her there, they are good-looking men.

The voices resonating from the hallway are growing closer by the second until they're suddenly upon us and the door is thrown open.

"That was fucking awesome! One of the best shows we've done this entire tour. The outdoor venues are so much better. Don't you guys think so?" As they talk amongst themselves, I'm drawn in by their enthusiasm.

Seeing these men come in on their post-performance high is captivating. Their happiness is almost contagious. Belle and I are taking them in, watching in fascination. It's been a long time since I was a part of this kind of excitement. I almost forgot how much goes into pulling off a successful show. They've got a posse of people with them. The PA I saw earlier is trying to wrangle them up while I assume their stylist is the one carrying a few extra shirts.

The cute one with the dimples takes one of those shirts. When he pulls his sweaty shirt off over his head, I'm absolutely mesmerized by the way his muscles move. His abs are screaming for me to come and lick them, the beads of sweat crying out my name. I want to taste his essence on my tongue. Sadly, as fast as the mini porn played out in my head, it's over as his shirt goes on. He catches me looking at him and flashes me a sexy smirk again. The flush I feel spreading over my face is nothing, I'm sure, compared to how it looks.

Hoping to suppress the flush, I open my water bottle and try to cool myself down from the sudden heat enveloping my body. He's eying my lips as they wrap around the rim of the bottle, and I wish I were wrapping them around him instead. I drink as slowly and seductively as possible, knowing he's watching me. When I raise my eyes back up to his, he licks his lips. *Holy hell.*

This is foreplay, yet, at the same time, couldn't be anything further from it. The spell is broken when one of the crew calls for him. It's just as well, musicians aren't my thing... *anymore.*

After about twenty minutes, they dismiss the posse surrounding them and finally sit down across from us. Their manager is an older man with a gentle smile who begins the introductions.

"I'm Warren, BAD's manager, and these are the bastards themselves."

Belle and I laugh at his joke, which also serves as an ice breaker.

"Warren, it's nice to meet you. Thank you for extending this opportunity to *Slammed*. We're honored for the exclusive. I'm Belle Dixson and this is my good friend Amelia Greyson, but we all call her Mel."

The cute one snorts out loud, and it's kind of a dick move.

"Amelia and Belle. Look, guys, we've got our own Disney fucking Princesses for the night."

"Shut up, Sawyer," their frustrated voices reply in unison.

"Dick." The single, snarky word escapes my mouth before I have a chance to stop it, and Belle is horrified. *Rightly so.* Sawyer actually shuts up, and a hush falls across the room. Sometimes, the old me creeps out when I least expect her to. *Shit, this is so bad.*

"That was fucking AWESOME! I've never seen anyone but family call Sawyer out on his shit and I've known him all my life. I'm Noah Weston, and I'm very pleased to meet you, Amelia."

Belle exhales and flashes me a smile. "Nice to meet you, too, Noah," I answer, relieved they can overlook my foot-in-mouth moment.

"I'm with Noah, that was epic. I'm Darren, and the guy at the end of the couch with his head in the book is Wyatt."

Wyatt peeks up from the book in his lap and smiles.

"Sorry, I'm behind. I promised my wife I would read this book and I haven't had much time. I wanted to at least try and squeeze in a chapter before we Skype later."

"You're such a pussy, Wyatt. What man worth his balls would actually read *The O Factor*?" Sawyer laughs at Wyatt, and my stomach plummets fast as Belle tries to hold in her laughter. That's my book, and this is about to get really uncomfortable.

"One who loves his wife. Why don't you just go find a chick to hook up with already so you'll stop being such an ass?"

"What do you think of the book so far, Wyatt?" Belle asks, ignoring their exchange. I could kill her!

"On or off the record?"

"Off," Belle replies casually.

"It's interesting. I mean, I've never read a girl's point of view on sex before, it's crazy. It's definitely keeping me reading for sure."

"Well, it *has* been number one on the New York Times bestseller list for three weeks, so it's got to be good."

Couch just swallow me up now, please.

I close my eyes and take a breath, hoping to ease my nerves.

"What's wrong, Princess Amelia? Are you too prude to talk about a sex book?" Sawyer taunts.

Belle laughs so loud and so long, tears are beginning to pool in her eyes.

"Why do I get the feeling I'm missing something here?" Noah asks, intrigued by what they're obviously missing.

Belle finally loses her composure and wipes the corner of her eye as she shamelessly outs me. She's officially off my Christmas list. "Who wrote that book, Wyatt?" Belle asks sweetly.

Wyatt flips the book over, and a huge smile breaks out across his face. I don't have a photo on the book, but how many Amelia Greysons are out there walking around? My guess is not many.

"I think Sawyer is about to eat his words. This night keeps getting better and better." Wyatt grabs a pen off the table and brings his book to me. He's going for dramatic. Lovely.

"Ms. Amelia Greyson, will you please autograph my book for my wife? And before you say no, just keep in mind she's a huge fan, and if I tell her I met you and didn't get your autograph, I won't be getting any Os, either. Her name is Annabeth but we just call her Anna."

I can't even bring myself to look at the rest of these guys. Belle's giggling again, and I make a mental note to kill her when we leave here. But Wyatt asked so nicely, how could I not sign his book? I reach out, taking the pen and book from him, and autograph it quickly. Looking up when I hand it back to him, all eyes are on me.

"Never judge a book by its cover, Sawyer," Noah says to him smugly, but his eyes and smile are focused solely on me.

Noah's beautiful. I know it's odd to describe a man that way, but he is, and so is Sawyer, which only makes sense because they're practically identical. Their eyes are as green as a forest after the rain. They've got strong, chiseled jaws, and both are easily over six feet tall and equally fit. Sawyer has dimples where Noah is lacking them, but Noah has personality where Sawyer is just an ass. Noah's coppery-brown hair is perfectly styled, as is Sawyer's, but his is black as sin. Sawyer has his lip pierced; Noah, his eyebrow. Both have tattoos. I wouldn't kick either out of my bed.

"Thanks, Amelia! My wife is going to love this!"

His happiness is infectious, making it easy to return his smile. "Of course, I'm glad she enjoyed the book."

Belle takes his presumed slip as a chance to dive into her interview. "I didn't realize any of you were married."

They exchange knowing glances, and Wyatt nods his agreement to the group of men. "Wyatt and Anna have been together since we were in high school. Rumors always have us portrayed as big playboys, but that's not necessarily the truth. Anyway, I don't know how it flew under the radar, but they were married six months ago in a private ceremony and *no one* has picked up on it yet. It's beyond bizarre. We're thinking someone misplaced the paperwork or misfiled it at the courthouse for it not to be out by now," Noah answers Belle, but his eyes never leave mine.

"So this is off the record, too?" Belle asks them.

"No, you guys can announce it. Wyatt even has a few pictures he'll email you to print." Wyatt nods his head in agreement with Warren's statement, but he's once again engrossed in my book.

"If I can just be blunt here, I have the feeling this isn't going to be a typical off-the-cuff interview. Why don't you guys tell me why we're here and then I can build from there." That's Belle, she loves to get to the point as quickly as possible.

"We're done with this leg of the tour in a week. In three weeks, we're releasing an acoustic album. It's something we've been working on for a few years now. This is vastly different than anything we've ever done, but it's good. Might even be the best album we've ever done." All the guys nod and murmur their agreement with Sawyer.

"Now that might be something I would be interested in listening to." *Damn, I said that out loud. Where the hell is my brain tonight?*

"What's that, Princess? Why *wouldn't* you be interested? You're here now, aren't you?" I don't know why Sawyer throws me off my game so much, but I'm blushing from head to toe, I'm sure of it. They're all looking at me, eagerly awaiting my answer. Belle only laughs; she's getting way too much enjoyment out of my discomfort tonight.

"Well, if you want the truth ..."

Noah nods, and I can tell his curiosity is at an all-time high.

"I'm not a fan. Tonight was the first time I've ever listened to more than one of your songs in the same sitting."

Sawyer's offended. "You're fucking lying. The way you were checking me out earlier said differently."

"Look, asshat, I'm not a fan. Your music is too much for me. I've got eclectic tastes, but I grew up in the Hollywood club scene listening to loud rock bands my entire childhood. This kind of music just doesn't appeal to me. Was I checking you guys out earlier? Sure, because you're attractive men, and I'd have to be dead not to notice. It wasn't because I was fangirling all over you, you can trust me when I say that. I'm only here because Belle asked me to come. If you'd prefer for me to wait outside, I'll be happy to."

Sawyer starts to speak, but Noah cuts him off. "No, Amelia, don't go. It's a rarity we meet anyone who doesn't know us and doesn't enjoy our music. Actually, I don't think anyone has ever admitted to not being a fan. Not ever. It's kinda cool."

"Can I continue?" Sawyer asks. He's frustrated, and it makes me want to fuck all his frustrations right out of him.

"Go for it," Noah replies.

"As I was saying, we've got the new album dropping. In four weeks, we're starting a new tour. Worldwide. We have the schedule, but these venues are going to be smaller and more intimate. There are going to be less tickets available but more shows. The U.S. tour is going to last a year. We'll have a few breaks, a couple of weeks off at the holidays, but that's it. It's going to be a hard schedule, but we've all agreed to it."

Belle is taking copious notes, her eyes sparkling brightly as she writes furiously.

"The reason for our exclusive announcement is because at the end of this year-long tour ... we're retiring."

Belle gasps, her eyes glancing from member to member, and all of them are nodding their heads in affirmation.

"Why?"

Darren speaks up to answer her, "We've been best friends since junior high school. We're always going to be best friends. Our success has been beyond our wildest expectations, but it's been ten years, twelve if you count the two years before we were signed, fourteen if you factor in when we actually first started. Nine of them were spent touring and in and out of the studio after our first album dropped and took off. It's time. We want to enjoy life. Wyatt wants to settle down and have some kids. Anna has been so gracious putting his needs first, but they're married now, and she should be his top priority. That's hard to do when you're constantly on the road."

Belle nods. "Any chance she'll go on tour with you?"

"No. I don't want that life for her. She comes sometimes, but she has her own career she's trying to build. I don't want to come in the way of her dreams. She's never tried to get me to give up mine," Wyatt answers softly.

"It's not to say in five or ten years we won't miss the hell out of this or have more music to put out. We're just not touring anymore, but the band is *not* breaking up," Noah clarifies.

"This is huge, you guys. *Slammed* readers are going to freak out. The whole world is going to freak out. Why did you decide you want us to run this story?"

"When these guys told me they wanted to quit touring, we got together and tried to come up with a game plan. You're right, this is huge, and we wanted to do it with dignity and grace. *Slammed* is the only magazine out there that has never printed any rumors about BAD. We had a whole team on it for months, and everyone else out there, at one time or another, has printed something untrue. *Slammed* has integrity, and we admire that." Warren smiles warmly at us.

"So much so, we want to work with *Slammed* exclusively over the next year. We want *Slammed* to run a monthly post with the upcoming venues and ticket sales information. I know it's old school, but I think the Internet has taken all the fun away from concerts as far as ticket sales are concerned. I remember, as a kid, waiting in line with my dad at the local music store, hoping to get there early enough to be one of the lucky ones to get tickets. The people you meet in line, the camaraderie, it should all be part of the experience. We've got a deal with Top Hitz Music and they're going to join with Ticketmaker to sell tickets for us. If people want them, they're going to have to wait in line for them." *Wow, that's actually really cool.* Sawyer almost sounds like a nice guy when he's all business.

"We'll give *Slammed* access to any shows they want, and you'll be in constant contact with Warren to set it up. You'll be able to give an insider's view into all things BAD." Noah smiles at Belle, who looks like she's about to pass out. This is major for her career.

"Ladies, if you could step outside for just a minute, I need to run something by the guys. Mac!" Warren bellows loudly.

The door opens, and their grumpy bodyguard pops his head in. "Yeah, boss?"

"Mac, can you keep an eye on these beautiful ladies for just a few minutes out in the hall? I'll come get them when we're ready for them to come back."

"You got it, boss. Ladies, please come with me."

Mac glares at us as we follow him outside.

"So what did you two do? Did you hit on Wyatt?"

22

Belle looks up at him, craning her neck because she's all of five feet tall and Mac is at least six foot four.

"We didn't do anything to them. Maybe you should start giving people the benefit of the doubt and show your naturally sunny disposition every once in a while."

Mac laughs, and it makes me smile. He doesn't seem like a bad guy anymore, just protective, and he should be.

"Maybe you're right, little lady. I'm Mac, head of BAD security, and you are?"

"I'm Belle, and this is Amelia," she replies with a warm smile. Mac takes her tiny hand into his big one and gives her a firm handshake.

"It's nice to meet you both."

Mac is quiet, and so are Belle and I. There's a lot of noise coming from inside the green room. And by noise, I mean raised voices and yelling. Nothing we can make out, but it's enough to make us both uneasy. After about fifteen minutes, Warren comes out to get us. He's smiling so big you'd never know there were raised voices in here. In fact, they all look happy, except for Sawyer, but I'm beginning to think the brooding looks he shares are all part of his charm.

"How would you girls like to come and have a late dinner with us? We have lots more we'd like to discuss with you, both of you, actually, but we're starving and Sawyer can't function like a normal human being without food." Noah's invitation is warm and welcoming. It's not like we actually have much choice in the matter because Belle is nowhere near done gathering information for her article.

"Sure, that would be great. Where do you want to go? I'll let the driver know and we'll meet you there," Belle tells Noah.

"We're going to our house in Malibu. The food is already there waiting for us. Our housekeeper loves to feed us when we're in town. She's a great cook. Trust me, you'll love whatever she makes. Darren and Wyatt can ride with you guys, if you don't mind. Sawyer, Warren, and I have a few things to discuss on the way there."

Belle is over-the-moon excited; she's covering it well, but I know that expression. Between the BAD interview and Darren eye fucking her all night, it's a dream come true for her.

Once we're all in the car and on the road, Wyatt asks me for a favor. Wyatt is cute, no doubt. But he's one of those guys whose cuteness factor is boosted because of his adorable smile. It makes you instantly want to say yes to whatever he asks for. I would never want to be the one responsible for taking that smile off his face.

"Amelia, would you do me a huge favor?"

A favor for a rock star—even though he seems mild enough, I'm still cautious. "Depends on the favor, Wyatt," I reply, smiling right back at him.

He laughs. "Smart girl. I knew I liked you. I have to Skype Anna, and I brought the book to show her you signed it, but would you mind saying hi, too? It would make her night. I'd consider it a personal favor, and I *always* return favors."

Hmm, a rock star in my back pocket, now that can be useful for sure. But that's not why I agree to do it. It's romantic, and as a romance writer, this is something books are made of. I'm happy to help him woo his wife and think it's great he still tries after all these years.

"Of course I will, it'll be fun."

Wyatt pulls out his phone to start the call. I scoot over a bit to give him what little privacy I can so he can catch up with his wife. Eventually, he gets around to the *Slammed* interview and tells her about Belle and myself. It's then I hear her squeal.

"Wait, Wyatt, back up ... Did you say Amelia Greyson was with the *Slammed* interviewer? *The O Factor* Amelia Greyson?"

Wyatt laughs. "That's exactly what I said, babe, and she autographed my book for you, too."

"Shut up! Wyatt, oh my God! That is so freaking awesome. Why am I not with you tonight? I could kick myself."

"Well, I thought you might feel that way, so ..." He motions for me to scoot closer now, which I happily do.

"Babe, meet Amelia. Amelia, this is my beautiful wife Anna."

"Hi, Anna! It's so nice to meet you. Wyatt said you enjoyed my book. I'm flattered. Thank you for reading it."

"Me? *You're* thanking *me*? Good God, girl, you're *amazing*! That book is amazing! The things I realized we were missing out on or could be ... umm ... enhancing ... Well, let's just say I've been enlightened."

We chatted a few more minutes before saying our goodbyes. As Wyatt ended the call, her parting words were, "You're so getting laid the second you walk in the door."

I only got to observe them for a few moments, but that's all I needed to see how in love they are. I've also been discretely watching Belle and Darren. There's some serious sexual chemistry brewing between the two of them. They've had their heads together, whispering back and forth, since we left the venue. This is going to be an interesting night.

To Tour Or Not To Tour

Their house is beautiful. It's up on a bluff in Malibu, overlooking the ocean. When I exit the car, I inhale deeply, letting the salty Pacific Ocean air fill my senses. I should really take more time to come out this way. It's not too far from my apartment in Encino, and if I could find a place to write, I'm sure I would be inspired.

Once we're inside, I'm slightly disappointed; it's fairly lacking in here. Don't get me wrong, it's *gorgeous*, but almost ... I don't know ... Perhaps, medicinal feeling? The walls are all white; the furniture, again, all white. At least the kitchen is filled with all stainless steel appliances and dark granite, which gives it some contrast. Darren and Wyatt give us a tour, and I'm relieved to find the rest of the house has more personality than the entrance and living area. It looks like everyone has decorated their own bedrooms, but no one has done anything with the common area. It's a shame; it could be beautiful.

"Do you all live here?" I ask Wyatt.

"Sometimes. This is our inspiration house. We come here when we're writing or recording. We have a full studio downstairs instead of a garage. It's been used a lot lately. Our album is supposed to drop in a few weeks, but Sawyer is still working on the title track. So we're all here for the weekend between venues, trying to inspire him and finish it up. Officially, it's Sawyer and Noah's house. We each have a room because we're here a lot and it's not like there's a lack of space. Anna and I actually live in San Diego, and Darren lives in a house up on Mulholland Drive."

"Why do you live so far away from the rest of the band?"

"It's only temporary. Anna's job sent her there for a two-year project. She's helping launch a sub-division of SOS Publishing and has already been in San Diego for a year. If it goes well, she'll be finished and back in the Los Angeles office late next year."

The O Factor is self-published, and SOS was the first publishing house I sent it to for consideration. I sent it to them a year before I published it myself. It's been about sixteen months, and I'm glad I didn't wait for a response; the book is doing very well on its own.

"That's a fantastic opportunity for her. You must be so proud."

Wyatt flashes me that adorable smile of his. "I am, but I worry about her being down there alone, not knowing many people. Anna's a strong, determined woman. Ultimately, I know she can take care of herself, but I'm grateful Sam, he's Warren's husband, is there with her. They keep each other out of trouble." He winks at me and leads the way back into the living area since Belle and Darren seem to have taken a temporary pit stop in his room. I see a date with a rock star in her future.

Warren, Sawyer, and Noah enter through the garage, talking excitedly. I notice even Sawyer is wearing a smile, but I have a feeling it's a rarity for him. I'm not sure what it is about him, but I can tell Sawyer is guarded. I can spot a fellow wall builder a mile away, and his are up so high I'm not sure a bulldozer could even knock them down. It took me five years of therapy to try to bring mine down, but I still have my moments.

"Excuse me, Amelia, I'm going to go get Belle and Darren before they get a lecture from Warren. He's got his business hat on tonight, and I don't want him getting pissed off at Darren." With a slight nod, I take the opportunity to admire the view from their floor-to-ceiling windows. The moon is full tonight, and its reflection illuminates the ocean below. It's breathtaking.

"Princess Amelia," Sawyer greets me as he creeps in on my personal space.

"Asshat," I toss back, countering his annoying greeting with one of my own.

The laughter rolling out of Sawyer is surprising, but not as surprising as the heated look he's giving me when I finally turn to acknowledge him. We're the only two in here, and the sexual tension is so thick you could cut it with a knife.

"You know, Princess, not too many people speak their minds to me. I haven't decided if it makes me want to take you over my knee and spank you for your disobedience, or if it makes me want to fuck you until you submit to me. *Or both.*"

My breath escapes me, but my lady bits know who's boss here and they're hot, wet, and wishing for all of the above. I'd give anything to pull his lip ring into my mouth right now, tug it lightly with my teeth, and tease it with my tongue. I'm so turned on and he hasn't even touched me.

"Sounds like you've been reading my book, and yet I know you haven't, or you *definitely* wouldn't be calling me Princess."

A sinfully sexy smile spreads across his face, and I know I'll never see a smile again that makes me feel the way his does. I want him as much as I want my next breath, but I know getting involved with Sawyer is not only next to impossible, it's extremely dangerous for my health. Bastards and Dangerous suddenly takes on a whole new meaning.

Thankfully, we're interrupted by everyone else on their way to the dining room. Sawyer winks as he passes by me, letting his fingers graze mine as he goes. His touch is searing, and a warning goes off in my head. Messing with Sawyer is like playing with fire—in the end, you'll *always* get burned.

"Amelia, come and sit by me." Noah flashes me a smile, which is similar to Sawyer's, except his is friendly and sweet. There's no sin pouring from his lips. I'm relieved I'll be sandwiched between him and Belle and nowhere near Sawyer's heat.

Someone has already plated the food. It looks and smells amazing. Lasagna, salad, and garlic bread—it's even still hot. As I blow gently on my fork, Sawyer stares at me with a hooded gaze. I savor the flavors. The food is incredible; their housekeeper cooks as well as my grandmother used to. Sawyer licks his lips—never breaking eye contact with me, nor I with him—and he finally takes a bite. Thankfully, the conversation begins and I have a legitimate reason to turn away from him.

"So, Belle, I know we haven't talked many details yet, but from what you've heard so far, will *Slammed* be up for what we're offering?" Warren asks.

"Absolutely, and I'm going to do this assignment personally. I'll add a few reporters to work under me if needed, but I don't want anyone messing this up. I'm honored you researched our reputation and picked us. It will be my sincere pleasure to cover this story and follow the tour for the magazine."

Warren nods his head, obviously pleased. "That's wonderful news. I was hoping it would be you. I've read some of your work, and it's very good. We'll be in touch on Monday to work out all of the official details. I'll also email you the photos from the wedding and the general information we want in next week's issue. We'll get you some exclusive interviews later down the line."

Belle is blushing but readily agrees. She's smiling so big you'd think she won the lottery. She may as well have; working one-on-one with BAD for a year is a music journalist's equivalent to winning a Grammy.

"Now, Amelia," Warren says, turning his attention to me. "The band and I would like to extend an offer to you as well. It's a bit unconventional, but we're hoping you'll be receptive to it."

I'm intrigued and nod for him to continue. Glancing around the table, all the guys seem excited.

"Your being here tonight was extremely favorable for us. We've been looking for an author who might be interested in touring with us this last year."

Holy ...

"It's been a difficult search because most of the authors we've considered have been fans of the band. Normally, it isn't a bad thing for the interviewer to be a fan when they're creating an article. *But* to actually share living quarters and tour with the band in hotels, on planes, and on the buses, it can present a problem. We don't want the person glorifying the book from a fan's point of view."

The guys are all nodding, and Belle looks as if she's about to fall off her chair. That makes two of us because I'm about to pass out.

Stay calm, Amelia.

You don't have to say yes.

"You are the first person we've met who is not only *not* a fan, but you have no issue putting Sawyer in his place. I'll be frank, that was a big concern of ours. Sawyer can be a little rough around the edges."

"No, I'm a *lot* fucking rough around the edges," Sawyer confirms with a smirk.

"Case and point." Warren counters, nailing him with a steely glare before turning back to me. "I know you're just launching your own career and trying to get your book published. I also happen to know SOS publishing has been preparing a proposal for you, in hopes you'll sign with them."

What the ... How does he even know that?

"I'm sorry, I don't understand. I haven't heard anything from SOS." My heart is running sprints in my chest. Could this *actually* be for real?

Warren smiles warmly at me. "Amelia, my husband is Sam Owen Stevensen. He *is* SOS publishing, and when he personally read your book last month, he put the wheels in motion."

Anna is in San Diego with Warren's husband Sam. Wyatt's words come flying back to me.

29

"What exactly are you looking for this book to portray?" I'm barely able to choke out the words.

"Well, we'd like the author to put their own unique spin on it, but we also want it to be an insider's view of all things BAD. The good, the bad, *and* the ugly. We want the fans to understand how exhilarating it is to be on tour but also how time consuming. We'd like to show how sweet *and* how aggressive the fans can be and how overwhelming it all is at times. Most of all, we want them to get to know *us*. You'll be allowed candid shots, a basic point and shoot camera, nothing fancy. You'll have an all-access pass into everything they do. By extension, you'll be the fifth member of the band. Where they go, you go."

"Sixth member, Warren, you always leave yourself out," Noah corrects firmly.

This could be the biggest career opportunity I ever get, but one major fact remains. "I'm not an autobiographer, I write fiction. I'm not sure if I'm the right choice for you."

"Amelia, you self-published the number one book on the New York Times bestsellers list. Do you know how rare that is? I've got a feeling you can do anything you set your mind to. SOS has agreed to use this tour as an opportunity to promote you as their newest author, if you're up for it. Instead of sending you on a standard book tour, they're going to set you up with signing opportunities in select cities."

"Wait … They want me to do a book tour?" This is beyond my wildest expectations.

"Of course they do, and we'll work the schedule around rehearsals or down time for the guys so you're not missing too much of what we want documented in the book. The contract details between you and SOS are between you and them for your books. They've already signed on to publish the BAD story, so I would assume that would be an extension of said contract."

Two publishing deals, one for me the romance author and one for me the BAD autobiographer.

"You'll be independently contracted to BAD for this tour, and we'll be covering all of your travel and food expenses. You'll share royalties on the book and earn two hundred and fifty thousand dollars for giving up your life for a year. There will be no days off unless it's an emergency, but since you're mostly an observer, you'll have tons of time to yourself. You'll be on their schedule. When they have downtime for holidays and vacations, that'll be your prime opportunity to really see into their lives."

My head is spinning. I'm terrified to take this offer, but I'm also ecstatic they chose to extend it to me. Who in their right mind would turn this down? Could I give up my life for a year for this? I'm not sure I'm strong enough yet to jump back in with the demons.

Maybe, just maybe, they don't have those demons.

Belle is beaming with pride. I know she's happy for both of us, and if I turn this down she may never speak to me again. "I don't know what to say. How long do I have to give you an answer?" I ask, clutching my napkin for dear life under the table. Belle's jaw drops, along with Darren's and Wyatt's. Sawyer looks perplexed. Noah reaches out and grabs my free hand.

"Warren, Sawyer, and I were working out the details in the car on the way over here. Unfortunately, Amelia, you don't have long to decide. We leave day after tomorrow. We need someone who can start in four weeks, and by the time we get the paperwork going and finalized, that's about how long it's going to take. We have two other authors to choose from, but you were our *only* unanimous choice." Noah brushes his thumb across mine, and it's comforting. More comforting than it should be. These brothers sure do exude sexual pheromones. Could I be in close quarters with them for that long and have a platonic relationship with them?

I'd have to.

I swallow over the lump in my throat as the butterflies take flight in my stomach. Could I do this? I would be living the dream again, but that dream was my nightmare—the cause of my sadness and the road to my eventual heartbreak. But BAD *is* living the dream. They aren't flailing after falling from grace into the abyss of rock stars past. It might be a way for me to let those demons go. *Exorcise the bad by doing something good.*

"I need to think about it for a while. Do you have beach access here?"

"Sure, I'll show you to the backyard. There's a staircase leading down to the beach from there. Let me just grab a flashlight."

Everyone is quiet while Warren is gone. I'm sure they're shocked I'm not jumping on this. Only Belle knows why, but she won't tell. What's in the vault stays vaulted.

Warren returns with a flashlight and a smile. "Come on, I'll show you the way."

We're both quiet as he lights the path in front of us.

"Amelia, I don't want to pressure you, and I'm sorry you don't have much time to make this decision, but I think this can be a really

31

good thing for us all." He sighs and runs his hands through his hair, obviously needing to say more.

"Sawyer and Noah started this band when they were just kids. Sawyer's had some bad experiences with women, and he's closed himself off. Tonight, for the first time in years, he showed genuine emotion toward a woman. I think you can help him, Amelia. I'm not sure how but I just have a hunch. Please give it some serious thought. You're a writer, and the best thing about being a writer is you can do it from anywhere. Hell, I'll even throw in movers and a packing crew if it helps."

After he pleads his case, he passes me the flashlight, pats me on the shoulder, and goes back inside. Taking my time descending the stairs, I finally come to a plateau at the bottom and take a walking trail down to the sand. Guess they want to make sure people don't realize they have access to the house. But then again, this is probably a private beach.

It's a beautiful night out, but it's cold. I'm glad I wore a sweater, but even that isn't helping much against the chill. Just when I decide to go back inside, Belle plops down into the sand next to me and wraps a blanket around us.

"This place is amazing, isn't it?"

"Yeah, it really is," I reply.

"Talk to me, Mel. Tell me what you're thinking."

"I'm wondering if five years of therapy battling my demons has made me strong enough to do this and come out unscathed. I'm thinking I would be a fool to take this job, and I'd be a bigger fool not to."

"Oh, sweetie, don't let this be about him and the past. Let this be about you and what an amazing opportunity this would be. You've always wanted to start traveling again, and this is your chance. People would *kill* for this job, and while I understand it would mean immersing yourself into a musical world you've fought hard to get away from, it's going to be a whole different side than you've ever seen before. One that doesn't include demons and self-destruction."

Tears begin to fall from my eyes. She's being truthful; this is everything I've ever wanted, just with a different kind of writing.

"Besides, it's not like you're going to be missing much. You hate your job and you've wanted to quit for a long time. The money is phenomenal, and all your expenses will be paid. Aside from me, you have nothing holding you here, and I'll be there with you often. I'm already figuring a once a month spotlight will be awesome for the magazine."

She's making valid points, and thinking about it is almost liberating. I can get out of my crappy apartment and be able to promote my book with the full backing of a publisher. It's a dream come true.

"You're right, Belle. It's everything I've always wanted. Well, except being packed in a tour bus with BAD. *That* was never my fantasy."

"Oh, Mel, but it's such a good fantasy to have." She falls into laughter, and so do I.

"You can do this, Mel, you just have to choose to. But if you're in, you know you have to see it through to the end. I know you've never quit a job easily, even the bad ones, which is why you still work for bitch face. But if it gets to you out on the road, you have to stay. You *have* to fight your demons. I'll help you get through it."

She's right about everything. I can do this; I know I can. You're not living until you push yourself out of your comfort zone, right? Well, this is *definitely* beyond the scope of mine.

"Excuse us, ladies, but we were wondering if we could cut in on your alone time?"

Noah and Darren have come down to keep us company. Darren has a blanket and is holding out his hand to Belle. I think I know exactly what he has in mind for their night.

"Do you mind if I steal your friend for a walk down the beach, Mel?" Darren asks sweetly.

I shake my head. "No, not at all." So far, other than Sawyer, they all seem to be really nice guys. I haven't seen much yet to make me think they deserve the reputation they have.

Noah sits next to me, and I throw the blanket over his shoulder. Neither of us says anything for a long time as we look out at the ocean. He smells good, and the feeling of his body heat wrapped under this blanket with mine is nice, comforting.

"Do you prefer Amelia or Mel?" he asks, eventually breaking the silence.

"I don't really care. Either is fine, just don't start calling me Princess or we're going to have a problem."

He roars in laughter. "I wouldn't dream of it. Sorry Sawyer can be a bit of a dick at times, but he's got a good heart."

"Who's older, you or Sawyer?"

"I'm older by six minutes. We're fraternal twins."

"I always wished I was a twin when I was younger. That must have been fun growing up."

"It had its moments. It was much better when our mom stopped dressing us alike." He smiles in fondness.

"Aw, I bet those are the cutest pictures." I can imagine him and Sawyer, young and adorable.

"I'll show you sometime if you come with us."

With a raised eyebrow, I turn to look at him. "So you're resorting to blackmail?"

He pushes his shoulder against mine in a playful gesture. "Not blackmail, just another incentive for you to come with us."

"Noah, why do you guys want me?"

"Mel, you're different, especially compared to the other two candidates. And frankly, you're a better fit for us. Aside from being smart and motivated, you're not a fan. It might be disappointing to my ego but really is a breath of fresh air to my soul. Best of all, you have no problem putting Sawyer in his place, which is awesome and exactly what he needs. Lastly, although this has absolutely no bearing on why you were offered the job ... you're beautiful."

He says "you're beautiful" in a whisper, and goose bumps spread over my body. I need to be careful here; I haven't been in a relationship in over a year. Noah or Sawyer could have me falling for them easily, but this needs to stay professional.

"*If* I do this, we need to be friends. I need to get to know you guys. You'll all have to let me into your world. Do you think you'll be able to do that?"

An excited gleam sparks in his eyes. "Absolutely. I'll have to work on Sawyer. We'll *all* have to work on Sawyer. This is something he wants, too. I can't promise he'll be easy, but he'll eventually let you in. He's got trust issues, so you're going to have to earn his trust, but I'll help however I can."

Great. Between my demons and Sawyer's trust issues, we're going to make a great pair.

"Alright," I reply with a resigned sigh.

He jumps up, pulling me with him. "Alright you're in?"

I nod my head. "I'm in."

He picks me up and spins me around. "Thank you, Mel. This is going to be the greatest tour yet. You know fate brought you to us tonight, don't you?" he asks excitedly.

"You believe in fate?" I ask as he slides me down his body, still holding me close once my feet are firmly planted in the sand.

"Of course. I wouldn't be where I am today if fate didn't have something to do with it. We worked our asses off to get here but so did thousands of other bands who failed. There had to be a stronger force at play and I'm thankful, for whatever reason, we were the chosen ones."

He releases me and bends down to pick up the blanket and flashlight, then takes my hand in his and starts walking back.

"Fate and I aren't exactly friends," I confess, letting my guard down a bit. If they have to let me into their lives, I suppose I'll eventually have to let them into mine. Might as well start with baby steps.

"Are you sure about that? Maybe she's trying to make amends now. You've got a bestselling novel and were just offered a job most people would kill for. Sounds to me like she's trying to make things up to you."

"You're pretty optimistic. Are you always like this?"

He shrugs his shoulders. "Yeah, I guess so. My life is crazy, but I don't have many complaints. Once this tour is over, I probably won't have any. There are a lot of people having a hard time out there, and my issues are small in comparison."

"Under your bad boy exterior, you're not really such a bastard, are you, Noah Weston? I'm going to enjoy getting to know you." My candid confession surprises me.

"I'm looking forward to it." He squeezes my hand in his, and I'm not sure what to do. I'm normally a pretty standoffish person and holding hands like this is pretty far out of my comfort zone.

"Is this making you uncomfortable?" he asks, holding our hands up in front of us.

"It's that obvious?"

He chuckles and releases my hand. "Sorry, I'm a pretty friendly guy, and I haven't been around a girl in years who would be uncomfortable holding my hand. You intrigue me, Amelia Greyson."

"I get it. You've had no shortage of willing women at your disposal for a decade at least."

"It's true, but just because they were there and available doesn't mean they're what I wanted. I'm not one of those guys who gets off on having a different chick in his bed every night. I'm not sure any of us are, or ever were."

"Not even Sawyer?"

He pauses and inhales deeply while running a hand through his hair. "Sawyer is complicated. Something happened when we were kids that changed him. He's deep and deeply affected by everything around him. I think it's what makes him such an amazing songwriter, but sometimes he needs to find solace in whatever girl is closest."

Noah drops down and sits on a step, holding his head in his hands. I feel completely out of place, but I get the sense he really needs someone to talk to, so I take a seat next to him and awkwardly pat his shoulder.

This is so not my thing.

When he looks up again, his eyes lock on mine. "There are things we don't talk about to anyone, not ever. You're going to be on the tour, so there are things you should know. Sawyer is rough around the edges. You've already witnessed that for yourself. He copes by having meaningless sex, and it works for a while. Sawyer was burned badly once by a girl, and he took it really hard. Ever since, he's been completely closed off."

"I'm sorry, Noah."

"Don't be," he replies with a smile. "For the first time in ages, tonight, the old Sawyer was present. I think you could be the key to getting him to open up again."

"You don't think I'm going to hook up with Sawyer, do you? I'm not ... I can't ... just no," I say, scrambling to my feet.

Noah's laughter follows me as he gets to his feet. "No, we aren't bringing you on tour to pimp you out to Sawyer, Mel. God, you're adorable. We're bringing you on tour because you're the perfect person to get him to tell his story. He responds to you, and he hasn't responded to a woman in a long time. At least, not for longer than it takes to get laid."

"Okay." My voice wavers in hesitation, but he isn't fazed.

"It will be fun, you'll see."

I second-guess my decision the whole way up the stairs and into the house. It's surprisingly quiet. Guess they're pretty mellow when they want to be.

"Is there a restroom I can use?"

Warren glances up from the table and points at the hallway. "Use Sawyer's. He's in the garage, and honestly, it's the cleanest one in the house. He's a neat freak. Second door on the left, bathroom is inside to the right, you can't miss it."

The hall is dark and only illuminated by their earthquake nightlights. I find Sawyer's room easily and head to the bathroom. Just as I'm about to knock on the closed door, it opens and a hand reaches out and pulls me into the darkness.

"What the fuck?" I cry out softly.

"Fucking hell, Princess."

Sawyer.

The room is steamy; he must have just gotten out of the shower. Before getting the chance to tell him where to shove his Princess comment, his lips crash against mine. One hand finds the back of my head and he tugs me close as his free arm wraps around my waist, pulling me even closer.

It's fucking hot, and when his tongue glides across my lips, I open to him. I can't help it; my body succumbs to his instinctually. As our tongues meet, I moan in absolute pleasure and wrap my arms around him.

Fucking hell, can he kiss.

Then I do what I've wanted to do since I first laid eyes on him. Pulling his lip ring into my mouth, I tug on it with my teeth. Even if his pleasurable moans didn't tell me how much he enjoys it, his hard length growing against me would be a dead giveaway.

I *want* to fuck him.

Thankfully, my conscience chooses this moment to remind me this is not even in the realm of possibilities. I don't do this anymore, especially not with people I work for.

Reluctantly, I push him away. "We can't," I whisper breathlessly.

"Oh, Princess," he says, placing my hand on his cock, "I'm pretty sure we can."

I laugh, I can't help it, and when he flips the light on, I blink repeatedly. When my eyes focus on him, he looks offended and determined at the same time. My eyes take him in slowly, and I'll be damned if I don't lick my lips. He catches it, too, and smirks like the devil.

All he's wearing is a towel. He's nothing but well-defined muscles and tattoos. His nipples are pierced, and my breathing becomes rapid. There's nothing separating us except his towel and my clothes.

And your conscience, Amelia, don't forget about that.

"I'm sorry, but I can't do this."

"Your body says otherwise."

So does the beating of my heart, but this is wrong.

"Maybe it does, but I don't think with my body anymore, I think with my mind. We can't do this if I'm coming on tour with you."

He's frustrated. I don't blame him; I am, too. That may have been the hottest kiss ever. But there's something else lingering in his gaze, I just can't pinpoint what it is.

"Alright. I've never had a woman turn me down before. I'm not sure I like it. It's your call, Princess. You know where to find me if you change your mind."

With those words, he turns and walks out, closing the door behind him. I take a few moments to calm myself before using the facilities and when I finish, he's nowhere in sight. It's just as well.

As I walk back into the living room, Warren shoots me an apologetic look. "Sorry, Amelia, I didn't realize Sawyer had come back up."

With a shrug of my shoulders, I reply, "It's alright. It's not like I've never seen a man in a towel before. Besides, I'm sure I'll end up seeing a lot of that on the buses."

"About that … I know tomorrow is Sunday, but would you mind coming by my office and filling out all the paperwork? The quicker we move on it, the better. Sam and Anna are coming down for the day tomorrow, and he'd like to speak with you as well while he's here."

"Of course. What time is good for you?"

"How about noon? I'll have some sandwiches brought in as well."

"Sounds great."

"Hey, Mel, want to watch a movie with us while you wait for Belle?" Noah smiles from across the room. He, Wyatt, and Sawyer are debating between *The Avengers* and *The Goonies*. Considering Belle is sure to be a while, it's not like I've got anything else to do.

"Sure, why not?"

I've got a feeling this is going to be the first of many movies I watch with these guys.

NDAs Go Both Ways

Last night was surprisingly fun. Even more surprising, I fell asleep with my head on Noah's shoulder. Belle and Darren took their time on the beach, and then she had a million more questions about her article. By the time she dropped me off it was almost five in the morning.

Watching *The Goonies* with the guys was fun. They're the kind of people who know all the lines and ad lib their way through. I usually find that annoying, but they were completely into it. One of the things I already love about them is how much of a family they truly are.

Now—after three cups of coffee and a forty-minute drive—I'm in the elevator on my way up to Warren's office.

I'm so nervous.

It's silent in the elevator. What the hell kind of record company doesn't have music piping into their elevator? One that is closed on the weekends, I guess.

"Amelia," Warren calls out, waving me down the hall with his hand, "come join me in my office. Sam will be here in a little while with our lunch."

All morning, I've been trying to figure out how to tell Warren who I am. I'd like him to keep it confidential, but I know it's a lot to ask of him. However, I just don't feel right accepting this job until he knows all the facts.

His office is huge, and I can see the ocean sparkling in the sunlight through his windows. What a gorgeous view. The walls are covered with gold and platinum records, photos of BAD, and other industry plaques and paraphernalia. It reminds me so much of my dad's office, but I won't go there—not today.

"Please, have a seat. Can I get you something to drink?" He motions to a plush leather chair across from his desk, and I make myself comfortable.

"A bottle of water would be great, thank you."

After he hands me the water, he sits across from me and looks at me thoughtfully.

"You're the perfect combination of them." My mouth drops with his words. He chuckles and leans back in his chair.

"I was going to tell you," I stammer softly.

"I'm sure you were. Last night, it gnawed at me for a long time. I knew I recognized you from somewhere. You probably don't remember me. You couldn't have been more than five or six the last time I saw you."

"Sorry," I say, shaking my head.

"Eh, some things are best left in the past. It came to me on my way here this morning. Now, I realize why you're so hesitant to join us. So what I have to ask you is, are you sure you can handle this?"

"No, but I won't back out once I'm in. I'm sure their issues aren't the same, but you could tell me that for sure. Are their lives as dramatic as my parents' were?"

He leans forward and steeples his fingers, thinking long and hard. It's not the response I was hoping for.

"Amelia, no disrespect, but I don't think anyone is as dramatic as your parents were. That isn't to say they don't come with their own drama because they do. This lifestyle always brings drama in one form or another. However, I'd prefer for you to form your own opinion of them without me pointing out their weaknesses."

"Fair enough."

"You know, for what it's worth, as bad as things got with your parents, they did love each other, and they loved you. Sometimes, as adults, you lose yourself in someone else so completely you don't know where they end and you begin. It's not a bad thing unless you let it become toxic, and unfortunately, that's what they did."

I'm quiet. I've got too much anger and sadness within to comment on his thoughts. Instead, I nod my head in understanding, even if I don't agree.

"You go by Greyson now, and you've been out of the public eye for what … eleven, twelve years?"

"About that," I answer softly.

"I'm assuming, then … you'd like to keep your identity secret for as long as possible."

The pointed look he gives me has a clear meaning, and it's something I've been thinking about since last night.

"Yes. I realize my anonymity won't last very long, especially if I take the deal from SOS, but I'd like to hold on to it as long as possible. I hope that doesn't put you in an awkward situation."

"You know, NDAs work both ways. What they don't know won't hurt them, and they won't hear it from my lips. Once upon a time, your parents were good friends of mine, but when things got bad ..."

"When things got bad, Joey Triton shut out the world, including me, so you probably shouldn't take it personally."

"This is inappropriate of me to ask, and you don't have to answer, but is it true about the money? The rumors have been circulating for years."

This makes me smile. "It's true. Every single penny goes to charity. I've never taken a dime of it. I consider it fruit of the poisonous tree and all that."

He nods in complete understanding.

"There's something else I need to address before we go over the paperwork."

He releases a sigh, and I'm intrigued.

"Most of this tour will be by bus. This tour is smaller, there are no sets, it's all acoustic and very few instruments. There's not even an opening act. We'll have a total of two trucks and five buses. Two buses for the band, one for workout equipment, and two for the crew. We meant it when we said it's intimate."

Sweet Jesus, that's a small crew for a band of their caliber.

"Most of the time, I travel with them, and that won't change on this tour. Typically, I travel with Wyatt and Darren. We wanted to put you with them, but then I realized it would be extremely inappropriate to have you on the bus with Wyatt."

I see where he's going with this, and I'm not sure I like it.

"So I'd have to bunk with Sawyer and Noah," I finish for him, and he nods.

"The buses are large and luxurious. There are two bedrooms in the back. Essentially, it's one large bedroom split down the middle with a wall, so Noah and Sawyer could have some space. Just outside the rooms on the left is an almost full-size bathroom, including a spa tub. On the right are two twin-size bunks. It's spacious, and of course there's a kitchen, small office area, and a lounging area."

"So I could use the office space to write?"

"I'm sure you're going to be the first person to use the office space for anything."

This is overwhelming.

"Look, here is all the paperwork, feel free to review it. It includes your contract, standard NDA, tour schedule, and potential book tour schedule. Sam will be here with your other paperwork shortly. Go over it, take it to your attorney and have them go over it, and get it back to me by Tuesday at the latest."

"I thought you needed it finalized by Monday?"

"We thought so, too, but it seems Sawyer has been inspired to finally finish the title track of the album. They'll be working in the studio all day tomorrow."

The elevator dings and Warren rises. "That must be Sam. I'm going to see if he needs any help." He pats me on the shoulder as he passes. "I really do think this will be good for all of you."

It's easy for him to say, he didn't live through it the first time around … I did. It doesn't matter because my mind is already made up. I'm going to do this, and I'm going to enjoy it if it kills me.

"Amelia, join us in the conference room, won't you? Sam brought entirely too much food to eat in here."

I follow Warren to the conference room, which also has a spectacular view of the ocean.

How do they ever get any work done here?

"You must be Amelia. I'm Sam Stevenson. It is such a pleasure to finally meet you. Your book was phenomenal. I read it in one sitting."

"Thank you," I answer while taking in the massive spread in front of me. He brought three different kinds of bread, at least five different kinds of meats and cheeses, veggies, condiments, fruit, and chips. It's enough food for thirty people, let alone just the three of us.

"Please, help yourself and let's get to know each other a bit. Business can keep until a bit later, don't you agree?"

"Of course."

If it keeps me from talking about my parents, I'll pretty much agree to anything. Sam pulls out a chair for me, and I sit. He and Warren both take chairs opposite of me. They're an interesting couple. Warren is easily in his mid-fifties while Sam is probably mid-forties. Warren has salt-and-pepper hair, a little bit of a belly, and the kindest smile I've ever seen. They both look to be a little under six feet tall. Sam, on the other hand, is bald and well-built. Where Warren seems to be more of a casual dresser, Sam is in a suit, even on a Sunday afternoon.

As we pass around the different trays of food and make our plates, Sam and Warren catch up on their morning.

"How long have you two been married?" I ask, hoping to break the ice and continue to divert the discussion away from myself.

"Five years this month, but we've been together for twelve. Believe it or not, we met at one of BAD's first shows down at the Whisky."

"Wow. Twelve years, that's impressive."

"You don't believe in romance, do you, Amelia?" Sam asks bluntly, and I know I'm blushing.

"I believe in it for some people. I'm just not sure I believe in it for myself."

"You write it extremely well for someone who doesn't necessarily believe," he counters.

"Life wouldn't be as fun if we didn't give the world fairytales, even if we don't buy into them ourselves, would it?"

"You've got me there," he answers with a hearty laugh. I like him; he doesn't beat around the bush.

After a bit more chit chat, and entirely way too much food, I push my plate away.

"Should we get down to business?" Sam asks with an excited gleam in his eye, and I nod in agreement.

"Warren says you might not want to be in the public eye …"

"It's true, but it's also a little too late for that, don't you think? Soon enough, someone will point out my past. I'm just hoping to stay under the radar for as long as possible."

"Glad to hear it. If you sign with SOS, we will not be revealing any of your personal details you don't want the general public to know. Once your secret is out of the bag, we'll decline to comment on anything. If and when you're ready to talk, it will be your choice and not guided by any of our publicists."

"Sounds fair enough." I'm keeping it cool on the outside but relief is pouring through my veins. I know I'm going to have to talk about them eventually, but it's not something I want to think about now.

Sam reaches for a folder on the table. "These are the contracts which contain all the details of the publishing deal SOS would like to offer you. It encompasses *The O Factor*, the currently untitled official BAD biography, and first right of refusal for your next book, as well as any potential sequels to any of these books. It's a fairly standard contract, but please have your attorney look it over and get back to me in the next few weeks. I'll need the BAD contract back in the next few days, as Warren has already advised you."

"Thank you." I'm pretty speechless at the moment, so I'm lucky to even squeak out those words.

"I should be thanking you. It will be nice to get a fresh, younger author into SOS. I'm hopeful this can be the beginning of a long-term relationship. And, of course it goes without saying, the sooner you decide, the better, since we will be coordinating the book tour with the BAD tour."

"About that, how would that work exactly?" I've been wondering about this because I can't imagine doing as many signings as they do shows.

Sam leans back with a smile; he's happy I'm interested. "Actually, it wouldn't be bad at all. You'll be on tour for a full year, and you're going to be busy working. The tour is five stops for you. Los Angles, New York, Chicago, Boston, and London."

"London?" *He wants me to go international?*

"Of course London," he replies with a hearty laugh. "You are an international bestseller, Amelia, and your fans want to know you. London is the perfect place for your first signing abroad. If it goes well, we'll set up more for when you complete the BAD story. Who knows, maybe they'll even travel with you next time."

The twinkle in his eyes is mischievous, and I'm not entirely sure he's joking.

"Don't look so fearful. This is a great opportunity for you," Warren says in a fatherly tone. If only my own dad had been more like him.

"It's a lot to think about, but I'm thrilled to have both offers to go over. I could never thank you enough, either of you."

"The pleasure is ours. Do you have any further questions?" Warren asks as he and Sam stand to walk me out.

"Just one. I'm still allowed to put Sawyer in his place when necessary, correct?"

Warren roars in laughter and responds once he composes himself again. "Amelia, not only are you allowed, but I think it's going to be the best part of the entire tour. Sawyer, more than anything, needs someone to set him straight."

"Perfect. I'll be in touch once I've gone over everything with my attorney. Have a good day, gentlemen."

The elevator door opens and once inside, I'm frantically emailing my attorney. I know he'll respond within a few minutes, and the sooner I can get in to see him, the better.

Leaving On A Tour Bus

"So that's everything," Belle says excitedly, surveying my empty apartment. The movers took the last box down to the truck and are taking everything to the storage unit Warren set up for me.

"I guess so," I reply sadly.

"Hey, don't be so glum. This is a good thing. It's time to let go of the past, including this apartment. It's been your shield for far too long."

Belle pulls me into a hug, and I nod. "I know it is, but this was the first place I ever had that was mine, and I fought like hell to get here on my own."

"Amelia Greyson, you listen to me. Everything in your life has changed. You're not the girl you were back then, and your financial future is completely secure. Between the money you're getting from the tour, the royalties from the book, and your new publishing contract with SOS, you're set for a very long time."

"I'm going to miss you so much."

"Girl, please," she says, pushing me out at arm's length, holding on to my shoulders. "You're not going to have time to miss me. You've got a book to write, a band to document, and fun to be had. Plus, you'll see me in a week *and* at least once a month. You've got this. Just give in to it."

She's right. I'm just scared of what's going to come from all of this.

"Come on, let's get you to the buses before they're ready to leave. I'd like to say goodbye to Darren alone, anyway."

"I can't believe you're dating a rock star," I reply, shaking my head.

She clears her throat. "Fucking and dating are two very different things. I'm fucking a rock star like there's no tomorrow. I'm not dating anyone who's going to be gone for a year. There are too many hotties in my life for that."

"Whatever you say, Belle."

She turns to me with her hands on her hips. "Mel, what exactly are you implying?"

"I'm not *implying* anything. I know for a fact you like him more than you want to admit, and I'm curious to see how this all plays out. That's all."

"That's funny coming from the girl who has *both* Weston brothers salivating over her."

"They are not!" My protest is weak and we both know it.

"We'll see. Come on, *Princess*, or you're going to be late." Her laugh follows behind her as she runs down the stairs. She should run, too; she knows I can't stand that Princess shit.

Once we're on the freeway, she asks the question I knew was going to come eventually, and I'm utterly shocked it took her almost four weeks to get it out.

"Seriously, Mel, what was it like when Sawyer kissed you? You haven't talked about it at all, but damn ... he's Sawyer fucking Weston, and the first thing he did was nickname you. From everything I've heard, that's extremely out of character for him."

Do I tell her the truth? I've never lied to her before, but if I tell her she's going to make fun of me. And if I don't, she'll know I'm lying.

"In the vault, Belle. This is off the record and in the best friend files, got it?"

She nods enthusiastically and nibbles on her bottom lip while she drives, waiting for my answer.

"I can't believe I'm going to tell you this."

After a long pause, I finally give her what she's waiting for.

"Being kissed by Sawyer made me believe in the devil. There's no way someone can make me feel that good and turn me on that fast without being completely damning to my soul. I've never felt like that before, and I'm sure I'll never feel it again."

"Babe, if someone makes you feel *that* good, you need to believe he came from God because that kind of pleasure can *only* come from heaven above."

She looks at me and we both burst into laughter. Once we've calmed down a bit, we fall into silence. As Belle exits the freeway, she turns to me. "Seriously, Mel, don't push him away if he makes you feel good. Maybe you're what he needs, too."

"What I need is to focus on my job and not on screwing band members."

"If you say so." She shrugs her shoulders. "I just hope you eventually figure out you can work *and* have fun."

She turns into the parking lot of The Forum and pulls into the lot where all the trucks and buses are lined up and getting ready to go. Belle parks next to the first bus, which I was told is their bus. I guess Noah and Sawyer are always in front of the procession, or whatever you call it.

My bags are already on the bus. Warren took care of that as well. The only things I have with me are my purse and my backpack which houses my laptop and a few other necessities.

This seems so normal. Everyone is lingering around outside the buses just chatting away. Darren is the first to approach us, and he immediately pulls Belle into a hug and spins her around.

"Mind if I steal your friend for a few minutes?" The devilish smile on his face tells me it's going to be more than a few minutes, but I don't mind.

"Not at all. Have fun, you two, and be safe," I call after them as they laugh their way into the second bus.

"Is this really her?" a female voice squeals from behind me, and I turn to see if she's talking about me. She is because about a half second after I turn around, I'm being hugged like I'm this chick's long-lost friend.

"Sorry, Mel," Wyatt says sheepishly. "This is Anna. She's a little excited to meet you in person."

With a laugh, she pulls back. "Sorry, sometimes I'm overly friendly. I'm just so excited to finally meet you. I can't wait to read the book you write about these guys. I know it's going to be absolutely incredible." She's gushing and I'm blushing. I'm not used to this kind of attention.

"Princess," Sawyer says as he slithers up next to me.

"Well, if it isn't Prince Charming himself," I mutter.

Anna and Wyatt snicker, and Anna whispers to Wyatt, but it's loud enough for us all to hear. "You're right, they're going to be really fun to watch."

"Don't worry, Mel, I'll save you from the big bad wolf," Noah says, slinging his arm around my shoulder. Once again, he's a little too close for comfort, but I'm beginning to understand this is just how he is. His parents were probably very loving—although, that doesn't explain Sawyer.

Anna gives me a knowing glance, reminding me of Belle. I'm not going to be in a Weston brother sandwich, so I duck out of Noah's arm and lean up against the bus instead.

Anna giggles, and I really take a good look at her. We couldn't be more opposite, that's good. Hopefully, she'll never worry about me wanting her husband. She's about five-foot-two, curvy, and has short, red, spikey hair and piercing blue eyes. She actually kind of reminds me of Pink. Considering I'm about five-foot-eight, with long, wavy, brown hair, hazel eyes, and a sarcastic attitude, we probably couldn't be any different.

Thank God.

"If you need the real scoop on these guys, you can feel free to call me anytime. I've known them for years, and I know them best. I know what makes them tick."

Sawyer surprises me by scooping her up in a big bear hug. When he sets her down, she's misty-eyed.

Noah must notice my surprise because he points between the two of them. "They've been best friends since we were kids. It's actually how Anna and Wyatt met. All of us met in junior high school, but Sawyer was the first one to meet Anna our eighth grade year."

"Correction. I *dated* Anna in eighth grade," Sawyer retorts smugly, and Anna promptly slugs him.

"Stop telling tales. We dated for about a day. I met him over the phone through a mutual friend. You know how it goes. Once we met in person, we knew we were going to be friends, but that was it."

"Hey, I wasn't telling tales. I said we dated. Now, if I said I almost had you coming in your pants with just a kiss, *that* would be telling tales."

He's smirking, and I'm doing my best not to blush.

"Eww, Sawyer, stop being gross. Wyatt is the only one of these guys who's ever made me come with his tongue," she clarifies for my benefit. I like her already.

"Come on, Mel. Why don't I show you the bus and get you your entry code?"

"Entry code?"

"To the bus. Everyone has their own entry code for security purposes."

"Oh, sure, that makes sense." I follow behind Noah and wait while he punches in his own code to get onto the bus. The door opens and we step inside.

It's gorgeous.

With a quick glance around, I already know we won't be lacking for luxury. This is far nicer than any other bus I've been on. The floors are hardwood, the appliances stainless steel, the counters granite, and the furniture is all black leather. It's sexy as fuck in here. As we walk further inside, we pass the office and Noah opens the door to show me the bathroom.

Warren wasn't joking; it's pretty awesome.

"We figured you'd be happy with the bathroom. That's the biggest perk of the nicer buses. You actually get a full-size tub and shower."

"This bus is beautiful."

"Well, you might not want to say that too soon. Here are the bunks."

Even the bunks are nice. They aren't super small cubbies with a flat mat posing as a mattress. These are full-size twin mattresses, with super plush bedding and black-out curtains. There are built-in lights above so you can read if you want to and since there are only two of them, I won't have to worry about bumping my head. They're spacious.

"They're bigger than I'd imagined. Can I have the bottom, or is someone else traveling with us?"

"Nope, you can have my room. I'm taking the bunk."

What? No fucking way.

"Sorry, that's not the deal. I'm fine on the bunk, really."

"I don't feel right about it. You're the only girl on the bus, Mel, and you should have the room."

"Noah, I appreciate the offer, but this is more than enough. I knew what I was getting into, and I'll be fine. This is your job, and you need to be well-rested in your own bed."

With an adorable smirk, he replies, "You know, I could say the same about you."

"I've slept in worse places. This is fine, I promise."

An unhappy look flickers across his face with my words.

"Well, maybe I'll eventually be able to convince you to rotate."

"Um, I think that's going to depend on the number of skanks who go in and out of your room and Sawyer's. No offense."

He's taken aback, and I feel awful.

"Is that what you think of us?"

"I'm sorry, Noah, I shouldn't have assumed. This isn't my first rodeo with musicians, so I just lumped you in with what I know."

"Care to elaborate?" he asks, intrigued.

"Not now, but maybe someday. Again, I'm sorry if I offended you." I turn to walk away, and he pulls me back.

"Not so fast. I still have more to show you."

He opens Sawyer's door; the room is spotless. They weren't kidding when they said he was a neat freak. Then again, the buses haven't left yet, so we'll see. There's soundproofing on all the walls in here. With a raised brow, I look to Noah and he chuckles, pulling me into his room, where there's also soundproofing on his walls.

He sits on the bed and pats the spot next to him. I'm hesitant to sit, but at least I know the sheets are clean—for today.

The room is large enough for a full-size bed, a flat-screen TV mounted on the wall, and a dresser that runs across the wall under the TV. Yet it's small enough for him to reach over and kick the door shut with his foot. My heart speeds up a bit.

"Amelia, I'm not into random hookups, and I haven't been for a few years. I've always been more of a relationship kind of guy. It's important to me that above all else you know that about me, okay?"

I nod, not really able to find my words.

"Sawyer is a different story. He doesn't bring different girls in every night, but once in a while, he needs to let off steam, and having sex is how he does it. We have a rule on this bus and always have. Sex on the bus is only allowed in the bedrooms, and we've *never* broken that rule. Hence the oh-so-decorative soundproofing on the walls. It's not pretty, but trust me, it's necessary. It also helps mute freeway noise."

"Trust me, I already know the scene."

"I know I've said this before, but I'm looking forward to getting to know you."

"Me, too. I mean, you know, getting to know you."

He's shaking his head and laughing. "Has anyone ever told you how fucking cute you are?"

Now it's my turn to laugh. "I've been called a lot of things in my life, but I'm not sure cute has *ever* been one of them."

"Well, maybe it's time to change that," he says, taking my hand and pulling me to my feet. As we exit the bedroom, Belle runs up onto the bus with Darren and Sawyer is right behind her.

"You're leaving now!" she squeals as the engines fire up.

She runs up to me and hugs me tightly. Belle is so petite; I always feel like a giant next to her. I'm about six inches taller than her, and I swear she can't weigh more than a hundred and five pounds.

"I'm going to miss you."

"I'm going to miss you, too, but I'll see you in a week, and I'll be texting you constantly. I love you, Mel. Live today like there's no tomorrow." She kisses me on the cheek and runs off the bus. *Typical Belle.*

Belle's First Tour Update

Slammers!

It's your girl Belle here, and I literally just got off the BAD tour bus as they embark on their farewell tour. If you read my last article you know the deal, but in case you missed it, I'll forgive you this once and recap it for you.

Bastards and Dangerous are heading out on their farewell tour for their final album. The Just an Illusion tour is like nothing you've ever seen. All your favorite Bastards getting all acoustical and shit on you. It's the fucking bomb. *Just an Illusion*, the album, goes live tomorrow, and tickets for the first show go on sale on Monday.

Tickets will be released three days before each show and will only be sold at the nearest Top Hitz Music locations to the venue. These venues will be smaller than ever, and the crowds more intimate, so be sure to click the link at the bottom of the page for all the deets on upcoming tour locations.

Trust me, this is one you *don't* want to miss. If you do, no worries because my girl Mel is covering the entire tour from the first day to the last in the only official book to ever be written about BAD. That's right. My best friend Mel is spending 365 glorious days with the Bastards herself. Imagine the secrets she'll be able to tell!

That's all for now.

Don't forget, live today like there's no tomorrow!

Xs and Os,

Belle

On The Road Again

The last time I was on a tour bus, I was sixteen years old. I'm twenty-eight now, and I've recently discovered all the guys are the same age as I am. I knew we were close in age, I just didn't realize how close.

Yesterday was our first day on the bus, and everyone mostly kept to themselves. I'm assuming it's a routine of some sort, getting acclimated to life on the road again. Or maybe they were being mindful of me because I slept a good part of the day and into the night.

Tour buses were my home for a long time. The lull of the bus as it moves along has always been comforting to me. Our tour bus was pretty much the only home I ever knew. We spent more time on it than we ever did at our actual home. I never realized how much I missed it until yesterday.

Now, it's five in the morning, and I've already successfully brewed a cup of coffee in the Keurig. I'm sitting on the couch in my pajamas, with my feet curled up under me, watching the sunrise over the desert. Belle always tells everyone to live as if it's your last day, but my favorite thing is waking up in the morning and watching the sunrise with the knowledge yesterday wasn't my last day. It's what brings me hope.

One of the guys is up; I heard him stumble to the bathroom a minute ago, but I'm selfishly hoping whoever it is goes back to bed.

No such luck.

Sawyer walks out in his boxers and nothing else and works on making himself a cup of coffee. His body is so perfect; it takes everything I have not to stare. Even still, it's impossible not to flick an occasional glance his way.

When his coffee finishes brewing, he sits at the opposite end of the couch and sips it slowly, looking out the window the same as I am. I wouldn't have pegged him as a morning person.

"Good morning," I whisper softly, hoping not to make too much noise and wake Noah.

"Morning, Princess," he says before sipping his coffee again. I hate the nickname, but what I hate even more is how much I love hearing *him* call me Princess.

"Are you ever going to call me by my name?"

He flashes me a smug grin. "Nope."

"Great," I mumble, and he laughs. "Shhh. Just because you're up doesn't mean you need to wake up Noah."

For some reason, he laughs even harder. "Noah could sleep through one of our concerts. He doesn't wake until he's had enough sleep. Most days that's about ten a.m."

That's weird. I would have pictured them completely opposite.

"I wouldn't have pegged you as a morning person."

"Never used to be, but it's something about the bus."

I nod in understanding but don't elaborate. Sawyer fumbles around and opens a cabinet next to the couch.

"Want one?"

He's holding out a pack of Pop-Tarts.

"You eat Pop-Tarts for breakfast?"

"I eat Pop-Tarts whenever I want a fucking Pop-Tart, and Noah always steals them, so I hide them all over."

This is probably the first normal thing I've learned about him, and I decide then and there it must go in the book.

"What flavor?"

"The only one that matters … cinnamon."

"Yeah, I'll take one." He's about to toss me a pack and thinks better of it.

"Toasted?"

I feel like this is a quiz, but toasted Pop-Tarts aren't my thing.

"Eww, no."

With a smile, he passes it to me. "I knew I fucking liked you for a reason, Princess." His words give me the feels but I can't let them. He and I are *not* going to happen, no matter how fucking sexy he looks sitting next to me in his boxers.

"So what do you usually do in the morning?"

"Read, write, sing, practice, whatever I feel like. At some point, usually around lunchtime when we stop for a break, all the guys will get on one bus for a few hours and practice or just hang out."

"What do you like to read?"

"Different things, I guess. Biographies, books on history, mystery or suspense, I guess whatever grabs me when I'm browsing."

I bet he looks sexy as fuck while he's reading.

"What do you like to read? Romance?" he teases.

"Not really. Sure, every once in a while, I might want to read something with a happy ending and romance is usually where it's at. I'm more of a paranormal or suspense girl."

"But don't you write romance?" he asks, surprised.

"Yeah, but that doesn't mean I'm a huge romantic. Quite the contrary, actually."

He turns to face me. "How does that work? I figured all these romance chicks all had this fairytale idea of life and shit."

"Hardly. I mean, who knows, maybe some of them do. I don't really know any other writers. For me, growing up, things were different. Real all the time, shitty some of the time, and romance pretty much never, or at least never in a functional way. I'm sure most relationships aren't so loving and sweet, which makes reading about people who *do* have that an escape for people who don't and never will."

"Anna likes your book," he counters.

"Ah, but I'd assume Anna is happy and in love, and Wyatt is probably pretty romantic. It's the other side of the coin. Happy people don't want to read sad stories, they want to read happiness and happily ever afters so they can stay in their happy bubble."

"So happy people want to stay happy, lonely people want to believe it's out there for them, and people who aren't happy want to escape to happy every once in a while?"

"Pretty much."

"But if you take that analogy to music, it doesn't work."

"Doesn't it?"

He wrinkles his nose a little as he thinks. "No, it doesn't. If it did, people would be listening to love songs all the time."

"Not necessarily. Music is different. It's filled with memories and emotions. Certain songs and beats trigger good and bad memories. Blues can make you swoon, love songs can make you reminisce or even cry. Rage metal and grunge are both great outlets for any aggressions you may have, rap … Well, oddly enough, rap encompasses it all. R & B and soul allow you to unleash your inner Whitney. No matter what the fuck she sings, Adele just gives you the feels. Don't even get me started on Prince, Michael Jackson, and Madonna … they're fucking gods. All of it makes you want to dance. Think about how you feel when you write. Do you think that reflects in your music?"

The skeptical look on his face makes me smile, but at least he answers the question.

"At times it does. Other times, my lyrics are based on the past or maybe even thoughts about the future. You might actually know this if you ever listened to my music. If you knew *anything* about us. Why are you so opposed to our stuff anyway?"

His question hits too close to home for me to give him an entirely truthful answer. But the fact of the matter is, I want to be open to them because they're being open with me for the book. It only seems fair.

"Number one, I'm here to get to know you. I'm sorry if I bruised your delicate ego by not already knowing enough to be able to write my own tell-all book on BAD."

His brow raises with my sarcastic answer, but this is me and he'll just have to get used to it.

"Number two, I'm going to answer your question, but I'm not going into details about the whys of my ways, okay?"

With a lifted brow, he nods and continues to drink his coffee while awaiting my response.

"The music you play takes me back to a part of my life I've been trying to bury for years. It's not your songs in particular, so I'm not singling you out. It's the entire heavier rock category as a whole."

"You should listen to our practice today. We're focusing on the new album. Some songs are new and some are old, but all of them are acoustic. I'd really like to know your thoughts. Maybe see if we might be able to make a fan out of you yet."

I thought Sawyer would be the last one of the guys to want to have a conversation with me. But we're actually sitting here conversing over our morning coffee. I could get used to this.

"Sure, I can do that, but calling me a fan is reaching. I'm not typically a fangirl over anything."

"Why doesn't that surprise me?"

"What's that supposed to mean?" My tone is light, but I'm genuinely curious.

"You're just not like anyone I've ever met, Princess."

"Is that bad?"

"I'm not sure. When I figure it out, I'll let you know."

We fall into silence, each of us lost in our own thoughts. I'm already realizing there's so much more to these men than I ever thought possible.

A short time later, Noah emerges from his bedroom wearing a pair of athletic shorts and a t-shirt, his hair is messed up, and he flashes me a sleepy smile.

"Sawyer, what the hell?" he suddenly yells across the bus.

Sawyer looks up, obviously confused, and Noah uses his hand to gesture up and down his own body.

"Clothes, dick. Have some manners and put on some clothes."

"Are you seriously giving me shit for walking around the way I do every single day of my life?" He shakes his head, obviously frustrated.

"It's okay," I interject before they really start fighting. "Really, I'm used to it, and it's not like I've never seen a man in his underwear before. It doesn't bother me. To be truthful, it actually makes me feel better to know you're not acting differently because I'm here. I don't want to intrude on your lives any more than I have to."

"See, Noah, she doesn't care."

"Dude, *I* care!" Noah exclaims.

I'm pretty sure there's more to this than just me, so I'm going to excuse myself and let them work this out.

"Since everyone is awake, I'm going to go take a shower. Excuse me."

Noah moves into the kitchen area as I pass by. When I reach my bunk, I grab my toiletry bag and the clothes I pulled out last night for today and duck into the bathroom. I hope Noah can get over trying to act differently with me around. The last thing I want is for him not to be comfortable enough to be himself for the next year.

After showering, I feel much better. The shower on this bus is better than the shower in my apartment.

There's a knock on the door; I figure it's my cue I've taken too long. Noah is waiting outside the door.

"Sorry to bother you. I just wanted to let you know the second drawer on the left is all yours."

"You're giving me a drawer?"

"Well, yeah, I don't need too much stuff, and you can't be on the bus for a year living out of your suitcase."

I've actually got two drawers under my bed, which are a godsend because they're super deep, but I know what he means. It's still hard to believe the two of them are brothers. Other than their similar looks, they're nothing alike.

"Thanks, Noah, that's really sweet of you."

"Nah, I'm just a guy with two sisters and I know how I'd want them treated."

"You guys have sisters?"

"Yup, one older and one younger. I reminded Sawyer of them when you got in the shower. I'm sure he wouldn't want some guy walking around in his underwear around our little sister."

"Really, it doesn't bother me."

"It bothers me," he states firmly, leaving no room for discussion.

He's so stubborn, but his gesture is appreciated. When I turn to unpack my toiletries into the drawer, I catch him smiling at me in the mirror.

"So Sawyer says you're going to listen to us practice today. We're working on the new song since we just finished it. I think you'll like it, even if it's probably the saddest song we've ever done."

"I'm looking forward to it, actually. We had a nice talk this morning. It's nice to get to know Sawyer a little bit without his guard up."

"I'd like to say you'll see more of that, but the truth is, he's been guarded for a long time, and you should relish those moments when you get them."

"Well, maybe that will change," I answer softly.

"We can only hope."

He steps back so I can put my stuff back in my bunk, but it's not far enough, and I end up brushing against him. His hand finds its way to my hip briefly before he releases me and steps further out of the way. I could get used to his touch; for some reason, it exudes safety, security, and comfort. Too bad musicians aren't on my to-do list anymore.

"Warren mentioned there's a fitness bus. Is there a specific time you get to use it?" *I've got to work out my sexual frustrations somehow.*

"Nah, not really. We all like to exercise at different times, so if one of us wants to get on, we just radio the bus and tell them to pull over for a minute while we swap. It's also got the biggest bathroom out of all the buses, which is kind of nice after a hard workout."

"Cool. What kind of equipment is on there?" He's so cute with his bed head and lopsided grin. Noah follows me back to the sitting area and Sawyer is nowhere in sight. He must have gone back to his room after Noah chewed him out.

"The usual … a treadmill, elliptical, weights, bike, rowing machine, pull-up bar, and some yoga stuff Anna and my sisters use. I usually go after practice if you want to come with me."

Working out with him will only increase my sexual frustration, but his offer is so sweet I can't say no.

"Yeah, sure. Thanks."

"So how do you feel about the photoshoot tomorrow?"

"Ugh, don't remind me. I'm not fond of having my picture taken, and SOS is insisting it be put on the book now."

"You're beautiful. You should have your picture taken, and often. Besides, it will be fun. They're doing it with all our promo shots, so you're not the only one who has to go through it. We'll be miserable together."

Isn't it sad I can't tell if Noah is being nice, flirting, or both? I haven't dated in so long, I'm completely out of touch with men and their ways.

"True. At least I won't have to suffer alone."

"Alone is one word we don't use often on tour. Wherever you go, there's always someone underfoot."

It's not like I'm not fully aware of what he's saying, but I don't want to raise suspicion, so I nod in agreement and leave it at that.

"Okay … well, I'm going to get in the shower. I'll see you in a bit?"

"I'll be here, but I'll try not to be underfoot," I reply with a wink, but he's suddenly Mr. Serious.

"You could never be underfoot, Mel. Just the opposite, in fact." He turns and walks away quickly, leaving me in a shocked silence. I'm not wondering anymore. Noah Weston obviously likes me, and I have no idea what I'm going to do about it.

A few hours later, the buses stop and we all get off and have lunch. When it's time to get going again, everyone piles onto our bus so they can practice. Darren and Wyatt bring over an acoustic guitar and a set of bongos, and both Sawyer and Noah pull acoustic guitars out of their rooms.

I know enough about guitars to know the different colors of the wood create acoustical variations. Their guitars are gorgeous and easily cost ten thousand dollars or more.

"What are you thinking?" Noah asks as he sits next to me making some minor adjustments to his strings.

"I'm actually thinking what beautiful guitars those are, but there's no way you're going to use those at the venue, right? You have to have an electrical acoustic to play for a crowd that big."

"You know a good amount about instruments. Have you been doing your homework?"

"Something like that." I'm not going to tell him my dad owned more guitars than any normal person had the right to.

"Yes, these are our guitars. They're our babies, we've played on these for years. They're the closest thing we have to kids," he adds with a laugh. "When we first made it big, these were our major purchases. They're all we ever use to practice with on the bus. The equipment truck transports all the equipment for the shows. All of our equipment is good, but these are special."

Leaning in closer, I whisper in his ear, "So what's with the bongos? I really don't get why you have those."

Goose bumps rise across his neck, and it's obvious I've affected him. Noah doesn't lose the moment, though, as he throws his arm over my shoulder and whispers back, "They're fun and a lot easier to practice beats on in the bus. Darren knows his shit. As long as he's getting the beats down, we don't care what he plays."

His eyes are locked onto mine, and all I see is a pure heart reflected back at me through them. With Noah, what you see is what you get. He's the kind of man you dream of, and if I wasn't on this tour, he'd be the kind of guy I could fall in love with.

"Alright, let's get this going," Sawyer calls out and sits down across from me.

"Ready to listen with an open mind, Princess?" he teases and tugs his lip ring into his mouth. I swear he did that on purpose to remind me of our kiss. What's worse is it worked.

"I'm ready, but I'm *not* going to fangirl all over you."

"You say that now, but you haven't heard us yet," Wyatt teases with an easy smile.

"Well, you know, if anything, I might fangirl over Darren. I mean, he *does* have those awesome bongos."

"You can bang my bongo anytime you'd like, Mel."

I know he's joking, but it makes me feel sleazy since he and Belle are doing ... well, whatever it is they're doing.

"Such a sweet offer, but I think Belle likes banging your bongo enough for the both of us."

He actually blushes slightly and laughs. "Well, the feeling is mutual because I like the way she bangs my bongo, too."

"Jesus, just because there's a chick on the bus doesn't mean we have to come up with euphemisms for everything, does it? Grow some balls and call it what it is. You like the way she—"

Noah cuts Sawyer off, "Freaks you."

"The way she makes you cream," Wyatt throws out.

"How she takes you deeper and deeper," I add, and Sawyer is trying hard not to laugh.

"Stop. You guys are stupid. You like the way she fucks you! Damn, can we move on now? This is what I get for trying to talk sex with a bunch of musicians. And you ..." Sawyer says, pointing to me, "you know your music, which intrigues the hell out of me. You might just fit in after all."

Is it wrong that his compliment flushes my body with need? I hate this. I don't want to be attracted to Sawyer he's ... He's like the sin I don't ever want to repeat.

They start strumming a few chords, and I lean back against the couch, pulling my knees up to use as a makeshift desk in case I want to take some notes.

They sing their new song a few times. Noah was right; it's sad, but it's also beautiful. Their harmony is on point, and I'm blown away. If they kept doing this kind of music, they could tour another ten years and no one would tire of them.

Their lyrics trickle down to the end as their singing becomes even softer.

Your love is an illusion
Not given without strings
You can't be mine forever
Not while wearing his wedding ring
You're just an illusion
From a place deep in my mind
Where your love surrounds me
And withstands the test of time

"I think we've finally got it, you guys. That was great!" Noah exclaims, jumping up and high-fiving them all.

"Wow, I'm impressed, guys. I would have never known you had it in you to sing like that."

"Thanks, Mel. It's the title track to the album. It took Sawyer forever to write it, but he wanted it to be perfect, and he succeeded."

Noah beams like a proud brother should as he sings Sawyer's praises.

"You mean that was the song you wrote just after we met? Warren told me you had a breakthrough."

"Shouldn't surprise you, Princess. I mean, come on, from one writer to another, don't you ever get inspired at the most random of times and end up with your best work in just a few hours or days? It's the same for songwriting. Once you're inspired, it's all that matters."

"I guess that's true. So how do you decide?"

"Decide what?" Noah asks, inching closer to me.

"Correct me if I'm wrong, but when you're inspired, you write. And since you're artists and spend a lot of time traveling, I would assume you get inspired a lot. So how do you decide which songs are good?"

"They're all good," Sawyer states simply.

"Okay ... how do you decide which ones are good enough to go on your album and which ones sit in a vault of your undiscovered work fifty years down the road?"

"Sometimes, Sawyer comes up with a concept and we all decide we like it. Then we put our heads together and make it a song. Other times, Sawyer writes music and we do a blind vote to see if it's something we want to work with." Darren's explanation sounds simple enough, but they're artists, so there has to be more to it.

"And that's it? You just agree or you don't do it?"

"Pretty much, unless it's personal and one of us feels strongly about it, then we'll reassess," Wyatt adds with a shrug.

I'm jotting down notes here and there, enjoying the fact they're opening up to me fairly easily. Then I remind myself this is something they wanted, so it's not like they're being forced into it.

"Can I ask one more question, and then I'll be quiet so you can get back to practice?"

"Sure, Mel, ask away," Wyatt replies.

"Why Just an Illusion? What is the significance of it that you titled your tour, album, and title track all the same?"

Sawyer won't meet my eyes, and Darren and Wyatt turn to Noah, deferring to him.

"Our cousin Jordan had one of the most fucked up childhoods you could ever imagine. By the time he was seven, he was living with us. Growing up, he, Sawyer, and I were beyond tight."

He pauses and sets down his guitar with a sigh.

"Anyway, after all the shit that went down with him, he had this uncle on his dad's side of the family who kept in constant contact with him. He was a real cool dude, but he passed away a few years ago. He owned a bar, and the name of the bar is Just an Illusion."

Now we're getting somewhere.

"When he passed away, we bought the bar and gave it to Jordan."

"Sold," Sawyer corrects him.

"Yeah, I guess we technically sold it to him. He refused to accept it as a gift, so he makes monthly payments on it. So when we first started out, it's where we got our start. We worked our way up to

61

places like the Whisky and the Troubadour, but Just an Illusion was always our home, and our favorite place to play."

"So essentially, you're paying homage to your roots," I add for my own clarification.

"Pretty much. The big, private party in California in November is at the bar. Kind of a welcome back and a farewell all at once."

"Exactly. Now you know the big secret and we need to practice." Sawyer cuts us off, obviously uncomfortable with the topic.

For the next few hours, I sit and listen to them play. As much as it pains me to admit it, I think they've definitely got a new fan. All of the acoustic stuff is incredible.

Belle's Colorado Update

Slammers!

It's your girl Belle and I've got the 411 on last night's AMAZING BAD concert. It was off the hook! I'd been prepared for a different kind of BAD, and let me tell you, the Bastards did not disappoint! The teenage girl deep within me broke free and the grown-up, professional version of myself was nowhere to be found. I think I fangirled harder than I ever have before.

On a positive note, I found out there's a show in California that is going to be filmed and uploaded for free so you all can watch this tour again and again. It's BAD's way of giving back to all of you who have supported them throughout the years. Especially for those of you who aren't able to get one of the elusive tickets. Speaking of tickets, you will no longer be able to purchase more than two tickets per person for the shows. Originally, the limit was four, but due to the ridiculous amount of scalping going on at outrageous prices, BAD and their label have decided to put an even bigger cap on sales.

I can't wait to get back on the bus in a few weeks; a few days is not enough time to spend with my girl Mel! I miss her like crazy, but you all should know I got a sneak peek at her notes and this book is going to be HOT!

That's all for now.

Don't forget, live today like there's no tomorrow!

Xs and Os,

Belle

Getting To Know You

I've been on the bus for about three weeks now with the guys. We had our photo shoot which I was stressing over for nothing. It was a blast to watch the guys taking their photos; they're seasoned pros and know how to make it entertaining, for sure. Once it was my turn, every time the photographer went to snap my photo, Noah got behind him and did something to make me laugh. The pictures were some of the best I've ever taken in my life.

A few days later, they kicked off the tour in Colorado, and to say it was epic is an understatement. All five shows were completely sold out, the meet and greets were each filled to capacity, and the parking lots were overflowing with tailgaters who were content to listen to the music from afar when they couldn't get seats. The photos from the parking lots are some of the best I've taken, and they're really going to add another layer of depth to the story. This band is loved more than I could have ever imagined.

After Colorado, we went to New Mexico for another five days, and we just stopped in Arizona. Tonight and tomorrow, we're actually in a hotel so we can have some space, relax, and do our laundry. Well, technically, the hotel does our laundry, but it will be nice to have my own room for a couple of days.

Warren sent me a text a few minutes ago telling me he has me all checked in and needs to speak with me for a few minutes in my room.

"Hey, Mel, wait up!" Noah calls, running to catch up to me as I enter the hotel. I pause for a second until he's by my side.

"What room are you in?" he asks, bumping my shoulder a bit. The two of us have really started bonding the past few weeks. I think we're going to be friends long past the tour.

"2034. What room are you in?"

"2036. We have the whole floor, and there's security at all of the entrances and exits to the floor, so you'll need to keep your all-access pass with you."

"Warren already told me, but thanks for the reminder. I'm so excited to have some actual space to stretch out."

He looks at me with a frown. "Mel, if you want space just say the word. My room is yours whenever."

I'm not sure I'll ever get used to his sweet nature, but I love him for it. He's one of the few people I've ever met who doesn't have an agenda. He's genuinely a nice guy who likes doing things for people.

"It's okay. I mean *real* space. Your room is nice, don't get me wrong, but it's all of what … an eight-by-five-foot space?"

"About that," he answers with a grin.

"I'm looking forward to the thousand-foot suite I'm about to step into."

"Totally get it. We all usually keep it pretty low-key and enjoy our time apart, but sometimes it gets boring, so if you want to hang out just text me or knock on the wall or something."

"Thanks, I'll do that. And you, too. I mean, you know, if you're bored or want to hang out or something."

God, I'm an idiot sometimes.

"Thanks. Well, maybe I'll see you later," he says, leaving me at the open door to my room as he waves hello to Warren.

Warren actually hasn't been with us much. He came to the first show in Colorado and then had to fly back for some business, but from what I understand, he's here with us at least until we get back to California for Thanksgiving break.

"Amelia, how are you doing?"

I drop my backpack and purse down on the chair and sit next to him at the table.

"I'm doing well, how about you?"

"Couldn't be better. I won't take up much of your time, I just wanted to discuss schedules a bit. It's been decided that Thanksgiving will be at the Malibu house this year. It's large enough, and since everyone's family is local, it's an easy enough place to have a few days of down time."

"What does that mean for me?"

"Excellent question. You'll be staying there as well, and since it is the holidays and Belle is your family, she is going to stay there, too."

My answering smile alerts him to my happiness.

"I thought that might make you happy. We want you to enjoy the holidays, so even though you're working by observing, you are also under strict orders to enjoy yourself."

"I think I can do that."

"Great, now on to more business. Sunday, when we get back on the bus, I want you to start a rotation and keep it up until the end of the year."

"What kind of rotation are you looking at?"

Kelly

"I think it would be in all of your best interests to get to know each other better. Monday through Thursday, I want you to spend at least two uninterrupted hours a day with one of the guys."

"Alone?"

He can't be serious.

"Yes, alone. We'll juggle the buses if we have to so you have one bus for two hours with whatever band member is assigned that day. I've emailed you the schedule, that way the guys see it's coming from me and stick to it."

So much for safety in numbers. Two hours a day alone on a bus with Sawyer or Noah is going to be difficult to juggle, but I can do it.

"Alright, anything else?"

"Yes, I ... uh ... Well, I wanted to talk to you about sex."

"Sex?" I bust out laughing. "Warren, I've known about the birds and the bees for a long time. I'm pretty sure I've got sex down."

His cheeks turn crimson as he laughs with me.

"Amelia, I just wanted to say there are no rules in place with you and certain band members. I know them and there would be no point. However, I wanted to put it out there that if you should get involved with any of them, you need to be mindful of the consequences. You'll still be on the tour. If it should turn sour, it could make for an uncomfortable situation, as you well know."

His subtle reminder of my parents stings a bit, but I shake it off. I'm not them.

"Warren, above all else, my professionalism will remain intact no matter what may or may not happen with the guys. But for the record, I don't have plans to actively pursue *any* of them."

"Never thought you did, but I'm not so sure the same can be said for them. I should go, but I'll see you tomorrow at the show."

As Warren closes the door behind him, I flop down onto my bed and wonder what in the world he's been hearing through the grapevine to make him have that discussion with me. I pull up my email and review my new schedule. After practice each day, I'm slotted to spend two hours or longer—at our discretion—with the guys. Wyatt is Monday, Noah is Tuesday, Darren is Wednesday, and Sawyer is Thursday. There's also a note saying I can use the same time slot on Fridays to ride with the crew for a while if I'd like to talk with them.

Crew interviews are definitely on my list, along with interviewing Warren and the bus drivers. I'd bet my ass the bus drivers have some juicy bits they can contribute. Those would probably be for my enjoyment only.

My phone rings, and I practically jump off the bed. I'm still holding it in my hand, looking through my email, and wasn't expecting it to go off.

"Hey, Belle!"

"God, Mel, I miss you so much. Can I just live on the bus with you for the next year?"

I feel bad for her, touring with BAD would be her dream job.

"Actually, I've been thinking about that because I miss you like crazy."

"Okay, Lucy, what kind of scheme are you cooking up now?"

I laugh. Ever since we were kids, my grandma always called us Lucy and Ethel. Since I was the one way ahead of my age and full of bad ideas, I was forever getting Belle into trouble.

"Well, why don't you sell *Slammed* and Warren on a three-month end of the U.S. tour exclusive edition magazine? You can tour with us the last three months before we head overseas. *Slammed* would be exclusively covering all of the crazy excitement."

"Oh my god, Mel, you're fucking brilliant! I'm going to come up with an awesome pitch as soon as we get off the phone."

"I'm sure if you mention it to Darren, he might put in a good word for you as well."

"You're so sneaky. I love it! Oh, by the way, did they ever get that whole international part of your contract worked out? I can't believe it slipped through the cracks like that."

"Yeah, we did. Just this week, actually. So the way it works is the U.S. tour runs from October to October, which is what I was contracted for. The international part of the tour will go from January to March, so it's definitely shorter. I agreed to extend my contract for the three months for another sixty thousand *and* I'll get to do my London signing while I'm there."

"I'm so fucking proud of you, Mel. Have I told you that lately?"

"So many times, Belle," I answer softly.

"Hey, don't get all quiet on me. You're my sister in every way that matters, and I am forever going to be your biggest cheerleader, just like you'll always be mine."

"Always. Enough with the nostalgia. Have you talked to Darren lately?"

She sighs on the other end of the line, bringing a smile to my face.

"I like him way too much for my own good."

"Well, if it helps any, from what I've seen so far, he's a good guy."

"I know he is, and that's the problem. We text and talk every day, and tonight we're supposed to Skype since he'll have a bit more privacy in the hotel."

"Belle! Phone sex???"

"No, Skype sex. He's so amazing, Mel, I can't help it. I want him even when I can't have him. Don't get me wrong, I'm not in love with the guy or anything, but honestly, he's probably the best lover I've ever had."

Eww. Lover ... I hate that word. It's almost as bad as moist.

"I'm going to say two things. First, stop saying lover. That word makes me cringe. Second, in my opinion, it's a good sign a man would rather Skype sex with you than go out and get laid by an actual person. All he'd need to do is go to the lobby and point. I think he likes you, Belle."

"We'll see how it goes. I'm not sure I even want to fall in love with a rock star."

"Yeah, I hear you on that one." I've yet to fill her in on Noah's obvious affection toward me. There's no point. Nothing can happen.

"How are you *really* doing, Mel? I know it's only been a few weeks, but are you having flashbacks or nightmares or anything?"

"I'm fine. Really, this is nothing like it was before. I'm pretty sure I was freaked out for nothing."

"Good, but if anything happens, you let me know. I love you, and I'll see you next weekend!"

"Love you, too."

My afternoon flew by. I got my notes in order and typed up, went through all the pictures I took and sorted them into files, and was able to relax in a long, luxurious bath. Now I'm starving because I was enjoying my alone time so much I forgot about eating lunch.

Room service could be nice, and I've been dying to see *The Hunger Games* which is on demand in the room. I'm already comfortable in a tank top and some loose pajama pants, and the thought of getting dressed and seeing the sights really isn't high on my to-do list.

As I reach across the desk to grab the room service menu, there's a knock at the door. When I go and look, there's no one there. Now my phone's going off. *What the hell?*

Noah: Other door

With a laugh, I cross the room and open the adjoining door between the rooms.

"Are you bored yet?" he asks with a grin, and I motion for him to come in.

"What I am is starving, but I'm too comfortable to get dressed, so I'm thinking room service and a movie."

His eyes take in my attire quickly, and mine return the favor. He's barefoot in athletic shorts and a loose t-shirt.

"You do look pretty comfortable."

"So do you. Do you want to join me? Although, I do need to warn you, I've got my heart set on watching *The Hunger Games*."

"Cool. I've been wanting to see that, too. I'm down for a mellow night, especially since we have a show tomorrow."

After we order, he runs back to his room to be sure he locked his door. I can hear his voice, but I'm not trying to eavesdrop. He's most likely checking in with his guard or letting the guys know he's in for the night.

"So did you get Warren's email with the new schedule?" he asks when he comes back over.

"Yeah, I did. We had a talk about it earlier as well. Are you guys okay with it?"

"Of course, Mel. You need to relax. You're our employee, but you're also our guest. We want you here, and we know you're going to do a kickass job on this book. I can't wait to see how it turns out."

"Why did you decide you wanted to do this now? I'm sure people have wanted to tell your tale for years."

"We were waiting for you," he states simply.

"Are you going to ask me if I fell from heaven next?" I reply with a laugh.

He shakes his head. "Fate, Mel, it's all about fate. You were the one who was supposed to write our story. Other than that, if you want the other reasons, I guess it boils down to the timing was never right."

"Because you were young?"

"That's part of it. I mean, hell, we're still young but we're definitely more level-headed now than we ever were before. In the beginning, it was learning the ropes and the tricks of the trade, then we spent a few years flying high on fame, after that it was learning how to be who *we* wanted to be and not who everyone *else* wanted us to be. Does that make sense?"

"More than you could ever imagine."

"You're always so cryptic. Tell me about you. You don't have to tell me your deep, dark secrets yet unless you want to. But give me the cliff notes version of Amelia Greyson."

Talking about myself is not my strong suit.

"I'm pretty boring compared to you."

"Maybe I like boring, maybe boring is my thing, *maybe* boring really turns me on."

Why does he always make me laugh?

"Okay," I say, catching my breath. "Let's see how much I can turn you on. Growing up, I spent a lot of time with my grandma. My parents were always traveling for work, so when I didn't go with them I was with her."

"Keep going."

"Belle lived next door to my grandma, so we've known each other since about the third grade. She was pretty much my only friend because most of the time I was homeschooled or had tutoring."

"You never went to school?"

"Not until high school, and even then, only for a year. It was quite the adjustment. Belle had my back, though."

"College?"

"Yes, we both graduated from USC. I was an English major, and she majored in journalism. Since then, I've worked random administrative jobs while writing, and she did a few internships and finally landed at *Slammed*, where she's worked her way up."

"Do you see your parents and grandma often?"

"No," I answer, shaking my head. "My grandma passed away a few years ago, and my parents were both dead by the time I was sixteen."

"Mel, I'm so sorry." From the look on his face, he feels awful for asking.

"It's okay. My grandma was old and she lived a full life. My parents were reckless and suffered the consequences."

A knock on the door interrupts our discussion in the nick of time. After signing for the food, another room service cart arrives.

"I think you have the wrong room," I start to tell him, but Noah pays him and ushers him out.

"When did you order more food?"

With a wink, he pushes the second cart to the side of the bed and plugs something into the wall from under the cart.

"When I went back to my room to check my door. I'll show you what it is after we eat."

That explains who he was talking to.

70

As we're eating, we talk about random things. He talks about his sisters, Rory and Diane. Diane is married with two kids, and Rory just graduated college. His parents are still together and deeply in love.

"It must be nice to have your parents as sort of a role model for relationships," I say as I move over to the bed and grab the remote so we can start the movie. I pick the far side so he can sit next to his mystery electrical cart.

"It is. I think I have more romantic ideals about love and friendship. Sawyer used to, believe it or not. He just had a bad experience and closed himself off. Eventually, he'll find the right girl and open up again ... I hope."

"What about you?" I ask, turning toward him.

"I'm always open to love, but finding someone isn't exactly easy, you know?"

"Actually, I do. I've always wondered how celebrities find love and hold on to it. It's got to be difficult to figure out who's real." There's a sadness in my words. I feel like we've become friends, and I want more for these guys than fake-ass bitches.

"I've actually developed a pretty good bullshit radar these past few years," he quips, pulling me easily from my sudden funk.

"Good to know. I'll put it in my notes. Never bullshit Noah."

"So are you ready to see what's in my magical cart?"

Ready to be wowed, I nod enthusiastically as he stands, pulling off the tablecloth covering the cart with a flourish. There's a microwave and bags of microwave popcorn, Red Vines, Raisinets, and a variety of other movie-themed candy.

"The perks of being rich and famous," he says with a laugh.

"That's pretty awesome."

"Want something?" His eyes are twinkling with happiness.

"No, we just ate! How in the world can you still be hungry?"

"I was smart and saved room for dessert," he answers easily.

"Well, maybe if *someone* told me there was dessert, I would have saved room for it, too."

"Sorry, I wanted to surprise you. I'll tell you next time. Or maybe, in the future, you should always just assume there's a dessert option."

Next time ... He's totally flirting with me.

"Okay. Are you ready to start the movie? I'll let you know when I'm ready for dessert."

He nods and props himself up on the pillows next to me while eating sour straws.

About halfway through the movie, I decide I'm ready for some candy. I'm a sucker for licorice; I eat it all the time when I write.

"Noah, can you pass me the licorice?"

"You mean these Red Vines?" He's already got them in his hand and is bringing one to his mouth. "I guess I could share," he says as he takes a huge bite out of one and then feeds me the bottom of it.

His finger grazes the bottom of my lip when he puts it in my mouth. At first, I'm surprised, and when he does it again with the next piece, his finger lingers a bit longer, and my heart beats *a lot* faster. When I finish chewing, I turn my head toward him, and he reaches for the remote and pauses the movie.

For a brief moment, his piercing green eyes lock onto my mouth. He leans forward and briefly brushes our lips together.

They're soft and warm, and as he lowers his forehead against mine, he whispers, "Can I kiss you, Amelia?"

My heart races. No one has *ever* asked permission to kiss me before. It's the sweetest thing.

"Yes," I answer breathlessly as his hand weaves through my hair, pulling me closer to him by the back of my head.

Again, his lips brush against mine so softly I can hardly breathe with the anticipation of what his kiss will feel like. Gently, he tugs my bottom lip into his mouth and sucks. He tastes so good, and I want more of him. His tongue traces the outside of my lip before I open enough to let him inside. When our tongues finally meet, our kiss is soft and sweet as we learn our rhythm. The deeper I'm pulled into our kiss, my whimpers fill his mouth as his pleasurable moans fill mine.

After a few moments, he pulls back. We're both breathless, exhilarated.

"Thank you," he whispers softly, looking deep in thought.

So deep I begin to panic. Maybe he regrets kissing me, or worse, maybe he knows Sawyer kissed me already and he feels guilty. *Shit.*

"Was that okay, Mel? Tell me the truth, you won't hurt my feelings." His words pull me from my own panicked thoughts, and I realize I never replied when he thanked me.

"Yes, it was perfect," I answer truthfully. I'm not sure I've ever been kissed like that before. So passionately and yet not rushed or overly sexual, it was … dare I say … romantic. Shit it *was* romantic. My heart pounds in my chest, not from the exhilaration of the kiss but from fear of blowing a good start on this job before it even really gets started.

"You're tense," he says, pulling back a bit from me. "Shit, Mel, I'm sorry ... I wasn't thinking ... I've just ... Never mind, it doesn't matter. I've obviously crossed a line, and I'm sorry."

"No, it's not like that, really. That was nice ... really nice."

He relaxes a bit and sighs. "I've wanted to kiss you since that first night on the beach. Hell, I wanted to kiss you when you told Sawyer off."

Again, he makes me laugh, and it lightens the mood a bit.

"Noah, I'm not a random hookup kind of girl. I used to be a long time ago, but I've worked hard to try and grow into someone who has more self-respect."

He leans back onto his pillow and pulls me into the nook of his arm. It's awkward and comfortable all at the same time.

"Being on the road is hard. We're propositioned more than any normal person. Inevitably, at some point tonight or tomorrow, some bold fan will make her way up to our rooms and Mac and the rest of the security team will have to kick them out of the hotel. It sucks. We never want to have fans removed, but we're regular people and we'd like regular lives."

I love that he's comfortable enough to confide in me. So much, in fact, I relax in his arms.

"I can understand that."

"I'm sure you can, and unfortunately, you're going to see it. And you're bound to get some haters because you're with us every day. It's absolutely ridiculous, but it also comes with the territory."

"Don't worry about me, I can handle petty women and haters."

He looks down at me with a small smile. "Somehow, I don't doubt that at all. The truth is, Mel, I like you. I like you more than anyone in a long time. I'm not sure how that makes you feel, especially with your job, and if you say the word, I'll back off."

I let his words ruminate for a minute before answering him, but my silence doesn't seem to bother him at all.

I'm positive he doesn't know about Sawyer kissing me, and I don't know if I should tell him. I'm sure it was just Sawyer being Sawyer, and while it was hot and gave me the feels, I knew right away it could never be more than a hot hookup.

With Noah, on the other hand, it *could* be more. Since we met seven weeks ago, we've progressively gotten to know each other. Our personalities click, and there's no lack of attraction. On the contrary, he's one of the most beautiful men I've ever met—inside and out. But this is my job, and I don't want to screw it up if I'm making a mistake.

Belle's voice creeps into my mind, telling me what she always does. *Live each day as if it's your last, Mel. You never know when it will be.*

"I like you, too, Noah. More than I should."

"Do I hear a but coming?" he asks lightly.

"Maybe. I do worry about my job, about causing tension on the bus, about our feelings being fleeting and the possibility of eleven months of hostility between us if it doesn't work out. In fact, that's my biggest fear."

Honesty is the best policy, but I need to talk to Sawyer. I'm not sure it's my place to tell Noah he kissed me. I do find it odd Sawyer didn't mention it or brag about it. He seems like the type who would gloat over kissing "the princess." Then again, since he didn't actually nail me, maybe it's a loss in his book. Either way, Noah should know.

"That won't happen. I'd never be hostile to you, or anyone for that matter, unless you gave me a reason to. And by reason, I mean crazy things like stalking or sleeping with my friends or brother," Noah adds in a serious tone.

"Oh my god, I'd never do that!"

Kissing isn't the same as sleeping.

He chuckles lightly. "I didn't think you would, but some girls are happy to hop between us. We don't let them. At least, not anymore."

He doesn't even need to explain that one; I totally get it.

"The truth is, I'm tired of being alone. I want a relationship, I want to find someone to love, who loves me for me. That doesn't mean I'm in love now or you need to be my girlfriend. It just means I'm looking for someone who wants the same things, no matter how long it takes to get there, *even if* it doesn't work out in the end. I just don't want a fling."

"So, in other words, we can take this slow and there's no pressure."

Why am I even considering this?

Because he's amazing.

"None whatsoever," he confirms.

"Okay, we can try, but we need to be cautious. I can't have this backfire on me, and my reasons go far deeper than just my job."

He pulls me in a little closer and grabs the remote. Before unpausing the movie, he lightly kisses the top of my head.

"I'm happy to go as slow as you want, Mel. But for this to work, someday you're going to have to let me in. Whatever your past is, it's not going to change what I think of you. Whatever happened back then contributed to who you are now, and I happen to like this girl."

74

He doesn't wait for me to reply, just presses play and snuggles me close.

The next thing I know, my phone is ringing and the sun is streaming in through the slit in the heavy curtains. Except I quickly realize it isn't my phone, and I'm still tucked into the crook of Noah's arm. I can't believe we fell asleep like this and slept all night without waking up.

I shake his arm gently, but he's dead to the world. Sawyer was right, not much wakes him up. After sitting up, I push him harder, and his phone stops ringing.

"Noah, wake up. Come on, wake up." I'm half laughing and half groaning trying to get him to rouse, to no avail. Just when I'm about to give up, his arm wraps around me and pulls me back down to him.

I glance over and see his eyes are still closed but he's grinning.

"I'm a sound sleeper, Mel, but not that sound. I was comfortable before the phone started ringing, and what I'm doing right now is more important than answering Darren's call about breakfast."

"A ... How do you know it was Darren, and B ... what are you doing right now?"

"A ... I know it was Darren because he's the only one who calls me to go eat breakfast while we're in hotels, and B ... I'm enjoying getting to know my future ex-wife."

He said that with such a straight face, but I can't stop myself from laughing hysterically.

"Don't tell Darren you're laughing about breakfast. He takes it pretty seriously."

Oh my god. How is he funny this early in the morning?

"So if I'm your future ex-wife, why do we split up?"

"Well, after many years as my beautiful trophy wife, you fall into the arms of a former boy band phenom, Eli Watts, when he sings your favorite teenage love ballad to you at our twentieth anniversary party."

My body stiffens; I know he's joking, but I can't breathe. There's no way he could know about me and Eli, but it hits a little too close to home.

"Mel, hey, you know I'm kidding, right? If I ever were lucky enough to make you my wife, there's no way I'd let you fall into Eli's skeevy clutches."

Fuck, my eyes are tearing up, and all I can do is squeeze them shut and take a few deep breaths. Noah shifts and rolls me to my side.

"Hey ... I'm sorry. I'm not sure what it was, but I didn't mean to upset you and make you cry. Please look at me." When I open my eyes, my eyelashes are wet but only a single tear falls. Noah is lying on his side, facing me, with a concerned look on his face. Gently, he wipes the tear from my face. "Can you tell me why you're upset?"

I don't want him to know about me and Eli. He might piece more of my puzzle together than I want him to. But I can't hide forever, and it's only one small part of a bigger story. I really don't want him thinking Eli broke my heart—even if he did—or I'm some stupid fangirl of Eli's stupid band, either.

"No matter what happens with us, Noah, if we ever date, or if anything goes further, you should know I'd never, *not ever*, leave you for Eli fucking Watts."

"Do you know Eli, Mel?" he asks softly, never breaking his gaze from mine. I've always been a sucker for eyes, and Noah's are no exception.

"Yeah, you could say that."

"Do you want to elaborate?"

"No."

"Would you anyway?" His pleading tone is my undoing.

"If I do, will you promise me you won't Google anything or tell anyone about it until I'm ready to talk about everything else?"

"I'd never tell anyone anything you tell me. Our talks are between us ... always. I'm not a fan of Googling anyone because I know how bad even I look on the Internet."

"So you're a saint?" I say, teasing him, trying to lighten the mood a bit.

He shrugs his shoulders. "Depends on what you believe, I guess."

Noah runs his arm down mine softly, and his hand lands on my hip. He pulls me a little bit closer and whispers, "Tell me why I made you cry because I don't ever want to be the cause of your tears again."

I've never met anyone as considerate as Noah.

"About fourteen years ago, I used to date Eli Watts. It lasted for a bit, and then it was over."

The wheels are turning in his head. He doesn't seem surprised, but he's definitely thinking over what he just heard.

"You dated Eli Watts when you were fourteen? For how long?"

"Long enough."

"Mel, did you ... I can't even believe I'm about to ask you this, but did you sleep with him?"

This is the embarrassing part, although back then it was pretty awesome.

"Yes, Eli was my first. But just to clarify, we didn't actually sleep together until I was fifteen."

He releases me and rolls onto his back. His eyes flutter closed, and for a while, all I do is watch the rise and fall of his chest as my bombshell sinks in.

I'm not sure how much time passed—it could have been five minutes or it could have been an hour—but eventually, he asks me the one question I knew was coming and didn't want to answer.

"I'm sorry, Mel. I know this is going to make me sound like a total and complete dick, but I have to know. Do you make a habit of sleeping with and dating musicians?"

Ouch. His words sting, but they're not surprising. I'd ask, too.

"I'm not the person I was back then, but to answer your question, Eli was the only musician I ever dated, but he wasn't the only one I ever slept with."

"You lost your virginity to a *pop star god*. Shit, I can't even believe I'm going to ask you this, but was it your best sex ever?"

"The first time, no, we were kids. He was almost year older than me, but I looked older than him. I'm not sure if he was *the* best, but he was one of the better partners I've had."

"You know, if we ever sleep together, I'm going to blow that little twat out of the water, don't you?"

The huskiness of his voice turns me on. He flips back on his side and pulls me toward him, wordlessly crushing his lips to mine. This time, there's no hesitation, and I open to him immediately. While his tongue leads mine in a sexy game of chase, his hands slide under my shirt and across my breasts. My body arches into his touch and my leg wraps around his hip instinctively.

When he flicks my nipple, I groan even louder, wanting so much more of him than he's giving me right now. His mouth leaves mine, traveling down my neck as he lifts my shirt higher. When his soft lips gently meet my nipples, I'm lost, and when his tongue dances around them as he squeezes my breasts, I'm in ecstasy.

Sadly, as quickly as it started, he pulls away, gently pulling my shirt back down. He places a soft kiss on my lips and leans his forehead against mine.

"I want you," he whispers softly.

"You've got me," I answer back breathlessly.

"Not like this. Second base is enough for today. You're not some random girl for me, Mel. I meant what I said last night. I want to get to know you. We should take this slow."

"Okay."

"Are you disappointed?"

"Yes ... no ..."

"Yeah. Me, too." He pulls back and adjusts himself in his shorts. He's got a nice package.

"Perv," he says as I wiggle my eyebrows at him.

"Can't blame a girl for checking out the goods."

"Thankfully, I have some nice goods for you to check out." That's sexy. He's confident in his size and doesn't need an ego check to confirm it's as big as he assumes.

"Yes, nice goods are definitely a perk."

Out of nowhere, I begin feeling guilty I haven't told him about Sawyer. After the comment he made last night about girls friend and family hopping, it bothered me. But now that he knows about my past with musicians, I *have* to tell him. I can only pray it doesn't cause an issue. Even if it does, it's better to do it now before I'm in too deep.

Or before it bites me in the ass.

"Noah, there's something I need to tell you. I wasn't sure if you knew already, and I didn't want to wreck the mood, but I don't feel right keeping it inside."

"Should I be worried?"

"Not about me, but maybe? Honestly, Noah ... I don't know ... I wish I'd said something last night."

As I pull myself up and prop myself against the back of the headboard, he follows my lead.

"Why do I have a feeling I'm not going to like this?"

Because you're not.

"I'm not the girl I used to be before. You have to believe me when I say that."

He nods but doesn't reply.

"The first night we met, after we came back from talking on the beach, do you remember when I went to use the bathroom?"

"Yeah, and Warren sent you to Sawyer's room?"

"Yes. Sawyer kissed me in the bathroom."

"What?" He jumps up and starts pacing the room.

"I didn't even know he was there. He pulled me into the dark room, called me Princess, and the next thing I knew, his lips were on mine."

"Did you kiss him back?"

"Yes, but I was caught up in the moment, and I stopped it after a few seconds."

"Shit, Mel, this is bad. I mean, *really* bad. Fuck!"

"I'm sorry. At first, I thought maybe you knew, and then the more I thought about it, I realized you didn't. The kiss didn't mean anything to me, but I still didn't feel as if it were my place to tell you. But now that you know some of my history, I didn't want you thinking I was still that girl ... because I'm not."

He softens somewhat, but he's still upset.

"I know you aren't, Mel, but this is ... Well, there's no other way to say it. This is fucked up. I've got to go talk to Sawyer. I'll see you later."

When he walks out, I know I won't be seeing him anytime soon.

After their show, I went to the hotel bar and had a few drinks. Three wonderful margaritas later, I figured I better get to my room before I surpassed pleasantly drunk. Unfortunately for me, before the elevator doors could shut, Sawyer and a random groupie stepped in.

Great, this is all I need.

It's no big shock she's draped all over him, practically fucking him in the elevator. He lifted his eyebrow in greeting when he got in but never took his lips off of hers. It doesn't bother me, but this is the first time I've seen Sawyer with a woman, so I guess I'm just a little surprised.

Where is his bodyguard, and why are his eyes open? My random, drunken thoughts occupy my mind while we ascend to our floor and help me keep my eyes and ears off of them.

As the elevator doors open, they walk out ahead of me and he turns his head, perversely eyeing me up.

"Could have been you, Princess." The girl laughs, assuming he means tonight.

"Thanks for turning him down," she tosses over her shoulder as they make their way down the hall. Never have I been so glad I've been out of this scene for years than I am right now.

Once I finally get my door open and make it inside, I realize I'm a little bit drunker than I thought. When I trip over my own feet and start to fall fast, I know it's going to hurt and pray the tequila numbs the pain. Except I never hit the ground. Instead, I'm caught just inches from the floor by colorful, tattooed arms.

Noah.

"Jesus, Mel, are you okay?" Is it wrong the concern in his voice makes me swoon a bit? In a good way, not in a drunk way, although

I'm probably doing some of that, too, since I fell as soon as I walked in the door.

"Sure, I'm fine. Thanks for saving me, but why are you in my room? Actually, how are you in my room? Is this your rock star influence again?"

"Are you drunk?" he asks, leading me to the bed so I don't fall again.

"Maybe a little bit?" I hold my fingers to his face, spread apart an inch so he can see how little drunk I am.

"What did you drink?"

"Geez, dad, relax. I only had three margaritas down at the bar."

"The ones that come in fishbowls?" he asks incredulously.

"Well, they didn't seem *that* big after the first one."

"You're going to hate yourself in the morning. Why did you go drink alone?"

"You never came back," I tell him flatly.

Shoot, I probably shouldn't have said that.

"I know," he says softly as he removes my shoes.

"It's okay, I didn't think you would. You don't owe me anything."

When he stands, he turns around and walks to the mini bar. Maybe he's going to get drunk with me.

"Damn, you have a nice ass." Drunk Mel apparently has zero filter on her mouth.

"Nice to know it's appreciated." He walks back over to the bed and hands me a bottle of water and some ibuprofen. Then he opens a beer and drinks it quietly while sitting next to me.

"I'm sorry." I can't make eye contact with him; I'm too ashamed, but he needs to know how bad I feel.

"You don't have to be sorry. You shouldn't have been in this situation in the first place."

"You didn't come back," I repeat like the drunk girl I am, and his chuckle makes me smile.

"You said that already. I wanted to come back. It took me forever to find Sawyer and even longer to talk to him. Once we'd worked through it all, it was time to rehearse and I thought I'd see you there. That's when I realized my phone was dead. As soon as the show was over, I came back here. I've been waiting for you ever since."

"You came back—" His mouth covers mine, and I open for him eagerly. His hands cup my cheeks while we kiss. It's slow and decadent, and I feel myself falling into an abyss. One I haven't traveled into in a very long time. One which always leads straight down the road to heartbreak, but this time I don't care. Noah Weston can break my heart into a million pieces if it means I get to feel like this along the way.

When he breaks off the kiss, he stands and takes off his clothes down to his underwear. He walks to my door and locks it, turning off the lights on his way back. Then he goes to his room and I assume does the same. Upon his return, he helps me stand and carefully undresses me down to my bra and panties.

"Lie down, Mel," he tells me firmly as his gaze follows my curves from top to bottom. I do as he says, and he climbs into bed after me and turns off the bedside light. I'm surprised when he pulls me into a spooning position and kisses the top of my head.

"Go to sleep."

"Aren't we going to have sex?" I'm so disappointed.

"Absofuckinglutely, but not tonight. You're drunk, and tomorrow I need to tell you about *my* past. Until then, we sleep. Sweet dreams, Amelia."

Amelia ... I love when he calls me that.

"Sweet dreams, tight buns." I feel him chuckling behind me as I close my eyes and drift off into never never land.

In the morning, I'm awakened by Noah's fingers tracing a line softly up and down my arm. My head hurts but probably not as bad as it should.

"Good morning, sleepyhead."

"Morning," I reply before promptly covering my mouth and jumping out of bed. "I'll be right back."

As I run into the bathroom to brush my teeth and use the facilities, his laugh trails behind me. While I'm in there, I throw on my pajamas I left on the counter from the morning before, too.

"Better?" he asks when I walk back out. It's only now I notice he's already back in his clothes from last night and there's a room service cart in the doorway between our rooms.

"Much."

"Good. Let's get some grease in you and make sure you start your day off right. I ordered coffee, orange juice, pancakes, waffles, sausage, bacon, eggs, and fruit." When he walks over to get the cart, memories from last night wash over me.

"Oh God, I talked about your ass last night." I'm mortified. I really didn't think I was that drunk.

"Among other things, but don't worry, I won't hold it against you. Just promise me next time you won't drink without me. I think we could have a lot of fun getting drunk together."

Next time ...

The first thing I do is pour myself some coffee.

"Do you remember last night, or should I refresh your memory?"

"I'm good. I'm pretty sure I remember everything. Ugh ... Including Sawyer and his groupie."

"You saw Sawyer?" Nodding, I fill him in on my brief but disgusting encounter with his manwhore brother.

"Well, that's Sawyer." His demeanor is off; something is bothering him.

"You said you wanted to talk today. Now is probably the best time since we have to be back on the bus in a few hours."

"Let's eat first, and then I'll tell you everything."

We mostly eat in silence. Ever since I mentioned Sawyer, his attention is fleeting. The food is good, but I'm dreading the conversation. After I can't eat another bite, I lean back in my chair and continue to nurse my coffee.

"Sawyer and I tend to be attracted to the same type of women, and about seven years ago, we were almost torn apart by one."

I guess it's time to talk.

"I'm sorry. It must have been difficult for the two of you."

"It was difficult for everyone. We thought we were going to have to give up the band at one point."

"So what happened to drive the two of you so far apart? You seem pretty close to me."

"We are now, probably closer than we ever were before Marilyn. See, back then, we probably deserved a lot of the things that were said about us. We were twenty-one, flying on the wings of fame, and at times, alcohol and an illicit substance or two."

I nod for him to continue, and he pauses. "This is for you ... Mel, my friend. Not for Amelia, the author."

"Noah, I'd never put anything in the book without your permission. Besides, I thought we clarified yesterday our talks are between us."

"Yeah, I know, but this was ... no, it *is* something extremely personal to us all."

After this, I might feel obligated enough to tell him my story.

"Don't worry, your secret is safe with me. I promise."

When he pulls me from the chair and leads me to the bed and spoons me, I realize how hard of a story this is for him to tell.

"Marilyn used to be a bartender at Just an Illusion. She was a good friend, and she always had our backs when we used to play there. When we got our record deal, we ended up staying in touch. She and I would text often, and one summer we decided we wanted more, so I brought her on tour with us."

I already know this is going to end badly; the sadness in his voice is unmistakable.

"Back then, all of us were on one bus and we reserved the back room for hookups. I knew by the time Marilyn started touring with us I was in love with her. Once we started spending every day together, I fell deeper and deeper in love. I *thought* she was in love with me, too."

I pull his hand off of my waist and lace my fingers through his. He sounds like he needs all the support he can get.

"Anyway, what I didn't know was she and Sawyer had history. They'd hooked up a few times, and he had legitimate feelings for her. Every one of us were friends with her, even Anna. So if someone offhandedly mentioned talking to her or having texted her, nobody thought anything of it.

"Sawyer had changed when she came on the bus. I thought he was just irritated at being even more cramped, or maybe it was because he was using more drugs." He squeezes my hand a bit harder. "One night, we'd all been out partying, and Marilyn and I had a huge fight. I was drunk, but she'd been doing coke with Sawyer and Darren. I'm not even sure what we were fighting about now, that's how fucked up we were. I ended up sleeping on a different bus with one of the other bands. In the morning, when I got back on our bus, I could feel the tension. Darren and Wyatt wouldn't even look at me. Then, when I walked back to my bunk, I heard the two of them going at it in the bedroom."

"That's awful, Noah."

"It was. I was so furious I kicked the door in. When I saw them with my own eyes, it was as if I'd been sucker punched. My own brother, my fucking twin, was going at it with my girlfriend. I made the bus stop, and I got out and walked for miles. We were in New Mexico at the time, but we all shared a condo back in Santa Monica. I took a cab to the airport and flew home. By the time the guys found me the next day, I'd lost it. I'd been drinking non-stop and cried more tears than I'll ever admit."

"Because of Sawyer," I state matter of factly.

"Exactly. As much as I loved Marilyn, she could never cause the kind of pain Sawyer did. It wasn't until Darren and Wyatt sobered me up a bit that I started asking questions. Marilyn lied and told Sawyer I broke up with her. She was so high, maybe she thought I did. Who knows? She and Sawyer were so coked up they fell into old patterns. Patterns I never knew existed because neither of them ever told me. I felt betrayed, and my heart was broken. It took a week before I could even talk to Sawyer." His words are heavily weighted with the residual pain and anger he must still feel when he thinks about it.

"Why didn't Sawyer tell you he had feelings for her? That they had a past? I thought you two were close."

"Sawyer has a hard time expressing his feelings to anyone, including me. Admittedly, he's gotten much better at communicating with me since all of this happened. When the two of us finally talked, he explained how resentful he'd been when Marilyn and I started dating. He'd been angry with both of us, and it's why his drug use became more frequent. I never knew he'd had feelings for her. If I had, I would have never pursued her. Unfortunately, Sawyer assumed I had figured it out and put my feelings for her above us. That's how everything turned into such a clusterfuck."

Finally, I flip over so I can see him when he talks to me. "Didn't he know you'd never do that to him?"

"I thought so, but the drugs clouded his judgement. After that, we both got clean and our relationship has only gotten stronger. We've always been close, connecting at a deeper level than just brotherly love or best friends. I'm guessing it's because we're twins because he's the only person I have that kind of bond with. Eventually, we both realized how that bitch played us against each other and swore we'd never let another girl get between us."

"So we'll be just friends then?" *Damn, those words are painful to say.*

"Well, that's what I had to find out yesterday. If Sawyer had feelings for you, there's no way I could get involved with you."

"What happened when you found him?"

"After he kicked the groupie out of his room, we talked. I could tell I caught him off guard when I asked him if he kissed you. He said he did and it was hot, but it was only something to do in the moment. I didn't believe him. There's something about the way he said how hot it was that made me think it meant more to him."

It was off-the-charts hot.

"It didn't mean more to me, but I don't want to come between the two of you. It's better to nip it in the bud now before it goes any further. I'm sorry, Noah, but I'm so glad I told you when I did."

"Hey now, don't write me off just yet. Sawyer and I talked for a long time, and what finally convinced me it didn't mean anything to him was the fact he didn't tell me. Sawyer isn't a bragger and he hooks up with girls all the time. We never know about it unless we see them together. If it would have meant something, he would have told me."

"So what does that mean?"

His finger traces my lip slowly before he moves in closer. "It means I like you, Amelia, and with Sawyer's blessing, I'm going to enjoy getting to know you."

My stomach flutters as his lips meet mine. I've got a feeling Noah Weston is about to spin my whole world on its axis.

Breaking Routines

Yesterday, when we got back on the bus, Sawyer went straight to his room and didn't come out for hours. I think his extra-curricular activities the past few days wore him out. Noah and I hung out and watched a movie, but I spent most of the day working after that.

This morning, I woke up a bit later than normal and decided to shower before relaxing with a cup of coffee. Noah's door was still closed when I put my clothes away, but Sawyer is up and writing furiously in a notebook. He must be feeling inspired this morning.

"Good morning," I tell him as I pick my coffee and grab a mug.

He nods his head as a greeting but doesn't say a word. I know what it's like to be inspired like that, so I keep quiet and think about my upcoming day with Wyatt.

Normally, Noah and I work out after their practices, but that's my scheduled meeting time with the guys now, so maybe I'll start going in the morning instead and shower on that bus.

About an hour later, Sawyer is still writing. Noah said a brief good morning to us and hopped in the shower. As I'm looking for my headphones on my bed, Noah comes out of the shower. Still wrapped in his towel, he pulls me into his bedroom and closes the door.

"How long has Sawyer been writing?" His demanding tone catches me off guard. I was excited about him being half-naked.

"He was writing when I got up … so at least two hours that I know of. Why?"

Frustration fills his features but he shakes it off. "No reason, really. Sometimes when he gets intense like that it means he's upset about something. Most likely he's just journaling."

"Sawyer journals?"

"Yeah, all the time. His therapist taught him how to journal as a coping mechanism. All part of what he went through when we were kids."

"Oh … Well, if it helps."

"Hey," he says, grabbing me around the waist and pulling me close. "I'm sorry I can't tell you more, but this one is his story to tell, not mine."

"It's fine, Noah, really. I don't expect you guys to tell me all of your secrets."

"Oh yeah?" he says, leaning in so close his lips are just a breath away from mine. "What if I *want* you to know all my secrets, Mel? What if I said I want you to know every single thing there is to know about me?"

I raise my arms above his head and wrap them behind his neck, closing the miniscule gap between us. When I bring my lips to his, he pulls me tighter to him, close enough to feel him harden under his towel.

I want him so much.

As his tongue meets mine, I let my hand slide down his arm and then between us. His dick is hard, and my body aches for his touch. With a deep inhale, he pulls away slightly, dropping his head against mine.

"Amelia, what are you doing?"

"I'm getting intimately acquainted with one of your biggest secrets."

"Well, I did say I wanted you to know me." His breathing increases when I wrap my hand around him and begin stroking his cock.

"You did." I'm excited to know this part of him.

With more willpower than I've ever seen, he gently pushes my hand away.

"I'd say this qualifies as third base, wouldn't you?"

"Mmhm."

Fuck third base. I want a home run.

Noah tips my head up and locks his gaze onto mine. "Our first time isn't going to be on this bus. I want more than this for our first time. How about we go to the gym and work off our frustrations instead?"

My eyes peruse his body again. It would be so easy to flick his towel open and see him in all of his glory.

"Don't even think about it," he says, backing away and reaching into his drawer for a pair of boxers, which he puts on like a kid in gym class under his towel.

"You're taking all the fun out of this." I'm pouting, but I don't care. I like Noah, and I haven't had sex with a man in a really long time.

"That's where you're wrong. I'm bringing the fun into this. Think about the anticipation, about how badly you want this, about *how many* orgasms I'm going to give you when we finally do have sex."

"Not if B.O.B. has anything to say about it," I reply with an exaggerated sigh. His eyes twinkle in understanding as he inches closer to me until I'm leaning against the bed.

"Sit," he commands, and when I do, he straddles me, pushes me down flat on the mattress, and holds my hands above my head.

"Do you have a vibrator on this bus, Mel?"

"Maybe you should read my book and tell me what you think," I counter while enjoying this fully submissive position he has me in.

"I've read your book, but I'm still not sure I think you're bold enough to pack a vibrator on a bus full of rock stars."

"You've read my book?

That's such a turn on.

"Oh yeah. I started it the day after I met you, and I read it in one sitting. It was good, it was real, and it was sexy as fuck."

"You're sexy as fuck," I whisper breathlessly as he continues to hold me down. A few minutes of silence pass as he keeps me locked underneath him.

Finally, with a raised brow, he speaks, "You *do* have a vibrator on the bus. Damn, that's hot."

"I'm not sure about hot, but it's totally necessary. No straight woman could be on tour with four seriously attractive men and not have one. Especially since you really should be off limits. I *do* have a job to do after all."

He leans down and gives me a quick kiss, and then releases me so he can finish getting dressed.

"And you'll do it amazingly, I have no doubt. As for your friend B.O.B., I suppose he can stay on the bus for now, but I'd prefer, sometime in the very near future, *all* your orgasms come from me."

Me, too.

"Well, maybe B.O.B. can join us on occasion."

"Don't tease me with a good time unless you mean it, woman," he says, groaning as he finishes tying his shoes. "Go put your shoes on if you want to come with me. The bus is going to stop in a few minutes."

"How do you know?"

"This is when Wyatt and Darren work out."

"Okay, I'll go change really quick. I can't exercise in jeans."

Fifteen minutes later, we're all on the training bus. I've never been on here with all of them before. This should be interesting. Normally, I listen to music on my iPhone when I exercise, but since

I've been working out with Noah, he puts his phone on the Bluetooth system.

He keeps the mix pretty good, so I don't really mind. Today, Sawyer is controlling the music, and from what he's played so far, he must have some serious aggression to work out. Even the guys notice, but they simply exchange glances and shrug it off. Apparently, no one wants to mess with Sawyer when he's in a bad mood.

One good part about everyone being here at the same time is being able to observe them. Typically, I work up to a run pretty quickly on the treadmill, but today I'm enjoying a nice brisk walk while listening to them talk.

"Darren, did you invite her to the party yet?" Wyatt asks as he spots him on the weight bench.

"She's going to be there already, dipshit. She's the one writing the articles. Why would I need to invite her?"

"Uh, maybe so she'll realize you're into her?"

"This isn't high school, Wyatt. I'm sure from the way she screams my name she knows I'm into her."

"Mel, what do you think? Should he tell Belle he's into her?"

Oh hell, why am I getting dragged into this?

"Yeah, Princess, why don't you tell him the *proper* way to show a girl you're into her?" Sawyer is extra snarky today, and I'm starting to take it personally. He's probably pissed at me for telling Noah about our kiss.

"Sorry, guys, I'm not a relationship guru."

"No, but you are a Belle guru. If anyone knows her, you do," Noah kindly points out.

"Alright, you want my opinion? Here it is … Belle likes to have fun, so if you're having fun, keep it the way it is. If you want more and you seriously want to attempt a relationship, then show her. Ask her to the party as your date. Let her know you want her there *with* you and not just so she can write an article."

"Then what?" This time, it's Darren actually asking.

"Then let her know how you feel. She's not a mind reader, and you're a famous rock star. She's going to assume this is fun until you tell her otherwise. She's not a deluded fan who's going to jump to conclusions and assume you want to date just because she's banged your bongo a few times."

"For someone who wrote a book about sex, you sure do have issues with saying fuck," Sawyer growls.

"Fuck you, Sawyer." The words fly out of my mouth without a second thought. At least he grins this time, but it's more menacing than pleasant.

"Already missed your chance at that, didn't you, Princess?"

"Dude, Sawyer, what the hell?" Now Noah is pissed and in Sawyer's face, and that is the last thing I want.

"Relax, Noah, I'm just kidding. Sorry, Princess, I didn't mean anything by it." He almost looks sincere. Noah's eyes dart back and forth between Sawyer and me.

"It's fine, Sawyer. I know you're just being you," I concede.

"See," he says turning back to Noah. "You need to lighten up, Noah. She might be a princess but she doesn't need *anyone* to save her."

Without giving Noah a chance to reply, Sawyer stalks off into the bathroom. A minute later, the shower turns on.

"He's in an exceptionally bad mood today," Wyatt comments, shaking his head.

"Yeah, totally, and I saw him with at least three different chicks at the hotel. Getting laid usually calms him down for a few weeks. What gives?" Darren saw him with three different girls? I'm not really surprised, but damn.

This is a conversation I'm not getting into. It's up to Noah if he wants to say anything. When he looks at me, I shrug in response.

"Look, guys, Mel and I are sort of seeing each other," he confesses. They exchange knowing looks and laugh.

"We kind of thought so, but what's that have to do with Sawyer?" Wyatt asks, confused.

"Sawyer kissed Mel the night we all met."

"What the hell?" Darren bites out, obviously pissed. At least I know Belle didn't say anything, not that I ever thought she would.

"It's fine. He and I talked it out and we're all good. I think it just brought up memories of Marilyn, and you know how he gets when he thinks about her. He's been journaling all morning, too."

"Ah, okay. We'll just let him work it out of his system for the next few days then."

"That's probably a really good idea," Noah tells Darren, even though he seems a million miles away.

It's Thursday—my first official one-on-one interview with Sawyer. I'm nervous. He's still keeping his distance, but he was a bit nicer to me yesterday. So far, the individual interviews are going great; I'm learning a lot about the guys. My day with Noah was half interview, half making out. It was fun, but next time it needs to be more professional.

Today is also the fourth day in a row we've all worked out on the bus together. Each day they rotate whose music we listen to. I don't think they wanted to hear Sawyer's angry music all week.

"Hey, Mel, give me your phone." Noah holds out his hand and I pass him my phone, curious as to why he wants it.

"Where's that playlist you're always listening to when you work?"

"Why?"

"Because today is your playlist day," he says, scrolling through all my different lists.

"You guys don't want to hear my playlist, trust me. It's just a mix of random stuff."

"Doesn't matter, it's your turn," he counters.

"Tit for tat, huh?" I ask him with a wink.

"Exactly," he replies as he turns the phone to me and waits for me to pick the right one.

"Alright, but don't say I didn't warn you," I caution as I press the list.

With a smile, Noah messes with my phone until he gets it synced to the Bluetooth on the bus. When he presses play, the first song is NSYNC's *I Want You Back*. I thought for sure they'd make fun of me, but instead, what unfolded next is probably one of the best things I've ever seen.

All four of them, including Sawyer, started singing along. Wyatt, Darren, and Noah even popped off some pretty impressive dance moves. I'm pretty sure I stood there the entire time with my jaw on the floor.

Once it was over, I even clapped.

"You guys actually like boy bands?" I'm amazed, especially after Noah made his distaste for Eli known.

"We like *a* boy band," Wyatt corrects me.

"Enough to dance like them?"

Noah shakes his head. "Not exactly. We did it for our sisters … they were huge fans. One year, my parents said we spoiled everyone with gifts that could never be repaid. So the following year, they deemed Christmas a 'themed holiday.' We could only give something we could make or perform. They loved it, though, completely ate it up, and then Rory and Diane posted it to YouTube. We didn't count on that, but they wanted everyone to know they had the best brothers in the world. They count Wyatt and Darren as family, too."

"Well now, that is definitely something worth Googling."

The song changes from NSYNC to The Eagles, and Darren seems to think it's hilarious.

"Damn, Mel, is your playlist bipolar? Talk about one extreme to the other."

"What? I told you guys I'm eclectic in my musical tastes. Actually, this is probably the biggest playlist I have. One day I started adding music and didn't stop until hours later."

"There's no better way to get to know someone than through their playlist. I'm curious to see what you've got, Princess."

"Sawyer's right, music is like the key to your soul. You can learn a lot about a person from their playlist," Wyatt says as he leans back on the weight bench.

"Great, now I'm a little freaked out."

"It's all good, Mel, we already like you," Darren adds, throwing a cautionary glance at Sawyer. Out of them all, I think he and Darren are the closest as far as friendship goes. Sawyer and Noah are, of course, the closest, but when they pair off to do things, Noah and Wyatt seem to team up. I'm sure it's because Noah is pretty calm and Wyatt is married and likes to chill.

The next thirty minutes pass seamlessly, and the guys ruminate over my playlist, making random comments here and there. They laughed especially hard when my list went from a slow country song immediately into a DJ Quik song. When I hear the beginning beats of the next song and the first few lines come through the speakers, I almost fall off the treadmill.

When the sun rises up in the sky
She wakes up with a twinkle in her eye
Her smile is the light of my life
She's my Mellie sunshine

I've turned the treadmill off and I'm frozen in place. I don't know how I forgot I loaded this song onto this list. Probably because most days I skip over it; only when I'm sentimental do I ever listen to it.

"Holy shit!" Sawyer exclaims.

"That's Joey Triton!" Darren cries out as he jumps off the bike.

"It's not *just* Joey Triton …" Noah begins, only to be cut off by Wyatt.

"It's an unreleased, long-lost Joey Triton song. The one he wrote for his little girl."

At least their excitement blocks some of the lyrics from reaching my eardrums. Not like it matters at this point. I grab my water and practically stumble over to the couch. It's over. There's no way I'm getting out of this without telling them everything.

My heart is pounding out of my chest. Suddenly, there's complete silence, and all eyes are focused on me.

"How do you have that song, Mel?" Wyatt asks excitedly at the same time Sawyer points out the obvious answer.

"You're *her*. Amelia Triton. Your parents are Iris and Joey Triton. Holy fuck." If I didn't know better, I'd say there's actually admiration in his eyes. Noah sits next to me and grabs my hand, but his eyes are filled with unanswered questions they all want answers to.

"Yes, I'm their daughter, but I'm not that girl anymore. I'm not *Mellie Sunshine*, and I never will be again."

"No way," Wyatt says, shaking his head. "This whole time we've had a legend's daughter touring with us. This is unreal!"

They're stoked. I get it, I truly do. It's exciting for outsiders to meet a celebrity. Even though I'm not actually famous, everyone groups me in "celeb status" because I came from them. Even celebrities can be dazzled by other famous people; it's such an odd dynamic.

"You look so different," Noah says softly.

"Yeah, well, I was a wild child back then. I dyed my hair a different color every few weeks. I dressed a lot more rock and roll and I partied as hard as I could. After they died, things got crazy, first with her death, and then with his. No one wanted to give me time to grieve. Interview requests were out of control, the phone rang constantly, and everyone wanted a piece of me. I was sixteen, I was just a kid, and I wanted to get away from it all, so that's what I did."

"Didn't you have to go through a background check to get this job? How do we not know this already?" Sawyer actually seems upset about this, but I guess I can't blame him.

"NDAs work both ways. Warren knows who I am, but we decided it would be up to me to tell you, when I felt ready. I was working up to it, but it's a hard subject for me."

"Now it makes so much more sense," Noah says with a half grin. I know he's talking about Eli, but the rest of them don't.

"You suspected something was up?" Sawyer snaps.

"No, I just knew something, but I couldn't put it together."

"Look, guys, there's no more secrets from here on out. I'll tell you whatever you want to know."

"Good, start with what Noah knows," Darren replies diplomatically.

"Do you guys have tequila on this bus?" They laugh, and Noah goes into the kitchenette area and pulls a bottle out of the cabinet, along with some shot glasses.

"Mel, there's tequila on *every* bus," he says as he comes back over and pours me a shot. I toss it back and hold it out for a refill and down that one, too, before leaning back and preparing myself to tell them my story.

Confessions

A few minutes pass while I let the tequila settle into my system. They're all waiting patiently, eagerly, to hear all about Joey and Iris Triton. I don't blame them; they were the power couple of rock for decades.

"Alright. I'll tell you what Noah knows about my past so you don't feel left out, and then I'll go back to the beginning. Noah knows I used to date Eli Watts."

"Really, Mel? He's such a skeezy fuck." Darren almost sounds sad.

"Yeah, I know. That seems to be the general consensus. Now, let's go back to the beginning. This could take a while." They nod their understanding and settle in around me—Noah on the couch and the rest of them sitting on mats on the floor.

"When my parents met, my mom's career had just taken off. She ended up being the opening act for my dad on his tour for a while. There was a time where my mom described their love as magical. Maybe it was because I was a little girl, or maybe it's because at that time they really felt that way."

"I've heard their love story was pretty epic," Sawyer says softly.

"Yeah. Me, too. There's no denying they had an amazing amount of chemistry. When the two of them were in a room together, their love filled it … at least when things were good. When things were bad, their hate was equally prominent.

"The first few years after I was born, my mom continued working on her music. Her albums kept close rank to his on the charts and the labels milked their love story for all it was worth. It was the best of both worlds: mutual success, getting to tour together, and having the chance to stay together as one big, happy family. When I was about six, her career was running on fumes. Her label gave her an ultimatum: leave Joey's tour and go into the studio and record a new album so she could do her own tour, or lose her contract."

I feel the tequila settling in over my senses; it makes it a bit easier to continue.

"That's harsh," Wyatt says softly, and I nod.

D. Kelly

"She loved him with everything she had, and she believed him when he said he would help her succeed. So she told her label she was staying with her family. For the first year or so she was content, waited out the tour, and when we got back home, she wanted my dad to keep his promise. He didn't.

"They were one of those couples who loved so hard and so much they absolutely lost their individual identities in that love. It was like they were the same person, neither of them could work without the other. The problem when your identities blend like that is no one's ever happy. Their relationship was controlled by passion, and when they weren't consumed in their sexual bliss, they were miserable and hateful to each other."

Noah looks like he wants to say something but then shakes it off. I wonder what he's thinking.

"I started spending more time with my grandmother, which is how I know Belle. They were next door neighbors. She was my only friend, probably until I met Eli. We met when we were eight, and we've been best friends ever since. She's *my* sister. One summer, when I was ten, my mom finally had enough, and we stayed with my grandma the entire summer while she recorded a new album."

"Good for Iris," Darren calls out, and I smile with the memory. She was so proud of herself.

"She had a hard time with it, but she finished it and she was proud of it. The problem was the content. The entire album was essentially a love song to my dad. It flopped, and no one was interested in signing her again. Her label only released it because it was the last album she owed them and they could write her off after that. Personally, I think it was her best music, but you can't sign an artist whose most recent album was filled with twenty sad love songs.

"My dad was the exception. He loved it, and the album brought them closer together, so we went back on tour with him. My mom struggled daily with her fleeting fame. She didn't like being known only as Joey's wife, or the second half of his soul. She wanted her own musical identity. She'd been bit by the itch and was willing to get fame, whatever the cost."

"Mel, it's okay. You don't have to keep going. This is obviously upsetting for you," Noah tells me as he squeezes my hand in comfort.

"No, I owe you guys. I can't expect you to open up to me and not reciprocate. I want you to trust me, and if anyone would appreciate this story, it's the four of you."

"Okay," he whispers as the others wait with baited breath for me to continue.

"Anyway, by the time I was thirteen, we had The Savages touring with us. They were almost as popular as my dad by then, but since Ryland Savage was my dad's best friend, the tour was fun for them. Slowly, my parents started getting along better. My mom was extremely loving, and my dad was inspired beyond belief. They even wrote a duet, and she got to start performing with them occasionally.

"Shortly after my fourteenth birthday, my parents got into a fight, a big one, and my mom started sleeping on The Savages' bus. My dad knew she was safe there since Ryland and he had been friends since they were teenagers. And honestly, I think he enjoyed a break from her at times. Their love was suffocating them. It was like the attraction was so great their bodies were like magnets. They were always touching, kissing, and more, but it didn't always look sweet."

"What do you mean? How else does attraction work?" Sawyer asks with a genuine interest.

"I'm not sure, but at times it just looked painful. Like they *hated* each other but still couldn't keep their hands to themselves, even if they wanted to. They were that physically drawn to one another."

Sawyer's expression changes to a scowl, and I return to my story.

"Around this time, I met Eli at an industry party. He was sweet and funny and honestly the first boy I'd ever had a friendship with. His band had just been signed, and their tour coincided with ours on most of the major cities, so we were able to spend a good amount of time together.

"One night, a few months after my mom started riding on the other bus, Eli and I were hanging out on my bus playing video games. My dad came in screaming and yelling. I'd *never* seen him so angry. We were stopped in L.A. for a show at The Forum. After the show that night, we were supposed to go home for some down time. I was really excited because Eli and his parents were going to crash at our house over the Thanksgiving break."

"But the show never happened," Darren fills in for me.

"No, the show never happened. My parents and Ryland got into a massive argument. It was the day my dad found out my mom had been having an affair with Ryland. It had started even before she moved onto their bus.

"At first, she was screaming at him, telling him he drove her to it. Then she was dropping to his feet and begging him to take her back. It's fucked up as a kid to watch your mom tell your dad no one can make her come like him. Listen to her cry about how no one can fuck her like he does, how no one *owns* her the way he can."

97

My skin crawls even repeating the words, and what's worse is Eli heard it, too.

"Ryland convinced my mom to go with him so everyone could calm down. Eventually, she agreed, and they left. From what the police could tell after they compiled all the witnesses' statements, my mom and Ryland were fighting in the car. Somehow, he lost control of the Corvette, took out the center divider on the 405 freeway at ninety miles an hour, and the car flipped multiple times. They'd been driving erratically for some time, and other drivers were holding back because of it. If they hadn't been, it wouldn't have been just the two of them killed."

"God, Mel, that's so messed up." Wyatt's voice is filled with sympathy.

"Yeah, pretty much. My dad went off the rails after that. He couldn't cope. Losing his wife and his best friend after learning of their betrayal ... it fractured his soul. Eli became my rock. He'd seen it all unfold and knew what I was going through. *He* got me through it all. He stayed with me over the break, called off a few tour dates for the funeral, and when he was forced back out on tour, he called every chance he could. I fell head-over-heels in love with him. My dad took a few months off to regroup after everything that happened, but I couldn't take it. The sadness was just too unbearable, so I hopped on Eli's bus and toured with him."

"I still can't believe you slept with Eli," Wyatt says, shaking his head.

"Looking back on it now, even after how it all ended, I wouldn't change it. The two of us crashed and burned, but what we had was real while it lasted. If it weren't for Eli, I would have never made it through that time. He saved me from myself. Even Belle couldn't get through to me the way he could."

"So what happened? Why aren't you still with him?" Sawyer asks, genuinely interested.

"Sawyer, you know as well as I do, these relationships have a hard time surviving. Tack two fifteen-year-olds into the mix and it's a recipe for disaster. We dated almost two years. I got pregnant, Eli freaked the fuck out, and he cheated on me to cope. I'm not sure if I would have kept the baby, probably not, but I miscarried a few hours after I found out he cheated. Back then, I blamed him, but now I know better. It was just something that happened because it wasn't our time. Not because he stressed me out by cheating."

"That bastard cheated on you while you were pregnant?" Noah's less than pleased, and from the scowls on the rest of their faces, he's not the only one.

"Yeah, it's why we don't talk. He tried, he felt horrible, but I couldn't hear it back then. I knew he loved me, and that's what made it hurt so bad. By the time I realized I forgave him, years had passed. It wasn't his fault. He was sixteen, I was fifteen. We were babies."

Noah's hands are balled into fists. I'm not sure I even thought such a sweet-tempered man could get this pissed. So I quickly continue with my story, hoping he'll relax.

"After the Eli mess, my dad was back on tour. So after a short stay with my grandma, I went with him. He was all I had left, and this was our life. It wasn't the same, it was *never* the same. He partied hard. Harder than I've ever seen anyone go. Coke, alcohol, speed, heroin here and there, but nothing numbed his pain. I was helpless to stop it, but I couldn't leave him alone in the state he was in.

"I'd been on the road with him about six months. He had a random chick here and there, but my mom still had his heart. Anyway, one night after a show, he was at it again, fucking and drugging. I was thankful we were staying in a hotel that night so I didn't have to be on the bus to watch him self-destruct even further. So many people tried to get him help, and yet others just chalked it up to grief. I guess I fell somewhere in the middle. I loved him, and I wanted him back to normal, but I knew without my mom he never would be, and I didn't want to see his pain anymore.

"The next morning, I went to wake him up so we could get breakfast. We'd yet to celebrate my birthday, which was a few months prior, so we were supposed to have a daddy/daughter celebratory breakfast. He wasn't answering my knock, so I used my key. I'd gotten used to sobering him up in the mornings, so I figured this would be no different, but it was. I'm the one who found him lying on the bathroom floor, cold, lifeless, *dead*."

By now, tears are streaming down my cheeks as I'm transported back to that moment in time. The moment my entire world crashed in around me and the all-consuming grief set in with the knowledge I had officially become an orphan. The moment I realized neither of my parents loved me enough to stay with me instead of self-destructing. It was the moment I stopped believing love could conquer all because I knew the only sure thing about love was that it had the power to destroy you.

D. Kelly

"Shit, Mel," Wyatt says as Noah pulls me into his embrace. I'm rapidly swiping at my tears, trying to stop crying. It's been twelve years and what's done is done.

"When the police had finished cleaning out his room, they brought me his belongings. At least I knew he was planning on keeping our date. There was a birthday card and a gift for me. After the funeral, I disappeared for a while. Dyed my hair back to its normal color, dodged all the reporters I could, declined interviews, and by the time I came back to stay with my grandma, things had died down. Occasionally, we'd have to get rid of a reporter or two looking for a story, but it wasn't too bad. I wasn't the famous one, I was just what was left over of an iconic couple."

"You're the best parts of them, Mel. You need to remember that," Sawyer says, surprising me with his kind words.

"Thank you, Sawyer."

He simply nods, and Noah continues to hold on to me.

"That's pretty much it, you guys. My story in a nutshell. I finished high school, went to college, all under my grandmother's maiden name, Greyson. When I turned eighteen, everything reverted to me. Assets, royalties, musical library, you name it. The only money I kept was my college trust fund, and that had been set up before things went bad with them. Now, every penny of whatever royalties come in are donated directly to charity. Every few months I change it up so lots of causes can benefit."

"What about the rest of the money? There has to be a fortune sitting somewhere," Darren asks excitedly. I can't blame him; it's almost like finding One Eyed Willie's treasure.

"There's definitely a lot of money sitting in an account accruing daily interest. My grandmother convinced me to hold on to it until I was thirty so I'd be old enough to make a truly informed, grownup decision on what to do with it. So I'm honoring her wishes. She'd always hoped I'd at least set up trust funds for my future children's futures. She thought it would make my parents happy, and she's right. I'm just not sure if I consider their money a blessing or a curse.

"I'm sorry, you guys, I've totally killed your day. It's long past lunch. You should be getting ready to practice. Plus, I've got my interview with Sawyer in a few hours."

They all exchange a glance. I've gotten used to their expressions pretty well lately, but this one is a new one for me.

"I don't feel like practicing today. I think it's a movie day," Wyatt says with a smile.

"Yup, total movie day, and I even think it should be Mel's pick," Darren adds.

"I just texted Warren. He's got pizzas ordered for the next stop. We'll be there in ten minutes." Sawyer fist bumps Noah, and Noah hugs me close, kissing the top of my head.

"Thanks for letting us into your world, Mel," Noah whispers sweetly.

"Well ... I will say one thing. This completely explains how you became acclimated to the bus so quickly. Most people get sick and whine about being cooped up, but you looked like you felt at home."

"That's because I *do* feel at home, Sawyer. The bus was my home for most of my childhood. I missed it. My biggest fear about coming with you was not knowing if you guys were as dramatic as my parents."

"Nah, the most drama we get up in here is when Noah eats the last Pop-Tart. Darren and I have finally started stashing them on our bus so when we're in the middle of nowhere, we can tame the beast."

"Look, I ask for one thing on the bus and that's to leave my Pop-Tarts alone. It's not like Noah's broke. He can afford to buy his own."

"True," Noah adds. "But *your* Pop-Tarts taste so much better."

"Yeah, because *you* aren't paying for them. Everything's sweeter on someone else's dime."

"Jesus, would the two of you kiss and make up already? I don't know how you put up with them all day, Mel, for real," Darren says with the shake of his head.

"So what movies do you want to watch?" Noah asks, lacing his fingers through mine.

"Movies as in plural?"

"Sure, why not?" he answers with a shrug.

"I still have Sawyer's interview to do."

"Do it in the morning while I'm sleeping. It's not like the two of you don't get up at the crack of dawn. Warren won't care, if that's what you're worried about, Mel."

Warren is probably going to be happy he doesn't have to keep my secrets anymore.

"Alright, then. Let's watch *Boomerang*." That movie always makes me laugh; it's one of my all-time favorites.

The buses come to a stop, and we all switch over to our bus. Warren is waiting inside and pulls me into a hug. "I'm glad you told them. I think it will be good for you all. Especially you, Amelia. Maybe now you can let those bad memories die and make new, better ones."

Everyone on this tour is so huggy and close-knit. It's a little disconcerting at times, but in the best kind of way.

"Maybe I can." I pull back, and Noah is patting a spot next to him on the couch.

"So is *Boomerang* good? We've never seen it," Wyatt asks as he searches for it on the movie app.

"What? None of you have ever seen *Boomerang*? Like, never?"

With a mixture of shrugs and heads shaking, I find myself laughing. This is going to be fun. I know the movie is a bit old, but still I can't believe they haven't seen it.

"You guys are going to love this movie. Belle watches it with me whenever I need cheering up."

"So I get to be a substitute Belle today?" Noah whispers in my ear as he wraps his arm over my shoulder. I shake my head.

"Why not?" he asks, seeming truly offended.

"Because I don't let Belle kiss me the way you do. And I sure the hell haven't gone to second base with her."

A wicked smile plays across his lips, and for a brief second, it reminds me of Sawyer.

"Third base, Mel, remember?"

"How could I forget?" I murmur as his lips meet mine.

"Get a room, you two! I thought we were supposed to be watching a movie?" Wyatt chuckles at his own words. "Sorry, they always say that to Anna and me. I just wanted to see how it felt for once."

Mac—their head of security—enters the bus, arms loaded down with pizzas. He sets them on the table and heads back out, Warren following behind him. I'm learning he's a man of few words, but he's one of the best bodyguards I've ever met. Too bad my mom didn't have someone like him. Maybe she wouldn't have gotten into the car with Ryland if she had.

"Pepperoni, or ham and pineapple?" Noah asks.

"Or sausage and peppers, or cheese?" Darren offers, and I've got a feeling this is more of a test. There are four of them and four pizzas.

"Sausage and peppers," I reply, glancing at their faces to see whose favorite I just picked.

"Looks like Sawyer has to share," Wyatt taunts as Sawyer puts a couple pieces on a plate for me.

"I don't mind sharing with the princess. It's the rest of you fuckers I have an issue with." His words make me giggle. It's nice to see Sawyer being sweet, and I've got a feeling this is about as sweet as he gets.

After we're all settled and the movie starts, I'm immediately sucked in. They all seem to be enjoying it, too, and as soon as Halle Berry pops up on the screen, someone pauses the movie.

"That's it!" Wyatt jumps up excitedly.

"What the hell are you talking about?" Sawyer snaps.

"Halle Berry! That's who Belle reminded me of. I kept telling Darren I *knew* her from somewhere and I couldn't figure it out. She's like Halle Berry's frickin' doppelganger!"

Belle gets this a lot.

"I hate to admit it, but he's right," Noah concedes.

With a slight nod, even Sawyer agrees. "Yeah, she really does."

Darren smiles wide. "I'm one lucky SOB, but for the record, Belle is *way* hotter than Halle."

"Someone's whipped." Sawyer's snarky comment doesn't surprise me, but what happens next does.

"So what? I like her, there's nothing wrong with finding someone, Sawyer. You're the only one of us who is still content to have sex with random women. Even so, you've slowed down, too. You've realized you want more but you won't admit it to yourself. We're almost thirty. It's time to grow up."

"Just because you've had sex with someone a few times, now you're a relationship expert, huh?" Sawyer's snarky reply obviously irks Darren.

"No, but that's the thing, man, it's not just sex. We talk, we text, we Skype and email. I *like* her, more than I have a right to with her home and me on the road, but damn, I can't stop thinking about her. *I want more, Sawyer.* Don't you ever just want more?"

Darren's impassioned words hit hard. Sawyer lowers his eyes. His feelings are hurt. It's as if I can feel his pain seeping out of his heart and into mine. I ache with him, and for him, but it seems like I'm the only one.

"Maybe *more* isn't in the cards for everyone at the same time, Darren. After all the shit Marilyn put us through, maybe I'm not ready to take a leap like that. At least not now," Sawyer reluctantly answers.

"Noah is," Darren retorts nastily, and I'm starting to feel uncomfortable with the growing tension around us.

"Noah has a fucking reason to! Stop pushing this, Darren. You're *not* going to win." Sawyer is sitting on the chair next to me at the end of the couch. Instinctively, my hand covers his as my gaze locks on his.

"So do you, Sawyer. You deserve to be happy." Electricity pulses through me, and I pull my hand away. I've got no idea why he affects me like this. It makes me uneasy because I don't want him that way, and I shouldn't touch him so intimately.

Even if I'm drawn to him like a moth to a flame.

"Thanks, Princess, but I'm not looking for a fairy tale right now."

Someone turns the movie back on and about halfway through, Sawyer pulls out a pack of Pop-Tarts.

"Want one, Princess?"

"I want one," Noah says, holding out his hand.

"Is your name Princess?"

"Nope, and it's not Mel's name, either."

"Well, it's what I call her and she answers, so she must not mind as much as she used to."

"Uh, hello? Right here … Yes, I want one and no, unfortunately, your stupid nickname has grown on me."

With a killer smirk, he passes me a pack. Once I've got them open, Noah whispers in my ear, "Are you going to offer to share?" His words make me laugh, and Sawyer knows exactly what's going on.

"No sharing," he warns.

"But he asked so nicely, I can't say no."

With a raised brow, he flashes me a devious look and I know he's remembering me telling him no. At least he doesn't seem angry.

"Traitor," he says with a smile when I hand one to Noah.

Darren and Wyatt watch our exchange while failing to hold in their laughter.

"I'm not a traitor. I'm just showing you how easy it is to share with your brother. You should try it sometime."

"Sure, once Noah starts sharing with me, I'll share with him. Until then, get your own snacks, baby brother, and stop guilting your girlfriend into giving you hers."

I feel the blush creep into my cheeks as I stutter over my words "I … I'm not his …"

Noah places his hand over my mouth so I can't speak. "Yes you are. Now hush, watch your movie, and eat your toaster pastry," he says as he slowly releases my mouth from the cup of his hand. I want to say something, but honestly, I'm stunned silent. Instead, I do exactly what he said and bite into my Pop-Tart. All the guys snicker at us and turn back around to watch the movie.

This is really fun. I love hanging out with them and doing normal things. It's so much better than watching girls trail them at every freaking stop. So far, no one has said anything directly to me, but I feel their eyes and know they're curious about the author on tour with the band.

Once the movie is over, they want to know what's next.

"*Empire Records?*"

"Jesus! Noah, you lucky SOB. Mel, you've got to be the coolest chick ever." Wyatt plops down by my feet and searches for the movie.

"If you guys have all seen it, we don't have to watch it."

Wyatt holds up his hand. "Stop right now before you lose your cool chick status. *Empire Records* is a cult classic, and my teenage self spent many nights picturing Liv Tyler's pouty lips wrapped around my dick."

"TMI, Wyatt!" I'm laughing so hard I can't even pretend to be offended.

"Well, you know, not all of us get to be romanced by our teenage idols, even if they do turn out to be first class douches. Let me have my fantasy."

He crosses his arms and pouts a bit, but I know he's joking, so I don't let his Eli reference bother me … too much.

The fact of the matter is, I probably owe Eli an apology. He's tried to contact me many times over the years, even long after we broke up. Losing our relationship was painful, but losing our friendship crushed me, and I reacted in the way I always do: I ignored it and pushed it away. I never once considered how cutting him off may have affected him. Back then, he needed me just as much I needed him … at least until he cheated on me.

Someday I'll make things right with him.

We spent the rest of the night laughing, joking, playing video games, and taking tequila shots. It was the most fun I've had in I couldn't even tell you how long.

The buses stop for gas around midnight, and Wyatt and Darren head back to their bus. Sawyer had called it a night about a half hour ago, so that gives Noah and me a chance to finally talk.

He pulls me to my feet and wraps his arms around me.

"Sleep with me tonight."

"I don't think that's such a good idea. We've been drinking and …"

He captures my lips with his and kisses me breathless. My body tingles from head to toe until he pulls away, leaving me wanting so much more.

"Just sleep, Mel. I miss having you in my arms."

"Okay, let me change and use the bathroom first."

He flashes me a huge smile and kisses me on the forehead. "Don't take too long."

The pitter-patter of my heart feels more like a stampede of horses, but I can't shake it. I haven't liked a guy as much as I like Noah in a long time. It's so cheesy, but he really does make my days better.

Once I finish up in the bathroom, I put my clothes away and head into his room. He's not wearing anything but his boxers. *God, he's sexy.* His skin is a colorful canvas I've yet to fully explore, and right now the *only thing* I want to be doing is licking that V until I can suck his essence off his gorgeous cock.

"My eyes are up here, Mel," he says with a slight chuckle. I'm biting my lip so hard I actually taste blood.

"Sometimes waiting is overrated."

He closes the door and pulls me into bed, flipping off the light. "And sometimes anticipation is the sexiest foreplay of all."

With those words, my panties are soaking wet and those damn horses are stampeding across my heart again.

"Mel?" he whispers in my ear as he spoons me from behind.

At least I know he's not immune to me because I can feel his hardness bumping up against me.

"Mm, yes?"

"Will you be my girlfriend?"

I flip over to face him and can barely make out his facial features in the dark room. "I thought I already was?" I'm teasing him and he knows it, but it's so hard for me to be serious sometimes.

"Well, I realized that was kind of a jerk thing to do to you in front of everyone. I don't want to start our official relationship off being an ass. So I figured you should have some say in the matter."

"I see. Since you're applying for the job, could you explain to me what kind of boyfriend you're going to be? Some examples of your skills would help make this decision easier."

"Sure, I can give you examples. First example ..." He kisses me softly, passionately, until I'm breathless once again.

"I'd kiss you like that every chance I got. Second example ..." He lowers his head and kisses a fiery trail down my neck as he slides his hands under my tank top and pulls it off over my head. His mouth latches onto my nipple as he fondles my breasts in his hands. I try and keep my moans quiet, but it's no use as he rotates between my breasts, licking and sucking so deliciously, it's only a matter of time before I come.

His hands slide into the waistband of my loose pajama pants and inside my panties. He's moving slowly … too slowly, so I push his hand down further, letting him know I want this. His thumb circles my clit as he slides one, then another finger inside of me.

My hands latch onto his head, my fingers gliding through his hair. He's fingering me as if he were fucking me, and when his mouth drops back to my nipple, I cry out and pull his hair.

"Oh, Noah, yes!" My walls clench around his fingers as I ride out this wave of euphoric bliss. I don't think I've ever been this turned on and we haven't even had sex. *Lord have mercy on my soul.*

"Third example," he says huskily. "Third base seemed appropriate."

"I'm pretty sure that was a home run."

"My darling Amelia, didn't you ever play baseball? You need a bat for a homerun."

"Well then, batter, maybe it's time for you to swing."

He laughs and pulls me close. "Are you going to answer me, or do you need more examples?"

"Well … I like your examples, so I'll put you out of your misery. Yes, Noah Weston, I will be your girlfriend. But there are a few things you should know about me now that I have the official title."

"Lay them on me."

"Well, for starters, I grew up on a tour bus which means I know how crazy fangirls are. If someone goes too far with me, *or* with you … I *will* take them down."

"Noted. Keep bail money on hand at all times to bail sexy girlfriend out of jail for protecting what's hers. Next."

I climb on top of him and kiss him deeply before pulling away from his lips and sliding down his body.

"I believe in tit for tat."

My tongue swipes across his abs and slides down his happy trail. He writhes underneath me, and it turns me on even more knowing I have that effect on him. I pull his underwear down enough so his cock springs free and let my tongue circle around the tip like I'm licking an ice cream cone.

"Fucking hell, Mel."

My hand wraps around the base of his cock as my tongue takes a journey down to his balls. When I gently suck one in my mouth, he practically jumps off the bed and more pre-cum leaks out.

It turns me on even more knowing this is something he likes. When I release him and finally slide him down my throat, he pulls my hair. Softly at first, but the more I get into it, the harder he pulls. I'm so fucking turned on I want to ride him until dawn, but I know he wants to wait.

"Damn, Mel. Fuck, I'm about to come."

What a sweetheart, giving me fair warning, but this is the best part. Not always the taste, but the rush of a man losing control inside of me is one of my favorite feelings.

"Mel, I mean it, babe. I'm going to …" I groan excitedly as I suck harder and faster. When he finally expels his release, it's incredible. His whole body shakes.

"Oh shit, damn … holy hell."

He still pulls my hair, but gently now as I finish sucking every last drop. He doesn't taste bad, either; just a little salty. As he cracks his toes, I laugh and crawl back up his body. He pulls me into a passionate kiss, licking his own essence off my lips, and I think it's the hottest thing I've ever seen.

After he kisses me senseless and pulls me close, he asks a question which sets the tone for a long time to come. "What are you thinking?"

"I'm thinking I'm glad you asked me to be your girlfriend," I say with a smile he can't see.

"Really?"

"Of course. What are you thinking?"

"I was thinking I've never been as turned on by anyone, mind, body, and soul, as I am by you, and how lucky I am that fate brought us together."

"There's that F word again."

"Yes, but it's a good F word, unlike the other one my brother says more than anything."

"We'll see. I'm still reserving judgment on that one. You know, it's usually women who are believers in fate, not the other way around."

"Yeah, I know, but sometimes in life, bad things happen, and if you don't believe in the good that can come from them, then evil always wins. I don't have a place in my heart for the bad things. There's too much good in the world."

"Are you trying to make me swoon, Noah Weston?"

"Not intentionally, but if it's happening, then hell yes." His laughter makes me happy.

"Keep it up and I'll be head-over-heels for you in no time."

He kisses the back of my head and pulls me closer, wrapping his arms even tighter around my waist. I'm so tired I can barely keep my eyes open, but as I drift off to sleep, I hear his whispered words plain as day.

"Good, it's about time you catch up. I've been head-over-heels since the night we met."

Present Day
Amelia

The persistent ringing of the doorbell eventually pulls me from the overflow of memories racing through my mind. I haven't let myself go back to the beginning in a very long time. It just hurts too much.

Something's changed, though. Perhaps enough time has passed to allow me the strength to look back with fond memories. Or maybe it's the entire bottle of wine I drank tonight that's numbing my pain. Whatever it is, I'm actually somewhat happy I'm finally doing this.

The doorbell rings again, and I finally rise up off the couch to answer it.

"I'm coming," I call out, hoping whoever it is doesn't ring the bell again.

When I open the door, Anna looks me up and down, nods her head, and pushes her way inside.

"Come on in, Anna," I say with a chuckle as I close the door behind her.

"My God, Amelia! Are you alright? I've been ringing that bell for the last fifteen minutes. I was about to break in to make sure you were still alive!"

She's practically frantic, and it makes me feel bad.

"I'm sorry. I was sucked into writing and I didn't even hear it."

"So it's true," she says softly, and I reply with a slight nod.

"Wow, I mean, Wyatt mentioned he thought you were finally going to try and write their book, but I didn't think you would."

"Oh, no. Sorry, Anna, I misunderstood. I thought you meant his ultimatum ... that was true. I'm not writing their book. I'm not sure I ever will."

Her expression falls slightly. She's not the only one who's been anticipating the official BAD story I was supposed to write nearly three years ago. But she is one of the few who understands fully why I haven't.

Why I can't.

"So what are you writing?"

"Just a new story that came to me. It's not much of anything right now, mostly an outline."

I feel bad about lying to her, but *no one* can know I'm writing this story. Not even Anna.

With a broad smile, she nods. "Well, I'm just happy to see you working on something new. It's been a long time."

"It has been a long time. We'll see if it ends up being anything."

"So you're okay, though?" She gestures to the empty wine bottle and empty glass next to my computer.

"I will be."

"Do you know what you're going to tell him?"

I shake my head, and she pulls me into a hug.

"Sometimes, the bravest thing we can do is let go of our past. The present is now, Mel, and you only get one shot at it. Happiness, pain, love, life, it's all a fleeting speck of emotion. But when you look at the bigger picture as a whole and remember the good, bad, and everything in between and realize everything really *does* happen for a reason, only then will you find peace."

"You sound like Noah," I tell her somewhere between a laugh and tears. Stupid wine always makes me so emotional.

Keep telling yourself that, Amelia.

Denial has worked so well for you so far.

She flashes me a beaming smile. "I'll take that as a compliment."

"You absolutely should."

"Alright, I'll let you get back to it," she says, releasing me and pointing to my computer.

"Thanks."

"No problem. It's late, but I just finished reading the biggest piece of shit submission on the planet. I needed to get out of the house for a bit. Normally, I can find something redeeming in any manuscript, but not this one. Make some magic on that computer and send it my way. You're far too talented to only have released one book. Even *if* it was a game changer."

"I'll see what I can do. Have a good night, Anna. Thanks for coming over to check on me."

"Anytime. You've got this, Mel," she says with a squeeze of my hand as she walks out the door.

I wish I had the kind of faith in myself she has in me.

The kind of faith they've all had in me since day one.

D. Kelly

Slammed Blog Post

Belle's Utah Update
Three Years Ago

Slammers!

It's your girl Belle again, and I've got news for you! Haha. Okay, not really, but I am off for a weekend with BAD and my girl Mel for their show in Salt Lake City! I'm loving the hell out of this tour and hope you all get a chance to experience it. Have you actually paid attention to the lyrics for *Just an Illusion*? *Swoon* Talk about making a girl's panties wet and her body tingle in *all* the right places!

I've got a plane to catch, so I'm keeping this short and sweet. Be sure to check out my post on Monday. I've got an epic giveaway for a lucky Southern California *Slammed* reader. You're not going to want to miss this. But if you do miss the post, it will be front and center on slammedinc.com by Monday afternoon.

Ta-ta for now.

Don't forget, live today like there's no tomorrow!

Xs and Os,

Belle

The Real Sawyer

Last night, I had one of the best nights of sleep I think I've ever had. When I woke up a few minutes ago, wrapped in Noah's strong arms, it was *the* best feeling. I pick up Noah's phone from the side of the bed and look at the time. It's six a.m. and my bladder says it's time to wake up.

I carefully extricate myself from his grasp, and he doesn't even flinch. It's actually pretty cool he's such a sound sleeper. I'd love to sleep through someone moving around. I bet he sleeps through earthquakes. I'd give my right tit to be able to do that. Earthquakes freak me the hell out.

I opt to take a quick shower before coffee so I can clean up from last night. When I come out and make my coffee, Sawyer is up and gazing out the window.

"Good morning," he says as he lifts his coffee cup in greeting.

"Good morning. Ready for our interview?"

"Sure, let me just get a refill when you're done."

"Of course." I look around the kitchen and grab a banana and a granola bar.

"Don't want to share my Pop-Tarts today?" he teases wickedly.

"You seriously eat them every day?"

"No, I'm just kidding. Sometimes I will, but there's cereal and breakfast food on the bus for a reason. I actually like them more for a snack. Then sometimes, believe it or not, I actually get the urge to cook."

"Interesting. Are you any good at it?"

"Princess, I'm good at everything."

"Everything, huh?"

"*Everything.*" There's so much sexual innuendo in his tone, but I started it, so I'm going to let it go this time.

"Hmm. I'm now going to make it my mission to find something you suck at."

He comes closer and brushes against me as he reaches for a coffee pod.

"Truthfully, I suck at making coffee. That's why we have this nifty machine." He points to the Keurig and then opens up the cabinet under the sink and points to another brand new Keurig still in the box.

"Two?"

"Hell yeah, because if this one goes down in flames and we're miles from civilization, I need a backup."

"Makes complete sense, now spill. You have to be bad at more than one thing."

"Not that I can think of. What are you bad at?" he asks, throwing the question back on me. I take my coffee and my food and sit down at the table.

"Art. I can't draw to save my life, not even a straight line with a ruler. Dealing with anything emotional, I'll avoid it like the plague. Drinking, I always hit my limit sooner than I think I will. I bypass pleasantly drunk and end up shit faced more often than not. I think the worst is apologizing, I've recently come to realize I owe someone a huge one, sooner rather than later."

"I'm pretty bad at apologizing, too," he says, taking the seat across from me. "As a matter of fact, I probably owe you one for kissing you the night we met. I thought ..." He shakes his head slightly and continues, "Well, it doesn't really matter what I thought. The point is, I'm sorry if I made you uncomfortable."

"You didn't. I was caught off guard for sure, but that kiss was not unwelcome."

"Then why?" His question is a plea for answers.

"Why did I push you away only to turn around and start dating your brother?"

He nods but doesn't look me in the eye. Instead, he fiddles with his coffee cup.

"Look at me, Sawyer ... please."

When my gaze locks on his beautiful green eyes, my heart melts. I'm not sure Sawyer allows himself to be vulnerable with anyone the way he's being with me right now.

"I've got a bad history of dating and sleeping with musicians. You and I ... we're combustible, and our chemistry is off the charts. But that night I had to go off the only information I had, and that was my past and your bad reputation. I'm sorry I misjudged you."

"You think you misjudged me?" he asks softly.

This time, I cross my own comfort zone when I reach across the table and take his hand in mine.

"Yes, I know I did. You put on a brave front, Sawyer, but underneath your bad boy persona, you're a *good* man. There's so much more to you than what you let people think."

"Thanks, but it doesn't matter now. You're with Noah, and he likes you a lot."

"I like him, too."

"Enough to risk your job, apparently." His words are like a dagger to my heart, and I finally realize how much my rejection hurt him.

"At first, no, and I'm scared to death about what this could mean for my job. My number one goal is to tell the best story I can and be able to shed light on the real men of Bastards and Dangerous. Noah managed to work his way into my heart, and it's not an easy thing to do. I never saw it coming until it was too late."

"So you love him?" His face is solemn; the look makes my palms sweat. I've got an overwhelming feeling my answer could hurt him.

"I'm not sure." My reply is hesitant, so I do my best to expand on it the best way I can. "You all have become like a second family to me, and considering Belle is really the only family I have anymore, it means a lot to me to have you in my life. I love you all in that aspect."

"Did you just friend-zone my brother?"

"No, not at all, Sawyer. It's not in my nature to let people into my heart easily. Noah is pushing past my defenses for sure. However, when and if I decide I'm in love with your brother, he's going to be the first to know. Okay?"

"Fair enough."

My hand is still covering his. I'm surprised he didn't pull away when my palms began to sweat.

"Can you sit on the couch with me? I'd like to tell you a story. This isn't for the book, but after you shared with us yesterday, and now knowing your feelings about us all, I think you should know something about me and my family."

"Of course," I answer with a small smile and release his hand to grab my coffee. Instead, he takes it and carries it over for me. It's such a small gesture, but for him, it's huge. Sawyer is opening up to me, and my insides are doing a happy dance. That in itself is concerning. I can't like Sawyer as much as I do because I'm falling head-over-heels for his brother.

"Look, I know you won't print this, but I need to make sure you won't tell anyone, either. This isn't only my story, my whole family is involved, especially my cousin Jordan. He's a brother to me, and I don't trust just anyone with this."

"I'd never tell your secrets, it's not my place." I hope my reassurance is enough for him.

He's wringing his hands together but eventually nods.

"I don't trust many people, but I trust *you*, Princess." My heart patters with his words. But I convince myself it's only because he's letting me into his world.

"Thank you."

"When we were seven, our aunt and uncle lived around the corner from us. It was cool because Jordan was our age, so we got to play all the time. Jordan had an older brother, his name was Carl, and a baby sister, Carly."

The fact he said "was" while referring to children, coupled with the fact he's still wringing his hands together, already says this is going to be a horrible story.

"Jordan was supposed to come over so we could go to the movies. Carl was thirteen and had a girlfriend, so he didn't want to hang out with us. He was going to go hang out with her instead. We waited as long as we could for him, but we were going to be late for the movie. No one answered the phone when we called over there. My mom figured Aunt Carrie was in the shower and Jordan was busy helping with Carly since she was only a year old.

"I'd been on this kick to see how fast I could run, so I offered to go so my mom could time me. When I got there, no one answered and the door was locked, so I ran around to the back door. I saw Uncle Javier in a pool of blood, he'd shot himself straight through the heart. I didn't know that at the time, though."

"Oh, Sawyer." Instinctively, I reach out for his hand and he squeezes my fingers in his.

"The door was unlocked, so I slid it open and went in. I was in shock. My hands were shaking and tears were running down my face, but I *had* to see if everyone was okay. I didn't think there could have been an intruder or that I could have been in any kind of danger, I just had to find my cousins and my aunt. The phone was on the kitchen counter, so I called 911, told them my uncle had been shot and I was trying to find my family. The operator kept telling me to go outside and wait, but I couldn't, so I put the phone down and went to find everyone.

"In the living room, Carl was lying in his own pool of blood. His eyes were wide open, and I knew he was gone. I guess it was then I started screaming, I don't really remember, but from what they could piece together from the neighbors, that's what they came up with. I kept going toward the bedrooms, and my aunt was out in the hall in front of Jordan's room. She was gone, too. I had to jump over her to get inside the bedroom, and that's where I found Carly in Jordan's bed, and she was gone, too."

Tears are streaming down his cheeks, and I reach out and pull him into my embrace. The way he hugs me back fills me with sadness. It's as if he's needed this hug his whole life. After a few minutes, he pulls away, leans back into the couch, and wipes away his tears.

"By then, I was screaming for Jordan, I heard a tapping noise in the closet, so I opened the door. There was so much blood, but he was still alive, gasping in pain. I remembered when I fell off my bike and cut my arm open and my mom had wrapped a shirt around it to stop the bleeding, so I grabbed something off the closet floor and held it to his head.

"There was blood on his side, too, but I didn't have enough hands to hold them both, and his head was the worst. The police were there soon after I found him and since I hadn't stopped screaming, they found us quickly. By then, my mom had arrived with Noah. She was freaked out because I hadn't come back, but the police had already roped off the house and wouldn't let them in. Thank God, because no one should have to see what I saw that day."

My heart aches for the innocence they lost that day. For the whole family they lost.

"So Jordan is okay?"

"Jordan is a fucked up mess, like me, but he's alive and functioning. Like me, he doesn't trust many people and rarely lets anyone in deeper than surface level. His mom had shoved him in the closet and begged him not to come out. She put Carly down on his bed and was trying to get out of the room when she was shot. Uncle Javier shot at Carly a few times from a distance. I guess one of the bullets went through the wall and caught Jordan through his side. It went through his ribs and had partially collapsed a lung, but when he was hit, he fell and hit his head hard on the bottom of his ice skates and that's why he was bleeding so much from his head.

"We found out later Javier used a silencer. The assumption is he killed Carl and my aunt saw and rushed to try and save Carly and Jordan. She did save Jordan, and even though he didn't see what happened, he heard it all. We both have to live with that day forever. Between the two of us, we spent years in therapy learning coping mechanisms and shit."

D. Kelly

"Did they ever figure out why he did it?"

Sawyer releases an evil laugh.

"Yeah, he'd met a woman at work and had fallen in love. She convinced him they'd be better off if his family was out of the picture. It was supposed to be staged as a robbery, but I guess Javier felt guilty and killed himself instead."

"God, Sawyer, I'm so sorry."

"It's alright. I didn't tell you so you could pity me. I guess I just wanted you to know my story since you shared yours."

"You're brave. Not many kids could have done what you did. Hell, not many grownups would have walked into that. You're a hero, Sawyer."

This time, his laugh comes from deep within. "Thanks, Princess, I needed that."

He's deflecting, but I let him. Lord knows, I don't want him wallowing in his thoughts any longer than he has to. It must have been hell to open himself up to me like that.

"So when is your first book signing?"

"In the new year, when we get back on the road. The first one will be in New York."

"Are you nervous?"

"Terrified. Once I'm seen at that signing, everyone will know who I am."

"You should be proud of who you are. You aren't your parents. It's okay for you to live your life outside of their shadow."

"I know, but once it happens, there are going to be tons of questions, interview requests, not to mention ..."

"The singing?"

I nod and pull my knees to my chest, wrapping my arms around them.

"Is it true? Your voice is even better than your mother's? Rumor back then was you were about to drop a solo album when your dad died."

"Well, you know why they're rumors. My voice is decent, but the album was his idea. I think it was his way of keeping her close. He wanted me to put out the album and tour with him, but it was never my dream."

"Seems to me you're living your dream now."

"I'm trying to."

"I'm glad you're here, Princess."

I've never seen Sawyer's eyes sparkle the way they are right now. I think we just officially became friends.

"Me, too."

"God, I've missed you!" Belle screams out as she runs across the parking lot and wraps me in a hug.

"I've missed you, too! I'm so glad you're here."

"Aww, how sweet. It's a princess reunion," Sawyer says as he leans up against the bus.

"You *know* you want a piece of this princess action," Belle retorts.

"Is that an offer?" Sawyer asks with his classic smirk.

"Hell no, it isn't," Darren and Noah answer in unison.

"You guys take the fun out of everything. We still on for Sully's tonight, or are you pussies backing out of that, too?"

"Have we ever backed out of a night at Sully's?" Noah asks indignantly.

"Okay, then."

"What's Sully's?" Belle asks as Darren pulls her away from me and into his arms.

"Only the best bar with the best karaoke night on the planet."

"This might be a stupid question, but don't you guys get noticed at a karaoke bar?"

Noah wraps his arms around my waist and kisses the top of my head. Not exactly the answer I was looking for, but I'll take the affection.

"Nope, or at least if they do, they've never outed us. We do keep our hats on and sing music totally different than our own, so that might help." Darren answers the question while Noah distracts me with a trail of kisses along my neck.

Belle's phone rings and she doesn't even say hi when she answers the phone. "Oh shit, sorry! I'll tell him right now."

She hangs up and puts her phone back in her pocket. "Wyatt, you need to go to your bus. I left something there for you from Anna, and Warren said it's in his way, so you need to go take care of it."

Wyatt shakes his head and walks toward his bus muttering something about how Sawyer and Warren deserve to be on the same bus since they're both so anal.

"What did you bring him?"

Belle's grinning like a fool and watches Wyatt enter his bus before answering my question.

"*Who* would be a better question. Anna and I flew in together."

"Anna loves Sully's. This is perfect!" Sawyer is obviously excited his best friend is here. I also realize this makes him odd man out in terms of a date. Hopefully, he won't feel like a third wheel. I know he'd never say as much, but I'm starting to get a good read on Sawyer, and I think he's a lot lonelier than he lets on.

With Belle and Anna here it would have been nice to be in a hotel tonight, but tomorrow morning, the guys have some radio interviews and Warren didn't want to have to round them up. Especially Sawyer, and since we're heading out after the show Saturday night, there's really no point.

Due to a scheduling conflict with the Utah venues, we have to split our time here. They're doing one show tomorrow night, and then we'll be back around before the tour ends next fall.

"We're going to go work out. Do you girls want to come, or do you want to go gossip?" Noah asks with a knowing smirk.

"I can hit the gym on my own time. Come on, Mel, let's go talk about the good stuff while we can." Belle pulls my arm, and Noah pulls me back toward him, popping a quick kiss on my lips before releasing me.

"That was the cutest non-romantic kiss I've ever seen," Belle teases.

Noah pulls me away from her completely and wraps his arms around me. One hand is lingering on my ass while the other weaves through my hair, pulling me to his lips. My heart races as the smell of his cologne reaches my senses. He always smells so spicy and clean.

His lips linger on mine briefly, and his tongue parts my lips, meeting mine slowly, passionately, as he pulls me further into his embrace. Wrapping my arms around his neck, my fingers grasp onto his hair, and I fight to keep my feet on the ground instead of around his waist.

Darren's snicker finally pulls me back to reality, and we part slowly, reluctantly, and as always, breathlessly. This man could kiss me into my dying breath, and I'd let him. I couldn't imagine a more wonderful way to go.

"Romantic enough for you?" Noah teases back at Belle.

"I'd say. Now I need a cold shower. Holy hotness, you two were on *fire!*"

"Anticipation," Noah whispers into my ear, his hand dropping from my head, caressing my side until landing on my hip.

"Torture," I whisper back before adding, "I may need my friend B.O.B after that."

"No way. I'll take care of you tonight when we get back from Sully's, and I'll make it worth the wait."

"Homerun?" I ask hopefully, but he shakes his head with a slight smile.

"Soon, I promise."

Darren kisses Belle on the other side of the bus, and I look around, noticing Sawyer is nowhere to be found. He must have gone to the other bus to exercise. I hope we didn't make him uncomfortable. It's the one thing I really wanted to avoid.

Belle and I finally get on the bus, and she immediately pulls me down on the couch, crosses her arms, and gives me one of the fiercest looks I've ever seen on her.

"You're in love with him," she states matter of factly.

With a slight shake of my head, I reply, "I'm in *like* with him."

"Amelia Greyson, I've only ever seen the gleam in your eyes once before, and that was with Eli. You're in love with Noah Weston."

"I'm not ... not yet."

"Alright, you keep telling yourself that, but I think we need to talk about the bigger picture here."

"What bigger picture?"

"Sawyer."

"What about him?"

"He's seriously crushing on you, Mel."

I practically choke on my laughter, even though deep down inside, I don't necessarily think she's wrong.

"He's not, he's just going through some shit right now."

"Let me guess, you've been his shoulder to cry on?"

"Not exactly."

"Mel, I know the look a man gets when he's infatuated with a woman, and Sawyer Weston is as hot for you as his brother is. You need to be careful."

"Belle, I wouldn't ..."

She holds her hand up to me. "Sweetie, I know you wouldn't, but I also know what an amazing person you are and how easy it is to fall for you. Trust me, if I were playing for the other team, you'd be my girl already."

We're both laughing, but there's a lingering hurt deep down inside of me. I don't want to lead Sawyer on, and I definitely don't want to hurt him. There's no way I can deny we have sparks, but if anyone is going to get my heart, it's going to be Noah.

"Remember how my parents had that chemistry?"

D. Kelly

She nods. "Their heat could spark a fire in any room when they weren't fighting."

"Yeah, it could," I reply sadly.

"You always swore you'd stay away from anything that ever made you feel like that."

"And I will. I'm never going to lose myself in something where passion rules my heart and my mind."

"Where's this going, Mel?"

"When Sawyer kissed me, it confirmed what my parents had could exist in my world."

"Is that why you ran from him?"

I nod and bury my head in my hands.

"And you don't feel that for Noah?"

"It's not even comparable. Noah lights me on fire from the inside out. He's adoring, sweet, and one of the most genuine people I've ever met. I'm falling for him hard, and I'd never do anything to hurt him."

"So what's the problem? I don't get it."

"It's not a problem per se. It's just, Sawyer and I are getting closer, we're becoming friends, and I like it. He's deep, and there's so much more to him than people give him credit for. If he has feelings for me, I don't want to hurt him, and I can't ever let it get any deeper than the one kiss we shared."

"Then don't."

"I won't."

If only I felt the conviction in my words. Sawyer Weston terrifies me; he's dangerous in the best kind of ways. Right now, the only truth I know is I'm falling hard for Noah, and as tempting as Sawyer can be, he's not his brother.

"So how does it feel to be Noah Weston's official girlfriend?" She easily changes the topic to readjust my comfort zone. God, I love her.

"So surreal. After Eli, you know I swore off musicians as a viable long-term option, and after my parents … I swore them off for good. But Noah is special, Belle, and as hard as I tried to fight my feelings for him, I'm not sure I want to anymore."

"I'm glad. You deserve some happiness in your life, and if it comes to you in the form of Noah Weston, mega hot, super sexy, famous rock star, then so be it."

"What about you? Have you pitched your plan to tour with us to *Slammed* yet?"

122

"I did, and they're all for it. I'm going to run it by Warren this weekend. Darren is completely on board with it. I hope they all go for it because I miss the hell out of you. At least they arranged for us to spend the holidays together."

"I know. It was really thoughtful. With your mom out of the country with her new boy toy until the new year, the timing couldn't have been better."

She giggles and shakes her head. "You know I'm all about living each day to its fullest, but I never imagined my mom dating a man my age!"

"So true, but your mom is gorgeous and she had you so young. She's not even fifty yet. You'll be lucky if you don't end up with a baby brother or sister."

Belle shudders at my words, but she knows I'm right. Veronica is beautiful, sexy, and relatively young. At forty-six, it's not completely impossible for her to have another child.

"Alright, enough talk about my mom. Let's figure out what we're going to wear tonight! Pull up Sully's online and see if it's casual."

A Rare Night Out

Belle, Anna, and I all got ready on our bus while the guys got dressed and waited for us on Darren and Wyatt's bus. Sully's is casual but we're still looking good. It's rare to get a night out, so we're taking advantage of the opportunity. Belle opted for heels while Anna and I chose high-heeled boots. Where Belle and I stuck with jeans and sweaters, Anna went with a red dress which accentuates every curve on her body. Wyatt's going to be one happy man tonight.

Anna texted Wyatt to let him know we're on our way out to meet them. They rented two Escalades to take us to Sully's. Mac is driving one, and Ryan—their second in charge of security—is driving the other. It seems whenever they split up, Ryan is always with Noah and Sawyer, and I wonder if there's a story there.

Strong arms wrap around me from behind. Without looking at them, I already know it's Noah by his scent.

"You look incredible," he whispers, lightly nipping on my ear.

"You haven't even seen my face. My makeup could be hideous."

His chuckle vibrates against my skin. "You couldn't be hideous if you tried."

He twirls me around so I'm facing him and cracks a smile. "See? Absolutely gorgeous."

"You don't look half bad yourself."

"So are you ready to experience Sully's?"

"Sure. I mean, what could go wrong with tequila, karaoke, musicians, and a public bar?" I only half-tease him.

"Oh ye of little faith, you'll see this isn't the place where people care about who we are. In fact, I'm pretty sure they know but choose to ignore it."

"Do you think Rhymin' Rieanne will be there?" Anna wonders aloud.

"Isn't Rhymin' Rieanne always there?" Sawyer asks rhetorically, and they all start laughing.

"Who's Rhymin' Rieanne?"

Darren turns to Belle and answers, "She's this local chick who has been at Sully's every time we're there. She turns karaoke night into a freestyle and she …"

It's as if he's at a loss for words, so Sawyer tries to explain, "She's an eclectic mix of inappropriate and rap versus spoken word."

"Nah, it's definitely more rap," Noah says, shaking his head. "At least I *think* that's what you'd call it. You'll see, she never ceases to amaze me. Each time, her rhymes are crazier than the last."

"Well, let's go! I want to see for myself, and I need a few shots of tequila if you think you're getting me on stage," Belle squeals excitedly.

"Oh, we're definitely getting you on stage, and when we come back here, I'll let you ..." Darren pauses and looks directly at Sawyer, "bang my bongo."

I'm trying to hold in my laughter, but Noah isn't doing as good of a job at it. Sawyer throws his arms in the air and shakes his head. "I give up!" he exclaims before hopping into the SUV. Noah and I follow behind him while the others climb into the SUV next to us, still laughing.

"You guys are assholes."

Noah reaches over and throws his arm across Sawyer's shoulders. "Oh, come on, little brother, you know we love you. It's just so easy to annoy you, we can't help ourselves sometimes."

This is the first time I've really witnessed the two of them being brotherly. Sawyer actually hugs him back before pushing him away. They're adorable together, and I can imagine how cute they were as little boys. I can't wait to see them with their family at the holidays.

The drive to Sully's is short, and Mac lets us out at the door, which is great because it's freezing outside. Noah laces his fingers in mine and brings my hand to his mouth and kisses it. My heart flutters; I feel like a teenage girl.

"So this is our first official date," Noah says to me as we follow behind Sawyer to our table.

"You don't consider our movie night in the hotel a date?"

"Nope, you weren't my girlfriend then."

"Well, no, but people have to date before they become exclusive, don't you think?"

"Not always, sometimes, like with us, friendship turns into more. I want more with you, Mel." He says the words confidently, with no hesitation.

"I want more with you, too, Noah." And I mean it.

"You guys are sickeningly sweet. I'm going to need lots of shots if you're going to act like this all night." Sawyer doesn't seem mad, but there's an underlying tone to his voice which makes me think he might be. Noah isn't fazed by it at all, so maybe I'm reading something into it that isn't there.

Unfortunately for me, since we're the first to arrive, I end up between Sawyer and Noah in an extra-large booth immediately to the left of the stage.

Sully's is interesting. It's dark and sexy like a blues or a jazz club. Each table has a lit candle in the middle next to sign-up sheets, pencils, and a massive song list notebook. A waitress stops by with menus, and Sawyer orders a bottle of Don Julio and seven shot glasses.

Wyatt and Anna reach the table first. Belle slides in next to Anna and Darren takes up the end. She is shooting me warning glances. As if I don't already know it's bad I'm stuck between Sawyer and Noah.

There's a table to our right with what looks like a similar situation to ours. There are two couples and one single girl. She's a pretty blonde, and she's eyeing Sawyer up.

Great.

It's not that I don't want Sawyer to have fun; I'm just not looking to watch a fangirl experience tonight.

Sawyer passes the bottle around and soon we all have full shot glasses. Noah's free hand rests on my thigh, and I relax. This is going to be fun. Sawyer deserves to have fun, and I deserve to be relaxing on a date with a perfect man.

Sawyer lifts his shot glass in the air. "To friends, old and new, cheers."

"Cheers." We all echo his sentiment and toss back our shots. Darren fills his glass again and immediately passes the bottle back around. After three more rounds of shots, I'm thankful a busboy brought bread to the table.

"What's the matter, Princess, can't handle your tequila?"

I turn to Sawyer with a smile plastered to my face. "I puke to the right, so if you'd prefer I drink on an empty stomach, you'll be the one who gets it in his lap."

Noah snickers in my ear as his hand grips tighter on my thigh. "Have I told you how much of a turn on it is when you put Sawyer in his place?" he whispers.

"She's not lying, either. I've been on her right more times than I'd like to admit," Belle tells him while shaking her head at the memory.

"Fine. By all means, eat, Princess, but you're still drinking until I can get you on that stage."

"Hell yeah!" Darren high fives Sawyer across the table and Belle's gaze catches mine. She knows I won't sing.

Noah's arm wraps around my shoulder. "It's okay, Mel. We can sing a duet, or a quartet, and you can have the smallest part. But the one rule they have at Sully's is, no one leaves without singing."

He points up to a sign above the stage I didn't notice before and it says exactly that.

Shit, I'm going to need a lot more tequila for this.

A couple of random people have gone up to sing, but between my shots and my bread, I haven't paid much attention to them. Noah just ordered some appetizers for the table, and I know he did it so Sawyer wouldn't talk shit to me.

They're all excited, filling out their songs from the song book, even Belle the traitor is totally into this. Belle slides me a piece of paper with a song for her, me, and Anna to sing, and I nod in agreement. It's not like I'm getting out of this, and we'll likely be up later anyway because this place is packed. That gives me plenty of time to consume more tequila.

There are a few monitors around the perimeter which list singers' names and songs. I don't have any idea what names the guys use here to know when they're up.

About a half hour later, I'm nibbling on some fries and just finished my fifth or sixth shot of tequila and I'm feeling no pain.

As I bring a fry to my mouth, Noah leans over and pulls it away with his teeth. When he swallows, he pulls me close and kisses me deeply. It's not a good idea. I'm definitely drunk, and tequila makes me horny. If he kisses me much longer, I'll straddle him here and ride him to oblivion. I pull back and raise my eyes to his.

"Homerun?" I ask hopefully, and he shakes his head.

"Then stop because tequila makes me a freak."

He leans forward again and bites my lip. Sawyer groans next to us, but we ignore him.

"Told you it would be fun to get drunk together."

"Not if you're not knocking one out of the park, it's not," I tell him with a pout, and Sawyer snickers, muttering under his breath.

"I can't believe you two haven't fucked yet."

"Me, either," I say, turning toward him, and they all laugh.

With a shrug of my shoulders, I turn back to them. "What? It's true. We're being good, getting to know each other. Doesn't mean I'm not sexually frustrated."

"She's so drunk," Belle replies through her laughter, and Noah takes it like a champ. He pulls me all the way to him and kisses me on the forehead.

"Soon," he says sweetly, melting my heart. I'm pretty sure I've fallen in love with him, or at least the tequila-imbibed me thinks she has. It's while I'm swooning over him I remember my promise to not make Sawyer feel bad he's alone. I pull back and grab another fry and take a sip of my water.

"Oh shit, look who's up next!" Wyatt whispers excitedly.

The monitor says *Rhymin' Rieanne – freestyle*, and they all seem excited.

"This is going to be the best thing you've ever seen, you guys." Even Anna is excited to see her. This chick must be really good or really crazy. Belle looks at me and shrugs; she doesn't get it, either.

A few minutes later, after an adorable elderly woman finishes singing a song from the Roaring Twenties, a young girl takes the stage. She's got to be twenty-one since she's here, but she doesn't look it at all. Her dark black hair is cut into a bob, and her massively large black glasses take up at least half of her face. She's tiny as can be. In fact, I think she's smaller than Belle, and I'm starting to lose faith in these men who swear we're in for a show.

She looks up at the audience as if she's hesitant to begin, when suddenly, she starts beatboxing into the mic. Belle and I both watch her in drunken awe. How could so much sound come from such a small girl?

"Wait for it," Noah whispers into my ear just as she begins adding words to her beats. And holy fuck … they are *words*.

"I … love big balls in my face
Big balls in my face,
I love the way they jiggle
And I love the way they taste."

I can't hold back my laughter, but I'm trying hard and cover my mouth with my hand as she keeps up her rhyme.

"Big balls in my face,
Big balls in my face,
Just lean right over
And let them shake, baby, shake."

I'm going to die. I literally can't breathe, and Belle isn't far behind me. This is the most entertaining thing I've ever seen in my *entire* life.

"Put them in my mouth
And move them all around

Let me lick and suck
Your big balls, I'll go to town.
I love big balls in my face
Big balls in my face
Then lean your cock down
And slap it all around."

That's it, I'm crying. Tears are streaming down my cheeks, and my chest heaves up and down. I can die knowing I've seen the funniest thing on earth and it exists in Salt Lake City, Utah.

"Big balls in my face
I love big balls in my face
I'll fuck them with my mouth
Then suck your big dick down,
When you finally come, I won't even frown.
I ... love ... big balls!"

"Thank you," she whispers, strolling off stage as if she just recited *Mary had a Little Lamb* and wasn't talking about her love of cock and balls.

"What was that?" Belle whispers loudly.

"Rhymin' Rieanne is *who* that was. We told you two she's been worth the trip every single time we've come here." Darren is smiling like the Cheshire cat at our awe.

"Does she do the same song each time?"

"Hell no, what would be the fun in that? I think last time we were here she did something called *If I were a Penis*," Sawyer says with a straight face.

"No way. You're just messing with us because we're drunk."

"Hand to God, Mel, she really did," Darren says as he passes a new bottle of tequila around.

"That was awesome but not as awesome as we're about to be. Come on, guys, we're up." Sawyer slides out of the table, and I follow to let Noah and Wyatt out. I glance up at the screen. They're listed as Sully's Crew—how original—and they're singing *Whip It* by Devo. This ought to be good.

I'm surprised they didn't do something a little more like their own music. Then again, even though they can lay low here, they're going to be outed if they bring the house down.

Belle, Anna, and I do our due diligence as fans, cheering and catcalling them while they're onstage. We're not the only ones; blondie at the next table is eyeing up Sawyer. They're really good, but of course, that's a given. When they come off stage, the blonde distracts Sawyer on his way back to the table.

129

D. Kelly

Next up: Belle's Bells. How creative. Then, I see the song and know they tricked me. Instead of *Rock Lobster* by The B-52's, we're now doing *The Boy is Mine* by Monica and Brandy; it's a highly lyrical song.

Damn her!

"Hey, guys, I decided to do a duet with Wyatt, so I'm going to sit this one out." Anna is smiling, and when she looks at Belle, I know they did this on purpose.

"Come on, Mel, it will be fun!"

"You're *so* lucky I'm drunk," I tell her as I take another shot before standing.

"I was counting on it. Drunk Mel sings her ass off."

"You're the worst best friend ever."

She wraps her arm around my waist as we head for the stage.

"You'll forgive me. You love me too much not to. Besides, this song used to be our jam, Mel. Let's have some fun. We only live once, you know. And to top it all off, you know my voice sucks and you're going to sing me under the table, leaving me utterly humiliated."

She does sort of have a point. Belle is really tone deaf.

"Makes you feel better, doesn't it?" she teases.

"Marginally," I answer as we take the microphones and the music starts. It's as if we're teenagers again; she takes Brandy's part while I take Monica's. We must have practiced to this video a million times in her living room. The whole time we look at each other so I don't have to admit we're doing this in front of a crowd.

When we finish, she hugs the crap out of me and we're met with cheers. I still keep my head down until I get back in my seat.

"Holy shit, Mel, you've got pipes!" Wyatt high-fives me from across the table, and Noah pulls me in close.

"That was seriously sexy," he says, guiding my hand to his cock under the table. He's hard, and I want nothing more than to go back to the bus and fuck his brains out.

Sawyer slides in next to me, and his blonde friend squeezes in on the end. He doesn't even bother introducing her.

Real classy.

"Princess, that was the shit! You were so good we didn't even pay too much attention to your pitchy princess pal."

Belle makes a pouty face, but Darren sticks up for his woman. "It's okay, Belle, I've got enough musical talent for the both of us. You just focus on playing my bongo, babe." Belle sticks her tongue out at Sawyer like she's twelve years old, and he groans at Darren's words.

"Why can't you guys just say fuck, or cock, or dick? Hell, I'd be happy with penis at this point!"

"I can say penis, cock, dick, *and* fuck, so what does that get me?" His blonde bimbo addresses him in a fake, sexy, husky voice, and the rest of us girls at the table all groan at the same time. Especially Anna. She's his best friend, and you can tell from the smirk on her face she's got something to say.

"That gets you me for the night. Let's go." Sawyer throws down a huge wad of cash on the table as the blonde wraps her arm around his waist. She knows *exactly* who he is.

"Hey, Sawyer," Anna calls out before he gets too far away.

"Yeah, Bethie?"

Bethie? That's new.

"Make sure you triple bag your dick. Your tramp seems a little looser than most."

Blondie doesn't say a word. If someone said that about me, I'd be pissed. Just goes to show what fans will go through for a celebrity fuck.

"Always do, Bethie," he replies.

"Hey, Sawyer!" I shout, and he pauses again.

"Yeah, Princess?"

"Make sure that triple stack comes from *your* condom stash, not hers. Groupie tricks always seem to travel with pin holes in their condoms."

Now that seems to get her attention, and while she fumes, Wyatt and Darren snicker. Noah pulls me even closer, whispering in my ear, "So fucking hot."

"You got it, Princess. Anything else?"

"Have fun," I add with a smile.

"That's the plan," he snaps back. I guess I pissed him off. *Oh well.*

"That was hilarious, Mel. Sawyer sure does get pissed when you put him in his place. It's quickly becoming one of my favorite things to see." The twinkle in Wyatt's eyes confirms the sheer pleasure he gets from my knee-jerk reactions to Sawyer.

"I second that," Darren says, lifting his shot.

"Didn't she look like trouble?" Anna asks Wyatt.

"They all look like trouble … most of them *are* trouble. But my heart belongs to you, so you don't have to worry about me."

"I know, babe, but I worry about Sawyer. He can be so self-destructive."

"He's a grown man, Anna. He's going to do what he wants, when he wants. It's why we have the sex in the bedroom only rule on our bus. I don't want to see him with his groupies." Noah's sigh indicates he's more concerned than he's letting on.

"Oh man, we're going to hear them tonight, aren't we?" I groan inwardly at the mere thought of listening to Sawyer and blondie all night.

"Nah, it's not as bad as you'd think. The soundproofing does help. As long as he closed his door, we're good."

We stayed at Sully's a few more hours. Anna and Wyatt finally sang their song, which was more laughing than singing since they did *Baby Got Back* by Sir Mix-a-Lot.

We had a few more shots, and by the time Noah called the car, we were all drunk. The ride back to the buses is quick, which is good since we're all drunk and horny. After saying our goodnights, Noah and I finally enter our bus. My feet are killing me, and I can't wait to get inside and take my boots off.

The one thing neither of us were expecting was to walk in on blondie riding Sawyer on the couch. This girl is something else. She turns her head and looks Noah and me up and down, while she's still riding Sawyer's cock, no less.

"You guys want to join in? Or maybe switch partners? I'm not really into chicks, but we can make it a foursome if you want."

I'm about to go off on this trick, but Noah holds me back. He's just as pissed as I am.

Their clothes are all over the place; her bra is hanging off the Keurig, of all places. There's a bottle of tequila on the table and two shot glasses. Sawyer is so drunk his eyes can't even focus but he's trying because he hasn't taken them off me since we walked in.

"Go to bed, Amelia. I'll be there in a minute." I've never heard Noah this angry, not even when I told him Sawyer kissed me.

Noah doesn't wait for me to make it into the room before he flips.

"What are you on, Sawyer? I can see it in your eyes, you fucking took something! Get your whore and take it to your room. We don't *do* this, Sawyer! *Never*! So what, you just assumed *now* would be a good time to start when we have Mel on the bus?"

Sawyer doesn't say a word, and Noah stalks toward the bedroom, turning around halfway down the hall.

"Blondie, you need to be off this bus when you're done. Not after the sun rises, either. As soon as his dick goes limp, you're out. Don't make me throw you off myself. There will be a cab outside in fifteen minutes, and it will stay there until you get inside of it."

He slams the bedroom door, strips off his clothes, then strips off my clothes and throws me my pajamas. He begins texting furiously on his phone, and when he gets a reply, he tosses it onto the dresser. Sawyer just killed whatever sexual buzz we had going on from our night out. Noah turns off the light and pulls me down onto the bed and spoons me.

"I'm sorry, Mel. He's never done this before." He's trying to tamp down the anger in his tone, but he's really worked up.

"It's okay. You can't control your brother."

"It's not okay, but I'll deal with it in the morning. Goodnight, Mel."

"Goodnight."

I hate that he's so short with me, but when he pulls me in as close as possible and hugs me, I know it's not me he's angry with. His heart thumps rapidly against my back but slows after a few minutes. Only then, when I know he's alright, do I allow my eyes to droop shut.

I've got to pee, and I'm so thirsty. Noah is sprawled out on his back, so I can slip out of bed pretty easily. After using the bathroom, I stumble into the kitchen and grab a bottle of water. It's only four a.m., no wonder I'm so tired. We've only been back here for about three hours.

Blondie's bra isn't hanging off the Keurig anymore, but I'm opening the new one tomorrow and throwing this one out. Sawyer can buy another one.

"No, no, no, no, NO!"

The yelling is coming from Sawyer's room, and before I reach his door, he screams bloody murder. I flip on his light, but he doesn't wake up. Obviously in the middle of a horrendous nightmare, he's thrashing across the bed.

"Sawyer, wake up." I'm shaking him, but he isn't waking.

"Don't close your eyes, Jordan. Stay awake!"

D. Kelly

It feels like someone is squeezing my heart. He's dreaming about his cousin, about finding him in the house. About finding all of them.

"Sawyer, come on. Wake up, WAKE UP!" I'm yelling and shaking him, and he finally opens his eyes. Tears are streaming down his cheeks, his eyes filled with fear. I've never seen anyone so vulnerable before.

"Princess?"

"It's okay, Sawyer. You're okay," I whisper as I lower myself next to him on the bed. He pulls me into his embrace and hugs me so tightly it's hard to breathe. His whole body is clammy and sweaty.

"Oh God, Princess, they were … It was …"

"Shh, it's okay, Sawyer. I know. You're here and you're safe. Jordan is safe. It's okay. Everything is okay now." He sobs into my chest and begins to cry. Whatever drugs Sawyer did tonight have him completely fucked up.

He lies down and pulls me with him. I'm not comfortable with him like this, but I don't want to leave him, either.

"I'm so sorry for tonight. Thank you for being here." He continues to sob as I run my fingers through his hair.

"It's okay, Sawyer. Shh, it's okay."

"I'm sorry about the girl. It won't happen again, I promise. Don't leave, Princess, please. We need you." I pull back slightly and brush his hair from his eyes. My breath catches because they're so much like Noah's.

"It's going to take more than a skanky girl to get me to leave. I made a promise and I intend to keep it. This job is important to me … you're all important to me. I …"

"What, Princess? You what?"

"I feel like I'm home with you guys. I'm attached, and I didn't intend for it to happen, but I'm so glad it did. You don't have to feel the same or anything, but …"

Sawyer chuckles, and a small smile appears on his lips. "It's okay. We're pretty attached to you, too. We don't find new friends, *real* friends, often. It's nice when it happens."

I move back a little, but Sawyer clutches me harder, trying to keep me in place. "Please stay. I just need someone here for a little longer until I can come down."

"So you did do drugs tonight?"

"Yeah, but I swear I didn't know. She offered me a mint before she kissed me in the car on the way back here. I didn't think anything of it, but I fucking know better. It was Ecstasy, she admitted it when

134

we got here. I was pissed, but I was so fucking turned on I just couldn't care."

"Are you going to be okay? Do you need a meeting?"

"No," he answers, shaking his head softly, brushing my hair off my face. "Coke and meth were my drugs of choice. I've been able to control everything else. I've only done E once, and it was almost as bad as it was tonight. I'll be fine, I promise."

"Okay … Speaking of tonight … I know it's your bus and all, but your skank's boob-sweat-filled bra was all over the Keurig. Can we open the new one tomorrow?"

His eyes immediately begin to twinkle. "I think Rhymin' Rieanne could make a song from a mixture of those words, but sure, I'll replace it and order a new backup, no problem. It's the least I can do."

"Thanks."

A silence falls between us, and I feel like I'm teetering on a precipice. Sawyer is running his fingers up and down my arm, and he hasn't taken his eyes off of me. Nor have I taken mine off him. I'm worried about him, but I've got no clue what he's thinking about me.

"Sawyer?"

"Yes, Princess?"

"Does this happen often? The dreams, I mean."

"I'd like to say no, but I can't. It happens less than when I was younger. Usually, drugs bring them on. But sometimes it happens when I'm really stressed, or when the anniversary comes up. Even around big family gatherings."

"And Noah usually helps you?"

"He used to when they got bad enough to wake him. Most of the time he sleeps through them, especially with the soundproofing. I didn't want him to continuously keep getting dragged into my nightmares."

"I thought it was to block out the sex?"

He laughs so hard the bed shakes.

"Do I look like the kind of guy who wants to block out sex noises? I mean, if she gets ridiculously loud, I could cover her mouth or something. And Noah doesn't bring back girls often enough to make a difference."

"So you were protecting him?"

"No, I'm not that noble. I was protecting myself. It's my drama and I need to deal with it alone."

"Sawyer! I'm sure Noah would want to help you, and what about Jordan?"

"J deals with his demons by fucking. Must be a family trait. And Noah … He's helped long enough. It's easier for me to keep this to myself."

"So what about me?" I whisper softly, feeling guilty for even asking the question.

"You were in the right place at the wrong time, but I'm glad you were. You helped me tonight, and I'm thankful for that. You should go back to Noah. You guys are good together. If you ever fuck someday, you might even make me some cute nieces and nephews."

He releases me. For a quick minute, I'm disappointed. But in the next breath, I'm relieved because Noah's bed is the only place I want to be.

"I'm years away from kids, thank you very much. But hopefully, sometime soon, your brother will hit a grand slam and finally cross home plate."

As I stand, Sawyer reaches out and grabs my hand. "Hey, Princess, if Noah is waiting, it means he really likes you. Don't take that for granted."

"I won't. I could never. He's practically perfect."

"Practically?" he asks with a raised brow.

"Well, you know … he doesn't buy Pop-Tarts. That's a big brownie point loss."

His answering grin sets my heart on fire.

"Don't worry, Princess, you're the one person I don't mind sharing with."

"Goodnight, Sawyer," I say as he releases my hand.

"Night. Thanks again for tonight."

With a nod, I head back to Noah's bed, wondering how in the world this became my life and thanking my lucky stars that it is.

The next day is rough. Sawyer and I shared a pack of Pop-Tarts and our morning coffee in silence. True to his word, he threw out the Keurig and opened the new one for me. He even let me brew the first cup of coffee in it. Our time together last night still lingers in my thoughts and I wonder what I should tell Noah. Well, maybe not what … but when.

A little later on, everyone comes over to our bus. Tensions are high between brothers and bandmates. The guys end up spending most of the day behind closed doors in a meeting with Warren. I can only imagine how they're all laying into Sawyer right about now.

Thankfully, with Belle and Anna here, I'm pretty distracted with our girl time. We do our best to avoid talking about the elephant in the room, and the remainder of the day flies by in their company. We part ways when it's time for me to work the venue.

Tonight, I'm not in a people kind of mood, so I decide to focus on photography. During their set, I browse through the photos I've taken so far. They're raw and emotional, and I know just by looking at the thumbnail view, I'll never share them. They're hands down some of the best photos I've ever taken. Maybe it's because I have a soft spot for a vulnerable man or maybe it's because I'm feeling melancholy tonight.

After the show, the girls and I say our goodbyes with promises to spend time together over the holidays in a few weeks. They head back to their bus with Darren and Wyatt to enjoy their last few hours together before leaving for the airport. Heading back to my bus, I curl up into my bunk and work for a few hours. I'm not sure where Sawyer and Noah have been, but they just got back to the bus and they look exhausted.

Wordlessly, Noah reaches out his hand to me on the way to his room. Taking it, I follow him. I've been in my pajamas for hours already and even though I know nothing will happen between us, I feel a small twinge of disappointment when Noah strips down to his boxers and throws his own pajama pants on.

He lies down and pulls me to him before flipping off the light. Noah wraps his arm around my waist, my back to his front, and softly plays with my hair.

"Mel?"

"Hmm?" I answer softly, enjoying the feeling.

"Why don't you ever come in here before I have to come and get you?"

"Because it's your room, silly."

He releases a sigh and pulls me tighter. "Do I not make you feel comfortable enough here?"

"What? Noah, no …" I answer and flip over in his arms. "What's going on?"

His finger traces along the bottom of my lip. "I'm not sure. It's been a long day and I don't want to fight."

Fight?

"Noah, you should know I'm the kind of person who doesn't like to let things fester if I can help it. Why would we fight?"

"I don't do this, Mel. I don't hook up with random girls. You're the first woman in a long time I've been interested in. I get you're going to need your space sometimes, but why would you come to bed with me only to sneak out in the middle of the night? Why not just say you'd rather be alone?" His exasperated tone lingers between us.

"Is that what you think? That I ran out on you?" I pull myself to a sitting position and sit Indian-style up against the wall. "Jesus, Noah, Sawyer was right … you could sleep through anything." I try to stifle my laugh, but it's no use. He sits up and turns on the light, practically blinding us both, before crossing his arms defensively.

"Why is this funny to you?"

"Because the *only* place I wanted to be last night was in your arms. I thought that was plainly obvious. I woke up to use the restroom and get some water. You were knocked out. On my way back to bed, Sawyer started screaming." I shudder just thinking about how awful it was.

"He had a nightmare?"

"Yes, a really bad one. I woke him up and pulled him out of it. He needed comforting, so I stayed with him. He refused to let me wake you, said you'd done your share of taking care of him."

"He's such a stubborn ass," he answers with a frustrated sigh.

"I think it runs in the family."

He turns his green eyes to mine and smiles. "Oh yeah? Why is that?"

"Just a feeling I have," I reply with a sigh. "Look, Noah, I don't do this, either. Letting you in as far as I have has pushed past every single comfort zone I have. I know better than to date musicians."

"Mel …" he cautions.

I hold up my hand so he'll let me finish. "But you're not like any other man I've ever met. I like you, *a lot*. However, this is still new, and we agreed to take things slow. Which is why I don't push myself into your personal space."

"What if I like you in my personal space?" he asks, lying back down and pulling me on top of him, his hardness underneath me impossible to miss.

"Then do what you did tonight and ask me to come be with you. I don't push myself on people, Noah. You're going to have to let me know when you want me in your space, or when you want to be in mine." I emphasize the last few words by grinding my pelvis against his.

"Do you always have to make everything hard?" His double entendre isn't lost on either of us. He pulls my lips to his and kisses me softly. I've never been kissed before the way Noah Weston kisses me. His kisses are sensual, loving, and filled with comfort. It's almost as if with every stroke of his tongue he's claiming a piece of my soul.

"Think of it this way," I reply once he has me tucked into the crook of his arm, "I'll never be the crazy fangirl lying in wait in your hotel room."

"Maybe not, but could you be the sexy girlfriend waiting in lingerie to reward her star-studded boyfriend after a show?"

"I think I could probably arrange something like that." I begin to drift off in his arms, still exhausted from last night with Sawyer. I'm pretty sure Noah thinks I'm asleep because his next words are whispered so quietly I barely hear them.

"I don't ever want to sleep without you again."

I've never had to try so hard to pretend to be asleep before. Every part of my being wants to freeze up. Those words are frightening to me, and although I like Noah and really want to make a go of this, I'm not ready for a forever kind of commitment.

Belle's Post-Utah update

Slammers!

It's your girl Belle, and do I have news for you! Over the weekend, I got to see another BAD show, and let me tell you, it keeps getting better and better. I wish I could give you all the gift of witnessing BAD in person, but even I can't pull those kinds of strings.

So here's what I can do. I've got a set of passes—one for you and one for your lucky guest—to join us at BAD's super-secret holiday show. This is where the free concert will be filmed, and it's going to be a blast.

How do you enter?

At the bottom of this post, there is an entry link. You need to fill out all of the questions. Don't skip any or it will void your entry. One winner will be drawn at random. You do have to be twenty-one to enter per the rules of the venue hosting this event.

Now, to hold you over until the next update, my girl Mel and Wyatt Smith have put together an album of photos from Wyatt's wedding to his longtime girlfriend Anna. That's right, ladies and gentlemen, if you missed my announcement a few weeks ago, (or if you were in denial) I'm reconfirming it now. Wyatt is off the market. Don't shed too many tears. True blue BAD fans know Wyatt and Anna have been together since before BAD existed. This is a bona fide match made in heaven, a real life happily ever after.

Congratulations once again, Anna and Wyatt!

Don't forget, live today like there's no tomorrow!

Xs and Os,

Belle

Repercussions

It's been a week since Sawyer brought the girl back to our bus. Things have been tense. Noah is still pissed at him, even though I really believe he didn't take the drugs on purpose. Most mornings, Sawyer doesn't even come out to get coffee and when we work out, he's seriously working out his aggressions. I'm wondering if he's pissed at himself or struggling because he wants to use again.

Now, he's fifteen minutes late for our getting-to-know-you session. That's what I've started calling them. Noah is on the other bus with the guys, and it feels strange to be out here by myself. When I've finally decided I've waited long enough, Sawyer comes strolling out of his room.

"Sorry, Princess, that took longer than I thought," he tells me as he grabs a bottle of water and sits in the recliner.

"No problem. Were you stuck on a call?"

"No, I was watching porn and jerking off."

My eyes immediately drop to his hands and quickly dart back to his face. His smirk is ridiculous, but he's obviously telling the truth.

"Good for you. Feel better?" I snap, not exactly sure why I'm so pissed off, other than ever since that night he's been more and more inappropriate with his comments to me.

With a shrug, he answers, "It helped to blow off some steam, but what I really need is a willing fuck. How about you, Princess? Want to help me out?"

"What the hell, Sawyer? What's wrong with you?!" *I can't believe he just said that to me.*

"Oh, come on, why are you acting all high and mighty? It's not as if you haven't ridden the musician train before. And it's not like my brother is giving you any. Let's work out our frustrations together. I promise you'll feel better."

He moves from the recliner to the couch, and his hand creeps up my thigh. I shove it off of me and jump up.

"Are you on drugs again?" I demand, but his eyes look fine—pupils are normal, they're not glassed over or anything.

"No, I'm just an asshole who wants what he can't have."

My heart races and my voice drops lower than anticipated. "What's that supposed to mean?"

He stands and wraps an arm around my waist, pulling me to him. "What do you think it means, Princess? It means I want to fuck you."

Without thinking twice, I slap him across the face—*hard*—and pull away from him. He cups his face with a stunned expression, one that would make my heart ache if I weren't so pissed.

Shit, that hurt.

I'm shaking my hand out and slowly back away from him. At least he has the decency to look remorseful, if that's what you'd call it.

"You love him," he whispers softly, and my heart beats faster.

"What? No."

"I was testing you, trying to gauge your feelings for him. I had to know if you could be swayed back to your old ways."

He's lying. I know he's lying, but I want to believe him because anything else is unthinkable and unforgivable. And I don't want to hate Sawyer.

"I like him, a lot. I'm not that girl anymore, Sawyer, and you testing me or whatever the fuck it was you just did is *not* part of my job description. You don't get to talk to me like that, and if it *ever* happens again, I'm going straight to the label. Sexual harassment is real, Sawyer, and you are an asshole. We're done for today."

After storming off to Noah's room and slamming the door behind me, I throw myself on the bed. I hear Sawyer scream "Fuck" and then there's nothing but silence. This is exactly why I didn't want to get involved with any of them. Close quarters and sexual tension don't mesh well. And I can't tell Noah what happened. He and Sawyer are already at each other's throats. Maybe he was telling the truth and he was looking out for Noah. I couldn't blame him if that's what he was doing. God knows it's hard to trust anyone in this industry.

I've earned his trust by now, haven't I? He's told me things he's never told anyone outside their circle. I'd never break his confidence. Maybe he's regretting his choices, maybe he thinks I'm going to betray him. I don't know if I should try to get closer to him or stay far, far away. Whatever happens, Noah can't know what just went down. I don't want to be the girl who comes between them; they can't go through that again.

It's been two weeks since my falling out with Sawyer. The first few days, I pulled away from Noah, mostly feigning sick. He was beyond attentive, insisted I take his room, brought me soup, and completely doted on me. Then the next few days, I claimed I had lots of work to catch up on to explain my distance. I even pulled the whole "I could be contagious for up to ten days" line to get him to agree to sleep in his room after I scrubbed it down—not that it needed it. I was fine, just emotionally drained.

Finally, when he was as fed up as possible about me sleeping in my bunk, I blamed my period. Last night, my period stopped—perfect timing since we pulled into Las Vegas a few hours ago.

"Mel?"

I look up to see Noah standing in front of me with a dozen beautiful red roses in a crystal vase. I can't help but smile at him.

"Yes, Noah?"

"Are you feeling better?"

It's his way of politely asking if I'm done being a bitch and off my period.

"I am much better. Thank you for asking."

"Good," he says, finally handing me the flowers and taking a seat next to me.

I pull them to my nose. "Mmm, they smell amazing."

"I'm glad," he answers with a small smile, and I take them and set them on the desk in the office area. When I come back, he's squeezing the edge of the mattress with his hands. I take the seat next to him and turn toward him, giving him my full attention. "So I was wondering ... would you be okay sharing my suite while we're here? I mean, we can totally get you your own, but I was just hoping ..."

I place my finger against his lips. "Shh," I tell him and lean in for a quick kiss. "I'd love to share a room with you. I don't need my own."

"Are you sure? Because it's not a problem. I know things have been strained between us lately."

"Noah, I want this with you. Truly. I'm sorry things have been off. I've just been working through some things, but those things have nothing to do with my feelings for you. I'm sorry if I gave you that impression."

He nods and a grin peeks up from the corners of his mouth.

"Mel?" he asks again.

"Yes?"

He pulls me close so our lips are only a whisper apart. "Can I make love to you tonight?"

"God, yes." His mouth captures mine, and I exhale softly when our tongues meet. Noah kisses with every ounce of his being. I pull away before I climb up into his lap and take him here and now.

"Noah?"

"Yes, Mel?

"Is that suite ready yet?"

He laughs loudly and pulls me into a hug while walking backward into the living area of the bus. "Not yet, but soon. Pack your stuff so we can go have some fun first. Besides, I want to take you on a date tonight. Bring something sexy."

"Can I bring B.O.B.?" I ask, teasing him.

He growls and pushes me onto the couch, climbing atop my body. "After tonight, you won't even remember B.O.B.'s name."

"Poor B.O.B.," I whisper softly.

"Indeed, because when I'm through with you, the only thing you're going to crave is my cock. B.O.B. will be a distant memory."

Fuck if his dirty mouth doesn't turn me on like crazy.

"I'm going to hold you to that, Weston. You better be able to back up your game." He pushes against me, hard and ready, and I wrap my legs around him and pull him close just as the guys all walk onto our bus.

"Uh, we came to tell you the rooms are ready, but maybe you don't need one after all," Wyatt says, avoiding looking me in the eye.

"About fucking time. If Noah and Princess don't fuck soon, their sexual tension is going to blow this bus apart," Sawyer tells them. He's not making eye contact with us, either, but his underlying tone indicates he's happy we're together.

"Tell me why Belle isn't flying out here this weekend again? Vegas is only a forty-five-minute flight from L.A.," Darren grumbles.

"Because ... she's wrapping up the next issue so she can have the whole week to spend with us ... well, mostly you ... at Thanksgiving next week. Would you rather have two days or a whole week?" I ask sweetly.

"Both, I want both."

"Here we go again," Sawyer groans.

"Darren, Belle likes you, and if you want something serious with her, you have to make it clear. She's not the kind of woman who is going to assume a man wants something more with her. She's happy to have variety in her life. But that's not to say she won't be in a committed relationship, either. You're the rock star, so the ball is pretty much in your court."

"Is that like saying Belle wants a man to tell her what to do?" Sawyer asks, and I finally sit up and shake my head.

"No. It's basically like this. Darren could have any woman on the planet he wants. Belle knows this. She's not going to put her heart into a game where she's one of many players. That's not how she works. If you want her, you have to show her the only players in this game are the two of you."

"That makes sense," Wyatt tells him with a pointed stare.

"Sometimes it sucks having to be the guy. Why can't a girl just say what she wants?" Darren whines.

"Darren, you *do* realize you're a mega star, right? I know deep down you're just a guy. But Belle has her head on straight. She isn't going to jump in heart first for you, as much as she may want to. You've got to guide her to you so she knows you want her as much as she wants you."

Wyatt nods in agreement. "Yeah, what she said. Besides, haven't you always complained about wishing you knew a girl wanted you for you and not because of what your status might be? I'm pretty sure Belle wants you for you or she wouldn't be keeping you at a distance."

"That's true," Darren mumbles as he types furiously on his phone.

A few minutes later, his phone goes off and right after his, mine does as well.

Belle: Booyah! Skype sex tonight!

There's no way I can hold back my laugh, and from the blush that creeps up Darren's cheeks, he knows exactly why I'm laughing.

"Good job, Romeo," I tell him as I type a message back to her.

Mel: You're not the only one excited. Keep doing whatever it is you're doing, it's working.

Belle: I'm just being me. Love you! Can't wait to see you next week. Xoxo

Mel: Love you, too. Miss you bunches.

"Are you done yet?" Noah asks, peeking over my shoulder with a smirk on his face.

"That depends … are we getting out of here?"

He nods, and I hop up and start walking to my bunk. "I'll be ready in ten minutes."

Their laughter follows me to the back of the bus.

"You're whipped, man. And I can't even say you're pussy whipped because you haven't hit it yet." Sawyer's words are said in jest, but based on Noah's reply, Sawyer has pissed him off again.

"So what, Sawyer? Maybe you should stop being a douche and let someone into your life. Then maybe you'll get it."

I look up in time to see Sawyer storm off the bus.

"Yo, Noah, you've got to let this go," Darren cautions him.

"Yeah, I hate to be the one against you, but Sawyer didn't get high on purpose. If you keep pushing him, he might just get high to piss you off," Wyatt adds.

"It's more than that, but it's not something I want to discuss right now," Noah whispers to them, but I can still hear him. This bus isn't that big.

"Alright, man, you know where to find us if you want to hash this shit out," Darren says, standing and patting him on the shoulder as he exits the bus.

"Later, dude. I'm off to pick up Anna," Wyatt adds as he leaves. After grabbing some things out of the bathroom and throwing them into my bag, I zip it up and throw it over my shoulder.

"Ready," I call out and flash Noah a smile. We're going to have fun tonight if it kills us. Enough with this heavy stuff lurking over our heads.

Noah stands and pulls the bag from my shoulder. He's always the gentleman.

"Ryan is going to be our security for the weekend. I'm sorry, but Vegas can get out of control real fast. It's also a place where we might go unnoticed the entire weekend. It just depends. He'll keep as much distance as he can."

Bodyguards—it's been a long time since I've had to deal with them, but I understand their importance.

"It's okay. I get it." We exit the bus and walk out to the waiting SUV. The entire time, Noah keeps his hand on my lower back. It's the best feeling in the world, so subtle but so intimate. The Vegas sunshine beats down on us, and I pause for a minute to pull my sunglasses out of my bag. While I'm at it, I grab my lip balm and swipe it across my lips. Noah leans down and kisses me softly when I'm finished.

"Tasty," he says with a smile.

"Melon," I toss back over my shoulder while climbing into the SUV. They've got tonight off and then they have shows the next four days. I'm thrilled to have some alone time with Noah this weekend. Maybe it can help me sort out all the uneasy feelings I've had about keeping what Sawyer did away from him. I know it's for the greater good. I just have to keep reminding myself of it.

Vegas Vacation

We're staying at the Hard Rock Hotel. When we arrive, we're ushered into the VIP registration area. They're expecting us, and everything is ready and handed to Noah in a matter of minutes. We're in the Nirvana Suite which is a penthouse suite. The woman checking us in bats her fake eyelashes at him but remains professional.

Ryan leads the way, and once again, Noah guides me with his hand on my lower back. It takes a few minutes for Ryan to check out the room, but when he returns, he gives us the all clear. Our bags are already inside, and Noah lets Ryan know we'll be here for a little while and he'll call when we need him.

I've been in nice hotel rooms before, and this one is no exception. It's massive, over two thousand square feet, with two bedrooms. Floor-to-ceiling windows give us an incredible view of the strip. I bet it looks amazing at night.

Noah comes up behind me as I'm looking out over the city and wraps his arms around my waist.

"Do you like it?" he asks, softly nipping at my neck.

"Mmhm, it's gorgeous, but are we sharing it? It's huge!"

"Hell no. I wanted something where we could be together but you could still have your own space if you needed it."

I relax in his arms and lean into his kisses. His warm lips feel so good against my skin. "The last thing I want right now is space. I'm excited to be here with you."

"Me, too. I mean, I'm excited to be with you, Mel."

I turn around in his arms and wrap my arms around his neck. He lowers his mouth to mine and kisses me softly.

"How about lunch? We can order some room service and go sight-seeing or get a movie?" he says hopefully.

"Are you a gambling man?"

"That depends. Do you want to gamble?"

I nod excitedly. I love Vegas and the excitement in the casino. He laughs and pops a quick kiss on my lips.

"Okay, room service for lunch and then gambling before our night out."

We quickly browse the menu and order lunch. While he takes care of that, I explore the suite. There's a massive shower; it could fit probably six or more people with room to spare. It's all glass and has multiple knobs and showerheads. You could shower and look out at the strip. Outside, on the terrace, it's fully furnished and there's a heated plunge pool which could be fun, but it's pretty cold outside. Even heated, I think I'd still freeze. My body does not like the cold; probably a side effect of being a California girl. Three bathrooms, a large great room, a bar—the only thing missing is a kitchen.

This entire situation is still so surreal to me. Somehow, I ended back where I started. It's like karma is saying, "You can run but you can't hide." But this time around, it's different. I'm with a functional band on a farewell tour. This isn't my future, only my present, and in a way it's my chance to say a proper goodbye to my past.

"What are you thinking about?"

I turn around and go sit next to him on the sofa. "Just about how strange life can be sometimes."

He nods. "I get that. I thought I was going to want to do this forever. Be in a band with my friends, my brother, and travel the world. Then suddenly it stopped being my dream. Stopped being enough."

"What's your dream now? I mean, you've accomplished more in twenty-eight years than most people do in a lifetime."

"I want a life. A domesticated one. My sister Diane and her husband Rob are happily married. My nieces are the light of their lives. I want that. I want a legacy, kids to love and carry on my life cycle. I want to grow old with someone and take care of them during all the shit life throws our way, knowing she'll take care of me, too. I know it sounds morbid, but it's easy to love someone through the good times, but the ultimate test of love is making it through the bad and coming out on the other side stronger than ever."

"It's not morbid. That's as real as it gets. Too many people give up, they don't fight, and they let go of the best part of their lives so easily. In the heat of the moment, everything seems so black and white, but life isn't black and white at all. It's in those shades of grey where we all get lost, question our morality, make the bad choices that affect the rest of our lives. Those make-or-break decisions are the crux of our being, and having the right person by your side is *everything*."

Noah leans over and crushes his mouth to mine. I open to him immediately, and our tongues meet stroke for stroke. He releases my mouth and tugs my head back by my hair, lowering his lips to my throat. Biting his way down my neck, he soothes the sting with the swipe of his tongue, fueled by my needy whimpers.

"I need you, Noah," I cry out just at the doorbell rings. He pulls away breathlessly and cracks a grin.

"Saved by the bell," he says, jumping up.

"What do you mean, saved?"

He smiles down at me as the bell rings again. "Coming!" he yells.

"I wish," I mutter, and Noah laughs as he walks to the door. He answers and signs for the food. The delivery guy is probably in his early twenties. You can immediately tell he knows who Noah is, but he remains professional. When Noah hands him the payment pouch, the kid checks it quickly but discretely to be sure he filled it out.

"Have a good day, Mr. Weston. Please let us know if you need anything."

"Hey, kid," Noah calls out, and the delivery boy stops in his tracks and turns around.

"Yes, Mr. Weston?"

"Are you a fan?" He looks torn, like he wants to answer but is afraid to.

"Yes, sir, who isn't?"

Noah laughs and points to me. "See my girlfriend over there? She's not a fan, but I think she's slowly coming around."

His mouth drops as if surprised there could be such a thing as a non-BAD fan.

"That was pretty much our reaction when we found out. Anyway," he says, pulling something from his pocket and handing it to him. "Here are two tickets to our show. They're my personal tickets so you can use them whichever night works for you. The date is open."

"Thank you so much. I don't know what to say."

"Just do something nice for someone else someday when you can," Noah tells him, and my heart melts into the biggest puddle of mush.

The guy nods up and down excitedly. "I can do that. I can definitely do that."

Noah pats him on the back and walks him out. His excitement still lingers when he's gone.

"Why did you do that?" I ask as he wheels the cart over to the couch.

He shrugs. "I always try and do stuff like that. Especially for people who work jobs where they take care of others. Sometimes it's a meal, sometimes it's more."

My heart flip flops in my chest. Any chance of not falling in love with Noah Weston is officially gone. I'm pretty sure I'm head-over-heels already.

"What's the biggest thing you've ever done?"

A blush creeps into his cheeks as he chews his French fry.

"The biggest, or the most meaningful?" he asks thoughtfully.

"Both." Now he has me intrigued.

"I have a good financial planner who's made good investments over the years. I'm a planner, always have been. So I guess the most meaningful are the accounts I've set up for my family. My nieces will never have to worry about college, and no one in my immediate family will ever have to worry about retirement. They don't know it yet, but when it's time, they will."

"That's amazing, Noah."

"It's nothing. Family should always help family."

"And the biggest?" I prompt, anxiously awaiting his answer.

"I guess the biggest thing I ever did for someone else was pretty meaningful, too. I saw a story on the news one day about a family whose insurance denied a heart transplant for their fifteen-year-old son. They had a huge fundraiser for him, and I donated a million dollars."

"Oh my God, Noah! That's incredible, but that's a lot of money."

He laughs softly. "Now, it's a drop in the bucket, but back when I did it, I didn't have nearly what I do now. But it didn't matter. You shouldn't be able to put a price on someone's life. Even if I never earned another dime, I still had my health and I could still work. Money has never really mattered to me."

"I understand that. I've got more money in the bank than I know what to do with, but I don't want any of it."

He shakes his head. "You're doing good things with it, Mel. But I agree with your grandma. Your parents would have wanted you to have it, to never struggle, and to make sure you and your children have a good life someday. It's all about balance. You can give it away *and* secure your future."

"So what, now you're a financial planner?" I ask, hoping to lighten the mood.

"Probably would have been if I didn't tour with the band. I've always been cautious and prepared. I was probably the only thirteen-year-old I knew who had a retirement account."

"You didn't."

He nods sheepishly. "I did," he confirms, and I can't stop laughing.

We continued to chat about random things over lunch, and then he called Ryan to follow us down into the casino.

"I've got to stop at the ATM," I tell him as I grab my purse.

"Uh-uh. Today is my treat," he states firmly.

"Noah, I don't spend money on much, but I love to gamble. I can easily drop a few grand in a matter of hours. That's not something I'm putting on you."

"I can afford it."

"That's *not* the point," I protest.

"How about you let me pay, and if you win, you can pay me back?" he asks with a smile.

"How about I pay and you pay me back if you win?" I toss back at him.

He reaches around my waist and pulls me to him. "You are frustrating, and if I wasn't secure in my manhood, I'd go as far as to say emasculating. Do you know how many women have ever offered to pay for anything?"

"Probably none, but the sooner you learn I'm not every woman, the better. You pay for you, and I'll pay for me. Then, tonight I'll put on a sexy dress and let you buy me dinner. Deal?"

He releases a frustrated sigh, but the twinkle in his eyes betrays him. He's irritated and happy at the same time.

"Deal," he concedes.

"Good, let's go!" I take his hand and pull him out of the room. He's laughing behind me, but I can't help it; Vegas is fun.

"What do you play?" I ask him as the elevator takes us down to the casino.

"Poker, usually. Sometimes video poker or roulette. When I'm feeling adventurous, I might try the craps table, but I'm not very good at it."

"Okay, so let's start with a drink and some video poker and work our way up to adventurous. How does that sound?" I ask, taking his hand in mine and leading him off the elevator. Ryan follows us, and I inhale deeply as I lead Noah to the ATM. Las Vegas has the most ridiculous stench of cigarettes, cigars, alcohol, and desperation in the casinos, but I love it. It's part of the experience, and for whatever reason, it makes me happy.

Noah uses the ATM first and turns to me before punching in his code. "Are you sure I can't sway you into letting me pay?"

"I'm positive. I like paying my own way, Noah. It's just who I am. You need to accept that if you want to make this work."

With a shake of his head, he turns around and makes his withdrawal. I make sure to look the other way as to not invade his privacy.

"Your turn," he says as he moves to the side. After making my withdrawal, Noah leads me to the closest bar. After we're both seated, Ryan stations himself about three feet behind our barstools—close enough to intercept a fan but far enough away to let us talk with a semblance of aloneness.

While the bartender is taking my order, Noah quickly slides a twenty into my machine. "Noah!" He raises his hands in mock surrender and leans over, placing a quick kiss against my lips.

"For luck," he answers huskily against my lips.

Hell, how can I argue with that?

"Thank you," I reply gracefully, and his answering smile is worth letting him have his way. The two of us talk easily, transitioning from one topic to the next.

"Come on, baby," I say as I hit max bet and wait for the cards to flip. Noah raises a brow at me, and I squeal as four aces pop up on the draw. I save the aces and hit draw again and receive a King as a high card.

"That's right. Come to mama!" I cry out as my available balance grows on the machine. Noah chuckles next to me and shakes his head. "What? I won!" He reaches for me and pulls me to him, parting my lips with his tongue. After he kisses me senseless, he pulls away from my mouth and leans his forehead against mine.

"I've never seen anyone talk to their machine before. It must be lucky."

"Just wait until I have a few more drinks. I talk to them like they're my best friends. But that's not why I won. I'm pretty sure that was all on you and your lucky money."

He brushes my hair back and cups my cheek. "I'm pretty sure it's the two of us, Mel. We're incredible together, and the universe knows it."

My heart flutters, and I suddenly need air. "What do you want to do now?" I ask him, hoping we can go straight to the room and ease this ache between my legs.

"Anticipation is a wonderful thing, Mel. How about we hit the poker tables?"

I nod and hop off my barstool, pressing the button to collect my ticket. There's a woman on the other side of the bar eyeing us suspiciously, and I've got a feeling Ryan is going to be dealing with her very soon.

There's only one open spot at the poker table, but I'm not great at real poker anyway, so I tell Noah to take it and I sit one table over and buy in for some blackjack instead. I play a few hands against the dealer and then let him know I'm going to wait a few minutes to see if any more players show up. It's not fun playing alone, and I'm honestly too busy watching Noah to want to play.

As Noah is dealt his cards, he takes a quick look and places his bet. His table is full and no one recognizes him. He's dressed casually in dark blue jeans and a black t-shirt. The colorful ink on his arms is set off against his shirt and the casino lighting. He's incredibly sexy, and I wish the casino was empty so I could straddle him at the table and ride him until we both tremble with exhaustion. He peeks up at me and winks, and even though it's the sexiest fucking wink in the world, I decide I've ogled him enough and have the dealer go ahead and deal me in again.

Ryan is trying to stay in between me and Noah. I'm pretty sure Noah told him to stay close to me, even though I'm not the one who needs him. And when the dark-haired girl from the bar and her friend come up and tap Noah on the shoulder, Ryan steps into action.

Noah holds up his hand, probably trying to diffuse the situation himself, and folds out of his game. We're less than three feet apart, and since I know how fans can get, I refrain from betting another hand. Instead, I tip the dealer so he knows I'm done for good.

"I told you it was him!" she squeals to her friend, and Noah flashes her his fan smile—the one that melts panties worldwide but never touches his eyes. I don't think many people would ever pick up on it, but my dad had the same smile for his fans.

"Hello, ladies," Noah greets them kindly.

"We're going to be at your show tomorrow," the dark-haired girl's friend tells him as she bounces up and down excitedly, giving him the perfect view of her fake, bouncing tits. *Ugh.* I will admit this is intriguing to watch. I've avoided the VIP meet and greets so far just to be able to focus on them and not their fans. I wanted to wait until I had a handle on their personalities before integrating myself into those events. Mostly so I didn't judge them unfairly while we were still getting to know each other.

153

"Great, I hope you both enjoy it. I'm glad you were some of the lucky ones to get tickets."

"We're here alone," the one with the dark hair tells him. "Maybe we can take you out for a drink?" *Oh, she is a bold one, isn't she?* Is it wrong that part of me is really eager to see how he handles this?

"I'm sorry, ladies, no can do. Have a great day," Noah answers firmly and stands. He tips his dealer and pockets his chips. She isn't ready to take no for an answer, though. Instead, she slips her arm through his and tilts her head up to him, giving him the ultimate pouty face.

Ryan jumps into action as soon as she links her arm.

"Release Mr. Weston, NOW." His tone is commanding and firm. Her friend stands back, looking embarrassed, but this bitch isn't letting up.

"Oh, he doesn't mind. This is all part of the game. He plays hard to get, and I convince him I'm worth it," she replies, pushing her chest up onto his. Part of me wants to do something, and part of me is enjoying seeing how Noah handles his fans.

Ryan looks to Noah for guidance, and Noah nods subtly. Ryan pries Noah's arm away from hers carefully and professionally. Noah moves closer to me without ever taking his eyes off of the demented woman. His arm wraps around my waist, and I stand up, allowing myself to be pulled into his firm grasp.

"You're picking *her*?" she squeals incredulously.

"My girlfriend," Noah counters proudly. "Yes, every single time I will pick her. No doesn't just mean no when a woman says it to a man. It also means no when a man says it to a woman. You'd do yourself a favor to remember that. Have a nice day, ladies."

Her friend snickers and shakes her head, clearly enjoying that her overly anxious friend just got told off. Ryan keeps close to us as Noah wordlessly moves us toward the elevators. Once we're safely inside, he pushes me up against the back wall, leaning his head against mine. Ryan faces forward, ignoring us. Or trying to.

"I'm sorry, babe," he whispers softly against my lips. I reach my hands up and wrap them around his neck.

"You've got nothing to be sorry about. I know how this goes, and to be honest, we got to hang out down there longer than I thought we would. Besides," I whisper conspiratorially, "I'm more excited to start getting ready for our date tonight."

He groans and pushes his hardness against me. "Me, too," he answers with his eyelids fluttering. The elevator door opens, and Ryan checks up and down the hall.

"The hall is clear, Mr. Weston. I'm going to check out the room and give it the all clear."

"Sure thing, Ryan," Noah tells him, keeping me pinned against the wall. But when we hear a girl screaming at Ryan, Noah releases me as we both exit the elevator to see what the commotion is about.

"He'll want to see me," the woman's voice travels outside of the room.

"Highly doubtful," Ryan says dryly as he pulls her outside of our suite. The woman is gorgeous with her long, flowing, red hair, legs for days on end, perky, full tits that bounce like mother nature intended—there's nothing surgically enhanced there. *Lucky bitch.* She's wearing knee-high black boots, dark blue skinny jeans, and a light pink V-neck sweater. I'd almost consider playing for the other team for a shot at her.

"Sara? What are you doing here?" Noah asks, stalking toward her. His expression is fixed, and I can't tell if he's happy to see her or pissed.

"I wanted to see you. I'm here for your show this weekend and thought I'd come by and say hi and see if we could talk."

Noah runs his hand through his hair and exhales loudly.

"We don't have anything to talk about," he finally answers, her sadness at his reply evident.

"Please, Noah, I miss you," she pleads.

He shakes his head in disbelief, and she finally looks past him and realizes he's with someone. Based on the O her mouth just formed, she's surprised but recovers quickly.

"I thought you didn't do the groupie thing."

Damn, she went from sweet to snarky pretty fast.

"Not that it's any of your business, but I don't. This is my girlfriend Amelia. Amelia, this is Sara, a *long* ago ex-girlfriend of mine."

"I hadn't heard you were seeing anyone."

"We don't exactly travel in the same circles anymore."

She laughs. "The media *is* your circle, Noah. You can't do anything without someone documenting the moment."

"Well, now you know, and if you'll excuse us, we have plans. I hope you have a nice stay, Sara. I wish I could say it was good to see you."

"You're really not going to talk to me?" she asks emphatically.

I squeeze his hand gently to get his attention and place a soft kiss on his cheek. "I'm going to go inside and let you work this out."

"You don't have to go," he says, and the look in his eyes is obviously pleading with me to stay, but I can't.

"I do," I state firmly and walk inside, closing the door behind me so he realizes I'm really trying to give them the privacy they deserve. After pulling a big, bulky sweater from my bag, I walk over to the bar and mix myself a vodka and cranberry before going out onto the terrace and curling into one of the overstuffed chairs.

The sun sets over the Vegas skyline, and all the casinos light up in its absence. It's such a beautiful sight, and I wish I wasn't alone to see it. My mind wanders to Noah and Sara and I can't help wondering what went wrong in their relationship. Most men wouldn't let a girl like her fade into the background. Then again, Noah has shown me time and time again he's not most men.

I try not to let myself dwell on the fact they have history. Or the fact she's gorgeous, or the fact he could change his mind about us and decide to go back to her. Because even though I haven't had sex with Noah, I'm slowly realizing it's the last piece of myself I have left to give. He's already stolen my heart, whether I want to admit it to myself or not.

I'm not sure how much time has passed since I left them in the hall, but it's dark outside by the time Noah pops his head out. I'm just about finished with my jumbo-sized drink and am feeling the warmth of the alcohol spreading through me.

"Jesus, Mel," Noah says as he squeezes in next to me. "It's freezing out here." He pulls me close and rubs my arms.

"I'm fine," I assure him and hold up my drink.

"Great," he mutters. "Now I'm driving you to drink. Could this night get any worse?"

"That depends …"

He lifts me up and pulls me into his lap, making both of us a little more comfortable in this chair. "On what?" he asks, pushing my hair aside and placing soft kisses against my neck.

"Are you leaving me for her?" I ask boldly and unashamedly. I'm not going to wait and wallow in what ifs.

"God no," he whispers, picking up the intensity of his kisses along my neck, moving to the front of my throat. I move my head back onto his shoulder, giving him easier access.

"Are you sure? Because I wouldn't blame you. She's beautiful."

Pulling my head so I'm facing him, his eyes lock onto mine in a firm hold. "Only on the outside. Her beauty is only skin deep, and I don't want that kind of person in my life. She's malicious, though,

156

and I can guarantee you our relationship is about to be blown wide open for the world to know about it."

"It was bound to happen," I whisper, never breaking our intense gaze.

"Amelia, you're breathtaking. Your beauty far surpasses hers, both physically and internally. I've never in my life wanted someone as much as I want you."

"Oh." One single, disappointed-sounding word falls from my lips at his confession. It's not that I am disappointed; on the contrary, I'm elated.

"Don't sound so excited," he says with a slight chuckle.

"It's not that. I'm just surprised, is all."

"Why?" he asks, intrigued.

With a shrug of my shoulders, I finally break our gaze and lean back against his shoulder. "Because sometimes the past wins and sometimes we shouldn't stop it. I know I'm being superficial and extremely self-depreciating, but she is gorgeous, Noah, and she *did* come all this way to see you. I guess I didn't expect you to put me above her."

His arms wrap tightly around my waist, and we both stare straight forward at The Strip. After a few moments of silence, he begins talking.

"I thought tonight would go so differently. I still want it to, but I want to tell you a few things first. I was going to talk to you about this anyway, but I think now it's more important than ever to talk."

"Okay," I whisper as my heart begins to race.

"The first time I saw you was when you were heading toward the greenroom at The Greek. There was a twinkle in your eye, and I couldn't place it then, but after learning about your parents, I think I figured it out. You felt like yourself again. You felt like you were home. It's probably why you told Sawyer off because your filter was down. All your defenses were."

Wow. He completely nailed it. "Go on," I whisper softly.

"That night, on the beach, I wanted to know you. I wanted to know you in a way I'd *never* wanted to get to know someone before. You were mesmerized by the shine of the moon on top of the ocean waves, and I was mesmerized by you. I'm not sure I'd ever been happier about anything as I was when you said you'd join us on tour."

"Noah ..."

"Please, Mel, let me get this out." He pauses and then continues.

"The last few months have been the best of my life. It's like everything we've gone through as a band happened so I would end up here with you. I believe that with every fiber of my being. With every brush of your lips against mine, with every smile you give me, with every laugh we share, I fall deeper and deeper in love with you."

My gasp is audible, and he presses his lips against my neck.

"You don't have to say it back. You've made it abundantly clear you guard your feelings, and it's okay if it takes you longer to get where I am. I just wanted you to know how I feel because I don't ever want you to question how I feel about you should something like what happened today happen again."

"Noah," I say softly, turning to face him, "I love you, too."

"Seriously?"

With a nod, I answer, "Seriously. I'm not sure when it happened. Sawyer said something a little while back that made me question it, but when I left you with Sara tonight, I was suddenly sure. I hoped you wanted me as much as I wanted you, but I couldn't stay out there and sway your decision. You had to decide if you wanted me on your own."

Noah picks me up and carries me inside, planting us both on the couch. His hand caresses my cheek, and goose bumps cover me from head to toe—the good kind.

"You love me," he states simply.

"I do."

"And I love you," he replies, and I nod.

"You do."

"Okay, then. Let's get the rest of this out of the way so we can go on with our night. You owe me a sexy dress, if I remember correctly."

"Yes, and I have just the one."

With a frustrated groan, he pulls a blanket from the back of the couch and wraps it around us so we can warm up.

"Sara was my first girlfriend after Marilyn. We went to high school together and had been pretty good friends. She followed the band and came to all our shows at the bar and any others we played locally. When she heard through the grapevine what had happened with Marilyn, she sent me a Facebook message letting me know how sorry she was."

"That was nice. I'm surprised you even go on Facebook."

He smiles. "I don't usually. I had a Myspace account, and when most of my friends went to Facebook, I set it up. It's a look into normalcy for me, I guess. Every once in a while, I log in to check up on my old friends. It's nice to see how their lives turned out. When I started seeing people having kids and getting married while we were touring and living our dreams, it started to get to me, though."

"Seeing what you wanted and can't have. Yeah, I can understand that."

"So, anyway, Sara and I started talking. She said she'd tried to call my cell, but after the whole Marilyn thing, we all changed our numbers. We started talking, reminiscing, she came to a few shows, and we fell into a comfortable rhythm."

"Sounds nice, Noah."

"Yeah, it was, but I should have realized it was *too* nice. Anything I wanted to do, she was down for it. Anywhere I wanted to go, she was fine with it. She always let me decide, and she *always* let me pay."

I turn to him, asking pointedly, "Would you have let her pay if she offered? I've been there, Noah. You're not exactly easy to sway."

"Probably not, but she never tried. Which was okay. I'm rich and I like to treat the people in my life. It's the right thing to do."

"So I don't understand. It sounds like things were going well. What happened?"

His face contorts into a grimace with what must be painful memories.

"It's going to sound petty, and I'm not trying to, I swear. At first, it was little things. She'd come for a weekend and forget her shampoo. But she couldn't just use ours or Anna's, she had to go to the fanciest store and buy expensive stuff. Which was me buying it because, you know … that's what I do. Then suddenly, she was running low on cash to pay her rent and bills and needed small loans. I was happy to help, but in the back of my mind something nagged at me."

"You weren't sure if she wanted you for who you were or for what you could give her."

He taps the end of my nose with his finger. "Exactly. So then, when she'd come visit for the weekend, she started just bringing herself. Nothing else. No clothes, toiletries, not even a change of underwear."

"Oh," I answer softly, finally understanding where this is going.

"Still, I let it all slide until one weekend when we had a local show back home. It was a charity event, and even the band only had limited tickets. Two per band member, to be exact. Between Sawyer and I, we had enough tickets for our parents and sisters. Wyatt gave his extra ticket to Jordan because it was a gun violence event and we wanted it to be a united family front."

A bad feeling crawls over my skin as he continues his story.

"To say Sara was pissed is an understatement. She threw an absolute hissy fit. Apparently, she'd told a bunch of her friends she could get them in. Sara and twenty of her nearest and dearest were waiting at my house a few hours before the show."

"Oh no. Noah, I'm so sorry," I tell him, resting my hand on top of his.

"It was a nightmare, Mel. She'd convinced the housekeeper to let them in, and since we were dating, she had no reason not to trust her. When I got home to change, they were all drinking in my kitchen, listening to music, and having a good time. I asked to see Sara in private, and as you can imagine, things only went downhill from there."

"What a disaster." I feel so bad for him. How could anyone take advantage of Noah like that? He's got a heart of gold.

"There were tears and hysterics. She told me I was the love of her life and she never even considered I'd put my family before her. Mel, God's honest truth, we dated less than a year and saw each other one weekend, maybe two, a month during a good month. We never once used the L word. For me, it was casual. I mean, as casual as you can get in a monogamous relationship because I don't do the whole groupie thing."

"So it ended there?" I hate that I'm intrigued by his story, not because he went through hell, but because it's another chance to get to know him more.

"Oh no, I wish it had. She kept showing up at my house. I had to hire a security firm to guard it. She was essentially stalking me. Sending texts and creepy messages. It got so much worse. I mean, for me, it ended that night, but for her, I'm not sure she realizes even now how far of a line she crossed."

"And now she's back."

"And now she's back," he confirms with a frustrated sigh. "I ended up having to report it all to the police. Warren made me. I didn't take it as far as a restraining order, maybe I should have. I just wanted her to leave me alone. I already called Warren before I came and got you outside. Now, I have to get with my attorney tomorrow and give him a statement and decide if I want to press charges. To top it all off, we have to hire extra security for the venue because she already stated she was coming to the show."

My heart drops in my chest as I turn to face him. "Do you think you're in danger, Noah?"

He shakes his head. "I don't think so. But the fact of the matter is, she's crazy. So how hard is it to go from crazy to violent? I'm not sure."

"Wow."

"I do want to clarify I wouldn't have gone back to Sara, even if she wasn't nuts. We were never right together, and I think part of the reason why I was with her was because I knew she wouldn't fuck me over for Sawyer."

There it is—the elephant in our whole relationship, the crux of his issues with Sawyer. I know their stress lately has been because of me. I'm not sure why, but I can feel it.

"Noah, you know I'd never leave you for your brother, right?"

He diverts his gaze elsewhere, and I tenderly pull his face toward mine.

"Noah, I need an answer."

"No, Mel, I don't think you would. But I don't think that would stop Sawyer from trying something. I'm pretty sure he has feelings for you."

Shit.

It's not like I didn't feel it, but it makes our confrontation a few weeks ago even worse. Not to mention I hid it from Noah. But I don't want to give their feud any more fuel, either. I've got to stick to my decision to let it go, but if Sawyer does something like that again, I'll have to tell Noah everything.

"I care about Sawyer and what happens to him. I consider him a friend. Plus, he's your brother, and that means something to me. I'm a strong woman, Noah, and although your brother may exude sexual greatness to some women, I'll never be one who falls under his spell. If you truly love me, you have to trust in *me*, not Sawyer."

"Mel ..."

"Look, Noah, I'm not telling you to cut your brother off or not believe in him. Sawyer loves you and would do anything for you. I have no doubt about that. *None.* Sometimes, our hearts and our libidos want what we can't have. I think Sawyer falls into that category often, not because he doesn't love you, but because he sees what you have and he wants it, too. I just don't think Sawyer realizes he can get it on his own."

"What do you mean?" he asks thoughtfully.

"I think Sawyer assumes it has to do with the woman someone has versus finding one and making that for himself. He needs to feel love, Noah, but for whatever reason, he feels he isn't worthy of finding a woman on his own who can give him that. Hence all the one-night stands."

Noah stares at me as a heavy silence wraps around us. Maybe I went too far. I should have just kept my opinions of Sawyer to myself, but I'll be damned if my relationship is going to be condemned because Sawyer can't keep his dick in his pants.

Noah reaches his hand around to the back of my head and crushes my lips to his. It takes me by surprise, and when I open my mouth and let out a yelp, he invades me with his tongue. He meets mine mercilessly, and then pulls his other arm up to hold my head steady. His fingers are laced into my hair, his lips moving against mine with so much passion I can't catch my breath, and I don't want to. I'll willingly drown in Noah's kiss one delectable stroke at a time.

When he pulls away, we're both breathless. "I fucking love you, Amelia. More than you can ever imagine."

"I think I've got a small idea," I answer as I brush my fingers against my lips, silently willing his to come back.

"Go shower and get changed. Text me when you're done and don't leave the bedroom. I'll pick you up at your door."

"Okay," I reply, still in a daze from that kiss.

As I walk into the bedroom and close the door behind me, I let my excitement kick in.

Noah Weston loves me, and I love him.

Date Night

After an amazing shower, I moisturized my skin, applied my makeup, dried and curled my hair, and got dressed. I'm hoping we're staying inside of the casino because although I have the perfect dress, I don't exactly have a warm jacket with me to go over it.

As I slide on my black heels, I take a final look at myself in the full-length mirror. My long, brown hair cascades past my shoulders in big, bouncy curls. My royal blue halter dress is tight on top and flares on the bottom. It rests about mid-thigh, and it's nothing but bare legs until my heels. I've got on a small diamond pendant necklace my dad gave me for my fifteenth birthday and a matching tennis bracelet. He was so proud when he gave it to me. He said he and my mom had picked it out together before she passed away. They're the perfect accessory for any occasion and a way of keeping them both close to my heart.

When I'm satisfied with my appearance, I grab my phone to text Noah. My hands are trembling. *Why am I so nervous?*

Mel: I'm ready when you are.

A soft knock against the door indicates he's seen my text. As I swing the door open slowly, he takes his time looking me over from head to toe, and I return the favor.

"Jesus, Amelia," he whispers softly as he wraps his arms around my waist. "What did I do to deserve you? Because I want to keep doing it for the rest of my life."

My cheeks flush with his words, or maybe it's because of how sexy he looks. Noah's wearing a charcoal suit with a grey button-up shirt and a deep purple tie. His dress shoes are shined to a polish as well.

"Fucking gorgeous."

"Me or you?" he asks with a smile, and I can't believe I said that out loud.

"Uh, you, definitely you," I reply, and he smiles wider.

"Why are you smiling at me like that?"

"Because you lose your filter when your defenses are down. And I love that your defenses are down right now."

I'm thrilled with his words, glad my defenses are down, too. It doesn't seem to happen very often. "So what are your plans for the night?"

"Do you dance?"

"Of course I dance. What kind of rock star's child would I be if I didn't dance?" I ask with a laugh.

He shrugs. "An uncoordinated one?"

"Do you want to dance with me, Noah?" I ask in what I hope is a seductive tone. By the way he pulls me tighter to him, I think he'd agree.

"Very much so." He laces his fingers in mine and walks me into the great room. The whole room is flickering in candlelight, and soft music is flowing through the speakers in the corners of the room. There's now a table set up with fine linens and champagne on ice. Covered containers of food await us on the table, and there are dozens of roses in vases decorating the room.

"Noah, this is everything. It's perfect," I whisper in awe.

"Are you sure? We could go out, but I thought after the day we had, maybe a night in would be more conducive to expressing our feelings."

Oh, I want to express my feelings all right. Too bad dropping to my knees and sucking him off as an appetizer would probably wreck the romantic vibe he has going on tonight.

"I love it. Seriously, it really is perfect. Thank you."

He presses a few buttons on the remote for the sound system and pulls me into his arms. I rest my head on his shoulder as we sway together. Then Noah does the unexpected and sings along to the music, giving me my own private concert. His voice is magic, and the tingling between my thighs grows with each word he sings. Sawyer and Noah often split the vocals, but Sawyer is always the front man.

"Please tell me you've considered going solo with that voice," I whisper in his ear.

"Nah, that's not my thing, but I'll sing to you anytime you'd like."

"Promise? Because I'll never tire of you singing your heart out to me," I tell him candidly.

"Promise, Mel. Whenever you want, whatever you want to hear."

I nod and rest my head against his as he sings along to *Open* by Rhye, and I relish the sound of his voice against all of my senses.

Being with Noah is effortless. I've never felt more comfortable around anyone, except maybe Belle. I thought my relationship with

Eli was perfect, but this puts that one to shame. We continue to dance through a few more songs. I'm not even sure what they are; I'm just hypnotized by Noah's voice as he sings along.

"Are you hungry?" he asks softly.

"Hmm, for food?"

A massive smile spreads across his face. "Yes, for food. After we eat dinner, *then* we can have dessert."

I turn my head, looking around for the dessert cart. "Where's your magic cart?"

There's a wicked gleam in his eye as he pulls me back to him. His mouth descends to mine as he places soft kisses against my lips, my cheeks, and makes his way to my ear, where he whispers huskily, "I thought I'd sample you tonight instead."

"O-kay, let's eat." With a soft laugh, he leads me to the table and pulls out my chair for me. Before he sits, he uncovers our meals—steak, lobster, and loaded potatoes. "This looks amazing, Noah."

"Thanks. It was pretty hard ordering, actually. I've been paying attention to what you eat lately, but I wasn't sure if the lobster was okay."

"Lobster is *always* okay," I tell him emphatically, and he laughs.

"Well, that's good to know. I put a cheeseburger and fries behind the bar in case you didn't like it."

He's so damn sweet.

"Maybe that can be our midnight snack."

"I love the way you think," he says. Reaching across the table for my hand, he pulls it to his mouth and places a soft kiss against it. When he releases me, we both start eating. A comfortable conversation flows as we eat our meals, but I barely manage to eat half of mine. The butterflies fluttering around my stomach are wreaking havoc on me. I'm looking forward to our after-dinner activities way too much.

Noah pushes his plate away and crinkles his eyebrows at me. "Do you not like it? I won't be offended if you want the cheeseburger instead."

He tops off my champagne glass and refills his own. I take a sip before answering and let my eyes flutter closed with the decadence of it. "It's wonderful," I answer, turning my gaze to his, "but I'm not hungry for food anymore." His pupils dilate as I rise to my feet. Standing with me, he takes my hand and leads me into the bedroom.

When Noah opens the door, I can't help but gasp. "Noah, this is incredible." I'm in complete awe as I look into the room. He's set up a star projector. It's so realistic, I can't imagine how much it cost him. There are a few candles flickering for ambiance. It's perfect.

He pulls me close and tenderly kisses my forehead. "We don't get much time outdoors, and I'd give anything for a night under the stars with you. Until we get our chance, I wanted to bring the stars to you. But someday, Mel, I'm going to make love to you under the stars. Just like I wanted to the first night we met when we were down on the beach."

His mouth captures mine in a sweet, heart-fluttering kiss. He cups my cheeks in his hands softly as his tongue swipes along my bottom lip. Wrapping my arms around his neck, I open to him, letting his passion for me ignite us both. Noah takes his time with this kiss, knowing tonight there's no rush and we can take things as fast or as slow as we want to.

When he pulls away and releases me, I spin around and take in the rest of the room. Roses in vases are strategically placed on each dresser and nightstand just out of reach from the flickering flame of the candles. Chilled champagne and two fresh flutes are next to the bed, and a single red rose lies atop one of the pillows. There's nothing he hasn't thought of.

Noah pops the champagne and pours us each a glass. Nobody has ever done anything like this for me before. *Not ever.* When he passes me my glass, he raises his in a toast.

"To love. May we be blessed with it deeply, every single day of our lives," he toasts.

When his glass clinks against mine, I echo his sentiments, "To love." As I take a sip of the bubbly deliciousness, I can't take my eyes off of him. He places his glass on the dresser, and I follow suit, allowing him to pull me into his arms.

"I love you, Amelia," Noah whispers against my lips.

"I love you, too, Noah." I softly caress his cheek with my hand. His mouth lowers to mine in slow motion, the taste of champagne still lingering on his lips. His tongue sweetly parts my lips, and I whimper at the sensation. No one has ever made love to me before, and so far, Noah is knocking it out of the park before we've even really started.

His hand glides from my hips up toward my breasts. I lean into him, enjoying every touch. My hands roam his back, softly caressing his broad shoulders and feeling the flex of his muscles each time he moves. When his mouth leaves mine and drops to my throat, to my neck, and finally to the sweet spot on my ear, I call out his name, "Noah."

"Say it again, Mel," he whispers as he pushes his hardness against me. I'd call his name out forever if it comes with that response each time.

"Noah, please ... I can't take anymore anticipation."

He chuckles lightly against my skin and leads me to the bed. I'm not waiting any longer. As we walk, I begin ridding him of his clothes, starting with his jacket that falls to the floor.

"Oops," I murmur as my fingers begin working on his tie while he pulls the halter over my head and unzips the back of my dress. As it falls to the floor, Noah groans when he takes in my black lace bra and matching thong. Of course, I'm still wearing my heels.

"I wish I knew how to paint because this moment deserves to be captured for all time. Your photo could hang in museums for centuries to come."

There's a rush of heat to my cheeks, and I'm surely blushing from head to toe. Awkwardly, I try and shake his words off with a joke. "You know I'm a sure thing, right?" He's not having anything to do with my jokes. Instead, he pulls me to him and brushes his lips against mine.

"I'm not kidding, Mel. You're the most beautiful woman I've ever seen."

"Thank you," I whisper softly while trying to get his clothes off. While I work on the buttons of his shirt, he draws a trail against my skin with his fingertips. His touch is so light, goose bumps spread across my skin. He stops touching me when I pull each arm out of his shirt. I'm fascinated as I watch him finish what I started. First, he toes off his shoes and then unbuckles his belt. When he drops his pants, I suck in a much-needed breath. His erection is straining against his Calvin Klein boxers, but when my eyes drop down to his socks, I can't help but chuckle.

"What, the black socks aren't sexy?" he asks with a grin.

"You look like the dink," I reply honestly.

"The dink?" he asks, confused.

"Please tell me you've seen *Stealing Home* with Mark Harmon and Jodie Foster. It's only the best movie of all time."

"No, I haven't, and it's a baseball movie?" he questions, and I nod. "I'm usually all over baseball movies."

"It's old. It came out in 1988, the year after I was born. I used to watch it at least four times a year with my mom. Anyway, we'll watch it and you'll understand. Until then, take off the socks."

"Just the socks?" he asks as he reaches down to peel them off. Once he has them off and looks back up at me, I pull him toward the bed.

"For now. Heels on or off?" I ask as he checks me out again from head to toe.

He gestures for me to sit on the bed and kneels down, removing them one at a time. "Off. But someday soon, I want them wrapped around my head while you're screaming my name."

Holy shit.

His words drench my panties even more than they already are. Noah Weston has a sexy fucking mouth. I only nod my agreement because there's no comeback to that, and from the predatory look he's giving me, the conversation is over anyway. I scoot up on the bed and move the rose from the pillow. After taking a long inhale, I place it delicately on the side table, careful to avoid the candle. Noah sits up on his knees and lifts my foot into his hands. He massages my arch and the rest of my foot, then switches to the other one.

"Noah, that feels amazing." My eyes practically roll into my skull from the pleasure. When he releases my foot, he begins to deeply knead my calves. With a loud sigh, I allow myself to enjoy the pleasure he's giving me. As he reaches my thighs, his hands are replaced with his mouth, his lips searing their imprint onto my skin. With every single kiss and swipe of his tongue, a tingling sensation encompasses me from head to toe. I'm on cloud nine and we're barely getting started.

As he spreads my legs and kisses my pussy through my panties, I begin to whimper. I can barely keep still beneath him as he sears a trail of kisses from my abdomen to my breasts. He shows attention to both breasts, catching my nipples with his teeth through the fabric of my bra and tracing the edges of the lace with his tongue. At least he's close enough now so I can get some friction by rubbing myself against him. I wrap my arms around him and massage his back, his biceps. God, he has nice arms. When he reaches my neck, my body arches off the bed, closer to him. He chuckles softly, but firmly pushes me back down. He wants me at his mercy.

I want to be at his mercy.

When we're finally eye to eye, he reaches his hand up and caresses my face tenderly, never once breaking eye contact with me. His striking green eyes move closer and closer to my hazel ones as he peppers kisses across my forehead, over my cheeks, down the bridge of my nose, and finally to my mouth.

Anticipation.

I'm so worked up, I cry into his mouth as soon as he parts my lips with his tongue. His kiss is slow, calculated. When I wrap my arms around his neck, he pulls back, taking me with him. Reaching around and popping my bra open, he slides it from my arms without once breaking our kiss. I'm pretty sure Noah Weston is a sex god.

After he pulls away, he drops his head down to my breasts. My hands instinctually drop down to his head, where I can glide my fingers through his hair. He's cupping both of my breasts, one in each hand, kneading and massaging them, caressing them as his body moves against mine. Then he's dropping his lips to them, rotating his mouth between the two, sucking, licking, and biting. With each bite, I cry out and tug his hair. He's creating an incredible balance between pleasure and pain, and I want more of him. *I need more of him.*

He releases one of my breasts and slides his hand down into my panties.

"Fuck, baby, you're drenched for me." The fire in his eyes as he slides a finger inside of me ignites my fire even more. I buck into his hand and cry out his name.

"Noah, please ..." My whimpering fuels his passion even further as he slides a second finger inside of me and sucks harder on my throbbing nipple. His eyes meet mine again as he flicks his thumb against my clit.

"Noah! I'm going to come!"

He increases the pressure of his thumb and the pace of his fingers. "I know, Mel, and I can't wait." He drops his mouth back down to mine as his fingers work their exceptional magic. When he adds a third finger inside of me, my walls clench and spasm as I'm taken over by one of the strongest orgasms I've ever had. He keeps his mouth against mine, catching every last cry, and when my orgasm subsides and I've finished arching my body against his, he pulls back.

Noah's predatory gaze moves down my body. His hands make their own path down along my curves, finally hooking on to my panties. Seductively, he slides them off and tosses them to the floor. His tongue takes a journey across his lips in anticipation as he spreads my legs and nestles his head between them. When his tongue swipes against my sensitive flesh, my body arches off the bed. It's been so long and his mouth feels too damn good. He takes his hand and places it against my abdomen, holding me in place as he licks and sucks, bringing me to the brink yet again.

"Noah!" I scream, unable to hold back a second orgasm. His tongue darts into my channel as my walls convulse around him. His hand still presses me in place but it doesn't stop me from writhing in pleasure. When he finally comes up for air, he looks damn proud of himself. Swiping his thumb over his bottom lip, Noah crawls atop my body. When he reaches my mouth, he rubs his thumb against my lip—coating it with my essence—and lowers his mouth to mine. I never used to be a fan of this move, but tasting myself on Noah's lips is a complete turn on.

He reaches across to the bedside table and grabs a condom. "Are you on the pill?"

I wish I was because Noah Weston is the first and only man I've ever considered letting go in bareback. "I'm allergic to birth control."

He looks at me quizzically as he removes his boxers. "I didn't know that was a thing."

"Unfortunately, I'm one of the small percentage of the population affected."

"That sucks," he says as he works the condom on.

"You're telling me," I reply with a laugh. This is such a random conversation we really should have had before, but somehow, even now, in the middle of the most romantic night of my life, I still feel comfortable talking about this with him.

Noah's naked body in front of mine pulls me from my thoughts. My eyes peruse him for the first time from head to toe, and my libido lights up again. His body is incredible, not like I didn't realize it before, but he's seriously perfect. Leaning forward, I place my hands against his chest, allowing myself to explore his body. His abs are taut under my palms. He hisses as my fingers follow along his happy trail. I divert them momentarily to trace a path along his perfectly cut V. My pulse quickens as my hand lands at the base of his cock, which is sheathed and ready for me.

Noah leans forward just a little bit and cups the back of my head with his hand. Gently, he guides me back to the bed while exploring my mouth with his tongue. Kissing him never gets old. While he kisses me, his hands explore the curves of my body, and I return the favor. The flickering candlelight makes the setting beyond perfect as the shadows of our bodies do a sensual dance across the room with the stars. He pulls a whisper away and brushes his thumb across my cheek.

"Thank you," he says softly.

"For what?"

"Giving me you," he answers, kissing me again. As our kiss intensifies, he presses his cock against my entrance, teasing me, bringing me to the brink once again.

"Noah," I gasp as I pull my mouth from his. "I want you." With my words, he slides in further.

"You've got me," he replies, finally pushing all the way inside. He stills, pausing a moment to relish the feeling. "Jesus, Mel."

Spurred on by his words, my legs wrap around his waist and I pull him to me, bringing him as deep as he can possibly go. He groans, and I begin moving against him. Slowly, he begins moving himself. He raises one hand above my head and laces his fingers through mine. Our bodies move in a beautiful synchronicity; I can't believe we waited this long to have this. But Noah was right, if anticipation built up to this, it was beyond worth it.

My orgasm is building, and from the corded muscles flexing in his neck, I'm assuming his is as well. Noah is deep inside of me both physically and emotionally. Our lovemaking is beautiful.

"Noah, oh God, Noah ... Yes!" I cry out as my walls clench around him, my body riding out wave after wave of pleasure. And when I'm at the tail end of coming down, his orgasm shatters through us both, bringing me right back to an unbelievable high.

"Amelia."

My name falls from his lips as he collapses against me and wraps me into his arms. Our sweat-slicked bodies and pounding hearts become one. Neither of us speak, but I can't help running my fingers through Noah's hair. I've found my soul mate, of this I have no doubt.

He finally rolls us onto our sides and removes the condom, tying it and tossing it to the floor. "What are you thinking?" he asks as he brushes my hair from my face.

"No one has ever done that to me, Noah. No one has ever made love to me, not like that. It was amazing."

A sweet smile creeps across his face. "I have a confession."

With a raised brow, I let him know to continue. I'm pretty sure it's the only part of my body I can move right now. "I've never made love to anyone before. Not like that."

His words send my heart aflutter, and the shy look on his face confirms his confession is true. "Hmm, guess we were saving the good stuff for each other. Noah?"

"Yes, Mel?"

"In case you were wondering, since you asked before, you've definitely proven you can back up your talk."

"Is this your way of telling me I'm the best you've ever had?" I bite into my lower lip and nod. He smiles triumphantly and lays back, pulling me into the crook of his arm. "I already knew that."

"Then why did you get all macho man about it?"

"Well, maybe I didn't know it then, but I know it now. I figured if this was hands down the best sexual experience of my life, it had to be yours, too."

My fingers dance in circles across his chest as his heartbeat echoes in my ear. It's so strong and steady.

"You're so quiet, Mel. What are you thinking now?"

I love how he asks me this question as if he's waiting with baited breath because he really does want to know. When a man wants to know a woman, it's a special thing. Unfortunately, in my life, it hasn't happened all that often. If I'm honest with myself, the last person who ever wanted to know me—*all* of me—was Eli. How sad is that?

"Shh, I'm listening to your heartbeat. It's my new favorite sound, aside from your newly-discovered singing voice."

His heartrate increases, thumping harder and faster against my ear. My words are affecting him, which is good because he's affected me since the moment we met.

"I'm a lucky son of a bitch," he replies with a wondrous tone, and I smile against his chest. There's no reply needed because if he was listening to my heart now, he'd notice it's beating faster as well. We fall asleep under the stars, with me listening to his heart and his fingers dancing through my hair.

Rude Awakenings

I hear the ringing in my dreams. It's a rotation of tones and it's finally bugging me enough to wake up. The room is dark, thanks to the heavenly black-out curtains. The candles have long since flickered out, and I stumble from our bed to the bathroom. I don't hear a thing now, so it must have been my bladder's way of waking me up from a dead sleep. After quickly relieving myself and pulling on a robe, I walk out to the bar and grab a bottle of water.

The remnants of the cheeseburger we shared last night after our second round of lovemaking are still sitting on the plate. I throw the cover over it and smile as I remember how we worked off our late-night snack. Noah fucked me in the best possible way: up against the floor-to-ceiling window as we looked out onto the city glowing below us.

The phone to the room rings, and I grab it before it wakes Noah up. We had a long night, barely falling asleep when the sun was rising, and he's got a long night ahead of him still.

"Hello." My voice is groggy, and I try to clear my throat.

"Oh, Mel, thank God you picked up!" It's Belle and she's obviously crying.

"Belle, what's wrong?" This isn't like Belle. I haven't heard her cry since my grandma died.

"I'm downstairs, and I really need to see you. Can you please tell Ryan it's okay to let me up?" She sobs again. I drop the phone and grab mine, quickly texting Ryan to do whatever needs to be done to let Belle up to my room.

"Done. Now, talk to me until he comes to get you."

"No, he's already here. I'll be up in a minute." She hangs up the phone, and I rush to the other bedroom to throw on some underwear and pajamas. A few minutes later, I'm waiting in the doorway for her.

As soon as she exits the elevator, I know something is extremely wrong. Her hair is everywhere, she's in pajamas, she's not wearing any makeup, and she's even wearing slippers. Ryan follows behind her, and when she pulls me into a tight hug and sobs hysterically, he sets her bag inside the door, closing it behind him with a nod to me.

Because of Belle's strong-willed personality and love for life, I sometimes forget how fragile she is. Not only because of her extremely petite size, but also because when she hurts, it cuts her down to the core.

"Come on, let's talk."

We walk toward the great room, and as we pass the bedroom where Noah is sleeping naked on the bed, I quickly pull the door closed. It doesn't latch all the way, but close enough.

"Is Veronica okay?" It's the first thing I ask because the only thing I could imagine shattering Belle like this is if something happened to her mom.

"She's fine," she says, pulling a tissue from her purse and blowing her nose.

"Are you sick? Is something wrong?" Her normally glowing ebony skin is dull, and it concerns me. *Immensely.*

"Everything is wrong. Why didn't you answer your phone? I've been calling for a half hour. I thought they were going to have me arrested until I finally got hold of Ryan."

"We were sleeping, we ... We didn't go to sleep until pretty much sunrise. What time is it, anyway?"

"Dammit, Mel, I'm so sorry. I forgot last night was the night. I'm over here crying while you're positively glowing. Shit!" Belle's obviously frustrated, at herself or the situation, I'm not sure, but at least her anger brings a little bit of a glow back to her cheeks.

Moving next to her on the couch, I pull her into a big hug. "You're my sister, Belle. I don't care if I'm mid orgasm, if you need me, I'm there for you."

She snorts and tucks into my arm. "That's so fucking demented but in all the right ways."

"Alright, why don't you tell me what's going on? Let's start with how you got here?"

She pulls her knees to her chest, still staying tucked into my hug. "I flew, in my pajamas, looking like this. My plane landed at eight, and I got here about eight thirty. It's just a few minutes after nine now, to answer your earlier question."

Well, that explains why I'm so tired and why Noah is still dead to the world. At least Belle seems to be doing better, or at least I thought so until the tears begin to stream down her cheeks again.

"Belle, you're scaring me. Please talk to me."

She finally looks up at me. "That makes two of us. I'm so fucking scared, Mel," she sobs, her body shaking with each one. I couldn't hug her any tighter if I tried, but I want her to feel my love

174

and this is the only way I know how. Tears are pooling in the corners of my eyes, her grief having an effect on me, even though I don't know what we're grieving. I don't need to, though; her pain is enough to affect me.

"I'm pregnant, Mel," she whispers softly. It takes a minute for her words to bounce around through my sleep-deprived brain before they really sink in.

"What? How?"

She snorts and actually smirks for a brief minute. "I think you know how. When the penis enters the vagina—"

"Smartass, you know what I mean. Aren't you on the pill? You've always been on the pill."

"Yeah, of course, well … sort of. God, I'm so stupid! Not everyone can be a condom control freak like you, okay?"

"Hey," I say softly, pulling away and turning toward her. "I'm not judging you, Belle. I just want to understand."

She exhales loudly and puts her head in her hands. "I know, I'm sorry. I shouldn't take it out on you. It's not your fault you're allergic to the pill."

I leave her on the couch for a minute and go to the bar for a couple bottles of water. Handing her one, I sit back down. She scoots up to the end of the couch and turns to face me, tucking her arms around her knees. I mirror the pose. This has always seemed like our position for deep conversations.

"Sometimes, I forget to take my pill. I get swept up in life and work, so I end up taking it late some days or sometimes miss a day. It hasn't been an issue because I still *always* use condoms. But the night of the BAD concert, on the beach with Darren, I wasn't expecting to have sex. And apparently, he wasn't, either, because he didn't have any condoms. He thought he did, but he'd forgotten his wallet in the house."

I know where this is going and I really wish I didn't.

"Belle, he's a rock star and STDs are a real thing! What were you thinking?" I'm not trying to chastise her, I'm really not, I'm just concerned.

"Obviously, I was thinking I was about to fuck a dream guy. One who has been on my top ten list to cheat on my husband with since I was old enough to make that list and stick to it just in case I ever did get married."

I laugh, not at her, but with her. "I forgot about your 'celebrity crush I'm allowed to fuck' list. Go on."

"I didn't lie to him. Let me be crystal clear about that. When he realized he didn't have a condom, we had an adult conversation. I told him I'd missed a few pills but I had just finished my period which should mean we were safer than at any other time of the month."

I'm nodding at her, hanging on to her every word as she continues.

"He assured me he gets tested every few months for STDs as part of his contract. Which totally makes sense to avoid scandals and such."

Noah didn't tell me that part.

But then again, it never really came up because we used protection.

"He swore he always used condoms, and I believed him, Mel. I still do. We were so caught up in the moment and threw caution to the wind. It was stupid, so fucking stupid, but I'd never felt like that before, Mel, you know?"

"Yeah, Belle, I do."

"Darren's touch ignites my soul. How could I say no to my one chance to feel that? And yes, I know he was on my list, but if it hadn't felt right I wouldn't have done it … But it felt so right. I know this is going to be TMI, but he was supposed to pull out."

Oh shit. "And he didn't?"

"I sort of begged him not to."

Jesus, this just gets better and better. "Why? Why would you put yourself at risk like that?"

Her cheeks flush, and a small smile peeks up from the corner of her mouth. "Because I was on top, and I started to come. It was the most intense, most explosive orgasm of my *entire* life. I still can't really describe it, but it was like, at that moment, he reached in and grabbed a part of me that had never been touched. I didn't want to lose a second of that sensation out of fear I would never feel it again."

"What did he say when you told him not to pull out?"

She giggles with the memory of their first time together. "He said 'Oh, thank God, because I really wanted to bust a nut in you.'"

We both fall into a fit of laughter, her because of her memory, and me because I can completely picture Darren saying that.

"I think he felt it, too, Mel. Whatever it was that possessed me that night on the beach … I think it reached out and took him as well."

I think she's right, but it's not my place to say. I've signed so many NDAs I can't divulge our conversations, but I know Darren wants so much more with her. He just needs to figure out the right time to tell her.

"Was that the only time you two didn't use a condom?"

She holds up two fingers. "Scout's honor."

"So what are you going to do now, Belle? Did you come to tell him?"

She shakes her head sadly. "No, I came to beg you to go with me to have an abortion."

An abortion.

I get it. More than anyone else, I understand where she is right now. But she has to tell him; he has to know. Reaching over and taking her hand in mine, I give it a tight squeeze. I swear I heard a noise, but when Belle doesn't flinch, I assume I'm wrong.

"I will do whatever it is you need me to do. But you have to tell Darren first."

"I can't. I won't do that to him," she states adamantly.

"Do what? Tell him the consequences of a mistake you both made? This isn't all on you, Belle. It takes two to tango irresponsibly and make a baby. I've been there, remember? But I would have never *not* told Eli. That wouldn't have been fair to him. You have to tell Darren."

"How, Mel?" she squeals, standing up, throwing her arms up in the air while she paces the room. "How do I tell that beautiful man I'm pregnant and I'm going to fuck up his life with an unwanted baby because he decided to fuck a reporter who can't remember to take her birth control on time?"

"The same way you told me. He knew, Belle. You didn't lie to him, you didn't take advantage of him, and he damn well knew what could happen by having sex with you without protection, just like you did. You both made this mess, and you both need to decide what to do now. This is not only your choice. You need to hear him out, to see what he thinks, because if I know anything, it's that if you thought he loved you, there's no way you'd give that baby up without a fight. You don't need a man to be a mother. Your mother is the perfect example of that."

She flinches with my heated words as her hand drops to her stomach. She's close to three months along right now, and the longer she waits to figure this out, the harder it's going to be. Before she gets a chance to reply, Noah comes out of the bedroom fully dressed.

Shit. I knew I heard something, and it's not like we were being quiet. His jaw is tight as he marches straight over to the couch and sits down, pulling me into his lap and wrapping his arms around me tightly before dropping a kiss against the back of my head.

"You heard," Belle states sadly.

He nods, and in the coldest tone I've ever heard him speak in, he gives her a piece of his mind. "I did, and Mel is right. You have to tell him. If you don't, I will. Right fucking now."

Belle collapses into the closest chair, her eyes darting from me to him.

"He's my best friend, Belle, just like Mel is yours. He has a right to know, and I could never forgive myself for keeping it from him. I'm sorry I overhead your private conversation, truly, I am. But I did, and I can't *not* tell him. Although, I really want it to be you. I think he may surprise you, but you'll only know if you try." This time, his words are much softer, kinder.

"When did you take the test?" I ask.

"Last night after our Skype session. I was inputting deadlines into my calendar, trying to work around show schedules, and realized I missed my period twice. I don't know how I didn't notice it. I guess it didn't really dawn on me because you weren't around to eat Ben and Jerry's with me. When the test came out positive, I went to the all-night clinic. The test came out positive there as well, and since they were slow, they went ahead and did an ultrasound."

She crosses the room and grabs her purse, pulls out a photo, and passes it to me. Tears fall from my eyes as I look at it. It's just a peanut now, but that peanut is a part of my favorite person in the world, and I love it already.

"She's gorgeous, Belle," I whisper, holding the photo higher so Noah can see it. He traces the little nugget with his finger and then presses his lips against my neck.

"Don't do that, Mel. Don't get attached, don't cry, and don't personalize her." I direct a raised brow her way, and she shrugs. "You don't even have to say it. I know I've already personalized her, too. I mean, how could she *not* be a girl? Look how tiny she is."

Noah chuckles against my skin and brushes my hair to the side so he can rest his chin on my shoulder.

"I could call him down here. Mel and I could be your fluffers while you tell him."

Belle and I start cracking up. "You mean buffers, right?" she asks him.

"Well, yeah, but fluffers makes it sound way more interesting."

She smiles at us; it's possibly the most genuine smile I've ever seen on her. "You're good together, you two. Keep that shit up."

Then, with one of the most mercurial mood swings I've ever seen, she plops back in the chair and pulls her legs up. "I'll tell him, but not now. Can I just crash in the other room and talk to him after the show tonight? I promise I will, but I haven't slept in over twenty-four hours and I really need to sleep if I have to do this."

"Of course you can," Noah tells her warmly. "I'll go get Mel's things out of there and bring them into the other room. I'll take your stuff in so you don't have to carry your bag." He lightly pushes me off his lap and grabs Belle's bag on his way into the other room.

"That man is in love with you," Belle says after he walks out of the room.

"I totally am," he calls out from the bedroom, and she dissolves into laughter.

"You could have warned me he had supersonic hearing, though," she adds with a pout.

"I would have, had I known. Do you want me to lie down with you?"

"No, it's okay. I think I just need to be alone for a little while. Kind of let this all kick in and see how I feel when I wake up. I know I need to tell him. I just don't want to wreck his life, or just as bad, have him hate me for life."

Noah pulls up the stool next to her chair and takes a seat. "I'm going to break guy code and tell you what Mel couldn't because of her contracts. I'm not doing it for you. I'm doing it so you won't stress and hurt the little nugget in there," he says, pointing to her belly.

"Darren likes you. A lot. He might freak at first because finding out you're going to be a dad is pretty heavy for anyone. Especially in a new relationship."

"That's the problem. We're not even *in* a relationship, and I don't want him to feel obligated," Belle says with a loud sigh.

"He's not fucking anyone else. Are you?" Noah asks bluntly, and Belle shakes her head.

"Then it's semantics. It's close enough to a relationship to count. And trust me when I say Darren is a good guy, but obligated isn't in his vocabulary. He doesn't do anything he doesn't want to do … ever. And that includes deciding to fuck without a condom. He wouldn't have done it if he didn't want to. That being said, Darren loves kids, he comes from a *huge* family. His dad's side of the family is very reserved, uptight, and super conservative. They hate that he's a liberal in a band."

"Great," Belle mutters. "Even more fuel for the fire."

179

D. Kelly

"You didn't let me finish. They don't have much to do with his side of the family. They weren't too happy when his dad married the Mexican girl down the block with undocumented parents. From the stories his parents tell, it was love at first sight, immediate sparks, an undeniable connection. They didn't give a damn what anyone thought about how 'unconventional' their relationship was. They hadn't been together very long when Darren's mom got pregnant. Less than a year, if I remember correctly. When Darren's family demanded adoption, Darren's dad married her. To this day he says there was never a choice, he'd loved her from the start."

"What are you trying to say, Noah?" she questions, but I'm sure she knows. She just wants confirmation.

"That Darren is much more like his dad than he'll ever admit. Don't count him out, Belle, because if I had to place a bet, I'd bet everything I own that he's going to want this baby."

She nods and stands. "I'm going to go lie down for a bit. Thanks, you guys."

"She's got the right idea. I'm so tired," I tell him as he reaches for my hand and pulls me to my feet.

"Me, too, but I have rehearsal. Not to mention a conference call with my lawyer, and I'm starving. I'm going to let you get some sleep and go grab some food with the guys." He brings his lips to mine and kisses me softly. "Thank you for last night. It was one of the best nights of my life."

"Mine, too," I answer, and as he turns away, I reach for his hand. "Noah, you won't tell him, right?"

"Not now, Mel, but if she doesn't do it tonight, I will. Do you think she's mad because I butted in and told her his family history?"

"No, Belle isn't mad. She's just one of those people who won't allow her emotions to control her mind. Until she's living in the reality of the situation, she won't accept it's actually real. It helps her stay sane."

"That's understandable, then. I actually admire that."

"Me, too," I tell him with a nod.

"One last thing before I go. Just so we're clear … if I were to ever knock you up, I'd charter the first plane to Vegas and marry you. Because the one thing I want to be able to say when I have a baby with the woman I love is that my wife gave me the best present on earth."

He winks at me and leaves, closing the door behind him, not even bothering to let me respond. It's for the best because I wouldn't have known what to say. My fear would never be telling Noah; it would be getting married.

Hours later, I'm pulled from my dreams by the most delectable kisses against my neck. Noah's tongue trails along my shoulder blade, and he flips me over, removing my shirt in the process.

"You're back, and you're naked," I murmur as he places frantic kisses from my lips to my abdomen while he works my pajama pants off.

"Yes, very naked and ready for you. Shower with me."

He doesn't have to ask me twice. I've been dying to take a shower with him since I took one last night before our date. I follow him into the bathroom and he turns the water on and tosses a condom onto the shower step. I notice he transferred all my toiletries into the shower when he moved my stuff for Belle. It would have been an easy thing to overlook, but he didn't. It's all here.

When he steps into the shower, he holds his hand out to me so I don't slip getting in. I'm beginning to realize Noah is the perfect caregiver. Even when I was sick, he was constantly taking care of me. My heart fills with love at the thought.

After I wet my hair under the waterfall showerhead, I reach for the shampoo. "Let me," he says, and I pour it into his hand. He turns me around and gently scrubs it into my hair; the sensation is incredible. He reaches for the body wash and a washcloth and bends down, soaping me from my feet on up. I spread my legs wide open when he reaches my thighs, and his erection grows larger the closer his mouth gets to me. I brace my hands against the wall as he holds on to my thighs. His tongue licks a trail from my channel to my clit, where he pauses briefly before sucking me into his mouth. A loud gasp falls from my lips as he continues to suckle my clit. When he slides his fingers inside of me, he sucks harder, and my orgasm hits fast and hard.

Noah replaces his fingers with his tongue and releases his own pleasure-filled moan as he sucks my essence from me. My body is at his mercy and he knows it. As he stands, he slides up my body with his hands and pulls me in close so I can feel what's waiting for me. I do what I've been wanting to do since last night and drop to my knees, taking him deep into my throat.

His hands slide into my soapy hair as he holds my head, going with the rhythm I set.

"Fuck, Mel, your mouth feels so good."

I moan around him, letting him know how much I'm enjoying doing this to him, and when his moaning increases and his pre-cum becomes thicker, I know he's close. When he pulls away from me, I'm disappointed, but only for a second because he pulls me to my feet, turns me around, and bends me over with my hands against the wall.

The sound of the condom wrapper tearing makes my pussy clench, and when he lines himself up to my entrance and pushes in, I call out his name. He brings one hand around to my clit and the other to my breast, but it's when he bites my shoulder that I buck against him and come again.

"Amelia ... Fuck, Mel, I love you," he calls out as he explodes inside of me, throbbing as his release fills me.

I've been bent over long enough for soap to drip in my eye, and although it was worth it, I really need a towel.

"Noah, soap ... in my eye. Give me a towel, please."

"Oh shit, Mel. I'm sorry, babe." He reaches up and pulls down a dry hand towel that was hanging on the side of the shower, using it to wipe my eyes so delicately and sweetly, it steals my breath. I'm beginning to love how he takes care of me.

"It's alright. I'm fine, I promise," I reply with a light laugh, and he relaxes. We finish showering, each of us washing the other, taking our time getting to know each other's bodies. Noah turns off the shower and passes me two towels and then wraps himself up.

"Are you hungry yet?" he asks, and I realize I'm starving.

"So hungry. What do you want to do for lunch?"

He avoids my question and walks out of the bathroom, taking a seat on the edge of the bed, and puts his head in his hands. "Noah, what's wrong?"

He takes a moment before looking up at me with a sad smile. "I want this tour to be over, Mel. I want my life back. I want to take the woman I love to lunch without having to worry we might bump into my psychotic ex. I just want some fucking normalcy for a change."

"Sometimes, normalcy is overrated. And sometimes, you get lucky by loving a person who understands overeager fans and crazy exes more than most. I'd rather eat with you here, anyway, so I don't have to share you with your adoring public any more than I already do. Is that wrong of me?"

"No," he answers, pulling my mouth to his. "That's everything right about you." Getting lost in Noah's kisses is quickly becoming one of my favorite past times.

Just an Illusion Series

Once we're dressed, we both pick some things from the room service menu. I pick out a few things I know Belle likes in case she decides she's hungry, and I hope she is since she's eating for two.

"So do you want to tell me what happened at breakfast this morning? Or was it the sound check?" I ask Noah while we're curled up together on the couch waiting for the food.

"How do you know anything happened?"

"You just seem distracted. I figured it was a good guess."

He shakes his head in disbelief. "You already know me well. But I like it," he adds with a sly smile. "The four of us guys and Anna were all having breakfast downstairs. Mac and Ryan were on duty, and after Sara's stunt yesterday, Warren hired extra security."

"That makes sense if she's really that unstable. Besides, I know your crew is good, but you guys really don't travel with many guards."

He chuckles against the back of my head. "We're guys, Mel, we can defend ourselves pretty well. Besides, it's rare for a fan to get crazy out of hand."

He can laugh it off, but I'm allowed to be worried, aren't I?

"I just want you safe, Noah."

"I will be, Mel. She didn't do anything, anyway. All she did was stare at us. Oh, and she waved at the guys as if they were friends. It was really just irritating to be stared at the whole time. Then, of course, Anna had some choice words for her."

I knew I liked Anna for a reason.

"What did she say?"

"As we got up to leave, Anna made sure to pass her table when we walked out. Then, all of a sudden, we heard Anna call her a bitch and accuse her of having a staring problem. Then she went off on her about the money she owes me, ranting about how she should start a fundraising campaign to pay me back. I don't remember everything verbatim except what she told her to call the fundraiser. Loud enough for the entire restaurant to hear, Anna says, 'You can call the campaign Thieving whore needs a sugar daddy for Lasik surgery and more. Hmm, actually, it sounds like a better title for your Tinder page.'

"Sara jumped out of her seat and lunged at Anna, but Ryan was right there and moved Anna before she could reach her. Not that it would have mattered, Anna could take her down. There's no love lost between them, if you can't tell."

"Can you keep her from coming to the show?"

"Sure I could, but I'm not that vindictive. She bought her tickets like everyone else. We are going to have extra guards at the stage. The only saving grace I have is that these tickets are so hard to get. Unless she's the luckiest girl in the world, she won't be up front."

With his luck lately, she will be, but I don't voice my thoughts. There's a knock at the door, and Noah carefully climbs over me to answer it. When I sit up, I can tell it's the same guy from yesterday.

"Can I get you anything else, Mr. Weston?" he asks as Noah hands the payment pouch back to him.

"We're good, thanks. Hey, did you decide what show to come to yet?"

The younger man blushes a bit and nods. "Yeah, I'm actually going tonight with my boyfriend, he's a huge fan. Thank you again. Those tickets knocked me into boyfriend of the year status," he says with a laugh.

"Good, I'm glad to hear it. Are you working tomorrow?" Noah asks, and I wonder what he's up to.

"No, tomorrow is my day off." Noah looks between him and me for a minute and then smiles.

"Mel, would you be willing to do me a favor tonight?"

"Of course."

"Be in your seats by six, kid, can you do that? They'll give you early access because your tickets are officially coded to me," Noah says.

"Yeah, we were going to get there early anyway. We can do that."

"Okay. Mel will come find you tonight and bring you a surprise. You'll be boyfriend of the decade after this one. What's your name, anyway?"

"Evan … Evan White," he says as he reaches out to officially shake Noah's hand.

"And your boyfriend? What is his name?"

"Ethan Black." Noah raises a brow in surprise, and Evan laughs. "I know, all of our friends make fun of us."

"Alright, Evan, we'll see you tonight."

Evan practically runs out of the room, and as Noah wheels the cart to me, I wonder what he's going to do. I don't have to wait too long to find out because he holds a finger up at me and makes a call. He hits the speaker button so I can hear, too.

"How can I help you, Noah?" Warren answers with a knowing tone.

"I need two meet and greet passes for tonight."

184

"What are the names, and why do you always wait until the last minute? Never mind, don't answer that, I already know. You just did another good deed."

Noah laughs and shakes his head. "You should do more good deeds. You'll feel better."

"Yeah, yeah. Names, Noah."

"Evan White and Ethan Black, and I need autographed shit. Two bags, shirts, headshots, CDs, whatever, just have someone make them good."

"What is this all about, Noah?" Warren asks, suddenly intrigued.

"Young love, my man."

Warren laughs heartily. "I think you love gay men more than I do."

"Later, Warren," Noah says as he disconnects the phone.

"Is that true? Should I be worried?" I push against him with my shoulder so he knows I'm joking.

"Maybe I have a soft spot. My cousin Jordan is bisexual. He was fucked up enough with what happened to him as a kid. When he realized he was attracted to both men and women, it really messed with him."

"That must have been hard on him. Did he tell you?"

Noah smiles. "Not exactly, I walked in on him kissing a guy from our high school. I think we had just turned sixteen. At first, they didn't see me, and like a teenage pervert, I watched. I was so intrigued. They were making out just like I made out with my girlfriend. It struck a chord inside of me that Jordan must finally be happy. And Jordan finding happiness made it seem like everything was right in the world."

The more I get to know Noah, the more I want to know about him. *Every single detail.* "What happened when he saw you?"

"I gave him a thumbs up and backed out of the room."

My smile couldn't be bigger. "That's the best thing I've ever heard. Then what?"

"Don't you think we should get Belle?"

"After. The food will keep warm for a few more minutes. I want to hear the rest of the story."

He leans over and presses a soft kiss against my lips.

"About an hour or so later, Jordan came knocking on my door. He looked so embarrassed and apologized for what I saw. I remember thinking how fucked up it was he was apologizing for anything. I didn't care if he was gay, I just cared he was happy and told him so.

He sat at the foot of my bed and told me he was happy, but he was also confused and worried the past fucked up his sexuality somehow."

"That's so sad." My heart aches for that boy and for any kid who struggles with their sexuality.

"It was then that he explained he was attracted to men and women. I was always studying back then, and not too long before that, we had been talking about sexuality in biology. I was intrigued with the different species and their procreating patterns, so I continued studying human sexuality in my spare time. I knew being bisexual didn't have anything to do with his accident. I was so excited to finally be able to talk to someone about my 'research.' So I pulled out my computer and showed him it was actually pretty normal and told him I'd help him tell the family if he wanted."

"Were you really researching? Or were you being a horny teenage boy?"

"Both," he answers with a laugh. "I mean, I'd been having sex with my girlfriend for a while then, but there's so much more to sexuality than sex. That's what was intriguing to me. It took Jordan a while to accept the things I showed him. He asked me a lot of questions over the next few weeks, and then I sat down with him while he told my parents. They were so excited he was opening himself up. They called Sawyer and my sisters in and we had a family meeting about it right there."

"You guys are a really close family, aren't you?" It's not like I didn't know it; he calls his family a lot. It's a little strange for me because I never had anything like that … not really.

"We are, and we became even closer after Jordan moved in. It sucks what happened to him, and I wish it never would have, but he really did complete our family."

I squeeze his hand, just needing to feel him close for a second. "So what happened at the family meeting?"

"My parents used it as a teachable moment. Rory was only ten at the time. Diane was already in college, so nothing fazed her. My dad told us all that Jordan had a boyfriend right now and he made him really happy. But that someday, Jordan may have a girlfriend because his heart loves both boys and girls."

"Wow, that is really sweet."

"Yeah, Rory didn't get it exactly. She high-fived him and told him she loved boys and girls, too. But it wasn't about his sexuality, it was about being accepted. And in that moment, I knew Jordan's fate brought him to us for a reason because his dad would have never accepted him. It fucking sucks, but it's the truth."

"How about Sawyer? How did he take it?"

"Sawyer struggled with it … a lot, actually. Not because he's bigoted or anything. Sawyer doesn't care what your sexuality, religion, or political agenda is as long as you stay true to who you are. He struggled because he felt like Jordan had been through enough and he didn't need any more personal struggles on his plate."

"I can understand that, too." I can picture Sawyer being fiercely protective of those he loves. *Especially* Jordan.

"We came up with a plan as a family, with Jordan's approval, of course. He didn't hide it. He was open and proud of whomever he was with. If someone had a problem with it, they had a problem with us all. I think that's why I wanted to give to Evan … because he reminds me of Jordan. I admire when people are open and honest about who they are from the start. It says a lot about their character."

Unlike me.

"I think some people are bolder than others. We all grow at different paces, Noah. I get what you're saying but just because someone doesn't confess everything right off the bat doesn't mean they won't be some of the most amazing people you could ever meet in your lifetime."

I know I'm taking his words to heart, but I didn't tell him who I was when we first met for my own reasons. Not everyone wants or needs to throw their secrets out there for the world.

"Hey, I know that. Maybe it didn't come out right. I'm sorry, I didn't mean to offend you."

"You didn't. I know you have a split second to make decisions at times. I get your reasoning. Just don't forget you didn't know about me when we met and I'm quickly becoming one of your favorite people, right?"

He pulls me into his lap and immediately begins kissing me on my neck, pausing by my ear. "You're not becoming anything … you *are* one of my all-time favorite people."

"Good," I say just as he lowers his mouth to mine. He kisses me slowly, and I relish the feeling of his lips against mine. When he parts my lips with his tongue, I wrap my arms around his head and play with his hair while we explore each other's mouths. It's a long, passionate kiss, and when I'm at the brink of needing more, I hear Belle clear her throat.

Noah releases my mouth but not my body, and we both turn to greet her.

"Keep that shit up, you two. Seriously, Noah, this girl never relaxes. You're the best thing to happen to her since me."

D. Kelly

"I plan on it," he tells her as he gently pulls me up to a sitting position so we can eat.

"Are you hungry, Belle? I got you a few things I know you like in case you were and some ginger ale and crackers in case you weren't."

"I'm starving, but I'll take the ginger ale for sure."

"You got it. Chicken Caesar salad or cheeseburger and fries?" I ask as she looks over all the food. "Or you can have my club sandwich and I'll eat whatever."

"Can we split the sandwich and the salad? I think my stomach can handle that."

"Yup. So did you get some sleep?"

"I did," she says, looking directly at Noah. "And I sent Darren a text letting him know we're on for our Skype call tonight. I'd like to surprise him at the meet and greet just for shits and giggles before I blow his world apart after the show tonight."

"Cool," Noah says, but she's still staring at him. "Did you forget your pass?"

"Yeah, I left in a hurry. Is there any way you can hook me up?"

Noah pulls his phone from his pocket and puts it to his ear. "Hey, Warren, I need another pass. This one all-access. Can you have it discretely brought to my room and don't tell anyone else about it? No other band members. No, it's not another good deed. Belle came to surprise Darren and forgot her pass at home. Yeah, I know ... I'm a sucker for romance. Thanks, man, you're the best."

"I want to be you when I grow up," she tells him with a smile.

"Most people do. Good thing you have an in."

"Why are you over there smirking?" she asks me.

"No reason."

"Liar," they both accuse at the same time.

"Sometimes, a girl needs to keep her thoughts to herself."

Belle looks to Noah and fake-whispers, "She's happy we're getting along but she doesn't want to say it."

"I know. Isn't she adorable, though?" Noah fake-whispers back, and Belle falls backward in her seat, throwing her arm over her eyes.

"Fucking swoon worthy, too. I think God put you through hell with Eli so you'd appreciate the heaven he was going to drop at your feet with this one."

Noah laughs when I throw daggers at them both with my eyes. "It was fate, Mel. I told you."

"He even believes in fate? Where have you been all my life? Forget her, we can run off together and you can be mine instead."

188

"Have you ever seen Darren mad?" he asks Belle, completely seriously.

"No, should I be worried?"

"Only if you're the one running off with his girl. I won't be putting myself in that situation ... *like ever*. No offense."

"We're not serious enough for him to fight for me." She brushes him off, but I can tell he's got her thinking about more.

"You'd be surprised. When Darren wants something, he gets it, and lately, all he's been wanting is you."

Belle takes a sip of her soda, and our conversation flows smoothly. After Belle excuses herself to go shower, I pull Noah into our bedroom when I hear the other shower turn on.

"What do you think Darren is going to do? I need to prepare for damage control and freak outs."

"I think Darren is going to freak out at first and maybe even lose his temper. But he'll come around quickly, and that's going to be it. They'll both be off the market and planning a family."

"I hope so. Babies make things so complicated," I reply on a sigh.

"Babies are a gift from God, people make things complicated."

"There you go with that fate stuff again. Watch it, Weston, I might start thinking you want to make me a believer."

He pulls me close and hugs me tight. "Damn straight I do. Then you'd be nearly perfect."

"Nearly?" I push him back at arm's length. "What else do I need to do to be perfect in your eyes?"

"There's really only one thing."

His husky voice wraps around me and pulls me toward him until I'm standing inches from his mouth. "And what would that be?" I ask as his eyes fixate on mine.

"My last name. If you had my last name, you'd be absolutely perfect. Even if you didn't believe in fate because I'd believe in it enough for both of us."

My stomach lurches as if I'm on the world's tallest roller coaster. This is far beyond the scope of my comfort zone. "Noah ... I'm not, that's not—"

He places his finger against my lips to silence me. My terrified eyes meet his twinkling ones. He *can't* be talking about marriage.

"Mel, I'm not crazy, I just know what I want in life. A family is at the top of that list. So far, I don't see anything that would indicate we won't be together in a year, or even two. I'm not asking you to marry me yet because I'm *not* crazy."

D. Kelly

An uncomfortable laugh bubbles out of my mouth.

"But I'm also not crazy enough to be with you for an extended amount of time only to let you go. So one day, in the future, I'm going to drop to one knee and ask you to be my wife, and I'm telling you that now so you have time to prepare for it."

"Noah ..."

"I know you're scared to let people love you, Mel. But I already do, and it's too late to stop it. Unless you want to break my heart, that is."

The vulnerability in his gaze cuts deep into my heart.

"I'd never intentionally break your heart, Noah, but please understand I'm a long way away from marriage. I'm not actually sure I even believe in it."

His mouth covers mine in the sweetest of kisses, one so tender and filled with love I don't know where he ends and I begin. As he breaks away, he drops his forehead against mine. "Then I'll believe in it enough for both of us. We're not your parents, Amelia. Our love will be whatever we want it to be."

I bite my bottom lip and nod, fearful of saying anything that may hurt him.

"Besides, Mel, just food for thought ... I'm not sure being married was your parents' issue. Sounds to me like whether they had that paper between them or not, their love was intense."

"Maybe ..."

"Let me ask you this ... Do you think the paper makes the marriage or it's the people and what they put into it?"

"The people, Noah, of course."

"So why are you afraid?" he asks softly.

"Why does it make a difference to you?" I counter.

"I don't know. I just know I love the idea of sharing everything I am with the woman I love, including my last name."

This man and his honesty ... it's annoying and amazing. "I'm afraid of losing myself in someone else."

He tips my chin up with his thumb and kisses the tip of my nose. "I'll never let that happen. I promise you, Amelia, I'll never let you lose your identity."

"Someday, I may hold you to that, Weston," I reply with a resigned sigh.

"I'll be looking forward to it. Until then, can you do me a favor?"

With a raised brow, I ask, "What kind of favor?"

"Since you're bringing Evan and Ethan to the meet and greet tonight, will you please fangirl all over me? It's kind of a huge fantasy of mine, and since you haven't been to one before, it would make my night."

"Seriously?"

He nods shyly as I pretend to think about it.

"Can I touch you?"

"You better."

"Can I kiss you?"

He groans. "Fuck yeah …"

"Can I run my fingers through your hair, pull you close enough to feel your cock against me, and softly cry out your name?"

He pulls me close, his hardness already evident. "What do you think?"

"I think if I do all that, we will be officially outed to the world."

He shrugs. "Belle will be there, so she can have the *Slammed* exclusive on our official coming out."

"I'll see what I can do. In the meantime, you're going to be late for your sound check if you don't hurry up."

"Yeah, you're right. Warren will get all the passes to you and the swag bags. I wrote down Evan and Ethan's seat assignments on the pad of paper by the desk already. Anything else before I leave?"

"One more thing …"

He smiles and places his hands on my hips. "Name it."

"What would I be wearing in your fangirl fantasy?"

"You don't happen to have a sexy school teacher outfit with dark glasses and a ruler anywhere, do you?" he asks with a faraway look in his eyes.

With a laugh, I shake my head. "I'm afraid I don't have that on me, but I can make a mental note for the future."

He groans with the thought. "Wear anything you want as long as it comes with those sexy knee-high boots you've got."

"Done."

Noah releases me and smiles wide as he leaves the room. I lie down on the bed and let our conversation soak in. I can't believe he brought up marriage, and what's worse, I can't believe I'm not as freaked out about the idea as I was a half an hour ago.

chapter 15

A Night To Remember

Belle knocks at my door as I'm zipping up my boots. "Come in."

"Damn! You bringing sexy back or what?"

"You look pretty freaking hot yourself, mama."

A small smile spreads across her lips as she drops her hands to her belly. "Thanks. I figured it's probably good to make him want to get in my pants before I tell him."

I can't believe my best friend is going to have a baby. "Belle, no matter what Darren says, I've got you. We can do this if he's not in. Not that I think he won't be, but don't give up if he's not."

She nods her understanding and squeezes my hand. "Thanks."

"In other news … You get a *Slammed* exclusive announcing Noah's and my relationship tonight. He wants a fangirl fantasy fulfilled at the meet and greet, so …"

"You sexy bitch! I'm all over it. And for the record, I'm incredibly proud of you for letting him in and trying to have an adult relationship. I know it's not easy for you, but no one deserves it more."

"I'm trying," I tell her with one final look in the mirror. I'm nervous as fuck to put our relationship on blast tonight, but I want to do this for him. Belle spritzes herself with perfume as I grab the passes and gifts Warren dropped off a little while ago.

"Here," I say, passing her the all-access pass he left for her. We slip them over our heads and walk out of the room. I'm surprised to find Ryan waiting at the door.

"Ryan? Why are you here?"

"Mr. Weston's orders, Mel. I'm your shadow for the evening."

"Did something else happen with Sara?"

"Who's Sara?" Belle asks, obviously irritated she's missing out on something.

"No, and hopefully it won't. This is just a precaution."

"Okay. Thanks, Ryan."

"Who is Sara?" Belle repeats as we make our way to the venue.

"Noah's ex. She was in our room yesterday when we got back from the casino. I guess she's a bit crazy." I try and shrug it off, but Belle isn't having it.

"Jesus, Mel. Ryan, is she in danger?" she asks, pivoting around with her hands on her hips.

"Not as far as we can tell. Like I said, this is just precautionary."

"So Noah has a psycho ex and you pick *now* to come out to the world about your relationship? Do you think that's smart?" A worried glimmer simmers in Belle's eyes.

"It's fine, Belle. Noah believes if we don't come out first, she's going to try and do something to cause a scandal surrounding our relationship. It's better this way."

"If you say so." She remains quiet as we enter the venue. Ryan leads us to Noah's seats, where Evan and a man—whom I presume is Ethan—are talking.

"Hey, Evan!"

"Mel! This is my boyfriend Ethan. Ethan, this is Mel, Noah's girlfriend." Ethan is adorably cute—brown hair, brown eyes, baseball player build—and he's holding onto Evan's hand tightly.

"Nice to meet you, Ethan. This is my best friend Belle."

Ethan shakes my hand and then reaches for Belle's, as does Evan. "So I have some gifts for you both," I say as I hand them their swag bags. They have incredible restraint; neither of them even glances into their bags, even though it's probably killing them not to.

"Thanks, Mel. Please tell Noah thank you," Evan says as I turn to walk away. I'm totally messing with him, though; the best is yet to come.

"Hm … Evan, wouldn't you like to thank him yourself?"

"Well, of course" he answers with a smile, and I hold up their meet and greet passes. Ethan pulls Evan in for a quick kiss. "I fucking *love* you," he says when he pulls away and excitedly puts his badge around his neck. Their interaction makes me smile, and I can't wait to see their expression when they find out they're even getting a few minutes of alone time with the band.

"Follow me, gentlemen," I tell them and follow behind Ryan to the meet and greet area. I'm a bit anxious and do my best to keep Belle behind us so Darren doesn't see her right away. Not only am I nervous to come out to the world about our relationship, I'm also worried for Belle and peanut and their future. I can only hope Darren is the man I think he is and I'll have a niece or nephew in about seven months.

Ryan opens the door to the meet and greet room and moves to the side, allowing us to enter single-file. Evan and Ethan go first, and Noah is quick to stand and greet them. I reach behind me to grab

D. Kelly

Belle's hand and walk her over to Darren, who has his back to the door. Sawyer, Anna, Wyatt, and Warren are all smirking.

"What the hell are you guys all smirking at?" he asks in an irritated tone. When he turns around and sees Belle in front of him, the excitement on his face is unmistakable.

"Best surprise ever! Whose idea was this?" he exclaims as he picks Belle up and swings her around.

"It was my idea, you goof." she says as he slides her provocatively down his body. Darren leans down and kisses her while the rest of us turn our attention to Noah and the guys, letting them have their moment.

While everyone gets acquainted, I take the opportunity to snap some photos. This is the first time I've gone into one of these rooms on the tour. Usually, I take photos of the lines leading into the room, but I haven't wanted to be a part of the experience. Especially as Noah and I have grown closer. I strive not to be a jealous person but sometimes, even I have my days.

I'm able to get photos of Evan and Ethan and promise to email them after Evan puts his contact information into my phone. Sam steps in a few minutes before the meet and greet opens to everyone else, and after a quick hug, he and Warren step off to the side to observe.

The setup in here is a little different than I thought it would be. There are four tables spaced about three feet apart. Each guy is sitting behind a table, and each table has a cup of Sharpies. Each table also has its very own security guard. The fans are allowed in sixteen at a time, they do a rotation of four at each table, and between each group, the guys pause long enough for a group photo. It might take a bit longer, but it avoids crowding and gives them a little bit more one-on-one attention. About halfway through the meet and greet, I make my way over to Belle and Anna.

"So how am I supposed to do this?" I ask them, and Belle laughs at me.

"Just do what I do all the time. Get in at the end of the line, in your case, Noah's line, and stake your claim," Anna answers simply.

"I'm not making a claim," I tell her, and Belle smirks.

"You keep on telling yourself that," Belle says, and I pause. Am I making a claim? It wasn't necessarily my intention; I really just wanted to make Noah happy.

"Don't second-guess yourself, Mel. Who cares if you're making a claim? He's your man and he loves you. And from what Belle says,

194

he *asked* you to do this, he wants you to claim him. That's so fucking sexy. Don't you dare back down."

"Alright, here goes nothing." I pass my camera to Belle and get in line behind three extremely excited women. The one at the front of the line pulls her shirt down in Noah's face. He mouths "I'm sorry" to me and signs quickly. All I can do is roll my eyes because this is what comes with this job.

"Oh my God!" the next girl squeals at the top of her lungs. I'm surprised she didn't shatter the glass wall behind us with that shrill tone. "Noah fucking Weston, you are my *favorite!*" She's so excited, she's practically running in place.

"Well, thank you," he answers with a slight blush. My, my, Noah gets embarrassed even after all this time. He reaches down and signs everything she has with her: a shirt, a CD, a homemade scrapbook, and what looks like … a hand towel? He raises a brow to her when she hands him the towel, and she giggles. "You sweated all over that towel about two years ago and then threw it in the crowd after you wiped your face on it. I was lucky enough to be the one who caught it."

Oh my God.

It's taking everything inside of me not to bust out laughing, and when she moves on to the next table, I don't miss Noah's sleight of hand with the bottle of sanitizer that quickly disappears under the table. Can't say I blame him. Who knows what she's done with that towel since then?

Finally, the last girl is up before me. She's so shy she can barely speak. But Noah coaxes her gently and she finally talks to him. When she walks away, Noah leans back in his seat and looks up at me.

"And what can I do for you, pretty lady?" he asks with a flirtatious smile. I bend down in front of him just enough so my cleavage pops to the top of my sweater, and his eyes follow down to the girls, just like I knew they would.

"Well, Mr. Weston, I was hoping you could give me my first genuine fangirl experience. But since I'm a virgin to it all, I'm not sure where to start."

His eyes meet mine and shine mischievously. "Is that so?"

"Mmhm, it is." I step around to the side of his table and half sit on the edge, bringing my booted foot up to his thigh. Noah wraps his hand around the back of my leg and stands up, pulling me from the table with him. His hand drops to my ass while his other hand wraps around my waist and pulls me close.

D. Kelly

"I'm a fucking lucky SOB to be the one to pop your fangirl cherry, Mel," he whispers in my ear.

The next thing I know, his hands are weaving through my hair and his mouth is pressed against mine. I open to him and kiss him back as if we're the only two people in the room. But when I begin to hear angry growls coming from the crowd, I know our time is about up.

"Hey!" the girl with the shrill voice screams out. "That wasn't an option! I want to do that, too!"

With her words, I begin to laugh in Noah's mouth, and he pulls back laughing, too. His forehead is against mine; our hearts sound like drums they're beating so loud. "You are the best girlfriend ever. Keep those boots on. I want them wrapped around my neck tonight."

"Anything you want ... boyfriend." I walk back toward Belle and Anna, who are both looking at me in awe.

"See you later ... girlfriend," Noah calls back, loud enough for the whole room to hear. As soon as I sit down, Belle passes me her phone, which I gratefully accept so I can have something to look at aside from all of Noah's fans giving me the glare of death.

Slammers!

It's your girl Belle here, and do I have news! You know how they say a picture speaks a thousand words? Well, this one is worth a million ... *at least*. You're seeing and hearing it here first, and it's officially official. Noah Weston is off the market. His new girlfriend is none other than Amelia Greyson, bestselling author of *The O Factor* and also my best friend in the entire world. This relationship has been brewing for months, and the lovebirds finally decided now was the time to let the world in on their happiness.

The men of BAD are growing up and moving on. Let's wish Noah and Mel all our best on their journey into romantic coupledom.

Don't forget, live today like there's no tomorrow!
Xs and Os,
Belle

The photo Belle took of Noah and me is breathtaking. She captured the moment his lips hit mine. "I want a copy of this picture," I tell her softly, and she nods, rubbing her hand against my back.

"Are you nervous?" she asks sweetly.

"Terrified." Who I am is bound to come out anytime now.

196

"Don't be," Anna says firmly. "Noah deserves to be happy and so do you. This is his life, not theirs."

I let Anna's words resonate for a few moments. "You're right. We do deserve it."

We watch on in silence, each of us lost in our own thoughts. I know what's keeping me and Belle occupied, but when I turn to Anna to see why she's unusually silent, it's evident. She's sitting quietly, blowing kisses to Wyatt, without a care in the world. And Wyatt, true to his nature, is catching them from across the room in between fans.

Belle deserves that, and so do I. Every time I look up at Noah, he's got a dazzling smile on his face. I'm pretty sure he's thrilled with our announcement. I forward him the photo Belle took, and when his phone buzzes, he actually checks it right then. I didn't think he would do that, but it makes me feel special that he does. Even more so, his reply is instant.

Noah: Best picture I've ever seen.

Mel: It's already gone viral.

Noah: Well, that doesn't surprise me. You're gorgeous.

He winks at me and pockets his phone, turning his attention back to his fans. Once the meet and greet is over, the guys go straight into one final sound check before the venue begins allowing the regular ticketholders inside. When they're finished, the three of us give our men kisses for luck and begin to head out to our seats.

"Uh, Mel," Belle says, pausing as she's scrolling through her messages.

"Yeah?"

"You might want to read this. I'm sorry, babe." Her arm wraps around my waist as she passes me her phone. It's the comments on the *Slammed* blog; one comment in particular is pulled up.

Amelia Greyson, my ass. That's Amelia Triton – guess her bitch ass decided to come out of hiding where she's been ever since she broke my brother's heart. What happened, Mel? Did you run through your inheritance already? If Noah Weston is a smart man, he'll stay far away from her once he sees this comment. – CeCe Watts

"Mel, are you okay? You look like you're about to pass out." Anna grabs my elbow to help balance me.

"Come on, let's take her to the green room," Belle says, keeping her arm around my waist. CeCe never did like me; she was always jealous I got to go on tour and she had to live at home while her brother was living his life. *Dammit!*

D. Kelly

Once we're settled on the couch, I scroll through the responses to her revelation. They range anywhere from "awesome" to me being called a "gold-digging whore" and worse. "I didn't think it would come out this fast, and I sure the hell didn't think CeCe of all people would be the one behind it."

"Can one of you tell me what's going on? Please?" Anna asks sweetly, and I pass her Belle's phone. Her eyes scan the text while Belle continues to rub my back. I'm sure the guys are wondering why we're not in our front row seats since I can hear the strains of the first song kicking off.

"Oh, that's … unfortunate. But it's not true, right? Well, I mean, don't be mad, but Wyatt told me your story. It's just … we don't keep secrets from each other. It's how we survive being separated. We take it pretty seriously, but he wasn't intentionally trying to violate your privacy or anything, I swear." Anna's rushed confession actually brings a small smile to my lips.

"It's okay, Anna, I wouldn't expect anything less. And no, it's not true. At least, I don't think it is … exactly."

The two of them look at me like I'm crazy. "Explain," Belle snaps.

"Being on the road again has made me think a lot about what happened with me and Eli. Don't get me wrong, he's a cheating asshole and he broke my heart, but I've been playing devil's advocate lately, and I think I owe him an apology."

"The hell you do!" Belle screams.

"We were kids. And he did something he seemed to truly regret. Now that I'm older, I don't hate him as much for it, but what I do hate was how I treated him. How I cut him off and ignored his calls, texts, and emails for years. He tried, and I was so angry I refused to acknowledge his hurt, his pain."

"No. *He* doesn't get to make you feel like you should acknowledge his pain. *He* cheated. You lost *your* baby. It's *his* fault," Belle states adamantly.

"Belle, we both know I wasn't going to keep that baby. And we both know Eli did love me. You can't deny that any more than I can. I'm not justifying it at all, but I should have talked to him and given us both closure. We deserved that."

"He didn't deserve anything, but I will admit he looked like shit after you broke up. For a long time, actually," she says, biting her lip with the afterthought.

"You guys should go out there. They're expecting you. I'm going to watch from back here tonight and let all of this sink in."

Anna shakes her head and stands up, holding her hand out to me. "Nope, that's not going to work for me. Let's go sit in our seats and watch our men. We'll leave before the encore and the guys can meet us upstairs. Don't take this special night away from Noah because Eli's sister has her panties in a wad."

"She's right, Mel. You avoided the press because you wanted to be a normal teenager for a change. You're an adult and I know you're proud of who you are. You've been hiding in plain sight for years. You need to act like it doesn't bother you to be 'outed' because it shouldn't after all this time. You're the same amazing person you've always been. It's time to shine in your own light. If you want to release an official statement, I'll post it … but I don't think it's necessary. If people wanted to find you, they would have."

They both make a lot of sense. My parents were legends, but I've proven myself in my own career path. I'm not riding the coattails of their fame; I never have. I just happen to be their daughter, and even with everything that happened, I know they loved me.

"Let's go. You're both absolutely right. This is supposed to be a good night for us all." I link my arms in each of theirs as we head out to the main floor.

As we take our seats, the beginning verses of *Just an Illusion* start. Anna shoots Wyatt two thumbs up, and Sawyer shakes his head and mouths "geek" at her, to which she promptly blows him a kiss. Darren and Noah both look at me and Belle quizzically, but when we flash them a smile, they both seem relieved.

When Sawyer and Noah softly begin to sing and alternate verses, I lose myself in the song.

I'm looking out the window
Can't believe what my eyes see
His arm is wrapped around you
In the place where mine should be
Is this just an illusion?
A trick played by my mind
Or have you really found another?
One who gives you all his time?
Didn't sparks fly when your lips met mine?
Didn't you feel it?
It couldn't have been in my mind
Was it just an illusion?
The way you looked at me
How your body felt
Pulled so close to me I could hardly breathe

D. Kelly

Baby I know I'm not your typical kind
And maybe I know he's more worthy of your time
I can change for you if you'd open up your mind
It wasn't an illusion
This isn't just in my mind
Our love could last forever
I can see it in your eyes
You want me, but you're still with him
You touch me
But you're too deep with him to even try
Your love is an illusion
Not given without strings
You can't be mine forever
Not while wearing his wedding ring
You're just an illusion
From a place deep in my mind
Where your love surrounds me
And withstands the test of time

This song is the antithesis of their typical music, but somehow it fits. And their fans agree because everyone is giving them a standing ovation as praise for their perfect harmonies echoes through the building. But I swear, in the midst of it all, Sawyer only has eyes for me.

"Do you see that?" Belle leans over and whisper-shouts in my ear. I nod and shrug. I don't know what else to do. Noah has my heart, and Sawyer has been so strange lately I don't even know what to make of it. Thankfully, he turns away before anyone else catches on. When they launch into their next song, the crowd goes wild once again. It's a shame they're ending with this tour; the music really is their best ever.

During the last song before the encore, the three of us stand to make our way back upstairs. Ryan follows us immediately. Once we reach the lobby, we bump into Sara and a woman who must be the friend she said she was attending the concert with.

"Well, well, look who we have here. It's Noah's bitch and her posse."

I seriously don't know what this girl's issue is but I've had enough of crazy for the night. "Let's go," I tell them as Ryan positions himself so close he's actually rubbing against my arm with his.

"No, don't go. I wanted to thank you for fucking up. As soon as Noah finds out you lied to him about who you are, he's going to come

200

running back to me. *Especially* when he learns he's been banging Eli's sloppy seconds."

Her friend high-fives her and they laugh. But I'm done and so over this night.

"When you stop acting like a teenager, maybe you'll realize adults don't keep secrets from each other. We also don't try to steal someone else's boyfriend or force men who want to leave into staying. If Noah wants you back, he knows where the door is."

I swear I saw the corner of Ryan's mouth kick up into a smirk with my words, but he schools his features quickly and escorts us to the elevator. The look on Sara's face is a mixture of crazy bitch and "I just got told" but I couldn't care less. Belle and Anna are still laughing at our exchange as the elevator doors close.

"It wasn't that funny." My frustrated tone quiets them, but not for long.

"Yeah, Mel, it really was," Belle says with a warm smile. I decide to let it go because if this keeps her mind off the rest of the night, all the better. When the doors open a few floors below mine, Mac is waiting for Anna. She kisses us each on our cheeks.

"Night, ladies. Time to get my own fangirl experience ready. See you both tomorrow!"

Belle and I are quiet on the way up to my room and as Ryan checks the suite. As soon as we're inside, I make myself a vodka tonic and Belle looks at it wistfully.

"Sorry, Mama, I'll drink enough for you, too."

"If you did that, you'd be drunk before Noah even gets here." She walks over to the windows and looks out at all the lights.

"Nervous?"

"Terrified," she confirms as I wrap my free arm around her.

"It will be okay," I reassure her, and she leans into me.

"Yeah, I know. It's just getting to the point where it's okay is what I'm worried about. The in-between. I wonder how long Darren will need to process it all before he's ready to talk about it."

Me, too, but I keep that to myself.

"Have you thought about how you're going to do it?"

She nods. "If it's okay with you, I'd like to tell him here. If he gets pissed, I don't want to feel awkward sitting in his room, and if he kicks me out, I don't think I could handle it. I'm safe here either way."

"Sounds like a good plan. We've got you, Belle, no matter what."

"We?" she asks with a raised brow and a smirk. "I'm glad you love him enough to consider the two of you a we. That's progress."

"Whatever, bitch."

She laughs with my endearment and we take a seat, passing the time catching up on random stuff. It seems like we wait forever, but it's really only a little more than an hour before Noah and Darren show up.

Noah stalks straight toward me and pulls me to my feet, hugging the daylights out of me. Belle and I exchange quizzical looks over his shoulder. "I'm sorry, Mel," he says as he hugs me even tighter. Over his shoulder, I watch as Darren pulls Belle up and kisses her senseless.

"For what?" I ask, pulling back, still wrapped in his arms.

"For the world finding out who you really are, for Sara attacking you, for all of it."

"Hey! Sara didn't exactly win that battle of words," Belle cries out, pulling away from Darren. He lets her but holds on to her hand all the same. *Interesting*.

"No?" he asks, and Belle beams.

"Hell no. Your girl can take care of herself."

"Well, I'm sorry all the same." Noah sits down and pulls me into his lap.

"It's fine, Noah. I'm fine. I knew as soon as we announced our relationship everything would come out. I wouldn't have done it if I wasn't ready. Although, I did think I'd have at least a few hours before the news hit. And as far as crazy goes ... don't even worry about her. Eventually, she'll go away."

"Alright, you two, it's been real, but I'm taking Belle back to my room. Later." Belle looks at him, wide-eyed, and drops his hand.

"Don't you think you should ask me if I want to go to your room first?" she fires off. Darren looks to Noah for guidance and he shrugs.

"Sorry, I just assumed you wanted to spend time with me. That is why you came here, isn't it?"

"Not exactly," Belle whispers. Noah and I take that as our cue.

"We're going to let you two talk," Noah says, standing and pulling me with him. "If you need us, we'll be in the bedroom." We turn toward the bedroom, but Darren isn't having it.

"Hold up," Darren states firmly, and we turn back around. "You two stay," he commands, turning to Belle and then looking back and forth between us and her. She's like a deer caught in headlights, and my heart aches for her.

"Do they know what you came out here for?"

"Yes," she answers softly.

"Might as well stay, then, since your best friend and *my* best friend obviously know something I don't."

"Dude, look, we're going to give you some space. Just come knock on the door if you need us," Noah tells Darren diplomatically.

"Fuck this! If you want to break up with me, just do it, but don't bring my friend into it." Darren's backed up against the wall now, with his arms crossed over his chest. Belle looks like she's about to cry.

I turn around, determined to give them space. "Stay," Darren bites out sharply. "Or I'll go." When I turn back around to gauge what Belle wants us to do, she's not even looking our way. Her gaze is locked onto Darren, and she's pissed. This isn't going to be good.

"I had no idea you could be such a fucking asshole. And an assumptive one at that. Why do you automatically assume I'm going to break up with you? I saw you four hours ago and we made out like horny teenagers. What could have changed between now and then?"

Belle assumes his same stance directly across from him. She might be tiny, but she's fierce, and Darren looks like he might be a little worried now. He should be.

"Well, it's obviously something bad if everyone already knows but me." His response is weak but semi-accurate, depending on how he feels about being a dad.

"Whatever … This isn't how I wanted to tell you, but it's your own damn fault. And before you take what I tell you and run with it, just know Noah wasn't hiding anything from you. He had your back. He's the one who told me to tell you or he would, and he only found out a few hours ago."

"Found out what?"

"I'm pregnant."

Darren closes his eyes with her words, and the rise and fall of his chest becomes more frequent. The silence in the room is uncomfortable, and Belle is biting her lip so hard I'm surprised it's not bleeding yet.

"Say that again," he tells her, eyes still closed.

"I'm pregnant," she repeats, this time softer, the timber of her voice wavering.

"That's what I thought you said. I need to take a walk. Don't go anywhere. I'll be back. Noah, don't let her go anywhere." His words are as forceful as the sound of the door slamming behind him.

"Great … now what?" Belle mutters, taking a seat on the couch. Noah and I follow, sitting with her.

"Now we wait. I know it doesn't seem like it, but that was the best possible reaction you could have had from him," Noah tells her honestly.

"I guess it could have been worse," she admits. "What would you do if it were you?" she asks him, and I throw daggers her way. She doesn't need to jinx me with her hypothetical questions.

"Honestly, it would depend on who was telling me. If it were some girl I didn't have feelings for, I'd probably be pissed and freak out. I know better than to have sex without protection. But if it was someone I had feelings for … at this stage in my life, I'd most likely be happy."

"Really?" she asks, wide-eyed, and he nods.

"Yeah, sure. I mean, being a parent is scary as fuck, I'm sure. People always talk about the right time to have a baby. There's never a right time. You're always going to have to work, pay bills, want to get ahead in your career. There's all kinds of shit you can say to blame timing. I think babies come when they're meant to. Just like love and even death. When it's your time, it's time. Everything is destined by fate, so why not go with it and enjoy the ride?"

Belle laughs and points at me. "Oh, Amelia, you couldn't have ended up with someone more polar opposite than you, and yet, you two make perfect sense together. When she's forty and her eggs are drying up, you better have something more than fate as your Hail Mary pass to get her to agree to have kids."

"You don't want kids?" he asks incredulously.

Guilt washes over me with his words. "It's not that I don't … I'm just sort of indifferent about it. I'm not the kind of person who has ever pictured my life and planned out my husband and kids. I guess I figured someday, when I find someone I want to spend my life with, we'll have that talk then."

He nods but doesn't seem happy with my answer. Tough, because it's how I feel.

"Don't worry, Noah, if worse comes to worse, I'll share my rug rat with you because I've got a feeling Darren isn't exactly happy."

Noah laces his fingers into mine and squeezes. My heart feels like a weight has been lifted. I didn't even realize how worried I was about how my answer would affect him.

"He'll come around, just give it time."

A few hours later, just as we're all getting ready to go to sleep, there's a soft knock at the door. Noah leaves us on the couch to go deal with it. I squeeze Belle's hand in reassurance while we wait.

Darren walks in looking disheveled and carrying flowers. Looks like a promising start to me.

"I'm an ass," he states simply.

"That's yet to be determined," she answers, and he smiles.

"You warned me you weren't consistent with your birth control, but all I could think of was the fact that you were the sexiest woman I'd ever seen and you actually wanted me as much as I wanted you."

"I felt the same way. I don't make it a habit to sleep with anyone without a condom. *Ever*." The corner of his mouth kicks up into a smile as she emphasizes the word.

"The truth is, I've been struggling. Ask any of them," he says, pointing in our direction.

"About what?"

"You! I don't do the girlfriend thing, and I've got no idea what I'm doing with you on any given day. I've been trying to figure out for weeks how to ask you to be my date to the video party."

Belle chuckles. "I'm going to be there anyway."

Darren slides his hands into his hair and sighs. "I know, but I want you there with me, as my girl. Not as Belle, *Slammed* reporter extraordinaire ... not *only* as that, anyway. I don't know how to do this."

"Do what, exactly?"

"This," he says, pointing between them. "A relationship. It's not my thing, but fuck me, Belle, I want it with you ... so fucking much."

Her eyes are brimming with tears, and even though I feel like we're intruding on a private moment, I'm so happy I get to see this.

"Me, too," she whispers. "I want this with you and only you."

Darren pulls her into a hug and Noah smiles at me. Belle holds on to him for less than a minute before pulling away. "What about the baby?" she asks with baited breath.

"Our baby is going to be the cutest kid in the fucking world, and your pregnant waddle is going to be so damn adorable." Belle jumps up and runs into the other room. Darren looks to us. "Did I say something wrong?"

"I'll be right back!" she yells out, and Darren releases a loud exhale. When she comes back, she's holding her hands behind her back and smiling.

D. Kelly

"Close your eyes," she tells him firmly, and he complies. She positions herself in front of him and holds up the ultrasound level with his eyes. "Open them."

Darren's eyes open wide as he realizes what it is he's looking at. "Our baby's first photo. Noah, did you see this? That's my kid!" he exclaims proudly. Noah stands and pulls Darren into a big man hug.

"I did. Congratulations, man, she's going to be perfect."

"She? Is it a girl?" he asks.

"We don't know yet. Mel and I think it's a girl." Her excitement brings a smile to Darren's face.

"She'll be the prettiest baby ever. Dude, my parents are going to shit themselves. They'll be so excited."

"Your dad's family will just shit," Noah points out, and Darren laughs hysterically.

"Hell yeah, they will. Wait 'til they hear I'm going to bring another interracial baby into the family. My cousins are cool with it all. Just my grandparents are the stuffy ones and they'll be dead soon enough."

"Darren!" Belle chastises him.

"What? It's true. They're like ninety or some shit. It's not like I'm wishing them into the grave ... they've already got one foot in."

Noah laughs and clutches his stomach. "His grandpa volunteers with the fire department and his grandma runs like five different charities. They aren't going anywhere anytime soon."

Belle shakes her head and holds back her laugh. But then, Darren falls to one knee and pulls out a box, opening it to reveal a sparkling ring.

"Put that away," Belle tells him before he even gets started, leaning down to close the box. Darren pops it back open and she closes it again.

"Marry me," he spits out as he pops the box back open.

"No," she says firmly.

A quizzical look passes over his face, but he's determined. "Why not?"

"Because this isn't 1920 and I don't need a man to marry me for appearances. Marriage should be about love and only love."

"Monogamy."

"Well, of course."

"For family," he adds.

"In some instances," she replies.

"We're going to be monogamous, we already are and have been for three months now. We're a family in the making, and my feelings

206

for you are different than I've ever felt for anyone else. I'm sure it's because I love you, because I know damn well I don't ever want to be without you." His emphatic confession pulls at my heartstrings, and from the way Belle's hand goes immediately to her belly, I think he's pulling hers, too.

"I don't want to be without you, either."

"Marry me."

"No," she repeats.

"Promise you'll think about marrying me?" he asks softly, and she nods. Then Darren slides the massive ring onto her ring finger.

"I didn't say yes," she tells him as she starts to take the ring off. His hand covers hers, holding the ring in place.

"Not yet, but you will one day. That can be your promise ring until you say yes."

Belle closes her eyes and exhales loudly. She knows how to pick her battles, and I think Darren may have just crossed into no man's land.

"And what do I tell people when they ask about this ring? Because people will see us together and assume, then they're going to ask a lot of questions."

He laughs. "And you don't think they're going to ask questions when you're about five months pregnant and I'm constantly rubbing your belly? Get over yourself, Belle. Tell the world you're having my baby because I know I will."

"Are you serious?"

"Hell yeah. You sure you don't want to marry me now? It will make a much better story." His playfulness is such a change from how he stormed out of here earlier.

She rolls her eyes. "I'll think about it."

"Fine. Now, will you come to my room so I can persuade you to think about it in ways that don't include using my mouth for talking?"

"Get my bags, they're on the bed." She hugs me and Noah goodbye while he collects her things.

"I'm so happy for you," I tell her as she hugs me.

"Me, too. You're going to be an auntie."

"And you're going to be an uncle," she tells Noah as she hugs him. He looks pretty happy about that. When Darren comes back, Noah follows them out and locks the door behind them.

207

About an hour and three orgasms later, we're curled up together in bed. My eyes are drooping, and I'm barely awake when Noah whispers in my ear, "Someday we'll make a beautiful family, Mel. I'm planting the seed now so in a few years when I bring it up again you'll remember this night and know how long I've wanted that future with you."

My heart flutters in a way I wish I could ignore, but if I'm ever going to hope for a future like this, Noah is the only person I'd ever want it with. Not knowing how to respond, I tell him the only thing I can so he knows I'm with him, even if I'm not ready.

"I love you, Noah."

He tucks me closer into his body. "I love you, too."

Belle's Thanksgiving Announcement

Slammers!

After an unexpected and super exciting weekend trip to Las Vegas, I'm back home in the City of Angels. So much has been going on in the lives of BAD lately, it's hard to keep up! This is just a quick reminder post for you that our winner for the BAD holiday video show will be picked later this afternoon. If you haven't entered yet, what in the world are you waiting for? The lucky winner and their guest will be spending the evening at a table with myself, Amelia Greyson, and Anna Smith. Who better to fill you in on everything BAD than the women behind the scenes? Other than the Bastards themselves, that is. Plan on this being a quiet week for updates. I'm off to spend the holidays with friends and family and I hope you're all doing the same. Of course, if there are any major BAD updates over the holiday, we'll be the first to bring them your way.

Happy Thanksgiving Slammers!

Don't forget, live today like there's no tomorrow!

Xs and Os,

Belle

chapter 16

Home Sweet Home

"I'm so ready for this vacation!" Darren yells as he exits his bus.

Sawyer snickers loudly. "You're just ready for six months of condom-free sex." Darren flips him off and keeps walking toward the SUV waiting for him, Warren, and Wyatt.

"You did notice he didn't deny it," Wyatt says, patting Sawyer on the shoulder as he gets off the bus.

"Of course he didn't. Who wouldn't be excited to have sex without a condom? They're a pain in the fucking ass."

Noah looks at Sawyer as he heads back onto the bus and asks, "So are kids. Which would you rather have?"

Sawyer laughs and shakes his head. "Not a kid, that's for sure."

"That's what I thought," Noah answers with a laugh as he disappears inside.

"What about you, Princess? What do you think about the baby on its way?" Sawyer's question catches me by surprise. Not really because of the question itself; just because we haven't been talking much.

"I'm happy if they're happy. I'm just glad it isn't me."

"What, you don't like kids?" he asks, obviously surprised at my answer.

"I like kids as much as the next person. I just like them better when they have their own parents to go home to. I'll be a kickass aunt, though, for sure."

He shakes his head and pulls me to the side of the bus. "Does Noah know how you feel about kids?"

"Good God, Sawyer, I don't hate kids. I'm just not ready for any of my own, and yes, Noah is very aware of that fact."

He releases a breath and seems relieved. "Okay, good. I'd hate for him to finally have the girl of his dreams and have it go bust over a missed discussion. I'll see you guys in the car." He walks away as Noah steps off the bus.

That was weird.

"What was that about?" Noah asks.

"Nothing, just Sawyer being brotherly."

"Is that a good thing?" he asks hesitantly.

"For you, yeah. He loves you. Come on and take me home. I need to be drunk for the next twenty-four hours until I have to meet all your family."

Noah laughs and kisses me on top of my head as we walk to the car. "They're going to love you, and you'll love them, too."

Noah holds my hand all the way to his house, squeezing it every so often in reassurance. It's like he knows I need to feel wanted. It's strange being home and not having my own home to go to.

After we get out of the car, he leads me inside of the house. It's even prettier in the daylight. The sun glimmers atop the water, reflecting a million rays of light dancing on top of the waves. It's not early enough for dolphins and whales to be playing, but Noah says if I'm up as early as I am on tour, I'll definitely see them from his bedroom window in the morning.

When he opens his bedroom door, the first thing I see is an eight by ten photo Belle took of the two of us next to his bed. "Noah! When did you get that?" I ask, pointing to it.

"Anna made it for us and brought it when she came down last night."

"For us?" I repeat, and he pulls me in close.

"This is your room for now. What's mine is yours. Besides, if you think I'm going to let you go easily after the tour is over, you're mistaken. After almost a year in my bed, I figure when the tour is over you should just move in here with me."

"Noah ..."

"What, Mel? What is the problem?" His frustration is showing. The last thing I want to do is kick off this week with a fight. Especially since this is an important week for me to be documenting for the story.

"Nothing," I say, placing a quick kiss against his lips. "I'm fine. I'm just going to go take a walk and enjoy some sunlight. I'll be back in a bit."

He looks like he wants to say more as I take my sunglasses out of my purse, but he doesn't. I'm glad. I just need to get some air and think for a while. I was only here the one time back on that August night, but I remember my way down to the beach.

It's cold down here, but I grabbed a blanket from the couch on my way out, expecting it would be. After walking a little way down the beach, I wrap myself up in it and sit down. It's so peaceful here. The only sounds are the seagulls crying and the waves crashing against the shore. It's the perfect place to try and figure out what is going on inside of my head.

The last few months have passed at warp speed. I've been so wrapped up in Noah and the band, I haven't even thought about my upcoming book tour. And even though I'm building a great timeline with photos and memories from the tour, I haven't started their book yet. Which isn't a huge worry since it's not due to the publisher until a year after the tour wraps up, but I feel like I'm slacking. I just want it to be perfect, and I'm scared my relationship with Noah will compromise the story.

I really want to bring to light the Sara situation, even if I can't name her. If the fans can see how their favorite celebrities are stalked and taken advantage of, I think it will go a long way into understanding just how much people give up for their craft. And if it can bring awareness to a touchy subject, all the better. I'm just not sure they'll go for bringing this into their story.

As my fingers dredge through the sand, the tiny grains sifting through my fingers, I keep hoping my mind will slow. Work will always be there, but my biggest issue right now is the way I feel about Noah. I love him—more than I ever loved Eli—and it terrifies me. It's only been a few months and things still have so much time to go wrong. I'd known Eli for a year before I realized I was in love with him. How can I love Noah more, so much quicker? If he leaves me, it will destroy me. Yet, every time he talks about the future, it makes me want to run and I can't figure out why. At some point, if this is going to work between us, I have to start acknowledging the big things. Like eventually moving in together.

"Is this seat taken?"

Sawyer.

"It's a public beach."

"Actually, it's not."

"Figures."

"If you had Sara chasing after you, you'd be glad it was private, too."

"True," I answer, glancing at him, but his sunglasses are hiding his eyes as he looks out at the sea.

"He loves you," he says softly, almost as if the words hurt to say.

"I know," I answer on a sigh. "And I love him, but ..."

"He's moving too fast."

"Yeah, I guess maybe that's it."

"Noah has been ready for the rest of his life for a while now. He's always loved being part of the band, but if he had it his way, we would have quit a few years ago. After all the Sara shit happened the first time. Maybe to you he seems overly eager, but he's just excited to finally move on to what he's wanted all along."

"A family."

"Bingo. You know, Princess, you and I aren't so different. It takes us longer to let people in, but once we do, it hurts like a bitch to let them go."

I scoop up a handful of sand and let it funnel through my fingers while his words sink in.

"I don't want to let him go. I just don't know if I can give him what he wants." Why I'm confessing my thoughts to Sawyer, I'll never know, but it does feel good to talk them out.

"Look, I'm not one to give advice, but Noah is different. If you can't give him what he wants, do us all a favor and break it off now. I know my brother and he's in this for the long haul. Forever, if you'll have him. He won't break your heart, but you could easily break his. Marriage and a family have always been his dream. What he's saved and built up for his whole life. And to be honest, I've never seen him fall for someone the way he's fallen for you. You're his heart, Princess. Try not to break it."

"How do you know?"

Sawyer turns to me with a sad smile. "Because he told me. But even if he hadn't, I know my brother, and I've never seen him this happy."

Sawyer stands and bends down, placing a kiss on the top of my head before he walks away. Now I feel worse than when I came down here.

As the sun warms me up a bit, I ball up the blanket and put it under my head, quickly falling asleep.

When a darkness falls over me, I pry my eyes open. Noah is standing above me, throwing a shadow over my body. A sexy smile peeks up from the corner of his mouth as I reach for my sunglasses. Once they're on, he takes a seat next to me as I sit up and brush the sand from the backs of my arms.

"I'm sorry," he says, turning toward me. "I didn't mean to scare you or make you uncomfortable. That was never my intention, Mel."

The thing about Noah is there's never anything but sincerity in his words. I've never met anyone who is so utterly sincere all the time.

"It's okay. I've been down here doing some thinking."

"And sleeping," he throws in, and I laugh.

"Yes, and sleeping, but even in my sleep I was dreaming of you. So my subconscious was still thinking even if I took a timeout."

"Come to any conclusions?"

As I lace my fingers through his and squeeze, I rest my head on his shoulders. "Yeah, I think so. I know I love you and I want to be with you. Thinking about the future is scary, but thinking about a future without you ... it's terrifying."

"So what does that mean, exactly?" he asks with a hopeful lilt in his voice.

"It means I'm going to go with the flow. Is it absolutely crazy to think about moving in together in a year? Completely. But could I picture getting off that bus and moving somewhere without you? No, I can't."

He squeezes my hand and rubs his thumb over my ring finger. I'm going to try not to read anything into that. Enough freaking out for today.

"I know this seems like we're moving fast. Especially for you, when you weren't looking for love."

"Maybe a little."

"What do you believe in, Mel? Do you think people are meant to be together? That you fall in love with someone for a specific reason?"

"Like divine intervention?" I ask, trying to narrow down the topic a bit more.

He chuckles. "Maybe if you consider divine intervention like fate."

"I know you put a lot of faith into fate, but honestly, I'm not sure."

With a sigh, he kisses my forehead. "I've met a lot of women over the years. Some I've connected with on one level or another, but you're the first I've ever felt like this with."

"Do you think there's more than one person out there for everyone? That you can have these sparks with someone else?"

"Without a doubt," he answers firmly.

"Wow, that's ... comforting," I reply with a pout, and he laughs.

"Come on. If you think about it, there has to be. People break up, lose touch, are separated by any number of reasons, including death. Yet, somehow, they will eventually love again if they're open to it. There has to be more than one person out there for us. But finding one of them and making it work ... those are the stories you hear of ... people who are married for fifty years. The epic romances. Sometimes, the work isn't *in* the relationship, but it's spent in the time *before* the relationship, when you're still looking for the one who completes you."

"Don't you mean completes you for now?"

Noah pushes me down into the sand and rolls on top of me. "For now, for next month, next year, and for the rest of our lives. Maybe there's someone else out there for the both of us, but they're just going to have to keep looking for whoever else matches them because we're off the market."

"We are?" I whisper as his lips inch closer to mine.

"Most definitely." His mouth covers mine. Noah takes his time kissing me, drawing out the pleasure as his body moves against mine. My hands wrap around his neck to bring us even closer. As his tongue sinfully dances with mine, my body arches against his. Everything about this man sets my soul on fire. I'm a fool to try and convince myself otherwise because there's nothing more exciting than the thought of spending forever with him.

We're both breathless when we break apart.

"Did you send Sawyer out here earlier to talk to me?"

Noah stills at my words, rolls off me, and sits up.

"No, I didn't. What did he want?"

"Hey …" I reach for his arm and pull myself up, turning his head toward mine. "Why are you mad?"

"I'm not mad. I just don't want Sawyer making things worse."

I wish he wasn't so on edge about Sawyer all the time now.

"He made things better, Noah. Your brother loves you and he wants you happy. I felt better after talking to him, and I feel even better after talking to you."

His silence lingers between us as he turns his gaze back out to the ocean.

"If you want to do something that would make me happy, you could start by forgiving Sawyer. He's trying, Noah. Of all the weeks in the year, this is when you should be thankful for him most, even if he's a pain in the ass at times."

My own lies are eating away at me. I should have told Noah what Sawyer said to me on the bus before Vegas, but it would only make things worse. If I thought it was something to be worried about, I would, but the more time that passes, the more I feel like he was just trying to get a rise out of me. And the last thing I want to do is put a bigger wedge between the two of them. Their relationship is priority number one.

"Would that really make you happy, or are you trying to guilt me?"

"It really would make me happy. I'm sure your parents would love to see the two of you without picking up on any underlying tension as well."

He laughs and turns back to me. "Have you been talking to Rory and Diane?"

"Hell no. The thought of meeting your family terrifies me. I'm not jumping into that pool any earlier than I have to."

"They're going to love you. After you meet them, you'll feel better. One more day and you'll realize you've been worried for nothing."

"I hope so."

Just The Two Of Us

Later, Noah and I have the whole house to ourselves. When I get out of the shower, I'm surprised to find him in bed with a room service cart filled with candy next to the bed.

"A cart and everything?" I ask with a beaming smile I couldn't hide if I tried.

"Well, you know … you seemed a little disappointed it was missing from our Vegas vacation, and since I have your favorite movie queued up and ready to go, I figured it was a necessity."

"You didn't! You got *Stealing Home?*"

He waves the remote in the air, and I take that as my cue to pounce on him. When my lips meet his, he pulls me close and his hardness hits me in just the right spot.

"God, Noah … I think we should work up an appetite first."

"I think you're reading my mind." He pulls my shirt off, exposing my breasts. His hands move quickly to my waist and he flips us over, tugging my shorts down in record time. His shirt is off before he even stands, and he makes fast work of getting rid of his shorts and boxers.

The tip of his cock is glistening already, and I quickly lean down and suck him into my mouth. "Fuck … Mel, your mouth feels so good." I pull him in deeper. His hands weave through my hair as he sets the pace.

"Enough," he says, pulling back out of my reach. "I want to come with you tonight. Lie back."

I do as he says, and he opens the nightstand, searching for a condom. When he doesn't find what he's looking for, he moves to the top dresser drawer.

"Shit." He picks up a towel lying on the top of his hamper and wraps it around his waist. "I'm out of condoms. I'm going to go grab one from Sawyer's room."

He's back a minute later with a few condoms in hand, drops the towel, and climbs into bed. "Now, where were we?"

"I think right about here." I pull his mouth back to mine. Letting myself get lost in Noah's kisses is the easiest thing in the world. His hands caress every inch of my body they can reach, but his mouth never leaves mine.

Suddenly but smoothly, he flips us over so I'm on top of him. The hooded look in his eyes fuels my desire to make him scream this time. I scoot down enough that my head is at his stomach and take my time kissing and licking my way up his chest.

"Shit, Mel ... you feel so good." His enjoyment is obvious by the way his cock is pressing against my leg. When I flick his nipple with my tongue, he hisses. I do it again and he groans in pleasure, pulling me to him and taking my mouth with his.

"Uh uh," I tell him softly as I pull away. "It's my turn to play," I whisper into his ear before sucking his earlobe into my mouth. My lips travel down his neck, and for a minute, I consider leaving my mark, but we're not teenagers anymore and the press would have a field day. I suck just long enough to have him writhing beneath me, calling out my name.

"Jesus, Mel, what are you trying to do to me?" he groans as he rips a condom open and slides it on.

I position myself over him with my lips a breath away from his, answering him as I slide down onto his firm length, "Make you lose control."

An indecipherable moan of pleasure falls from his lips as I pull him into my heat. His hands move to my hips as he tries to set the pace.

"You can hold on for the ride, but this is my show," I tell him softly. His grip loosens, and my body curves to his. I'm riding him slowly, and as I lower my mouth to his, he opens to me immediately. Our kiss is slow, sensual, our tongues dancing to the pace of our bodies. Making love to Noah is an incomparable high.

While we're kissing, he moves his hands to my ass, pulling me tighter to him. Based on the increase of our collective moans, I can tell he's as close to coming as I am. But I want this to last a little bit longer. I shift my body, placing my hands on his chest and sitting straight up. His knees are against my back, and I lean against them, trying to pull him even deeper inside of me. Noah's hands go to my breasts as he arches into me.

"Noah!" I cry out as he hits my g-spot again and again. This is supposed to be my show, but damn, he feels good. I pull myself up, just out of his reach, and his cock hovers at my entrance.

"Mel ..." His breathless cry spurs me to slam back down on him, taking him all at once. His cries prove he loves the feeling, and each time I do it, he gets louder and louder as my orgasm builds to the point of no return.

"Come with me, Mel. Please come with me," he calls out as he takes back control, arching into me again and again. His fingers squeeze my nipples as my walls quiver around him.

"Noah!"

"Oh, baby, yes! Mel ... fuck!"

I love the sound of him losing control as our bodies come together. I fall against him, still pulsing around him, and his hands go right back to my ass, pulling me as close as possible as he fills me with his release. Our hearts beat as one loud drum until we both finally calm from the exertion.

He bends slightly and kisses my forehead. "That was incredible."

"Mmhm." My fingers dance across his chest. I feel his chuckle rumble through his chest as I continue listening to his heart.

A few minutes of silence pass as we lay together. "What are you thinking?" It brings a smile to my face. He asks this almost every time we have sex. Only this time, I don't want to tell him because it's embarrassing.

"Nothing important."

He carefully peels me off of him and takes off the condom and ties it off before coming back and scooping me into his arms.

"Bullshit. Tell me what you're thinking about. You know you can talk to me about anything, right?"

"Of course."

Except Sawyer. I can't be the one to wreck his relationship with his brother.

"I was just thinking maybe I should make an appointment to get an IUD."

Concern fills his features. "Is that something you want to do?"

"I think so. Being allergic to the pill sucks, but it's never mattered much before. After Eli, I focused on me. I had a couple of short-term relationships over the years but nothing that ever had long-term potential."

"And you think we have long-term potential?" he asks, unable to hide his smile.

"Yes, I do. What we have is incredible. Tonight, I realized I want to be able to feel all of you, to take all of you, and not have to fear getting pregnant. Then maybe, someday, when the time is right, we can revisit that topic."

Noah leans in and kisses me softly. "If that's something you want to look into, of course I'd be all in. I'm not a fan of condoms,

D. Kelly

but I'm a big fan of you, and I'll wear them for as long as I need to. I just don't want you to feel like this is something you have to do for me."

Could he be any sweeter?

"It's something I want to do for us. I'll call my doctor next week and see if they can get me in over the holidays when we're back for Christmas and New Year's."

He places a kiss on the tip of my nose and nods.

"Can I ask you something?"

"Anything, anytime, anywhere," he answers.

"Why do you ask me what I'm thinking after we have sex? Don't get me wrong, I don't mind, I'm just curious."

"I always want to know what you're thinking. I guess after we have sex it just seems like the perfect time. The world has slowed down and there's no one around but the two of us. There's nothing getting in our way, no interruptions … Well, hopefully." He chuckles. "I don't know exactly how to explain it, but it's when I feel the most connected to you, so I want to know what you're thinking in those moments."

"Okay, that's fair, but I might start asking you the same question."

"Anything, anytime, anywhere. I'm an open book."

I laugh and shake my head. "Maybe you need that tattooed. Or you can get three As."

"I'd actually need four."

"Why four?"

"Anything, anytime, anywhere, and Amelia. You're the only person I'm an open book for."

This man steals my heart one word at a time. As much as I hate the idea of someone having the power to hurt me more than Eli or my parents ever did, it's too late. There will never be anyone for me other than Noah.

"You still want to watch the movie?" he asks.

"Yup." I pop a kiss on his lips. "Just give me a few minutes to clean up and get dressed."

"Clean up and stay naked. We've got all night, two more condoms, and a locked door. Plus, all the snacks we could want."

"The only snack I want is you … and maybe some popcorn. We'll see." I duck into the bathroom and hear his laughter behind me. That sound will never get old.

While we watched the movie, I mostly watched him. I've seen it a million times, but seeing his expressions while he took it all in was priceless. He teared up where it was sad—even if no tears fell—and he laughed hysterically at the dink and promised never to be caught in shorts and black socks again.

When the movie finished, Noah is smiling at me.

"Well … what did you think?"

"It was really good. I'm not sure I would watch it four times a year because it's kind of sad, but I get the appeal."

"Would you watch it once a year?" I ask sweetly.

"With you?" he teases, and I nod.

"Of course I would. There's not much I wouldn't do for you."

"Would you buy my tampons?"

His eyes grow wide with my question, and I hold back my laughter. I would never ask a man to buy my tampons unless it was an emergency.

"Somehow, I would get you tampons if you needed them, but it might involve paying off a woman shopping at the same store or calling one of my sisters for help."

Finally, I let my laughter out. He just shakes his head at me.

"Don't worry, I try and stay well stocked. I think there are some things us women should get for ourselves."

"That's good to know." He pulls me into a hug.

"So is there anything I should avoid saying or talking about around your family?"

"Mel, just be yourself. I promise they're going to adore you as much as I do. My family is normal. I mean, they all have their ticks, but the most important thing you can do is just be you."

"Yeah, okay."

"Hey …" He tilts my chin up so my eyes meet his. "Is there a reason you're so worried?"

"I haven't met anyone's parents since Eli's. Like I said, there weren't really many other guys, and none of them with long-term potential. With Eli it was different because we were kids, meeting the parents was kind of mandatory. But this is …"

"What, Mel?"

"It's so grownup!" His lips meet mine as he kisses me through his laughter. "Laugh all you want, but you don't have to meet my family. *You* get the easy way out."

221

D. Kelly

"I would have been happy to meet your family. They couldn't have been too bad. They gave me you, after all." His solemn words calm my nerves.

"That's a good way to look at it. Thank you."

"Anytime." His lips begin a trail of kisses across my shoulder, up my neck, and eventually make their way to my mouth. "I think you need to be distracted from your thoughts, don't you?" His husky tone sends chills through my body.

"Distract away, Mr. Weston."

Meeting The Family

Of course, today of all days, I was up at sunrise as usual. Even three rounds of incredible sex with Noah last night didn't knock my sleep schedule off track. Thankfully, Sawyer has a Keurig here with a much more impressive selection of coffee. I'm the only one awake, so after grabbing a pack of Pop-Tarts and my coffee, I head back to Noah's room.

I'm curled up in a chair by his window watching the dolphins and the whales as the sun rises. I'm as excited as a little kid at Sea World watching them and wishing I could go down and swim with them. Maybe I can talk Noah into a trip to Sea World over the next break so we can feed the dolphins. Knowing him, he'd try and one-up me and plan a vacation to swim with them instead.

My phone vibrates on the table and I hop up to grab it.

Belle: I just finished puking my guts up. Come talk to me in the living room. I know you're up.

Poor Belle. I don't envy her.

Mel: On my way.

When I enter the living room, I notice the crackers and ginger ale on the table.

"You going to be able to sit at the table with all that food tomorrow?"

She looks up at me with a frown. "God, I hope so. I want sweet potatoes and mashed potatoes and rolls."

"Carb central. You've *got* to be having a girl," I reply with a laugh.

"Look, Mel, I have to tell you something. It's important."

"What's up? You look like your dog died."

"That would almost be better," she responds dryly. "When I woke up this morning, I had an email from *Slammed*'s PR team. They picked the winner for the concert Friday for the video shoot. She returned all the paperwork for her and her guest."

"I'm sure that's exciting for them." I'm still not understanding where she's going with this.

"For the winner, yeah, but for her guest, not so much. Look, Mel, I don't know how to say this except to just say it. The winner was Jessie, and she's bringing Eli as her guest."

"Eli's cousin?"

"Yes."

Holy shit.

"Jessie is a huge BAD fan. She always posts about them on her social media accounts, but I doubt Eli is."

Yes, I still talk to Eli's cousin on social media. She stayed out of our breakup and we remained in touch occasionally. When I set up my Facebook account, she was one of the first people to send me a friend request. I denied Eli's.

"You know he's only going for one reason. To see *you*, Mel."

"I have to go, Belle. It's one of the biggest angles for the story."

She reaches over and grabs a cracker to nibble on. "I know, babe, that's why I'm telling you now. You've got to tell Noah. For the record, I tried to get her disqualified, but *Slammed*'s PR team is eating it up that Eli is coming with our winner. They said as long as the forms were filled out correctly, it's a done deal."

"Thanks. I'm excited to see Jessie, but ..."

"Yeah. Eli, not so much." Belle tucks herself into the corner of the couch and nibbles on another cracker.

"You guys have a plan yet for breaking the news about the baby?" I ask, changing the subject from Eli.

Belle shrugs. "I think they'll see me throw up before Darren figures out who to tell first, or how, but we'll see. It's his family, and I'm nervous enough to meet everyone as it is, let alone having to explain to them I'm a slut who got herself knocked up."

"Belle, you know that's not true."

"But that's how they'll see me. Come on. Their mega famous, mega rich son just *happens* to knock up a reporter?"

Her frustration with the situation is apparent, but I know her heart, and it's not what she's describing.

"They're going to love you. And when they see that ring on your finger, they're going to know Darren loves you, too, and that there's so much more between the two of you than the peanut in your belly. Speaking of ... Have you given any more thought to his proposal?"

I'm being evil right now because Darren is standing in the hall listening to us with his finger pressed against his lips, asking me to keep quiet.

"Of course. It's all I think about when I'm not throwing up, worrying about his family hating me, and of course, keeping up with my job."

"I know you have a lot on your plate, but soon you'll just have to worry about work. Your morning sickness will be over in a few weeks and you'll meet the family today. So what did you decide?" My feet are bouncing up and down as I wait for her answer. Darren is leaning against the wall, smiling and waiting as well.

"I'm not ready. But after the baby, if it goes well and we still get along and can manage to live together amicably, I'd absolutely marry his fine ass."

She's going to kill me for this, but Belle will hold back her feelings until the end of days just because she can. "Do you love him?"

She taps her nails against her knees with a thoughtful expression. "Do you remember that summer when we discovered Jolt Cola?"

This is random, but I'll go with it. "Of course, how could I forget? It's what led to my coffee addiction."

"Exactly. You know how it was the best thing ever and it gave us tons of energy and we were completely addicted to it?"

I nod my head in affirmation.

"Then you remember how bad it sucked when we didn't have any? And how miserable we were that our parents wouldn't let us have it anymore? But we didn't realize how addicted to it we were until they took it away?"

"Yeah, that was a pretty rough transition." I understand her point, even though Darren looks totally confused.

"Darren is Jolt. Except I didn't realize it until he left that night when I told him about the baby. I know it was only a few hours, but it was enough to make me realize how much I would have missed him if he were gone."

A smile spreads across his face and mine. "So you love him."

She nods. "God help me, I do. Enough to wear this ridiculous ring for the next how many ever years it takes to get comfortable with the idea of marrying him."

"I love you, too," he says, stalking toward her. She shoots an evil glare my way before turning to him.

"I'm going to take that as my cue to go talk to Noah." Her expression softens with the thought of what I have to tell him.

"I'll deal with you later," she says as I blow her a kiss on my way down the hall. Those two are going to be fine. They'll probably be the happiest of us all.

Noah is still dead to the world as I crawl back into bed and wrap my arms around him and squeeze tight. He mumbles a bit and eventually turns over, facing me, slowly wiping the sleep from his eyes.

"Good morning, beautiful," he says in a sleepy, gravelly voice. "What time is it?"

"Early, too early for you, but we need to talk."

"Can I use the bathroom first?"

"Of course, I'm not sadistic," I answer with a laugh.

A few minutes later, he crawls back into bed with minty fresh breath and an empty bladder. His lips meet mine in a soft, lingering kiss. "What would you like to talk about?" he asks as he brushes my hair away from my eyes.

"Eli," I whisper softly, and he tenses in my arms.

"What about him?"

"He's going to be at the video shoot on Friday," I confess, watching his facial expression change from neutral to furious in less than five seconds.

"The hell he is," he bites out.

"It will be fine, Noah. I need to talk to him, anyway, and clear the air. It's time."

He sits up and leans against the headboard with his arms crossed over his chest. "After what he did to you? He's lucky he's still breathing. No way is he going to be at the show. I won't allow it."

I knew he was going to be mad, but this is worse than I thought. I crawl up into his lap and straddle his legs, reaching over his shoulders and holding on to the headboard for balance. "His cousin Jessie, who I adore, by the way, won the tickets from the *Slammed* promo. It's already been announced and their paperwork confirmed. She picked Eli as her guest. You can't punish her because he's her favorite cousin. Besides, I really would like to see Jessie and I'd hate to break her heart if you pulled strings to get them banned."

"Not her, then, just him," he says stubbornly.

"Noah ... for me, please let it go."

"You're the reason why I want to kill him," he states simply, and I shake my head.

"Don't do that. Don't let my past be a reason to bring hate into your heart. It's not worth it. *He's* not worth it. You are the man I love now. You're the only man I want."

With a raised brow, he exhales as I grind myself on top of him. "Really? Using sex to distract me?"

"Never," I whisper, bringing my lips to his, tasting his lips with my tongue before he opens to me and allows me to set the pace of our kiss. "This is to remind you I belong to you now, not Eli."

"*Fuuck.* That might be the best thing you've ever said."

"Well … now I'm going to kill your high. We need to get dressed and go to the store. We've got a Thanksgiving list to fill and condoms to buy."

"Martha already did all the shopping for Thanksgiving."

"Not from my list. There are things I need to make Belle's favorite sweet potatoes that you don't have. And I'm not borrowing condoms from Sawyer all week. Get dressed and let's go before the crowds start and all the women fawn and fondle you instead of their groceries."

The heated stare he's giving me sets me on fire. One look and Noah has my panties soaking. It's not fair, but I wouldn't have it any other way.

"You know, you're pretty sexy when you're bossy." He smacks my ass as I get up.

"Hmm, goes back to that teacher fantasy, huh? Maybe you want to be spanked by my ruler?"

"Kinky … Maybe I want to spank you with your ruler. Turn the teacher into the student."

"Well, I have been a naughty girl, Mr. Weston. Maybe I deserve detention."

Noah groans and wraps his arms around my waist. "Come on, dirty girl. Let's shower before you have me coming in my boxers."

"You need *all* of this for sweet potatoes?" Noah asks incredulously as he tosses the condoms in the grocery cart. "Bourbon, oranges, two forms of cinnamon, canned milk?" he questions with a turned up nose. "And two kinds of marshmallows? What else could you possibly need?"

He's laughing now, but wait until he tastes the magic. "Yams, butter, brown sugar, white sugar, and vanilla," I answer proudly.

"And this is a two-day process?"

"Absolutely, and they'll be the best you've ever had. Trust me."

"If you say so."

"You'll be begging for me to feed you more," I respond to his skeptical look.

D. Kelly

"Maybe I'll just eat them off of you," he whispers in my ear seductively. He's now standing behind me, with his arms around my waist, pushing the cart. It's completely awkward and totally fun.

"And you called me kinky. Do you have a food fetish, too?" I whisper back at him.

"No, I have a *you* fetish." His words fill my body with need.

"I don't think you have enough condoms." I'm looking down at the box in the cart.

"There's plenty on the bus, and if you think my family is going to give us enough alone time over the next few days to have sex more than forty times, you're high."

He captures my groan with a kiss, sucking the frustration straight from me. As we wait in line at the checkout, our faces are front and center on the cover of *Slammed*. This is awkward. I haven't been on the cover of anything since my dad died. Noah has a hat and a hoodie on, but I'm not disguised at all. I didn't even think about it, and apparently, neither did he. And like idiots, we ducked out without any guards. This is exactly why I wanted to get to the store early, but our shower took a little longer than expected and now the store is filling up.

"Relax, babe. We'll be fine." He pulls my hand to his mouth and kisses it softly.

Everything is fine until we're paying and the two women behind us start gossiping about the magazine cover.

"Can you believe he's with Joey Triton's daughter? That's got to be a couple destined for the lifetime love hall of fame. I mean, Joey and Iris had an epic love story."

The second girl clucks a disapproving sound. "I don't think so, girl. She used to date Eli Watts, and it's a long-known fact he's been pining away for her for years. In fact, I heard in one of his fan groups they may be reuniting soon at some secret event."

Noah's hands squeeze my hips hard, and I cover one of them with mine, rubbing him reassuringly as I use the other hand to punch in my PIN number on the keypad. I wish he could see inside my heart and know Eli isn't competition for him and never will be. Once our bags are into the cart and we're about to make a clean getaway, Noah turns to the women, whose mouths are now gaping open.

"You shouldn't believe what you hear in fan forums," he tells them with a smile. "True love always trumps old flames."

One of the girls covers her heart with her hands as the other girl flicks her on the shoulder and pops off her opinion. "See, I told you those fan forums are full of trash talk. Will you listen now? It's

228

obvious they're in love. They're even Thanksgiving shopping … Swoon."

Noah smirks at her words and eyes her purchases, dropping a hundred-dollar bill on the counter. "Happy Thanksgiving, ladies," he says and pushes our cart outside at a rapid pace. We hurry and load up the car and get out of there before they, or anyone else, can chase us down.

I can't stop shaking my head at his random act of kindness. "What?" he asks as we pull out of the lot.

"Nothing, I just don't think I've ever met anyone like you before. You're one of a kind, Noah Weston."

"Is that a compliment?"

"The best one I can give," I reply truthfully. He reaches over the seat and laces our fingers together. The drive back to the house is silent, but he's smiling the whole way there. Seeing him happy is the best feeling. I never realized how much of my happiness could depend on someone else's. Noah is teaching me a lot about life and love, and he doesn't even realize it, which makes the feeling even better.

When he pulls into the driveway, there are cars here that weren't here when we left, and my stomach drops rapidly. It's like we just crested a hill on a roller coaster and we're freefalling. Noah squeezes my hand reassuringly. "Breathe, Mel. They're going to love you."

I nod absently while I freak out internally. Before we even exit the car there's an enthusiastic girl banging on his window. Noah laughs with happiness and hops out of the car, scooping her up and swinging her around in circles while hugging her. She throws her head back and laughs, planting a big, loud kiss on his cheek when he finally puts her back on the ground.

Their resemblance is striking. Sure, she's younger, but she could be Noah's twin sister more than Sawyer is his twin. It's uncanny. Same eyes, same hair color, same smile. She's adorable. Before I know it, she's pulling me into a huge hug. "You must be Amelia! It's so nice to finally meet you! I've never heard the four of these guys rave about one person before, let alone a woman. You must weave some awesome magic." She winks at me, and I can't help but laugh; it's like her happiness is contagious.

"I don't know if it's magic. I just don't put up with anyone's shit," I tell her, and she bursts into laughter.

"My mom is going to drill you for your secrets. I think you're the only person who Sawyer has ever *let* put him into place."

A flash of irritation crosses Noah's face, but he covers it quickly. "It's what attracted me to her in the first place. She told Sawyer off and it was incredible. I was instantly in love … or at least like." He winks at me. "You should have seen the look on his face, Ror. I thought he was going to pass out."

"That's what he gets for calling me a princess." I help Noah start unloading the car.

"I've heard you've settled into your nickname nicely," Rory replies, and Noah snickers.

"Yeah, I guess so. For whatever reason, your brother seems to enjoy it. I don't think he means it maliciously, so whatever works for him."

Rory grabs the last of the bags and closes the trunk. Noah leads the way into the house, and we follow the endless stream of chatter into the kitchen.

"There's my boy!" I hear the scream before I see the face that goes with it. As Noah puts the bags down on the counter, he's wrapped up in a massive hug. "God, I've missed you!" Her voice is muffled against his chest because she's still hugging him.

"I missed you, too, Mom." She pulls his head down and smothers him in motherly kisses. Noah's blushing furiously, and I can't stop myself from smiling. He's loved, and it's the best feeling to know he's not just a good guy with me; his family thinks so, too.

"You must be Amelia." I turn around, meeting their dad for the first time. He's handsome and really fit for a man in his fifties. Now I know where Sawyer and Noah get it from.

"I am," I reply with a smile. "It's nice to meet you …"

"Owen," he fills in.

"Owen," I add, shaking his proffered hand.

Before I know it, I'm being flipped around and embraced in a huge hug. "You're her … and you're here! Welcome to the family, Amelia. We're so happy to have you with us." I'm a bit overwhelmed with her show of affection. I can see Sawyer laughing at me over her shoulder.

"Karen, I think you're freaking her out a bit. How about you stop squeezing her and introduce yourself first?" Owen tells her as he pulls one of her hands gently away from me.

She waves her hand dismissively, but she does release me. She's a pretty woman, with light hair and green eyes. Now I see where they all get them from. She's on the petite side and a bit curvy, with laugh lines that show a life well lived. She's pretty in an understated way, and her smile is sincere, just like Noah's. In fact, I definitely think he resembles his mom more in his expressions. Sawyer has more of Owen's reserved features. Wow ... meeting people's parents can be a trip.

"I'm sorry, Amelia, I was just excited to meet the woman who has stolen Noah's heart. I'm Karen, but I'm sure you guessed that all on your own," she adds with a laugh.

"It's nice to meet you." As I look around the room, I realize Belle and Darren are missing. Wyatt and Anna are sitting with Sawyer at the table, eating breakfast.

"Where's Belle?" I ask as I start unloading the bags.

"Oh, she and Darren went to breakfast with his parents. She's a sweet little thing, isn't she? She looked more nervous than you did when you walked in," Owen says with a chuckle.

I'm sure she did.

Thankfully, Noah is keeping close as I unpack the bags. When I get to the bottom of the second bag, I come across the condoms. *Shit.* After elbowing him in the side twice, he finally follows my gaze to the bag. When he looks inside, he laughs and pulls them out, setting them on the counter as if it's no big deal.

I'm mortified, and from the smirk on his face, he knows it and is enjoying pushing me out of my comfort zone. I move to the side, giving the condoms a wide berth, and continue unloading what I need to start the sweet potatoes.

Sawyer is watching it all unfold, and for the first time ever, I see him cover his mouth to hold back his laughter. I'm glad to see they're all enjoying my shame. Once the last bag is emptied, I swear all eyes are on me and the room is quiet.

"Oh, for heaven's sake, Noah. Stop teasing this poor girl and go put your condoms away like a gentleman," Karen says with a chuckle, and everyone laughs, finally easing the tension. Noah wraps his arms around me from behind and pulls me close, kissing me on the cheek.

"My parents know we have sex, Mel. My mom is always hounding me to be safe, so I was just making a point. This was about her, not you. But I couldn't love you any more right now if I tried," he whispers, and even though I'm mad, my heart melts.

"Yeah, yeah, just go put them away and come back so you can watch me make holiday magic."

"Sure thing." He picks up the condoms and takes them into his room. The doorbell rings, and Sawyer jumps up to get it. I'm not sure I've ever seen him smile this much. Being around his family has a calming effect on him.

"J! What's up, man?" Noah exclaims from down the hall, where he has a perfect view of the door. Sawyer, Noah, and Jordan walk in at the same time, and they take turns hugging. He's shorter than I imagined but just as built and tatted up as his cousins … brothers … hell, I don't even know what they consider each other, but I know they're close.

"Jordan, this is Amelia, my girlfriend."

Jordan offers his hand to me. "Nice to meet you, Amelia."

"You, too."

A quick look passes between him and Sawyer. Noah didn't see it; that's probably a good thing because I'm sure it had something to do with me.

As the family chats and catches up, I find two potato peelers and pass one to Noah. "You're putting me to work?"

"Hell yeah. This is the most I've ever had to make at once. Your family is huge! I need all the help I can get cutting and peeling."

"I'll help, too," Rory pipes up, so I show her how to slice the potatoes once they're peeled.

"Mel, is this normal?" Noah asks, looking down at his hands. His fingers are stuck together and they're turning a bit orange.

"Completely. It's all the natural juices seeping into your skin." He flashes me a devilish smile.

Rory bumps me with her hip. "You two are adorable, even when the conversation is not sister friendly."

"Don't encourage them, Ror. They're nauseating on a good day," Sawyer mutters.

"He's just jealous he hasn't found his 'one' yet. Ignore him. So how long have you been dating, exactly?"

"About two months now, Noah?"

"No, it's closer to three," Noah remarks, and I'm confused. He must notice because he clarifies. "Alright, I guess, officially, it's been two. But I knew the night we met she was all I wanted. And since we flirted constantly from the minute she got on the bus, I count from then, which puts us at about three months."

Rory smiles and continues peeling the potatoes. She and Noah switched jobs when she realized it's tiring cutting through uncooked sweet potatoes. They're harder than you'd think. While they finish up the potatoes, I start mixing all the other ingredients into big Pampered Chef baking bowls. Noah watches in fascination as I melt and stir and spice up each bowl. When they finish, I show them all the steps and laugh when they gasp at the amount of bourbon I use in them.

"Are those kid friendly?" he asks.

"Absolutely. It will all bake out between today and tomorrow."

"Don't tell Diane, she'll shit a brick," Noah remarks.

"No, she won't. Are you kidding, Noah? She'll give them double helpings and hope they'll pass out. Dealing with a two- and a four-year-old at the holidays isn't easy. Hell, *any* day. But it's what she wanted. Did you hear they're trying for a boy?"

"It's what I want, too," Noah says softly so only I can hear. Tingles flood my body, and for the first time ever, I can understand the appeal of romanticizing love and family. "No, I hadn't heard, but good for them. Diane's always wanted a big family."

"So have you," she points out, and he shrugs. I try and ignore their conversation and focus on mixing up the potatoes. The doorbell rings again while Noah is washing his hands and Rory goes to answer it. Everyone else moved into the living room when we started cooking. It's an open floor plan, so we can still talk to and hear them, we just have to speak up to do it.

The sound of running feet precedes two of the cutest little girls I've ever seen. "Uncle Noah!" the oldest one calls out, and he turns around and scoops her up, kissing her all over her face.

"Saylor! I've missed you." He tickles her belly. She giggles like crazy and squirms in his arms. Her little sister is standing in front of me, looking up at me with big, blue eyes.

I kneel down to her level and smile. "Hi, I'm Mel. What's your name?"

"Emme," she answers proudly. Noah puts Saylor down and picks up Emme, giving her more of the same treatment he gave her sister.

"Are you Uncle Noah's new girlfriend? My mommy said she's happy you're not … not a …" She's searching for the word, suddenly being scolded at the same time she remembers.

"Saylor!"

"A gold digger! What's a gold digger, Uncle Noah?" she asks innocently. Noah is furious, Diane is blushing, and I'm laughing. From the mouths of babes.

"Emme, Saylor, let's go see Uncle Sawyer!" Rory gets them excited again and leaves us to deal with the aftermath.

"Yay!" they cry out as they run to the living room. When I see how excited they are to jump into Sawyer's lap, and how happy he seems to see them, it gives me butterflies. I guess I never thought of Sawyer as a family man. I don't know why, other than he prides himself on being rough around the edges. It always surprises me to see a softer side of him.

D. Kelly

"Diane, what the hell are you telling your kids about my relationships?" Noah bites out under his breath so they don't accidently overhear.

"Nothing, Noah. She overhead me and Rob talking. Sawyer told me about Sara showing up in Vegas, and once you went public about your relationship and Mel obviously has her own money, I was just relieved. That's all." She raises her hands in surrender, and Noah thaws a bit. "Now, can I please have a hug? I missed you."

He pulls her into his embrace and they hug tightly. An attractive man walks in and watches them affectionately. He must be Diane's husband. When Noah releases her, she leans against the counter as her husband joins us. Noah wraps his arm around my waist and pulls me close. "Diane, Rob, this is my non-gold-digging girlfriend Amelia."

Diane shakes her head as she shakes my hand. "I'm never going to live that down, but I guess I deserve it. It's nice to finally meet you, Amelia."

"Likewise," I reply and shake Rob's hand as well. He seems quiet. Rob is one of those men who wears dark eyeglasses and looks hotter because of them. He's got the sexy geek look going on. Diane is tall like Noah and Sawyer, with dark hair like her dad and Sawyer. She doesn't have their green eyes, though; her eyes are hazel, but they're still gorgeous.

"Come on. Is Mel going to get all the attention today or what?" Sawyer asks as he walks into the kitchen. Diane rushes over to him, and he hugs the hell out of her. She actually has tears in her eyes.

"I've missed you, baby brother," she chokes out on a sob as Sawyer rubs her back to comfort her.

"I've missed you, too, but we haven't been gone that long," he reminds her subtly.

"Long enough," she retorts, wiping away her tears.

Noah squeezes my hand as I watch them in awe, my mind spinning on a way to work their family relationships into their book. I want people to know them, who they are inside and outside of the spotlight.

While everyone is catching up and the potatoes are in the oven, I take a moment and excuse myself to use the restroom. When I enter, the sight of the condom box just sitting on top of the bed for the world to see makes me laugh. If it were me, I would have tucked them into a drawer and covered them with socks or something. Not like I'm a prude when it comes to sex at all, but I guess I just don't need everyone knowing my business.

234

After using the restroom, I take a moment and sit on the edge of the bed. His family is nice, but it's all a bit overwhelming. There are a lot of them. I haven't been around that many family members since I dated Eli, and I was young then; it didn't faze me like it does now.

"Hey, are you okay?" Noah asks as he closes and locks the door behind him, his concern apparent.

"Of course. I'm just taking a breather." That might have been an inappropriate word choice.

"From my family or from me?"

"I feel like that's a trick question, but it's definitely not from you."

Noah lies down on the bed sideways and pulls me with him. "They're just excited to meet you and to see us. We're kind of a lot to handle because we don't see each other much, so there's always tons to catch up on."

"I'm not complaining, but you guys talk to them all the time. It's good, it's just different than anything I've ever known."

"Is it off-putting?" He seems concerned, but I wish he wasn't.

"No, it's just a little overwhelming. I'm happy you're close with your family, although it seems like you and Sawyer each have favorite sisters."

Noah brushes my hair away from my face and then his fingers dance a trail down my arm. "I guess we do. When everything happened with Jordan, Diane became a mother hen to Sawyer. And because my mom was so frazzled with everything going on with Jordan and getting his life straight, I helped out a lot with Rory. She was just a toddler back then."

"I guess we should get back out there. The potatoes are probably almost ready to come out of the oven."

"Not yet." He drops his mouth to mine. "Thank you," he whispers after kissing me breathless.

"For what?"

"Putting up with my family. Not hating me for torturing you with the condoms. For loving me. I could go on and on. There's an endless list, really."

"Is that so?" I remark with a laugh.

"It is. Well … maybe not endless yet, but I'm sure I could find enough things to go on about."

"Of course you can. I am pretty amazing, after all." He laughs and pulls us both into a sitting position. "But right now I could really use a drink. How about some bourbon and egg nog? Or will your parents frown at my needing a drink this early?"

"Are you joking? I bet my dad's cup is already filled with wine or whiskey. It's a longstanding joke we're not together often because we drive each other to drink. It's the only other thing we do as much as joke and hug."

He's kidding, but I'll take it. After he opens the door, he laces his hand in mine and we walk out to have more family time.

"Mid-morning nookie already?" Sawyer jokes, and I instantly blush.

"Nah, there was no screaming," Jordan pipes in.

"It was too fast. Noah doesn't move that quickly," Rob adds, and I'm officially disturbed and mortified.

Noah flips them off as Sawyer follows us into the kitchen.

"Where is everyone?" I ask while I pull the egg nog and bourbon out. Sawyer eyes my goods and pulls out two glasses.

"I came in for a beer, but that looks better." I nod as he hands me the glasses and get to work making the drinks. "They took the kids down to the beach to tire them out a bit so they'll nap."

"Do you want one, Noah?" I ask, but he's already got a beer and is tipping it to his lips. *Lucky bottle.* His eyes never leave mine, and only when Sawyer comes back in the room does he stop eye fucking me. *Barely.* It's sexy as hell and has me wishing we *had* taken time out for mid-morning nookie.

Sawyer tosses a pack of Pop-Tarts to Noah and then opens his and holds it out to me. "Pop-Tart, Princess?"

"Thanks." I pull one out of the pack. Jordan and Rob are watching the scene play out with sideways glances to each other. Guess they're not used to Sawyer being nice, either. Noah still seems surprised Sawyer shared with him, but as he rips open the package and takes one out, he actually acknowledges the olive branch Sawyer extended.

"Thanks."

"Don't get used to it. I'm just in a good mood. Holidays and shit," Sawyer grumbles back, and Noah laughs. It's the closest thing I've seen to normal between them since the drug incident. Sawyer leaves and takes his seat next to Jordan, who promptly points to the hallway, and the three of them disappear into one of the bedrooms.

I lean against the counter with Noah and squeeze his hand. "Good job."

He shakes his head and sips his beer, licking his lips before speaking. "I'm not going to stay mad forever. As much as he irritates me sometimes, we *did* share a womb. I'm pretty fucking attached to the guy."

"Is that what it is? Irritation?"

He releases a sigh. "No, it's also disappointment. We were in such a good place for so long and lately, I feel like we're slipping back into how things were after Marilyn. I just wish we could fix this rift."

An uneasy feeling settles into my stomach. I know their rift has to do with me, and other than giving Noah up, there's nothing I can do to help. Even then, we're too deep. It wouldn't work; there would always be some sort of blame. All I can do is encourage them to get past it and keep my mouth shut about the inappropriate side of Sawyer.

"Give it time and keep being nice."

Noah puts his beer on the counter, and then pulls my drink from my hand and sets it next to his. When he plants one hand on my hip and the other weaves into my hair, I know I'm in trouble.

His lips crash against mine, his tongue meeting mine with a passion I've never felt. He exhales into my mouth and breathes new life into our kiss. My responding whimper is met with his sensual moans. It's taking all my willpower not to throw my legs around his waist and fuck him through his clothes.

This kiss is everything.

Until it's not.

"Mommy, why is Uncle Noah eating Mel's face?"

I don't think having a glass of ice water being thrown on me could have cooled me off and made me pull away any faster than Saylor's words. At first, Noah groans and then he laughs as he crosses his arms and waits to see how Diane is going to explain this away.

Their parents are wearing matching smirks, and Rory is smiling broadly as she holds Emme and plays peek-a-boo with her. Diane looks uncomfortable until she finally smiles, too.

"He's not eating her face, sweetie. Uncle Noah was kissing Mel the way grownups sometimes do when they're in love."

She crinkles her little nose and walks over to Noah. "Uncle Noah," she begins, and he drops down to her level.

"Yes, ladybug? What can I do for you?"

Ladybug. My heart sighs.

"Um ... that kiss was kind of gross. Don't kiss me like that, okay? And not my mommy or my sister, well, just Mel, okay? Please?"

You can see Noah's heart melting with her words. "Promise, Saylor. Only Amelia, and I'll try not to do it when you can see. Deal?"

She exhales a huge sigh of relief, and I wonder momentarily if I'm looking at an Oscar win in her future. "Oh good," she replies, and then cups her hand around his ear and whispers loudly, "Because that was kind of scary."

Karen's hand goes over her heart as echoes of "aww" sound around the room when Noah pulls her into a hug. Maybe my eggnog buzz is contributing to the sudden appearance of motherly feelings stirring inside of me. But my biological clock can go suck a dick because my mental capacities are in control, and there's no way I'm ready for all this domesticity and all that comes with it. One step at a time, and right now I'm basking in loving Noah and him loving me back.

Suddenly, there's a commotion. The moment is broken up by Darren, Belle, and his parents as they come through the door. Belle looks like she could use some of this egg nog, and because sometimes I can be a bitch, I hold up my glass in a salute to her and down the rest of my drink.

She sneers at me and then rolls her eyes because she knows I'm joking and she can't drink anyway. Before there are any more introductions, I refill my glass.

"Did you hear the news?" the woman squeals incredibly loud as everyone looks at her with baited breath. "I'm going to be a grandma!"

Commence the cheering and many, many rounds of congratulations. People begin to come out of the woodwork. People as in Wyatt and Anna—who have probably been off having sex this whole time—and Sawyer and all the guys who disappeared with him a little while ago. Their whole mood seems somber, but Sawyer makes his way back to me and holds up his glass for a refill. I refill his and top mine off as well, even though I've only taken a sip since I filled it. But I can already tell it's going to be one of those days.

Later, after all the pre-made food was tucked away and we'd all toasted the new baby, new beginnings, health, and anything else possible you can toast and celebrate when a large family gets together, we all called it a night.

Belle seemed to get along with her future in-laws and she was glowing all night. I'm not sure if it's the pregnancy hormones or just the relief of finally getting her true feelings for Darren out in the open. He even joked about getting a tattoo that says "Jolt" but no one understood the reference except me and Belle. I think they all just chalked it up to too much booze and let it slide.

Now, I'm sitting on our bed after overhearing a conversation I definitely wasn't supposed to, trying to figure out what to do. Rory is in our shower, and Noah is in the garage studio with a few family members playing some of the live recordings from the tour. My heart aches, and all I want to do is scream into a pillow or something as I think about what I just heard out in the hall.

I walked toward Sawyer's room, hoping to use his bathroom since mine is occupied right now. The guest bedroom on the right side was dark, but the door was cracked and I heard hushed voices. Not loud enough to carry far but definitely loud enough to carry into the hall. I wasn't really paying attention to them until I heard my name.

"Amelia!"

"You must have misunderstood, Rob," Diane tells him, unconvinced.

"No, not at all. I know a man in love, and Sawyer is in love with her. He all but admitted it."

Her laugh echoes through the room. *"I'm sorry, but I know Sawyer wouldn't admit to being in love with his brother's girlfriend. Especially after what happened last time."*

"Okay, he didn't exactly say that, but still, after all these years, I can read your brother. He's got feelings for her."

My heart races. He's not saying anything I hadn't already thought myself, but it's nothing I want to acknowledge or be a part of. Knowing Sawyer has feelings for me makes me think my relationship with Noah has an expiration date, and that's not an idea I want to entertain.

"I'll talk to him," she promises.

"About his Princess?" he points out.

"Yeah, your point is noted. None of us can go through this again," she answers on a sigh.

And with those words, I turned around and came back to my room. God, I swear Rory is taking the longest shower known to man, but I know what to do. I get up and make my way into the kitchen. Thankfully, there's no one out here; everyone seems to have either gone to the garage or to their respective bedrooms.

Once I'm in the kitchen, I pull out the bourbon and a tumbler and fill it with ice. The only light is coming from the under-cabinet lighting. It's eerie for the house to be this silent, especially when it's filled with this many people. The bourbon is smooth and warm going down. It's exactly what the doctor ordered.

I know coping with alcohol isn't a solution, but right now it feels pretty damn good. Rory paddles out in a robe and slippers and joins me.

"Can I have some of that?"

"Of course," I reply, pouring her a glass.

"Can I ask you a question?"

She most definitely is Noah's sister. "You sound exactly like your brother. Ask away." I hand her the drink. She sips it slowly and winces a bit before setting it down. I guess bourbon isn't what most twenty-two-year-olds want to drink.

"Do you love my brother?" Her words are rushed, and she gulps down more of her drink as if ashamed of asking.

With a smile, I reply, "With my whole heart. He's everything I never knew I was missing in my life."

"Oh good. Noah deserves every happiness, and he seems to have found that with you, but after his last few girlfriends I wasn't sure. Well, I mean … it's just I'm not in the habit of asking women how they feel about my brothers."

"You should be. They'd protect you in a heartbeat. It's only fair you have the opportunity to protect them."

"That's why I don't bring just any guy around. I'll wait until I find someone serious before subjecting them to that interrogation. Can you imagine? Not only will they have to put up with my dad, Noah, and Sawyer, but Rob, Wyatt, and Darren, too. Whoever I end up with better have the patience of a saint."

"Hold that thought for about two minutes so I can use the restroom. I'll be right back." Rory laughs at me as I rush out of the room, but it's her fault I had to go so bad. I'm back in a flash, and she's snacking on homemade chocolate chip cookies when I return.

"Where did those come from?" I ask, snatching one up out of the tin. I moan in ecstasy with my first bite. "They're so good!"

She nods as she chews. "My mom made them. She's the best baker around. She hid these, but it's like she hides them in plain sight because she knows we're going to look for them and then, like magic, a zillion more of them will appear out of thin air tomorrow. She's pretty awesome."

I snatch another cookie and eat it while sipping bourbon. It would probably taste better with milk, but that's not in the cards tonight. "Alright, back to the overprotective men in your life. I think one thing you should consider is they've all been around. They have a good sense of what a good man is. I swear, Rory, they've got amazing bullshit radar. If you can get their seal of approval, you'll have a keeper. And if they weed the frogs out, all the better for you."

She giggles, and I keep rambling. "I mean, think about it. If you could just stick Joe Schmoe in front of all your brothers and say 'here, let me know if he's worth the effort,' it would save you so much freaking time and heartache."

Rory is in full-on laughter mode now and pushes her tumbler out to me for a refill. "God, Mel, you're right. Maybe I should let them vet all my dates from now on because some of the men in college were real assholes."

"Bring 'em on, Ror. I'll vet all those fuckers for you." Sawyer walks in and his eyes grow wide. "Mom's cookies? Were you seriously hiding those from me?"

"Does it look like I'm hiding them? I'm pretty sure I'm sharing them with Mel in plain sight, ding dong." She slides the tin across the counter, and Sawyer literally hugs them to his chest.

"Co-dependent on cookies?" I ask, amused.

"These things are life. I'd give up Pop-Tarts if I could have an endless supply of these cookies."

"That's pretty hardcore."

He nods enthusiastically with his mouth full. "You've got no idea." He pulls out the milk, pouring a glass to go with the chocolaty goodness.

"Where's Noah?"

"He's talking to our parents in the garage. Everyone else went to bed a little while ago. I think Belle was tired because she fell asleep on Darren's shoulder listening to the music. It wasn't on low, either. She must have been exhausted."

"Poor thing. I know this week has been hard on her. I'm hoping she'll feel better soon." As the words come out of my mouth, I realize how hard this pregnancy is going to be on her. Belle is usually the life of the party; falling asleep early isn't going to make her happy.

"So Belle is your best friend?" Rory clarifies.

"Yes, but we grew up together. She really is more like a sister than anything."

"Rory's jealous because she's got a huge crush on Darren," Sawyer says, and Rory's face falls.

"I'm not jealous. I'm happy for them. Childhood crushes have no place in the grownup world, and if you think I was under any illusion you would allow me to date someone in your band, you don't give me any credit at all," she fires back.

"Hell no, we wouldn't. I love Darren and Wyatt like my brothers, and if either of them had made a move on *either* of my sisters, I would have thrown them off the bus while we were flying down the highway, and they know it, too."

Sawyer shoots her a look, daring her to argue, but she just brushes it off. She definitely doesn't act like someone who's infatuated with a man who's about to have a baby with someone else. Voices trail in from the garage, becoming louder with each step.

"You found the cookies!" Karen scolds good-naturedly, and Noah reaches over Sawyer's shoulder to grab a few.

"Jerk," Sawyer scolds.

"Hog," Noah tosses back as their parents look on, smiling.

"It doesn't matter how old your children get, whenever they're together, they fight like kids," she says wistfully.

Noah wraps his arms around me from behind after he wolfs down his cookies. His parents won't stop grinning at us. It's weird.

"Mel loves you, Noah," Rory states proudly, bringing all eyes on her.

"I could have told you that." Noah squeezes me tighter. "What, did you give her the sisterly drill?" She blushes and nods in affirmation. "Glad to see you're not slacking on your sisterly duties." He places a kiss on the top of my head.

I feel a yawn coming on and cover my mouth quickly to stifle it, but it's no use. As soon as I yawn, everyone is yawning.

"Ready for bed?" Noah asks, and I nod.

"We're about to hit the hay, too. I've got to be up early to get all the food in the oven," Karen tells us.

"Do you need help?" I ask, not wanting her to have to do it all alone.

"That's sweet of you to offer, but you sleep in. I love cooking in the morning. I'm sure I'll take you up on your help in the afternoon, and I'm dying to taste those potatoes. They smell absolutely divine."

She's such a sweet woman. It shouldn't surprise me, but somehow it does. Noah and I say our goodnights and make our way to the bedroom, the conversation I overheard earlier temporarily forgotten as we make love before going to sleep.

As I'm drifting off to sleep, one very important thought comes to mind. It really doesn't matter how Sawyer feels about me because I'm head over heels in love with Noah. Eventually, Sawyer will get over it.

Thanksgiving

Thanksgiving starts off rough.

Really rough.

Between our sexcapades and my drinking, I was so exhausted last night I actually slept in with Noah today. It's nice waking up with him, feeling his fingers tracing my skin and his kisses on my lips. I should sleep in more often.

"Good morning, beautiful," he whispers.

"Good morning, sexy," I whisper back, allowing myself to get lost in his eyes.

"Do you know what I'm thankful for?" I shake my head, hoping he doesn't ask me what I'm thankful for because I'm pretty bad at verbally expressing my feelings. Especially before coffee.

"You. Every single day, I thank my lucky stars that fate brought us together."

My eyes begin to fill with tears, but someone banging loudly on the door interrupts our moment.

"Noah! You need to get out here now!"

Sawyer's tone is frantic, and we both rush out of bed, hastily getting dressed. When Noah throws open the door, Sawyer snaps, "Kitchen now," before stalking off.

As we enter the kitchen, everyone is crowded around the table, where a crazy-beautiful display of flowers sits. It's psychedelic looking; there's got to be one flower each of about fifty or more different varieties and colors in a vase. Next to the vase is a note, open and laid flat on the table.

"Don't touch it," Warren cautions. "Just read it."

Noah,

Roses are red,

Violets are blue,

Thanksgiving is mine,

Tell your whore toodle loo.

Tremors of terror flood my body. Everyone looks at me sympathetically, and when I turn to Noah, his eyes are wide. Belle is suddenly by my side, holding my hand tightly and rubbing my shoulder.

D. Kelly

"That handwriting …" Noah says, turning to Warren, who nods in confirmation.

"It's Sara's. We've already called the police, Noah."

When he turns back toward me, sadness floods his features as he pulls me close and hugs me. Tears are streaming down my cheeks unbidden. I don't care what she tries with me, but I'm terrified for Noah. She's bat shit crazy.

"The cameras?" he asks over my shoulder while continuing to rub my back, whispering "shh" into my ears.

"Got nothing. It was just a kid. She probably paid him to drop them off, but the police will look for him, I'm sure."

"Come on, Mel, let me take you to the bedroom while Noah talks to Warren," Belle offers sweetly, and Noah concurs.

"I'll come check on you in a few minutes, I promise."

I walk numbly into the room trying to listen to the rapid-fire whispering going on behind me, but the further we walk down the hall, the harder it is to hear.

"She's crazy, Mel. Maybe you should take a break from the tour. I want you safe. I *need* you safe," Belle pleads.

"Absolutely not. I'm probably safer on that bus than anywhere. If I were here, I'd just be a sitting target or I'd be flanked with security all the time. But Noah, my God, Belle, what about Noah?" I'm almost hysterical, but this is all such bullshit.

"He'll be okay. They'll catch her and put her away."

"Why today? What the hell makes Thanksgiving hers?"

"It's her birthday," Rory whispers from the doorway.

"Well, that explains that," Belle replies dryly.

More tears fall faster than I can wipe them away. Both Belle and Rory hug me—one from each side—and although having them with me is comforting, my sobs continue growing louder and louder.

"I've got it from here. Thank you both for your help." Noah's voice is like sunshine to my soul. Using the back of my hand, I rapidly swipe at my cheeks after he closes our door behind Rory and Belle.

Our room.

In the span of a few days, I've gone from being apprehensive about moving too fast to wanting everything he's willing to give me. Especially now.

"Baby, it's okay. Please don't cry." Noah lies down, pulling me into his arms.

"I'm worried, Noah. She's crazy and she's going to hurt you."

244

"Shh …" he whispers, rubbing my back. "She's not going to hurt either of us. We won't let her."

"You can't stop her!" I'm officially freaking out.

"Mel, we have an entire security team who will move heaven and earth to stop her. If you thought Vegas was bad, you've got no idea. We'll have no less than four guards around any of us at all times. The whole band is going to be covered."

"I can't lose you, too, Noah. I can't go through that again," I choke out through a sob.

"You're worried about losing me, but I'm worried about losing you. When you're not around, I struggle to breathe. You're my air, Mel. I'd die without you. You have no idea how important you are to me, how much I adore you, how much I love you."

My arms are wrapped around him, clutching him to me, holding on for dear life. I won't let this crazy bitch get to us.

"I love you, too. So much. What now? What's the next step?"

On an exhale, he fills me in. "The police are on their way, along with my attorney. We've already compared her note to copies of other notes she's left in the past, and they look like an exact match. Of course, the police will have to confirm that."

"They won't be able to do anything. Her note was vague, there was no actual threat, but those flowers …"

"I know. Those flowers are the creepiest things I've ever seen. So beautifully demented, just like her." He presses his lips against my forehead and holds them there.

"Does she have family? I mean, why today of all days? I know Rory said it was her birthday, but what specifically makes today hers as far as you're concerned?"

"She does have family, but I've never met them. In fact, the only thing I can even think of that would correlate to Thanksgiving is she spent it with us here not too long before I broke things off with her. She wanted to spend her birthday with me and that year, like today, it fell on Thanksgiving. I didn't think much about it. I should have questioned why she didn't want to spend Thanksgiving with her family, but I was relieved she didn't ask me to go to her house because I didn't want to lose what limited time I had with my own family."

"That's understandable. What about your family? How did they get along?"

He groans. "They didn't. I mean, they were decent to her, but Sara kept bragging about all the things I'd bought for her and instead

D. Kelly

of it proving I loved her, or whatever point she was trying to get across, it just made her look ..."

"Like a gold digger," I fill in with a slight laugh, remembering Saylor's slip.

"Exactly."

There's a light knock at the door, and Karen sticks her head in with a soft smile. "Noah, the police are here, and so is your lawyer. Go on and deal with it. I'll stay with Mel until she gets cleaned up."

He pulls my mouth to his and kisses me firmly. "Wash your face and come join us. There's nothing you can't hear, okay?"

"Okay," I answer as he jumps off the bed and kisses his mom on the cheek on his way out.

"Sweetheart, are you okay?" She's worried about me; the sentiment warms my heart.

"I will be."

She nods at my words. "Yes, you will. Nobody messes with my family and gets away with it. Especially not some two-bit hussy." Her words don't warrant a reply; she's made it abundantly clear she's not a fan of Sara's, either. I kind of love her for saying it, though. Needing to get rid of this headache, I go into the bathroom to look for some ibuprofen. She follows right behind me.

After finding what I'm looking for and swallowing the pills, I proceed to brush my teeth. It's only when my mouth is full of toothpaste that she speaks again.

"I'm sure you've heard my boys don't have the best track record with women." Her eyes meet mine in the bathroom mirror and she continues, "When they told us they were taking a hot, new sex book author on tour with them, saying I was concerned is putting it mildly."

After spitting out my toothpaste, I correct her, "Romance. Romance author, not sex books."

"Yes," she says with a hint of a smile. "So I've come to learn. I've read your book, Mel, you're very talented. But as you well know, all good romances come with good sex." Her sassy smirk brings a smile to my face.

"Yes, I suppose you're right. Thank you ... for the compliment."

She continues while I work on wiping off yesterday's makeup. "In any case, when Noah started talking about you incessantly, I knew he was hooked. And when Sawyer started talking about you often, I was scared of the past coming back to bite us. But then Darren and Wyatt started talking about you, and Anna, and Warren. Are you getting my drift?"

246

"I'm not sure." I turn around, forgoing any makeup for now. "It was then I realized you were different. You were making an impression on many of the people I love dearly. So I started listening harder, actually hearing what Noah was saying. When he told me you were his girlfriend, I knew he was already in love with you."

"Oh."

Yeah, that sounded dumb, but I really don't know what to say to her right now.

"As parents, you raise your kids to be everything they can possibly be. Letting them go is hard. My boys, as much as I love them, have put so much stress on me. I worry about them all the time. I'm sure that will never go away, but touring, performing, interviews … Well, you know as well as anyone what a toll that can take on a person."

"Unfortunately, all too well." My voice is thick with emotion. I've been missing my parents lately. With the holiday and watching all of them with their families, I guess it's getting to me. It's why I was so nervous yesterday, why I drank so much. It was a way to cope with missing my own family while letting a new one into my heart.

"But love, Amelia, that's always been my biggest fear with their fame. I've hoped and prayed for them to be able to find someone who loves them for the men I *raised* them to be and not the men they are under the public eye."

"I don't care about their fame. To be honest, I'm not even a fan of their music. Well, the new stuff is good, but the old stuff … To each his own, I guess."

She laughs a deep belly laugh and pulls me into a hug. It's not as awkward as yesterday, but I'm still not quite there yet.

"I heard you weren't a fan. I'm pretty sure you shattered Sawyer's ego." She releases me from her hug, but her eyes are still fixed on me with an all-knowing mom look.

"He got over it," I answer softly, not wanting to talk about Sawyer.

"Yes, I suppose he did. You've become a good friend to him. I want to thank you for that. Sawyer doesn't have many friends … not real ones. But I'm getting off track. All I really wanted to say to you is thank you for loving my son."

"You approve?" Blinking back my tears, the raspy words fall from my lips, and she nods.

"I needed to see it for myself. And if I had any doubts … Which I didn't, by the way. After this morning, I know the love both of you

D. Kelly

feel is mutual, and that makes me happier than I've been in a long time."

Her heartfelt words burrow into my soul, but I have one more question I need to ask her.

"You don't think it's too soon?"

She leans back against the bathroom counter and takes me in. "Your parents really did a number on you, didn't they?" It's a rhetorical question, but I'm positive I see her blink back her own tears.

"Amelia, love is infinite. It is the one constant thing that makes the world a better place. You come in with it and you hopefully die with it. There's no limit on love, not on the amount you can give, the amount you can receive, and surely never on how fast you can feel it.

"The only way I can explain how strongly I feel about that is by comparing it to having a child. For nine months, you walk around pregnant, rubbing a growing stomach and wondering what it will be like when that baby comes to you. How can you take the fears you have about becoming a parent, about all the things you can possibly do wrong to screw up an innocent life and earn the love and respect of this child? Even though you love being pregnant, love the idea of having a baby, you really don't know *how* that emotion is going to translate. Not the first time, at least."

I assumed all pregnant women loved their baby instantly.

"What I'm trying to tell you is that all the pain you go through in delivery is gone when you hear that baby scream, or if they don't scream, you're instantly concerned. Fearful. In a split second, your mothering instincts kick in, and that baby has just become your everything. You'd push your own husband in front of a speeding train if it meant saving your child without a second thought. And when the doctor puts that child in your arms, there is no love as pure as what you will feel in that instant.

"That right there is how I know there's no appropriate time frame for falling in love. If it's instant with your child, surely it can be instant with the man who will eventually give you that child, don't you think?"

Suddenly, Belle's words flash back at me.

"I still can't really describe it, but it was like, at that moment, he reached in and grabbed a part of me that had never been touched. I didn't want to lose a second of that sensation out of fear I would never feel it again. I think he felt it, too, Mel. Whatever it was that possessed me that night on the beach, I think it reached out and took him as well."

I know she wasn't talking about love, but after listening to Karen, maybe she was and didn't even realize it.

"Thank you for sharing that with me, you make some excellent points. You mentioned fear. Did one of the kids have issues?"

With a reflective look, she nods. "Sawyer did. Noah came out screaming away, making his presence in the world completely known. And six minutes later, when Sawyer was born, he didn't make a peep. I'd never felt fear like that before. It only lasted a few seconds and then suddenly, it was like he needed to out scream Noah. We got Noah in our arms first and he calmed immediately, but not Sawyer. It wasn't until we put him next to Noah, bodies touching, that he calmed down. They've been best friends since the day they were born, and I'm sure it's a bond that started at conception."

"That's beautiful." I wish I could see that with them. I'd give anything to see their true friendship shine.

After brushing my hair, I exhale loudly as Karen rests her hand on my shoulder.

"Ready?"

"As I'll ever be."

Karen leads the way to the other side of the house. She stops outside of an open door, and I hear him before I see him. There's a loud crash preceding his words. "God dammit, I want her safe! I don't care what you have to do to find the crazy bitch, just do it!"

Karen's eyes lock onto mine, and she squeezes my hand before going back to the kitchen. I duck into the room quietly and observe as Noah and Warren work out details and answer questions. There's a man taking notes, a man in a police uniform, two men in suits, and Mac.

After a few minutes, Noah looks up, his eyes softening. "Baby, come here." All eyes turn to me as I cross the room, feeling more uncomfortable by the second. "Gentlemen, this is my girlfriend Amelia Greyson. Mel, this is my attorney Tony Hastings, Detectives Marsh and Johnson, and Officer Lawrence. Officer Lawrence is the local PD liaison who will be working hand in hand with our security team and helping to coordinate local police backup."

I nod with each introduction—shaking hands as prompted—but refrain from exchanging pleasantries because there's no need. This is not a happy circumstance.

"Ms. Greyson, do you have anything you can add to Mr. Weston's statement? Any personal experiences you may have had with the suspect. Perhaps any past history you may have with her?"

D. Kelly

We quickly recap the two times I've seen Sara and the fact I was sleeping this morning. I let them know before Vegas, I'd never seen nor heard of her before. After a bit more information from Warren and Noah, they stand to make their exit.

"We'll be in touch tomorrow, Mr. Weston. Please try and enjoy your holiday. We'll have cruisers patrolling the neighborhood tonight and over the rest of the weekend as well. If anything else happens, or if you receive any more unexpected deliveries, don't touch them. Call us immediately and we'll get someone sent here as soon as possible."

"Thank you for all your help. Happy Thanksgiving." Warren escorts everyone out except for Tony, who remains seated. Noah motions for me to take the seat next to him now that the room has cleared.

"Alright, Noah, you don't need me to tell you this isn't a good situation, but it could be worse. My assistant got the judge to sign off on the emergency restraining order a few minutes ago, according to her text. It's effective now and will be filed with the courts tomorrow. It's up to you to get your PR team on this to do damage control. The second this gets filed, you know the media is going to be on you like flies on shit."

He looks at me apologetically. "Sorry."

"Don't be. I'm not easily offended."

Tony nods and looks back down at his paperwork. "I don't have to tell you it would have been better if you'd put this restraining order in place a few years ago. Your stalking evidence was much stronger back then. Right now, we only have a few unpleasant instances ..."

"She was in my fucking hotel room!" Noah roars, slamming his fist into the desk. I've never seen him so angry.

Tony runs his hands through his hair and drops his pen onto his paper. "Look, I get it. She's crazy. But you know the industry. She didn't leave any souvenirs in the room, she didn't come on your sheets, she didn't take anything, either. Right now, she's a nuisance. Let's hope the restraining order will be enough to keep her at that."

"Yeah, let's hope."

"I've got to get going. My wife wasn't happy I had to leave, and as much as I appreciate the reprieve from my in-laws, I do need to get back. Ten a.m. tomorrow, be at my office. We'll go over the official documents and take care of that other paperwork you asked me to draw up. It shouldn't take more than an hour. I know you've got a big night tomorrow. Now, so do I."

"I'll see you there. Go see my mom on the way out and she'll give you some cookies."

A smile lights up his face. "Don't tell my wife. The cookies are mine. She gets the concert tickets for tomorrow. It was nice to meet you, Amelia. I wish it would have been under more pleasant circumstances. I'll see you tomorrow night at the show. Maybe you can autograph my wife's book, she's a big fan."

"Of course. It was nice to meet you, too."

He leaves, closing the door behind him. In an instant, Noah is pulling me from my chair and onto his lap. His mouth covers mine as his tongue parts my lips with a desperate need. Our tongues meet in a forceful dance, our hands exploring and gripping each other's bodies as our kiss fuels our desire for each other. I'm desperate for him. I need to feel him inside me—a physical reminder we're okay.

"Stand up," Noah commands, and I comply. "Bend over the desk and pull your pants down." He walks quickly to the door and locks it, tossing his shorts off on the way back to me. My hands work triple speed to rid myself of my pants as I watch Noah pull a condom from his wallet on the desk. Knowing he needs this as much as I do completely turns me on.

He leans over my body with ease, lining his cock up against my entrance. "Are you wet for me, Mel?" he asks huskily against my ear.

"So wet ..." The words are barely out of my mouth before he slides in and fills me completely.

"This has to be quick or we'll be interrupted." He presses his thumb onto my clit. The eroticism of the moment, coupled with his movements, is enough to already have me on edge. Adding his finger to the fire brings me over the edge faster than I'd ever have imagined. Noah covers my mouth with his hand, catching my screams before they hit the air. With one final push into me, his release fills me while he chokes down his own cries.

His mouth meets my neck as he places decadent open-mouth kisses against my skin.

"If you're not ready to go for round two, you need to stop that because you're really turning me on." His chest moves against me as he laughs at my words. I can't hear his heartbeat with him pushed up against me this way but I can feel it, and for right now, that's everything.

"There's nothing I want to do more than lock myself away in our room and fuck away this day. But it's Thanksgiving and I want to spend time with the people I love most in this world and watch some football."

Noah stands up and disposes of the condom in the trash can under his desk. I wipe off with a couple of tissues and put my pants back on. Before we leave the room, he pulls me into a hug and we stay that way for a while. He's holding onto me tighter than ever. I understand the feeling; I don't ever want to let him go, either.

"Christ, Mel, can you make these on the bus? Like, every day for every meal?" Wyatt asks through his food orgasm.

"I'm with him, these are the best!" Darren wholeheartedly agrees.

Dinner is amazing. Karen pulled off a feast even amid all the stressors of the day.

"I'm not sure I can pull them off on the bus, but I'll make them for Christmas if you want. And if you're really nice, I'll make enough to freeze to take on the road. Karen, this meal is delicious. Thank you so much." I turn my attention to her, making sure she knows how much I appreciate her hard work.

A chorus of thanks echoes around the table, and she waves her hand like it's not a big deal. Her smile shows otherwise; she likes being appreciated and taking care of her family. Owen kisses her sweetly, his eyes dancing with mischief. I'm pretty sure someone is getting lucky tonight. It warms my heart seeing them so happy and in love after all their years together.

Darren's parents, too. They're frisky, hands constantly touching some part or another of each other. Anna and Wyatt's moms are both here, and Warren and Sam as well. I'm sure Belle is missing Veronica as much as I am tonight. She might be Belle's mom, but she's been a surrogate to me for twenty years.

I know Belle hates the idea of telling her she's pregnant over the phone, but she's got no other choice. This news is going to seep out faster than any of us can control it. Especially with the rock that graces her finger now.

"Grandma, can I have the wishbone now?" Saylor pleads in a sing-song voice with the excitement only a child could have for a bone that comes from inside a turkey carcass.

"Sorry, Say, but Grandma promised it to me tonight," Sawyer teases her, and for the first time, I wonder if Saylor is named after Sawyer.

"No, she didn't, Uncle Sawyer. My mom already told me you were going to try and trick me. You're being sneaky."

"He's just jealous, Say. He's worried you won't want to make a wish with him," Noah tells her, and she hops out of her seat and up into Sawyer's lap.

"I will share with you, Uncle Sawyer. But can I have the big side? I need to wish for a baby brother *really* bad for my daddy."

Diane and Rob watch the exchange like any adoring parents would, and Sawyer is like putty in her hands. I wish he wouldn't keep this side of himself hidden; it's the best part of his heart.

"How about even if I get the big side, I make the same wish so you have an even bigger chance of it coming true?" Saylor's eyes grow wide and she nods enthusiastically as she high-fives him.

"What if *I* wanted the wishbone tonight?"

"Grandpa, don't be silly!" she says, giggling hysterically. Noah's hand squeezes my thigh, and when I turn my attention to him, he's looking at me adoringly.

"That could be us one day." He leans over, speaking low in my ear so only I can hear. And maybe it's the day—or the wine we've been drinking with dinner—but when I reply, my words don't scare me.

"Mm, maybe it could be."

Those words spark a fire inside of him. His hands come up from under the table and grip my cheeks, pulling my mouth to his. He kisses me firmly in front of everyone, and my cheeks heat. Once he releases me, I'm flustered and the table around us is silent.

"That was much better, Uncle Noah, thank you," Saylor tells him thoughtfully and proudly, and I'm so grateful for this four-year-old right now as the embarrassment of the moment fades away. It's funny how outgoing and spontaneous Saylor is and how quiet and reserved Emme is. I realize Emme just turned two, and Saylor is actually going to be five next month, but they're like night and day. At least from what I've seen so far.

After dinner, Belle and I offer to clean up the dishes and put the food away before dessert. At first, everyone offers to help, but we convince them to go rest and have some time together. I think the two of us could use a little normalcy for a minute.

"How are you feeling?"

"Better. I told you I needed potatoes and rolls and all would be right with the world." She places a hand against her belly.

"I hid some for you. They're already in the freezer, disguised as a bag of okra."

"Okra?"

253

Her quizzical look brings a smile to my face. "Yeah, I know. Who eats that crap? But your future husband said it's been in the freezer for as long as he can remember, and he thinks it's because one of them got it from a random girl's house after taking a punch to the eye when her boyfriend came home and caught them in the act. He just couldn't remember if it was him or Sawyer who took the hit."

"Life of a rock star." She rinses a pan off and places it in the dishwasher.

"Speaking of … You're going to have to talk to Darren about releasing an official statement first thing tomorrow morning on the *Slammed* blog before the restraining order gets leaked from the courthouse."

"I know," she says with a sad look on her face. "Everything is going to be okay, Mel. They're going to get this crazy bitch."

"Yeah, I know. You know what's weird? Of all the crazy things that happened to my parents, random deranged fans and whatnot, there were never any stalkers who were clinging to my dad like this girl is to Noah."

I'm wiping down the counters when she finally answers me. "That's because there was never anyone for Joey except for Iris. And maybe because back then we didn't have the advantage of social media tracking our every movement all the time. It's a lot easier to stalk anyone now. As sad as that is, it's the truth."

"You've got a good point there."

"Oh, before I forget to tell you, I decided to tell Mom about the baby tomorrow. Darren and I are going to Skype her in the morning."

"Seriously? Why? I thought you wanted to wait."

"I did, but he pointed out something I hadn't thought about. Tomorrow night, we're making our first real appearance as a couple and I'm wearing this massive rock on my finger. We don't plan on confirming or denying any suspicions, but my mom is going to hear news of it and flip."

She would, too. Veronica wouldn't put up with not knowing her daughter is pregnant and engaged before the rest of the world does.

"So is *Slammed* getting the exclusive of the two of you?" I ask, bumping her playfully against her shoulder.

"Maybe someday, but right now we are kind of in love with the idea of letting people speculate whatever they want to. When I start showing, it will be pretty obvious, but until then, let them guess."

"Are you two done yet? I'm ready for my dessert." Noah comes up behind me, nibbling on my neck. Belle laughs at him and points her finger back and forth between us.

"You two, seriously, are the cutest couple ever. I know I keep saying it, but I can't help it. I think all that anticipation you made her go through was the best thing you could have ever done."

"Told you," Noah says to me. "Anticipation is key."

Belle wipes off her hands and leaves us alone.

"Well, Mr. Weston, I anticipate whipped cream and pumpkin pie making an appearance in our fun tonight after our door is locked and our clothes are off. Care to make that happen?"

My eyes travel down to the front of his slacks, where his cock is eagerly agreeing with my words. "I'm pretty sure we can manage that." He adjusts his pants around his package.

"Can't wait." I leave him standing there while I set up the kitchen island with all the preparations for dessert.

Belle's Post-Thanksgiving Announcement

Slammers!

It's your girl Belle again. Today, I have a post for you from BAD themselves. Things have been a little hectic for our favorite guys over the past twenty-four hours, and I know they could use your love and prayers if you've got them.

Dear Slammed Readers,

On Thanksgiving morning, we had an unfortunate incident occur. As part of our ongoing partnership with Slammed Magazine during the Just an Illusion tour, we wanted our Slammed readers and followers to hear about this from us first.

Sometimes in life, we come across people who have a different perception of reality than the rest of us. As of ten a.m. this morning, Noah Weston has obtained an official restraining order against one of his former girlfriends. This is not a decision he took lightly. We hope this restraining order will bring an end to the ongoing issues and the offender will realize the errors of her ways and find the peace and happiness she needs to move on with her life. At this time, BAD has no official statement as to why this restraining order was issued, and we hope you will respect our privacy during this difficult time. Rest assured our tour is still on track and no changes have been made to the schedule itself as of now.

Due to this unfortunate occurrence, we do want to advise if you have tickets to an upcoming BAD show to please allow time for additional security checks and expect an increased presence of security at all of our venues. Meet and greets will also be limited to autographs only. This is for your safety as well as ours.

We'd like to thank you for all your continued support through the years. We wouldn't be who we are without all of you.

With love and gratitude,

Noah, Sawyer, Darren, and Wyatt – AKA Bastards and Dangerous

The Aftermath

"Naptime is over. It's time to wake up, sleepyhead." Noah's soft words pull me from a desperately needed slumber. When my eyes blink open, they're met by his vibrant green ones staring right back at me.

"How in the world do you do it? You've slept about five hours less than I have and yet you're wide awake and about to go on stage."

"Years of practice. I enjoy my sleep as much as the next person, which is why I'm looking forward to retirement. Or at least retiring from touring."

Last night, Noah and I made love until the sun came up. I can't even begin to count how many times we had sex, how many orgasms we had between us, or how much our love seemed to multiply in those hours. We'd only been asleep for about three hours when he got up and went to meet with his attorney and to approve the statement Belle posted on the *Slammed* blog.

"How is the response to the statement?" I ask as I pull myself into a sitting position.

"It all seems pretty positive. Lots of pissed off fans at Sara. Her name was leaked within minutes of the restraining order being filed. I feel bad about that."

"Noah, that's her problem, not yours. Honestly, she probably gets off on it … everyone knowing she used to be with you. I'm sure in her mind, she doesn't even understand what she's doing is wrong. She needs psychological help."

"That's for sure."

There's a soft knock on the door. "Come in!" Noah calls out, and Warren enters carrying a beautiful blooming cactus.

"This was just delivered for you from one of the nurses at the hospital." Warren brings the card to Noah and sets the cactus down on his dresser.

"Do you have a thing for nurses I don't know about?" My teasing tone makes Warren laugh.

"Nurses, doctors, radiologists … I could go on and on," Warren deadpans, and Noah brushes him off as he opens the card. He passes it to me when he finishes reading it.

Dear Mr. Weston,
On behalf of all of us at UCLA Medical Center, we'd like to
thank you for your continued generosity. The holiday meals you
provide to our staff mean more than you could ever know.
Sincerely,
Joel Martin, M.D., Chief of Emergency Medicine

"You bought holiday meals for the hospital?" My amazement is profound.

"It's nothing."

"Don't let him fool you. He does it every year. Easter, Thanksgiving, and Christmas. Each department gets their own catered spread." Warren is beaming with pride. So am I, for that matter. "I'll leave you two alone. Don't be too long, we have to leave soon." He locks the door on his way out.

My eyes don't leave Noah's as I climb into his lap and cup his cheeks in my hands. "You are the most amazing man I have ever met. Your generosity and kind spirit are unparalleled. Seriously, Noah, I feel blessed to even know you, let alone love you and be loved by you."

My lips meet his eagerly, but our kiss is slow and sensual. Our tongues dance to a beautiful melody only our souls can hear. I want to breathe him in and make him a part of me. Going on this tour was the best choice I could have ever made.

"Mel," he gasps as he pulls back reluctantly, "we have to get ready to go." My forehead presses against his while we catch our breath.

"I know. I think I'm going to drive with Belle so I have a little longer to get ready."

"No," he answers firmly. "You can come later with Belle, but Ryan will come back for you both in the SUV. I don't want either of you driving anywhere on your own."

It's pointless to argue with him when I know he's right. Besides, Belle's been so tired lately, it would be good for her to have someone driving her around for a night. "Okay. It won't take me too long, so just send him back after he drops you off. That will give me an extra hour and a half."

"Don't dress too sexy tonight."

"Why?"

"I don't know … maybe you should dress extra sexy. Shit." He scrubs his face with his hands and sighs loudly.

"What's going on, Noah? Talk to me."

"Tonight, you're going to see Eli for the first time since he broke your heart. There are bound to be feelings bubbling to the surface on both sides. Part of me wants you looking hot so I can rub our relationship in his face, and the other part …"

"Wants me to look like shit so he won't want me anymore? I hate to break it to you, but he's seen me at my worst. Acne breakouts, awkward hair and makeup days, snotty nose and streaked cheeks, missing showers for days because my mom was gone. I'm not sure I could ever look worse than I did back then."

Noah groans as I take his hand in mine and squeeze it.

"I love that you're jealous, even though I shouldn't. I've already told you I want to mend fences with Eli. But this is yours, Noah." I pull his hand over my heart and hold it there. "For as long as you want it, my heart belongs to you. Whatever you see tonight, whatever you may think you see from the stage, remember you're the one I share a bed with, my heart with, my love with, and that I'm building my future with."

"So I can be your future ex-husband?" he jokes, and I remember back to that first morning after he stayed with me in my hotel.

"Of course. But instead of Eli, I'd like David Beckham as your replacement."

His mouth agape, he asks, "What about Victoria?"

"I know. She's perfect, isn't she? They're so adorable together." With a resigned sigh, I confess one of my innermost secrets "She's the only reason I've ever wished I had been a Spice Girl."

Noah laughs; it's contagious.

"You'll always be my Spice Girl." The devilish gleam in his eyes proves he's serious.

"I'll settle for being the love of your life." I meant for it to come out as a joke, but my tone couldn't have been more serious.

"That's a given, Amelia. There's no me without you. Not anymore."

"Ditto," I whisper softly across his lips.

In typical fashion, before we can take anything further, there's an incessant banging on his door. "Hurry up, big brother, we leave in ten." It warms my heart to hear Sawyer joke with him. I think the Sara thing is putting things into perspective with him as well.

With one final look at me before he leaves, Noah shakes his head and smiles. "Sexy, Mel. Make Eli wish he had what's mine tonight."

"You got it." I pull a trick from Anna's book and blow a kiss his way. He even catches it like Wyatt does, and we both laugh. Some things are just way too cheesy for us, even though it's adorable watching others do it.

As soon as Noah leaves, my phone starts ringing. When I look at the screen, I know I'm in trouble. It's Veronica, and she's Skyping me.

"Hey, Mama!" My excited greeting doesn't have her fooled one single bit.

"Don't hey mama me, young lady. Just how long were you going to keep Belle's secret for her?" She may be scolding me, but I can see the smile trying to peek through.

"Only long enough for her to tell you she fell in love and has a little peanut on the way."

"So in other words, forever," she adds with a laugh.

"Well, yeah, you know how it goes. They're excited. She just would have rather told you in person. But throw a rock star in the mix and everything goes public."

"I know, baby girl," she adds, a scowl crossing her face. "So tell me two things … is he good enough for my baby? And how are you doing today with all that's going on?"

I move up the bed and prop myself up on some pillows, leaning back against the headboard. "He thinks she hung the moon and stars just for him. Darren loves her, they just jumped into this a bit backward. Did you see the ultrasound picture?"

"I did, and I'm already in love. I trust your opinion, so I'll give her my blessing."

The smug look on her face makes me bust up laughing. "You didn't give her your blessing?" I finally choke out.

"Hell no. That girl waited weeks to tell me about the baby and months to tell me about her man. She can sweat it out a few minutes while I talk to you. Now, you didn't answer my question, baby girl … how are you doing?"

"I'm okay. I'm in love with him."

The thoughtful expression on her face makes me miss her so much right now. Belle, Veronica, and I are used to having weekly dinners, but since she met her new man and then went on vacation, those dinners fell off the map a bit.

"Amelia, you've kept your heart to yourself long enough. If you finally decided to give it, I know he must be worthy of it. Don't you succumb to crazy and let her get in the way of your happiness. You fight tooth and nail for what's yours, come hell or high water. You get me?"

"I got you, Mama. Thank you. When are you coming back? I miss you like crazy and would love for you to meet Noah."

Her gleeful expression shows me she's enjoying her time away. "We'll be back right after the new year. We'll have a big family dinner so you can all get to know Wesley as well. I think he's going to be in our lives for a long time to come."

"I'm happy to hear it. You deserve some happiness of your own. Now, I have to get ready for tonight, but do me a favor and call Belle back. She doesn't need any more stress on that peanut."

"Will do. Love you, baby girl. I'll see you when we get home."

"Love you, too." The screen goes blank.

True to his word, Noah sent Ryan back to the house for Belle and me. It's only been about three hours since he left, but I can't wait to see him again. I took his advice and went for a sexy look for tonight. But I did it for Noah, *not* Eli.

Just an Illusion is a trip. The whole outside is a graffiti-covered warehouse. It looks like a tagger—or a few crews of taggers—had the best day of their lives, but it's beautiful in an eclectic, artful way. It also meshes perfectly with Jordan's personality. The outside is bold and brave and the inside is subtle and kicked back.

Now I understand why they chose this location. It's spacious and dark, completely intimate. Perfect for a show. As I look around, I take some photos. The only people here now are friends and family. But that's what this night is about: putting on a show for the people who love them most. An intimate set for family and friends that their fans can watch later and feel a part of. It's one of the greatest gifts they can give them, and it makes me glad Jessie is the one who won the tickets. She and Eli will respect the vibe and the space. Even if Eli doesn't like them, he's an artist first and foremost.

"Come on, Mel! You've got all night to take in the details, let's go see our men." Belle's pulling me to the backstage entrance with such enthusiasm you'd think she hadn't seen Darren in weeks.

Judging by the raised voices, it's obvious we walked in on something bad.

"No, I'm not going to be a part of lying to her, Noah!" Sawyer yells with a fierce expression on his face.

"What good is it going to do her to know? Huh, Sawyer? Tell me, after everything that went down yesterday, how this is going to make it all better?" Noah screams back, getting in his face.

D. Kelly

Belle and I stay back against the curtains, an unspoken bond between us to hear what the hell is going on.

"Because she's a fucking target now, Noah, that's why! This isn't just some vague note. It's an obvious threat. Do you think Tony would already be working on an emergency restraining order for Mel now, too, if it wasn't? What the fuck?!"

Belle's nails dig into my wrist, her eyes wide with fear. My heart races, but I'm not ready to go in there yet.

"He's right, man," Wyatt concurs.

"Yeah, Noah. Dude, I love the fuck out of you, but if Mel's a target, that affects Belle. They have to know. I'm not risking anything happening to my baby by keeping them in the dark."

Noah drops into a chair and rubs his temple. "This was never supposed to happen. I gave Sara everything she could have wanted. Why couldn't she just move on like any normal person?"

Belle and I finally make our way into the room, all eyes instantly on us. Sawyer's linger longer than appropriate, then he shakes his head and points to Noah. "You two need to talk."

The pain in Noah's eyes is unmistakable. "You look beautiful," he whispers.

"You look like hell. What did she do now, and why am I taking out a restraining order?"

With slumped shoulders, he leads us over to a computer on the desk in the corner of the room. "I got this email when we got here. It's already been forwarded to the police."

Noah,

Tsk Tsk Tsk ... I didn't like spending my special day alone. I'm willing to forgive you, but you've given me no other choice but to take matters into my own hands.

Blood is red,
Murder divine,
Dead girlfriends can't love you,
Soon you'll be mine.
Until then, all my love. ~ Sara

"What the ever-loving fuck?" Belle screams.

I should be scared. I should be freaking out because as soon as this bitch has her way with me, she's going to try and go excessively crazy on Noah. It's only a matter of time. But right now I'm pissed. *Beyond pissed.* I reach for the keyboard just as about eight hands pull it from my grasp at the same time.

"There is *nothing* you can say to make this better, Mel. In fact, anything you say will only make it worse … guaranteed," Sawyer cautions, and Noah nods, agreeing.

"I'm not afraid of her. Let that bitch bring the crazy train to town. I'll throw her fucking ass off." My hands are trembling, and from the looks I'm getting, I'm sure I seem deranged, but I don't care. I'm so tired of this girl fucking with our lives.

"Before you rip off your earrings, how about you take a deep breath and calm down," Darren tells me with a slight smirk.

"We should cancel the show," Noah says suddenly.

"No … don't you dare." I hiss at him. "If you do that she wins, and she isn't *going* to win. Tonight is about your family, your friends, and giving your fans something many of them will never be able to witness. Don't let her take that from you … from them."

"Mel's right," Sawyer agrees as he admires me with a newfound respect. "Capitulating to her will show we're weak. Even if we feel it, half the battle is not letting it show."

Noah looks torn. Actually, he looks fucking miserable. "Fine, the show goes on. Ryan, I want you and no less than three back-up guards on Mel all night. And when I say on, I mean within eighteen inches of her."

"Noah, that is ridiculous …"

He interrupts my protest. "This is the deal, Mel, or I walk tonight. I'm not taking any risks, not with you."

"Give him that, Princess, it's a fair deal. Your safety for his peace of mind … and ours." They all nod in agreement.

"Fine, anything to get this night over and done with."

Noah stands and pulls me close. "Thank you," he whispers huskily as his lips meet mine in a brief kiss.

"You guys, I hate to break up the little moment you've got going on here, but it's starting to fill up out there. We should go mingle and greet guests. This is still our party, even if it is a show," Wyatt points out objectively.

Belle and Darren have been whispering quietly for the past few minutes. I'm sure she's completely freaked out about me and he's worried about her being too close to me right now. I don't blame him. He's got to protect his family.

"Look, I'm going to call Dad and fill him in on everything before they all get here," Sawyer says, turning to Noah. "Rob's sister is supposed to watch the girls, and I want to make sure there's a security team on her house, too."

"Do you think that's necessary?" My tone isn't nice and neither is his answering glare.

"Do you think I want to take a single chance with my nieces?"

"Sorry ... I'm so sorry."

His expression softens. "I know you are, Princess. We're all just flying by the seat of our pants here."

Isn't that the fucking truth.

"Alright, you guys. Tony got the restraining order approved. We're going to start about thirty minutes later tonight to allow a small buffer due to the increased security. You've got a good crowd out there already. Go have a drink and mingle. Act normal. Don't let her know she's frazzled you." Warren is going through his spiel like a well-oiled machine. It's why he's their manager.

"And Mel," he adds, "do me a favor and stay alert tonight. Have a drink but sip on it. Don't let yourself get wasted and don't let your drink leave your sight. We can watch for Sara, but we don't know if she has any accomplices. Just be safe."

When I see the fatherly concern in his eyes, the fear begins to set in. There's a psycho out there who wants to kill me.

When Past And Present Collide

The first thing Noah did was stop at the bar and order me a vodka tonic. "I'll be with you for the next hour. Drink this now and calm yourself. Before I go on stage, we'll switch you to water."

When he hands me the glass, my hands are trembling so hard some of the drink sloshes over the rim of the glass. Noah discretely steadies the glass as I bring it to my lips. After a few large gulps, I finish and put the glass back on the bar.

"Better?" he asks tenderly.

"Much, thank you."

With his arm around my waist, we make the rounds. The next forty-five minutes are a whirlwind of names and faces I'll likely never remember. Never once does Noah release me from his grasp. A familiar squeal catches our attention as Jessie Watts makes her way through the crowd.

"Oh my God, Amelia! I'm so happy to see you!" She effectively pulls me away from Noah and into her welcoming arms.

"Jessie, you look incredible!" As I pull away from her embrace, I take her in. She's always been a raven-haired, blue-eyed beauty.

"Amelia, it's great to see you." I'd know his voice anywhere. Hearing the timbre of it brings tears to my eyes, which I immediately blink back. I don't want Noah getting the wrong idea. But when Eli pulls me in for a welcoming hug before I even acknowledge his existence, I return his hug fiercely.

Without lingering too long, I pull away and duck back into Noah's embrace. "It's good to see you, too, Eli. It's been way too long." I mean it, too. I don't think I realized how much I missed my friend until right now.

"Well, it wasn't for lack of trying. At least, not on my part. Noah, how've you been?" Eli asks, turning his attention to my uptight man. I wish he'd relax just a bit.

"Better than ever," he answers, tight-lipped, and I take the opportunity to introduce him to Jessie in hopes of loosening him up.

"Jessie, this is my boyfriend Noah. Noah, this is my friend Jessie, Eli's cousin." She flashes him a mega-watt smile and extends a shaky hand. She's always been a fangirl at heart.

265

"Good to meet you, Jessie. Mel tells me you're a longtime fan."

"You could say that. I'm so excited to have won the tickets from *Slammed* and to be able to spend the night catching up with Mel and Belle. I haven't seen them in ages."

Noah stiffens. He's still not happy the contest winners are sitting with us, but it was arranged long before he knew Eli was going to be part of the equation.

"I'm sure you'll have a great time." When the lights flicker, that's his cue to head backstage. Before he leaves, he pulls me into his arms and hugs me tight.

"Be careful tonight," he whispers. "As soon as the show is over, I'll come meet you at the table. Don't go *anywhere* without Ryan. If you need to use the restroom, you have Ryan take you to J's private one in his office. Four guards at all times. Even while you pee. Outside the door, of course," he adds with a smile.

I catch a scowl on Eli's face over Noah's shoulder as he confirms his instructions with me. Too bad. He's got no clue what's going on and no place to judge what happens in my life. "I promise, I'll be safe." Noah lowers his mouth to mine and kisses me senseless, putting on a show specifically for Eli. I couldn't care less; I'd let Noah kiss me anywhere.

"Dude, we're up," Darren says, interrupting our kiss. When he notices Eli, he smirks. "What's up, boy band? Long time no see."

Darren and Noah leave, and judging by the intense look on Eli's face, just in the nick of time. He's always hated when people disrespect his music. Or give him nicknames related to it. Ryan steps into Noah's empty space and hands me a water bottle.

"Noah's orders," he adds sympathetically as he leads us to our table. Belle, Anna, and Rory are all already seated. Originally, we were supposed to be front and center, but now we're front and off to the side so the guards can surround the table but not block views.

Of course, since half the table is already sitting, I end up sandwiched between Eli and Jessie. Great. Noah is going to hate this. Sure enough, I can see his face sour when he looks down at us, so I do a repeat of the cheesiest thing I've ever done and blow him a kiss like I did in the bedroom this afternoon. He doesn't attempt to catch it this time, but I can see his chest rise and fall in a laugh as he mouths the words "I love you" to me. My heart dances in my chest as I say those words right back to him.

While Jessie catches up with Belle, Eli pulls my attention to him by putting his hand on my thigh. "You're going to move that before I have Ryan move it for you," I growl at him under my breath. He immediately complies and flashes me a classic, playful Eli smile.

"I just wanted your attention. I didn't mean any harm by it. Look, I know this isn't ideal, especially with your boyfriend watching, but can we please talk? There's so much I've needed to say to you for so long."

"You're not going to try and win me back, are you?"

"Nah, I know love when I see it. You're happy with him."

"Unbelievably happy and undeniably in love." My words confirm his suspicions, and he seems okay with it. I guess there's really no reason why he shouldn't be.

He scoots his chair closer to mine so we can talk. "I'm guessing this is about as private as we're going to get with the guards. Before we talk about the past, can you tell me you're okay? All this security isn't normal. Are you in danger, Mel? Does that restraining order extend to you?"

Such a barrage of questions so fast, and I'm hesitant to confide too much in Eli. Not because I don't trust him, but because I don't want to hurt Noah by saying too much to someone he isn't fond of.

"As of a few hours ago, it does. I'm okay, and it's all precautionary. Sorry, Eli, I can't really get into anything more than that."

While he contemplates his next words, I use the opportunity to take a good look at him. His blue eyes still sparkle like the ocean on a sunny day. His sun-kissed blond hair is styled to perfection as always. He's dressed casually in designer jeans and a button-down shirt that's tight enough to enhance his abs and muscular arms. Those are the arms that held me through some of the worst days of my life.

"I'm sorry, Amelia. I know you said my words are meaningless, but they're all I have. I've spent years trying to talk to you so I could somehow make this right. I understand why you denied my calls, letters, and emails. I just wish, more than anything, you would have talked to me. All I wanted was to show you how much I cared about you and what a huge void you leaving made in my life."

It's as if I can feel the pain that still flickers in his eyes. Maybe I can; I loved him once—more than *anything*. "Eli, if I could go back, I would change my actions. I've come to realize lately how losing your friendship hurt more than losing our relationship. The problem was, at fifteen, the only thing I understood was the boy I loved with all my heart betrayed me. I couldn't get past it."

His hand reaches for mine under the table and squeezes it comfortably as a friend would, and I let him. "If I could take it back, I would. I know those words don't mean much now and would have meant less back then, but they're the truth. I was terrified." His expression becomes sad. "We were kids having a kid. I wasn't thinking anything else when I had sex with that girl other than how much I wished she were you. I thought ... I guess I thought if I had sex with someone else I could get it out of my system."

"Get what out of your system?" My raised voice pulls Belle's attention to us, but I smile to let her know I'm fine.

"The fear of knowing I couldn't be with anyone else for the rest of my life. But hand to God, Mel, that was *the* worst sexual experience of my life to date."

He shakes his head as if he's trying to shake off a bad memory. "Men who cheat on their wives and girlfriends ... I don't understand how they can. The entire time, I felt dirty. I knew I was tearing apart everything I loved with every thrust into her, but I couldn't stop. And the rumors, they were true. I did cry, at least through half of it. I cried because I knew I'd just lost you. I've never felt so disgusted with anyone in my life and that disgust was all aimed at myself." With a disturbed chuckle, he adds, "I didn't even blame her for telling people I was a freak. I deserved the tell-all she gave. I was a fucking mess, and my indiscretion followed you like a black cloud. I don't think you'll ever know how heavily that weighs on my soul."

I look over to the stage as Eli's words ruminate through my mind. The guys are still huddled together, talking some stuff out. Knowing I have a bit of time, I turn back to Eli. I know, without a doubt, he's telling me the truth. As I try to push down my own regrets of that time of our lives, I offer him the one thing I can give him.

My forgiveness and the truth.

"I forgive you, Eli, and I'm sorry you felt so bad about what happened, and I couldn't hear you. Refused to acknowledge your pain and your fears. We were just kids and didn't make the best choices. It's exactly why we weren't ready for parenthood."

He shakes his head sadly. "If it weren't for me, you wouldn't have lost our baby."

His words are like a knife through my heart. We never had the abortion discussion; that was something I had kept to myself. I would have talked to him about it, but he cheated and I lost the baby so there was no point.

"Eli, I wasn't planning on keeping the baby. We were kids. We weren't ready. Your actions proved that more than anything I could have said."

"All my actions did, aside from push you away, was prove to me how much I loved you. If you would have forgiven me, I would have married you."

Time has jumbled his memory. "No, you wouldn't have."

"Yes, I would have. I had your father's permission. Mine, too."

My world spins on its axis. The sounds of the band warming up are an indicator of how little time we have to wrap up this discussion. "How?" I whisper, trying to hear him over the buzzing in my ears, through the pounding of my heart.

"After I cheated and confessed to you, I rented a hotel room for the night. I must have run a thousand scenarios through my head. The *only* one that made any sense was the one where we had the baby and made a family. Shit, I knew it wasn't ideal. But I loved you, and unlike you, I grew up in a small town. I'd seen teenagers get married and raise families happily. I had it so much better than they did. At sixteen, I had enough money to live off of for the rest of my life if I was smart with it. So I went and bought a ring."

No, no, no, this isn't happening.

My head moves in tandem with the words inside my head as Eli squeezes my hand, pulling me back from denial to the present. "Yes, Mel. I had a ring. Then, I found your dad and asked his permission. Only then did I tell my parents."

"My dad said yes?"

I'm still trying to work through why he would have done that.

"With some groveling. I told him everything. About the girl, about the baby, all of it. When he threw me up against the wall and cocked his fist, I didn't even flinch … I deserved what was coming. Just as quickly, he dropped me back down, deciding he was impressed I was willing to take the beating. Then he sat me down and said 'Tell me why I should give you my Mellie Sunshine.'"

My eyes brim with tears I'm trying desperately to blink back. Eli remembers the moment with fondness; he *loved* my dad.

"I told him the truth, and how I knew it at sixteen, I'll never know. I said 'There's no beat to my music without her because there's no beat left in my heart. I could go home now and the only thing I'll regret is that she's not with me, but I'll never regret leaving the music behind. It's what brought me to her, and in a way, what's taken her way. Fame isn't all it's cracked up to be. But beyond it all, she's the best of me. The best friend I've ever had, the best of my heart, and the best person I know.'"

When his eyes meet mine, there's a sadness that wasn't there before. "He gave me one of his classic Joey smiles, clapped me on the shoulder, and said if my words could sway him, he hoped for both our sakes they could sway you. He told me you had your mother's stubbornness and it might take me a long time to win back your heart. When I stood to leave, he looked me right in the eye and said, 'If you cheat on her again, I *will* kill you, and I know just the people who can make it *and* you disappear.'"

My laughter bubbles to the surface as I picture my dad putting the fear of God into Eli. Belle and Jessie are looking at us, both of them smiling, but Anna doesn't seem to know what to think. I'm sure her loyalty is with Noah, of course, and me joking with an ex doesn't look good. Right now, I couldn't care less. I need to hear the rest of Eli's story.

"Anyway, later that day is when I came to your house and your grandma told me you'd lost the baby. I knew I couldn't propose to you then, but I held on to that ring in hopes you'd forgive me. Once I'd had that future for us planned out, I couldn't stop thinking about it. Even after. I still have the ring, although I haven't had the girl for twelve years."

Why is this day such a mind fuck all the way around?

"What do you want from me, Eli?" I murmur softly.

"I only want your friendship, Mel. I miss the hell out of you, every day."

"Me, too. I miss my friend, Eli. But I can't be the woman you love. I have that with Noah in a way I *never* had it with you. He's *the one*."

Eli glances up at Noah and back to me.

"Does he know that?"

"We've talked about the future some, but you know me ... I hope he knows."

Eli pinches the bridge of his nose. He used to do that when he was stressed. Funny how I remember that detail about him, even funnier he still does it as a grown man. "Tell him. Don't make the same mistakes I did. Make sure he knows before you miss your chance."

This man sitting next to me isn't the same boy I used to know. He's changed, but I guess that's to be expected. With all the turmoil of the past few days, the one thing I feel good about is reconciling with Eli.

"Give me your phone." I hold out my hand. When he passes it to me, I use it to call mine and save the number. Handing it back to him, I pull mine out to send him a text message.

Mel:

Just an Illusion Series

1. I forgive you.
2. I'm happy you're back in my life. I've missed your friendship most of all.
3. Password protect your phone; it's for your own safety. Bitches be crazy.
4. Thank you for telling me the truth. I'm sorry I couldn't hear it sooner.

Eli's phone vibrates in his hand and he smiles first, then roars with laughter as he reads my words. My phone vibrates shortly after.

Eli: Thank you for hearing me out and for extending the olive branch. I'm excited to pick up our friendship. Please tell your boyfriend not to kill me. Boy bands don't teach you how to fight like rock bands do.

His text cracks me up and reminds me so much of my dad. That was a long-standing joke between him and Eli. My dad was forever telling him nothing would teach him how to fight like being in a rock band and all a boy band was going to do was pussify him.

Eli used to do kickboxing in his spare time, so I'm pretty sure he could hold his own, but the memories are priceless. He's one of only two people in my life who knew my dad and loved him as much as I did. To me, that makes him family.

"I'll talk to Noah. I'm pretty sure he loves me enough to work through this."

With a nod to the stage, Eli answers wistfully, "I'm pretty sure he's only got eyes for you, Mel. We may have our issues, but I know he's a good man. I've heard about all the random acts of kindness he does. It's actually inspiring."

"They've brought me to tears a few times. He really does have a heart of gold."

"Good, because you deserve someone who will cherish the fuck out of you."

The rest of the evening is spent catching up with Jessie and Eli. Even Belle seems to be thawing toward him. Anna and Rory are both huge fans, so once the initial awkwardness is out of the way, they are able to get to know him a bit, too.

Our conversations are flowing easily, and I'm having a great time, but my eyes never stray long from Noah. Since the concert is being recorded, it lasts longer than normal, but the guys seem into it and happy to be here with their closest friends. They're professionals to a fault because I know they'd much rather be figuring out our next moves. If we even have any.

D. Kelly

"Over the years, we've written and performed more songs than we can count," Sawyer speaks out to the crowd.

"And my brother, Noah, prefers to stay out of the limelight, never taking on lead vocals alone if he can help it. But recently, he met an amazing woman and fell in love."

The crowd is "oohing" and "ahhhing" as they listen to Sawyer speak, and I've got no idea what they're up to.

"So it turns out he tried some romantic move on her and it backfired on him because she fell in love with his voice. And being the romantic man he is, Noah promised her more words sung by him."

Noah is blushing as the crowd laughs lightly. "Now, he's in a bit of a predicament because he wants to give her the world. So tonight, for the entire world to see, Noah is going to sing for his love, Amelia. Give it up for Noah, everyone."

The girls at my table are squealing in happiness for me, and even Eli has a smile on his face. Noah catches my eyes and locks onto them.

"This was a decision made about five minutes after we got on stage tonight. If you noticed our pre-show huddle, this is what it was about. I hope you'll excuse the cover song, but the words couldn't express my feelings better. Amelia Grayson, this one's for you, baby. I love you."

I've never been so riddled with such emotional happiness. My heart is about to burst, and it's taking everything I've got not to let the tears pooling behind my eyelids fall. When Noah launches into a cover of *Make You Feel My Love* by Bob Dylan, I get lost in his voice and lose the battle of the tears. It's as if the words float on top of the smooth huskiness of his voice.

When the last lyrics fall from his lips, the deafening silence of the room explodes into a standing ovation. Except for me, because even though my vision is blurred by the many tears streaming down my cheeks, my eyes are locked solely on him. Eli is right; I need to tell him exactly how I feel because I've got no doubts about his love for me.

"Thank you all for indulging my romantic gesture. We'd like to thank you all for coming out tonight and for the love and support you've all shown us over the years. For those of you who aren't aware, *Just an Illusion* is more than an album and a song title. It's also the name of the bar we're filming from tonight. This bar holds many memories for us, and we wouldn't be where we are now without the chance we were given here. It only felt right to do this show here, where it all began. So please give a round of applause to my cousin Jordan for letting us invade once again. We love you, brother."

A round of applause breaks out, and Eli leans over my shoulder as the guys continue to talk to the crowd, expressing their love and thanks. "Amelia Triton, as much as it pains me to say this, you should marry him and never look back."

"It's Greyson now, Eli," I correct him harshly.

With a raised brow, he shakes his head. "You'll always be a Triton. Own that shit, Mel. It's who you are and who you were always meant to be. You're not hiding anymore. Write under Greyson but *be* a Triton."

He's got a point.

"And by the way, your book was outstanding. I'm proud of you."

It's strange falling into a friendship with Eli so easily after all this time. Sometimes, there are people in your life who you can pick up right where you left off with. I'd have never considered it before because I was so angry, but it makes sense Eli is one of those people.

"Thanks, Eli."

Before I know it, the guys have left the stage and the show is over. The camera crews are tearing down their equipment and the place is buzzing as everyone tries to talk to and congratulate our guys.

Noah's family makes their way over to us. They were on the other side of the venue, where their security could linger on the outer edges and out of view all evening. Belle makes introductions to everyone because my eyes never leave Noah. It seems like it takes him forever to finally get to me, but I stayed put like I told him I would.

Eventually, he pushes his way through the crowd of friends and label executives and finds his way to me. In a heartbeat, I'm out of my chair and in his arms.

"I take it you liked the show?"

"The show was good. You were sensational. You didn't have to do that, but I'm so glad you did." His hands rub against my lower back, and his head dips down against my ear. With a voice so low only I can hear, he whispers, "So you're not leaving me for Eli?"

His tone is one of joking insecurity. Turning around, I indicate to Eli and the rest of them we'll be right back before pulling away from Noah and grabbing his hand. "We need to talk privately. Now."

Noah pulls me back toward Jordan's office, determined not to let anyone get in our way. Ryan keeps up along with who knows how many other guards and he does a quick sweep of the office before stepping outside and closing the door behind him.

"What's going on, Mel?" Noah asks with a resigned sigh.

"You!" I cry out louder than I should while poking a finger at his chest. "We need to get a few things clear right now because there are obviously still some unresolved issues at hand."

Noah leans against the desk and crosses his legs in front of him, his arms follow. He's in a fully defensive position, effectively keeping me at bay. We'll see how long that lasts.

"First of all, I'm pretty sure I told you that you have no reason to be worried where Eli is concerned."

When he opens his mouth to speak, I hold out my hand. I'm not having any of his BS right now, not when there's something this important I need to get off my chest.

"There are things you are going to have to accept, Noah, if you want to be with me. One of those things is Eli. He's my friend, he was my *best* friend for a long time. One of only two I've ever had ... before you."

He relaxes, dropping his arms to his sides. "You consider me one of your best friends?"

"Of course I do. Which brings me to my next point. In case it's not completely obvious, I'm going to follow Eli's advice for once and come clean. I'm in love with you, Noah. *You're the one.* The only one for me."

His brilliant smile is automatic with my words, and he moves toward me at a slow pace. "Eli told you to come clean? About your love for me?"

I nod and pull him close by the front of his shirt. When his mouth is a whisper away, I drop the bomb, "Eli told me I should marry you."

Noah's mouth closes over mine and he takes complete control of our kiss. I don't know if he's claiming his dominance or me as his woman but whatever he's feeling right now, it's reflecting in his actions and is a complete turn on.

Reluctantly, he pulls away, leaning his forehead against mine. "I can't believe I'm going to say this, but Eli's a smart man. You should listen to him."

"Maybe, but how about we tour, co-habitate for a bit, and then talk about getting married?"

"I can live with that. But tell me the truth, was I hallucinating or did you really say I'm the one?"

A sudden shyness encompasses me, but I look him in the eye because he deserves that and so much more. "I did. Noah Weston, you own my heart. You better be gentle with it."

He groans in frustration. "I need to get you home so I can make love to you until the sun rises."

"Sounds like a plan. Let's go get the goodbyes out of the way."

After he opens the door, he pulls on my hand. "Mel, hang on a sec. How good of a friendship are we talking about with Eli?"

I pause and think for a minute so I can give him the best answer possible. "Probably the kind where he's going to call and text me often, visit when we're in the same towns and definitely at home, and maybe even earn a godparent spot with one of our kids someday."

Just when I think Noah is going to complain, he flashes a brilliant smile instead. "Alright, if Eli coming back into your life means you're finally willing to acknowledge our future children, I'll take it. Just don't make me sing his music in karaoke. Out of all the boy band music, his was my least favorite."

After a burst of laughter, I plant a firm kiss against his lips. "I can't promise anything, but I'll keep your request in mind."

Hand in hand, we walk back into the bar so we can say goodnight to our friends and family. The only place I want to be right now is in Noah's bed. *Our bed.*

Two ridiculously long hours later, the bar is empty. As much as we wanted to go home, there were so many friends and family members here supporting them we couldn't just up and leave. Always the gentleman, Noah insisted on shutting the place down and helping Jordan wrap things up for the night. It's one of my favorite things about him, so I'm not complaining. Being here with him is enough. Besides, for the last hour or so, I've been watching the best thing ever. Noah and Sawyer are sitting together at the bar, drinking and talking. *Really talking.* None of that gruff and quick stuff. They're reminiscing, joking, and acting like the best of friends. It's nice seeing them interact with Jordan on his home turf as well. The three of them really are brothers in every way.

I've been observing them from afar while sitting in a circular booth making notes on my phone about tonight and catching up on emails. I've got plenty to keep me occupied while they do their thing. Every once in a while, Noah glances over and flashes me a smile, which I return with one of my own.

"Princess, are you sleepy?" Of course Sawyer would walk up on me as I'm yawning, but when he yawns, too, it makes me laugh.

"I guess as sleepy as you are," I reply as he slides into the seat across from me. Jordan and Noah are still at the bar with Mac and Ryan, talking and laughing. I'm happy to see Noah enjoy himself after all the drama of the day.

"Hey, I really just wanted to say I'm sorry for earlier. I didn't mean for you to overhear us arguing about things." He pauses and runs his hand through his hair before looking back at me. "But, to be honest, I'm glad you did. You have the right to know what is going on. I couldn't forgive myself if anything happened to you because you were unaware, so ... please be safe, Princess."

Sawyer's expression stops my heart. He has the look of a man who has everything at his fingertips and lost it. It's heartbreaking. There's so much more to him than the bad boy reputation he lets rule his image. For a brief moment, my mind flickers with the knowledge of how easily it could have been the two of us ... if I'd fallen into his bed that night. I can't even wrap my head around it so I shake it off. I'm not sure if Sawyer could have handled an us. Hell, I'm not sure I could have, either. It doesn't matter, though ... things are as they should be. I love Noah with my whole heart and can't imagine my world without him. But Sawyer has *seen* so much, lost so much, and I know this Sara stuff is weighing as heavily on his heart as it is mine.

"You don't have anything to apologize for, Sawyer. You were right. I know Noah wants to protect me, but knowing your battle is half of conquering it. I appreciate that you care enough about me to want to protect me. It means more to me than you could ever know."

My pulse quickens with the hooded gaze he wears, but we both shake it off. We have to get past this bit of inappropriate sexual tension between us because it's not going anywhere and never will. I think he realizes it as well because he brushes it off and a crooked smile appears on his face. "Yeah, well, we're family now, so be prepared to understand how Rory and Diane feel. We're going to be in your business all the time, it's what brothers do. And when you and Noah eventually tie the knot, that's what I'll be ... your brother." He practically chokes over those last two words, and I can't say I blame him. The thought of Sawyer being my brother-in-law is ... unsettling. And that pisses me off most of all because there shouldn't be anything unsettling about it. I'm head over heels in love with Noah.

"Hey, you guys about ready to get out of here?" Noah asks, sliding in next to me, immediately stroking my thigh with his fingers.

Instantly, I feel better. The awkwardness of whatever vibe was between me and Sawyer has vanished.

We both nod, and Sawyer pauses. "How are we working security?"

They let all the extra security leave to ensure everyone else got home safe about an hour ago. It's only the three of us and the two guards left. It's also two a.m. and totally fine, I'm sure.

"Mac is going to take you and J to Jordan's house and stay on his couch. Ryan is going to take Mel and me back to our house."

With a nod, Sawyer agrees to the plan. I'm not sure why Sawyer is staying with J tonight, but I don't ask. I'm sure they want some time away from the family to catch up alone.

A few minutes later, we're all leaving out the back exit of the club. Mac went out first and got their car ready and Ryan stayed with us while Jordan locked up the club. They drove off as Ryan finished checking out our car for any obvious issues.

"What the fuck is that?" I turn my head toward the sounds of screaming and banging around the side of the building. It sounds like someone is being beat against a dumpster.

"I'll go check it out. Get in the car and call the police," Ryan orders, tossing the keys to Noah. He's out of sight before I even step up into the car. Noah's hand is resting on my hip protectively as I climb inside.

"Noah!" The scream leaves my mouth the second I'm in my seat enough to see him start climbing in behind me. Sara is right behind him with a gun, and fear shoots straight through my heart. Before he even has the chance to turn around—while his eyes are locked on my fearful expression—she takes him down, cold-clocking him with the gun in her hand. Noah's body crumples to the ground as I lurch toward him. Blood is rushing down his face, and when I move to jump out of the car, the muzzle of her gun is against my head.

Cold fear floods my system as her feral gaze meets mine. She's fucking insane. If I doubted it before, I don't anymore. This woman is going to kill me.

"See what you made me do? You're such a stupid bitch! Noah is mine, he always has been. But you *had* to get in the way, had to make him *think* he was in love with you. All he needed was a reminder he's mine. And he is. Noah belongs to me! The sooner you're out of the picture, he'll realize how much he misses me." The frantic words flow from her mouth, but my eyes are locked on Noah.

The puddle of blood around his head is growing. *Where the fuck is Ryan?* If he doesn't get help soon, he's going to die out here. With tears streaming down my cheeks, I take my chances and try pleading with her.

"Sara, I'm sorry. Please, help Noah and I'll disappear. I promise. Just help him." My words are stuttered, spouted through sobs I can't control. My eyes are still locked on Noah; he's so still, his breathing so shallow.

"Help him!" I plead with her and am met by nothing but an insane smile.

"He's fine, he's only sleeping. It will be just like a fairy tale. He'll wake up from his true love's kiss. But first ... I need to get rid of you."

The gunshot blast echoes through the silent night. The heavy impact slams me backward into the car, and my vision dances with red and black dots before everything fades to black.

Belle's Post-Shooting Announcement

Slammers!

It's Belle. Remember those positive thoughts and prayers I asked for yesterday? Please get them going. We need the best vibes we can get right now. It's with great sadness I have to tell you Noah Weston and Amelia Greyson, along with their bodyguard Ryan Goodall, have been involved in some type of altercation after leaving the private BAD concert tonight.

We're en route to the hospital as I type, and at this moment, all conditions are unknown. I'll update you hourly with more details as they come in. Please keep them all in your hearts. Love is a powerful thing.

Xs and Os

Belle

To Be Continued …

D. Kelly

acknowledgements

Thank you all for reading *Just an Illusion – Side A*. This book was difficult to write because in a lot of aspects, it's a very personal story.

With each book I release, the acknowledgements become increasingly difficult to write. The indie book world is a wonderful place. Authors, bloggers, readers—everyone ensconced within our community is so giving. Every day, I'm helped by more people than I can count. With a simple message, post, or cry for help, people come through. This is a beautiful thing, and a wonderful community to be a part of.

To try and narrow down everyone who has helped me in some way or contributed to my books is nearly impossible. Please know I appreciate every one of you. Every blogger who has helped me in any way, every reader who has picked up one of my books, my editors, designers, formatter, proofreader, and beta readers, I am so thankful for each of you and love you all.

Of course, I do need to give a huge thank you to my PA, Ashley Griffieth. She has been with me from the beginning and knows what I need before I even realize it. My street team—D's Divine Divas—and my fan group—Dee's Dirty Divas—you are all amazing. I love you guys!

Lastly, to my family and friends. You may be last on this list but you're always first in my heart. I wouldn't be writing at all if it weren't for your love and encouragement. Thank you for always believing in me, even when I don't believe in myself.

Just an Illusion – The B Side
D. Kelly

D. Kelly

Just an Illusion

Dedication

For my readers. You guys are the reason I wake up excited to put my words on paper. The messages you send, your posts in the reader groups, your excitement to pick your team … all of this makes me happier than you could imagine. I even appreciate the way you lovingly call me a sadistic bitch for pulling you into another series. I promise I'll always try to make the journey worth it.

"The world breaks everyone, and afterward, many are strong at the broken

places."

— Ernest Hemingway

Amelia

Present Day – Two Years After The Tour

Stories are meant to be told. Those six words continue to swirl around in my mind. What was I thinking? As my heart aches this morning, I'm leaning toward the mindset that stories should stay in the vault—the one between friends and acquaintances who witnessed them happening in real time. Some things don't need to be rehashed and reshared. Good memories will live on in our hearts, and the bad ones can burn in hell where they belong.

But … I made a promise to myself and to them I would do this. After all this time, it's important to stick to my word. Once this part of the story is written, I'm hoping the next one will come to me easier. Then maybe, I can finally wrap up this chapter of my life which has been hanging in the balance for far too long. Maybe someday I'll share these words with my friends and our family, but this isn't the story the public wants to hear. They want to know about the fame, the accolades, and the fun times. They don't want to know the down-and-dirty secrets of BAD's love life and intimate family moments.

Admittedly, it felt good to finally write again; maybe it was the wine. When I finally crashed last night, I was exhausted, and more than a little drunk. Even so, morning came quickly today and I was excited to greet it.

Truth be told, I had a breakthrough—one I felt with every fiber of my being. Physically, emotionally, and with a wide-open heart, I let it all in. It's been two years since I've let myself reflect on the tour with any fond memories. When I woke up an hour ago, I couldn't wait to dive back in and let myself go back to a happier place. Writing this story feels good, and I want to finish it while I have time, so I can finally give him an answer.

But then I booted up my computer and remembered where I left off.

The shooting.

And that's when my mood went to shit.

We were caught off guard. It's amazing how a split second can change *everything*. We'd been aware earlier that evening, diligent, responsible. And even with all the shit surrounding us, Noah and I found our place with each other that night. Nothing or no one could take that away from us. We were so naïve. Sometimes crazy things happen in this world, and sometimes crazy people do; that night, we suffered the misfortune of both.

I've spent the past few years blocking out the bad parts. I think that's why I passed out when I did last night; alcohol or not, it's a hard place in time to revisit. Today is a new day—albeit a rainy one—and with my coffee in hand, I'm ready to tackle getting the rest of this story down on paper ... or I guess computer is more accurate. My time is running out. I've only got forty-eight hours to give him an answer. I'm not any closer to one than I was yesterday, or the day before, or the months and years before that.

I've never been an indecisive person, but this decision isn't only about him and me. There are so many other people in this equation ... especially now. But our take on that is different, too. Which is why it's important I finish this story. Even though I'm writing it for me, it also feels like I'm writing it for them. If I can do that—write it for them—maybe when I'm done, I can write the book I actually *do* owe them. Hopefully, it will have been worth the wait.

Everything Has Changed - Three years ago

"Is she hurt?" Frantic cries meet my ears, but I can't move. There's something weighing me down, squeezing the life out of me. Breathing hurts, and my top is wet... *Why am I so wet?*

"I don't know! Fuck! Help me get this bitch off her."

Sawyer ... I'd know his voice anywhere. He's going to save me, help me breathe easier.

"Why did you shoot?" another voice screams, and it's not Noah.

"I had the shot. Even if I didn't, she would have killed her if I didn't try." Mac. *What is going on?* I try pushing myself up and a groan escapes me. My arm is tucked under my body; it fucking hurts.

Suddenly, air fills my lungs and the pressure is gone. Gasping heavily, I blink my eyes a few times, but everything is blurry, tinged in red. Someone pulls me free and begins wiping my face with a cloth. That's good, maybe I won't be so wet now.

"Princess ... fuck. Are you okay? The ambulance is on its way. Please tell me you're alright."

The cloth presses harder against my eyes, scrubbing at them. "Why can't I see, Sawyer? Where's Noah?"

"She's okay," he calls out. "Alive," he corrects as he carefully pulls my arm toward him, causing me to squeal in pain.

Fuck, that stings like a bitch.

"He's here, and he's still breathing. Help is coming, Princess. Your eyes are okay now, you just got ... something in them. We'll get them flushed and you'll be fine. Help will be here soon." Sawyer wraps me in his arms and hugs me close to him. He's not wearing a shirt; there's nothing but bare skin under my embrace. That doesn't hold my attention long because from the way he's breathing and the moisture dripping onto my cheeks, it's obvious he's crying. *Poor Sawyer, he must have been terrified. But why?*

Sara ... she was going to shoot me. Then, I remember the shot.

"She shot me?" *No, I don't feel shot ... I don't think. What the fuck just happened?*

My frantic cries are muffled as Sawyer tightens his arms around me. I'm trying to blink my eyes open and closed, but whatever is on me is sticky and my eyelashes keep sticking together.

"J, how's he doing?" Sawyer calls out, still holding on to me in the SUV.

"He's okay. He's starting to move. I think she just knocked him out." The relief in J's voice is shadowed in fear. Hearing the trepidation in his tone kicks me into gear.

"You left ... and she ... shit ... Noah!" The fear I felt earlier floods back into my heart.

"Ryan hit the panic button on his phone and Mac turned right back around. Thank God he did ... we were a split second away from her killing you. Jesus, Princess, what happened?" With his pleading tone, I pull away, blinking my eyes harder and faster, finally getting my lashes to separate and open fully. Sawyer glances from my face to my arm, but my arm wins his attention as he presses his shirt to it.

"Shit, that stings." I hiss.

"Sorry," he winces, "I think the bullet grazed you. It's not too bad, but you'll probably need some stitches or something. It's still bleeding."

"Is that why I'm wet? Why is there so much blood?"

He avoids my question and looks over his shoulder. "It's going to be okay," he reaffirms as the sounds of the sirens grow closer. Mere seconds pass before their lights are flashing in the window behind us.

"I need to be with Noah."

He nods reluctantly and carefully helps me out of the SUV. The paramedics are surrounding Noah, hooking him up to IVs and machines. My eyes take in the scene around us. Sara lies on the ground about three feet away from us. Her eyes are wide open, lifeless, and she's *covered* in blood. So am I, I realize, as I look down at my chest.

Oh my God.

The scream escapes my mouth long before it ever catches up to my ears. My body begins to collapse, but Sawyer catches me and holds me steady. Instantly, the rest of the memories flood my mind, but my eyes close and before I know it, I'm floating on a cloud.

The steady beeping of a monitor burrows itself into my head. My eyes flutter open and Sawyer is at my bedside, holding my hand. No longer covered in blood, I'm wearing a blue and white hospital gown and he's wearing scrubs. My head feels a bit heavy, but I'm calm. There's a bandage wrapped around my upper arm now, too, but there's no pain.

When our eyes meet, his pain is palpable. Sawyer wears every emotion he's got in the depths of his eyes. He looks like a broken man, and I'm terrified to ask about Noah. Tears gather in the corners of my eyes and as they begin to fall, he wipes them away.

"Noah?" His name falls from my lips like a whispered prayer. Sawyer's expression falls slightly, but he recovers quickly.

"He's okay ... as far as we know. He woke up briefly, and he's having a CT scan and an MRI. The doctors think it's just a bad concussion. He'll need some stitches and some time off, but he's okay ... both of you are." Squeezing my hand tighter, he chokes out the words as his own tears fall. I can't imagine what this was like for him.

"Sawyer, I'm sorry ... I know this must be your worst nightmare come true."

He shakes his head and scoots as close to me as he can get, leaning his head against mine. "No, my worst nightmare would have been if I'd gotten there a second later. You're safe, Princess, and so is Noah. That makes everything right in my book."

I feel safe curled up with Sawyer, especially since I can't be with Noah right now. "What about Ryan? Please tell me he's okay?"

"Yeah, Ryan is fine. He feels awful, but he's okay. It looks like Sara had a few friends helping her out. I don't know much, just that they've both been arrested pending further investigation."

"What kind of friends would help someone do what she did?" I'm furious—for all of us, Sara included. They should have gotten her psychological help.

"I don't know, I'm just glad Mac got her. I only hate you got shot in the crossfire," he says with a reluctant sigh.

"I was shot?"

"It's technically a superficial gunshot wound. The bullet went through her and grazed your arm. The doctors cleaned it, gave you a tetanus shot, and started antibiotics. You don't even need stitches ... just wound care. God, Princess, you were so fucking lucky tonight." His pained words send shivers through my body. We were *all* lucky, except for Sara.

"I heard the shot. She had just put the gun against my head. Then there was a flash of red and nothing but blackness. I thought ..."

Sawyer nods, understanding my unfinished sentence. "She almost did," he whispers reluctantly. "When we pulled up, she was

289

screaming at you. We used her distraction to inch closer. As soon as she put the gun to your head, Mac took the best shot he had. Fuck, I'm not sure I've *ever* been so scared." His hands tremble in mine with the wavering of his voice. Gripping my hand tighter, he continues.

"The blood from her wound sprayed you, and when her body fell onto yours, I guess it knocked the wind out of you, or you passed out from the pain and shock. I'm not sure, it all happened so fast. J and Mac were checking Noah … I couldn't." His tears begin falling again, but this time he shakes his head and pushes forward. "I had to maneuver around them all, but Noah was almost directly in front of the door. We didn't want to move him because of his head. I had to climb over Noah, without disturbing him, to get to the door so I could pull her off you. All the blood was hers, *not* yours. You're perfect, Princess, and you're still here with me."

"I don't care if Jesus Christ himself is in there with her, you're *going* to let me in to see my sister!" Belle's screams echo from the hall, and her tirade is the first thing to bring a small smile to my face.

Sawyer brings my hand to his mouth and kisses me softly, then drops another kiss to my forehead before standing to diffuse the situation so my pregnant best friend can calm down.

"Oh my God, Mel!" she cries out when she sees me. Her tear-streaked face tells me all I need to know about how scary this was for her. Darren waits by the curtain with Sawyer and gives me a small wave and a smile to match. The sadness in his eyes is unmistakable.

"I'm okay, Belle. Calm down, it's not good for the peanut."

"The peanut is just as worried as I am, and she's manifesting her fear through me. Don't ever do this to me again!" She climbs up and lies down next to me, crying as she hugs me fiercely.

"Belle, I'm sorry." My mind is still a bit foggy, and I want to cry, but for some reason the tears aren't coming.

"Sawyer, did they give me something? I feel … strange?"

He looks up with a half-smile and nods. "You probably will for a while. They gave you something to calm you down and it knocked you out immediately. Then they gave you some pain meds and antibiotics in your IV so they could clean your wound and run some tests. The doctor said you'll probably be a bit out of it until tomorrow." Sawyer is really keeping track of the details. I'm so thankful for him tonight.

"Belle, have you seen Noah?"

She looks up at me and wipes away her tears. "No, babe. I just got here, and you were my only priority."

"Can you get someone to take me to him? Please?" I need to see him and make sure they're not lying to me.

"His bed is right on the other side of yours, Princess. That's why the curtain is pulled back in the middle. They're supposed to wheel him back here after his tests. I couldn't be in two places at once, so I managed to convince them to keep you both together."

Darren wraps his arm around Sawyer's shoulder and squeezes him tightly. "You did good, man." Sawyer pulls him into a massive hug and sobs. The night is catching up to him; it's heartbreaking to witness.

"Where are Jordan, Ryan, and Mac?" I'd really like to get eyes on everyone who was there tonight. I think it would make me feel a lot less apprehensive.

"Jordan is in the waiting room with Ryan, waiting for everyone to get here. Mac is still at the scene talking to the police."

Poor Jordan, I hope this doesn't mess with him. The two of them have been through so much already; I hate they're going through it again. Sawyer runs his hands through his hair in frustration. He's getting anxious Noah's not back, too, I think.

"You have no idea how scared I was tonight, Mel. I can't lose you, and I'm glad that bitch is dead after what she did."

"Belle …"

"Don't Belle me! You're the other half of my heart and soul. I'd be lost without you."

"Eh hem …" Darren fake-coughs to pull Belle's attention to him.

"Don't be so easily offended … you know what I mean. You're all of that and a bag of chips for my romantic heart, but she's it for my family and best friend side. I'll never get another sister just like I'll never get another you."

Darren covers his heart and stumbles backward as if catching her love. It makes me giggle and for a split second takes my mind off what could possibly be taking them so long with Noah.

"I'm going to see if everyone is here and fill them in. Princess, do you need anything before I go?"

"No, thank you, Sawyer. I'm okay."

"I'm going to go with him and let the two of you talk." Darren says as he leans down and kisses Belle and then leans over and drops a kiss against my forehead. "Don't scare us like that again," he whispers before leaving.

"Are you really okay?" Belle asks softly after Darren and Sawyer leave the room.

"I'm not sure ... I think so, but I can't even think about myself until I know how Noah is doing. I poured my heart out to him tonight, Belle. Maybe I shouldn't have. Maybe this is a sign I'm not supposed to get close to anyone."

"Oh, Mel," Belle says as she softly strokes my hair, "you deserve love as much as anyone, even more so. I've never told you the real reason I live by the motto 'live today, like there's no tomorrow' but maybe it's time."

"I always assumed it was because that sums up who you are in a nutshell."

She nods and squeezes my hand. "In part, yes. But the reason I live that way is because of you."

"Me?" I'm surprised and more than a little curious.

With a sad smile, she continues, "You're my sister, Mel, and a part of you died when you lost your mom. It took a while to get you over that hump of pain and sadness, but then you picked yourself up and went back on tour with Eli. Then, when your dad died, it was worse, and it took a lot longer to get you to recover, but you eventually did."

"Okay ..." I'm not quite following her, but maybe it's because of the meds.

"I admired you for that, for picking yourself back up and moving on. I know you had a lot to deal with, but you made the best of it. It's just ... I also saw those dark days you lived before you moved on and the only thing I wanted for you was happiness. I promised myself, no matter what it took, I was going to try and keep your dark days to a minimum. So that's when I adopted my motto."

"Was I really that bad?" I whisper, leaning my head against hers.

"No, babe, you were that *brave*. I just wanted you to know that instead of dwelling on what you can't change, you have to live for now. You did that tonight, Mel. When you told Noah how you felt, you were living for the moment. And if things had gone differently, you'd be so glad he knew how you felt before either of you were gone."

"Thanks, Belle, I needed to hear that."

"Anytime," she says, snuggling in closer. "So how did Noah react to the news?"

A smile creeps onto my lips as I recall how happy he was. "He was thrilled."

"That's not a big surprise. He already gave you the stars, but if he could, I'm sure he'd give you the moon, too."

"Ms. Greyson, how are you feeling?" A tall doctor with salt-and-pepper hair walks in, and Belle scrambles out of the bed and into the chair.

"Okay, a bit loopy. Mostly, I'm concerned about Noah."

He smiles as he finishes putting on his gloves and walks to my bedside. He shines a light into my eyes and checks my monitors. "Do you remember me from earlier?" he asks, taking a seat on a rolling stool.

"No, I'm sorry."

"Don't be, you've had a rough night. I'm Doctor Martin, head of the emergency department. Mr. Weston and I are old friends."

"You sent the cactus." I state matter-of-factly, and he chuckles.

"Yes, I did. Now, let me fill you in on what's been going on while you were napping. Noah has been asking for you. He's as concerned for you, as you are him. But Noah is going to be fine, you both are. As a precaution, and as a favor, we're keeping you both overnight for observation. The two of you were extremely lucky tonight."

Noah is going to be fine; the doctor wouldn't lie to me. Finally, I feel like I can breathe.

"I've had Noah taken directly upstairs to a private room. Your nurse will be in shortly to move you up there as well. People are already trying to sneak into the hospital for updates, so the sooner you're out of the emergency department the better. Your vitals are stable and your gunshot wound is superficial. Once your medication wears off you'll be a bit achy, but a few days of pain medicine and antibiotics should fix you right up."

"And what about Noah?"

His eyes soften as they meet mine. "Noah received some stitches, staples, and has a pretty severe concussion. Fortunately, we found no brain swelling or bleeding on his scans, but he will need to take a month off from touring. Concussions are serious. Movement and light could aggravate his pain, he may be forgetful, irritable, emotional, anxious, have trouble sleeping, or sleep a lot. He may also become dizzy, especially during the first week or two. Plan on spending a lot of time with him and giving him more patience than normal. He'll likely be frustrated because there's nothing you can do to promote healing a concussion except taking it easy."

"Noah's going to hate that, but at least you two will get some one-on-one time," Belle says optimistically.

D. Kelly

"He can hate it all he wants. He's alive and that's all that matters. I'll tie him to the bed if I have to." My face flushes as I realize what I just said, but Dr. Martin only chuckles.

"You're not the first woman to threaten that. Tomorrow, one of the hospital psychologists will be coming up to speak with the two of you. After a traumatic incident all of our patients go through an exit exam. It's only precautionary. You'll be given signs and symptoms to watch for, as well as treatment referrals and options if you feel you may need them."

Great. Nothing like trying to figure out if I feel traumatized before what happened has sunk in. But Noah … he might be, so I need to keep an open mind.

"Okay, can I see Noah now? Please?" I'm not above begging at this point.

"Young love, I remember those days. You two take care of each other and tell Noah I'll see him tomorrow before he's discharged." Dr. Martin opens the curtain, and a nurse enters pushing a wheelchair.

Jumping from the bed, I get a little dizzy and have to grab on to the bedrail for support.

"Mel, let us help you!" Belle chastises.

"Sorry, I didn't realize I wouldn't be okay."

With their assistance, I get settled into the chair.

"I'll be okay, Belle. Go tell everyone I'm fine and they're moving me up to Noah's room."

"They already know." Sawyer appears in the doorway looking even more ruggedly handsome, if it's possible. And tired; he looks so freaking tired. "Darren is waiting for you in the lobby, Belle. Go home and get some rest."

Belle hesitates but finally agrees with him. She leans down and hugs me gently. "I'll see you tomorrow, get some sleep."

"You, too, Belle. Thanks for being here."

With a sad smile, she replies, "Thanks for not dying on me. That would have sucked."

After the nurse tucks my IV bag in my lap, we start our journey to Noah's room, with Sawyer walking alongside us. I'm used to his quietness, but it feels like Sawyer has a lot he'd like to say right now.

We take an elevator up several floors, when the doors finally open and we're let out into a dim hallway. This floor looks like a hotel, not a hospital. The nurse pauses at a door at the end of the hall.

"Let me go inside and get rid of the visitors. They've been here longer than hospital policy allows." When she steps inside, Sawyer releases a deep sigh.

"Sawyer, are you okay? You can talk to me, you know … about anything."

"I'm not ready to talk but when I am, I promise I'll talk to you. I'm so fucking grateful we got to you two in time. I don't want to even think about what would have happened if we hadn't."

Reaching over, I pull his hand into mine and squeeze. "Me, either. You saved me tonight, Sawyer. You saved *us* … and I'll never forget that."

Sawyer's parents come out of the room, and Karen immediately bends down and gives me a hug. "Amelia, sweetheart, I'm so glad you're okay." A fresh round of tears begins to trickle down her already tear-streaked face.

Owen pulls Sawyer into a hug and from the way Sawyer's shoulders slump, it must be the first time he's let his guard down all night. The overwhelming sadness pulling at my heart strings while watching them is surprising. This family has become *everything* to me in such a short period of time.

"Okay, time to get Amelia settled for the night."

Karen releases me with the nurse's words. "We'll see you both tomorrow."

Sawyer bends down and kisses the top of my head. "Night, Princess."

"Goodnight, Sawyer," I whisper softly, finding it hard to vocalize the words. All I want to do right now is see Noah, but part of me wishes I could stay with Sawyer to comfort him, too.

The nurse pushes me into the dim room and closes the door behind us. Only the soft glow from a nightlight and light seeping out from the cracked bathroom door illuminate our way.

"Amelia?" Noah's voice is barely a whisper, but my body floods with relief.

"Yes, Noah, it's me. Can I spend some time with him please?"

"Of course, but not too long, you both need your rest. I'm going to go get your medicine and we'll get you settled when I come back." She pushes my chair next to his bed, and I reach for his hand, immediately bringing it to my lips. My tears are falling freely now that it's just the two of us. I almost lost him tonight, and there's no world where that would be okay. He's my lifeline.

"Don't cry, baby. I'm okay, but are you?"

"I'm fine, Noah, I was just so worried about you."

Fuck the nurse. With one hand, I hold my IV bag and with the other, I hold on to the bedrail and climb into bed with Noah. I'm careful to squeeze in between him and the rail so I don't move him, but right now I have to feel him against me.

After tucking myself in next to him, I lay my head over his heart. Even after everything, it sounds the same—strong and steady. It's all I can do to choke down a sob; the last thing I want to do is upset him, but I'm so relieved.

"Mel ... what happened to us tonight?" His words are soft and unsure. Maybe it's for the best he doesn't remember.

"We had an accident, Noah, but we're both okay. What's the last thing you remember?"

"Leaving the club, I think. I remember saying bye to Sawyer and J, but it's all blank after that."

That's good, he hasn't lost much time. Maybe it will come back to him, or maybe not.

A painful hiss falls from his lips, and I try to get up, but his words stop me. "Don't, Mel, please stay. You're the only thing taking my mind off the pain."

It's not fair; after all he's been through, he can't even have medicine to numb the pain. His hand lies loosely on top of mine, but his breathing has slowed and I know he's already sleeping again. I'm glad; he needs his rest, and I'm more than content listening to his heartbeat until the sun rises.

A few minutes later, someone sighs behind me; this nurse isn't going to let me stay here any longer. "Come on, Ms. Greyson, I promise you won't even miss him once your medication kicks in. Tomorrow you can go home and recuperate together."

Her hand wraps around mine as she helps me out of the bed and into my own. At least we're together in the same room. "You'll be getting sleepy pretty quickly. If you need anything, just hit the call button here," she says, showing me where it is before turning and leaving the room. She wasn't joking; one minute I'm waiting for her to leave so I can crawl back into Noah's bed and the next my lids are so heavy I can't even keep my eyes open.

"Stop!"

"Shh, Princess, it's okay." Warm hands close over mine, and my eyes flutter open as my heart continues to race.

"Sawyer?" The room is barely lit, but my eyes slowly adjust to the lighting. "What are you doing here?" My mouth is dry, my voice scratchy. He releases my hands and hands me a cup of water from the bedside table. The water is cold and feels amazing going down my throat.

"I'm not going anywhere. I didn't convince them to admit you both for observation to leave you alone. I left you once tonight and look where it got us."

"This isn't your fault, Sawyer."

"No, it's not," Noah croaks out from behind him. "Are you okay, Mel?" he asks softly, and Sawyer turns around and lifts a cup of water to his lips. Noah sips it slowly, and Sawyer remains at his side, helping him until he's had his fill. Then they both turn to me expectantly.

"I'm fine. Just tired, I guess. I don't know what woke me up."

"You were screaming in your sleep," Sawyer whispers as Noah's eyes close again.

Poor Noah.

"I'm sorry. I don't remember, but I didn't mean to scare you, or wake Noah. I feel awful."

"Don't," Sawyer says firmly as he sits next to me again. "He's been awake off and on all night. His pain is keeping him up, not you. And even if you were keeping him awake, it's how he'd want it. But he can't be there for you in all the ways he'd like to be, so I'm the next best thing."

In the shadows, I see the outline of a small smirk creeping up on the corner of his mouth.

"Always so pompous and yet somehow still a gentleman."

He replies with a snicker, "I'm no gentleman."

"Keep telling yourself that, Sawyer, but I'm starting to see the light," I answer with a yawn. "What time is it?"

He reaches to the bedside table and clicks on his phone. "A little after four. Go back to sleep. It will almost be time to go home when you wake up." He continues to look down at his phone, and I study his profile in the shadow of the light. He's got the outlines of stubble growing in, and I bet he'd look even more handsome with a close beard. But it would cover that striking jaw line of his; that would be a damn shame. I may be in love with his brother, but Sawyer is still one of the best-looking men I've ever laid eyes on.

His eyes slowly meet mine and he looks at me expectantly. "Well?" he prompts, and I sit up a bit in bed.

"Does he know yet?" I whisper, hoping Noah can't hear me.

With a slight shake of his head, he answers, "I don't think so. He hasn't said much. He's mostly been moaning. It blows they don't

297

want to give him anything for pain for a few days other than acetaminophen."

"How do we tell him that? And what about the police? They're going to want to talk to him."

"Shh, Princess, we'll handle it. Tony is already handling the police. They won't get near either of you until he says it's okay. When Noah is ready, we'll tell him … together. Okay?"

"Yeah, okay."

"You know, Belle was right tonight," he says suddenly.

"About what?"

"About how bad it would have sucked if you would have died. Don't ever do that, Princess, okay?"

"I'll try my best."

I'm tired, but as strange as it sounds, I'm also enjoying this special time with Sawyer. I'm sure it makes me a horrible person, but I love his vulnerable side. When he gets like this, all I want to do is bottle our time together and make it last forever. Someday, I hope he lets someone in enough to see this side of him all the time. She'll be one lucky girl.

"Sawyer," Noah calls out softly. Sawyer swivels his chair around and faces Noah, giving him all the attention he needs.

"Hey, Noah, what do you need?"

"Do we have security set up outside?"

"No one is getting in here, Noah. The hospital is locked up tight. We're good. I'm not letting anything else happen to you. I promise." Sawyer reaches over and clutches Noah's hand. I can't see his face, but the way Sawyer's shoulders slump defeatedly tells me all I need to know. He blames himself for what happened tonight, but it's not his fault.

"You saved us, Sawyer. Stop thinking anything other than that because it's the absolute truth. If you guys hadn't come back, there would've been a completely different ending. One that would have sucked," I joke lightly. He nods but keeps all his attention focused on Noah.

"Is everyone okay?" Noah asks, sounding a little more clearheaded than before.

"Yeah, man, everyone is good. You two will be discharged in a few hours, and then we can focus on the two of you getting better."

I close my eyes and listen to the two of them talk about random things. The sounds of their voices comfort me as I fall back asleep.

"Sawyer, it's okay."

"I wouldn't do that to you, Noah. You have to know that." Sawyers words are desperate, and I wonder what they're talking about. I've got a feeling it has something to do with me, so I keep my eyes closed a bit longer.

"I do," Noah replies softly. "Aside from Mel, you are the most important person in my life, Sawyer. Don't ever forget that." His words aren't cautionary; they're pleading with Sawyer to realize how much he means to Noah.

"I know, and no matter what you might think, I'm glad you found her. The two of you are sickeningly perfect together."

"What I think, Sawyer, is you put up a brave front, but deep down inside you're ready to settle down, too."

Before Sawyer has a chance to reply, I yawn. I'm not sure why I feel the need to save him from answering Noah. When I finally open my eyes, the room is bright from the sun peeking through the blinds.

"Good morning, Sleeping Beauty," Noah says with a small smile.

"Morning," I answer, looking between him and Sawyer. Neither of them look great. "How do you feel today?" I ask, turning my gaze to Noah. He's got a big bruise on the side of his face I didn't see last night in the dark. It looks beyond painful, but I try not to focus on it because I'm sure he hasn't seen it yet.

"My head hurts but I can't sleep. I just want to go home and get into my own bed."

"Did you get any sleep at all?" I ask, turning my attention to Sawyer.

"Sleep is for pussies. I'll sleep when you two are home safe and sound."

"Did someone mention pussy?" Wyatt asks with a forced smile as he peeks his head inside the door.

"What are you doing here so early?" Noah asks him. It's only then I realize they're still talking in low tones. Noah's head must hurt worse than he's letting on.

Wyatt shrugs and puts his hands in his pockets, propping himself at the foot of my bed. "I didn't get to see any of you guys last night, and I didn't sleep for shit. My best friend and his girlfriend were almost killed. Can't blame a guy for wanting to see for himself they're okay."

Noah releases a frustrated sigh. "What aren't you guys telling me?"

"Nothing, Noah. There's nothing you need to know right now that you shouldn't try to let come back to you organically."

"Mel, I love you, but you're a bullshit liar."

Sawyer and Wyatt chuckle at his words and then Sawyer shrugs, deferring to me. "It's your call."

Great. Put it all on me. "Fine. But first, you two go out for a few minutes. Let me pee and make sure I'm not going to flash you all my ass. Then we'll talk."

"It is a mighty fine ass," Noah quips, making us all laugh.

After they step into the hall, I gather my gown around me and make my way into the bathroom. At least the last time they came in to check my vitals they removed that stupid IV, so moving around is much easier.

After relieving myself and washing my hands, I go to Noah's bed and climb in with him. He scoots to the side and wraps his arm around me, hissing with the movement. "Noah, it's okay, I'll go back to my bed. You really should stay still if you can."

"The hell I will. I might not be able to do much, but if I have to lie in bed for a week or more, I'm going to at least be able to put my arms around my girl."

"Okay," I reply, kissing him softly before reaching across the table and grabbing my phone. It only takes a second for them to come back in after I text Sawyer it's okay.

"It's bad, isn't it?" Noah questions after Sawyer and Wyatt perch themselves on my bed.

"It depends on your definition of bad," Wyatt answers truthfully.

"What's the last thing you remember?" Sawyer asks.

"Leaving the club with everyone. Mac and Ryan were checking the cars. After that, it's all a blur."

"We left. Me, J, and Mac. The cars were clear."

I pick up where Sawyer leaves off. "There was someone screaming. Ryan told us to get in the car and call 911 while he went to check it out. You had me climb in first, and you were right behind me, but then ..." I'm choked up even thinking about it.

"Then what?" Noah presses.

"Then she hit you on the back of the head with a gun. Split your head wide open and knocked you out cold." I absolutely hate having to tell him this.

"Sara?" he whispers as he clutches me tightly.

"Yeah, it was Sara," I confirm.

"Crazy bitch left you on the ground bleeding out." Sawyer picks up my slack and continues the story. "She had Princess at gunpoint when we got back. Ryan hit the panic button as soon as the screaming started, so we turned around and came back. Sara was ..."

"What, Sawyer?" Noah pleads.

"Damn, Noah, she was insane. She was about to kill her. Her finger was on the trigger, and the gun was pressed against Princesse's head. I thought we were too late. I thought we were going to lose you both." Sawyer takes a deep breath and moves to the window overlooking the city below. When he turns around, anger flashes in his eyes.

"She was almost successful. If Mac hadn't taken the only shot he could get, this would be a different conversation. Even so, it was a long few minutes before we knew if Princess was okay. There was so much blood."

Noah trembles against me as he begins to understand what Sawyer went through last night. Not only because of Sara but because of his past.

Sawyer continues, "After Mac shot Sara, her body flew into Princess with such force. There was so much blood everywhere. I had to get inside the car and pull Sara off her just to make sure she was alive."

Noah grips me even tighter, but I still feel him shaking. "I'm okay, though. Just a superficial gunshot wound. It's my battle scar," I say, trying to lighten the mood a bit.

"And Sara?" he asks tightly.

"She's gone, Noah. I'm so sorry."

Sawyer and Wyatt throw daggers at me with their eyes, and Noah exhales on a sob. He pulls me closer and kisses the top of my head repeatedly. "Don't you ever be sorry for living, Mel. If it weren't for me, you'd have never been put in that situation."

"Fuck no. Don't put that shit on yourself. Sara's death is Sara's fault. That bitch was crazy, and the tragedy here is she never got the help she needed before she died. But this isn't something *either* of you could have prevented."

"What he said," Wyatt agrees, pointing to Sawyer.

There's a knock at the door and Dr. Martin comes inside.

"Noah, you're looking a bit better this morning. How's the head?"

"Hurts but I'll live."

Dr. Martin smiles wide. "You sure will, which is a good thing because I need someone to feed me next Thanksgiving."

Noah chuckles. "I've got your back, don't worry."

"I have some good news, Ms. Greyson. We received all the labs back from the deceased, and her blood is clear of any infectious diseases and STIs. You won't need any long-term antibiotic therapy or drug protocols. You got lucky."

"I don't understand," Noah says, confused. Dr. Martin looks to Sawyer, realizing he may have said more than he should have.

"When Sara was shot, we were inches apart. Her body slammed into mine, that's how I got the bullet wound. Her blood basically drained out of her onto me. Until Sawyer got her off." I spare him the details about my eyes. He doesn't need to know any of that.

"Motherfucker."

I'm not sure I've ever heard Noah use that word in anger before, but I guess it's appropriate for the circumstances.

Dr. Martin tries to ease the tense atmosphere. "I've written out all your discharge instructions and went over them with your parents and Sawyer this morning. I gave Amelia a breakdown of them last night. If you have any questions, you know how to reach me. Someone from psych will be down to ask you each a few quick exit questions and then you'll be free to go home. Noah, you'll need to follow up with a doctor or neurologist in the next week, but if you need anything in the meantime, you know how to reach me."

"Thanks, Dr. Martin."

"Always a pleasure, Noah, but next time let's keep you out of my ER, okay?"

"Sounds like a plan."

Dr. Martin turns back to me. "Ms. Greyson, do you have any questions?"

"No, Dr. Martin, but thank you."

With a nod and a smile, he pats Noah on the leg and makes his exit.

"Sawyer, get Mel some fucking clothes and get us out of here. I'm done. Do whatever you have to do and get us the fuck out of here."

Wyatt and Sawyer exchange concerned glances. I've never heard Noah talk like that to anyone except Sawyer the night he did drugs.

"Mom's got clothes for you both out in the hall," Sawyer replies softly, obviously unsure how to deal with Noah's mood.

"I'll get them," Wyatt offers, and pops out into the hall.

"It's going to be okay, Noah," I try reassuring him, but he shrugs me off.

"None of this is even close to being okay, Mel. Not by a longshot."

When Wyatt brings the clothes back in, he and Sawyer leave quickly so we can get changed. Noah hisses as he tries to sit up.

"Here, let me help you." I offer him my hand, and he looks up at me with tear-filled eyes.

"I should be helping you, not the other way around. I fucking failed you last night. I'm so sorry." Noah's shoulders shake with uncontrolled sobs, breaking my heart. Crouching in front of him, I lift his head and cup it in my hands, carefully avoiding his bruise.

"Don't do this, Noah. You could never fail me. You pushed me into the car, you covered me with your body, protected me from what was coming, even if you didn't know it. This isn't your failure, Noah, it's just something that happened. We're still here and we're okay. A little worse for the wear, but both alive. Don't use this as an opportunity to push me away. Not after I bared my heart to you last night."

Pressing our lips together softly, I use my thumbs to wipe away his frustrated tears. I've never seen him like this. I know the doctor said he could be emotional, and I've got all the patience in the world for this man. "I love you, Noah, and we'll handle this together. Let's just get home, okay?"

He presses his lips against mine and hugs me close. I'm trying to not lose my balance as I let go of his face and reach around his waist to hug him back.

Belle's Post-Shooting Update

Slammers!

It's your girl Belle with your latest update on Noah and Mel. As you're well aware by now, Noah Weston and Amelia Greyson, were in an altercation last night, along with their bodyguard Ryan Goodall. Thankfully, they're all going to be fine with some TLC.

As you may have already heard, there was also a fatality at the scene. The identity of the person is being withheld until their family is notified, but rest assured it is *not* a member of BAD or anyone from their family or crew.

I'll give you more updates as they're available, but please take a few moments today to hug your loved ones tightly. Crazy things happen in this world, and none of us are exempt from them.

Live today like there's no tomorrow.

Xs and Os

Belle

We're In This Together

When we left the hospital, Sawyer and Wyatt pushed our wheelchairs side-by-side while Noah and I held hands the whole way to the car. Times like these are when I really *hate* the media. As soon as we're pushed outside, paparazzi and fans are screaming, yelling, and crying as they try to get Noah's attention. Poor guy is wincing like crazy. Can't they tell he's in pain?

Noah is one of the most generous celebrities I've ever met. He never has an issue talking to fans or stopping for selfies or autographs. He might be ready to live his life, but he knows he owes his success to the people who buy his albums, and he's never once acted above them. But today, for the first time in all this madness, I find myself wishing they would just leave him alone.

A few reporters are trying to get my attention because I'm a story now, too, but I'm good at ignoring them—I have for years—and the only person I want to give a statement to has a direct line to BAD's fan base at her fingertips. After security ushers us safely into the car and we pull away from the hospital, Noah releases a loud sigh of relief.

"Police escorts?" I say to no one in particular as I notice them all around us.

"After last night, they want to be sure you get home safe. I'm sure they'd like a statement, too, but Tony is waiting at the house to make sure that doesn't happen until you're ready," Sawyer answers as he drives.

"Why are you driving?"

"You're just full of questions, huh, Princess?" I catch his smirk in the rearview mirror, but he schools it quickly. "Mac and Ryan wanted to be here, but I told them to wait at the house. They both feel bad and they've been through a lot."

Noah squeezes my hand with a sad look on his face. I didn't really think about the fact Mac killed someone last night—someone he actually knew and spent time with, even if she was crazy.

"Do they have families? Mac and Ryan?" I don't know why I'm suddenly so chatty, but I feel like conversation is important right now.

"Not locally. Mac's family is in Washington, and Ryan's is in Arizona. Both of them have been with us for years, and I think they're looking forward to having some downtime to date and stabilize their lives a bit," Wyatt answers.

"Are they going to be out of a job?" My high-pitched tone makes even Noah chuckle lightly.

He brings my hand to his lips and kisses it tenderly. "No, babe, we'll still need security even if we're not touring. They've agreed to stay with us for the immediate future."

Knowing they'll be around makes me feel much better. That was one of the worst things about losing my dad: knowing everyone was out of a job.

"Penny for your thoughts?" Noah says softly, and I shake myself out of my funk.

"They're not worth that much."

He squeezes my hand tighter. "They're worth a million times that. Come on, Mel, tell me what you're thinking."

"I was just remembering how after my dad died the staff and crew were all suddenly out of work. I felt awful and made sure they were all paid for a full year."

"That was generous."

This topic is not my favorite; I'm going to get choked up if we keep talking about it. "No, it was necessary. They were family and they lost their patriarch. It was hard on everyone."

The car is suddenly quiet but not uncomfortably so. I enjoy the silence before we get back to the house and are bombarded with well wishes and questions. Sooner than I'd hoped for, Sawyer turns the car up the drive and he and Wyatt help us out of the car. I'm fine, I don't need help, but I accept it hoping Noah will be as gracious.

Tony is waiting on the front porch and when he sees the detective behind us step out of his car, he jumps into action. Tony walks briskly to the detective's car, engaging him in conversation. I'm beginning to see Tony is worth his weight in gold.

"You're here!" Karen exclaims happily with fresh tears running down her cheeks.

"Shh, Mom, my head," Noah tells her as he hugs her tightly. Rory, Diane, Owen, Mac, and Ryan are all sitting at the table, and they look exhausted. Belle, Darren, Anna, and Eli are all on the couch.

"Eli? What are you doing here?"

306

He rises and walks over to me, pulling me into his warm embrace. "I just got you back into my life and you almost get yourself killed. Where else would I be? Did you tell him?"

Eli being here makes this whole thing real. It suddenly hits me how lucky we were last night. My tears begin to fall as I hug him back. "Yeah, I did, and I should thank you for pushing me. If last night had gone differently …"

"Shh, it didn't, and that's all that matters. Noah, how are you feeling?" Eli asks as he steps back and Noah slides his arm around my waist.

"I've seen better days, but I'll live. Thanks for coming, I know it means a lot to Mel."

Eli shoves his hands in his pockets and shrugs; he looks so much like the teenage boy I fell in love with in this moment. "I'm just hoping for a fresh slate for all of us from here on out. I've missed my best friend."

Noah releases me and extends his hand to Eli in a warm gesture of friendship. "You're welcome anytime." After Eli and Noah shake hands, Noah turns to the group. "Look, I know you're all here because you love us and you were worried about us, but we're fine. I do want to go lie down and talk to Mel for a bit. We can catch you all up on details later. Ryan, Mac, will you come to my room with us for a minute?"

Mac and Ryan both wear impenetrable gazes, I've got no idea what they must be thinking or what Noah wants to talk to them about. Noah leads the way and kicks off his shoes the second he crosses the threshold into his room. *Our* room. I need to get used to that.

"Boss, I'm so sorry," Ryan begins with remorseful eyes.

"Stop. Don't even go there. I wanted a minute alone with you both to let you know how much I appreciate you putting your lives on the line for us. Last night was a situation we should have never been in. Both of you went above and beyond the call of duty, and I appreciate it more than you could ever know."

"But boss, if I wouldn't have left you, she wouldn't have gotten to you," Ryan counters, clearly upset by the evening's events.

"Or she would have gotten to you first. She caught us all off guard and we all fell into her trap. What if that hadn't been Sara's friends? What if some girl was being raped and murdered over behind that dumpster and we all ignored it out of fear for our own safety? I don't know about you, but I'd feel pretty fucking shitty about that."

God, I love this man.

"Now, stop feeling guilty. You're both getting raises. Sara isn't a threat anymore and while I'm out of commission, I want you both to take some time off. Especially you, Mac. Where's your head at after what happened last night?"

Mac looks him square in the eye, but his stoic expression never falters. "I did what I had to do. It's part of the job. Would I rather not have it on my conscience? Sure. But I'd do it again in a heartbeat. She was seconds away from killing Mel."

Noah pulls out two business cards from his pocket and hands one to each man. "Dr. Martin recommends this therapist. I'll take care of the bill, but you both need to go see her at least once, or as many times as you need to be okay with what happened. It's not a suggestion, either. I want a note from her stating you saw her and you're cleared for duty."

With mutual nods of understanding, they both turn to leave.

"Guys, wait," I call out behind them, and they turn back around. First, I pull Ryan into a quick hug. "Thank you." Tears flood my eyes as he squeezes me back and when I hug Mac, they're streaming down my cheeks. "You saved our lives last night ... somehow thank you doesn't seem like enough."

Mac clears his throat while hugging me back. "It's more than enough. The fact you're here to tell the tale is everything. I feel bad about Sara, but I wouldn't have been able to live with myself if something had happened to either of you," he manages to say over the lump in his throat.

When they leave, Noah releases an exhausted sigh. "Lay with me?"

As if I'd deny him.

"Can I get you anything first?" I ask as I kick off my shoes.

"Right now, I just need you in my arms."

After Noah makes himself comfortable, I climb into bed and wrap my arms around him. Noah's fingers glide through my hair as we lay together in silence. When Noah looks up at me with tears streaming down his cheeks, my heart breaks into a million pieces.

"Talk to me, Noah," I plead with him softly, staying mindful of his headache. He reminds me of a wounded child the way he clings to me and cries. I wish I could take all his pain away.

"I don't know how I'm supposed to feel," he finally admits as his eyes meet mine. "I'm relieved we're alive, I'm so happy you weren't hurt more than you were, I'm pissed at Sara, but even worse, I'm sad she's gone and I don't know how to process that fact."

"Maybe you just have to let it sink in. You're injured and your emotions are all over the place right now. But Noah, no matter what, you cared about her once, and even though she ended up having issues, you're allowed to grieve no matter what anyone thinks."

"I don't want to grieve for her, Mel!" As he screams, he grabs his head and I release him from my arms. Noah's never yelled at me before; I've only ever heard him yell at Sawyer. "Shit," he hisses through his teeth, and his eyes are closed when I look over at him. I know he needs time and I shouldn't take things personally, but I do.

There's a soft rap at the door. *Saved by the bell.*

Jordan pops his head in as he opens the door. "Hey, I just wanted to come by and see how you're doing." The relief in his eyes is evident, and I use the opportunity to get a few minutes to myself.

"Come in, Jordan. I was just going to go see Belle for a little bit. Why don't you keep Noah company for a while?"

"Sure, I can do that, no problem," he replies with a grateful smile. After closing the door behind me, I walk up the hall and knock on Darren's door before taking a chance with the masses.

"Come in," Darren calls out. When I open his door, he and Belle are sitting with their heads together, browsing a baby catalog. I'm so glad they're doing something normal and not hovering around like everyone else.

"What's wrong?" Belle asks, patting the bed beside her.

"Nothing," I answer on a sigh.

"Liar," she retorts, earning a laugh from Darren.

"It's nice to see her call other people out on their shit," he says, still chuckling.

"Seriously, it's not a big deal. Noah is emotional and he snapped at me. I know it's his injury but it hurt my feelings. I just needed a few minutes to regroup, that's all."

"Aww, you're emotional, too. You've both been through a lot in the past twenty-four hours. He loves you, babe, he just needs some time to process things. Speaking of processing, Mama and Eli want you to call them when you're up to it."

"Eli left?" I feel bad I didn't get to talk to him more.

"He *finally* left," Darren grumbles.

"Stop. Eli's a good guy when he wants to be. He came back here with us from the hospital. He wasn't about to leave until he saw you for himself." From Belle's tone, I can tell she's forgiven Eli, too.

"That's sweet. I'll text him later and thank him. Tell Mama I'll call her as soon as I'm up to it, but give her my love."

"Look, Noah's my boy, so I have to ask … you don't want Eli back, do you?"

The look of horror on my face must answer his question because he throws up his arms in mock surrender. "Okay, don't freeze me with your icy glare. I just wanted to be sure Noah didn't have anything to worry about."

Belle whacks him on top of the head with her baby catalog and answers for me, "You fool. Amelia would never leave Noah for Eli or anyone else."

"Not ever," I confirm, suddenly feeling emotional. "So … what are you guys looking at?" I ask, hoping to change the subject.

Belle smiles sheepishly. "Nursery themes. I love baby Winnie the Pooh and Sesame Street Babies."

"And I like the baby zoo animals and the celestial-themed one with stars and moons," Darren adds, pointing them out as he hands me the catalog.

"They're all cute," I say, flipping through the pages until I come to one that makes me pause. "If it were me, I'd get this one." I point at the one I like and pass it back.

"Dr. Seuss?" Darren questions curiously.

"I love Dr. Seuss, but that's specifically from *Oh, the Places You'll Go!*, the best Dr. Seuss book. It's all about how your future is what you make of it and how you can do anything you set your mind to. It's one of my all-time favorite books."

"I always thought his books were creepy. Just because you can rhyme doesn't make it less weird with all those imaginary characters drawn in them." Darren shudders while reminiscing.

"Well, maybe it will be easier for you to pick a theme once you know what you're having. When do you find out?"

"Next month," Belle answers excitedly. "But we already know it's a girl. I just feel it."

"What do you think, Darren?" I ask.

"I'll be happy with whatever, but the thought of a mini Belle running around is pretty cool."

"Have you guys talked at all about logistics? Where the baby is going to be born and where you'll live? What you'll do while the guys wrap up the tour?"

Belle bites her bottom lip; I can tell they haven't from the look in her eyes.

"What's there to talk about? Belle is touring with us the last three months for *Slammed*. The baby should be here then so the baby will be on the bus with us," he answers like it's a no-brainer. Belle doesn't look as thrilled with the idea. Since I opened Pandora's box, I'm going to excuse myself.

"Alright then, I'm going to let you talk and go check on Noah."

"Let me know if you need anything," Belle calls out behind me.

I pause outside our door and take a deep, steady breath. When I walk inside, I'm surprised to see Sawyer and Noah lying in bed together, both napping. Seeing them together reminds me what a huge part of each other they really are. The fact they're twins makes their relationship that much more intense. It makes me happy but sets me off-kilter a bit as well. I realize they've never been apart. And I wonder how that will work when they find love and get married. Will they always want to live together? How will they function being apart? It's too much to think about right now. Backing out quietly, I make my way into the kitchen for some water.

It's quiet out here; everyone must be recovering from last night. There's a large photo album on the table, and I take it with me to the couch so I can look through it. The opening page says "Noah and Sawyer" on it. It starts off with pictures of Karen and Owen when they were probably my age at a baby shower. God, her belly was huge!

It immediately moves into hospital photos of them with the twins right after they were born. They were so tiny. I bet it was almost impossible to tell them apart at first. Soon enough, you can see their differences. It seems Noah's hair has always been lighter, and Sawyer's smile looks like it's always had a devilish hint to it. Their matching outfits make them even cuter and although they aren't identical, I'm not sure I'd have been able to resist dressing twins the same, either.

I'm lost in the album when someone sits down next to me. When I look up, Noah puts his arm around me.

"What are you doing up?"

"Better question, why aren't you in bed with me?" he asks as his fingers trace a photo of him and Sawyer on their third birthday.

"You and Sawyer were knocked out. I wanted to let you guys sleep. You both had a rough night last night. I was going to come back to check on you in a little while, but I got distracted with these pictures."

"I told you I'd show you pictures that night on the beach. My mom must have been feeling sentimental and taken the album out of the office. I'd love to see your childhood pictures. Do you have any?"

That's a complicated answer but one I owe him. "I do … Some of them are in my storage, but the bulk of them are at the house."

311

"The house? Whose house?" he asks cautiously.

"Mine ... my parents' ... the one in Bel Air," I admit sheepishly.

"Jesus, Mel. You still have their house? Weren't you living in a one-bedroom apartment?" His shocked tone isn't surprising; I'm sure I'd react the same.

"I was. I haven't been inside the house since a few days after his funeral. Until she died, my grandma took care of the staff, the details. Now, I do ... sort of. I have a property management company I pay to keep up on everything. Landscaping, monthly cleaning, those kinds of things. But the inside is basically a museum. Nothing has been changed since my mom died."

"That long?"

With a shrug, I reply, "I know it sounds silly, but my dad couldn't bring himself to go there after we lost her. If we needed something, someone brought it to us. Then, after he died, I went back and dropped some things off and picked a few things up, but it was just so empty I couldn't stand it. We never spent a lot of time there, anyway. Well, *I* didn't. My grandma's house was where I spent most of my time. That house was more of a hideaway for my parents."

Noah lifts my hand to his mouth and kisses it sweetly. "I'd be happy to go with you, Mel. If you ever want to ... well ... just go and remember the good times."

"Thanks, I'll keep that in mind. I'm not ready yet, but someday I will be, and I'll need you by my side."

"Anytime, anywhere, you know that," he answers with a yawn, which is sort of funny since Sawyer walks in at the same moment yawning.

"You guys could have woken me up. I didn't mean to keep you out of your room," he says as he moves into the kitchen and starts taking food out of the refrigerator.

"You didn't. I woke up and wanted to see where Mel went. I found her looking through our baby pictures," Noah tells him with a chuckle.

"Tell him the truth, Princess. I was the cuter twin, don't you think?" Sawyer flashes a devilish smile my way, and I get the feeling by Noah's groan this has been an ongoing battle for a long time.

"Don't encourage him, Mel," Noah cautions.

"Hmm ... well ... let me see," I tell them as I look through some more pages. "You both were pretty cute, and those matching outfits are sort of like the icing on the cake. I'd say you're equally adorable."

"She's just being nice because she's your girlfriend. We all know I'm the hotter brother," Sawyer replies in a teasing tone.

"Hotter, I'm not so sure. Pain in my ass, most definitely. I'm going to go lie down for a while. You coming, Mel?"

Closing the photo album, I look up into Noah's eyes. We really need some alone time.

"You guys want some sandwiches? They'll be ready in about ten minutes," Sawyer offers before we leave.

"I'm pretty hungry, I could eat." I didn't realize it until he offered food, but I'm starving. Noah takes my hand in his and I stand quickly. I don't want him exerting himself by pulling me up.

"Yeah, come get us when they're done. I'm hungry, too," Noah adds.

"Sure thing," Sawyer answers, getting back to his sandwich making.

Once we're lying together in bed, I feel like I can finally breathe for the first time today. We're still holding hands, both of us lost in our own thoughts. I can't imagine how conflicted Noah must be. I want to talk to him about it, but I'd rather he heal physically before delving into the emotional mess he's likely struggling with on the inside.

"What are you thinking about?" he whispers, as if reading my mind.

A warm feeling rushes over me as I suddenly realize how blessed I am that he's even here with me right now to be able to ask me that question. "Too many things to even narrow down." My reply is evasive but truthful … to an extent.

"Yeah, I know the feeling," Noah replies as his eyelids flutter closed. After a few minutes, his hand loosens and soon falls from mine. A soft snore escapes from his mouth; even that brings a smile to my face.

With a soft knock on the door, Sawyer sticks his head in and whispers, "Come eat."

I hold up a finger indicating I'll be there in a minute, and he nods as he steps back out into the hall. I'm hungry but also enjoying watching Noah sleep. It's rare when I get the opportunity to do this. When he sleeps, he's truly peaceful; there's no fear or worry marring his beautiful features. Even though Noah is one of the most worry-free people I've ever met, the past week or so since Sara reappeared gave me an insight to how deeply he feels things.

Noah would do anything to protect the people he loves—they *all* would. Seeing the band and their crew jump into action and do all they can to step up and band together during all of this is enlightening. It's not often people have true friends they can count on like this. I've only had Belle for years, and now the guys—Eli, too, of course.

My phone vibrates in my pocket and when I pull it out, I have a text message from Sawyer. When I open it, it's a video clip of "Eat It" by Weird Al Yankovic. I carefully slip out of bed, covering my mouth to stifle my laugh.

When I walk into the kitchen, Sawyer is sitting at the table looking up at me with a knowing smile.

"Weird Al, really?"

With a shrug, he replies, "What? It worked, didn't it? You need to keep up your strength, Princess. After you eat, I'll help you swap out your dressing."

I hadn't even thought about my dressing.

"Thanks, I could use some help with that. This looks good … are you normally such a master sandwich maker?"

"Practice makes perfect. We fend for ourselves a lot on the bus, as you've seen firsthand. I've learned a few tricks over the years, I guess. Food on the road gets so repetitive after a while, but you know this already … you've lived the life." He takes a bite of his pickle and passes me a bag of chips.

Noah's plate sits waiting; I wish he were up to eating it. "It's really quiet still. Where is everyone?"

"I sent all the non-essentials home. They'll be back tomorrow. Everyone else is in their rooms catching up on sleep."

"Who do you consider a non-essential?" I ask, trying not to choke on my sandwich. I've never heard him refer to anyone that way before.

"My parents, Rory, Diane, anyone who is just going to sit here and hover over you guys. After what went down last night, I figured we all needed some time to regroup. J's in the room he has here. I wanted him close after it all. I'm pretty sure he took his anti-anxiety meds and crashed."

The look in Sawyer's eyes right now is hard for me to accurately describe. Maybe a cross of concern and love? He's different today, probably because he's in caretaker mode and his defenses are down. But I'm pretty sure I'm seeing who Sawyer could be if he'd only let people in.

"You didn't have to do that. We would have dealt with them. I'm sure they're just worried."

He throws his crumpled napkin onto his plate and leans back against his chair. "Maybe I'm selfish. I didn't want to deal with them, either. My mom started throwing the past into the present and I just can't handle that shit right now, you know?"

"Of course, but they only do it because they love you, Sawyer. You're lucky to have people around you who do." My words come out softer than I mean for them to, but for some reason, especially today, I miss my parents.

We sit in silence for a bit as I finish my sandwich. Sawyer is fidgety, like he doesn't know what to do with himself. "Sawyer, if you want to talk about it, you know … like, ever, not necessarily now … I'm here."

He tugs his lip ring into his mouth and quickly releases it. Memories of our kiss flood my mind as I stand up and grab Noah's plate. "Do you want to help me with that bandage now?" I ask, trying to take my mind off the sudden flashback.

"Sure, lead me to the exam room."

With a laugh, Sawyer follows me into the bedroom, where we find Noah sitting up on the edge of the bed holding his head. "Hey," he croaks, barely moving his head enough to look up at me.

After placing his sandwich on the nightstand, I grab his bottle of water and the acetaminophen next to it. "Maybe we should take you back to the doctor."

He reaches for the pills I just poured into my hand and takes them. "I'll be fine. Dr. Martin said the first few days would be rough." His firm tone leaves no room for argument. "What are you guys doing?"

"I'm going to change her bandage," Sawyer states and walks toward the bathroom. Noah's eyes are filled with sadness when they meet mine.

"Yeah, that makes sense. How often do you have to change it?" Noah reaches for his plate and takes a bite of his pickle.

"Twice a day until I have my follow-up appointment."

With a slight nod, he turns his attention to his food and I follow Sawyer into the bathroom, leaving the door wide open so Noah has a clear view of us. I really wish I could do this myself.

Sawyer hisses as he removes the bandage, as if it's hurting him. "You okay, Sawyer?" Noah calls from the bed.

"I'm fine," he grumbles as he quickly tosses away the old bandage.

I catch sight of my wound in the mirror. It's nasty looking— oozing and raw—with the surrounding tissues black and blue. It's going to leave one hell of a scar, I don't even know how many layers of skin are missing, but it's probably going to take a while to grow back. I decided not to take any of the pain pills I got from the hospital. My teeth clench, and I suck in air through them as Sawyer pats the wound and covers it with the antibiotic ointment.

"Why didn't you take your meds?" The pissed-off tone in his voice is evident and before I know it, Noah is standing next to me with his water and my pills.

"I'm fine. You two need to stop mothering me. I don't want the medicine, okay?"

"Nope, not okay," Sawyer snaps back as Noah takes a more human approach.

"Why, Mel? They don't just give out pain pills like candy anymore. You wouldn't have gotten them if they didn't think you needed them."

These two are impossible.

"If you can't have meds, I don't need them, either. Your injuries are worse than mine."

Sawyer wraps the gauze around my arm, and I can't help but flinch; it stings like a bitch.

"Different injuries, different treatment. Take the pills, Mel," Noah insists, and I give in. Not only because I really am in pain but because he's clutching the counter with white knuckles, doing his best to stay upright while trying to take care of me the only way he can right now.

After I swallow the pills, Sawyer tapes my arm and throws away the trash. Sawyer then helps Noah back to bed, and I close the door so I can use the restroom. When I'm finished, I look at myself in the mirror as I wash my hands. I look like death warmed over. It's only afternoon, but I suddenly feel like I could sleep for a week.

Sawyer is gone and the door is closed when I come out of the bathroom. "Do you need anything, Noah?"

"Just you. Come get some rest." With a yawn, I crawl in next to him and wrap myself in his embrace. "Next time, take the pills, babe. It will make it easier on Sawyer if you're not in pain while he changes your bandage."

"Easier? I didn't think I was being difficult."

"Did you ask for his help?" Noah's voice has an edge to it; if I didn't know better, I'd think he was jealous.

"No, he offered. Since you can't help right now, and Belle is squeamish, I took him up on it."

"So is he," Noah murmurs.

"He's what?"

"Squeamish, big time. Sawyer hates seeing even a papercut. He's been this way since before he ever walked into J's house that day. But Sawyer is good about doing things he hates for the people he cares about." Noah brushes my hair away from my face as I let his words wash over me.

"I feel awful. I didn't know ..."

"It's okay, Mel, he wouldn't have offered if he were unwilling."

Looking deeply into his eyes, I confess some of what I haven't told him yet. "Last night, when Sawyer pulled me from the car, there was blood everywhere. He pulled off his shirt and used it to clean my face, my eyes ... I couldn't see. Then he held it to my wound to keep it from bleeding. We were both covered in blood at that point. The whole situation was a nightmare, but now I know he's got issues ... I mean, I figured he might but not to this extent."

Noah hugs me close and kisses me gently. "I'm sorry I wasn't the one who helped you, and I'm so sorry my past nearly got you killed. I'll spend the rest of my life trying to make this up to you, Mel, I promise."

"Just love me, Noah, and never let me go. Last night wasn't your fault, but it was a wakeup call. I don't want to waste another minute of my life, especially where we're concerned. The next month is going to give us plenty of time to do things and get to know even more about each other, and I can't wait."

"That I can do easily. Not loving you has never been an option. I meant what I told Rory ... from the minute you told Sawyer off at The Greek I knew there was something special about you."

I nestle my head into the crook of Noah's arm and fall asleep to the sound of his heartbeat in my ear and his fingers playing with my hair.

By the time I wake up, it's dark outside. Noah is fast asleep next to me and even though I try, I can't fall back asleep. My mind is running a million miles a minute with no direct cause. It's all just a rampant mashup of fleeting memories of my parents, our house, my grandma, Eli, Belle, and Sara; it's making me anxious.

Finally, I reach over and grab my phone from the table. After propping myself up on some pillows, I adjust myself, hoping to block the glow of my phone from Noah. He finally seems to be resting peacefully, and I don't want to disturb him.

D. Kelly

As I browse through my emails, I groan in frustration. There are
so many media requests for exclusive stories from my perspective as
Noah's girlfriend, as the *New York Times* Bestselling Author, as the
daughter of Joey and Iris Triton, and of course, someone even pulled
the "official BAD biographer" card. I'm not even going to waste my
time answering them and likely never will. This is Noah's story to tell
if he ever decides he wants to.

Belle and I end up texting back and forth for a bit, but I'm still
restless. As I scroll through my earlier text messages, I realize I never
replied to the video Sawyer sent me with one of my own. "Thank
You" by Dido seems appropriate to get my point across. I'm
appreciative for him and how he's helping us *and* me. Between
saving me, staying with me, feeding us, and even helping with my
wound, Sawyer has stepped up again and again. Knowing Sawyer
cares about me enough to help me repeatedly comforts me in a way I
didn't expect. If there's anyone who surprises me at every turn, good
or bad, it's Sawyer. Life will never be boring when he's around.

When all is said and done, I spend most of the night reading
while curled up against Noah's side. He sleeps soundly through the
night; it's a relief after his painful night in the hospital. The rise and
fall of his chest keeps me calm as I watch over him. The man I love
was almost killed. I know I haven't even come close to processing
what happened, but as long as I have Noah by my side, nothing else
matters.

Sawyer never texts me back, but I didn't really expect him to. He
knows I appreciate him and I'm here for him if he ever needs the
favor returned. Who would have thought when all of this started that
Sawyer and I would end up becoming close friends?

Belle's Pre-Holiday Update

Slammers!

It's your girl Belle, and I've got the latest 411 on your BAD boys! Even though I'm your official BAD source, I'm not going to re-hash what has been filling your TV and computer screens for days. If you want details on the horrific events that happened over Thanksgiving, you can visit *slammedinc.com* and click on the exclusive on our home page.

That being said, let's get to the good updates. Noah and Mel are healing well, and the tour is on track to start up right after the new year. These guys are excited to get back on the road and pick up where they left off. On the plus side, because of the holidays, there are only two weeks of shows that had to be canceled while Noah heals from his injuries. Those shows will still be happening, but they're going to be tacked onto the end of the tour. If you were one of the cities affected, October will be your month for all things BAD.

Speaking of the holidays, since BAD is on a temporary hiatus, don't expect any new updates unless something major happens. Instead, take this time and step away from social media. Enjoy your friends and family and remember why they're so important to you. So many of us forget to slow down and take the necessary time to reflect on life and where we want to be as often as we should. Make yourself a priority this holiday season and take the time to enjoy every happiness. Life is too short to let it pass you by without being an active participant. Take time for you.

As always, don't forget ... Live today like there's no tomorrow.

Xs and Os

Belle

Making Amends

The past few days have been great. Visitors were kept at a minimum, Sawyer stayed true to his word and kept the "non-essentials" in check. Noah was having fewer episodes of dizziness and stayed awake for longer periods of time. Light still bothered him some, as well as loud noises, but we were all able to talk at a normal volume, including him. Last night, he even sat in bed and lightly strummed his guitar. He's been quiet and contemplative, but he never wants me to leave his side, either—almost like he's afraid I'm going to disappear into thin air. This morning, however, I awoke to an empty bed, which is exactly why I'm freaking out right now. I've checked the garage, his office, our room, the front and back of the house, and I can't find him anywhere. It's raining outside, so I know he's not at the beach.

"Jesus, Princess, what's got your panties in a wad?" Sawyer asks as he walks out of the pantry with a pack of Pop-Tarts.

"Noah! Have you seen him? I can't find him anywhere!"

He places his food on the counter and looks up at me. "What do you mean can't find him?"

I throw my hands up in frustration. "Exactly that. I woke up and he was gone. No note, nothing. There's no trace of him in this house. His wallet and keys are gone off the dresser. Where would he go, Sawyer?" Tears are building, and I'm trying to blink them back but it's no use. I'm scared.

Sawyer is scanning through his messages, typing furiously on his phone. Belle and Darren shuffle out of their room sleepily to see what the commotion is all about.

"What's wrong, Mel?" Belle asks softly as she wipes my tears away.

"Noah's missing," Sawyer snaps back angrily. "Wyatt and Noah aren't answering their texts." He puts his phone to his ear and makes a call. "Bethie … do you know where Wyatt is? Because him and Noah aren't answering their phones or their texts and Noah is missing. Yeah … okay, thanks. I'll let you know if they call me, too."

He slams his phone onto the counter, his frantic eyes meeting mine. "She hasn't heard from either of them, but she's going to try to reach them."

"Why would he disappear?" Squeezing Belle's hand, she winces. "Sorry, Belle."

With a smile, she replies, "It's okay, babe. Just remember this when I'm in labor and I need *your* hand." My hand drops to her belly and I rub it softly. She's got the tiniest little pooch, probably not even noticeable to anyone else except maybe Darren. Knowing the little peanut in there is growing safely away from her Auntie Mel's freak out calms me down a bit.

"When was the last time you saw him? Did he say anything strange?" All eyes are on me as I think about Sawyer's questions.

"We fell asleep in each other's arms last night, and he didn't say anything out of the ordinary. In fact, he was even playing his guitar last night."

With a frustrated groan, Sawyer picks up his phone again. "Mac, I need you to track Wyatt and Noah's phones. Target their GPS and let me know where they are ASAP. I'm sorry to interrupt your leave, but we really need your help with this … Yeah … Thanks, man."

Belle rubs my arm softly. "I'm sure everything is fine, Mel. He probably just wanted to get some air and he and Wyatt took a drive."

"But why wouldn't he leave a note? Or text me? Or answer my calls?"

"I don't know, babe, but I'm sure he has a reason. Trust him. He's never given you a reason not to."

Belle's reply sets me off. "You think this is about trust? I'm *worried* about him, Belle! Until yesterday, he almost fell over every time he stood up and now he's just out for a *joyride*? I don't buy it. Something's not right here."

"I'm with Princess. This isn't sitting right with me, either. Noah's more responsible than this. But Wyatt is a different fucking story. He'd take any of Noah's secrets to the grave if Noah asked him to." Sawyer is cut off by his ringing phone, which he promptly answers. "What did you find?" He's quiet for a minute and then his expression becomes furious. "Unfuckingbelievable. Yeah, I got it … No, it's not necessary. If he doesn't come back in an hour or two, I'll have you check it out. Thanks."

Sawyer grips the counter and blows out a breath before speaking. "They're at a shopping center, both phones pinged to the same location. Only Noah would fucking get up and go Christmas shopping this early in the morning without saying a word." Sawyer grabs his

Pop-Tarts and his coffee and storms off to his bedroom, slamming the door behind him.

"You okay, Mel?" Darren asks as he wraps his arm around Belle.

"Yeah ... sure. I'm sorry I snapped at you, Belle. I didn't mean it."

She looks up at me and shrugs "It's okay. I could have worded it better. I know Noah isn't like Eli, and I don't think he ever will be. Maybe he wanted to get you a gift and thought he'd be back sooner."

"Maybe. I'm going to go take a shower. You guys should go back to sleep. I'm sorry for waking you up like that."

After letting my frustrated tears pour out into the shower, I throw on a pair of yoga pants and a t-shirt. I'm so emotional since the accident and I can't shake it. I'm hoping it's just the pain medication setting my moods off track and it's not some sort of traumatic after-effect of what happened. Maybe I should make an appointment with the therapist just to be sure. If it doesn't go away after I stop taking the medication, I will.

The house is quiet once again, and I hesitate before knocking on Sawyer's door. The sounds of his guitar greet my ears and it's the sweetest music. He's singing along to the music, but I can't hear the words, which is a shame; Sawyer is one of the most talented singers I've ever heard, even if he spent the last nine years avoiding showing off how beautiful his voice can be. This acoustic album really highlights his voice. It would keep him in the business for decades to come if he would allow himself to follow a different path. Noah could be right there with him, too. Where Noah has a raspier effect like Bob Dylan, Sawyer has a smooth flow like Eric Clapton. Together they're a powerhouse but apart they could be legends in their own right.

Finally, I stop eavesdropping and knock on his door. "Come in," he answers immediately, smiling when he sees me. *His smile, when it's genuine and not sinful it's a sight for sore eyes.* "Hey, Princess, what can I do for you?"

Holding up the small bag of medical supplies, I ask for his help. "I was hoping you could help out a damsel in distress?"

Laughing, he lays his guitar down on his bed and stands up, motioning for me to sit down. "Of course. I was raised to never leave a damsel in distress. Any news from Noah yet?" he asks as he spreads the antibiotic ointment over my wound. It's slowly getting better but still stings. I think the pain is mostly from the muscle bruising now.

"Nope, nothing. And it really pisses me off. I've been with him night and day since before Thanksgiving and he just disappears as if everything is back to being okay? I'm actually thinking about getting a hotel until we go back on tour."

As Sawyer wraps the bandage around my arm, he remains quiet. After he tapes it down, he takes a seat next to me on the bed. "Look, Princess, I know you're pissed and you've got every right to be. I don't know what crawled up Noah's ass today, but I do know he loves you more than anything and if you leave he'll be devastated. Give him a chance to explain before you do something drastic, okay?"

He's so sweet when he's sticking up for his brother; it makes me feel like a complete bitch. "I'll try. What were you playing before? It sounded great."

Sawyer rolls his eyes at me. "You would think that since I was playing something that isn't mine. It was "So" by Ed Sheeran."

"I love him, he's so talented. Will you play it for me?"

Sawyer is suddenly blushing, and I want to tease him about it, but for some reason I have the feeling this is a big deal for him. "I don't typically do solo performances for people, especially on demand."

"Oh, come on. You sing in front of me on the bus every day while you guys are practicing."

"Yeah, but that's group rehearsal. Regardless of what you may think, I'm not comfortable going solo. The guys are kind of my buffers in a way."

Wow ... that's different.

"So what about for your girlfriends? You don't sing for them, either?"

With a slight shake of his head, Sawyer leans back on his elbows while I scoot back up against his headboard so I can see his face. "I've never had any."

"Any what?" He *can't* mean girlfriends.

"Girlfriends." He's blushing again, and there are so many questions I want to ask him.

"*Never*, Sawyer? Why?" My heart aches for him. Why is he so closed off?

"This is just two friends talking, right? Not author and subject?"

"Of course. Even when I write the book you guys are all going to have a final say. I'd never put something in it you didn't want the world to know. I know what that's like, Sawyer, it happened to my parents all the time. Anything you tell me, that *any* of you tell me, is safe with me. I promise."

He squeezes my ankle, almost as if reassuring himself.

D. Kelly

"It's not that big of a deal. In high school, I wasn't worried about having a serious girlfriend. I was into my music. There were always going to be girls, but music felt like a limited opportunity for some reason. And where there are boys in a band there are girls offering up their virtue, so I wasn't lacking in opportunities for sex."

I laugh at his words because no matter the age, groupies are all the same. He cracks a smile, probably relieved I'm laughing and not lecturing him.

"Then we got signed and there was no time and to be honest … no motivation to find just one girl to settle with. I mean, I saw Wyatt and Anna and how solid their relationship was. I wasn't going to find something like that on the road. Something like what my parents have, or Diane and Rob."

"Is that what you want? Something solid like that?"

Trailing his fingers down my foot, he sits up and props himself next to me. "Someday, sure. I thought maybe I could have that with Marilyn, I really did have feelings for her. After all that went down, I guess you could say I lost my faith I'd find a good woman out there at all while I was involved with this industry. She was our friend and she still did that to us … imagine what a groupie would do."

This is one of the best conversations we've ever had; I'm loving the way he's opening himself up to me. "Sawyer, you have to know all women aren't like that. I understand your fears, I swear I do. I've seen those girls, and women, my entire life. But there are good women out there and you'll find yours, I promise."

"I know. I've realized that more and more lately. Seeing Darren with Belle, and you with Noah, it gives me hope. I'm still young and I'll never have any regrets some people have about not doing all the fun things they wanted to in their teenage years and beyond. I'm not even thirty and if I died tomorrow I'd have few, if any, regrets. I'm not in a place where I want a wife and kids anyway."

My gaze locks onto his, as he tugs that damn lip ring into his mouth. I swear that's my biggest weakness with him. "What do you want, Sawyer?"

He releases his lip but not his lock on my eyes. For a moment, I'm certain he's going to confess his deepest desires, but he averts his gaze at the last second instead. "To finish the tour and readjust to life. Once I figure out who I am outside of BAD, maybe I'll have a better idea about what or who I want in my future."

"I get that. Finding normal after living years of an unconventional life isn't easy. It took me a long time to adjust after everything with my parents. You'll get there, Sawyer, and I'll help

324

you however I can." He looks leery, and it annoys me. "What? You don't believe me?"

"Nah, I believe you, Princess, but this," he says, pointing between the two of us, "is new to me. I've got acquaintances in this business but I haven't made any new friends since junior high. You're the first in a long time, and I guess I need to get used to that."

With a sigh, I lean my head on his shoulder. "You and me both. My list of friends consists of Belle, Eli, and you guys. I like it that way, though."

"Why?"

"Because I don't care about the quantity of people in my life, only the quality of them, and you guys are top notch. Plus, it's nice to be surrounded by people who understand what you've gone through. I wasn't the famous one, but I get it, Sawyer. The fans, the traveling, the constant need for security ... it's the price you pay for your craft. As much as you love your fans, it would be nice if you could just go to the movies alone one day, right?"

He leans his head against mine and we stay like that for a few minutes. When he finally answers, it's with a hint of sadness. "You're exactly right. Shopping, dinner, movies, none of that is something I can just do anymore. Our fans enable us to have this lifestyle but the price we pay for it is high. Don't get me wrong, I love it, and if everyone wasn't ready to settle down I'd keep going. But it gets to me sometimes."

"Any thoughts for what you might do after?"

We both lean back against the headboard. Even though we're friends, sometimes I'm afraid we're a little too close for comfort, too.

"Nope ... well, yeah ... lots of ideas. I'm going to enjoy some down time. Maybe write some music. I could go into songwriting for others, or maybe producing. I'm definitely taking Saylor and Emme to Disneyland often. I can't fucking wait for that, actually. One of the perks of being home will be spending time with my family."

Family—there's that word again. Something everyone around me has except for me.

"You miss yours, don't you?" I feel like his green eyes can see right into my soul. It must be a Weston brother superpower.

"I do, but my family was never conventional. I learned a long time ago family is who you decide it is, not who God assigns you to. Belle, Eli, Veronica, you guys, *that's* my family. My parents and I ... we didn't have what your family does. There was no hugging like

crazy, phone calls all the time, inside jokes, we were more of a …
I'll-see-you-when-I-see-you crew."

"That's sad," he replies softly.

"Not necessarily. To you, maybe, because you have this huge,
boisterous, family. I see the difference now, but back then I didn't
know any different, so I loved them for what they were."

He grabs my hand and squeezes it gently. "You're in for it now,
Princess. There's no low key with our family. Get ready to be part of
loud and boisterous."

"Am I interrupting something?" Noah and Wyatt are standing in
the doorway, their eyes locked on our hands. Sawyer drops mine like
a hot potato, but I have nothing to be ashamed of.

"Nope, you're not interrupting a thing. I was just keeping
Princess company since she's been freaking out the last few hours and
threatening to go to a hotel. Maybe next time you should let the
people who care about you know when you're going to fucking
disappear so we don't all worry someone kidnapped you."

Sawyer's letting his anger shine; I follow suit. "Or, you know,
so we don't think you dropped dead somewhere after getting dizzy
and cracking your head open. God, Noah, how inconsiderate could
you possibly be? I've been calling and texting you for hours!"

Noah is shooting daggers at Sawyer; it's a bit disconcerting.
"Mel, can I talk to you alone please?" I look back and forth between
the two of them, but Sawyer only shrugs and picks up his guitar
again. "Please, Mel, we need to talk."

I turn around and give Sawyer a hug. "Thanks for the pep talk
and for changing my bandage."

"Anytime, Princess."

When I reach the door, Wyatt steps aside as Noah places his
hand on my lower back and leads me into his room. I know what he's
doing. He's staking his claim on me in front of Sawyer and I've had
about enough of him being jealous of his brother. I take the chair far
across the room so he can't sit next to me. "Well? Talk, Noah, I'm
here."

"Were you really going to leave?"

He disappears all day and that's what he wants to ask me? "Still
might, so you better make this good."

With a frustrated sigh, he leans against the floor-to-ceiling
window in front of me, blocking my view. The handle to the bedroom
door jiggles followed by pounding on the door. "Noah! Open this
door now!" Sawyer is screaming outside while Noah holds his head in

his hands for a second before the pounding begins again. "I'm not kidding, Noah, open the fucking door!"

Noah walks calmly to the door and talks through it. "Sawyer, I know why you're mad. I need to talk to Mel first and then I'll come talk to you."

"I can't believe you did this! What in the world were you thinking?" Sawyer is seething; I don't think I've ever heard him so angry. "Fine, but come find me as soon as you're finished."

"I will," Noah answers softly through the door. When he comes back to me, he drops to his knees in front of me looking absolutely defeated. "Don't leave me, Mel. I need you."

"Do you? Really, Noah, I'm curious because this morning I woke up to an empty bed, no note, no text, no call, no nothing. I was terrified. I searched this entire house from top to bottom, inside and out. I woke people up because I was losing my ever-loving mind. I've been by your side every day since Thanksgiving as I've lived out this nightmare with you. You don't let me out of your sight, but then suddenly you wake up today and decide you don't need me anymore and poof ... you disappear?" I snap my fingers for an added flourish.

"What I had to do couldn't wait, and I made sure I didn't go alone. But I also knew everyone would be pissed at me. I figured asking for forgiveness was better than arguing beforehand."

Fucking hell ... doesn't he know me at all? "Noah, there isn't much I expect in a relationship, but honesty is important. I hate secrets, and I understand they sometimes should exist to protect people from things that would hurt them. But how would you know what you had to do would bother me? Where did you go, Noah?"

He drops his head into my lap momentarily and then looks up at me with puppy dog eyes. "I went to see Sara's family."

"Oh, Noah ... why?" I ask, running my hands through his hair.

"There were things I had to know. Like, if she was always sick, and if they knew about her obsession with us. I just had so many questions and I knew if I told you, you would want to come, but ..."

"But what, Noah? Talk to me. I'm not angry I just want to understand."

He squeezes my thighs and continues, "She was their daughter and no matter how misguided, she had feelings for me. I didn't want to disrespect whatever it was they knew to be true by bringing the woman I love into their home."

"Come on, let's go sit on the bed." I pull his hands and he stands up, following me to the bed. "What happened?"

D. Kelly

"Wyatt stayed in the car. I took him so if I felt bad I wouldn't be alone and he could help me." *Good, at least he was thinking somewhat.* "Her mom was a mess and she apologized over and over again about what happened. They knew she was sick. She'd had mental issues since she was a kid. She was on and off meds like crazy but since she was never consistent, nothing ever really worked."

"Nobody monitored her?" I thought there were safeguards in place for people with mental illnesses.

"She lived at home. Her parents tried their best, but Sara was an adult ... there wasn't much they could do. I guess she never told them we broke up, so when she saw us together, and the news broke we were an item, they called her out on it. It must have set her off somehow."

"Jesus, that's so sad."

Noah pulls me into his embrace and hugs tightly. Before he releases me, he kisses me tenderly. "I know you're angry with me, Mel, and I'm truly sorry. I didn't know if they were sane people, either. I wanted you safe, too."

"So were they? Sane, I mean?"

With a nod, he answers, "Yeah, they're just two heartbroken people. Sara was their only child. They understand why she was killed and they don't have any ill will. They're old, way older than my parents, and her dad is in a wheelchair. It didn't seem like they have much, but what they do have is well-loved and taken care of. Or so it seemed."

He yawns. I can only imagine how tired he is; this is the most he's been up and about in almost a week.

"Were you there a long time?"

"Long enough. About two hours, I guess. Look, I told Wyatt if Sawyer pressed the issue he didn't have to lie for me. I'm sure what I'm about to tell you is why Sawyer is losing his shit. I asked when Sara's service was and they told me they weren't having one. They wouldn't tell me why, but I kept pressing them on it. Her mom broke into tears and admitted they couldn't afford it. Sara was the only one who worked in the house. I'm sure they get disability or Social Security or something but still ..."

"How much did you give them?" This beautiful man has a heart like nothing I've ever seen before. "I'm sorry, you don't have to tell me that. It's not really any of my business."

"Not enough to bring back their daughter." The effects of that night are going to stay with him for a long time. Maybe this will help him heal in his own way. "I gave them a hundred thousand dollars. I

328

figured it's more than enough to bury her and help ease the loss of income."

"Noah, you're the most amazing person I've ever met. I could never be mad at you for doing that, and I understand why you wanted to go without me. I just wish you would have texted me or left me a note. I was terrified."

My sniffling brings his eyes back to mine, and he trails his thumb across my bottom lip. It feels like it's been such a long time since we've been intimate.

"Her dad was so stoic. After I wrote them the check, he asked why I would do that. He seemed so skeptical of me. I suppose I can't blame him."

"What did you tell him?"

"A mixture of the truth and a lie but one they deserved to hear. I told them I loved Sara very much at one point in time and I was incredibly sad she's gone. Then I explained had she come to me for help I would have tried to get it for her. So the least I could do is help them since she no longer can." He hangs his head in sadness "I wish I *had* loved her, Mel. I wish I wouldn't have had to lie to them about that, but Sara wasn't really loveable … she was too busy looking out for herself. After seeing how bad off her parents are, though, I can even understand that, too."

"You did a good thing today, Noah. I'm proud of you."

"Really?" He's shocked; I'm sad he thought I'd be anything but.

"Of course. Even if you didn't love her, you cared about her once and that counts for something. I know this has been hard on you. It's okay to grieve the loss of the girl you once cared for."

Noah lays back and pulls me with him, his mouth meeting mine in a slow, tantalizing kiss. His love pours through with every stroke of his tongue, and I let the emotion fill me from head to toe. After he pulls away, he leans his forehead against mine. "I'm sorry, Mel, can you forgive me?"

My heart is still racing from our kiss when I give him my answer. "Under one condition."

"Name it."

"Don't keep me in the dark again. I'm not just any girl, and I don't freak out easily. I don't need to keep you on a leash … I only need to know you're safe. What would you have done if I'd disappeared without a trace?"

A dark look crosses his face and he shakes it off. "You don't want to know. I promise from now on I'll tell you before I leave the house."

"Good. You should probably know that Sawyer had your phones traced. He's pretty pissed you were at the mall."

Noah swallows hard. "Yeah, about that … I wanted to get you a present, but I couldn't find what I was looking for so it was kind of a bust."

I trace a path down his cheek with my fingers before moving my hands back to play with his hair. "You should have come home and rested. I don't need anything, Noah. Everything I could want is right here in this bed." He moves his hand to my hip and pulls me close to him. My lady bits are screaming for attention but my mind is in control right now. "How much pain are you in today?"

The sheepish look on his face tells me all I need to know. "I know you felt like you had to do these things but all you have to do it take it easy. Your follow-up isn't even until tomorrow, you shouldn't be overdoing it." I roll over and take a bottle of water from the nightstand and hand him a couple acetaminophen tablets.

After he takes the pills, he sits up and gets off the bed. "I promise I'll take it easy after this until I see the doctor, but right now I need to talk to Sawyer. Alone."

"Alright, I'll be here. But he was really worried about you earlier, too. Try and remember how much he cares about you before you yell back at him."

"I'll do my best," he replies, giving me one final kiss before he goes to talk to Sawyer. I'm so tired I decide to rest my eyes for a little bit while I wait for him to come back.

I wake up a few hours later with Noah asleep next to me. It's early afternoon and I'm starving so I decide to go make us something to eat and surprise Noah with lunch in bed. When I make it into the kitchen, Sawyer is sitting at the table, alone, with a nearly empty bottle of scotch.

"I'm going to make some food. Do you want something to eat?" I ask, hoping he'll take me up on it and sober up.

"Are you really not mad at him?" His words are slurred but his tone is filled with hurt.

"For which part?"

"Going over there, giving them money, not telling us he was doing something so epically stupid." He refills his glass and downs it like water.

After opening the cabinet and pulling out a pan, I look around for what I need to make grilled ham and cheese sandwiches. "I'm glad he took Wyatt with him. I'm not happy he didn't tell me first, but I understand it more now." As the butter melts in the pan, I layer up the sandwiches on a plate next to the stove.

"What about the money?"

After popping the first sandwich in the melted butter, I turn around and cross my arms. "What about it? It's his money, Sawyer, not mine."

He eyes me up, assessing me, and I wonder what is going on in that head of his. I flip the sandwich then turn back around, waiting for him to say something. When I plate the first sandwich and put the second in the pan, he finally speaks. "It will be. Hell, it might as well be. You know he's going to marry you."

After grabbing a few paper towels from the roll, I walk the sandwich over to him. "Eat this, please, and I'll keep talking to you."

He looks down at it like it's the best thing he's ever seen. Even though it's hot, he devours the first half in three bites. Moaning in appreciation, he looks back to me as I flip the second sandwich.

"Look, Sawyer, I love your brother, but I'm not his keeper. The last thing on my mind is his money and what he does with it. I've got more than enough of my own to worry about his. But I do think what he chooses to do with it at times is admirable. A family lost their only child to mental illness, and their child also happens to be someone Noah used to care for. I don't see anything wrong with him helping them out and easing his conscience."

As I make the last sandwich, Sawyer puts his plate in the sink. "That was good, thank you. But you didn't answer me … What are you going to do when he marries you?"

With a laugh, I turn around, my laughter coming to a halt when I see him looking at me like a wounded puppy. "You actually didn't ask me anything about getting married. You pointed out he was *going* to marry me. I don't know the answer to that, Sawyer. If … Someday, when … Noah and I choose to get married, that will be his choice. Personally, I love the random things he does to make other's lives better because he's fortunate enough to do so. If he's financially stable enough to help others, more power to him."

Sawyer rubs his head and blinks his eyes. I think he's about to pass out for the rest of the day. "Do you think I should do that? Be more philanthropic?"

"Sawyer," I say as I turn off the burner and plate the last sandwich. "You should do whatever makes you happy. Most days I don't have a clue what I'm doing. The bulk of my parent's money is sitting in an account accruing interest. The rest gets donated. That makes me feel better about the rest since I have no clue what to do with it."

Placing my hand over his heart, I continue, "You have to do whatever makes your heart happy. Nothing else is worth it. You also have to stop comparing yourself to your brother. The two of you are completely different people, both equally amazing, both with huge hearts and an incredible love for family. Stop being so hard on yourself. You've got your whole life to do good things."

His eyes are glassy and he flashes me one of those genuine smiles again, where his dimple shows and his childhood innocence shines through. "Thanks, Princess, I needed that. Tell Noah I'm sorry for fighting with him. I was just ..."

"Worried," I answer for him, but he shakes his head.

"Not only worried ... I was being protective of you. I'm your friend and I don't like to see you in pain, but he's my brother and I should know better because Noah would rather die than hurt you. I'm going to go sleep this off. Thanks for the sandwich and the chat, Princess."

When Sawyer walks away, I lean up against the counter and catch my breath. How can I feel so much for a man I'm not in a relationship with? Sawyer is a wonderful friend, but there's so much of *something* between us lying beneath the surface. It's not only attraction ... it's deeper than that. I wonder if it's like a twin connection thing. I should do some research on twins and their spouses and see if I can find anything that alludes to what I'm feeling. It's the only explanation I can come up with.

After looking through their cabinets, I finally find the tray I'm looking for in the pantry. I also find some Oreos and put them on the tray with the sandwiches and a soda for Noah and some iced tea for me. Noah is rubbing the sleep from his eyes when I walk in. Eyeing the food, he smiles.

"Have I ever told you how sexy you are when you're being domestic?"

"Uh ... no, I can't say you have," I answer with a laugh.

"Put the tray on the floor, Amelia." Noah's words are commanding, his eyes smoldering. I do as he says and he pulls me to him, placing my hand on his cock. "So fucking sexy," he murmurs as he pulls me on top of him. His lips are pressed against my neck as he licks and sucks his way to the spot right below my ear that sets my body ablaze.

"Noah ..." I want this, but he hasn't been cleared yet. "We can't do this yet, babe. You need to follow up with your doctor."

He moves his hands to my hips and slams me against his raging hard-on. "What if I promise to lie back and let you do all the work? I'll be a good boy, Mel, I promise." Before I answer him, he's sliding his hand down the front of my yoga pants and inside my underwear.

Latching on to his earlobe with my teeth, his fingers slide through my wetness and circle my clit. My whimpers escalate to cries as he increases the pressure. "You're so fucking wet for me, babe."

I know this is a bad idea, but I also know he's feeling much better. Moving my hands to the hem of his shirt, I pull it off and slide off his knees and onto the floor to undo his belt. He beats me to the button and zipper of his jeans, freeing his cock, the head glistening with moisture.

Sucking him in slowly, I allow my tongue to circle the head while licking his essence off seductively. Following his pulsing veins down to the base of his cock and back up again, I tease the tip with my tongue before releasing him.

"Lie back," I instruct, turning to the dresser to get a condom.

Walking back to the bed, I begin stripping as he watches with a hooded gaze. He managed to remove the rest of his clothes while I was getting the condom and is now stroking himself. My pussy clenches as I stand at the foot of the bed watching him. We don't need to even have sex; watching him would totally get me off.

"Are you going to watch? Or are you going to come while you ride?" He snickers at the indecision on my face. "Come on, Mel, ride me like you own me."

Within seconds, I'm ripping the condom open and sliding it on his erection. I'm on top now, straddling him, but before I guide him inside me, I ask him a very important question. "Do I?"

"Do you what?" he asks breathlessly.

"Do I own you, Noah?"

As he moves his hands to my hips, he pulls me down onto his length and groans in pleasure. "You're the only person who ever has."

Leaning forward, I take his lips in mine. Noah moves one hand to the small of my back and the other remains on my hip. He guides our movements but I'm still in control. With every thrust he hits my G-spot while I cry out into his mouth, never breaking our kiss. Soon, I'm screaming as I clench around him. Noah doesn't miss a beat, his cock pulsing inside me as he finds his own release.

As I collapse against him, my head lands on his chest. Noah runs his fingers through my hair as I listen to the rapid beat of his heart begin to eventually slow back to normal. The last thing I want to do is move, but I know he needs to get the condom off before it falls off inside of me.

After I roll over, Noah throws away the condom and brings back a towel to clean me up. It's quiet between us when he finally asks, "What are you thinking?"

With a smile, I trace my finger across his bottom lip, not wanting to hold anything back from him any longer. "That was incredible, Noah. It's never ... I mean, it's always, but ..." Shit, I don't even know how to tell him, but he knows; Noah always seems to know everything.

"The best sex ever? Yeah, it was."

"It was more."

He looks down at me and kisses me tenderly. "It's because I'm the one." His answer isn't smug, just matter of fact, but it's also spot on. "You're not holding anything back anymore, Mel. You finally let me in and it shows. If I'd had any doubts you loved me ... which I don't, by the way," he corrects quickly, "they'd be gone now. We're absolutely fucking amazing together."

"We really are, aren't we?"

His response is a long, lingering kiss. Noah Weston manages to steal my heart again, one beat at a time.

Holiday Madness

Every day for the past three and a half weeks Noah has been disappearing into the garage, which has been deemed a Mel-free zone. I've got no idea what he's up to down there, but I almost don't care since he's feeling better and acting normal again.

Each night, we talk for hours as we try to learn everything there is to know about each other. Noah makes love to me every night, fulfilling my heart and mind in ways I never knew they could be. Everything between us since the incident with Sara is better. And after the doctor cleared him—with the standard precautions, of course—he's been extra vigilant about keeping the anticipation high between us.

In the daytime, while he's off working or whatever it is he's doing, I've been spending all my free time with Belle and Rory. The house is fully decorated, although I really can't take any credit for that; these Westons are beasts when it comes to the holidays. The whole family came over and took a big group trip to cut down fresh trees—one for each of their houses. Saylor and Emme helped pick out each one and loved every second of the big adventure. They were extra adorable in their jeans, sweaters, and mini Uggs.

After picking trees, the whole crew went to each house and helped decorate; it was like a well-oiled machine. There was homemade eggnog at Karen and Owen's house, freshly baked Christmas cookies at Diane and Rob's, and a variety of wines, cheeses, and meats at Noah and Sawyer's house. Being the amazing uncles they are, they even had gingerbread kits for Emme and Saylor. In between the eating and drinking, all the lights and decorations went up, inside and out. Every box was labeled, every ornament had a story, and every Weston participated willingly and excitedly.

Belle and I felt like we'd walked into some sort of alternate reality. It's not that we're not festive people—we love Christmas—but both of us are more of the hunt-and-search holiday goers. We decorate, tear down, and put away things here and there until it's eventually all gone. Then the following year we look for all those random things we put away that didn't make it into the main box on the first go around. Organization is not our key skill when it comes to the holidays and from the looks of things, we're going to have lots to learn.

Tomorrow is Christmas Eve and everyone is coming over to our house to spend the night. Santa delivers here for the kids, and the entire family has stockings hung by the fireplace, including ones for Belle and me. Anna, Warren, and Sam are all coming tonight. They truly are this huge, happy family.

I've been taking lots of notes, even though I'm not sure how much of this will make it into the book. It's sort of strange; I've got this part of me that has to be here for the purposes of telling their story, and this whole other part of me is here because she's being inducted into this family. The latter part of me doesn't want to share these details even though I know they want their fans to see who they really are on and off the stage.

"Are those done yet?" Darren asks, hopping onto the kitchen counter and pulling me from my thoughts. I'm making sweet potatoes a day early since I have to make even more this time around.

"Not even close. They won't be done until Christmas. I'm just giving them an extra day of marinating time."

"Come on, Mel, can't you just throw, like, a small amount into a dish for me to cook now? I promise I won't tell anyone you love me more than them." Darren pokes his bottom lip out into a pout, and I can't help but laugh.

"Nope, they would smell them. You have to wait like everyone else."

"Yeah, I figured, but you can't blame a guy for trying. So did you ever figure out what to get Noah for Christmas?"

"Not yet. I thought about going and getting one of my dad's guitars for him." That's sort of a lie. I have actually been thinking about giving a guitar to Noah, Sawyer, and Wyatt, but I wouldn't have anything for Darren and that somehow doesn't seem fair.

"What's stopping you?"

"A few things. It seems like something Sawyer would like more than Noah. I want something uniquely special to him."

Darren taps a beat out on the granite countertop as he thinks. "Noah is simple … he likes security and he loves you. Propose to him, that should make him happy."

At the mention of a proposal, the spoon I was using falls to the floor, and Darren thinks it's hysterical. "Okay … so don't do that since it obviously freaks you out."

As my heart comes back to a normal rhythm, I grab a new spoon. "You guys are insane with your quick proposals and stuff. I love Noah, but marriage isn't on my mind right now. Besides, I might not be old-fashioned about many things, but I'm not likely to ever ask a man to marry me."

"I totally get that. For me and Sawyer, something like that would be completely emasculating. We're manly men and shit, but Wyatt and Noah … they'd get off on it." He shrugs. "Just food for thought. I don't think Noah will blink twice at whatever you give him, Mel. He's just happy you're sticking around. That Sara shit would have scared a lot of girls away. You're kinda badass, you know?"

"Are you hitting on my best friend? Because she'd fuck me *way* before she'd do you," Belle teases sarcastically as she makes her way into the room. Darren's eyes glaze over as he looks between the two of us.

"Head out of the gutter," I tell him as he pulls Belle between his legs and leans down to give her a sweet kiss.

"Can't blame me … that's a hot-ass visual. I don't even think Noah would object to seeing that action."

Belle rolls her eyes at him before turning her attention back to me. "Are you sure you don't want to come?" she asks me again for the tenth time.

"There's nothing I want more than to be in that room when you find out if you're having a boy or a girl, but I really think it's a moment you two should share alone. I appreciate you asking, and I expect to be the first person to know after you let it soak in, but you guys go and enjoy this moment together."

They both kiss me on the cheek on their way out. I can't wait until we know what Belle is having. Pregnancy agrees with her—or maybe it's Darren—but whatever it is, she's been blissfully happy since she told him about the baby. And now that her morning sickness is over, she's eagerly looking forward to Christmas dinner.

After wrapping up the endless bowls of potatoes and putting them in the refrigerator, I pour myself a glass of wine and sit in front of the fire. It's almost late afternoon and Noah should be finishing up soon. A little over a week from now we'll be back on the road. We're flying into New York the day after New Year's and I've got my first book signing the next day. I'm so nervous but I'm trying not to let on. The guys are booked solid with publicity junkets the whole time we're there, on top of their shows. I'm pretty sure I'm going to be flying solo on this signing and that freaks me out. SOS is sending a rep to come with me, so at least I won't be completely alone.

"You're done already?" Noah asks, coming out of the shadows and stalking toward me like a lion to his prey.

"I am ... better question is, are you?" Suddenly, I know the perfect gift to give him for Christmas.

Taking my wineglass and placing it on the table, he flashes me a megawatt smile. "Lie down, Mel," he commands as he pulls his shirt off. The heated look in his eyes leaves no room for argument.

As soon as I'm in the proper position, Noah makes his way up my body. Starting with my feet, he caresses every bit of me he can get his hands on until he reaches my mouth.

"I missed you," he whispers a breath away from my lips, my legs hitched over his hips.

"Did you?"

"Can't you tell?" he answers, pushing his hard length against my center, flooding me with need.

I slide my fingers into his hair and pull his mouth even closer. "How much more work do you need to do? We leave in a few days, Noah. I'd like some time with you before we go."

"Wrap your arms around my neck."

I do as he requests as he wraps his arm around my waist and lifts us from the couch. He doesn't put me down until we're in our room, and even then he's got me propped up against the door. "Arms up," he demands, and I comply. When he sees my lacy red bra he groans and pushes himself into me harder. "You're so fucking beautiful, Mel."

Freeing my breasts from my bra, Noah sears a trail of kisses along my breasts until his mouth meets my pert nipple and bites down gently before sucking me into his mouth. My body hums in anticipation. All my senses are lit up like a fucking Christmas tree as he seduces my body with his mouth and hands, not to mention the sexy-as-all-hell sounds falling from his lips.

"Love me, Noah ... please."

He drops his hands to my waist long enough to pull my jeans and panties down to my knees, and I work on kicking them off as he fumbles with dropping his own pants. After he's sheathed in a condom, he pulls my hands above my head and holds them there. His blazing eyes meet mine as he lowers his mouth to mine.

"I'm going to love you forever, Amelia, but right now, I'm going to fuck you."

I choke on an inhale and absorb his words. No one has ever made me feel like this before. Noah slams his cock inside me, stealing my breath, and I exhale on a scream as my walls clench tightly around him. His lips take mine in a wicked game of chase. When our tongues meet, I surrender everything I am to him. My body shatters around him, loving the complete domination he has of me. When I call out his name, he bites down on my neck, making me cry louder for him.

"That's my girl," he answers with a groan. He releases my hands and wraps his arm around my waist as my arms immediately go around his neck. Now that his arm is securely around me, he slams into me hard and fast, pushing us both closer to euphoria. With his free hand, he places pressure on my clit. I'm already close again, but he's pushing me higher and higher as my body slams back against the door with each thrust.

"Noah!" When all the sensations become too much, I scream as I come again.

"Jesus, baby, fuck," he cries out against my ear as he sucks the skin of my neck into his mouth to muffle his cries as he finds his release.

After catching our breath for a minute, he waddles us backward to the bed, careful not to trip with his jeans wrapped around his ankles. Laughing as we crash down onto the bed, we both take a minute to clean up and then curl into each other's arms.

"So *that* was unexpected." I say as he pulls me closer and kisses me chastely.

"I've missed you lately, and since I'm done with my work I thought we should celebrate." He nuzzles into my neck and places lingering kisses in places that are bound to get me worked up all over again.

"For good, or for today?"

"Mm … for good," he murmurs against my skin.

"Good. I have to go out for a few hours tomorrow afternoon but after that I'm all yours."

Noah's eyes narrow in protest. "Tomorrow is a family day, Mel. What's so important that you have to leave?"

"Just one last Christmas present for you I have to pick up. I'll only be gone a couple of hours, and I promise it will be worth it."

"You're not going alone, and Belle and Darren are going to be at his parents' house. Do I need to get you security?"

Shit, I didn't think about that, but there's no way I'm taking security with me.

"No, I'm going with Eli." Hopefully, I can get Eli to come with me.

With a sigh, Noah rolls onto his back and looks up at the ceiling. He's mad. I prop myself up on his chest and place my hand over his heart. "I thought you were okay with me and Eli now?"

Moving his hand to my back, he tucks me in close. "I thought I was, too. It's one thing if he's here or we're all out together, but it's different to have the two of you go out together. Not because of why you think. I know you're not going back to him, but the paparazzi are going to have a field day with the two of you out in public together."

Sometimes I forget about all the drama that surrounds being with a rock star. "I'll be careful and try to avoid them. It's the best I can do, Noah. I'm not going to miss out on your present because of them. This is important to me. I only have to go one place, but it's kind of far so I'll try and duck in and out without being seen. I'm sure Eli's driver can take us."

With a soft kiss to my forehead, he relents. "I'm not going to change your mind so just be careful. If anything happens, call me. I'm serious, Mel."

"Okay, I promise."

"Mel!" I hear Belle call out before she begins banging on the door. "Put your orgasm on hold and put on a robe. I've got news!"

"Hold on a sec!" I yell back excitedly. "Get dressed so we can find out what they're having."

After popping a quick kiss on Noah's lips, I rapidly throw my clothes on. Strong arms wrap around my waist and Noah kisses me. "One day, I hope *you'll* be this happy finding out what we're having."

Me, too.

Noah opens the door to Belle and Darren. Darren has his arms wrapped around Belle's massively round belly. With a cocked brow, I wait for her to explain. They're all smiles as Darren pushes down on the top of her belly and out pops a pink helium balloon that says "It's a girl."

"Really?!" I exclaim, and Belle nods her head frantically. We're instantly a puddle of screaming, hugging, crying women while Darren and Noah look on in amusement after their whole guy-hug-pat thing they have going on.

"There's no chance it was wrong and the cord was in the way of anything?"

Darren laughs. "Her legs were spread wide open and she was showing off her hoo ha."

"Dude, maybe reword that for future conversations," Noah says, patting him on the shoulder.

"Aww, she just wanted you to have time to pick a cute name for her so she doesn't end up with something horrible like Sunbeam Stratocaster Miller. She already knows how rock stars roll." Belle laughs at my words as Darren pouts because he knows damn well I'm right.

"We should celebrate. You guys want to go to dinner?" Noah asks. "We can get the security crew here in less than an hour. Anna and Wyatt will be here before then, and Sawyer and J should be back by then, too."

"Hell yeah. What do you say, Belle? You up for food?" Darren asks as he pulls her to him and rubs her belly.

"I'm game. Nowadays, food *always* sounds good. Hopefully, I'll lose the baby weight as fast as I'm going to gain it."

"There's nothing wrong with a little cushion for the pushin'," Darren replies with a devilish smirk.

"You two are my witnesses that he said that. When my ass is as big as a doublewide, you remind him what he said."

Pointing between Noah and myself, I tell her, "We got your back, Belle. When are you going to tell Veronica?

"How about now? Noah, want to meet my mom? I know she wants to meet you. Let's Skype her."

"Sure, why not?" Veronica is the closest thing I have to a mother and he's not even the slightest bit fazed.

"Hey, Mama!" Belle says enthusiastically once Veronica picks up the call.

"Hey! To what do I owe the pleasure?"

"A few reasons. One being Mel wants you to finally meet Noah. Mama this is Noah, and Noah this is our mom, Veronica." Belle passes the phone to Noah and he flashes her that same panty-melting smile he gives me.

"Sweet Jesus have mercy. No wonder you stole my baby girl's heart. You're enough to give an old woman palpitations. Good thing I'm not really that old," she adds with a laugh, and Noah joins her.

Climbing behind him on the bed, I duck my head over his shoulder and wave. "Hey, Mama, we miss you!"

Veronica clucks her tongue at me and nails me with one of her motherly glares. "Girl, you don't have any time to miss me while you're keeping company with this good-looking boy, but I appreciate the sentiment."

"I always miss you, Veronica. But I am going to give the phone back to Belle because she has bigger news."

"It was nice meeting you, Veronica. I hope we can take you to dinner when you come back and our schedules line up," Noah tells her with such sincerity it makes me want him all over again.

"It was good meeting you, too, Noah. Take care of my girl."

Noah hands the phone to Belle, and I whisper in his ear, "That was so fucking hot." He smiles and shakes his head but pulls me around from behind him and into his lap.

"Alright, Belle, what is your news?" I hear Veronica now but I can't see her anymore.

"Darren has something he wants to show you."

"Girl, did you only call me to get me worked up? My heart can only take so many attractive younger men in a day, and I've already had my fill of Marcus today."

"Mom! Stop!" Belle isn't even mad; she's cracking up. This is Veronica and all of her sassy glory. "I'm turning the phone to Darren now."

Darren is standing by the wall holding the balloon to his chest. As soon as Belle turns the phone, Veronica screams. Only Darren can see her face, and he's smiling like a loon.

"Oh my goodness! It's a girl! Congratulations, Darren. Now, Belle, turn me around so I can blow you a kiss."

When Belle turns the phone around, I take a peek over her shoulder to find Veronica blowing kisses at the screen as tears stream down her cheeks. "You're making me feel old before my time, but I am so excited for this new addition to our family. I just knew it was going to be a girl. As soon as I get back, we're celebrating. I love you all, but we have dinner reservations and I have to go. Noah and Darren, you take care of my three girls."

After a round of "We wills" from the guys and "love yous" from me and Belle, she finally disconnects the call. Noah sends Belle and Darren out to get ready and texts everyone the plans for tonight. When he finally turns his attention back to me, he smirks.

"What?"

"Belle's mom is kind of hot."

Even though I know he's joking, and Veronica would never steal my man, a lick of jealousy pounds through my veins. "Too bad. You're already taken and I *don't* share."

"Do I sense a little jealousy, Mel? Because I have to say that is extremely sexy. And for the record, I don't share what's mine, either."

Damn, I don't know what it is, but he keeps turning me on today with only his words. "Am I yours, Noah?" I ask, teasing him, and he pounces on me.

"That's not even funny, but just in case you need clarification, you are one hundred percent mine. One day, when we say our vows, everyone will know it, too," Noah says as he pulls me into an utterly heart-stopping kiss.

Noah's words ran through my mind all night while we were out with our friends. I'm not sure why he is so fixated on marriage, but I also can't deny how much deeper our connection has become since the Sara incident.

But still, my inner self wants to know if it's more than Noah just being ready. Does it have to do with his relationship with Sara? Or maybe Marilyn? And if it does have to do with Marilyn, is he still afraid of losing his girl to Sawyer? Because that will never happen. My heart will always be Noah's; I just need to find a way to make him believe it.

"Noah is going to flip when he sees what you got him for Christmas. I have to admit, even *my* ego is wounded a bit that you're giving it to him and not to me." Eli was happy to come with me today, and he got his driver and his security team to go with us. We've had the best day; I'm excited our friendship has easily picked up from where we left off.

"I'm sure your ego can handle it. Besides, you and Rory seem to be hitting it off. What's up with that?"

He pushes my shoulder with his and then shrugs. "We're just getting to know each other. It's not a big deal. She's a cool chick, though. Would it bother you if I asked her out?"

"Not at all, Eli. I want you to be as happy as I am. Noah and Sawyer may have something to say about it, but you've got my blessing."

"Yeah, I'm sure they will. But anything worth having is worth fighting for. I guess I just need to figure out if it's a road I want to go down."

"You'll figure it out. They don't have to know right away. Take time to get to know her first before you let anyone try and talk you in or out of something that may not even take off."

Eli looks up at me thoughtfully. "You're the same Amelia, but you're different, too. We grew up, Mel. How the hell did that happen?"

"I don't know. Most of the time when I look at you I still see the same cocky, teenage boy staring back at me. But you're not him. Hell, you're not even in a boy band anymore. I should have told you this sooner, I really love your solo stuff."

Eli blushes at my words. No matter how famous he gets, he's still a small-town boy deep down inside. Rory would be lucky to have him.

"I'm surprised you even listen to my stuff."

"At first it was hard, I'll admit that. But after some time passed it was easier, especially once you went out on your own and it was all new. When there weren't any memories tied to it, it wasn't as hard."

He leans back in his seat and looks me over cautiously. "You do know "My Everything" is completely about you, right?"

Turning my attention to fiddling with my bracelet, I deflect his stare. "I wasn't ever sure … but I wondered."

The melodic notes pour from his lips and I shut my eyes against them, hoping they don't get to me.

She looked at me, her eyes filled with tears
That I wish I could unsee.
Why?
She screamed
Because I'm a bastard and I'm sorry but you're still my everything.

Thankfully, he only sings a few notes and then smiles sadly at me as he shakes his head. "I just wanted you to know, in some way, I was sorry and I loved you."

Squeezing his hand, I meet his eyes. "I knew, Eli. I was being selfish and guarded, but I knew. I wish I'd told you sooner I forgave you. But we're here now, and I still love you to pieces, just not in the same way."

He squeezes me back and flashes me his adorable smile. I'm not sure I'll ever be able to see the man Eli has become when so much of him reminds me of the boy I used to love. "Right back at you, Mel. So when are you going to give Noah his gift?"

"Tonight, hopefully. I don't want to do it with anyone around for obvious reasons."

"Could you imagine the conversation that would spark? Hell, I'd *pay* to be there for that."

"Shut up!" We're both laughing; it feels good.

His driver pulls the car into the driveway. Rory and Noah are sitting on the porch waiting for us. I wonder if he knows she's probably hoping to catch a glimpse of Eli.

"Do you want to come in?" I ask, noticing how his eyes dilated and locked on Rory as soon as he saw her.

Tearing his gaze back to me, he replies, "I probably should be going. My family is going to be at my house soon. You know how the holidays are."

"Sure, I get it. Make sure you give my love to your sister." I'm being snarky and he knows it.

"You know she feels bad about that. After all that shit went down with you, I lit her ass on fire for it. I'm not sure it makes a difference, but she's cool now. She's happy if I'm happy. Having you back in my life is all I ever could have wanted for Christmas."

"Careful there, I sent you a present that should be at your house now and it might be something you want more." The sparkle in his eyes makes me smile.

"Not possible."

"We'll see. Come on, at least get out and say hi so they don't think something strange is going on. We've been in here probably longer than Noah's comfort zone can handle. I see him bouncing around out there. I'm sure it's driving him crazy that we're in here."

"That man has it bad for you. It's a good thing you've got it bad for him, too. Let's put him out of his misery." Eli opens the door and helps me out of the car. Noah is striding up to us confidently, but Rory is hanging out on the porch. I wave her over and the hint of a smile turns up at the corner of her mouth. I'm sure she didn't want to seem anxious and now she has no reason to.

Noah wraps his arms around me and pulls me into a massive hug. "I'm sorry," he says, throwing me off guard.

"Why would you be sorry?"

After placing soft kisses against my neck, he whispers in my ear, "Because now I know how much it sucks to be waiting around all day for you. You've put up with me disappearing for the last three weeks without so much as a peep. I think you're the better half in this relationship."

"I think we're both a great half and that's what makes us work so well. But I'm back now, so why don't we go inside and do whatever it is your family does on Christmas Eve?" Rory and Eli have already struck up a conversation, but I interrupt long enough to give him a quick peck on the cheek and a hug. "Let me know when you get your gift," I whisper into his ear and then wink at Rory. Her face flushes an adorable shade of pink; she's got it bad for him.

Noah's eyes narrow as I pull him into the house. "What was that wink for, Mel?" he asks, stopping me as soon as we step through the doorway.

"You caught that, huh? It was nothing, Noah, don't worry about it."

He's not having it, and he pulls me down the hall, closing his office door behind us quietly. "Spill it, Mel."

With his arms crossed over his chest he looks sexy as can be. All his colorful tattoos are peeking out from underneath his t-shirt, and all I want to do right now is lick him from head to toe. But I can't.

"Noah, it's up to Rory to talk to you about this. Please don't force the issue."

He drops his arms and stalks toward me, caging me in against the door. He closes his eyes and inhales deeply before opening them and pleading with me. "Please don't tell me Eli is the guy she was talking to me about having a crush on. I'm not sure I could take it."

Pulling his lips to mine, I caress the side of his face. After a lingering kiss, I exhale contentedly. "Your lips were made for mine."

His eyes are twinkling, but he's still schooling his features into a scowl "Don't change the subject, Mel. Your perfect lips aren't going to distract me from what is going on with my sister."

"Fine, Noah, but I seriously don't know what is going on with Rory. You're going to have to ask her yourself because she hasn't talked to me about this."

It takes a second before the impact of my words sets in. "That means *he's* talking to you about her? Fuck me. No. Just no ... this is *not* happening. Over my *and* Sawyer's dead bodies."

Taking his face in my hands, I force his eyes to meet mine. "He's a good man, Noah. He's made mistakes like we all have, but he's grown from them. What if they have what we have? Let them see where this goes and stay out of it. I know you don't want to admit it, but your sister is a grown woman and she's having sex with assholes. At least we know Eli. We know he's a good guy, and we know where to find him if he fucks her over."

"Don't you mean *when* he fucks her over?" he growls.

"Nope, because I don't think he's that kind of man anymore." I can see the instant he gives into me—his eyes light up, his features soften, and he leans into my caress.

"Alright, I'll leave it alone because I trust your judgement more than anything. But let's not mention this to Sawyer or anyone because for now I'd like to pretend it's not happening."

"Sounds good to me. So what did I miss today?"

Noah pulls me to him, his erection obvious. "Well, I missed the fuck out of you. Can you tell?"

"Mm, I can, Mr. Weston." He moves his hands under my shirt, but I quickly push him away. "Nope, there's no time for that. I'm already later than I thought I'd be. I want the rest of today and tomorrow to be everything you hoped it would be. It's our first Christmas together, Noah."

His mouth crashes against mine, making my body tingle from head to toe. Who knew loving someone so much could change the dynamic of everything? As he pulls away, he hugs me in the way only he can: with his whole heart and soul.

"The first of many, Mel, don't forget that."

"Never."

"Alright, so we already made Christmas cookies, but my mom has some more homemade eggnog out there. We've all finished wrapping presents, and my mom is dying to fill the stockings. It's her pride and joy to do it every year."

"Well, come on, then, show me the true magic of a Weston family Christmas. Just give me a quick minute to put my bags in the room. You'd better not go in there and peek."

"I'm not a peeker. I love surprises. Sawyer, on the other hand, is a major peeker. I wouldn't be surprised if he's out there right now shaking presents under the tree."

Laughing, we walk hand in hand to our bedroom. Sawyer is sitting at the dining room table wrapping presents. Guess he didn't finish with the rest of them. "Hey, Princess, have fun with Boy Band?" Instead of answering him, I flip him the bird as I walk by, and he busts up laughing. "I might have deserved that," he calls out behind us, making me smile. Sawyer and I have definitely found our friendship groove.

"Stay," I tell Noah as I slip into the room and hide my bags in the bathroom. Hopefully, no one will go digging through a cabinet with tampons to find a present.

When I step out of the room, Noah takes my hand again and we go join Christmas Eve in progress. Eli must have already left because Rory is playing on the floor with the girls. Karen and Owen are in the kitchen making drinks.

"Amelia! Would you like some eggnog?" Karen is flushed; she's got a serious buzz going on already.

"Sure, I'd love some." She hands me a glass filled to the rim, bourbon floating on top. After taking a sip, I breathe through my newly cleared nasal passages. This is so strong it might as well be moonshine.

"Christmas secret, the drunker my wife gets the more liberal she is with the booze," Owen tells me in a mock secret all while pinching Karen's ass. My eyes didn't need to see that, but they're so fucking cute I can't even complain. I'd say Karen isn't the only one who is drunk.

"Come on, Mel, you don't have to watch my parents get frisky."

"Oh, Noah, you wouldn't be here if we didn't get frisky," Karen jokes with him, and even though I'm blushing, Noah is laughing good naturedly. No wonder he's so in love with the idea of marriage; he's got some pretty good role models.

As we make our way into the living room, his parents keep laughing behind us. Diane and Rob are sitting on the loveseat looking like they're ready to get frisky themselves. "Does Christmas make your entire family horny?" I whisper in Noah's ear.

He chuckles. "Maybe, or maybe it's the free-flowing alcohol and the lack of any hostility. Everyone is happy on Christmas."

The ringing doorbell overpowers the Christmas music playing lightly in the background.

"Pizza's here!" Saylor yells excitedly and runs for the door.

"I got her!" Sawyer calls out, and Diane sits back down with Rob. A few seconds later, Saylor runs back into the room.

"Mommy! Uncle Jordan's here and he brought a girlfriend!"

Jordan and said girl come in on Saylor's heels. Although the girl looks horrified at the thought, Jordan laughs it off. "Everyone, this is Allie. She's new to town and just started working at the bar. Allie, this is my family."

Introductions are made, and Karen couldn't look happier that Jordan brought a friend. Karen hugs Allie almost as ferociously as she did me at Thanksgiving. Sawyer brings his presents into the room and watches Jordan and Allie with an intense curiosity. If Jordan gets a girlfriend, Sawyer will be the only one of them without. The thought makes me sad, but then I remember our conversation a few weeks ago; he'll settle down when he's ready.

Warren and Sam are next to arrive, followed by Anna and Wyatt. Their arms are filled with gifts, and they even have to make a second trip out to get the rest of them plus their bags. Noah and Sawyer are quick to help. I take the opportunity to talk to Allie as we both gingerly sip on Karen's fuel-filled eggnog.

"Have you known Jordan long?" I ask, trying to break the silence. Out of the corner of my eye, I see Rory and Diane covertly turning their attention toward us.

"Actually, I started working at the bar the night of the show. I'm sorry for what happened to you guys. I'm glad you're both healing well."

"It was scary, but we're both perfectly fine now."

"So Jordan says you're a writer. Anything I might have read?"

Rory snickers and Rob tosses the couch pillow at her.

"She wrote *The O Factor*," Diane tells her with a hint of pride in her voice. I haven't even spent much time with Diane, but I'm guessing she's also read my book.

"Get out! That was you? I loved that book!" The guys come back in on the heels of her words, and she turns her attention to Jordan. "Jordan, you didn't tell me she wrote *The O Factor!*" The way she scolds him makes me think there's something a little deeper going on between them other than boss and subordinate, but it's not my place to ask.

"Like I knew what Noah's girlfriend wrote? I just knew it was some kind of sex book so it wouldn't be anything I'd probably ever read. Now you know."

Allie rolls her eyes at him and takes a huge gulp of her drink. That's gotta burn, but she seems to need it after Jordan sits next to her and places his hand on her thigh. She doesn't move it away, either. Something is definitely brewing between these two.

"So, Allie, does your family live close?" Karen asks, also noticing Jordan's hand on her thigh.

"No, it's just me and my dad these days, but he lives in Washington D.C. and is working over the holidays. It's the first Christmas I haven't seen him, so Jordan took pity on me and brought me here. I hope you don't mind."

"Doesn't look like pity to me," Sawyer pipes up, and Owen throws him a parental glare. "Just saying, they look cozy."

Karen also gives him a "shut up" look to which Sawyer actually pays attention. "Of course we don't mind, the more the merrier. And don't pay a lick of attention to Sawyer. You know these boys are brothers in every way it matters and it shows. You'll see in the morning ... I think the three of them get more excited for presents than my granddaughters do."

D. Kelly

"Like Rory and Diane don't get excited about gifts," Noah adds, defending the brothers.

"I'm pretty sure it was you and Sawyer who pushed so hard Jordan fell down and broke his arm one Christmas morning when you were about thirteen," Owen says with a pointed gaze, and Allie and I bust up laughing. The rest of them must have heard this already, but this is new to me.

"You didn't, Noah!" I say through my hysterical sobs.

"Oh, he *did*. They were so excited because they saw guitar-shaped silhouettes under the tree and it was all either of them had asked for the whole year. After that, we all piled into the car and spent the bulk of the morning in the emergency room."

Jordan smiles up at Karen. "Yup, and when we got home, Mom and Dad made Noah and Sawyer pass out all the gifts to everyone. As punishment, they had to wait to open theirs until the rest of us were done."

"That doesn't seem like too much punishment. My dad would have whooped my behind," Allie replies.

Karen continues, "Oh, that wasn't all. We didn't let them have their guitars until Jordan said they could. But Jordan has a good heart and he loves his brothers. They had those guitars opened before bedtime."

Someone is ringing the doorbell like crazy. It must be the pizza this time.

"I got it," Sawyer says, running to grab the door.

"Mel! This one is on you!" he calls out.

Noah gives me an odd look, but I have no clue who could be here. As soon as I'm in the hall, Eli catches sight of me and barrels past Sawyer, scooping me up and spinning me around.

"You crazy, amazing, wonderful, thoughtful best friend of mine! You made me cry in front of everyone, but I fucking love you, woman! Your friendship is still the better gift, though," he says, setting me down. I brace my arm against the wall so I don't fall from the dizziness.

"I take it you got your gift," I reply, letting his enthusiasm sink in. He pulls me in for another hug; he's crying this time. "I'm sorry. I didn't mean for it to upset you, Eli."

He pushes me back at arm's length while our audience watches. "I'm not upset. I'm so happy I could burst. Seriously, Mel, that gift is everything, and it means more to me than you could possibly imagine. I had to come thank you in person. I'm sorry for interrupting. My parents weren't too happy about me ditching out, but I had to."

350

"Damn, Mel, what did you give him?" Wyatt asks, and Anna shushes him.

"Alright, you guys, I'm sorry for interrupting your night. Amelia Triton, you have always been and always will be my all-time favorite person. Hold on to her, Weston, they don't make them much better." His eyes linger on Rory; I'm sure Noah notices the attraction between them this time.

Eli leaves as quick as he came and all eyes are on me. "It was nothing, you guys. I gave him a guitar."

"Boy Band plays guitar?" Wyatt's shocked tone doesn't surprise me. There's a lot more to Eli than what the public knows.

"He does, and he's really good, too. He learned from the best."

"What kind of guitar was it?" Sawyer asks. He and Noah are propped up against the wall next to each other now, both in defensive poses.

"Does it matter?" I ask, losing most of the crowd with my tone. They're pissing me off.

"Humor us," Noah says.

"Fine. It was a 1934 Martin 000-45."

Wyatt whistles from behind me, Sawyer looks pissed, and Noah seems downright hurt.

"Did you go home to get that?" Noah asks with an accusing tone.

"Home?" Wyatt and Sawyer echo, but I ignore them.

"No, Noah, I wouldn't do that without you. I called one of the property managers and had them pack it up for Eli and send it to him. I don't owe you an explanation, but I'll give you one because I don't have anything to hide."

The three of them wait with baited breath for me to continue, but I need a second to compose myself. "My dad taught Eli to play on that guitar. It was Dad's favorite guitar and he took it everywhere with us. He always intended to give it to Eli one day. After he was gone, I didn't think about it. Probably because I was so angry with Eli. When we started talking about the house the other day, I remembered. And since Eli did me a huge favor by going with me to get your present today, I figured I owed him one. This one just happened to be a long time coming. Giving Eli that guitar was the right thing to do, and none of you are going to make me feel bad about it."

On that note, I pivot on my heel and go back into the kitchen. After downing my eggnog, I have Karen give me a refill. They don't get to be in the Christmas spirit for some people and not others. Who do they think they are?

Noah's strong arms wrap around me from behind, but I don't let myself fall into them like usual. "I'm sorry, babe. I had no right to judge or be jealous. What you did was a good thing and I'm proud of you."

"Thank you," I say, allowing myself to lean back into his embrace as he kisses me on the top of my head.

"They're so cute," Allie says to Jordan from the couch, and he just shakes his head. I think Jordan is a lot more like Sawyer than he is Noah.

After the pizza finally came, I was completely buzzed and I'm pretty sure everyone else in the house was, too. We were all spread around the table and the bar, eating and having a great time.

"Uncle Noah?" Saylor asks, tucking a dangling strand of cheese into her mouth.

"Yes, ladybug?"

"My mommy says you're going to make lots of babies with Amelia. Will they be my cousins?" It was suddenly so quiet you could hear a pin drop. Diane covers her eyes with her hands, and Rob begins laughing uncontrollably, as does Noah. I must look like a deer caught in headlights, but when I see Sawyer's face he looks sad.

"Maybe someday, Saylor, but not anytime soon. But yes, when I have a baby they will be your cousin." Noah diffused that situation like a boss, and I suddenly find myself thinking about how sexy he is when he's around his nieces. I can only imagine how I'd feel if he was all lovey like that with our kids.

"My wife is going to have to stop talking where little ears can hear," Rob teases Diane, and Karen and Owen chuckle.

"It's a lesson we all learn at some point. They get to a certain age where they repeat everything," Owen tells Diane with a sympathetic nod.

Darren and Belle come in and Belle is practically drooling. "Want some pizza, mama?" I ask, passing her my plate.

"I'm not sure *I* do, but this baby smells cheese and dough and I'm suddenly starving. She's going to be a carbaholic." Belle takes a bite with an appreciative moan. And while she enjoys her pizza, Emme is tugging on Darren's pant leg with pizza-covered fingers.

"What's up, Emme buns?" Darren leans down and she feeds him a bite. He plops down on the floor with her and they babble about pizza and God knows what else. I think Belle's ovaries are about to explode watching the two of them. If she has this kind of reaction with him and Emme, she's going to be knocked up again in no time.

After the girls had their baths and were snuggled into their pajamas, they got things ready for Santa. Saylor and Sawyer picked out all the perfect Christmas cookies for Santa, and Emme picked out the carrots for the reindeer. My poor childhood reindeer must have been starving because we never left treats for them at our house. Diane and Rob finally put the girls to bed, and Karen took all the stockings to her room to fill after she and Owen said their goodnights.

Once the girls were asleep, the siblings jumped into action moving bikes, dollhouses, kitchen playsets, and more into the living room, surrounding the tree with them. It looks like a Christmas toy catalog. "This is too much, you guys! We're never going to fit all of this into our house!" Diane exclaims in awe.

Based on what everyone bought for the little ones, Santa has been extra giving this year.

"They can leave some of it here. They'll get a kick out of being able to come over and play with it. We'll be back at Easter, but you know you guys can come over whenever to hang out and go to the beach. It will give them toys for the summer." Sawyer makes a valid point.

We spend hours talking and drinking until Rob realizes it's after midnight. Knowing the girls will be up early and we're all drunker than we should be—except for Belle, of course—we decide to call it a night.

As soon as Noah and I make it into our room, he presses me against the wall, slamming his mouth against mine in a passionate kiss. His hands are everywhere all at once and so are mine. When my hands make their way to his cock, he groans in appreciation. "I'm so fucking hard for you right now."

"Do you want your present, Noah? It's technically Christmas and I'd like to give it to you in private."

"Is it sexual?" he asks with a wicked gleam in his eyes.

"Not necessarily, but I think it will be. Get naked and be ready for me. I'll be back in a minute."

"Don't take too long, Mel. I don't have much patience right now." He tugs on my bottom lip with his teeth and smacks my ass. Hm … drunk Noah is playful; this could be fun.

I pull three bags out from under the cabinet. One has part of my present to Noah, one has a present for Belle's baby, and the last one has Christmas wrapping paper and supplies.

Noah's present is a red lace camisole and a pair of low-riding panties. Once I have them on, I tape a piece of wrapping paper over my bandage as decoration. My heart begins to pound; I hope I did the right thing and this isn't about to blow up in my face. I'm so far out of my comfort zone right now I could cry, but I did this for Noah; I'd do anything for him.

When I walk out of the bathroom, he's instantly on his feet. "Damn, Mel, you look beautiful." He grazes his hands across the lacey material, pausing below my hip. Walking backward to the bed, he inches up my camisole and lowers my panties a bit, his eyes narrowing at the festively-covered bandage. "What's this, Mel? What did you do?" I'm biting my lip, and Noah brings his finger up and pulls it from my mouth. "Talk to me, baby. What is this?"

"It's something for us. I have a hard time letting people into my heart, Noah, and you are my polar opposite in that aspect. In everything you do, you're looking to the future, encouraging me and reminding me you have faith in us, even if I'm not ready for the big steps yet."

"And I always will," he replies sincerely, his hands still hovering around the bandage but not touching it.

"I know you will, and this is my way of showing you even if my logical mind isn't there yet, my heart has been with yours every step of the way and always will be, forever." My hands begin to tremble as I brace them on his shoulders. He sits down on the edge of the bed and traces the outer edges.

"Can I open it now?"

I nod wordlessly as he carefully pulls the bandage back. Since the ink is fresh, it's still covered in ointment, but the black script is bold and unmistakable. His eyes bounce back and forth between mine and the tattoo. He's speechless; I can only hope that's a good thing.

"Do you like it?"

A single tear escapes his eye and he kisses his way up my body, slowly and seductively. "It's the sexiest fucking thing I've ever seen and the best present anyone has ever given me."

"Really?" I ask on a sigh of relief, thankful I didn't just mess things up.

"Do you even have to ask? You tattooed my last name on one of the sexiest parts of your body where only I can see it. The name that will soon enough be yours, the name that will belong to our children. You just made yourself a part of my family legacy without me even asking you to. How could I not love it?"

"Um … yeah, about that … Eli has seen it. I needed someone to go with me and he was the lucky winner. But Noah, he's so fucking happy for us. And he knows, without a doubt, you're the man who holds the key to my heart and my happiness."

"Damn straight I do." Noah pulls off the camisole and my panties, kissing his way from my hips to my toes as he takes them off. My entire body hums with need. After grabbing a condom off the nightstand and rolling it on, he lies down and pulls me to him. "Love me, Mel."

With my legs spread over his, I position him at my entrance and slide down onto him slowly. His hands move immediately to my hips, with his thumb caressing the outer edges of the "W" on my new tattoo. He's careful not to touch it since it's still a bit pink and tender, but he's getting as close as possible. His eyes are locked on it as I ride him slowly, as if it's going to disappear into thin air if he loses sight of it.

I can't even be mad; it's obvious he loves it. Even without making eye contact with me directly, he's making love to me with every other part of his body.

"Kiss me, Amelia," he commands, finally moving his eyes to mine. As I take his mouth with mine, he pushes deeper into me. Lacing his fingers through my hair with one hand, he sits up on his other elbow and pulls me closer to him. With every stroke of his tongue and thrust of his hips he brings me higher and higher into euphoria.

Our passionate cries fuel the desire between us, each of us not able to get enough of the other. If I knew getting a tattoo would have this effect on Noah, I might have done it sooner. "Noah!" I cry when he hits that perfect spot inside of me again and again.

"Come with me, Amelia," he says, gripping my hip harder, trying to hold on as he waits for me.

My walls convulse around him, and I stifle my cries by taking his lips in mine. Noah's body trembles as he powerfully releases himself into me. He wraps both his arms around me and we tumble back onto the mattress together, both of us panting as if we just ran a marathon.

After he tosses away the condom, Noah climbs on top of me, resting his head by my upper thigh as he traces his fingers around and around my tattoo. "Thank you for my present." His sparkling eyes meet mine.

"You're welcome," I reply with a smile.

"I have to ask, have you always wanted a tattoo?"

"Nope, not really."

With my words, he comes back up to the top of the bed and tucks me into the crook of his arm. "So why now, Mel?" He seems concerned now that the endorphins are wearing off; maybe the alcohol is, too.

"That night with Sara was eye-opening for me in a lot of ways. My logical mind tells me it's only been three months, almost five if you count when we met. But the part of me my heart rules says it doesn't matter. Love is love. I love you, Noah Weston, and I don't need a calendar to remind me it hasn't been long enough, or that it's been just the right amount of time."

"So you're proving a point to yourself?" he asks with genuine curiosity.

"No, not even close. I'm reminding myself life should be lived to the fullest and you are the best thing that has ever happened to me. I put your name on my body because you're the only man I've ever wanted as a permanent fixture in my life. Ever, Noah. After what happened to us, I don't care what anyone thinks."

He kisses the top of my head, and I snuggle in closer to him. "So was the placement significant to you? It could have been your wrist, shoulder, low back, or forearm, but why here?" he asks, tracing the tattoo again.

"It's going to sound girly."

He chuckles against the top of my head. "I like girly, in case you haven't noticed."

"Okay, but don't laugh. So it's below my hip but basically right above my pelvic bone. I put it there so only you could see it. Even in a bathing suit, I'm pretty sure it will be tucked away nicely. I don't care if people know I have it, but this seems intimate somehow."

"Very intimate," he murmurs while playing with my hair.

"And I was going to get Noah instead, but I started thinking about it and realized Weston would be more appropriate because eventually … years down the line … those bones are going to move to make room for the babies growing inside of me. At least one or two Westons will come from these hips. I guess I thought … I don't know, I just loved their name being in the area they'll grow would be sort of special."

"It's so fucking special, Mel. But I don't know … one or two is calling it low. I picture at least four or more. Especially since twins run in the family."

I flip over and pop a kiss on his lips. "No way, Noah, these hips won't spread that far. No twins allowed."

"Tell that to the Weston powerhouse sperm. I'm only the delivery method, they're the ones who work their way to the final destination." He sounds so fucking happy.

"And that's why we're not having babies for years. Our sex life is way too phenomenal to give up on it this early. We need to practice for a long, long time."

With a yawn, he pulls me back into the crook of his arm. "Our sex life *is* pretty damn amazing. Merry Christmas, Amelia. Thank you for the best gift ever."

"Merry Christmas, Noah," I reply with a yawn of my own. As I fall asleep, the only thought in my mind is how extraordinarily lucky I am to be here.

The Holidays

Morning comes quickly. For someone who isn't a morning person, Noah is bright-eyed and ready for action. And when I say action, I don't mean the good kind. He's as bad as one of the kids, dying to go open his presents and give me mine.

We make our way out to the living room, where everyone seems to be gathering. The girls aren't even up yet, but I'm sure their uncles will wake them soon. Karen is brewing coffee for all; I've never been more thankful for her than the moment she passes me the first cup. Even Sawyer is smiling from ear to ear, not seeming to care I got a cup before him.

Belle pulls me aside and eyes me up with a curious glare.

"Morning, Belle. Merry Christmas."

The side of her mouth pulls up in a crooked grin "Mm hm, I bet it is. Noah must have given you some present last night."

A blush creeps up my face as I pull her into the bathroom. "Why do you say that?"

"Because I got up for some leftover pizza around one in the morning and the way you were calling out his name even got *me* hot and bothered. What the hell did he give you to deserve that performance?"

Shit, I didn't realize we were so loud, but we were pretty drunk. "Um, it's actually what I gave him."

"Well?" she prompts, her hands on her hips. I never intended to keep this from her. If Noah wants to tell anyone, that's his choice.

"In the vault, Belle, okay?"

She nods excitedly, and I pass her my coffee to hold while I gingerly lower my pants and peel back the bandage. Seeing her eyes bug out of her head is worth everything. I don't think I've ever surprised Belle this much. She places my cup on the counter and hugs me.

"I'm not sure I ever thought I'd see the day, but this is almost as good as a wedding ring. Shit, Mel, no wonder he made you scream like a banshee. He probably came once just from looking at that sexy ink."

"Hardly. He saved all that for me. And damn … it was all that."

"So I heard. What does this mean exactly?"

Her brown eyes twinkle with excitement. "It means *someday,* way down the road, I'm going to accept a ring, get married, and after years of phenomenal sex, be his baby mama."

"Good, that's exactly what should happen. For some reason I can't picture you or Noah having an oops baby like me and Darren. I could totally picture Sawyer having ten of them, though," she adds with a laugh.

"Honestly, I picture Sawyer more with paternity suits out of nowhere. Hopefully, that never happens. He deserves more than that."

Belle's mood turns somber for a minute. "How's that going?"

"We're friends, Belle. Serious, honest-to-goodness friends. I'm not sure how we got there, but we're in a great place. I love Sawyer, but he's not the one for me."

"Does he know that?"

"He does. Sawyer is constantly encouraging me to have patience with Noah and reminding me how much Noah loves me. It was rough in the beginning, but Sawyer loves his brother and would never do anything to hurt him."

A soft knock at the door interrupts our talk. When I crack it open, Noah is smiling at me. "Is this a private party or can anyone join?"

"I'll let you two talk," Belle says, ducking out behind Noah as he walks in and locks the door behind him.

"What was that about?" The knowing twinkle in his eye already tells me he knows what we were up to.

"She heard us last night, Noah!" I whisper-shout into his ear.

"Yeah, well … I wouldn't be surprised if anyone on that side of the house heard us last night, Mel. We weren't exactly quiet."

"I'm so embarrassed. How can I go out there knowing they all heard us?"

Noah laughs and pulls me close. "Everyone in this house, kids aside, has had sex. If they haven't been embarrassed at some point, they're not doing it right. We were on fire last night, Mel, and I'm not going to apologize for that. Were you showing Belle your tattoo?"

"I was. I can't hide that from her. She's the only other person who sees me in all stages of getting dressed. But I'm not telling or showing anyone else. It's your gift, you can shout it from the rooftops if you want to, but I'm not showing it off to anyone else."

D. Kelly

"I wouldn't expect you to, and I have no current plans to shout anything from the rooftops. But Sawyer is about to wake the girls up, so we need to go open presents." He kisses me quickly and opens the door.

Sawyer pauses as he walks by. "Last night wasn't enough for you two?" The glimmer in his eye tells me he's teasing.

"I'm never having sex again," I mumble.

Sawyer laughs. "Why would you punish yourself like that? From the sounds of it, Noah was doing everything right." Still laughing, he walks down the hall to get Saylor and Emme. Noah's even laughing, but I don't find it funny. After grabbing my coffee, I head to the kitchen for a refill.

Thankfully, everyone is already gathered in the living room and chatting excitedly. Rob and Diane both have cameras out, ready to record, and when the girls run into the room with Sawyer right behind them, I understand why. Talk about a priceless memory. I've only been the kid at Christmas; I've never seen the excitement of other kids at Christmas. Everyone in the room is beaming with every squeal and scream as the girls try out their new gifts from Santa.

Once it dies down a bit, Noah, Sawyer, Emme, and Saylor play Santa and pass out gifts to everyone. I excuse myself for a moment to get Belle's gift from the bedroom. When I come back, the whole room is in disarray with people opening gifts. As I hold Belle's gift in front of her, she reaches for it with grabby hands.

"Yours is in that pile somewhere at your feet, but this one is for the baby," I tell her, and she immediately pulls all the tissue paper out and holds up the pink and white onesie.

"Auntie Mel loves me most." She hops up and manages to avert the presents at her feet as she gives me a hug. "This is the cutest thing ever. Thank you."

Even Darren seems to think it's adorable. I make my way over to Noah where he's saved me a spot on the floor next to the couch. It's a full house in here and it still amazes me they all spend the holidays together.

"When did you get that?" he asks as he passes me a gift.

"Yesterday, when I was out. Once we found out it was a girl, I wanted to get something especially for her."

"That's really sweet. Sawyer has already claimed favorite uncle so you may have a fight on your hands."

"Sawyer can bring it. I've known Belle longer than he's known Darren. He can be favorite uncle but I'm all-time favorite anything."

Noah just chuckles and moves on to opening more gifts. Everyone is floating in a sea of presents. It's too chaotic to pay attention to what everyone is getting, but I make sure to call out my thank yous as I open each gift. Once I've opened them all, Noah hands me a square box.

"This is from me," he says shyly. As I open it, I feel everyone's eyes on me. Inside the box is a C.D. labeled "Mel's EP" and a USB stick. The back of the case says *Songs for Mel*.

"Noah, what is this?" I already know; my trembling hands and tear-filled eyes give it away, but I can't believe he would do this.

"That's what I was doing in the garage. Making you your own … mixed tape of sorts. These are all songs that remind me of you, or of us, in some way. I promised you more songs, Mel, and this time I stepped out of my comfort zone to give you exactly what you asked for."

"That is so sweet," Diane says from the love seat.

I put the present down, place both of my hands on his cheeks, and kiss him senseless. I don't even care that everyone is watching. "This is the best present ever. Thank you, Noah."

With a shy smile, he nods and laces our fingers together. Everyone is smiling at us like we're too adorable for words. Maybe we are.

"Noah is so fucking whipped," Sawyer says after our affectionate display. Of course, the little ears pick up on it.

"Daddy, what does whipped mean?" Saylor asks innocently, and Sawyer leans his head back and laughs.

"One day, Sawyer, it's going to be *your* kids asking questions and I'm going to have a ball making sure you get payback," Rob tells him as he tries to refocus Saylor on her toys and not her naughty uncle.

I know it's Christmas and everyone is having a great time, but all I want to do is go to my room and listen to the music Noah made for me. In a way it's like having a present I still can't open. As the hours pass and the day turns to night, the alcohol flows freely again. By the time we get to go to sleep, neither Noah or myself can walk a straight line.

"So … how was your first Weston family Christmas?" Noah's words are slurred as he pulls me down onto the bed with him.

"It was fun, but all I want to do is listen to my present."

"Is that so?" he asks, climbing on top of me. "Because I want to listen to my present, too. I think we can give them a run for their money on last night's show, how about you?"

With Noah's hardness pressed up against me, any thoughts of music are completely out of my mind.

"I think that can be arranged," I reply as he moves his mouth to mine.

It's New Year's Eve. Since Christmas, Noah and I have spent almost every waking second wrapped around each other in bed. In what little free time I've had outside of the bed, I've been constantly listening to Noah's music. Having the house to ourselves for a few days has been absolute bliss.

Darren took Belle away for a few days, Sawyer is spending time at J's before we go back on the road, and their family left the day after Christmas. Warren, Sam, Anna, and Wyatt went back up to San Diego for a few days before we go back on the road.

I thought they would be doing one last show for New Year's, but Noah said they left that scene behind years ago. He did say he has plans for us tonight and for me to dress casual and warm. For the last few hours, he's been running errands while I've been relaxing and getting ready. Noah's version of "Let it be Me" by Ray LaMontagne is flowing through the speakers, and like anything Noah does, it's amazing.

I'm trying to pick out what to wear. So far, I've got an emerald-green bra and panty set to match Noah's eyes. The weather is mild—in the upper sixties—but if we're going to be out it could get pretty cold. I just wish I knew if I was dressing for warmth from car to building, or like waiting all night to see the Rose Parade. Finally, I settle on jeans, a sweater, and a pair of Nike's. I can bring a jacket just in case.

While I wait for Noah, I go back through my notes from the holidays. I got behind in work after the accident, but I was able to catch up while Noah was working on my album. At some point, I'm going to have to start writing, but there's so much information to take in and organize. My photos help because they help me keep a timeline. Different cities each week, new fans, so much hype, and four men who are absolutely nothing like I would have expected them to be. Their public image isn't even close to who they really are. And that's what I want to showcase—them. These four amazing men who value family, friendship, and love over anything. I want their fans to get to know them as I have; maybe they'll have a better understanding as to why this is the end for them.

Luckily, I have a year to complete the book once the tour is wrapped up, but I'm so excited to begin the writing process I doubt it will take that long. I'm pulled from my musings when my phone dings with an incoming message.

Sawyer: Just wanted to wish you a Happy New Year, I know we won't talk later.

Me: Thank you! I hope you have a Happy New Year, too. What are you guys up to tonight?

Sawyer: No good, most likely the usual. Party at the bar, meet women, party with women after the bar.

Me: Well … be safe.

Sawyer: Enjoy your night, Princess, you're going to have a great time.

Me: You know what he's planning? I'm completely in the dark!

Sawyer: Of course, who do you think helped him plan? Noah is smooth but sometimes even he needs help.

Me: Thanks for helping your brother with his plans.

Sawyer: There's not much I wouldn't do for him, or you, Princess. Enjoy your night.

Me: You're sweeter than you let on, but I won't let your secret out of the bag. P.S. Don't forget to use your own condoms. Never trust a groupie.

Sawyer: Thanks for protecting my virtue and my image. No babies for me anytime soon, don't worry.

I send Sawyer the video link for "Red Solo Cup" by Toby Keith and wait for his reply. It comes pretty quickly.

Sawyer: Oh, Princess, you can do better than that. I would have thought this would be more your speed.

I click on the link; it's "Tonite" by D.J. Quik, and I bust out laughing. This song used to be my and Belle's jam.

Me: That song is so much more my speed! I'm beginning to think you know me too well.

Sawyer: Just well enough. Night, Princess, we're off to the bar.

Me: Night, Sawyer … stay safe <3

"What are you smiling at?" Noah asks as he walks in with a beautiful bouquet of red roses. Wearing a pair of dark jeans, black Vans, and a black long-sleeve Henley, he looks fucking scrumptious.

"Your brother. He wanted to say Happy New Year early. He also said he helped you plan my surprise and I should enjoy it."

363

"You are absolutely going to enjoy it, and he didn't exactly help me plan so much as help me *execute* said plan."

"So are those for me?"

"Well, I don't know," he says, stalking toward me. "You *are* the only smoking hot woman in this room with the name Weston tattooed on her skin. You tell me, are they for you?"

He's in a playful mood tonight. "They'd better be, or else I'm going to be sleeping alone tonight."

Noah pulls me close and tugs my bottom lip into his mouth "Not a chance. I'm not sleeping alone ever again if I can help it, and neither are you."

"Am I dressed okay?"

He makes a show of looking me over head to toe and then spins me around and smacks my ass. "You're perfect. Tonight is all about me and you."

"Should I bring a jacket?"

"Sure, but I'm not sure if you'll need it. We'll have to play it by ear. Are you ready to go?" His eyes are dancing with happiness; I can't wait to see what he has up his sleeve.

"Absolutely"

Locking my arm in his, Noah leads the way through the house and out the back door. The stairs down to the ocean are all lit up with tealight candles. When we reach their private beach, there's a white canopy tent set up. Like the kind they use for weddings but on a bit of a smaller scale.

"Noah, what is this?"

He pulls me into his warm embrace and kisses me tenderly. "I promised you a night under the stars and tonight is our night. Come see."

As he leads me to the tent, he points upward; it's then I notice the top of this tent is clear plastic. When I look around, I'm amazed at all he's done. There is a queen-sized air mattress topped with warm blankets and big, fluffy pillows. There are battery-powered heaters in the corners and lanterns next to the bed, as well as on the table where our dinner waits for us. Champagne is chilling on ice and roses are on the tables, accentuating the romance. The best part of all might just be the wooden floor underneath us so we're not plowing through sand.

"This is amazing. How did you manage to do all of this in only a few short hours?"

With a shrug of his shoulders, he pulls me back into his arms. "There's not much money won't do if the price is right. Not to mention Sawyer and J helped a lot. And just in case you're wondering, there is a security team in place in case some drunk partiers make it this far down the beach. It's unlikely, but sometimes it happens."

"I wasn't worried. I know you'll take care of us however you need to. Thank you for this, it's the most incredible thing anyone has ever done for me."

Noah trails kisses along my collarbone and works his way up to right below my ear. His hands are on my ass as he pulls me tightly against him. "This is our year, Amelia, and I wanted it to start off perfectly. The rest of our lives begins now." Noah fumbles in his pocket for a second as soft music begins piping through the tent. "May I have this dance?"

"Of course." As I tuck myself into Noah's arms, the beauty of this moment sinks in. The soft, jazzy music, the stars looking down on us from above, the ocean waves crashing against the shore—nothing could be more perfect.

We spend some time dancing under the moonlit stars, enjoying each other's company. Noah's taste in music is exceptional and before I know it he's leading me to the dinner table. When he uncovers shrimp scampi I moan in appreciation. Noah's learned pasta is the way to my heart. After dinner, he leads us outside our tent where there is a bonfire and blankets ready for us. Once we're snuggled together I lean my head against his shoulder.

"What are you thinking?" he asks while we gaze at the stars above us. It's a perfectly clear night; the view couldn't be better.

"A few things, actually." Sitting here with him reminds me of the first night we met. The night I never even wanted to go to their concert in the first place.

"Okay, so start with the biggest."

With a sigh, I continue to look up at the stars—letting all my emotions run wild—and give him exactly what he asks for. "I didn't plan for this, and I never thought I would be this kind of girl."

He tightens his hold around my shoulder. "What kind of girl is that?"

"That night when we met, I didn't want to go. I was happy to stay home, curled up in my pajamas, and talk to some of my readers on social media. Did you know Belle and I actually got into a little tiff because I wouldn't wear the BAD shirt she brought over for me?" I laugh at the memory. "I told her it was me or the shirt, and at the time I was wishing the shirt would win, but she picked me."

"Remind me to thank her," he adds with a chuckle.

"So we went to the show and it was a flashback of everything I'd been running from the past few years. As much as I didn't want to enjoy it, especially since I'm not fond of the band's music ... sorry, I know, sensitive subject."

"It's okay, Mel, you like our new stuff and you seem to enjoy *my* music, so I'll forgive you."

Placing a light kiss on his cheek, my eyes meet his. "I adore your music. But back to the story. That night, I felt this anticipation." He raises his brow, and I tuck myself back into his shoulder. "Yeah, I know, there's that word again. I should have understood something bigger was at work. As we went from our seats to being led through the halls at The Greek ..."

"That's where I first saw you. Did you notice me looking at you?" he interrupts.

"No, I felt you, though. I felt eyes on me, but when I looked up, no one was looking at me. You must have turned away. Then I felt eyes on me again so I turned around, but it was Sawyer then, watching as we walked away."

"That's not surprising at all. Sawyer has always had radar for good-looking women, he's just lacking the necessary execution to do anything more than have them for a one-night stand."

Noah's abrupt words surprise me, and I find myself quickly defending Sawyer. "He could if he wants to, Noah, but he doesn't. This is what he wants for now. He seems perfectly content with that. But I do hope, for his sake, he finds someone after the tour who makes him reconsider keeping himself shut off."

"You two have talked about relationships?"

"Don't act so stunned. Sawyer and I have become friends, and I have interviewed each of you for the book, so of course we've talked. But we're not talking about him right now, we're talking about us."

Noah smiles and places a brief kiss on top of my head. "Of course we are. Please continue."

"From the moment we met you guys, I was intrigued. You just ... weren't what I was expecting. And after we got to your house, I just had this excited but uneasy feeling. When Warren hit me with your offer, I was stunned and came down here to think. The last thing on my mind that night was finding a man or going on tour. It was terrifying to think about getting on a tour bus again. The last couple tours I was on didn't end so well, you know?"

"I'm sorry, Mel, we didn't know." His soft words are comforting, and he squeezes my hand in support.

"I know, Noah, it's okay. I'm happy I came so I could put those things behind me once and for all. But I was still reveling in the fact I was an independent woman. I didn't want nor need a man. I had BOB for the times when he was needed, and for the first time in my life I was making real money and could see a future beyond being someone's assistant. Then you happened."

"And is that a bad thing?"

When I look at Noah, his brown hair is blowing in the breeze, the moonlight shimmers off his eyebrow ring, and there's a grin poking up from the corner of his mouth. I wish I had a picture of him like this because he's never looked more handsome.

"No, it's a good thing. From the moment you sat down on the sand next to me, I never stood a chance. I was this independent, kickass woman, who didn't need a man in her life, and then you came along and kind of blew my world apart."

"I'm pretty sure *you* blew *my* world apart," he replies, letting his lips caress mine for the briefest of moments.

"But here's the thing … I don't feel like we rushed things. Isn't that strange? It's like the whole time we were friends and getting to know each other, but my heart kind of raced ahead to the finish line while the rest of me caught up. I'm sure there are things I don't know about you, probably more things I don't know than things I do know. But every time I find out something new, my heart beats faster and I get excited to know more. That night I didn't want this, but now I can't imagine not having it. So now, my question for you is this … You could have any woman in the world, Noah. Why me?"

Noah moves his arm down to my waist and flips me so we're face to face with me straddling him. "I wasn't looking for you, either, Mel. Not exactly, anyway. I knew I wanted the tour over so I could work on settling down. Because that's where I'm at right now. I want what Anna and Wyatt have, but I want kids in that equation. Dating on tour is next to impossible, so I knew once it was over I'd finally have a shot at finding more. Then you came along with your sassy mouth, pouty lips, sexy mind, and beautiful body and soul and I realized … Why *not* you?"

Noah's lips find my collarbone, and he blazes a trail of kisses up along my neck and works his way slowly and seductively to my mouth. After a sensual kiss, he continues his story. "When you came down to think, I followed because Darren wanted Belle, and because I was hoping to get to know you better. I didn't have any clue my heart was going to be stolen by yours right here on this beach. Once that happened, I was a goner. Every day from the night we met until the tour started, I waited in anticipation of seeing you again. Yet I knew if we got involved it could be problematic, to say the least. When you got on the bus and I offered you my bed and you turned me down because you thought I was a manwhore, it really bothered me. I didn't want you to have that opinion of me, and I was damn well going to prove to you I was a man worth taking seriously."

"Yeah, I could tell from the expression on your face I really hurt you when I said that. I'm sorry for ever assuming the worst about you."

"I forgive you," he says solemnly. "The bottom line is you make me happy, Amelia. Happier than I've ever been. When I wake up in the morning, I'm excited to have a whole new day with you. And when I fall asleep at night with you by my side, I sleep easier knowing you're tucked safely in my arms. I wasn't looking for you, either, but fate knew it was our time and she brought you to me."

The sounds of fireworks popping pulls my attention from Noah. Looking over my shoulder, I witness a gorgeous display. He turns my face back toward his. "Happy New Year, Amelia."

"Happy New Year, Noah," I reply before he takes my mouth and kisses me sensuously under the moonlit sky. Once he releases me, he turns me around and tucks me between his legs so we can watch the fireworks.

"This is amazing. Do they do this every year?"

He murmurs against my ear. "Do you want me to have them do this every year?"

Oh my God. He did this for me.

"Noah, you didn't?"

"Enjoy the show, Mel." His whispered words wrap around me like a cocoon. And as the grand finale begins, with me still tucked between Noah's legs, he reaches into his pocket and presents a box in front of me. With his mouth still pressed against my ear, his husky words wrap around me and fill me with fear and a simultaneous comfort the likes of which I've never experienced.

"Amelia Greyson, I know people will say it's fast, but sometimes you just know. I've known since the first night on this beach with you that what we had was vastly different than anything I've ever experienced. Last month, when I almost lost you, it brought my whole life into perspective. Every moment we have is a gift and I don't want to miss any moments with you. Marry me, Mel. We can move as fast or as slowly as you like. I want to know that one day you'll be my forever, no matter how long it takes to get there."

Any rational thought is gone from my mind. "I don't understand. When did you ... Noah!"

He chuckles against my skin as if he already knew he was going to throw me off guard. "The day Wyatt and I were shopping. I lied. I found exactly what I was looking for. If you don't like it we can get something else, I won't be hurt."

"Before the tattoo?"

"Yeah, baby. Before the tattoo."

He wanted me before he knew. He wants me forever. God help me, I want him, too. I flip back around and straddle him again, pulling his face to mine. He fumbles with the ring box for a second before finally getting a grasp on it again.

"Yes, Noah Weston. I will absolutely, with my entire heart and soul, marry you." And before he can even slip the ring onto my finger, I seal my promise with a kiss I'll remember my entire life. I'll never be able to watch a fireworks display again without remembering this night and this kiss.

After I've kissed him breathless, he pulls the ring from the box and holds it up in front of me. "Did you even look at the ring?"

"I didn't before, but I see it now and it's gorgeous. Thank you."

It's perfect. A single, solitary round-cut diamond on a band made of smaller diamonds all the way around. It's a little flashy for everyday Mel, but considering I'm going to be a rock star's wife, it's extremely understated.

As he slides the ring on my finger, I'm amazed it fits perfectly. "Did Belle know?"

He shakes his head. "Why do you ask?"

"The ring fits like it was made for me. I figured she gave you my size."

"Darren told me what size he got Belle and I got two sizes up from that. I was going to just get one but Darren reminded me how tiny Belle really is, so I went up one more."

"Good call. So do all the guys know?"

A sheepish looks crosses his face. "Well ... yeah. I needed their help, and they were happy to give it once they figured out why. Even Sawyer went out of his way to make sure all of this went off without a hitch. I owe him a lot for tonight."

"He loves you. Just remember that when you have to return the favor for him one day."

Noah holds my hand up and lets his fingers caress the ring, then he brings it to his mouth and kisses my hand.

"Can I make love to the future Mrs. Weston now?"

"Yes, please" I murmur, allowing him to help me up from the sand.

Amelia

Present Day

That night was hands down one of the best nights of my life. It was also the calm before the storm. Even now, looking back, there would have been no way to pinpoint all the changes to come. The first of many started a mere few hours before we left to go back on the road. I'd love to write about that night; maybe someday I'll come back and add to this part of the book. Right now, it's a private memory between the two of us. What I will say is our lovemaking hit a higher plane of existence that night. One of which our relationship continued to thrive upon.

It seems like everything after that night was in fast forward. The new year brought new challenges, but Noah's and my love never faltered, but I'll get to that.

Moving back over to the window, I look out at the dreary day. The waves crash furiously against the shore, lashing back at mother nature in anger for disrupting their calm, lazy approach. It's even been thundering and lightning, which is rare for Southern California. Normally, I'd be worried about the boys since they're camping, but they're really glamping. Their idea of camping is a three-bedroom luxury cabin up in Big Bear where they can play in the snow, talk shit with each other, and drink. They need this time away, too. Since the tour ended, it's only the second time they've had a boys' weekend and the first one didn't go too well, but I'll eventually get to that, too.

The chime of my inbox reminds me there's still lots of work to do if I'm going to finish this book in less than forty hours. Speaking of … it's a message from him.

Hey,

This storm has wreaked some havoc up here. The roads are all closed and they don't anticipate them being open until Monday morning. Looks like you've got yourself an extra day to make a decision. I know this isn't easy, but nothing worth having ever is. All you really need to know is I love you, and I always have. Everything else is just details.

I've been considering sending him the pages I wrote yesterday. I thought maybe I'd let him read them when he came home, if he was still interested after hearing my answer. But now that he's going to be gone an extra day, and I'm still no closer to an answer than I was when they left, maybe it's the perfect time to let him into my thoughts. If anything, maybe he'll empathize with me and understand my hesitation if he knows what's going on in my heart and in my mind. Before I second guess myself to death, I reply.

Hi,

Thank you for the update, please stay safe up there. I know how you guys can be at times and since you're snowed in, please don't go snowboard off a cliff and break a leg or anything. I'm thinking about your question, but I'm never really *not* thinking about it. I know you feel like I blow you off a lot, but this situation is so much bigger than us. Actually, I've been writing. I know you thought I might and you were right. It's the only way to find my way through to the answers I need. I'm going to send you what I've written so far. If you want more, I can send you the rest as I continue to write. Don't worry about me; one way or another I'll have an answer for you when you come home. I love you.

A little while later, he replies.

Thank you for trusting me with your words. I'll take good care of them. Now, all you need to do is trust me with your heart. I won't let you down, not this time. I love you, too. Always.

His words resonate with me long after his email. I've never feared him letting me down. My fear is losing him forever.

Belle's New York Announcement

Slammers!

Happy New Year! Yes, I fully realize that was yesterday, but today is our first BAD announcement for the year and it seemed appropriate. Alright, let's get down to business. After spending the holidays home with their family and loved ones, our BAD boys are once again on the move. Under the cover of night, BAD will arrive in New York for a week filled with interviews and shows. Hopefully, you're one of the lucky ones who get to see them. But if not, or if you're not in the New York area, please see the list of interviews below and where you can watch them.

This year is going to be one for the records, folks! Our BAD boys are on their way out, but who's coming in? Check out the list of emerging new artists on our homepage and see if you can pick the next up-and-coming legacy. Who knows, maybe once our boys retire they'll start mentoring some of these new groups and won't be completely lost to us. It's all wishful thinking and speculation, but a girl can dream!

On another note, meet and greets. BAD and their security teams have decided meet and greets will remain modified to autographs only. In light of recent occurrences, I'm sure you can all understand why this is the new rule. Anyone in the meet and greet will now receive a group photo of BAD which you can have autographed while you're there to help make up for the inconvenience. Isn't that sweet of them? I swear they are always considering their fans' feelings, which is why BAD is truly one of a kind.

That's all for now!
Don't forget - Live today like there's no tomorrow.
Xs and Os
Belle

One big façade

"Earth to Mel, where are you?" Noah's teasing tone pulls me from my frantic thoughts. Our plane is taking off and even though it's a private plane, I still don't want to tell him what's really on my mind.

"I'm right here, sorry. I get a little nervous on planes. I'm more of a bus girl."

He laces his fingers in mine and nods in understanding. "You've been off since you got back from the doctor. Did the procedure go okay? Do you need some pain meds or to lie down or something? I read," he takes note of the people surrounding us and whispers, "that getting an IUD can be uncomfortable."

Leave it to Noah to research IUD placements. I'd kiss him if I weren't so nervous. "I'm okay. A few days and I'll be good as new. I've just got a lot on my mind, especially with the signing tomorrow and everything."

"I'm sorry I can't be there. I'm still trying to get out of my interview, though. I really want to be there to support you. I'm so proud of you, Mel. All your dreams are coming true."

"Hey, lovebirds," Wyatt calls out from across the aisle. "You guys pick a wedding date yet? You know that's going to be *the* most-asked question as soon as the paparazzi get a look at that rock on Mel's finger."

Thankfully, Noah takes the lead on this one. My head just really isn't in the game right now. "There's no rush. Whenever Mel wants to get married, we'll get married."

"So, like, never?" Sawyer retorts from the row behind us.

"Don't be mean," I call out.

Noah reinforces his faith in my love for him with his response. "She wouldn't have said yes if it was a never, she's not that cruel."

I crack a smile at his words. He's not wrong, but this conversation is making me queasy. Or maybe it's the fact we're in a smaller plane than I like and there's turbulence. Take your pick. Sawyer starts humming a tune behind us, and Darren and Wyatt are chatting between themselves. Belle was so sad when we left, but she gets it. She also joked about their pregnancy-hormone-induced reunion sex and I tuned her out about there. The good thing is Veronica should have been touching down with her boy toy as our flight was taking off, so Belle won't be alone while we're gone.

Sawyer begins humming a tune I haven't heard before, and Darren catches on and starts hitting some beats to go with it against the arm rest.

"Hell yeah, man. What is that? Do you have words for it yet?" Darren's enthusiasm catches up to the rest of them and they all pop out of their seats and head for the sitting area to chew his brain a bit more.

"Are you coming?" Noah asks, holding his hand out to me.

"Nah, I'm going to rest I think. I'm really tired." It's been a long few days. Ever since I said yes, Noah has been insatiable in bed. Not that I haven't enjoyed it, but I think it's catching up to me. We didn't sleep at all New Year's Eve, and not much last night, either.

Bending down, he plants a sweet kiss against my lips. "Get some rest. We'll be there before you know it."

The sounds of them talking excitedly lulls me to sleep. Even though I hate planes, their voices calm me enough to make me feel safe.

As the plane begins its descent onto the runway at La Guardia, I wake up. I can't believe I slept the whole flight. It's about nine in the evening New York time and all I want to do is curl up in bed with some room service and get a good night's sleep.

"Are you feeling better, Sleeping Beauty?" Noah asks softly as my eyes blink open.

"Yeah, I'm just tired. You wore me out the past few days."

"Seriously didn't need to hear that," Sawyer mutters from behind us. The rest of them laugh, but I feel my cheeks heat up; I didn't mean for him to hear that, either.

"You're cute when you blush," Noah replies with a kiss against my cheek. "We'll check in and get some room service, sound good?"

"Sounds incredible. Thank you." I pull my phone out of my purse and turn it on. There are a bunch of missed calls and messages from Belle.

Belle: I know you're on the plane but call me before you deplane if you can. URGENT

After hitting her speed dial number, I pull the phone to my ear.

"Oh my God, Mel! Have you gotten off the plane yet?"

"No, why. What's going on, Belle?"

"Hey, you're talking to Belle? Tell her I'll call her in a bit," Darren says, leaning over my shoulder.

"Mel, the paparazzi have pictures of your ring. Someone must have caught you guys at the airport earlier. All hell is breaking loose. Right now, it's all speculation, but you know how fans get. You need to figure out what to say and stay safe. Bitches be crazy, you know."

"Hang on, Belle. Hey, guys, uh … the cat's out of the bag about me and Noah. Someone got a picture of my ring before we left L.A. Belle wants to know what we want to do, if anything. Right now, it's just speculation."

I knew this was going to happen; we should have gotten in front of it from the get go. This is what I don't miss from this public life. Everyone thinking it's okay for them to be all up in your business.

"Whatever you want to do, Mel, it's up to you. I'm happy to let it be known, but you need to be comfortable," Noah says with a sympathetic look.

"I agree with Noah, Princess. Mac and Ryan have the SUVs already running and ready to go on the side of the building. Perks of flying private is they get to basically pull up to the plane's door. Have Belle put out a release, and as long as there's no stake-out squad at the hotel, you'll be good to go until tomorrow. We'll confirm it in our interviews and take the pressure off you. But Noah, you should send Mac with her tomorrow to her signing and hire someone else for us." Sawyer's words make sense.

"I agree, Mel. Let me announce this right now on the *Slammed* blog and we can sort of get ahead of it. Send me a selfie of you and Noah and a close-up of that ring."

"Okay. Thanks, Belle."

"What are best friends for? Be careful, and I'll talk to you tomorrow."

Noah and I snap a photo; considering I just slept for hours, I don't look bad. My makeup is still even in place. Ten minutes later, my phone beeps with an incoming message from Belle. A link to the *Slammed* post.

Slammed Blog Post

Slammers!

It's your girl Belle, and I've got some juicy and exciting information to share with you. You may have seen a photo circulating of Amelia Greyson wearing a new piece of jewelry. I'm here to put the rumors to rest. Noah Weston and Amelia Greyson are indeed engaged.

The lucky couple spent a romantic New Year's Eve together, where Noah and Mel decided to take the next step in their relationship. I know there are probably some sad Noah fans out there tonight, but trust me when I say they really are a match made in heaven. Just a few weeks ago, Noah and Mel were staring death in the face; who could blame them for wanting to live each moment to the fullest from here on out? Don't they look happy as can be?

Let's give Noah and Mel our best wishes and congratulations on their upcoming nuptials.

Follow their lead and my advice – Live today like there's no tomorrow.

Xs and Os
Belle

"This was the perfect way to announce it. Belle selling our love to the world. I bet she was a kickass Girl Scout and probably sold more cookies than anyone." Noah's words make me laugh. Belle was indeed a super cookie-selling Girl Scout.

"Ask her to show you her Brownie uniform. She's got more badges than anyone I've ever seen. Although, to be fair, I was pretty sheltered and she's the only Girl Scout I ever knew. But I agree, this was perfect. If it had to be public, letting my best friend do it tastefully and get a career boost at the same time was a great way to go."

Noah, Sawyer, and I get off the plane and into the truck with Mac. Wyatt and Darren go with Ryan. Warren is flying in later because he decided to stay an extra day in San Diego with Sam. Unfortunately, although the ride to the hotel was peaceful, the outside of the hotel is anything but. BAD fans are lined up all along the sidewalk. At least the hotel is keeping them outside.

"Guys, that's a pretty big crowd. Is hotel security on standby, Mac?" Sawyer asks, concern lacing his tone.

"This is why I can't wait to be retired for a few years. I hope some of this craziness dies down. This is insane. They don't even know we're staying here … every hotel in town probably looks like

377

this right now." Noah may be voicing his irritation, but I know he'll be as nice as possible to the fans. He always is.

Mac lets Noah finish venting before answering, "Yeah, we're set with security. We'll park in front and get you guys in. Their valet team is going to take the cars right away. Check-in is ready for you, but there are some fans staying in the hotel. They can't make them leave since they're just lounging in the lobby. You know the drill."

"Mel, we're going to tuck you between us and move fast. Whatever you do, don't let go of me and Sawyer."

"Yeah, Princess, these New York girls don't play. Hold on tight," Sawyer says, looking just as worried as Noah.

"You guys *do* know I've been through this before, right? Believe it or not, I can hold my own." I'm not a damsel they need to save.

"Alright, then, show us what a badass you are," Sawyer snaps.

Noah rolls his eyes. "Don't be a dick, Sawyer. Let's just get in and get settled," Noah says firmly as the car pulls to a stop. As we wait for Mac to get out and open the door, I see all the chaos. It's not just fans, it's paparazzi, too. Flashes go off one after another, fans are holding up posters; some of them are already crying. Sometimes I think I was blessed to grow up in the industry so I never went through one of these excessive fangirl phases. And another part of me thinks maybe I missed out on something special. A feeling you get when music touches you deep down in your soul and you become so invested in the maker you'd move heaven and earth for even the slightest glimpse of the people whose words make your life make sense.

When Mac opens the door, their screams become deafening. My heart races as all their grabby hands reach out, trying to get a small piece of these men. Ryan, Wyatt, and Darren are right in front of us. They've already stopped for a few autographs, but Noah and Sawyer aren't having it. They're waving and yelling hello, but they're not stopping … until they have no choice.

One of the girls escapes the blocked off area and manages to jump onto Noah's back.

"Whoa!" he exclaims as she throws her arms around his neck. Sawyer keeps me in his firm grasp, but a few other girls get loose while Mac tries to extract Noah. One of the bolder ones grabs my free hand—the one with my engagement ring on it.

"This was supposed to be mine, you stupid bitch!" she screams at me, tears streaming down her cheeks. I try and pull my hand back, but she's trying to pull my ring off.

I've had enough. Yanking my hand from Sawyer who, even though he's still holding on, is under siege himself, I try and reason with the girl. They love their fans, and I don't want to fuck this up for them.

"Let go." My tone is calm but firm.

"No, bitch, not until you give me my ring," she snaps.

Calmly, as I see NYPD pulling up, I warn her again, "You're not going to like what happens if you don't let go right fucking now."

She manages to get my ring off my finger, and while she looks down at her prize, I punch her in the face. She falls to the ground, her nose gushing blood everywhere as I yank my ring back from her. At the same moment, Mac lifts me up and runs with me like I'm a football into the hotel. It's embarrassing, but whatever … I've got my fucking ring and that's all that matters.

The lobby has been cleared of all guests. Darren and Wyatt watch in awe as I shake my hand out.

"Holy shit, Mel, you clocked her!" Darren yells with a proud smile.

"Bitch stole my ring," I tell them as I slide it back onto my finger.

Sawyer and Noah finally make it inside with a few policemen trailing behind them.

"Baby, are you okay?" Noah asks, pulling me into his arms.

"Yeah, I'm fine."

"Uh, Princess, I think you need some ice for that hand. But holy shit, next time I'll take you at your word. You don't have to punch someone to prove a point," Sawyer says, but even he's smiling like a proud papa.

"Ma'am, the woman you assaulted is screaming she wants to press charges. We're going to need a statement." The officer sounds annoyed, but it's a good sign he isn't rushing to arrest me already.

"Officer, she assaulted me first. She grabbed my hand, told me my engagement ring was supposed to be hers, and then ripped it off my finger. I punched her, but not until *after* she'd stolen my ring. Then I took it back while she was crying on the ground."

"I'm sorry to have to ask this, but what is the estimated value of the ring?" he asks, taking notes in his notebook.

"Is that necessary?" Noah asks.

"Yes, sir, if there's video of her stealing the ring, it's a crime."

"It's fine, Noah, let it go. You don't have to tell him if you don't want to." I don't know what Noah spent on the ring and I don't care.

But he's a private person; the whole world doesn't need to know, either.

"Fuck that, Mel, she needs to pay for what she did. The ring was just over forty-five thousand dollars. My attorney can get you the receipt for your records … here's his card." Noah hands him Tony's card from his wallet while all of us are in a stunned silence. I knew the ring was nice but I didn't realize *how* nice. I'm not comfortable with this. At all.

"Well, in the state of New York that's considered grand larceny. Do you want to press charges?" the officer asks.

I shake my head. "If she agrees to not pursue assault charges in court, and she agrees to not pursue them in a civil court, either, I won't press charges."

"Mel …" Noah cautions, but I've had my fill.

"No, that's my deal. I don't want anyone going to jail."

Sawyer walks up to me and hands me an ice pack. My hand is sore and swollen; it's going to be a bitch to sign autographs tomorrow. I take a seat on one of the chairs in the lobby and Wyatt sits next to me while Noah and Sawyer finish with the cop.

"Who would have thought you were a scrapper?"

His words make me laugh. "Yeah, well … when you grow up as Joey Triton's daughter, you learn early on that girls and women can be crazy."

He leans close to me and whispers, "We went to five stores that day. It's why we were gone so long, but Noah couldn't tell you the whole truth. At the last store, he finally found a ring he thought you would love. Never once did he look at a price tag, not at any of those stores. And when she gave Noah the receipt he didn't even blink when he signed it."

"Why are you telling me this?"

"Because Noah never does anything he's not sure about. What he spent is nothing compared to what he's getting in return. The only thing he was thinking about was you. He wanted something that wasn't going to be too gaudy, too flashy, but it also needed to fit your personality. When people look at it, not only will they know you belong to him but they will know he loves you enough and knows you well enough to pick something uniquely you."

"Thanks, Wyatt."

"Yup," is all he says before we stand and are escorted to the bank of elevators. We're all quiet as we ascend to our floors; everyone seems a bit weary. Mac and Ryan clear the rooms one by one. Noah and I are the last to be cleared.

"Food?"

"Yes, please." I open up my suitcase, pull out my pajamas, and get dressed while Noah calls in our order. When I come out, Noah is standing in front of the mirror looking at his neck.

"Oh shit, Noah, are you okay?" I didn't notice before because he had his jacket on, but his neck is covered in scratches. No one is supposed to leave scratches on my man but me. "We need a first aid kit."

"I'm fine, Mel, it's just some scratches."

"Yeah, from some bitch in heat who probably hasn't had her rabies shots recently."

He smirks at me, leans back against the dresser, and turns toward me. "You're quite the foul mouth tonight."

"Yeah, well, stupid women bring out the best in me, can't you tell?" I'm so angry looking at his scratches and when he lifts my hand to his mouth and kisses my swollen knuckles, I realize he feels the same.

"Just a few more months and this will all be over."

"You mean just another year?" I reply with a sigh.

"Yeah, but the U.S. tour is done in October, and then we'll have a break before going overseas. The international fans are excitable but less violent. Who knew you had such a right hook, though? Maybe I should hire you to protect my virtue."

I laugh; it feels good to let out some of the tension. "I'd prefer for all of us to stay low key from here on out if possible."

"Sounds good to me," he says as someone knocks on the door. It's room service. Noah is quick with the guy and wheels our food in.

"That was really fast," I remark as he takes the lids off a couple of cheeseburgers.

"Yeah, I find when we have incidents like what just happened, the hotels are usually on top of everything concerning our stay from that point forward. Even with everything going on down there, our luggage made it to our rooms long before we did."

The reality of their world weighs heavily on my shoulders, especially tonight.

"Look, Mel, can we talk about the elephant in the room for a minute please?" I nod, and he continues, "I don't want you to be angry about the ring. I even told you when I gave it to you we could trade it."

"Noah, I love the ring ..."

"But?"

"It's so expensive."

He pulls his chair next to mine and holds my good hand. "How long do you think you're going to wear that ring?".

I don't know where he's going with this, but I'll play along. "I don't know … forty years?" Considering we're almost thirty, that seems like a good estimate.

"I'd say at least fifty. After tax and insurance, that's basically a little over a thousand dollars a year for you to have a piece of my heart on your finger. Two thousand if you count the matching wedding band I already bought."

"Noah …"

"No, Mel, stop," he says, bringing his finger to my lips. "Two thousand a year is nothing. I pay more than that for insurance, for groceries, in gas, randomly gifting people stuff. You get my point. But our love is priceless. If it will make you feel better, we can skip a vacation, or not get the fancy room, but if you like the ring, it stays."

And that right there is how, the first and only time in my life, Noah Weston made me feel like an asshole.

"Okay, the ring stays. But can you make me feel better and let me call for a first aid kit? Those scratches are nasty."

His answering smile is all I need to feel like everything is right in our world again.

Nausea plagued me when I woke up this morning, and I felt like I hadn't slept at all last night; yesterday was exhausting. I hate the fact Noah isn't coming to this signing with me. My nerves are out of control, but I try to snack on some toast and coffee while Noah tries to ease my mind.

They all head out shortly after breakfast to start their interviews, leaving me to twiddle my thumbs in anticipation. Belle and I have texted all morning, Anna has texted wishing me luck, and even Warren sent me a text to let me know if he can let Noah ditch out for a little bit, he will. My signing is from noon to three, but I plan on showing up thirty minutes prior.

I wish I knew what to expect. SOS said the response has been better than they expected, but I have no clue what that means. I listened to BAD's first interview where Noah got grilled like crazy about everything—the fan who attacked him last night, the one who attacked me, how I punched her, about our engagement, and they want to know when the wedding is. I know all his interviews are going to go like this; there's no way he's going to make it to my signing. It's a relief because I'm terrified, but I'm also slightly disappointed.

When Mac knocks on my door, I'm trembling.

"Nervous?" he asks from the front seat when we're about halfway to the bookstore.

"Terrified. I don't know how the guys do it every day."

"It's different in a way. Equally terrifying, but they just have to perform and bail. *You* actually have to talk, smile, and be personable. It's a different kind of beast, if you ask me. Did you think about this part when you published the book? That one day you would have to do this?"

It's why I almost didn't publish. "In a broad aspect, I guess. But I don't think anyone who publishes independently believes their book will be picked up by one of the biggest publishing houses within weeks of release. If anything, I thought this was something I'd have to worry about years down the road."

"Well, you're here now, so you might as well enjoy the ride. You're tough, Mel, you'll get through today and come out on the other side stronger than ever."

"Thanks, Mac."

After he parks the car, we enter through the rear door of the store. The store manager is waiting for me and after introductions are made, she leads me into a room to wait until it's time. Mac waits outside the door and a few minutes later, the door opens once again.

"What are you guys doing here?" I exclaim when Anna and Sam walk through the door.

"Well, we couldn't let our newest star go to her first signing alone, could we?" Sam asks as he gives me a quick hug.

Anna moves in for a hug and squeals, "Yeah, superstar, no way would I have missed this."

"I'm so glad you guys are here! Thank you."

Sam comes closer. "So how is your hand? Can you sign today?"

Lifting it up, I show them the slight bruising. "I'll be fine, I took some acetaminophen a little while ago. I'm sorry about that, I didn't mean to jeopardize today."

We all take a seat and they both look me over.

"We heard you guys had quite a night trying to get into the hotel. Someone assaulted you, Mel, you had every right to defend yourself," Sam points out, clearly in my corner.

"I'm glad you did it. Those girls take way too many liberties with these guys. Just because they're famous doesn't mean they don't

D. Kelly

deserve human decency. I'm so glad it's almost over," Anna says emphatically.

Sam nods in agreement. "I know it's going to be a change, but I'm looking forward to having my husband around more. We're not getting any younger and life on the road is getting harder for Warren. He loves it, but I think he's ready to retire with BAD, at least from touring. I'm sure he'll always scout new talent."

It's an end of an era for these guys. It almost makes me sad I missed so much, but I'm thrilled I got to be here for the best part.

"You okay, Mel?" Anna asks, concern coming over her face when I start to fan myself.

"Sure, I just need some water." As I stand up to get it, the room spins rapidly and their voices sound like they're underwater. Slowly, I'm lowered back down onto a chair with Anna and Sam hovering above me. After a minute or two, the buzzing in my ears goes away and I feel fine.

"Maybe we should cancel." Anna's worried expression matches her tone.

"No, I'm fine. I just need some water."

Sam hands me a bottle of water and after they're convinced I'm not going to fall over, they sit back down.

"We can cancel if you're not feeling well, Amelia," Sam assures me.

"It's okay. I saw my doctor yesterday, I'm just a little anemic. She gave me some iron pills to help. I'll be fine. You know how it goes … stress, lack of sleep. I was so nervous I only ate a few bites of toast this morning."

"Anna, run out and see if there is somewhere on this street where we can get her some fruit or some juice. Anything with a little natural sugar."

"I'm on it."

After Anna leaves, Sam keeps me chatting. After spending the holidays together, I feel like I've gotten to know him more as a friend and less like a boss. Anna makes it back in record time with a fresh bowl of fruit. She opens it up for me, and they both glare at me until I eat it.

When I finish about half the bowl, I put it down on the table.

"Much better," Anna declares triumphantly.

There's a soft knock on the door and the manager pokes her head in. "Ms. Greyson, it's time. There's quite a crowd out here." She's smiling from ear to ear, surely hoping for the day's sales to be phenomenal.

When we get to the signing table, the first people in line are Belle and Veronica. I'm absolutely stunned and my eyes well up with tears. Looking past them, I observe the line goes all the way out the door. I had no idea this many people would show up for my book.

"What are you guys doing here?" I ask incredulously, giving each of them a hug before sitting down in my spot to sign their books.

Veronica fills me in as I personalize their books. "That beautiful man of yours insisted we come. It was his Christmas present to us both. We're staying at your hotel for a few days. We'll be here with you today for moral support but no way in hell were we not going to be first in line for our girl's very first book signing."

"Thank you. This means more to me than you could possibly know."

Veronica smiles wide. "We know, baby girl, we always know."

Belle smirks when she hands me her book. "You can sign it with your left hand if that helps."

"I'm good, but thanks for the offer."

"You must not have hit her hard enough," she replies with a laugh as she takes her book and heads off to pay.

The readers are all so nice. I've even been able to meet some I chat with often on social media. The amount of requests for selfies throws me for a loop; it's comical how many years I spent hiding in plain sight to only be thrown back into the spotlight, so to speak. Between touring with the band, being Noah's fiancée, and now the book, I'm right back where I started.

We're halfway through the signing when some of the fans start asking more personal questions. Now it's my turn to be asked about Noah and our relationship. Women are swooning over the fact he's a rock star and I'm an author. They swear it's a real-life romance novel in the making. I can see how some people may think of it that way, but to me, Noah is just the man I happened to fall in love with.

Many of the women have admired my ring longingly, as it sparkles under the fluorescent lighting in the store. They've gushed over Noah's excellent taste in jewelry and each time it brings a smile to my face. Noah would be so proud knowing how much everyone loves this ring.

We're down to the last half hour of the signing now and the line has dwindled to just a few people scattered here and there. What amazes me is how busy the store still is. Most of the readers are sticking around, chatting, making plans to get together for drinks and dinner, even forming book clubs with some new local reader friends. It's a beautiful thing to witness and be a part of.

Suddenly there's a spark of excitement as loud whispers and squeals make their way through the store on the heels of four BAD men and their security guards. Unlike the hotel, no one has rushed up to them, or even followed too closely behind them. But the smile on Noah's face as he steps up to my table is one I'll never forget in my entire life.

When he hands me a copy of my book, I decide to play with him. "Who should I make this out to, sir?"

"I think, 'To my future husband and future father of my children, I'm sorry this book wasn't dedicated to you, but the next one has your name all over it. Or something like that," he adds, still beaming. That was pretty good, though, so I write it word for word, promising myself my next book will indeed be dedicated to him.

Sawyer is next up and plops his butt right on the table as he hands me his book. "Please dedicate it 'To my future brother-in-law, who I'm finally willing to confess is the hotter twin. All my love, Princess.'"

And because they're in such goofy moods, I inscribe it almost exactly as he described, adding my own twist. Instead, I put:

I'm finally willing to confess you're one of the hottest twins on the planet.

The least I could do was give him a slight ego boost, right along with his brother.

Wyatt is next. "So this one is for me this time, not my beautiful wife," he says, looking right at Anna. "You can inscribe it:

To Wyatt, Never forget to bring your O game.

Anna is cracking up at her husband, but her eyes are filled with nothing but love for him.

Next up is Darren, and he passes me his book as he stares at me solemnly. "Put whatever you think is good, but make it out to Jolt."

I can't hold back my laughter as I write in his book.

Dear Jolt, Thank you for being a good friend and for making my best friend the happiest she's ever been. Also, thank you for making me an auntie, but don't you fucking dare name your kid Jolt.

Reading what I wrote, he's laughing hysterically and calls out, "If it were a boy that would have been perfect!" as he walks away. Belle peeks around his arm at the inscription and laughs along with him. Just when I thought I was done, Warren places a book down in front of me.

"Anything special?"

"Just make it from your heart," he replies.

> *Warren, Thank you for taking a risk on me and encouraging me to take the path less followed. My entire life has changed for the better and it's in large part because of you. I love you, big guy.*

When he looks up at me, he blinks. "Damn it, Mel, don't you know men aren't supposed to cry before happy hour? We don't have any liquor to blame the tears on. Your parents would be extremely proud of you."

His words bring me comfort. He knew my parents and since they can't be here, having him to remind me of them is priceless.

"Speaking of drinks, you ready to get your celebration on, Princess?" Sawyer asks as we pack up.

"Don't you guys have somewhere to be?"

Noah wraps his arms around me from behind, and a few lingering readers snap a quick photo. I don't mind, though; pictures with Noah I can handle. "Nope, we've got the night off to celebrate your success."

I'm overcome with emotions but try not to let them show. "Let's celebrate!"

The Truth Will Set You Free

We had an amazing time at dinner last night. Great food, great company, and the love of good friends are all anyone ever needs and we had it in spades. Sawyer was on his best behavior and spent most of the night catching up with Anna. It was evident from the look in his eyes how much he's missed his friend. I overheard him saying how much he was looking forward to the tour being over so they could spend more time together. Anna seemed sad as she apologized for spending all her free time with Wyatt, but Sawyer brushed her off. It's hard to fault your best friend for spending her limited time with her husband. It made me realize Sawyer has made a lot of progress since this tour started. He seems more mature and I wonder if it has anything to do with Noah and me settling down.

Veronica spent the night getting to know Darren and Noah; she seemed to enjoy it immensely. The three of them were thick as thieves all night. Belle and I sat back and watched them with mild amusement. Neither of us could have hoped for a better outcome.

This afternoon, us girls spent the day shopping, and she let us all know how perfect she thinks they are. A sense of relief flooded through me with her words. Veronica is the only parent I have left; her approval means a lot to me. More than I even realized.

The afternoon passed quickly and now we're all in a limo heading to a hotel across town. After tonight's show, the guys were swooped up and brought to a private suite Warren rented to entertain some people from the label and local friends. In other words, an industry party. Warren thought a new location for the party would be good since our hotel is still under siege by adoring fans. I hope he's right.

"Why are you so nervous, Mel?" Belle asks, eyeing me up suspiciously.

"I'm not nervous, I just don't like these kinds of events." If it's a true industry party, there are going to be high-class women who want to get their claws into our men.

388

"I'm with Mel ... these parties blow. Do you know how many women I'm going to have to politely extricate Wyatt from tonight?"

"He doesn't do that himself, honey?" Veronica asks Anna, who smiles sweetly.

"Oh, he does. I get the sly ones who think they're being sneaky with a brushed finger or accidental bump to the thigh. These girls are piranhas."

"Yeah, I'm not doing that. If Darren knows what's good for him, he'll stay far away from them. And if he doesn't, I know where the door is."

Anna laughs. "Just wait until he looks at you across the room with the biggest 'help me' expression on his face. You have to remember their label is going to be there and just because they're retiring doesn't mean they don't still have to play by the rules. *They* have to be nice and polite to everyone, but I'm not on contract, so I can do whatever I want to, and they *won't* kick out a wife."

"Guess that means Mel shouldn't punch anyone tonight," Belle teases.

"It's not like I randomly go around punching people. That bitch ripped my ring right off my hand." The same ring I've been spinning in circles for the last ten minutes on the ride over here.

The limo stops in front of the hotel, and Mac steps forward and escorts us all inside. There aren't any crowds here, which is good. This should stay low-key, at least for a while. The elevator takes us all the way up to the top floor and opens into the party. For a minute, I thought Mac was going to leave us to fend for ourselves, but he stepped out after us and led us to our men.

They're all tucked away in a corner with four guys in suits. After making the introductions, we're encouraged to have a seat with them. They continue to talk shop, but one of the men keeps staring at me. I glance down quickly to make sure my skirt is low enough and I'm not flashing anything I shouldn't be—I'm not, but he continues to stare.

Noah seems to catch on and laces his fingers through mine. Even his eyes begin to flit back and forth between me and Bob, if I remember his name correctly. Once their conversation dies down and everyone goes off to mingle, Bob stays behind.

"You don't remember me, do you, Mellie Sunshine?" His voice is kind but he's giving me the creeps.

"I'm sorry, should I? By the way, I don't go by that name anymore."

"I suppose you wouldn't. You're all grown up now. When I was in my younger years, I toured with your parents. I left your tour for an office job when you were about nine years old. Your dad was a close friend of mine."

I call bullshit on his memory—close friends attend funerals—but maybe in his mind he was.

"I'm sorry, Bob, I don't remember much from that time. You should reminisce with Warren ... he still remembers all the good old days." I've effectively shut him down without being rude. Noah gives my hand an encouraging squeeze.

"Maybe I will. It was good to see you again, Amelia. Take care of this one, Noah, she comes from good stock."

After Bob leaves, I turn to Noah, eyes flashing in anger. "Good stock? What am I, a fucking dairy cow?"

Noah laughs and kisses me tenderly. "I don't think he meant it that way, but Bob has always been sort of a creeper."

"Maybe that's why he stopped touring with us. Enough about Bob, how was your night?"

"Actually, my head really hurts."

This is what I was worried about. He's been better, but this was his first show since the incident; with the fans and the music, it must have set him back. "I'm sorry. I've got some acetaminophen in my purse, do you want some?"

"I took some after we finished our show. I'm hoping it will kick in. If it doesn't, I've got the pain medicine the doctor gave me back at the hotel. In the meantime, why don't we stay here in our dark corner and make out like teenagers?" Noah's free hand slides up my thigh, but I push him away.

"Down, boy. We can people watch, but no way am I going to neck with you in front of your bosses. If you're feeling better, we can do that later back at the hotel."

"Promise?" he asks, pressing his lips against the base of my neck.

"Mm, I promise."

Noah and I sit in the corner for a few hours with surprisingly few interruptions. We watch as Sawyer takes way too many shots, Anna takes down wicked trolls one smile at a time, and Belle, Darren, and Veronica talk the night away. The way Darren stands behind Belle all the time with his hands around her belly, it's only a matter of time before they're outing themselves to the world.

As most people begin to leave, Sawyer convinces Warren and Sam he'll shut everything down here so they can enjoy their last night together. Sam and Anna fly home tomorrow, as do Veronica and

Belle. It's not a wise decision, but Warren probably figures Sawyer is going to stay here with a girl and use the suite to his advantage.

"Babe, are you ready to go? I need to go take those pain pills."

Poor Noah, he's flinching at the light. I hope by morning he's better, but they may have to postpone more shows if this keeps happening.

"Of course, let's get out of here."

We share a limo back to our hotel with Belle, Darren, and Veronica. Wyatt and Anna already left with Sam and Warren. It's a quiet trip back, everyone being sympathetic to Noah's pounding head.

Since it's late there's not much of a crowd, but after what happened the first night, they don't get too out of hand anymore. The first thing I do when we get to the room is get Noah his medicine and help him strip out of his clothes. After putting my pajamas on, we curl up together and lie down.

"Thank you for taking care of me," Noah whispers as his eyes begin to droop.

"I love you, Noah. There's never a time I won't take care of you."

An hour later, just as I'm dozing off, Noah's phone rings. I answer it when I see it's Sawyer.

"Hey, what's going on?" I ask sleepily.

"Princess, I need to talk to Noah, it's important." His words are slurred and I pray he's not in jail.

"He's sleeping. His headache got worse and he had to take those pain pills."

"Shit. Can you come over to the hotel? I sent everyone home and now I don't have a ride. Can you come and get me?"

"Can I send Ryan or Mac?" I ask, not understanding why I need to go.

"No, Princess. Well … yeah. Make sure one of them drives you, but I need you to come up to the room and get me. Please …"

"Okay, I'll be there soon."

"Thanks, Princess."

Quickly, I throw on a pair of jeans and a sweater, along with my boots, and write Noah a note in case he wakes up. When I look out into the hall, Ryan is standing watch a few doors down.

"Ryan, we need to go get Sawyer." A confused look flashes across his face, but he only nods in agreement as he calls Mac to make the necessary arrangements for backup. A few minutes later, I'm in the back of the SUV on my way to the other hotel for the second time tonight. The whole way there I'm imagining why Sawyer needs someone to come, and I wonder if he got himself tied to a bed or something. The thought makes me chuckle because that would be something I could see happening to him.

When Ryan and I get to the room, Sawyer is sitting up at the bar drinking. It doesn't look like there's anyone else here.

"Sawyer, are you ready to go?" I ask as I cross the room.

"Princess! What are you doing here?" Sawyer is grinning like a loon, but I can smell his whiskey-laden body three feet away.

"You called Noah, remember? I told you he couldn't come and then you asked me to."

"Oh yeah, I remember. Hey Ryan? Can you give me and Princess a few minutes alone? I need to talk to her about something."

"Sure thing, boss," Ryan answers, stepping into one of the other rooms.

"What's going on, Sawyer? How long have you been here alone?" This isn't my first experience with drunk Sawyer, but something is going on with him for sure.

"Not sure. I kicked the last girl out a little while after you left. She wasn't happy with me, though, she cussed me out something fierce." He's laughing like he said something hysterical.

"I thought you were keeping the room for just the occasion?"

"Yeah, well ... some things are bigger than pussy, you know?" Alright, now I *know* he needs to talk. He exhales loudly and pours another drink, which I promptly take from him. "Sorry, Princess, I should have offered you one. Fuck ... I wish Noah would have come."

"You can talk to me, Sawyer. What did you want to tell Noah? Maybe I can help."

The devilish gleam in his eyes brightens and he smiles. "Nah, I don't think so. I was going to tell Noah not to marry you." Those words hurt more than anything he could have possibly said to me. "Do you want a drink?" he asks as if he didn't just rip my heart out.

"No, I want to know why you don't want Noah and me to get married."

He looks at me like a lightbulb just went off in his head and smirks. "Now *that* I can't tell you. It's a secret."

"People shouldn't keep secrets, Sawyer. Secrets only bring hurt."

He laughs again. If he weren't being mean I might think it was funny. "Like you don't keep secrets. You never told Noah I propositioned you on the bus."

"Alright, some secrets are better to keep because the end result can hurt more."

Sawyer gets off his stool and crowds my space. "And that's why I can't tell you. It would hurt too much."

I grab his wrist when he starts to turn away from me. "Sawyer, please ..."

He turns back to me, suddenly more somber than I've ever seen him. "Amelia," he whispers, pulling my face to his and pressing his forehead against mine. He's never called me Amelia before ... I like it. The look in his eyes is sorrowful, as if he's apologizing for something he hasn't done yet. The nerves in my stomach flutter like butterflies hatching from their cocoons.

"Sawyer," I whisper softly as he places his finger against my lips. I hate how much his touch lights me on fire.

"Pick me, Amelia. I'm a selfish bastard, and it will tear my brother apart, but he doesn't need you like I do. I need you, Amelia. You're the only one who has ever brought me to life." His lips capture mine, softly, lovingly. Without a second thought I open to him, briefly lost in this moment, in his vulnerability, and in his beautifully tragic words. Only when the pleasureful moan releases from deep within does it hit me that everything we're doing and saying is so utterly and completely wrong.

This can't happen. I'm in love with Noah. Sawyer and I can never—*will* never—happen.

"Sawyer ..." I pull away breathlessly and bend over, gripping my stomach to keep myself from throwing up, my anxiety getting the best of me. When my eyes meet his, they fill with tears. He's wearing his heart on his sleeve; he's never looked more beautiful.

"It's okay, Princess. I know you're in love with him, but I had to try, right?" he asks with a discouraged shrug of his shoulders.

"It's not only that," I whisper softly, and a brief flicker of hope flashes in his eyes before I distinguish it with my words, my secret. "Sawyer, I'm pregnant."

Sawyer stumbles back onto the bar stool and hangs his head. "Out of all the things wrong with this situation, that makes me the biggest asshole on the planet. Fuck. Mel, you need to go."

Mel?

He's never called me that before, either, and I don't like that he's starting now. It feels like something has irrevocably shifted, but I guess it has.

"I'm here to take you home, remember?"

He shakes his head. "Call Darren, will you? Have him come and get me. I need to talk to him. Fuck, Mel! Does Noah even know?"

D. Kelly

"No, he doesn't. I only found out before we got here. I wanted it to sink in a bit. This is all he's ever wanted for his future, but this dream isn't mine."

This time, he looks at me with a mixture of hope and fury. I get that emotion because I've been feeling something similar for a few days. It's why I haven't told Noah. I want to be happy about this when I tell him. He deserves that and so much more.

"You are keeping the baby, right?" he manages to choke out.

"Yes. How could I not? All I ever want to do is make Noah happy, and this will be the best gift I could ever give him … but I'd be lying if I said I'd wished for it to happen. At least not yet. He only just asked me to marry him. And now … boom … built-in wife and kid. We won't ever know what our life could have been like together before building on our love. Besides, I'm not quite sure I'm mom material, but I guess I'm about to find out."

"This is so fucked up," he mutters into his arms as he lays his head over them on the bar.

"Please don't tell him, Sawyer. Let me be the one to give him the news."

He looks at me with a dare in his eye. "Which part, Mel? Don't tell him you're having his love child, or don't tell him I just begged my brother's fiancée and baby mama to leave him for his fucked-up twin? Jesus, what's wrong with me? I fucking love Noah more than anything yet I can't get you out of my head!"

Sawyer grabs the whiskey on the counter and takes an enormous swig from the bottle. As soon as he sets it down, he repeats the action two more times. He was already drunk when I got here, which is why I was supposed to be taking him home. Tears are streaming down his cheeks; I hate that he's hurting so much. I swore I'd never keep another secret from Noah, but this one isn't an option.

"Don't tell him about the baby, Sawyer, please. As for what just happened between us … Noah will never know. It would kill him and your relationship, and I don't ever want to be the cause of that. I love you both, you're my family. Promise me, Sawyer, we'll move forward, but Noah can never know this happened because as far as I'm concerned, it didn't."

He wipes away his tears and looks up at me. He's completely shattered. "You'd do that for me? I don't get it, Mel, why?"

Lacing my fingers through his, I squeeze him tightly. "Because you're my family, Sawyer, and just because I'm in love with your brother doesn't mean I'm not allowed to love you, too. This baby is going to need its uncle and if Noah finds out you kissed me and I let you, there is nothing good that can come from it. This will never happen again, Sawyer. I'm madly and deeply in love with Noah and even though the timing sucks, we are having a baby. Babies deserve happy families all the way around, don't they?"

It's not just a question; my words are pleading for his understanding.

"They do, and regardless of how you feel right now, you're going to be the best mom, Mel. Never doubt that for a second."

"We'll see, I guess. But Sawyer, this is important. I need you to know Noah means everything to me. He's what is right in my life and I adore him. I care for you and let myself get sucked into a weak moment, and I'm going to have to live with that, just like you are, but this can't happen again. Promise me."

With a resigned sigh, he agrees, "I promise, Mel. Noah will never know. Can you please get Darren over here?"

"Yeah, let me see what I can do."

A few minutes later, a reluctant Darren is on his way over. Sawyer and I wait in a mutually uncomfortable silence. When Darren finally arrives, he's pissed—we interrupted his last night with Belle—but as soon as he sees us, he stops in his tracks.

"You told her, didn't you?" Darren asks, but the question is redundant and he knows that. I'm surprised Sawyer even mentioned it to Darren, but Darren's loyalty is to Sawyer like Wyatt's is to Noah. I give Darren a hug, thank him for coming, and ask him to find Ryan for me. Then I turn around and hug Sawyer, placing a kiss on his cheek.

"You're my family, Sawyer, and my friend … for life. Please don't let this moment in time mess that up for us. I'm not angry, I just want you to have what Noah and I do, and I know someday you're going to find it with the perfect girl for you."

Tears fill both our eyes, and before I walk out the door, he calls to me softly, "You're my family, too, Mel … always."

When I get in the car, a text message arrives from Sawyer. It's just a link to a song, of course, because it's how he talks to me. It's the video for "What We Can Never Have" by Fuel. That's when I lose it and cry my eyes out all the way back to the hotel. I cry for Sawyer's pain and my own. I cry for our betrayal of Noah. No matter how you cut it, we betrayed him, and that's something—no matter what I said to Sawyer—I will never get past. And I cry because I have this beautiful life growing inside of me, made from the best parts of me and Noah, but I'm still struggling to be happy about it. I wanted

D. Kelly

time to enjoy my life with the love of my life, but I guess fate had other plans.

Somehow, that gives me comfort. Fate is such a large part of Noah's life; it makes sense that's how our first child is going to be brought to us.

The Morning After

I've been awake for hours, barely sleeping a wink last night. I've never felt so guilty and ashamed in all my life. In a way, I hope Sawyer forgets what happened; it would lessen the burden somehow. Even then, Darren knows, and now he's being forced to keep secrets from Noah *and* Belle.

Belle and I said our goodbyes last night; it will be weeks before I see her again. She's my best friend, but I'm keeping her in the dark about so much. At first it was only to have time to process, but now … *I* don't even know what I'm doing.

Noah's alarm goes off, and I reach over to silence it. Blinking sleepily, his eyes flutter open.

"How are you feeling?" I ask, hoping at least something will go right and his headache will be gone.

"Okay, I think. Just tired … those pills really knocked me out."

"You need to rest when you can, Noah. I know it's hard but try for me, okay?"

He presses his lips against mine and pulls back, smiling, "Anything for you. What's wrong? You seem sad."

What I seem like is a lying, cheating, brother-kissing, backstabbing, whore, who hates herself with every fiber of her being for what she did to her future husband. But it's not like I'm going to tell him that. "Yeah, I just didn't sleep well. I think I'm coming down with something. Probably this cold New York weather getting to me."

Pressing his hand against my head, he nods, "You do feel a bit warm. Sam and Anna said you weren't feeling well at the book signing, either. Maybe I'm not the only one who needs to rest. Take today off, Mel."

"You're sweet, but I can't."

"It wasn't a suggestion. If you're sick, you rest. End of story. We don't need you catching pneumonia. Order some room service, sleep, watch some movies, and rest up." Noah is a caretaker at heart, it's one of the things I find so endearing about him. There's no doubt in my mind he's going to be the best father to our child.

"Alright. Tell everyone I'm sorry."

"They'll understand, Mel. No one likes to be sick," he replies as he gets up and heads for the shower.

After he leaves to meet the guys for breakfast, there's a knock at the door. Darren's tired face meets mine and I let him in.

"Hey," I say as he collapses into the chair.

"Hey. I'm so fucking tired. I'm sorry to bother you, but we need to talk about last night and get our stories straight."

Taking a seat on the bed, I sigh and nod in agreement.

"So look, I know you're pregnant, let's just get that out of the way. Congratulations?" he questions with a quirk of his eye.

"Thanks?" I reply with the same questioning tone. "How's Sawyer?"

"I'm not even sure. I woke him up before I came here. He's sad and embarrassed. We're going to try to keep this as close to the truth as possible. Lies get people into trouble."

Oh, he's preaching to the choir there.

"So we're going to tell Noah Sawyer called him but you went to get him since Noah was out cold. Once you got there, Sawyer decided he wanted to stay and since he was completely wasted, you called me for help."

"So pretty much the truth minus a few heartbreaking details. Sounds good." My tone is flat; Sawyer isn't the only one sad today.

"Look, Mel, I have to ask because Sawyer is my best friend and we've been through a lot of shit together. Are you sure you want Noah and not Sawyer? I won't judge, I swear, but if you don't … well … I can't believe I'm even going to say this, but I can … uh … try and help you with this baby situation if it's not what you want."

I look at Darren for a long moment. Part of me is really pissed off he'd do that to Noah. Especially after Noah vehemently defended Darren's parental rights to Belle. But … the other part of me who understands the stuff we do for our best friends completely gets where he's coming from.

"Darren, I love Noah with everything I am. Letting Sawyer kiss me last night was the biggest mistake of my life. I pushed him away but not fast enough. I let *all* of us down last night."

"Nah, you're only human, Mel. I've been kissed by enough random girls to know it takes at least thirty seconds or more for your instincts to kick in. You can't blame yourself for this."

One thing about Darren is he can be playful, but it's an act; he's one of the smartest people I've ever met.

"I love Sawyer. He holds a special part of my heart because he's Noah's brother but also because we've become really good friends. Or at least I thought we had. We had an incident before … nothing happened … but I thought we were past this thing between us. Noah is the love of my life, Darren, and I'm terrified I'm going to lose him by keeping this secret. Even so, I'm willing to risk it if it keeps their relationship intact."

Leaning back in his chair, Darren puts his hands behind his head and looks up at the ceiling. When he looks back at me, he sighs. "Noah and Sawyer have always been attracted to the same kinds of women. When Sawyer fucked up with Marilyn he swore, come hell or high water, he'd make it up to Noah. After Sawyer kissed you that night, he told me the next day. But when Noah woke up, he couldn't stop smiling or talking about you. Sawyer knew Noah was hooked, but he had no clue taking a step back was going to make him regret it every single day."

"Darren …" I'm at a complete loss for words.

"Look, Mel, I'm not telling you this because I want you to feel bad. I think you deserve to know how deeply Sawyer's feelings go and how long he's had them. Sawyer tends to self-destruct and after a blow like this, he's bound to act out. Be his friend, but try not to take it personally if he pulls away. He's going to need time."

He stands up and stretches, then yawns before continuing, "For what it's worth, I love the fuck out of Noah. I'd jump in front of a train for any of them, they're my brothers. You and Noah are right, not that you and Sawyer wouldn't be, but I'm not quite sure he's where he needs to be in his head yet to open his heart up to love. Noah is, and he's right about that fate shit, too. Look at me and Belle. We met, had instant fucking chemistry, and *bam* … baby on the way. It's by far the best thing that's ever happened to me. *They* are the best thing that has ever come into my life. And while we're speaking of babies, Belle is gonna lose her shit when she finds out you're pregnant."

For the first time today, I smile. "I know. One perk is our kids can grow up best friends like we did."

"I know you're scared and that's why you haven't told Noah yet. Swallow your fears, Mel, because you guys are in this for the long haul. You can't change the inevitable and that baby is coming sooner than later. I promise you, you will never see Noah happier than when you tell him. He's waited for this his whole life. His happiness might just make you feel better, but there's only one way to find out."

D. Kelly

Darren runs his hand through his already messy hair and in this moment, while he's being the best kind of friend there is to all his friends, I appreciate why Belle fell in love with him even more.

"I'll think about it. Thank you, Darren."

With a shrug, he moves to the door, yawning again. "Fuck, I need some coffee. One last thing … the sooner you tell Noah, the sooner Sawyer can breathe again by not holding in another secret that is going to rip him apart. Hiding his feelings for you has been hard enough, and frankly, he's not very good at it. Even Noah suspects Sawyer's got a thing for you. Once the baby becomes a reality to everyone, it will become reality to Sawyer, too, and he'll realize there's nothing left to hold on to."

Fuck me sideways. I'm pretty sure Darren just crammed into fifteen minutes what would take me six months to work out with my therapist.

"I'll consider everything you said, Darren, I promise. Please be careful and don't slip to Noah. He needs to hear about the baby from me."

Darren chuckles. "If you haven't figured it out yet, I'm pretty good at keeping secrets. I just prefer not to."

"I hear you. Thanks for the chat."

"Anytime, Mel. It goes without saying, I was never here."

"Of course."

Before leaving, he turns around. "For the record, what I offered about the baby if you weren't sure … I did that for you because you're Belle's best friend and she's not here. But it would have killed me if you'd said yes. Noah would never do that to me."

"Thank you," I whisper softly as I place a kiss on his cheek before he walks away.

I close the door and crawl back into bed feeling even worse than I did when I woke up. This will all blow over and we'll get past it, I just need to give it a chance. But when someone knocks on the door not even five minutes later, I'm hesitant to answer.

When I do get up and open the door, it's a freshly showered Sawyer. At least he smells like his normal self and not like a whiskey distillery. Opening the door wide, I motion for him to come in, although part of me wishes I could leave the door open.

"Morning, Mel," he says softly, and I cringe at the lack of his nickname for me. Guess that's something I'll need to get used to. "Noah sent a text that you're sick. Are you? Or are you hiding because of me?"

Taking a seat on the bed, I point to the chair Darren vacated just a short time ago, wordlessly asking him to take a seat. "I'm not hiding, Sawyer. Noah says I have a fever. It's probably just a cold, I'm sure I'll feel better tomorrow." For someone who spent his night in misery, he looks better than me or Darren. "How are *you* feeling, Sawyer?"

His sad eyes meet mine. "Like a fool."

"No, Sawyer, don't. You followed your heart and you should never feel foolish for that. I wish I could be who you need me to be. I want that for you. Someday you're going to find someone, and when you lay your heart on the line, she'll be ecstatic you chose her."

"Can I ask you something?" His soft words flow straight to my heart.

"Always."

"Was it just in my head? We have ... *had* chemistry, right? Please, Princess, tell me I'm not delusional."

And we're back to Princess. Sawyer wears his heart on his sleeve more than anyone actually realizes.

"No, it wasn't in your head, Sawyer. It just wasn't meant to be. If things had worked out differently, you're exactly the kind of guy I would have fallen head over heels for. But Noah, he stole my heart and, temporarily, my uterus." My dry laugh is met with a tiny smile.

"Yeah, well, if I had to lose out to anyone, Noah is the person I'd fall on my sword for every time. I'm sorry about last night, I overstepped. I'm willing to tell him so we don't have to keep this secret between us. About the kiss, not the baby ... that one is all you." His smile is genuine this time even if his eyes are still sad.

"I'm not a deceitful person, and I try to live by the truth in everything. But sometimes keeping secrets in extreme circumstances is the best thing. Your brother worships you, just as much as you do him. I'm the first to admit I don't understand the twin connection, but I see it every day. You guys have this irrevocable bond that is going to be with you for the rest of your lives, but if you tell Noah we kissed, you'll never get it back. He might forgive us, but things would never be the same. I could handle it. I'd be devastated, but if your relationship remained intact, I'd be okay. But I don't think it will."

Sawyer leans down, propping his arms on his knees. "Me, either, Mel. It won't happen again. And now I know it wasn't in my head, and Noah is your choice, I'll leave you alone."

"Hey, I still need you in my life. As my friend, as my child's uncle, and as my family. You and I will get past this, too. And not to make this anymore awkward, but if you're going to stop calling me

Princess, you should probably ease into it. It's the only thing you've ever called me before last night."

The surprised look on his face is amusing. "That can't be true."

"Except for the night we met when you called me Princess Amelia, yeah, it is."

Sawyer laughs so hard his eyes fill with tears. "I'm pretty sure that makes me the world's largest dick. I've got two sisters who consider pet names degrading and condescending. I'm sorry, Mel, really."

"Me, too, because I really grew to love it."

Sawyer stands with my words, probably needing a quick exit. "Well, I'm really late for breakfast and I'm sure I'm going to hear all about it. I just didn't want the day to pass without clearing things up between us. You're one of a kind, Mel. Noah's a lucky man. Not too many women would put family bonds above their own morals. Thank you."

"We're family now, too, Sawyer. Morals go out the door when you need to protect them."

He leaves without another word, but his shoulders are straight and he doesn't look like his puppy died anymore. I'll call that a win.

Noah walks into our room carrying a cold care basket, catching me on the tail end of a yawn. I'd just woken from a long nap when he came in. He hands me the basket filled with flowers, cold medicine, throat drops, menthol rub, the works.

"You're so sweet. How did you even have time to get all this?"

He's laughing as he takes the seat next to me. "I'd love to take all the credit but I'm just the idea maker this time. I pay people to do the legwork when I'm too busy to do it myself."

"Well, it's always the thought that counts, no matter how it's executed."

"How are you feeling? And why didn't you tell me you got dragged out to help Sawyer last night? It's no wonder you're sick."

Que the first lie. The second if you count me hiding what Sawyer did on the bus—a lie of omission is still a lie. "I'm feeling okay. I'm pretty sure it's just a cold. Sawyer is family, I'm assuming this isn't the last time I'll be called to bail him out. I just forgot to mention it this morning. You were in a hurry and I was tired. I left you a note last night, it's still sitting right there." I point to his bedside table, and he reaches for the note.

"Thanks for leaving a note, I never even noticed it." He places it back on the table and continues. "Sawyer on a bender is never any fun. No wonder you called Darren in for reinforcements. Thank you for trying, but next time you might as well send one of us first."

"If I can, I will, but Anna and Belle were both leaving so early this morning I didn't want to interrupt everyone's last night together."

Noah squeezes my hand and releases it. "As much as I'd love to lay here with you, I've got to get ready and get to the venue. We don't have any interviews or anything tonight so I'll come back as soon as we're done, hopefully without another headache."

"Are you sure you don't want me to come? I can get ready." I'm not sure if I'm sick or just pregnant and feeling blah. I'm also not sure I want to be left alone with my thoughts for the next eight hours.

"You know I love you with me, but I think it's more important for you to rest." He places a kiss to the top of my head before changing his clothes.

Once Noah leaves, I decide to take a shower and order some food. After eating, I feel much better. I think I'm emotionally exhausted, and until I tell Noah about the baby, I'm going to continue to be. Resolving to tell him tonight, I pull out my computer and start doing some internet searches. The one great thing about New York City is it never sleeps and anything can be delivered for a price.

I found a local shop that can make personalized, stainless steel guitar picks in an hour and deliver them. The front says "Soon-to-be Dad" with a little music note and along the side it says "ETA August." I ordered a dozen of them and then I ordered a dozen pink and blue frosted cupcakes. I had both deliveries addressed to Ryan, since he's standing watch over me tonight, and told them to leave them at the front desk.

No matter my mixed feelings, this should be a special night for us. A few hours later, Ryan brings the packages up to my room. The guitar picks are perfect and after carefully placing one on top of each cupcake, I realize I'm actually excited.

I thought about dressing up, but Noah would know something is up and I want this to be a surprise. Pajamas and one of his t-shirts isn't exactly the most flattering outfit, but the element of surprise will be worth it. When he finally texts me to say he's on his way back, I order a pizza from room service.

When Noah comes in, I'm lounging on the bed with the TV on. Not that I even know what's on. The nerves in my stomach are dancing like crazy. I can't believe this is my life right now.

"Hey," he says, smiling. "You look like you feel much better."

"I do, and I just ordered a pizza. Are you hungry?"

"Starving. Let me shower and change, then I'm yours for the rest of the night."

His lascivious gaze has me trembling. We haven't had sex since New Year's and even though it's only been a few days, I miss his touch something fierce. "Sounds good."

"Hey, what is that?" he asks, walking toward the table where the box of cupcakes is sitting.

"Back away, Weston. It's a surprise you can have after dinner, if you're good."

"And if I'm bad?" he asks with a devilish gleam in his eyes.

"I'll withhold sex," I state firmly, and his mouth drops. Yeah, two can play this game.

He throws his arms up in surrender. "I'll be good. Give me ten and I'll be out."

As soon as he closes the door, there's a knock on ours. After signing for the pizza and setting everything up, I grab Noah a beer and me a bottle of water. He steps out of the bathroom wrapped only in a towel, and my gaze locks on the rivulets of water dripping down his perfectly sculptured chest.

Noah dries off slowly, his eyes never leaving mine. It's a seductive game, and he's playing it purposefully. He slides into his boxers languidly, and I bite my bottom lip, my heart racing as he walks toward me.

"What's in the box, Mel?"

"Pizza," I reply, knowing damn well that's not the box he means.

"Other box."

"Not until you eat. Trust me, anticipation is key here."

On a groan, he turns around and puts on his pajama pants and t-shirt.

After he pops open his beer, he points at my water. "Still not feeling well? You love beer and pizza."

"I feel better, but I don't want to risk it. How was your show?"

"You know, it was a show." He runs his hands through his wet hair and takes a long draw on his beer. "I'm ready for it to be over. But I am enjoying the fact these aren't high-energy shows. I'm only breaking a sweat because of the stage lights."

"Well, I guess that's a perk."

"There's an even better perk, though," he adds, leaning back in his chair.

"Oh yeah? What's that?"

"You being here to go through it all with me." His dazzling smile sets off those nerves in my stomach again.

"You're sweet. I'm glad I'm here, too. But you have Sawyer and your friends … you're all family."

He finishes chewing and looks thoughtfully at me. "Sure, but it's not the same, you know? I don't curl up in bed with them at night. There's an intimacy missing from your life when you're single, and I don't even think you realize how much you miss it until you find someone."

"Yeah, that I can understand. How was Sawyer today? He was so drunk last night. I'm not sure I've ever seen him that bad."

"He was a grumpy fuck. Sometimes he gets like this. It's going to be a long week, but at least we don't have to hop on the bus for a few more days. That will give us some cushion from his piss poor mood."

That's what I was afraid of. Even more reason why it makes sense to tell Noah tonight; after he tells everyone, Sawyer is probably going to need some time.

"This pizza was really good," he says, pushing his plate away, "but I think I'm ready for dessert." He suspiciously eyes the box over on the other table.

It's time. I can't put this off any longer. Taking his hand, I lead him over to the table jump up on it, sitting next to the box. "Are you sure you can handle what's in this box?"

With a quizzical gaze, he reaches for the box, and I smack his hand softly. "What kind of dessert do you have in there, Mel? Is it kinky?"

Laughing, I push myself back on the table and grab my phone so I can record him. Then I push the box toward him. "You are so going to regret asking me that. Open your present, Noah."

"This must be some kind of dessert if you want to capture the moment for all time." He almost looks afraid to open the box; it makes me laugh harder.

"It won't bite you, I promise. Open your gift, Noah."

With a gentle ease, he opens the top and looks into the box. His eyes light up as he pulls one cupcake close to his face so he can read the guitar pick. The biggest grin I've ever seen spreads across his lips, and his eyes light up brighter than on Christmas morning.

"This is real?" he asks hopefully.

"Yes"

"This is why you've been sick?" He's carefully putting the cupcake back in the box.

"I think so."

"We're having a baby?" His hopeful tone is filled with happiness.

"We are." My eyes begin to fill with tears. Darren was right; this is what I needed, too.

"Holy shit, Mel! We're having a baby!" he screams and pulls me to him, turning my phone around so we're both in the shot. "Hey, Baby Weston! Your mom just gave me the best news I've ever gotten. We're expecting you in August! I'm the happiest man alive right now and we can't wait to meet you."

A tear falls down his cheek as he pulls me in for a quick kiss. I turn off the camera; I got what I needed for our first photo collection. Noah pulls me off the table and into his arms, where he kisses me with more passion than I've ever felt. Maybe I'm on a baby high, too.

"I'm so fucking lucky and I have so many questions. Can we tell people?" His excitement is contagious.

"It's really early, but it's your call. I wouldn't announce it to the world, but to family, the guys, and security … I don't see why not."

He pulls us to the bed, leaning me up against the headboard. "How did you find out?"

"When I made the appointment with my doctor, she had me do some pre-screening labs since I was combining my annual exam with the IUD placement. Then, when she came into the office, she told me she couldn't do it because I was pregnant. I'm also anemic, so I have to take iron pills and prenatal vitamins."

"What about all the drinking we did over the holidays? And an ultrasound … did you get one?" Noah is talking a mile a minute, but I suppose I wouldn't have expected anything less.

"That worried me, too, but she said it happens all the time and as long as I wasn't fall-down, pass-out drunk, everything should be okay. Especially since this is really early. She estimates conception at Thanksgiving, which I don't understand because we've been so careful. And no, no ultrasound. Her machine was down and we were leaving too fast for her to get me in somewhere. She did give me the name of a doctor here I could try to see."

Noah's fiddling with the drawstring on his pajama pants. "Um, Mel, there's something I need to confess."

"If it's another woman, Noah, this is not the time."

His hurt expression meets mine. "How would you even think that?"

"Well … usually, when men say they need to confess, it's about an affair."

"Okay, I'll give you that, but no. This is so stupid, but it's also my fault. So those condoms I got from Sawyer were groupie condoms."

"Groupie condoms?"

"Darren and Sawyer have this game they play to see who ends up with more condoms at the end of a tour. They unload the bus, bring them inside, count them, and then they give each other bonus points if they find one that's been tampered with."

Holy shit.

Pulling my knees to my chest in my typical defensive position, I ask what I really don't want to know. "And *how* does that affect us?"

"With the last tour ending and the new tour starting right after they unloaded the bus, they didn't tally the results. They were going to do it over Thanksgiving. I don't pay attention to that stuff so I didn't know I was grabbing groupie condoms. I found out a few days later when I saw Sawyer emptying the drawer, but by then it was too late to take any precautions anyway. And besides, what were the odds? Not every girl messes with the condoms, it really was just a fluke."

Just a fluke ...

"Or just fate."

Noah covers his heart with his hands. "Be still my beating heart. Did the word fate just come out of your mouth, my love?"

Sighing, I lean into his shoulder, and he wraps his arm around me. "I've been struggling with this since I found out. This wasn't exactly my dream, at least not like this, in this order, with us having so little time to be an us. That's the one word that kept coming back into my mind. It was like I could hear you whispering it over and over."

"I love you, Mel, and I'm sorry this wasn't your dream, but that doesn't have to take away from the happiness of this occasion, does it?"

The last thing I want to do is take any happiness away from him. "No, it doesn't. We're having a baby, Noah, and babies should always be celebrated. They come on their own timeline, when they're meant to."

"Good. I have one more confession and no, it's not another woman. It will never, ever, be another woman. I'm not that kind of guy."

"I know you're not. So let me hear it."

He pulls my face to his and kisses me softly. "Right now, I can't decide if I want to call everyone in here and pass out cupcakes or if I want to strip you naked and eat cupcakes off of you."

"I'd vote for the latter, but I know you're dying to tell them. How about a compromise? We'll tell them now, and when they leave we'll use the left-over cupcakes to play."

He groans and attacks my neck with his lips. "That sounds like the perfect plan." The huskiness of his words light my hormones on fire, but he pulls away so quickly those flames die out pretty fast. With one group message, he's summoned everyone to our room. I hope to God Darren and Sawyer can fake their surprise.

Less than five minutes later Wyatt, Darren, Sawyer, Warren, Mac, and Ryan are all in our room crowed around us.

"What the hell are we all doing here, Noah? I'm fucking exhausted." Sawyer is in a shitty mood, but Noah doesn't let it dull the light in his eyes.

"I thought you'd like to know you're going to be an uncle. Mel and I are having a baby!" Noah exclaims. Everyone immediately cheers and hugs us both. Sawyer blinks like he's in a daze but then a big, dimple-filled smile spreads across his face. No matter what is going on behind the scenes, he's excited for his brother.

While they're chatting, I decide to send the video to Belle. I haven't told her yet and now that everyone is in the know, it's time. Since it's only about ten her time, I know she'll be home. It seems like the guys are getting a kick out of the guitar picks, and Warren is even taking a picture for Sam.

Shit, Sam ... I hope he doesn't freak out and think I won't get my job done. Being pregnant isn't going to stop me from writing this story. Nothing will.

My phone rings with a Skype call from Belle. I excuse myself into the bathroom so I can have a little privacy.

"Hey, Belle."

Tears are streaming down her face. "Mel, oh my God, are we really having babies together?"

"Yeah, Belle, we really are."

"How long have you known?" she demands. That's my Belle.

I smile. "Since the day we left for New York. I needed to let it all sink in. I'm sorry I didn't tell you, but I wanted Noah to be the first to know." Not exactly a lie. I *did* want him to know first; it just wasn't how it ended up working out.

"He's ecstatic, but how are *you*?"

"The verdict is still out on that. I'm happy, but disappointed and terrified. *So* terrified. I'm going to mess this kid up, Belle."

"Stop that," she scolds. "You're going to do no such thing. I know you're scared ... hell, *I'm* scared ... but Noah adores you and there's nothing he won't do for you. Everything is going to work out fine for both of us. I'm happy for you, Mel, and I'm so fucking proud of you."

"Thanks."

I don't know why, but I don't have much to say, maybe because I'm in the bathroom. "Cute execution, by the way. I'm glad you thought to record it. It was almost as good as being there. When are you going to tell Mama?"

"Soon ... after it sinks in a little bit more. I wish you could have been here. If Noah hadn't had that headache last night I might have done it then. But I'm glad it ended up this way because I was able to make it special for him."

"Well, there's always next time," she says with a loud cackle.

"Bite your cursed tongue, woman. This one is coming a few years early as it is."

"True. Take me out of the bathroom so I can congratulate Noah myself."

"Noah," I call out as I come of out the bathroom, "Belle would like to talk to you." I point the phone in their direction and they all call out a round of hellos to her. After handing the phone off to Noah, the only spot available for me to stand that makes sense is next to Sawyer. I notice he's flicking something in his fingers—the guitar pick from the cupcakes. I can't help but wonder if it's from nerves, anger, or habit.

"Good job, Mel," he whispers. "Telling Noah in a special way was the best thing you could have done. Wait until my mom hears she's going to be a grandma again. If you have a boy, watch out for Diane ... she might try and take him from you."

"I hope it's a boy. I've got not a clue in the world what I'd do with a girl."

"Careful what you wish for," he flashes that sinful dimple again, "Weston boys are a handful to say the least."

"Everyone say bye to Belle," Noah calls out.

Sawyer is the first to leave, followed by Darren, and everyone else funnels out one by one until only Wyatt is left. He already called Anna and broke the news to her. Noah had interrupted their nightly phone call and he wanted to fill her in on the important news.

D. Kelly

"I'm so fucking happy for you two. Between you and Belle, you might just give Anna baby fever yet."

"You, too?" I ask, surprised he's on the baby train.

"Eh, I definitely wouldn't object. I want Anna to be settled in her career and stuff so she feels she's accomplished everything she wants, but I'm all for making some babies whenever she's ready."

"I'm sure you won't have to wait long. Once you're back from tour and Anna has unfettered access to you, she'll be pregnant in no time," Noah tells him as he not-so-subtly leads him to the door.

Wyatt laughs. "I get the hint. Enjoy the rest of the night, you two."

"Oh, we will," Noah tells him as he practically closes the door in his face. I can hear Wyatt laughing as he walks away. When Noah turns to me, he has a predatory gleam in his eyes. "I want to do some pretty wicked things to you right now, Mel, but can we call my parents first?"

Of course he wants to tell his parents. "Sure, why don't you Skype your dad and have your mom open her email. That way we can watch them while they watch us?"

I forward the video to Karen while Noah gets Owen on Skype. They're so cute, always side by side in bed together, usually watching TV. This time, Noah and I are side by side in bed as well.

"Hey, Noah!" Owen answers happily as he adjusts his computer screen. "Hey, Mel! I didn't see you there, too."

"Dad, tell Mom to get next to you and open up her email. We have something we want to show you guys."

"I'm right here," Karen says. "I'm pulling my email up now. You guys didn't get married, did you?"

"By the look of terror on Mel's face, I'm going to call that a no," Owen replies before we have a chance to.

"Dad, make sure you put the computer so we can see you both watching the video."

"Yeah, yeah, I'm not that old yet, son. I know how to work a computer." Owen adjusts the screen again so we can see them both looking at Karen's computer.

"Alright, I'm hitting play," Karen calls out.

Noah and I exchange glances as he squeezes my thigh. He's so excited to be able to share this with them. The video isn't very long; within seconds, Karen is screaming.

"What? I'm going to be a grandma again! Noah … Mel … Owen, did you see this? We're going to be grandparents!"

410

"Yeah, Mom, you sure are, and I'm going to be a dad. Hopefully, as good of one as the one I have." The pride in Noah's voice brings his parents to tears. Owen's trying to blink them back, but I see them. Karen doesn't even bother; she lets her happy tears flow freely.

"You're going to be an amazing father, Noah," Owen says proudly.

"We're so happy for you guys. An end-of-summer baby will be perfect. The tour will be almost over and you can enjoy being parents without the constraints of touring after that. Have you told your sister's yet?" she asks.

"Not yet, Mom, I'll tell them tomorrow. It's late here and I'm tired, but we wanted the two of you to be the first to know aside from the band."

"Congratulations! I'm so excited, we'll talk soon. Let us know when you tell your sisters. Love you guys."

Oh wow, he just included me in that. Noah squeezes my leg again sensing the significance of this moment for me.

"We love you, too. Goodnight," Noah replies.

"Goodnight," they say in unison as Noah turns off his phone and tosses it to the bedside table.

"See, Mel, I told you they'd love you. But now I'm going to show you how much *I* love you."

Noah lifts my t-shirt off and quickly rids me of my bra. "Lie down," he commands, standing and stripping himself naked in record time. Leaning over the bed, he pulls my pajama pants and underwear off, tossing them to the floor.

His hungry gaze travels up my body, followed slowly by his lips. Noah blazes a trail of kisses up my legs as his hands wrap around them, traveling the path his lips don't reach. His tongue flicks against my core once, leaving me needy for so much more.

When his mouth reaches my stomach, my heart skips a beat. He leaves tender kisses all over it while rubbing gentle circles with his hands, as if he's hugging the baby from the outside. Kissing his way upward, his hands capture my breasts, pushing them close. His tongue flicks only the tip of each nipple before blowing on one, then the next, bringing my nipples to hard, taut peaks. As his mouth descends against my breast and he sucks me into his mouth my body arches into his.

He slides one hand lower until he's cupping my pussy. Releasing a nipple, he asks, "Are you wet for me, baby?"

411

D. Kelly

"Yes!" I cry out, pushing myself into his hand, trying to get his fingers inside of me.

His kisses become frantic as he makes his way from my breasts to my neck. I love when he nuzzles against me and groans right below my ear with his lips against my heated flesh.

"Please, Noah," I whimper, begging him for relief.

Bringing his mouth to mine, he moves between my legs, hitching my leg up over his hip as he positions himself at my entrance. "I've never done this before." His emotional words land straight on my heart.

"Me, either, but I'm glad we're doing it together."

"Me, too," he answers as his lips catch mine. His cock slides in the moment his tongue meets mine, and it's an explosion of senses. My arched hips meet his thrusts in synchronicity. Our kiss a long, seductive journey to bliss. With my arms around his neck, our bodies are fused together in every way possible.

Words aren't necessary; everything is being said with the movements of our bodies. When my walls begin to clench around him, his body trembles above mine. With each thrust, he becomes more determined to make this last, but when my orgasm hits and I contract tightly around him, he loses his battle and comes with me. The twitching of his cock feels so intense; as he fills me with his essence, I feel it all—each pulse, each thrust, every decadent sensation.

Noah falls to the side and pulls me to him, my head against his heart. His heart thumps wildly against my ear as he combs his fingers through my hair. "That was …"

"The number one reason people get pregnant. After feeling that, who would want to go back to condoms?"

He chuckles and kisses my head. "Exactly, it was incredible. It always is with you, but I could feel you around me, clenching me, holding me, and pulling me into you. Fuck, Mel. It was euphoric."

"Just think … we can do it like that for the next seven, eight months."

With a growl, he pulls me to his mouth and kisses me relentlessly. "I'm never going to want to go back to condoms."

"Me, either. I'll get the IUD put in as soon as I can after the baby."

"Or we can work on number two right away."

"Keep dreaming, Weston."

Noah pulls the blanket up over us and tucks me into his arms. "Thank you for tonight, Amelia. It's one I'll never forget. I still can't believe we're having a baby. She's going to be perfect, just like you."

"Really? You want a girl? I kind of hope it's a boy."

"I want whatever is healthy. I wouldn't mind either. Do you have a feeling like Belle did?"

I can already tell Noah is going to be extremely hands-on during this pregnancy. But it's a good thing; he'll help me keep it together.

"No, I don't. I'm just not sure I'd know what to do with a girl. Boys seem easier. But whatever it is, I'll love it, just like I do their daddy."

"Goodnight, Mel," Noah whispers, almost asleep.

"Goodnight, Noah. Sweet dreams."

Belle's Pregnancy Post

Slammers!

It's your girl Belle, and boy do I have news! Listen up, *Slammed* family, because this time I need to ask for your forgiveness. We all know there's been rumors about myself and Darren Miller from BAD. I'm finally going to put those rumors to rest. Yes, I'm wearing an engagement ring and yes, I am also pregnant. We are *not* having a shot gun wedding; in fact, we haven't even discussed a date.

So why am I telling you this? Because you, my loyal readers, deserve the truth. At first, we kept things quiet because with any new relationship you never know how things are going to work out. As time passed, our love has only grown stronger. Now with the new photos emerging of Darren with his hands around my ever-expanding belly, it seems like the right time to come clean once and for all. To be fair, we never denied any rumors; we just didn't go out of our way to confirm them, either.

Forgive me, Slammers, for keeping this blessing from you. We just wanted to keep this little miracle to ourselves as long as we could. She's going to be something special, you just see.

That's right, I said she. *Slammed* readers are getting the exclusive gender reveal right here. Rest assured the upcoming baby won't affect any of your BAD updates. I'll still be bringing you all the exclusives as they happen.

My apologies, *Slammed* family, I never meant to deceive you. I always meant to tell you in my own way, when the time was right.

Don't forget - Live today like there's no tomorrow.

Xs and Os,

Belle

On The Road Again
Three months after New York…

Since New York, everything has been a whirlwind of activity. How in the world they managed to set up most of the eastern states in the dead of winter, I'll never understand. I suppose this was the most efficient way in order for them to end the tour in California, but still … the cold weather is not my friend.

When we pulled out of New York on the buses, Noah sat down and made a ton of calls. He singlehandedly scheduled each and every prenatal appointment with a doctor in whatever city we were going to be in at the time. And he scheduled them against his schedule so he could always be there. I have to admit, it was a huge relief. The only downfall is when the baby is due we'll be on the road, so my doctor won't get to deliver it unless I go home, which I can't do because Noah wouldn't be able to be there. Now, every month, a different doctor gets to see all my lady parts in all their pregnant glory. Did I forget to mention every doctor is a woman? I'm sort of grateful, but that was Noah's way of waving his man card loud and proud.

At least now that it's April, it's warming up, so I get to watch all the spring blooms in full effect. We're also inching closer to the end of the tour, and my excitement for going home grows with each day that passes. The band is in Florida this week and two exciting things are happening today. First, Belle is flying in for the weekend. And second, Noah and I are finding out the sex of our baby. I'm officially at the halfway point of my pregnancy and haven't had any morning sickness which was the greatest blessing of all. Belle is at the end of her pregnancy with only four weeks left to go, give or take. They've picked a name for the baby, but they're being impossibly stubborn and not telling anyone what it is.

"Morning, Mel," Sawyer says as he makes his coffee.

"Morning."

The two of us still have our morning routine while Noah still sleeps like the dead. Sawyer has stopped calling me Princess completely, and no one batted an eye. Guess I was the only one keeping track.

"So today is the big day. Are you excited?"

"I am, but I'm also scared."

His gaze travels to the window before looking back at me. "Are you even excited?"

His question catches me off guard. "I'm getting there. After today, I think I will be." What I really want to say was *I'm excited Noah is getting everything he wants, but I'm not sure I'm completely on board with the whole thing yet.*

"That's good, I was just curious. You seemed completely overwhelmed with all the attention at Easter."

"Your family was excited, I get it. But my emotions are on high right now, and I *was* overwhelmed. I'm not sure I've ever met anyone as excited for babies as the people in your family."

"Ha! You think *that* was bad, you should have seen when Diane was pregnant. Mom would show up at her house almost daily with new magazines, books, gifts, you name it. Rob finally had to talk to my dad to make it stop. Be glad you're on tour and she's not your actual mother."

I bite down on my lip when he says that. "Shit, I'm sorry, Mel, I didn't mean it like that. Is that why this is so hard for you? Because your parents aren't here?"

Here come the tears. Pregnancy hormones are the absolute worst.

"That's a loaded question I try not to give much thought to. Of course I wish they were here for this, but if they were, I most likely wouldn't be where I am now. I'd probably be singing and touring, and my book would have never been written. At least, if my dad had gotten his way."

Sawyer drops the subject and pulls a pack of Pop-Tarts from his secret stash. "Here, you know this will make you feel better." He hands me the pack with a smile.

For whatever reason, eating Pop-Tarts while pregnant is almost a transcendent experience. After moaning in appreciation, I lick my lips.

Sawyer rolls his eyes. "Stop making it sexual or I won't give them to you anymore. Fuck, I need to get laid."

"Well, we're in The Sunshine State, so I'm sure you won't have a lack of willing participants. Especially since we're in hotels once we get to Orlando. One more hour and you can … scratch your itch." I laugh at my own joke and even Sawyer joins in.

"What are you two laughing about?" Noah asks sleepily.

"Nothing," Sawyer says at the same time I tell Noah the truth.
"Sawyer needing to get laid."

Noah is immediately irritated when he hears the difference in our answers. This is what it's been like the past few months. My relationship with Sawyer is fine. But a good part of the time, Sawyer is an ass to Noah for no reason. I want to talk to him about it, but I don't want to make it worse. Darren has tried, though, and it works for a bit and then he's back to being angry.

Sawyer goes to his room and Noah leans down and kisses me and then like he does every morning, he leans down and kisses the baby good morning too.

"Do you know why Sawyer seems so angry with me all the time?"

God, does that question hurt my heart.

"Not for sure, but if I had to guess, I think he feels left behind. All of his best friends are married or getting married, and two of the three of you are starting families. I think, deep down inside, Sawyer wants what you have but he doesn't know how to get it."

"I miss my brother, Mel. What can I do?" Noah's sad eyes make me want to cry, but I don't because I'm a contributor to that sadness; I won't give myself an easy out on my guilt.

"What you're already doing, Noah. Take his smartass comments and love him anyway. But maybe try and find some bonding time with him this week. The two of you should go to Disney World or something and act young and dumb. Or go to Harry Potter World and drink some Butterbeer."

Noah stands up, smiling away. "Great idea. I'm going to go talk to him about it right now and then I'm taking a shower. Our appointment is in two hours and I want to be off the bus as soon as it stops. The sooner we get there, the sooner we get to see Baby Weston."

Our appointment. Never once have I felt like I'm in this alone. My emotions about this pregnancy might still be mixed but my love for its father has never faltered.

While Noah showers, I take the opportunity to type up my notes from yesterday's interview with Harold, one of our bus drivers. I had a feeling they'd have some good information for this book and I wasn't disappointed. I recall our conversation with a smile.

"Hey, Harold, mind if I keep you company up here and interview you for my book?"

Harold motions to the seat next to him with an easy smile. "I'd be a fool not to spend an afternoon with a beautiful lady. Don't go

417

falling in love with me, though ... my wife's had my heart for thirty years now."

"Wow, thirty years, and you're on the road so much. How do you keep it together?"

"Everyone's got to make a living. It can be hard at times, but Noah and Sawyer make it a point to fly my family out when we have extended days off. They're good bosses, and my kids are the envy of their friends for not only knowing BAD but also having the opportunity to hang out with them."

Damn, Noah and Sawyer strike again. I've never met anyone who cares like they do. Even if Sawyer is a bit more low-key about it all. "That's a great job perk. Are there any other's you'd like to share?"

"This job has lots of advantages. I love driving and seeing the country in all its seasons. It's my pride and joy to keep these guys safe and keep the tour running without interruptions if possible. I'd have taken this job in a heartbeat even without the benefits because the pay is good and the company is excellent. But my favorite perk of the job is for each year I drive, my kids get one year of college paid for. I've got two kids and I've worked here eight years. Neither of them will ever have to take out a student loan."

Blinking back my hormonal tears I scribble my notes furiously. I wonder if they have this deal with other people on the tour as well?

"How old are your kids?"

He points up to the visor. "You can take that picture down and look at it. My daughter is fifteen and my son is seventeen."

They're cute kids, and his wife is gorgeous.

"What does your wife do?"

"She's a stay-at-home mom. We decided it was important for them to have her home full-time when I took this job. She loves it and sends me videos of everything, so even if I can't be there I never truly miss things."

He's got such a laidback attitude; it's rare to meet someone with such an ease about them. I'm sorry I haven't made the effort to get to know him sooner, but I'm glad the guys make an effort to spend time with the drivers when they can.

"Okay, Harold, time for the down and dirty. What's the most outrageous thing you've had happen on the bus? Maybe something to do with the fans or something the guys did ... inquiring minds want to know. But rest assured they have final say on what goes in the book."

He releases a belly laugh and shakes his head. "Girl, I thought you were trying to get me in trouble for a minute."

"Oh, come on! I wouldn't do that. I'm just doing my job same as you."

"These guys are good guys. In the beginning, they were a bit rambunctious. It's really the fans who are out of control, or who can be. There was one time when we were stopped for groceries and it was right when BAD had become famous on their first tour. One of the guys forgot to lock the bus."

"Oh no ... "

Laughing, Harold looks at me quickly before putting his eyes back on the road. *"Oh yeah. We came out of the store and there were at least four women just lounging in their underwear waiting for them. Poor Noah, he was trying to avert his eyes and stay sweet but firm. They were all on the same bus back then. As soon as Wyatt saw what was going on, he turned around and got off the bus. Called out 'later' behind him and just bailed."*

Harold is laughing so hard he's wheezing. *"Darren and Sawyer ... well, let's just say they enjoyed themselves. Noah followed Wyatt pretty quickly. They were outside discussing the pitfalls of life on the road while Darren and Sawyer were inside enjoying what they considered the perks of the road. Just goes to show you, no two people see the same situation quite the same. There was a lot of that over the years ...girls sneaking onto the buses. Back then they didn't have the fancy digital doors like we do now. It's easier for them to get into the hotel rooms now than it is for them to sneak onto the bus."*

Isn't that the truth? Shaking away thoughts of Sara in our room, I turn my attention back to him. Harold begins to slow the bus so he can park at our next stop.

"Okay, last question, what is your favorite memory out of all your time with BAD?"

"That's easy, Wyatt and Anna's wedding. Finding balance in a life like this isn't easy, but those two have juggled their love, schedules, and careers since they were practically babies. Knowing love won in the end, and being able to witness their union, was one of my favorite days." He pauses and turns back to me after we're fully stopped.

"You and Noah have that same kind of love. It's visible to anyone, even if they don't know you. Don't let anyone take that away from you because most people are lucky to find a love like yours in their lifetime. Finding it a second time ... well, it's next to impossible."

"*Thanks, Harold, I think we're pretty lucky, too. Speaking of Noah, if I don't finish getting ready, he's going to freak. He owes me a lunch date today ... one that isn't on the bus.*"

"*Well, you two have fun and enjoy your date. I'll see you when you get back.*"

"Are you ready, Mel?" Noah asks, freshly showered and looking sexy as ever.

"Yeah, let me put this stuff away and I'm all yours."

"Are you two ready to see your baby?" the doctor asks with a bright, happy smile. Dr. Walter is a younger woman, probably mid- to late thirties at the most. It's obvious she's a fan of Noah's. So far, they all seem to be, but no one has crossed any boundaries yet, so it's all good.

"We are *so* ready!" Noah exclaims, squeezing my hand. I want to record his reaction, but it's not possible with the way we are situated. I'll have to write about it as soon as we get back. One thing I have started is a journal for the baby to have when it's older. It's silly, but I would have liked something like that, especially now, with my parents gone.

After taking all her measurements, the doctor shows us the heartbeat—my favorite part of these appointments. It's so strong, just like Noah's. But this 3D ultrasound might be my new favorite thing. The baby's features are so prominent already and it's only the size of a bell pepper. *How crazy is that?*

"Do you see this? she asks, pointing to the monitor.

"Is that what I think it is?" I ask, suddenly completely excited.

"If you think it's a penis, then yes. Congratulations, you two, you're having a boy."

"Noah! It's a boy, we're having a boy!" I'm screaming while he's still got his eyes locked on the monitor.

"Let me get the pictures that printed out and I'll give you a few minutes alone." She hands me a towel to wipe off the ultrasound gel; Noah helps me up as soon as it's gone. After buttoning up my pants, Noah lifts me off the ground and spins me in a circle.

"We're having a boy, Mel! Do you know what that means?"

"Diane is stealing our baby?"

"No way in hell. It means I can teach him to play guitar, and baseball, and how to treat women right, all like my dad taught us. And I can read stories to him and search for monsters and have mud fights." His eyes are dancing and he's still looking at the screen over my shoulder.

"You get to do all of that. You're also in charge of baths after those mud fights."

"Deal." Then he pulls us to the ultrasound machine and takes out his phone. "Crouch down here," he says as he moves to the other side of the machine to take the same pose. He takes a few pictures of us with the monitor between us and then shows them to me. "Look, our first family photos."

And fuck me sideways if the waterworks don't start falling from my eyes out of fucking nowhere. This is my family. Mine.

"That is the sweetest thing I've ever seen. You should caption it and send it to our friends, but don't tell them the sex. We need to do something unique for that tonight."

"Good idea." He's already typing and texting.

"Noah, when we go home for Fourth of July weekend we should do a maternity photo shoot. Nothing big, but it can be the next stage of our family photos."

"I fucking love that idea, and I love you, too." Of course, as soon as he lowers his lips to mine, the doctor comes back inside the room. After she officially tells us everything is right on track and there's nothing to worry about, we're on our way.

That night, the band didn't have a show. Noah and I invited everyone to our room so we could tell them about the baby. At the same time they were supposed to be with us we had deliveries made to Anna, Sam, Veronica, Jordan, Eli, and Noah's parent's and sisters. They all got a bouquet of blue tulips with a card. We wanted to go all out with balloons but since no one outside of the immediate family knows we had to keep it low key in case the reporters are out lurking.

For our room, we found this big round black plastic ball. It's got a latch in the middle you can easily open. We filled it to capacity with blue confetti and Noah hung it from the ceiling. We decided to let Sawyer be the one to open it and make him part of the process. Housekeeping is going to hate us but Noah promised he'd make it worth their while.

Everyone is here except for Belle and Darren, but when they walk in, I almost lose my shit. "Belle! You're all baby!"

Her waddle is the cutest thing, and I'm surprised she was even willing to get on a plane to come here. With an exhausted sigh, she

D. Kelly

takes a seat. "I know, and it's getting hard to breathe and hard to move. The doctor said she's already in position, so it's just a matter of when she wants to come. He said her size is good so she shouldn't have any issues if she's a couple weeks early."

Darren sits next to her, pulls her legs into his lap, and rubs her ankles. Those are huge, too, but I'm not saying anything about that. I'm sure that will be me in another three months or less.

Noah takes a quick second to position a fan at the ball, and turning it up to high. Wyatt gives him a quizzical look but doesn't say anything.

"Can you two stop being so secretive and tell us already if I'm having another niece or a nephew finally?" Sawyer's excited, even if he's acting huffy and puffy.

"Actually, little brother, why don't you do us the honors and open that latch on the ball?"

Sawyer cautiously looks up. "I'm not going to get slimed, am I?"

"I wouldn't do that to you, Sawyer," Noah says solemnly, and Sawyer opens the ball.

Just as we hoped, the fan blows the confetti everywhere as it's falling. Everyone is covered in blue.

"Look! They're having a Smurf!" Darren quips, making me laugh.

"Yes! You're the man, Noah! Diane is going to kick your ass, but I don't care because I finally get a nephew!" Sawyer, along with pretty much everyone, brushes away the confetti while Noah turns off the fan. For the first time in months, Sawyer looks genuinely happy.

"Mel! Our babies are going to grow up and get married!" Belle screams from the couch as I lean down to hug her. I had the exact same thought.

"I'm not so sure I want my daughter dating a Weston. I was never allowed to date a Weston, so maybe I should return the favor," Darren teases.

Belle socks him. "My best friend's son can date my daughter any time he wants to. Especially if he treats her the way his daddy treats his mama."

Warren gives me a big hug. "Your parents would be so happy for you. Your dad always wanted to try for another baby, but your mom never thought it was fair for you to be raised on the road. She couldn't bear to do that to another child. Although, I don't think you turned out half bad. I can't wait to meet him, Mel. You guys are making me proud."

We end up ordering drinks and food and celebrating with our family for hours. The proud look on Noah's face never left. I know he said he wanted a healthy baby, even mentioned he wouldn't mind a girl, but based on his reaction there's no doubt in my mind he was wishing for a boy, just like I was.

Today, Sawyer and Noah are spending the day at Disney World. Noah said when he asked Sawyer to spend a brothers' day together, he lit up. He also said Sawyer is a sucker for amusement parks, so he wasn't sure if he was excited to spend time with Noah or to be going to Disney.

Throughout the day, Noah has been sending me the best selfies of the two of them, and Mac having a blast. Noah and Sawyer look completely carefree. It makes my heart happy to see them bonding, and I can only hope that from here on out the animosity between them will be gone.

He's also been sending me random texts to check in, show his affection, and warn me about the barrage of packages about to hit the hotel. Apparently, he and Sawyer went a bit overboard shopping for Saylor and Emme; not that I'd expect anything less.

After moving all the photos into a file on my computer, I start uploading them to a printing site. I've been printing pictures like crazy and having them sent to the house. When we get home from tour, I'm going to start making photo albums. Some people think it's old school, but I loved looking through Noah and Sawyer's childhood memories; I want that for our kids one day.

My phone beeps. Expecting it to be another picture from Noah, I'm surprised when I find one from Sawyer. It's of the two of them on a boat in It's a Small World with the song attached as well. It makes me smile.

I fire off a link for "Hakuna Matata" to which Sawyer immediately replies with a smiley face emoji.

It's long after dark by the time they made it back to the hotel. Sawyer came to the room with Noah with a huge stuffed Winnie the Pooh in tow.

"Sawyer, do you have a plushie fetish we're not aware of?" I ask. His horrified look is priceless, and Noah is cracking up.

"Mel, my only fetish is sexy women with flexible limbs. Now the first gift to my nephew is going to be tainted with the words from your dirty mind."

"Really? It's for the baby?"

He puts the bear into my outstretched arms. "Yes, from his favorite uncle. I got Darren's baby a big stuffed Eeyore. Saylor and Emme got Tigger and Piglet. I don't know why, but Piglet seemed perfect for Emme."

"And did Uncle Noah try and outdo your shopping spree?" Quirking my brow at Noah, he shoots me a look of pure innocence.

"I did not," he states proudly

"Bullshit," Sawyer says, coughing into his hand. "I'm pretty sure he brought every princess doll in the park, along with matching costumes."

"Yeah, well, you know you play it off like you only bought stuffed animals. Tell Mel what else you bought."

My curiosity is piqued, and Sawyer replies with a resigned sigh, "I might have bought a family Disney World package for next summer for a week with the VIP experience."

That is a Noah-level good deed. Maybe Sawyer took our talk to heart, or maybe he's always like this with his family. "That's awesome, Sawyer, I'm sure they'll love it."

"We'll *all* love it," Noah corrects. "When he says family, he means everyone. Us, my parents, sisters, Jordan, Darren's family, Wyatt and Anna, Mac and Ryan, Warren and Sam. Everyone, Mel. Babies included. Hotels, tickets, everything bought and paid for."

Holy shit, I can't even imagine the price tag on that. "That was so thoughtful of you, Sawyer, thank you. I'm sure everyone is going to have a blast. Imagine the pictures we'll be able to get. It will be our first family vacation courtesy of their favorite Uncle Sawyer."

"Alright, well, I'm going to go crash. It was nice not having any shows for a couple of days, but tomorrow it's back to the grind, and I need some sleep."

"Thanks for coming with me today. We need to do this more often. Maybe after the tour we can make it a priority to take a brothers' trip at least once a year. Us, J, Wyatt, and Darren. I know we see each other all the time, but a guys' weekend is something we haven't done in I don't know how long. Not to truly hang out and relax, at least."

Sawyer's eyes soften with Noah's words, and I think hearing that Noah is looking toward the future and not abandoning him makes Sawyer feel better. "That sounds good, Noah, we'll make it happen for sure."

When Noah closes the door, my eyes are filled with tears. "Are you going to cry again?" he asks softly.

"No," I answer with a sniffle as I'm met with his loving arms.

"It's okay, Mel, you cry all you want to. I know they're happy tears."

"Did you have a good time?"

"We had so much fun. I meant what I said, I need time with Sawyer. When we're out of sync, I feel off. Like my equilibrium needs to be reset or something. I've been trying to give him space. I know he's lonely and trying to figure out what life has in store for him."

"He'll be okay, Noah." As I caress his back, he keeps me tightly in his embrace.

"He'll be better than okay. Sawyer was meant for great things. He's the most talented person I've ever met. I wish he'd go solo and showcase his voice like he's doing now. At least go into songwriting, something. This industry gives him life."

Noah has opened up a door I've been wanting to knock on for a while now. Pulling him over to the couch, I take this opportunity to delve deeper. "Why rock? Don't get me wrong, you guys are at the top of your game. Coming up on the heels of Linkin Park, A Perfect Circle, Incubus, bands like that ... I see the appeal. But I've heard your vocal ranges and you could have far surpassed any of that."

"We were kids in a band who wanted to make music. Darren loved Metallica, and Wyatt was a Korn freak. Sawyer and I didn't really care what we sang, but we loved the way you could go at it with a guitar in rock. Sawyer loved being able to scream out his aggressions, and we both wanted to be wherever our friends were."

I love getting new insight about them—for the book and for myself. "So when did the song writing come into play?"

His face softens at the memory. "I've always thought that came after what happened with J. Once Sawyer started journaling, he had this funnel where he could let his concentrated thoughts pour free. When the words started speaking to him, I think it was only natural for it to flow onto the paper in the form of a song."

"And what about you? Where do you see your future career taking you?"

Noah blushes. "I'd love to manage Sawyer. Make him an independent artist and watch him rise to the top. I've never imagined not working with Sawyer in some capacity for the rest of our lives. Darren and Wyatt as well. Maybe even think about opening a small boutique label one day for indies. Who knows?"

"But no singing for you?"

D. Kelly

"I'll sing for you anytime, Mel, you know that … and to our kids, but it's hard to have a career singing and not tour. I'm done touring. Life awaits us and we're going to enjoy it. Come on, let's go to sleep. I'm tired."

After Noah falls asleep, I think about what he said about being Sawyer's manager. I know Sawyer loves Noah, but I wonder if he realizes how much faith Noah has in him. It makes me realize, for the first time ever, the importance of siblings.

Welcome To The World

April eleventh is a day I will never forget. It was a Friday, and Darren woke Noah and me up pounding on our door at three in the morning.

"What's wrong?" Noah's frantic tone pulls me from bed.

"Belle's water broke and I have no idea what to do. She's not supposed to have the baby here!"

Noah jumps into action. First, he pops his head into the hall and tells Mac to pull the car up. Then, he tells Darren we'll meet him in their room in five minutes.

"Get dressed, Mel, we're going to see our niece make her way into the world. I'm going to call Dr. Walter and ask if she'll meet us at the hospital and take Belle on as a patient. I'm sure she will, I'll make it worth her while." Noah has this smile when he's plotting a good deed, or trying to get something he wants. I can imagine it goes all the way back to preschool and he even swayed many a teacher with it.

"Yeah, that sounds good. Oh my God, I can't believe the baby is coming, Noah!"

Placing a tender kiss against my lips, he replies, "Soon, it will be us."

Thinking about labor terrifies me, but imagining our baby after seeing him, not so much. I'm getting used to the idea; he's coming soon so I'd better be. I officially graduated into my own maternity pants this week.

Minutes later, Belle is laughing at Darren as he paces the floor in their room.

"Are you okay, Belle?" I ask, wondering why she's not freaking out right now.

"I'm fine, but Darren isn't. I don't even feel anything yet. One minute I was sleeping, the next I thought I'd pissed myself."

"Alright, guys, let's get downstairs. Mac brought the car up while I called the doctor Mel went to for her ultrasound. She's got the best reputation in Orlando, her name is Dr. Walter and she's agreed to deliver your baby. Grab your extra tickets for tonight, Darren. We've got a doctor and a nurse who are going to appreciate your thoughtfulness."

Darren rushes to his dresser mumbling, "Good idea, Noah. Good idea."

Belle looks at me and shakes her head, but she's watching Darren freak out in complete adoration. I can't believe she's so calm; it's got to be because the pain hasn't started yet. After exiting the room, we're waiting for the elevator as Wyatt, Sawyer, and Warren come running down the hall to catch up.

The guys help Belle into the SUV, where Mac has already laid out towels. I climb in, followed by Noah and Darren, and the other guys wait for Ryan to pull the other car up.

Twenty short minutes later, Belle is in a hospital room, gowned and hooked up to a fetal monitor and an IV. Talk about the VIP treatment. This room is a suite, and the nurse said we can all stay until Belle tells us to go. Darren takes one side of her bed and I take the other.

"Hey, Belle, we don't want to interfere with your special moment, so if you want us to leave just say so, okay?"

"Actually, Mel, I'd love for you to stay for the birth. Darren and I already talked about it and it's only right my sister is here. Especially since my mom isn't. She's going to be so pissed. But if I can wake her up in the morning holding a bundle of joy, I'm sure she'll forgive me."

I'm touched by her offer and a little fearful. Seeing her give birth is going to be a scary wake-up call for me. It will be worth it to see her baby come into the world. "I'm honored, Belle, thank you."

"You're welcome, but the other guys ... yeah, they'll have to go when the action starts. This is only a show for us three."

"Consider us gone. I don't think my player mentality can handle watching a woman give birth," Sawyer calls out, making the guys laugh.

Dr. Walter comes in right then and pauses in her tracks. When her eyes make their way across the room and she realizes she's got the entire band here, she's starstruck. Unless you were looking, though, you'd never know it; she recovered like a boss.

"You must be Belle. Seems like congratulations are in order because today is going to be your baby's birthday. I'm Dr. Walter ... and you must be dad?" She extends her hand to Darren.

"Yes, I'm Darren Miller. Thank you for coming and taking care of the two most important women in my life."

I start crying again. After this tour, I'm going to invent a pregnancy patch that somehow blocks the sporadic waterworks in pregnant women.

"Alright, let me wash up and we'll see how you're progressing. Mel, Noah, it's good to see you again. Thank you for trusting me with your friend."

Dr. Walter makes me wish if I were going to deliver anywhere, it would be with her. Noah's research has paid off in spades; I'm so thankful for him right now.

"Alright, guys, you heard the doctor, time to get out. We'll call you back in a few minutes." Darren gets up and ushers them all out the door in protective papa mode.

Belle giggles from the bed. "I'm pretty sure not a single one of them would want to see this, except for maybe Noah, and only because he'd want to know what to expect."

"Belle, put your feet up on the bed and spread your legs for me. You're going to feel some pressure, but it's only me feeling with my fingers to see how dilated you are."

"Ugh ..." Belle groans, squeezing my hand. The monitor lines start moving rapidly, and Dr. Walter pulls her hand back, removes her gloves, and goes to wash her hands again.

When she comes back, she smiles up at Belle. "You're in active labor. Right now you're about four centimeters dilated. That contraction you had while I was checking you was pretty mild in intensity, but every woman is different. How do you handle pain? Do you want an epidural or any pain medication? The hospital was able to get your records, but I didn't get a chance to review the birth plan yet."

"I'm not sure. I was still trying to figure that out because she wasn't supposed to come for another month." Belle is understandably upset; this wasn't how she was expecting her baby to enter the world.

"Yes, well, we find babies come when they're ready. You have time to think about it, but don't wait too long. It can sometimes take a while if you opt for an epidural and lots of moms end up missing the window and going natural. We can give you something to take the edge off if the contractions get bad, but it will wear off before you deliver. I'll check back with you in about an hour. If you make a decision about the drugs before I return, press the button for the nurse. Try and rest, it could be a long night."

For the next hour, Belle powers through her contractions amazingly well. Once the guys saw how much pain was involved they

D. Kelly

all decided to go into a private waiting room the hospital set up for them. Except for Noah, he was fascinated with everything.

In the end, Belle opts for drugs but not an epidural. It's shortly after eight in the morning when Dr. Walter checks Belle for the final time and announces it's time to bring this baby into the world. Noah goes to the waiting room, leaving me wishing I could go, too. This is the scariest thing I've ever seen.

With one hand wrapped around Darren's and the other around mine, Belle begins to push. When the baby's head comes out, Darren looks down in amazement. "Belle, I can see her head. She has so much hair." His excitement is palpable, but I'm not even sure any of what he said registered with Belle. She's exhausted, in pain, and trying to push a watermelon out of her hoo ha.

Three more pushes and the baby is all the way out. Dr. Walter suctions her mouth, allowing her to release the loudest scream I've ever heard. I get it; it was probably just as traumatic for her as it was for her mom.

"Happy Birthday, baby girl!" Dr. Walter announces, holding her high for Belle to see. Belle's bawling at the sight of her baby.

"Oh my God, Darren, we made that beautiful little girl," she sobs hysterically.

Darren kisses her sweetly. "We sure did, Belle."

"Dad, would you like to cut the cord?"

Darren looks horrified. "Um, I think I'll pass on that one, but thanks for asking," he tells her, watching with rapt attention as she cuts the cord instead.

"Let the nurses check her scores and her oxygen levels. She seems perfect, but we'll want to be on the safe side since she's pre-term. Then they'll clean her up and give her back, it will only take a few minutes. In the meantime, lets finish up with you first."

While Dr. Walter is tending to Belle, Darren is hovering over the nurses, making sure the baby is okay. The nurse calls out scores, oxygen levels, and weight before Dr. Walter gives her the green light to bring the baby to mom and dad.

"I'm going to step out now. Enjoy these precious moments. Darren, come get me when I can hold her and learn her name." Belle seems like she wants to say something, but I cut her off. "You did good, Belle. I'm so proud of you." With a kiss to her cheek, I go find the guys to give them the good news.

"She's here and she's perfectly healthy. They're going to take some time to bond and call us in. She's so cute, you guys. Tiny like Belle, but boy does she have a mighty cry."

430

"Seems appropriate, another crying woman to add to the mix. Between you and Belle, there's been nothing but tears the past few months." Sawyer's response might have made me laugh if I weren't so tired.

"How was it?" Noah asks earnestly as I take a seat on the couch and curl up against him.

"It looked like torture, but I'd say the end result was absolutely worth it."

"Are you scared now?" he asks, concern on his face.

"I've been scared but even though it looks horrific, she also sailed right through with no problems. I think I'll be okay. I'm not a fan of pain, so I might go for the epidural option. Seems like it would make the whole thing a bit more peaceful, or at least less stressful. But I don't want an audience, Noah. Just the two of us."

He nuzzles his head against mine. "That sounds like an excellent plan."

After about a half hour of waiting, Darren comes to invite us all back into the room. The guys all hug him, and he and Sawyer seem to have a moment of sorts before we go in to see Belle. She's beaming at her baby girl in her arms.

"Everyone, wash your hands if you plan on touching this baby," I announce firmly as I lead the way to the sink. My grabby hands are itching for a turn. Once I'm finished, Belle kisses her softly on the head and passes her to me with a smile.

"Meet the newest member of our family. Cadence Melody Miller."

"You picked a musical name, but it's not a messed up one at all, it's absolutely perfect. Happy Birthday, Cadence, I'm Auntie Mel." Noah is smiling down at her over my shoulder and I pass her to him next.

"How do you feel, Belle? Can I get you anything?" I ask, feeling useless after what I just witnessed her go through to bring Cadence into this world.

"I'm okay, Mel. Thank you for being here with me. We already called Veronica and she's trying to make plans to see her already."

Darren speaks up as the baby makes it into Wyatt's arms. "Hey, guys, I need to ask you something important. Especially you Wyatt and Warren." All eyes are on him except for Wyatt, who's entranced by Cadence. "Now that Cadence is here early, Belle has to go on maternity leave. It will push her all the way up to when she was supposed to come on tour with us anyway. Not trying to put you on the spot or anything, but would you mind if they just came now? I know it will be an adjustment and …"

"Darren, stop," Wyatt commands as he passes the baby straight to Warren. "It's your family, and your bus, too. You don't even have to ask, at least not me. You already know Mel and Noah don't care."

"I don't care. I think a baby might be just what the doctor ordered to end this tour right," Warren says, passing Cadence to Sawyer.

Sawyer cradles her in his arms, never breaking his gaze on her. "Hell, I'm her all-time favorite uncle already. She can be my sidekick anytime. I might even change diapers if you're lucky."

"Alright, it's set then," Warren announces. "Welcome to the tour. Speaking of … you guys need to get some sleep. I'll push the interviews back to after the show. Darren, rest as much as you can, but we need you there tonight."

"I'll come back and sit with Belle while you guys are at the show. You can relieve me when it's over, Darren," I say, with the hope of relieving the conflict crossing his face.

With relief in his eyes, he agrees. I get one more chance to hold Cadence before passing her off to her daddy. I've never seen Darren look so in love.

Once we're back at the hotel, instead of going straight to sleep, Noah gets on the computer and starts making calls. In under an hour, he's hired a company to come out and redesign Darren's bus. Nothing major, just making it baby friendly. They're supposed to figure out the ways and hows of fitting essential nursery items in tight spaces. They bring all the furniture and Noah pays them on completion.

After that's taken care of, he looks at me with a beaming smile. "Let's do some shopping, Mel."

As I curl up into his side, we look at a wide variety of items. Eventually, he places an order for a car seat, a stroller, a bouncy chair, and some essentials like clothes, diapers, pacifiers, and baby toiletries. Belle didn't have a shower and she's so last-minute, I know she doesn't have anything yet. It's another one of Noah's good deeds, but it's also fun to shop and browse. As a bonus, we now have an idea of all the stuff we still have to do as well.

We debated themes, colors, and styles of things we'd eventually like to get for our nursery once we're home from tour. He loves the Dr. Seuss crib set so much he ordered the whole thing now and had it shipped to our house. My husband-to-be is amazing.

"If that company does a good job setting up their bus, we'll have them come back out and do ours," Noah says, putting his laptop to the side and tucking me into his arms. With a contented sigh, I curl up into him as my eyes become heavy with sleep.

Later that evening—after bonding with Belle and Cadence for hours—I'm on a baby high. When Noah and I get back to the hotel and climb into bed, he pulls me into his arms.

In the sweetest tone, he asks, "Can we talk about something important to me?"

"Of course, what's going on?"

"Do you remember in Vegas when I told you if you ever got pregnant I was going to want to marry you immediately?"

Uh-oh, I know exactly where this is going. "Yes, I remember."

"Let's pick a day, Mel. We can have any kind of wedding you want. Big, or just the two of us, but I want to be your husband before our baby comes."

"Noah, isn't the whole pregnant bride thing a little cliché?"

His body tenses against mine. "Maybe if it's a shotgun wedding, but this isn't that." His firm tone leaves zero room for argument. "You know how I feel about you, and we got engaged before we knew about him. But he's coming, Mel, and I want us to be a married couple when he's born. It's important to me."

It's important to me. Those four words did me in. I won't deny him this; I really have no reason to.

"Would your family hate us if we had a ceremony with the two of us? We could video it for them and have a big reception once the tour is over. I hate the idea of the pregnant bride thing, but I'd feel better if it's only the two of us."

He quietly ponders my request. "I think they might be hurt at first, but I know my family and they'd understand. I'm sure it's hard for you to think about a wedding without your parents there, on top of them not being here for the baby. But it will have to be a really big reception, followed by an over-the-top honeymoon with lots of sex. I'm sure Diane and Rob would keep the baby for us."

And it's settled. Even though I feel massively guilty for Noah not having his family at the wedding, he'll be happy with us. This is why I hate secrets. I don't like having to think ahead to potential disasters. Noah will never know I had to weigh the pros and cons of Sawyer being hurt and getting drunk at our wedding. I don't trust drunk Sawyer to keep secrets, and I'm *not* going to lose Noah over one stupid mistake. As long as Sawyer doesn't have to suffer through a wedding, I'm sure he'll be fine at the reception, especially because the baby will be here by then.

But Noah is also right about something else. I've never wanted a big wedding because I don't have my dad to walk me down the aisle. This way I don't get hurt, either.

"Deal, one intimate wedding, one massive reception with an unforgettable honeymoon."

Noah's lips meet mine briefly before he asks another question. "Have you been thinking about names?"

"Some. I guess it's something we should start talking about." After meeting Cadence tonight, I can fully appreciate the value of a good name.

"What do you think about Nathaniel?" he asks tentatively.

"I like it. It's one I looked at in the baby book, actually. I have a list with a few names and I'm pretty sure Nathaniel is on it. I remember thinking we could call him Nate."

"Makes sense. I looked at the book after you and you had marked a few pages. I wasn't sure what name on the page you liked, but that one stuck out at me. Do you know what it means?" He's rubbing circles against my low back and it feels really good.

"Mm … no, what does it mean?"

"Nathaniel means 'Gift of God' or 'God has Given' and I think, in our case, it couldn't be any truer."

"It's perfect. Nathaniel, it is. What about a middle name?"

"What if we wait to meet him for that? We can make a list and see if his personality or his looks match?"

"That's perfect, Noah. Did we really just name our little boy?"

He chuckles at my excited squeal. "Yeah, Mel, we sure did. I love you."

"I love you, too. Always."

The next evening before their show Noah and I go over to the buses to meet with the baby company guys and put away the deliveries. Noah even arranged for a twelve-hour laundry service to come so they can take all the clothes and bedding and wash it in baby soap. Everything will be perfect by the time Belle and Cadence get on the bus.

The boss from the retrofit company shows us all the work they did; it's spectacular. They took the unused office space and turned it into a changing nook. The bottom of the changing table has dresser drawers and there are two smaller dressers on each side to make plenty of room for clothes.

In the bathroom, they hung a hook that holds the baby bathtub and toiletries. In Darren's room, they replaced the long dresser with a tall one and used the extra space for a small version of a crib. He shows Noah all the safety features of how the crib and bouncy seat latch and lock into the floor. They also added the appropriate kinds of safety harnesses to the couch so they could lock the car seat in place.

Noah is impressed and takes the guy's card so he can schedule them to come back in a few months. After he leaves, we get busy sorting all our purchases, which doesn't take very long. Noah runs outside to put the car seat in the car for tomorrow and while we're here, I decide to grab a sweater.

When I enter our room, I don't know what to think.

"Noah! What is this?"

"Did you call me, Mel?" he asks, climbing into the bus.

"What in the world is this?" I ask, pointing to the wall next to our bed. It's more like up at the top by the headboard—or where the headboard would be if there was one—but it's all soundproofing and a massive metal bar. Like the kind in handicapped bathrooms.

"I had them put that in for you."

"What the hell for?" I'm angry as fuck.

"Don't yell," he says, pressing his finger against my lips. "There are times when I'm not here and the further along you get, the harder it's going to be for you to get out of bed. Or it might be," he says, backtracking a bit. "I thought it would be better to be safe than sorry. I also had them put one against the wall next to the bathtub in case you wanted to soak and not have to ask for help."

And there's that sweetness I love so much, which makes my anger dissipate. Even though he's making me feel elderly, I understand his reasoning. "Thank you, it's very sweet. I hope I don't need them, but I'm happy you were thinking of me."

"I was thinking of you both, and you're welcome. They can come off later as easily as they were put on."

"Yeah, they're definitely coming down. Sawyer is going to have a field day with this one." I can just imagine the jokes now.

"Actually, he thought it was a really great idea. He saw how hard it was for Belle to move around at times."

"Are you two always going to be this overprotective?" My smile belies the frustration in my voice.

"Forever and ever, that's our job. Especially mine. Come on, let's get to the hospital so I can get to the show on time."

D. Kelly

"Need a baby fix, Mr. Weston?" He can't fool me; he's jonesing for Cadence.

"Is it that obvious?"

"Probably only to me. I need my fix of that cuteness, too. Let's go."

Noah pulls me close and as his lips meet mine, all thoughts of Cadence are temporarily forgotten as I fall into his love.

"You guys *do* realize you missed the baby store, like, five miles back, right? I know Darren said there's some stuff on the bus, but seriously you don't have any clue how much stuff we need." Belle's mama instincts are working overtime. I think it's mean they're making her worry, but I understand the element of surprise.

Veronica was able to fly in for a day but she had to get back to work. She'd already missed time for her vacation and Christmas, but they let her come since it was her grandchild. If she didn't have a massive deadline, she would have stayed longer. Darren arranged for a car to take her back to the airport when we all left the hospital this morning.

"Belle, make me a list and Noah and I will go. You need to rest and Cadence doesn't need to be in any store right now, she's too small." The softness in my voice makes Belle cry.

"I know, Mel, but I was supposed to have all this ready for her. I'm already a failure."

Wow, talk about post-partum hormones; Belle never talks like this.

"Stop that. It's not your fault she came early. She's impatient like her mother. Let's go get you settled and you can make me a list. It will also help me see what I need to start preparing for."

Once she hears she'll be helping me out, she nods her agreement. "Okay, come on."

Darren already took Cadence onto their bus, where everyone is waiting. When Belle is a few feet inside the bus, she notices the subtle changes. "What did you guys do?"

Noah wraps his arm around my waist. "Nothing you wouldn't have done if you could. Go take a look around and tell us if we're missing anything and we'll get it."

"You had a bottle station installed?" she squeals as she passes the kitchen area. "Oh my God, she's got her own dressing area!" she cries as she passes what used to be the office. "You guys!" she screams as she enters the bedroom.

Everyone is smiling, enjoying her incredible happiness at what she sees. We hear drawers and cabinets opening and closing all through the bus. "You even bought formula!"

"Well, you know we can be sadistic now and again, but we prefer for babies not to starve to death," Sawyer answers, and she uses her middle finger to blow him a kiss.

"Did we miss anything?" Noah asks as she walks back into the room. Belle goes to move Cadence's seat and she's caught off guard when the seat won't move. Looking under it, she notices it's latched in.

"I'm pretty sure I can say you didn't miss anything. Hell, I don't think I would have known about half of this stuff."

"Us, either," Wyatt adds. "Noah is so analytical when he researches things. I wouldn't be surprised if he learned his best bedroom moves from a step-by-step internet guide."

"Shut up, Wyatt, you're just jealous Susie French popped my cherry instead of yours."

Susie French sounds like a whore.

"Oh man, Susie French. Now *that's* a name I haven't heard in a long time. She was smoking hot. Why she picked Noah over me I'll never understand."

"Dude, why would I want her instead of Anna? And damn, Sawyer, do you have amnesia or what? You were banging Susie's best friend … what was her name?"

"Lola Martindale, and she was as hot as Susie," Darren adds.

"Susie French, huh?" I say quietly to Noah.

"Well, you know, we can't *all* lose our virginity to pop royalty."

"Touché, Mr. Weston."

"Besides, all of that is behind us. No more Susie or Eli. Just me and you." Noah kisses my neck, and Darren groans.

"Not in front of my kid."

Darren shoots daggers at Sawyer when he starts laughing. "Darren, we have luxury buses but they're still not huge. Are you not going to fuck in the room with your kid? Because if not, you're going to have to start scheduling babysitters so you can get laid."

I wish I had a picture of Darren's face right now. The sheer look of horror at the thought of having sex with Cadence in the room is probably his first official parental challenge. I'm sure he'll figure it out.

D. Kelly

"How about we change the subject? Mel and I picked a name for the baby," Noah tells them.

"This is a subject I can get on board with," Warren replies, finally joining in the conversation.

"Yes! What is Cadence's future husband's name?" Belle asks excitedly.

"You tell them," I tell Noah, knowing this is one of those important moments for him.

"His name is Nathaniel. It means 'Gift of God.'"

"That's awesome. I like it a lot," Sawyer says, nodding.

"Little Nate, that's the shit," Wyatt says.

"Cadence and Nathaniel. It already has a ring to it," Belle adds, earning another groan from Darren.

"You're going to put me in an early grave, woman. Let's get her into high school before talking about dating."

"Fine, we'll put it on hold for now. Actually, we have something else to talk about before we take off," Belle replies, looking directly at me and Noah. "That baby bump is getting big. You guys need to announce your pregnancy."

"Pot calling kettle much?" I toss back at her.

"That's why you should listen to me. I caught hell for that, and I'm lucky I still have my job. *Slammed* is supposed to get the exclusives, and anyone seeing you walk down the street who is paying two bits of attention is going to notice you rocking that bump. In two weeks, you're going to be five months along, it's time to spill the beans."

"She's right, Mel," Noah says against my ear. "We could release our first family photo. Just not the gender. It would be cute and the fans would eat it up. Maybe it will ease some of the haters, too."

"The haters will hate me even more, but I can handle that. Go ahead and announce it. Vague details, baby is due later this year, family photo, obviously we're thrilled with the news. Scroll in on the photo, if there's any identifying info on there at all … name, date, etc., edit it out."

With a worried bite to her lip, Belle replies. "Are you mad at me?"

"No, I'm not mad at you. I was being ridiculous thinking I could fly under the radar longer. After the book signing in Chicago, when I thought someone saw Noah kiss my stomach, I've been on edge. At least now it will be out in the open."

"That's the spirit! Don't worry, I'll make the post super cute and super vague. I'll send it to you to proof in a few minutes and then I don't have to work again until my next BAD update."

I kiss Belle and Cadence goodbye and Noah, Sawyer, and I make our way to our bus. At least now I'll have Belle with me. Maybe I'll interview her for the book; she's a huge part of all of this now. Not only as Darren's future wife and mother of his child but also as the lead reporter for this whole tour. It could be a great angle.

"Hey, Luther, how's it hanging?" Sawyer asks the bus driver as we all load on the bus.

"Doing good. Ready to get on the road and see some action."

"Sounds good. I'll come up and talk with you later after I get a nap."

Noah and I exchange greetings with Luther and follow Sawyer inside. I haven't had a chance to interview him yet. Maybe I'll do that this week. Sawyer is always up here talking to one of them during the day when he has free time. I wonder if he's always done it or if he does it now because Noah is occupied by me.

"Has Sawyer always taken time to sit with the drivers, or is that new?"

"Nope, not new, he always has. I used to try, but there's something about the curve of that front window that gives me motion sickness. Instead, I do my catching up when the buses are stopped. Sawyer loves to watch the world fly by. There's something about the open road in front of him that calms him."

"Yeah, I've noticed that in the mornings. It's always been my habit to drink coffee and watch the scenery. I was surprised when I first got on the bus he had the same habit."

Noah leans back onto the couch and looks up at me. "Why do you have that habit? Sawyer's always been an early bird, but what about you?"

"Well, my dad wrote "Mellie Sunshine" for me, but the nickname actually came from me being an early riser. He said even as an infant I was always up with the sun, as if I knew not a second of the day should be wasted. He used to get up in the morning and sing, and there was nothing I loved more than sitting with him in the mornings while he was being creative."

"You loved him a lot but you hardly talk about them. Maybe now it will be easier to let the bad memories go and focus on the good ones."

Maybe he's right. "He would have liked you a lot. You're exactly what he always wanted for me."

"How do you know?"

"He used to tell me to find a man who valued me more than his passion in life. He said that's where he messed up with my mom. He thought he could balance both of his true loves equally, but he was never able to find the balance. You've never seemed to have an issue finding balance, Noah."

Noah pulls me to him and kisses my belly, then stands up and pulls me in for a kiss. "That's because *you* are my passion, Mel. And you always will be."

With every word from his mouth, every kiss from his lips, and every thoughtful thing he does for me, Noah has more than made me fall in love with him. He's taken the girl who wrote a romance novel—the same girl who doesn't believe in fairy tales—and given her one of her very own. I'm in so much trouble and I couldn't be happier about it.

Belle's Baby Announcements

Slammers!

It's your girl Belle and do I have NEWS!

First of all, let's give a big Congratulations to Darren Miller (and me) on the birth of our new baby daughter. Cadence Miller was born on April 11th and she's perfect in every single way. We're not ready to show her off to the world just yet, but you can catch a glimpse of her in the photo down below. With her fingers wrapped around Darren's, she's already got daddy in her tight little grasp.

And more breaking BAD news. Hold on to your hearts, ladies, because this one is a doozy. Noah Weston and Amelia Greyson are also expecting their first bundle of joy later this year. The duo couldn't be happier and it shows in their very first family photo below. Could they be any cuter?

There's only one bachelor of BAD left, ladies. Who's going to be the lucky girl to grab Sawyer Weston's heart? You never know, it could be any one of you. Sawyer says he's happy to be single, but I don't know, ladies, I feel like that's a challenge. Anyone want to help me prove him wrong?

Just kidding, even *I* don't have those kinds of superpowers. Sawyer will pick his leading lady when he's good and ready. Sawyer may be picky for a reason; this BAD boy has a heart of gold. I should know … I've recently seen him coo at a newborn baby girl and it was all that and a bag of chips.

My love to you all. Until next time.

Live today like there's no tomorrow.

Xs and Os,

Belle

Unexpected Surprise

It's been a little over a month since Cadence and Belle came on tour with us and everyone seems happier. Who knew having a baby around was like a constant anti-depressant? Belle was able to recover easily with so much help, and Cadence is the best baby. Granted, I've never been around babies, but I'm spending a lot of time with her so I can learn fast. She rarely ever cries and if she does, there's a purpose behind it.

The guys have taken to rehearsing on Darren's bus because Cadence seems to love the sound of the guitars; she just sits in her bouncer and stares, wide-eyed. She has these expressive brown eyes that seem to be getting lighter by the day and the curliest dark-black hair. Unfortunately, Darren's parents haven't been able to come see her yet. Darren's dad had the flu when she was born, then his mom got it, and they couldn't get time off after missing work. They were going to come last weekend but we were traveling, so they're hoping to come next weekend. At least with technology, all the grandparents have been able to see her via video calls whenever they want to.

"Mel!" Noah calls out excitedly. I've been in the bedroom napping. I'm six months along now and my stomach is a big round basketball. I'll never admit it to Noah, but I'm so fucking glad he put this bar in. His foresight there was a blessing in disguise. "Babe, how fast can you pack a bag?"

"Why? Where are we going?" We're supposed to be on our way to Kansas for their shows this week.

"I was thinking Vegas so we can get married," Noah announces proudly.

"What about your shows? I don't have a ring for you, or a dress or anything." My panicked voice brings a soft smile to his lips as he sits next to me.

"Slow down, one problem at a time. Sadly, the area we were playing in was severely affected by tornadoes that touched down there this morning. We're moving the shows to the end of the tour and the band has already made a donation to the town's disaster relief fund."

"That's awful. I hope everyone is okay."

"Me, too. There were a few fatalities, we've been talking about doing a benefit show with some other bands who were supposed to play here. Warren is working on coordinating it. That would bring in a lot of money."

They should have called themselves PAK—Philanthropic and Kind. Bastards and Dangerous only suits their physical image, but not them as people—not at all.

"Belle and Darren are flying home on a private plane with Cadence to see Darren's parents so they can keep her off a commercial flight. Sawyer, Wyatt, and Warren are all going with them, and so is Ryan. Mac agreed to come to Vegas with us and be our witness if you're on board."

"Really? Just the two of us and Mac?" My racing heart must be noticeable to the baby. I've been feeling him kick a lot lately but last night, when Noah was on the other bus, I could actually *see* my belly move. Like it is right now. "Noah, look!"

His eyes immediately go to my belly and he lifts my shirt. "This is the coolest thing I've ever seen. Hey, Nate, do you want your mommy and daddy to get married tomorrow?"

"Ugh … I've never felt him kick that hard." It's like he knew exactly what Noah said and is putting his two cents in.

"That's my boy," Noah cheers him on, and he kicks again. I absolutely love the feeling.

Whenever the baby is active, Noah sings to him; right now is no different. As he sings a lullaby, Nate keeps on swimming around in there. He must have gotten my appreciation for his daddy's voice.

After he finishes singing, he looks back up at me. "What do you say? Will you do me the absolute honor of becoming my wife?"

"Of course I will, but what about a ring, and a dress, and …"

"Shh … It's okay, Mel, one thing at a time. We'll get a ring when we get there. Vegas probably has more jewelry stores than anywhere and we won't stop until we find whatever it is you want me to wear."

"I want you to wear what *you* like, Noah, not what I like."

"Perfect," he says with a beaming smile, "because I'd really like a simple platinum band and we can find that anywhere."

"Okay, that's the easy part."

"It's all easy. The two of us are in this together, right?" With his fingers laced through mine, he squeezes my hand. I've realized he does this to calm me down when I'm stressed.

"Right."

"Good. Do you want a dress and the whole shebang? Or do you want to keep it simple and wear whatever is comfortable?"

I've never even pictured myself in a wedding dress and since this is about me and Noah and our love, there's no reason not to keep it simple. "You answer that first. What do you want?" If he wants to see me in a dress, I'll put one on to make him happy.

"As long as you're at the altar saying yes, I'd even go naked, Mel. It truly doesn't make a difference to me."

"Good, because a dress makes it feel even more like the whole cliché pregnant bride thing, and since it's only us, there's no need. I can find something slinky, white, and sexy for the reception if you want."

Noah lowers my hand to his cock; he's rock hard. "I think you have your answer to that question."

And now I'm horny. I'd heard your sex drive while pregnant was enhanced but damn, I had no idea it was like this.

"When do we have to leave?" I ask, attempting to take off his shirt.

"In the next thirty minutes. There's a shared private charter leaving for Vegas in less than two hours and I booked the last three seats." He pulls me off the bed and kisses me deeply.

"If it was a sure thing from the start, why even ask?"

"We're a partnership, Mel. I may think I know what you want, but you'll always have the final say." I kiss him again, even though I'd rather be tearing his clothes off.

"Noah?"

"Yes, Mel?"

"Can we have cake?"

"You want a cake?" he asks with a knowing smile.

"Um … yeah. I mean, who gets married without a cake? Wouldn't that be sacrilegious or bad karma or something?"

"You know what? I'm sure it probably is. What kind of cake do you want? I'll make it happen."

"Maybe you shouldn't give me a choice because right now they all sound good. Chocolate with banana, chocolate with raspberry, vanilla with champagne, lemon with raspberry mousse. Noah, make it stop. I'm going to be so fat." Groaning, I look at Noah with pleading eyes.

He grabs my ass and pulls me as close as he can with this belly between us. "You aren't going to be fat. You still work out every day, but even if you do get fat, so what? You're having a baby, Mel. It's a good reason to gain weight and it will come off after the baby."

"What if it doesn't?"

"Then it doesn't. I love you, Mel, and it doesn't matter what you look like, that will never change. The vows we're going to exchange tomorrow pretty much mandate that. Are you going to love me if I go bald?"

"Of course, but …"

"Nope, I'm not done. What if I start rocking a dad bod? I hear they're all the rage right now."

"You'd still be hot, even with a dad bod."

"Damn straight I would. So stop worrying about your appearance. I love your heart, your mind, and your soul. And your body, to an extent, but your body isn't who you are, it's what you live in. Now, pack or we're going to be late. I'll work on the cake and surprise you."

He puts the suitcases on the bed and starts packing his clothes. "How long are we going to be gone?"

"We get a whole week, Mel. We'll just meet up with the buses in Oklahoma."

"What are you telling everyone? They're going to know something is up." My stomach clenches and rolls with even the thought of Noah lying to his family.

"I told them I was going to steal you away for a private vacation since it's the only chance we'll get for one before the baby comes."

"And, of course, because it came from you they fell for it hook, line, and sinker."

He zips up his suitcase and begins tossing stuff in mine. Guess I'm not moving fast enough.

"It wasn't a lie. We *are* going on a vacation, and it *is* the last one we're going to get alone before the baby comes. I just left out one important detail. Mac would have come with us regardless."

"You're slick, Weston."

"And you're slow, Greyson, get a move on."

It only took us two hours to get to Vegas and now I'm stretched out on the bed in our suite at The Aria while Noah runs errands. Because Mac is a good sport, Noah got him a suite as well, with instructions to enjoy his trip. Other than today and tomorrow, Noah told him we probably won't need him much.

On the way here we talked about splitting the trip between Vegas and somewhere tropical for a few days, but the last thing I want to do is lounge on a beach, pregnant, so the paparazzi can post unflattering pictures of me everywhere. It wouldn't matter if I were the sexiest pregnant person on the planet, they'd find a photo where I had a wedgie or something and post that one.

The only thing I'm hoping for right now is that Noah is keeping a low profile while he's out or the jig is going to be up fast. He knows what he's doing, though.

The next thing I know, I wake up with Noah curled against me. His arm is wrapped around my belly, his unique Noah scent filling my senses. The security I feel in his arms is indescribable.

"You awake?" he asks softly.

I roll over so I can see him. "I'm awake. How long have you been back? You could have woken me up."

"About a half hour, but I would never wake you up. I know you have a hard time getting comfortable on the bus lately and you're sleeping for two."

"Did you do everything you needed to?"

An excited gleam enters his eyes. "We have an appointment in the morning at the courthouse. I managed to get them to approve use of the back entrance and a private room so we can fill out the paperwork for the marriage license. Tony helped. He's got a lawyer friend here who put me in contact with the right people."

"So Tony knows we're getting married?"

"Yes, but he's a lawyer, Mel. He won't say anything. He is flying in on Friday, though, and I'm going to have to spend a few hours with him. I have to sign off on my final statement because they decided to prosecute Sara's friends as accomplices. You signed off on your statement after the accident, but I never did. I kept putting it off, remember?"

"Yeah. How do you feel about it?"

The sadness pours off him in waves. "I'm conflicted. I think they should face some consequences, but Sara most likely lied to them and they didn't realize what was really going down. Tony says they have a good lawyer, so I'm hoping it won't be too bad. I don't remember all the charges, but Tony said they could be facing five years or more."

"Will we have to testify?"

"Tony thinks they'll get a good plea deal. I'm going to also write a personal statement requesting a plea for them. They lost their friend, and I think we've all suffered enough. It's time to move on."

We both laugh when Nate kicks Noah's hand. "I think Nate wants everyone to move on as well."

"Oh, speaking of ... grab your phone and check it."

His excitement piques my curiosity, so I roll over to get my phone and then back again. When I see what he's excited about, I bust up laughing.

After pushing a few buttons, his phone dings. "I'm not sure how that hadn't happened already, but consider yourself my newest Facebook friend."

While I'm at it, I pull up the one friend request I've ignored for a long time and accept it. Eli is now also my Facebook friend. Eli and I text often now, and he's coming over for our big Fourth of July get together. Seems like he and Rory are really making a go of their new relationship, but they haven't announced it to anyone yet.

"Now that you're my official Facebook friend, I was hoping you won't mind if I start making updates."

I remember him talking about how sad he felt watching all his friends move on with their lives. Now he can have his own story to tell. The funny thing is his friends probably would have been excited to see all Noah's music stuff. Knowing Noah, he probably never posted much because, even though it's his life, he'd feel like he was bragging.

"You can do whatever you want as long as Belle gets her exclusives first."

"Yup, she'll get to go first but within seconds of her posting to *Slammed*, I can post to my page. My first post is going up now."

My phone dings with a new notification. He tagged me in our first family photo, and his post is so completely Noah.

You've probably seen this photo already, but I decided to start posting important updates to my page instead of letting only the media run with them. This is my fiancée, Amelia Greyson, and as you probably already know, we're expecting. I've never used this page for much more than keeping up with my friends who I rarely get to see. I'm hoping that will change after our tour ends. If you're on this page, it's because you're my friend and you're important to me. I've never posted much about the band because what I do with my life isn't who I am. This photo portrays me to the fullest. I'm a family man and always have been. This is your first look into my new family, but not your last. #BabyWestonComingSoon

D. Kelly

"That is so sweet, Noah. What's your second post going to be?"

"Our wedding picture, tomorrow night, seconds after Belle posts it to her blog. We're going to have some tough calls to make tomorrow night, but it's worth it for what I'm getting in return."

His excitement, his willingness to make all of this happen for me—the way I want—is too much to handle. As worried as I am about Sawyer, his twin missing his wedding is even worse.

"What is the plan tomorrow?"

He grins. "We have our appointment in the morning, and don't be mad, but I got a ring today while I was out. You said I could pick it and I knew you were tired."

"I'm not mad."

"Good. Tomorrow at four we're getting married at the chapel downstairs. I thought about doing something off the strip but doing it here leaves less chances of us being discovered."

Perfect. It might take a miracle for me to get everyone here … but if I can, the rest will be easy.

"Would you be mad at me if I said I changed my mind?"

With wide eyes, he chokes out his reply, "Changed your mind about what?"

"I can't picture marrying you in regular clothes. You can probably order a suit from any shop downstairs. What do you think the odds are of getting a cute, white maternity wedding dress? Nothing poofy or long, just short and sweet?"

He jumps up out of bed and grabs my computer. "I'm pretty sure those odds are fucking fantastic. Do you know how many pregnant chicks get married in Vegas every day? Probably more than anywhere else in the world."

As his fingers fly quickly across the keyboard, I want to smack myself. How I ever thought it would be okay to take this away from him, I'll never know. Within minutes he has a local boutique pulled up and a page full of options for me.

"What do you think about this one?" I ask, pointing to a dress that is everything I just described.

"I think you'll look beautiful. Is this the one?" I nod. He picks up the phone and calls the shop to be sure they have it in stock and asks them to hold it for him. Well … for Mac; nothing ever goes in their names. Then he does a search and finds out there's a suit shop adjacent to the dress shop.

"Did you order the cake?" I ask when he closes the computer.

"A few of them, in all the requested flavors." He's beaming. I'm beginning to think making people happy is some kind of addiction for him.

"What are we going to do with all the leftovers?"

"I figured we could box them up for a shelter or something. Or you can eat every single one and exhaust any cravings you have."

"Sounds perfect. Whatever my big ass doesn't eat, we'll donate."

Within minutes, he's off again with Mac to pick up the clothes, and I suck up my pride and call Sawyer.

"Hey, Mel, sick of my brother already?" he quips, but he's not going to be laughing in a few minutes; he's going to be pissed.

"Not quite. Sawyer, I need your help. I really messed up."

"What can I do, Mel? Anything you need." His words crumble my heart.

"Here's the thing. Noah and I are getting married tomorrow." I suck in a breath and wait for his response.

"The hell you are. Not without me. What were you two thinking?"

"Noah was respecting my wishes. This doesn't have anything to do with him." I hear a door close and Sawyer exhales.

"Do you hate me so much that you don't want me at your wedding because of what I said?" he asks softly.

"I don't hate you, Sawyer. I was trying to spare you … and myself. I was worried you'd be upset and get drunk and it seemed like a recipe for disaster. I know I hurt you that night and I'm sorry, but Noah needs you and I'm trying to make it right."

My words are met with silence, but he eventually speaks. "We really fucked this up, didn't we? I'm over it, Mel, I promise. You guys are perfect together and you're having a baby. I don't want my nephew ever finding out how reckless I acted. But it would shatter me to miss Noah's wedding."

His emotional words tear at my soul, and I start crying. "Can you help me, Sawyer? Can you get everyone together and here by tomorrow? Including Eli. I know you don't like him, but other than Belle he's my only family."

"You've got us now, Mel, don't you ever forget it. Tell me how this is going to work and I'll make it happen."

For the next few minutes, we go over all the details. I'm supposed to text him a photo of what Noah bought to wear so he can match it as close as possible and be his best man. I'm going to work out a plan with Mac to get everyone in the chapel before Noah and I go down to get married.

When we hang up, I call Belle.

"Amelia Greyson, I can't believe you would be so stupid to think you could do this without me there. I understand why you did it, though, so I forgive you."

"Thanks, Belle. So you'll come?"

"You couldn't keep me away now if you tried. I'm not thrilled bringing Cadence into a casino with all the smoke, but we'll make it a quick overnight trip and spend most of the time in the room. It will be fine."

I'm so relieved. When I told Belle about what happened with Sawyer and me, she hugged me and told me to forget about it and reminded me that people make mistakes. I'm reminding myself of that now and am glad I realized it before it turned into a bigger one. "Thanks for having my back in all of this, Belle. I know I'm a mess."

"I've always got your back, that's what sisters do. And you're not a mess, you're just in fucked up hormone land. It will get better, I promise. I almost feel like new again. But I'm going to let you go and go help Sawyer. I'm sure he's got a lot on his plate I can probably help with."

"Good, and I know it goes without saying, but this needs to be a complete surprise to Noah. Remind Sawyer to make sure no one updates any social media with any clues they might be going to Vegas or anything. As far as Noah knows, it's just us until he sees all of you in the chapel."

"Got it. See you tomorrow!"

I feel lighter than I've felt since New York. Everything is going to work out fine.

I Do

The Las Vegas Courthouse is a crazy busy place. If Noah wouldn't have made alternate arrangements, we would have been seen in seconds. They were extremely accommodating and got us in and out in less than fifteen minutes.

We spent the rest of the morning and afternoon together in the room. We ate, shopped online for some baby things, made love, ate lunch, had sex in the shower, and then it was suddenly time to get ready.

Sawyer has been emailing me updates on the off-chance Noah sees my text messages. Everyone is here; they got in this morning around two so they could sneak into the hotel unseen. I don't know how he managed it, but he did; I owe him big time.

My hands tremble as I try to fasten the diamond tennis bracelet my parents gave me. Noah's steady hands calm mine and he clasps it for me. "They're looking down on you today, you know that, right?"

"I hope that's true."

"You look beautiful. I'm glad you changed your mind. I didn't think the clothes mattered, but this feels more special somehow." He's melancholy, but he's putting on a brave face. Wait until we get downstairs—he's going to be thrilled.

"You're looking pretty handsome yourself."

He went with a black suit and red tie and looks even more handsome than he did the first night we had sex at The Hard Rock.

"Where did you go? You kind of zoned out there for a minute."

Leaning over, I kiss his perfect lips. "I was thinking about the suit you wore the first night we had sex. Funny, that was our first Vegas trip."

He kisses the top of my hand and laces our fingers together. "One of the best nights of my life, and this is going to top it. Are you ready?"

"I'm ready."

Mac is waiting outside the door and greets us with a smile. Mac's smiles are rare since he's paid to look intimidating. The hotel gave him alternate directions to the chapel to greatly reduce our chances of being seen. At this point, it doesn't matter other than Belle will lose the first notification; she'll still scoop them all with inside photos. But since Noah doesn't know this, I keep quiet.

Pausing for a minute outside the chapel, I tug on his hand. "Are you okay?" he asks.

"I'm fine. I hope you know how much I love you, Noah." For some reason, I need him to hear that before we go inside. Residual nerves, I suppose.

"And I love you, Mel, but I'm excited so let's go inside."

Mac follows the plan and ushers us in quickly like someone was trying to follow us in so he could take Noah's attention away from the people inside until the doors are closed. Once they are, everyone stands with smiling faces.

"You did this? When? Why?" he asks as he cups my face, kissing me fiercely.

"That was a good kiss, Uncle Noah!" Saylor calls out, and we laugh.

"That's why. Because when I saw how excited you were to share our wedding photo to Facebook, I knew I couldn't take this away from you … from us. This is a moment to be shared and remembered forever."

The happiness on his face is identical to how he looked when he found out he was going to be a dad. "And how?"

"Sawyer. I called him and let him chew me out a bit. Then I called Belle, and she chewed me out some more. Then they fixed my mess and here we are."

"This is the best wedding gift ever," he says, kissing me again.

"Alright, enough with that," Belle calls out. "You've got wedding party logistics to work out."

I had Belle bring a bouquet for her and flower petals for Saylor and Emme. Diane got them little flower girl dresses and they were supposed to be practicing down here.

"I've got two adorable flower girls and Belle," I tell him.

"And you've got me," Eli says, coming up to the two of us.

"You're going to be a bridesmaid?"

"No, Mel. I'm going to walk you down the aisle if you'll let me. Once upon a time, your dad gave me permission to marry you. I think he'd be okay with me giving you to who you really belong to, don't you?"

As my eyes fill with tears, Noah reaches out and pulls Eli into a hug, at which point I choke on a sob.

"Nope, none of that. Stop it right now. No crying on your wedding day!" Belle calls out as she pulls Cadence out of her car seat and walks over to us. She's wearing the cutest fancy dress.

"Yes, Eli, I'd love that. Thank you."

"Sawyer, Jordan, Darren, Wyatt, you know where to stand. We've done this once already," Noah calls out, and they all fall in line.

A few minutes later, the music is playing, the photographer's flash is flashing, and the flower girls are making their way down the aisle. The chapel is set up with video so this is all being recorded. It's perfect. Belle goes next, and it's just me and Eli left. He squeezes my arm and we're off. And the funny thing is, after all my hesitation, I'm not the least bit nervous or scared. This is where I'm supposed to be and who I'm supposed to be with. I couldn't be happier.

Most of my favorite people are lined up in front of me, and the rest of my favorite people are witnessing this beautiful day. But when Noah's tear-streaked face meets mine, I lose all conscious thought; he is my only focus.

He says his vows, and I say mine. Even though I'm aware of them and I mean every single, word more than I've meant any other words I've ever said, I don't hear them. I'm in this time lock where it's only Noah and me and our love.

If everyone feels like this on their wedding day, why would anyone get divorced?

We exchange rings; it feels so good to put his ring on. I still haven't seen my wedding band, but my eyes can't focus on anything but him. All I see is sparkle; I hope that's a positive metaphor for our future.

When the chaplain pronounces us husband and wife, Noah looks up quickly and says, "Close your eyes, Saylor," before devouring my mouth with his. I feel like I should be embarrassed and we should come up for air, but this kiss is the most powerful magic I've ever felt; I don't want to let it go.

When Noah finally pries his lips from mine, we're wearing matching smiles. Everyone is clapping, and he pulls me in for a hug. "I love you so much, Mrs. Weston."

Hearing him call me that sends chills through my body—the good kind.

"I love *you* so much, Mr. Weston." I observe the blush creep through his cheeks. He's just as turned on as I am.

"If I can have everyone's attention for a moment," Sawyer calls out to the room, and all eyes turn to him. "Thank you. I just wanted to

453

tell you the fun doesn't end here. After Mel called last night, Belle and I decided it wouldn't be a wedding without a reception. If everyone will head out to the steakhouse, it's reserved for us for the night."

"That is so sweet, but I hope he didn't order any cakes."

Noah laughs at my joke and puts his arm around my waist. Sawyer effectively got everyone moving, so we follow them all out. When we get to the steakhouse, Belle pulls me and Noah aside for a second.

"We're in a casino … this is going to be breaking news in two point five seconds. I'm your best friend, but I need to post this first. I wrote it before the wedding and attached a picture. All you need to do is say okay."

Slammers!

It's your girl Belle here and I've got major breaking news! Lift your glasses high and join me in toasting the newlyweds. Noah Weston and Amelia Weston (formerly Greyson) just got married!

I know hearts are breaking all over the world that it's all become officially official, but follow Eli Watts' lead and put on a happy face. That's right, ladies, you heard me. Mel's former flame, Eli Watts, was not only in attendance … he gave the bride away. If Eli can be happy for Mel and Noah, so can you.

The small, intimate ceremony was attended by family and the closest of friends and just narrowly at that. The bride and groom thought they could sneak off and elope but with careful consideration, the bride changed her mind and flew in their nearest and dearest to surprise her groom. The Weston family bond is strong and is now one family member bigger. For your first glimpse at the married couple, check out the steamy wedding kiss photo below.

Congratulations, Mel and Noah. No one deserves happiness more than the two of you.

Be sure to follow Noah and Mel's lead – Live today like there's no tomorrow.

Xs and Os
Belle

"It's perfect, Belle. Post it and then forward me that picture so I can post it on my Facebook."

"Not so fast, Weston. If you don't add me as your Facebook friend right this instant, you don't get the picture. This guy had a Facebook and no one told me?"

"Don't look at me, I just got a friend request yesterday."

Eli comes up and kisses me on the cheek. "Well, I've been in Facebook purgatory for years, but someone finally accepted my friend request yesterday."

"Done. Sent a request to you, Belle. Eli, too. What you did for us today was a class act, and I'll never forget it. Besides, Rory hasn't taken her eyes off you so far." Eli looks uncomfortable, and Noah chuckles. "Your secret is safe with me. Mel cushioned that blow months ago."

Eli's eyes dart to mine. "Sorry, but he guessed, and I wasn't going to lie," I say with a shrug.

"Uncle Noah!" Saylor cries out, running into his arms.

"Hey, ladybug, thank you for coming to my wedding and wearing such a pretty dress. You dropped those flower petals like a pro."

She nods excitedly. "I know. We practiced a lot while we were waiting for you. My mommy says that Mel's my aunt now. Do I get to call you Auntie Mel?"

"If you want to you can."

"Yes. Now I have two aunts and two uncles. Are we going to have cake?"

Noah laughs. "Oh yeah. Auntie Mel was having a cake craving. We're going to have lots and lots of cake."

"You already ordered cake?" Sawyer asks, coming up and putting his arm around Noah. "Shit, so did I. A big one, too."

"Looks like some shelter will get cake after all." I focus on the two brothers in front of me and how happy and handsome they both look tonight.

Karen taps me on the shoulder. Turning around to face her, I'm a bit worried she's going to be upset with me, but she takes the opportunity to pull me into a massive hug. "Now that you're officially my newest daughter, you get a proper Weston hug whether you're ready for it or not."

I'm ready for it this time and hug her the way she deserves. When she releases me, her hands immediately go to my belly. "He's going to be here soon, our first grandson."

While Noah and Sawyer are talking to Owen, Karen pulls me aside. "Thank you for changing your mind and letting us all come."

Of course she knows Noah would have never kept them away. "Karen, it wasn't about you guys. I hope you don't think that. It's just today, all I have of my parents is this jewelry I'm wearing. I wasn't sure if I could handle it."

She places her hand on my heart and blinks back her own tears. "Amelia, what you have of your parents is right here. You have their love, and they must have loved you something fierce for you to be the woman you are today. I couldn't have picked anyone better for Noah, and I'm so proud to have you in our family. I'm sorry they're gone, but Owen and I will be happy to fill in for them whenever we can."

The reality of what else I've gained from marrying Noah hits me. Not only did I get a husband, and a new last name, but I got a family full of loving and accepting people. "Thank you. Thank you so much, Karen." This time *I* pull her in for a hug—the first of many, I'm sure.

The night is filled with toast after toast, laughter, tears, and family. Listening to the speeches the guys gave about Noah had us all in stitches, but they are stories told with lots of love. Now it's Sawyer's turn, and the butterflies in my belly take flight.

"Yesterday, when Mel called to tell me what was happening, I lost the ability to breathe. When I heard the words 'we're getting married' it was like my heart stopped beating. I was sad, and angry, and couldn't understand how my twin brother was getting married and I wasn't going to be there.

"Noah and I have always been thicker than thieves. Sure, we've had our independent friendships, but my big brother has always been my best friend. In the last year or so there was this rift between us that seems to have resolved in the last few months. It was a rift neither of us could really put a finger on exactly why it existed. I think it goes back to Noah wanting his life back and us announcing our retirement. That's where I can say I first felt a change.

"You see, unlike Noah, I'm unsure what comes next. I've got no idea what I want to do or how I'll get there. It's scary. But before Noah ever met Mel, he knew what he wanted in life. He's known since we were kids. Noah is a family man.

"It's been eight months since Mel climbed aboard our bus, ten since the night she called me out on my shit."

Everyone laughs at his memory, but he continues.

"In that time, I've never seen Noah happier. Ever. Noah has always believed in fate, and some of us have been skeptical, to say the least. But looking at Noah and Mel, there's nothing I believe more. Fate brought them together for a reason. Maybe it's because Mel needed a family, or maybe it's because our family desperately needed Mel.

"Whatever the reason, Noah has made me a believer. Love, marriage, kids …those have never been my goals in life. Living each moment to the fullest is all I've ever done. Noah, you guys make me want it all. I'm so proud of you for catching your dream and making it a reality. In two short months we're going to meet the next generation of Weston men. We've already got the women and they're a force to be reckoned with. I'd expect nothing less from Noah's son. Hopefully, someday in the not-too-distant future, my son will be playing with yours. I can't imagine our kids not growing up together like we did.

"Mel, welcome to the family. We all love you and are immensely proud to call you a Weston. Congratulations to you both!"

By the time Sawyer finishes his speech, I'm crying buckets. Everyone is just smiling at me like it's the most adorable thing they've ever seen. Out of the corner of my eye, I see Veronica nudge Belle, who stands up to make a toast of her own.

"Mel and I have been best friends since we were little girls. We quickly adopted each other as sisters because we didn't have any siblings and we loved each other something fierce. Over the years, I've seen Mel go through a lot of heartache. She's lost every single family member she ever had, all within a few short years of each other. Mama and I swore we'd never let her feel like she was alone in this world, and we've kept our word.

"Mel is my sister in every sense of the word, so that means you are all my family now, too, like it or not."

They're all laughing with her; everyone already loves Belle and she knows it.

"Mel and I make each other face the hard truths. When I got pregnant with Cadence, she and Noah made me suck it up and tell Darren right away. And when Mel fell in love with Noah, I made her do the same. You see, for some of us, loving people and accepting their love comes as easily as breathing. And to people like Mel, it's the scariest thing in the world to allow love into your heart. When you've suffered as much loss as she has, it's easier to lock your heart up and throw away the key.

"That's where Noah came in. He didn't come on strong, he didn't try to woo her, nope. Noah's slick like that ... he tried to be her friend. Can you imagine? I knew my man Noah had a long-term game planned the first night he laid eyes on Mel. It was like he could see right into her soul. But Mel never saw it coming until it was too late. Mel fell in love with her new best friend.

"Relationships worth anything have to have an element of friendship. Some start with chemistry, like me and Darren, and some start with a slow, simmering burn, like Noah and Mel. You see, in all my years as Mel's best friend, she's never really talked about marriage or family, and now she's got both. Noah took every one of her fears and extinguished them with his love, one heartbeat at a time.

"Noah, Mel, I've told you before but I'm going to say it again. You two are good together, you keep that shit up. Keep living each day like there's no tomorrow. I love you guys. Now hurry up and bring Cadence her future husband. Cheers!"

There was no point in trying to stop crying after Sawyer's speech because Belle just made me a blubbering mess.

"Shh, baby, it's okay. Everyone just loves you a whole hell of a lot. Including me." Noah's husky words caress my soul as he wipes away my tears. "Dance with me, Mel, and then we'll have cake and that will make all your tears go away."

No rock star wedding would be complete without a DJ, and Sawyer didn't disappoint. Earlier, I saw Noah and the DJ with their heads together and figured he had some sort of surprise up his sleeve. He extends his hand to me and guides me to the makeshift dance floor. "Sad Song" by We the Kings begins to play. I know some people would think it's odd, but I can't think of a more perfect wedding song for us. I've surrendered all of my fears to Noah, accepting his love in exchange.

After our dance, Noah leads me to the cake table. We cut the first cake and let Saylor come help us cut up the rest. Karen takes over once she sees Saylor's excitement, playfully admonishing me as she ushers us away. "No cake cutting in the dress."

Noah, already showing his true colors as an adoring husband, makes sure to bring some of each flavor to me. There's no way I can eat this much cake, but a bite of each is a distinct possibility.

Saylor and Emme are the first back to the dance floor and they're having a blast. Soon everyone is up joining them, including Noah and me. The two of us spend some time making sure to dance with everyone who wants one. By the time it's my turn for a spin around the floor with Darren, I have a very important question to ask him.

"How's he doing? The truth, please."

"Good, Mel, he's really okay. After Disney World, it all seemed like water under the bridge. I'm not sure, but maybe it was the rift more than you." Neither of us believe that, but if that's his story I can stick with it. "You made the right call last night. They both needed this."

"I'm so glad I realized it in time. I couldn't imagine it any other way."

"Time to give my wife back, Miller," Noah says, butting in, and Darren releases me with a smile.

"Miss me already?"

Noah pulls me close, singing a few bars of "You Got What I Need" by Joshua Radin in my ear. This is one of the songs on the EP he made me. "I miss you whenever you're not in my arms, Mrs. Weston."

"Right back at you, Mr. Weston," I reply, resting my head against his shoulder.

"Would it be rude to bail on our own wedding?" he asks wistfully.

"After all the hard work it took getting them all here?" I lift my lips to his and break away with a smile. "No, I don't think it would be rude. We did all the stuff we're required to, I think. Ask them. I'm sure they'll be honest with you if leaving would be offensive."

"Hey, everyone!" Noah calls out, making me giggle. This isn't what I meant, but he took me at my word. "Anyone care if Mel and I head out and get a head start on our extremely short honeymoon?"

"Man, I've been sitting here for at least thirty minutes wondering why the hell you're still here," Wyatt yells back.

"Right? I thought they would have bailed as soon as Mel got her cake," Sawyer quips.

"So, in other words, you don't care. Great, meet us at the door if you want a hug because we're leaving."

"Oh, baby girl, I'm so proud of you! I know I'll see you before, but you better not forget to call me when you go into labor. I'm not planning on missing another grandchild making their way into the world," Veronica gushes and then releases me from the comfort of her arms.

"You'll be my first call, Mama, right behind Belle."

Warren and Sam pull me into a group hug next. "You know," Sam whispers conspiratorially, "I feel like a modern-day fairy

459

godfather. My writer and Warren's rock star are writing their own fairy tale ending."

"See why I married him? He's an incurable romantic." Warren kisses me on the cheek and releases me. "See you in a few days, Mel. Have fun and enjoy every second ... you only get one honeymoon."

Rory pulls me into the next hug. "I feel like we didn't get to talk at all, but I'm so happy to have you as my sister. We'll catch up on Fourth of July, there's so much to tell you."

"It's a date."

"Get over here, Mel, and give me a hug before your husband swoops you off your feet." I wrap my arms around Eli and hug him tightly. "Thank you for letting me be a part of your big day, Mel."

"I wouldn't have had it any other way. I love you, Eli."

After making it through the line, Sawyer is last. He hugs me like a best friend, and I return it with equal force. "This was one of the best nights of my life. Thank you for letting me be here."

"You are exactly where you belong, Sawyer. Thank you for making it perfect."

"My two favorite people ... Bring it in, bro," Noah says to Sawyer and before I know it, I'm in a Weston brother hug sandwich. "I love you, Sawyer. Thank you for being my best man."

"Love you, too, Noah. Go enjoy your vacation. I'll see you back on the bus in a few days."

With a final wave as we leave the restaurant, Mac escorts Noah and me back to the room while Ryan stays behind with the family. Once Mac clears the room, Noah sends him back to enjoy the party. Then he picks my pregnant butt up and carries me through the door and to our bed.

"Such a romantic, Mr. Weston."

"Always for you, Mrs. Weston. Today was the best day of my life, Mel, and look at all the well wishes we got on my Facebook post."

Noah's sudden love for Facebook is really cute, and when I see his post I get teary-eyed. It's Belle's photo with a caption from Noah.

I married the absolute love of my life today. She completes me in places I never knew there was a void. Fate brought her to me but love keeps us tethered. She's my one, my only, my Mrs. Weston. #MrandMrsWeston #BabyWestonComingSoon

"Your friends are happy for you. I'm glad, Noah, but I think it's time to put the phone down. We're both wearing entirely too many articles of clothing."

Noah tosses the phone onto the table and turns me around to unzip my dress. "I couldn't agree with you more, Mrs. Weston."

We spent all night sharing our bodies, our love, and our hopes and dreams. It was as perfect as I can imagine any wedding night could possibly be.

Amelia

Present Day

I'm exhausted; for the second day in a row I've written the entire day. I forgot how therapeutic writing can be, but unlike a romance novel, this one is about our lives. Plus, I miss them. They only go away one weekend a year but I still feel isolated while they're gone.

It's more than that, though. I'm scared this time. What if I don't have the right answer for him when he comes back? Will he leave me for good? I can't imagine he would; if it were reversed, I'd never be able to make that impossible decision.

The sky is dark and you can't see the moon through the clouds. It's the perfect night for a fire and cuddling, but the only thing I get to cuddle with tonight is my computer. There's a bottle of wine mocking me from the kitchen counter. I've been trying to write without liquid courage today, but it's late and I'm lonely, and I think it's just what the doctor ordered.

When I reach the kitchen, there's a knock at the door. It's late, but whoever it is had to go through Ryan already, so I answer it.

"Mel! Sweetheart I've been calling you for hours. Are you okay?" Karen pulls me into a hug and releases me quickly so she can look me over.

"I'm fine, I've just been distracted. Actually, I'm about to have a glass of wine. Would you like to join me?"

With a smile, she removes her coat, "I'd love one."

She follows me into the kitchen, where I pour us each a glass. "Come on, let's go sit in the living room and we can talk."

Her eyes roam across the boxes of notes, photos, and articles, before landing on my computer. "Looks like you've been busy."

"Well, ultimatums will do that to a person," I reply dryly.

"Good, maybe he should have given you one before."

"Karen ..."

She reaches with her free hand for mine and squeezes my fingers. "Life changes in the blink of an eye, Mel. We are all players in a rapidly changing game. But family always sticks together, sometimes in the most unconventional ways. Remember that. You'll always be our daughter, no matter what you decide. Now, tell me what you're doing."

She releases my fingers, curls her feet up under her, and settles in with her wine. I love this woman, even when she tries my patience.

"I'm writing our story." Her mouth drops and I shake my head. "Not *their* story, *our* story."

"Explain the difference."

"Their story is for their fans. The one with all the things they wanted the fans to know, to see how their lives were … you know, day-in-the-life-of-a-rock-star … but the real version. The crazies, the stress, the love, the fans, the media, the good and bad."

She sips her wine and motions for me to continue. "Our story is about us. How we met, what it was like getting to know them, intertwining our lives, and falling in love. It's so much more than their story, it's our lives. The good, bad, and everything in between."

"Well, if I were a BAD fan … which, you know … I'm not or anything … the second story you described is the one I would want to read. Because, in one form or another, everything you mentioned in the first story is out there already. People just have to search for it. But what you're describing in the second book, that's the *true* untold story … the one everyone would love to get their hands on."

"It's so personal. I can't even picture it right now. I sent it to him, though. You know they're snowed in, right? I'm assuming that's why you've been trying to reach me?"

"They called and we talked. It was mentioned you might want someone to talk to. But I was worried when you weren't picking up your phone." Motherly concern fills her features and I know Karen would never lie to me anyway.

"Anna came by last night and I lied to her. I couldn't even tell her I was writing about us. I'm a horrible person."

"Amelia Weston, you are not. And no matter what guilt you carry around about what lies were told when, and to whom, you don't have to tell anyone anything before you're ready. Including my son. But I do believe he's serious this time, and those are consequences you will have to face."

I swallow a long draw of wine and exhale. "I know. It's why I'm doing this."

"You mentioned it's personal, but would you consider letting me read it?" She looks hopeful and I know she loves me enough not to judge me.

"Would you promise to keep it to yourself? You'd have to read it here, I don't want it leaving the house. And Karen, there's sex in there … maybe it's not such a good idea."

With a delighted clap, she finishes her wine. "Let me text Owen I'm staying here tonight. I will keep it to myself and I'll skip the sex. I'm all for a good romance but not when it involves my son. I'm assuming it's a romance?"

"It is, until it isn't, but you already know the story."

She smiles lightly. "You mean it is, until it isn't, until it is again."

"Well, that's the million-dollar question, isn't it? I'll send it to my Kindle for you. I need my computer to write. I finished the first part and sent it to him earlier. I'm almost done with the second part now, and tomorrow I'm going to wake up with the courage and determination to finish the third part if it kills me. Which it just might, hence the wine."

"What doesn't kill you makes you stronger, Mel, now get the Kindle ready for me. I'm going to go put my pajamas on."

Owen and Karen will probably always have a room here. Living in this house with so many people over the years hasn't always been easy, especially when it comes to making it feel like a home instead of a house, but we're working on that, too. One step at a time.

When I go to my email to send the document to my Kindle I notice he emailed me about an hour ago.

Hey,

I read your pages and they're incredible. All your thoughts and your feelings ... How come you've never been able to convey them to me that way? I guess this is you doing that now. I'm proud of you for making this effort. For putting your family's needs first. For putting your own needs first. I know you didn't see it before, but maybe you do now. I don't just need your answer, Mel. I need you with me in every other way. It's time to let the past go as best we can and live for tomorrow. Please send me the next part when you're done. I love you, and I'm so fucking proud of you.

Before Karen finishes changing, I type out a quick reply.

Hey,

I miss you. I didn't think I would miss you this much, but I do. The house is lonely without you guys, and tonight is the perfect night for wine, fire, and cuddling. Your mom is here now; thanks for sending her my way. She's always a comfort when I'm stressed, but you already know that. Writing this book makes me feel like I'm in a dark, padded room trying to find my way to solid ground. It's hard, so fucking hard, but the only way out is through, right? I'm working my way through for you, for me, and for us. I love you, too. Come home to me safely.

When Karen comes back, I pour us both another glass of wine and turn on the fire. After handing her my Kindle, I settle back into the couch with my laptop.

"Be truthful," I tell her softly as she opens it up.

"Aren't I always?"

She is, and she always has been, even when I haven't wanted to hear it.

Fourth of July

I've decided to never be pregnant again in the summer. It's only the beginning, but some of these Southern states we've gone through have been so hot and humid. Arriving home to our beach house is the biggest blessing right now.

"I've got a surprise for you, Mel," Noah announces as we walk inside. The cool air greets me like a long-lost friend. I'll follow him anywhere as long as the air conditioner follows, too. He walks past our room to the guest room between his bedroom and Sawyer's, flinging the door open with a flourish.

Inside the closed door is the most amazing nursery I've ever seen—whitewashed maple furniture, glider rocker, bookshelves, toys, monitor, and clothes. But the best part of all is the paintings. Each wall is painted like a scene from a Dr. Seuss book. As I move closer, I see the bookshelf is filled with a Dr. Seuss library collection, as well as other classics like *Goodnight Moon, Where the Wild Things Are*, and many, many more.

"Noah, this is perfect."

He smiles as he takes the room in. "I saw pictures, but experiencing it in person is even better. I was going to do the paintings just like the bedding but *Oh, the Places You'll Go* has some of the creepiest illustrations. So I pulled some of the happier, kid-friendly ones instead."

One wall has a scene from *One Fish, Two Fish, Red Fish, Blue Fish*, and one has a scene from *The Cat in The Hat*, the third wall is from *Green Eggs and Ham*, and the last wall is from *Oh, the Places You'll Go*.

"Nate is going to love this room, and we're all going to spend a lot of quality time in here. Thank you for getting this done. It's so hard to think about it all, especially since he'll be almost three months old by the time we get home."

"That's how big Cadence is now, Mel. Look how fast it goes by and she's not even our baby."

"Yes, but at least he'll be small enough he won't remember where he spent the first few months. I loved growing up on our bus, but I'd never want my kids to grow up on one."

"Where there's love, there's family, Mel. You didn't turn out so bad for being raised on a bus. Not that it's what I want for our family, but there are worse things."

Wanting desperately to change the subject, I lace our fingers together and pull Noah into our bedroom. "There's something I want to show you, but I need to get off my feet." My ankles are swollen bigger than Belle's ever were, and I wonder if it's the heat or if I just don't do pregnancy well.

Taking a seat on the bed, I point to all the packages from the photo company. "Bring those over here and come sit with me. I want you to help me work on a project."

Noah's eyes light up. I swear the word project turns him on. "What kind of project?"

I point to the biggest box. "Open the big one first and you'll see." As he opens the box and pulls out the photo albums, he smiles. "When I was going through your and Sawyer's album that day, I was reminded how nice it is to have physical pictures. So much is digital these days. I've been printing every picture we've taken along this crazy journey so far and I thought you could help me organize them into chronological order."

He begins opening the other packages excitedly, removing the photos and making a pile of all the boxes and wrappers. "Noah, there's one more box on the floor by the dresser. There's something in there you asked for once upon a time."

He drags the box over to our bed and lifts out a few photo albums. "Your childhood photos?"

"They're supposed to be. I'm not sure there's one album dedicated to me, but there's your glimpse into my life."

Noah kisses me sweetly and settles in next to me, flipping through pages.

"Wow, look at that crazy spark between your parents. You can see their chemistry lifting off the photos. Do you think we look like that?"

"I'm not sure. All I see when I look at us is happiness, and it's rolled over into every aspect of our lives. If you listen to Belle, though, she'll tell you there's chemistry in our photos. She loves putting the kissy photos on the blog."

Noah laughs. "Whatever makes her happy, as long as it doesn't make you unhappy, is a win."

"See, that's what makes you the perfect husband. You care about my best friend's feelings, too."

"Well, you care about my best friends as well, and I have more of them. Come on, let's get you comfortable and we'll start our project."

Noah helps me find a position and takes off my shoes. When he starts rubbing my ankles, I sigh in bliss.

"That feels so good. You're the best husband ever."

"I'm the *only* husband ever," he growls, turning me on. Possessive Noah is always sexy.

"Damn straight you are. Now let's work on this project so you can spend the rest of the night ravishing my oh-so-sexy, pregnant body."

Leaning down, he kisses my belly and makes his way over the hump and to my lips. "Your pregnant body is extremely sexy, Mel. He presses his hardness against me as his tongue meets mine. Our passionate kiss leaves us both breathless—me a little more than him these days, since Nate is crowding my lungs a bit.

After our kiss, the ever-efficient part of Noah takes over. We spend the next few hours sorting pictures and making our first two albums. One consists of mostly candid shots of the two of us and the other is everything baby, including pictures of us with Cadence, with our family, and even some wedding photos. We received the album of pictures from the wedding photographer last week; it's still on the bus. We love looking at them when we're on the road.

There are some incredible pictures of the guys looking all sexied up in their suits; I want to use them in the book. But some of my favorite photos of the day are candids of Noah and Sawyer together. Even their Disney World photos had nothing on their happiness the day of our wedding. And Noah, being true to form, makes sure to leave some blank pages where he thinks it will be best to highlight the photos from our maternity photo shoot. We're doing that tomorrow morning before our doctor's appointment. Falling into married life with Noah has been effortless. I'm so excited to see what else our future holds.

Noah and I have been in bed for a while. He insists on sleeping with me even if he's not tired. My nights have become restless because I'm uncomfortable. When Noah gets out of bed and begins rustling through things, I open my eyes to see what he's up to. I watch in fascination as he sits on the floor next to the cracked bathroom door and thumbs through the pages of my photo albums. As he looks through them, he chuckles and even releases a few groans—I bet those were caused by the photos of Eli.

What I love best about it all is knowing Noah couldn't wait until morning to know more about my childhood and adolescence. Nobody has ever loved me the way Noah does, but I'm going to make sure Nate knows we love him this way. Noah pulls out his phone and my phone pings with a notification. I'm sure he just updated his Facebook page again; I'm dying to see what he posted. A few minutes later, he goes into the bathroom. I reach for my phone, my curiosity getting the best of me.

Spent the day making memory books for #BabyWeston and surprising my wife with his new nursery. So happy to be home for the Fourth, but the best part of my day so far has been watching my wife sleep while going through her childhood memory books. I wish more than anything we'd met sooner, but I'm happy to have the next fifty years of happily-wedded bliss. Fate brought her to me but it's my job to keep her happy. It will be the best job I've ever had. #MrandMrsWeston

One thing I love most about Noah is even though he knows this is going to go viral, he still posted it. He's proud to show his love to the world, one hashtag at a time.

As we're leaving the doctor's office the next day, Noah is walking on air. I'm excited I finally got to see my doctor for once and feel so much better knowing she said everything is right on schedule.

"Did you hear her, Mel? She said he could be here any day!"

I can't help but laugh at his enthusiasm. As excited as I am to get Nate here, I'm equally terrified to deliver him.

"She also said I could even go *past* my due date, and just because I'm one centimeter dilated doesn't mean anything other than we're getting closer."

The baby's due date is still targeted for August eighth, which leaves us just over a month to go. It's hard to believe everything that's happened in the last year.

"Next month, it will be a year since you came into my life. It's been the best year I've ever had." Noah's driving but he squeezes my hand in his, letting his fingers caress my wedding rings. If my fingers get any fatter we're going to have to cut these puppies off and try again.

D. Kelly

"It's been a great year, Noah, but what about the year you guys got your record deal?"

"First of all, you underestimate your worth if you're even asking me that question. And secondly, that year sucked donkey balls."

"Noah!" I laugh. "I've never even heard you say that before. Why?"

"We were eighteen, just out of school, we were idiot kids, Mel. It was exciting but it was also lonely. We were all crammed into this tiny tour bus on a shoestring budget, playing gritty clubs to see if we'd resonate with the crowds. It was only for a summer but the record company loved the response, so we went in to record the first album."

He looks like he's shaking off a bad memory but eventually continues. "The constant flow of alcohol, drugs, and women was beyond anything I could have imagined. You think to yourself it will be cool to be famous and have your dream come true but the reality is more like a nightmare. I started drinking too much, and I watched Sawyer and Darren fall into drug patterns I was terrified would take them away from us for good."

"I'm sorry, Noah, I had no idea it had affected you so deeply."

He pulls my hand to his mouth and kisses me reverently. "It wasn't all bad, but it was a lot to take in and get used to. Maybe it's why I started doing so many good deeds. I wanted to keep myself grounded. It's also why I created the no groupie rule. I didn't want to knock some girl up who I didn't even know and be stuck in a bad situation for the rest of my life. Most of those girls are with a different guy every night, and while I don't judge them for that, it's not the kind of person I was looking for."

I think back to after Eli and I broke up, when I spent a good six months randomly fucking men on tour at each stop just so I could feel something. Back then, I was one of those girls he wouldn't have looked at twice and I've never told him.

"What if I told you that was me? That I was one of those girls?" My tone is soft, and Noah senses the seriousness of this moment because he pulls the car off the road and puts on the hazard lights.

"What are you talking about, Mel? I know you mentioned you had a history of fucking musicians, but that was a long time ago, right?"

I've got his full attention so there's no backing down now.

"Yeah, after Eli and before my dad died. It was what I knew. That was the industry … fucking random people at each venue. For me it wasn't all about the sex. I was looking for something I never

470

found, something to make me feel better. It wasn't until I was on my own I realized the only thing to make me feel better was to become a better version of myself."

Noah looks at me thoughtfully as he figures out what to say. "I love you, Mel, not because of who you were in the past but because of the amazing woman you are now. You were a teenager when you made those choices. The women I'm talking about were long out of their teen years. You don't think I had my own ridiculous amount of teenage sex?"

Noah's a good-looking man; I've never doubted he lacked for women. "Would you be angry if I said I never really thought about it?"

"Ha! No, because I don't like thinking about you with other men, either. Especially Eli," he says with a shudder. "But I wasn't a saint. At one point, Sawyer and I had this ... sort of competition, I guess you could call it. We were sixteen at the time and it didn't last more than six months, but I'll tell you, we made a lot of people extremely angry."

I can only imagine. "Who won?"

He laughs. "Sawyer did. I gave up. It was clear he needed to win, and I was starting to feel bad. Before we started it, my girlfriend and I had recently broken up. Sawyer saw it as an opportunity for me to live a little. We were bastards back then, definitely deserving of the reputation. Are we okay now? Done purging our sexual regrets?"

"Absolutely. Now take me somewhere and feed me before your son kicks his way out."

The Fourth of July is another big Weston family event. It's funny how at Thanksgiving I was so nervous to meet them and now I can't imagine my life without them. These Westons really have a way of getting under your skin.

The entire family is taking advantage of the beach but there's no way in hell I'm going down all those stairs. Well, going down isn't technically the issue, it's waddling back up. Especially if I need to pee; my bladder may not hold out long enough for me to make the climb.

Instead, we decided to hang out on the back deck. Which quickly turned into hanging out inside where I could enjoy the air conditioning. Belle was happy to chill inside, too; she doesn't want Cadence exposed to a lot of sun at such a young age.

"This time next year, the babies will be big enough to take in the water," Noah says as he bounces Cadence on his knee. She's smiling up at him and cooing away. It's amazing how much personality she already has.

"Next summer we should do those mommy and daddy baby swim classes with them. If you guys are going to live this close to the ocean, our kids need to know how to swim," Belle states.

"Darren and I could do it, and you guys could watch us from the sidelines and talk about how adorable we are." Noah's teasing because he says when either he or Darren have Cadence, Belle and I look like we want to eat them alive. It's true; there's nothing on the planet hotter than a man taking care of a baby. Nothing.

"Yeah, I can just picture it now. Us in the pool and Mel punching out other baby mamas because they're eyeing up her man," Darren quips, and I throw my pillow at him. "See? She just proved my point. This one is violent ... you'd better tame her, Noah."

"There's a difference between needing to be tamed and protecting what's mine. Besides, I think Noah likes me untamed."

"Hell yeah I do, and I'll show you just how much later on tonight."

Darren looks between Noah and me and shakes his head. "You know what's funny? We spent *years* trying to get Noah laid, but he was always content to be alone and wait for the right situation. I seriously can't imagine life without you two together."

"Me, either," I say softly as Noah passes Cadence off to Belle.

"Speaking of being together ... we have some news," Belle says as Sawyer walks in the back door.

"Is this private news? Or does everyone get to hear?" he asks.

Belle waves Sawyer over. "Not private at all. We're going to announce it later, but we wanted you guys to know we've set a wedding date."

"Belle, that's awesome! Noah, help me up so I can hug her."

She laughs and gives Cadence to Sawyer. "I'll come to you ... it's quicker and easier."

This is a huge step for Belle; I'm so happy for her. After I practically squeeze her to death, Sawyer asks the big question. "When's the wedding?"

"Thanksgiving weekend. We figured everyone would be around and it would make it all the more special. Plus, the tour will be over and we'll have had a few weeks to recover," Belle replies.

"Do you know where you're going to do it yet?" Noah asks.

"Yeah, we're going to do it at my house. After the tour is over, we figure we should probably move in there for good and get out of your hair. We spend so much time here because of the band, but if we're all growing up and shit, I guess I should start enjoying the house I paid for," Darren explains.

There are mixed emotions of happiness and sadness lingering in the air. It's like the beginning of the end in a way. Especially since Wyatt will be heading up to San Diego after the tour as well.

"Well, you know you guys are welcome here anytime, and your room will always be here. Sawyer and I bought this house for all of us to have as a sanctuary and that will never change," Noah replies firmly, but he's a little shaken. It's another reminder we really never talked about plans for our family. Deep down inside, I know until Sawyer gets married Noah is always going to want to have his brother around. It will be good for Nate, too. There can never be too much family in a baby's life.

Later in the afternoon, we all gather out back for a barbecue. With Owen at the grill, all the guys surround him while drinking beer and shooting the shit. Even Eli seems to be accepted into this crazy family of theirs. Sawyer never even gave his relationship with Rory a second thought, which surprised us all.

"How are you feeling, Mel?" Diane asks kindly.

"Hot, tired, and fat, but ready to meet the little guy."

"I remember those days. The last few weeks are the hardest, but you won't even care once he's here."

"You guys are going to call as soon as you go into labor, right?" Rory's so excited. I think she's asked me this five times already.

"You guys will get a call from someone, just not me. I'll be busy birthing a watermelon."

"And that's why I'm not having kids anytime soon." Rory shudders. I try to picture her and Eli together long-term and I can't for some reason. Hopefully, I'm wrong; they're cute together.

"Are you all really going to fly in for it?" I ask.

Karen nods excitedly. "You're back on the west coast for the most part now. No matter where you give birth, you're just a few short hours by plane. Unless he comes in record time, we'll make it to see him right after he arrives."

At dinner, Belle and Darren make their big announcement and Veronica is beside herself. Her boyfriend Marcus is here and they seem to be getting serious. It's been over a year now that they've been together, so it makes sense. Belle likes him a lot, but I think she'd like anyone Veronica decided to let into her life. She's been alone for a long time.

Wedding chatter fills the air as their news is received by nothing but happy, smiling faces. After dinner, Noah brings out some contraband sparklers for the girls, and they run around the yard with their flaming sticks laughing and screaming with their uncles. It's a shame fireworks are illegal here; I bet this family would go to town with a huge display. At least they get to admire the fireworks at the beach; their house is in the perfect spot for that.

"What are you smiling at?" Noah asks, squeezing in behind me on the lounger and wrapping his arms around my belly.

"I was thinking about the last firework show I saw on this beach on New Year's Eve."

With a groan, Noah presses his lips against my neck. "If I remember correctly, we made some better fireworks of our own that night."

"Mm, we sure did."

"I think," he says, catching my earlobe in his teeth, "we should make some more of those fireworks tonight."

"Anything you want, Mr. Weston."

His hardness presses up against my backside, and he pulls me tighter.

When the fireworks begin, the recently-turned-three Emme comes over and climbs up into Noah's lap. "Look, Uncle Noah, fireworks!" she exclaims as she points to the sky.

"Aren't they pretty, Em?" he asks as he hugs her close. She nods, never taking her eyes off the sky. Emme sits with Noah the entire show, and Saylor spends the show sitting on the back of Sawyer's shoulders. It seems like the sisters have picked their favorite uncles. But I think that was a given with Saylor already.

Instead of watching the fireworks, I watch my friends and family. Anna and Wyatt, Sam and Warren, Rory and Eli, are all cuddled with their partners. Then I realize so is everyone else. There is more love in this backyard than most people see in a lifetime. It makes me proud to officially be one of their tribe.

It's a little before eleven when the show ends. I'm so tired all of a sudden; I've been yawing for about twenty minutes now.

"Noah, go put your wife to bed, she's tired," Karen scolds him softly.

I'm exhausted, but Noah promised me fireworks and I'm not going to miss them.

"Good idea, Mom. We'll see you guys in the morning," he says as he passes a sleeping Emme off to Rob before helping me up and leading me to the bedroom.

"Sorry, Mel, with Em curled up in my lap I didn't even notice how tired you were getting."

Reaching around him, I lock the door behind us. "I may be tired, Noah, but I'm pretty sure you promised me fireworks."

With a passionate gleam in his eyes, he reaches down and lifts my dress over my head. "If my wife wants fireworks, who am I to deny her?"

When Noah's mouth meets mine, I lose myself in his kiss, one delectable stroke at a time.

Belle's Oregon Update

Slammers!

It's your girl Belle here! Today is August 1st and baby watch is officially on. Anyone with eyes who has seen Amelia Weston lately knows she's about to pop!

Let's wish her and Noah all the best for their upcoming delivery. Now, back to the tour. This week, BAD is bringing the house down in Oregon. Next week, we'll be back in Utah to finish the rest of their gigs there.

Only two more months left of the Just an Illusion Tour. I can't believe it's been almost a year since we started this journey together, *Slammed* family. We've had a lot of fun, haven't we? Your comments and jokes keep me on my toes and constantly laughing. Maybe once the tour ends, we'll have to start our own "We miss BAD" fan club. On the plus side, the internet is a fabulous thing and pretty much anything BAD you want to see, read, or hear, you can find. EXCEPT, the upcoming BAD story Mel is creating for all of you. This book is going to be the shit. Everything you think you know about BAD may just be an illusion. What does Mel know that you don't? Well ... I can't tell you, but I *will* keep you updated with all the release info once it's set.

I'm off to spend some time with my baby girl while her daddy brings the house down in his first Oregon show tonight.

Talk to you later, Slammers.

Don't forget – Live today like there's no tomorrow.

Xs and Os

Belle

Utah

#BabyWestonCountdown

Tomorrow is the baby's official due date. Poor Mel, she's such a good sport, but being nine months pregnant doesn't look very comfortable at all. I have a whole new level of respect for all women, especially the love of my life. We're both exhausted and ready to meet Baby Weston. I wish the tour was over and I could move straight into fatherhood, but we all have a job to do and this one is mine. Send some positive thoughts and prayers our way over the next few days if you can. I can't wait to share the first picture with you all!

"I can barely breathe. How did you do this, Belle?"

Today is August seventh—the day before Nate is due to arrive—and I'm miserable. Let's not even talk about how hard it is to sleep. I know Noah's exhausted because I keep him up with my tossing and turning. I offered to sleep in the bunk, but he refuses to sleep alone. He said he'd rather be tired than be apart.

"I didn't, Mel. You've been pregnant a whole month longer than I was. I've got no idea how you feel right now, but you look like a fucking miserable bitch." She laughs and kisses Cadence. "Auntie Mel is uncomfortable. Maybe she'll give you a playmate in the next day or two."

Cadence giggles and drools. We're not the only ones who haven't been sleeping—teething babies don't make the best bed fellows. Belle's here so the guys can try to get some sleep before their gig. Tonight, after the show, Belle is going to sleep here so she can finally get some sleep since they don't have a show tomorrow night.

"Are we still going to take a detour to see Rhymin' Rieanne?" she asks.

"I guess we are. I'd love to go, but there's no way I'm singing, and I'm seriously not up to it. But I don't want to be a buzzkill for everyone. I'll keep Cadence so you can go, too."

"Didn't Noah tell you? He already offered to keep her. He said there's no way he's taking the chance of leaving you alone while he's in a bar when you're about to deliver. I swear, Mel, I've said it before and I'll say it again. You hit the husband lotto."

Nate kicks with Belle's words, and she's laughing because she can see it through my shirt. "See, even Nathaniel agrees his daddy is a good guy."

As I watch Belle with Cadence, it's hard for me to believe we're really this old and married with kids. "Well, Darren is a pretty good guy, too, Belle. I'm not the only one who got lucky. Going to that BAD concert with you last year was the best thing that could have ever happened to either of us."

"Finally! She admits it out loud. I've been waiting a *year* for those words to leave your stubborn mouth." Belle raises Cadence's arms in triumph and Cadence giggles.

"Whatever, you knew it even if I didn't say it. But if you *need* more validation, I'll give it to you while I'm weepy and hormonal. I love you, Belle. Thank you for introducing me to the love of my life and my new family."

The happiness on her face says it all. "I love you, too, Mel. Now I can officially brag about being the one to set the two of you up."

"As if that's ever stopped you before."

She laughs. "I know, right?"

The bus door opens and Noah walks in with a sleepy smile. "Did you sleep? You look like you feel better."

He leans down to kiss me "Five blissful hours. I feel like a new man." Noah crouches between my legs. "Hey, Nate, come on and kick your way out of there today. Daddy is ready to meet you, little man." Noah laughs when he's met with a kick to the cheek. "Well, at least he knows my voice. That's a good thing."

"Was Darren up yet?" Belle asks.

"Yeah, he said he was going to come over as soon as he brushed his teeth."

"Did you hear that, Cadence? Daddy is coming to see you." As if Cadence knows exactly what Belle said, she wiggles around excitedly. When Darren walks on the bus a few minutes later, and Cadence sets eyes on him, it's obvious she wants her daddy by her excited squeals.

Darren kisses Belle and then takes the baby from her, smothering her with kisses and love. Cadence is definitely a daddy's girl. "Did you miss me, baby girl?"

"See, Mel, this is what happens. You carry them for nine months, push them out of your vajay like a boss, and all they want is

Daddy." Belle's watching them adoringly as she complains. She wouldn't change it for the world.

"We're just lightening your load and doing our part," Noah replies wistfully. He is so excited; he jumps up and asks if he should call the doctor every time I moan because I'm uncomfortable.

"So Belle said you're not going to the bar?" I ask.

Noah looks at me, shocked. "You thought I was going? Why would you think I'd leave you alone? I don't even like going on stage right now even though I know you're right outside on the bus. You silly girl, my time is much better spent with you and Cadence."

Sawyer comes out of his room, where he's been the past few hours playing his guitar. "Finally, there's some fucking testosterone on this bus. It's about time you guys got up, we have to be at the venue in less than an hour."

"Shut up, asshole, you're just jealous you don't have some estrogen in your life," Darren retorts.

"If it means I can sleep like a normal human being, I might be okay with that. And speaking of sleeping, you going to let my nephew come out and play anytime soon or what, Mel?"

"Yeah, what's up with that?" Wyatt says as he climbs onto the bus.

"You guys have any ideas? I'm open to anything at this point." I ask, and Sawyer's reply is the last thing I expect.

"Go fuck your husband."

"Excuse me?" I manage to choke out.

Belle laughs. "He's not wrong, they say sex can induce labor. I just never got far enough to utilize the option."

"Alright, it's on tonight. Mrs. Weston, be ready after my show because we're going to give it the good old college try."

"Dude …" Wyatt says with a groan.

Noah chuckles. "Too much? I kinda figured, but there's not really a romantic way to say 'let's fuck to induce labor.'"

"Well, if anyone can figure it out, it's you, Noah. Why don't you think about it while you're onstage and come home and seduce your wife? I promise not to listen." Belle holds up her fingers in a scout's honor pledge.

"And on that note, I'm sleeping on your bus tonight, Darren. Since Belle needs rest, she can have my room." Darren and Wyatt seem excited about a guys' night and ask Noah to join them, but he politely refuses.

D. Kelly

After the guys leave for their show, Belle yawns as she's feeding Cadence. "Is it wrong of me to be excited to sleep alone tonight? I haven't slept by myself since I was in the hospital with her."

"Not at all. You haven't slept through the night in months. I'd imagine it sounds heavenly right now. I'm excited to be able to sleep on my stomach again."

She laughs. "Even more of a reason to give it the college try with your man tonight."

After Cadence falls asleep, Belle and I eat some pasta and afterward, she paints my toe nails for me. You know you have good friends when they'll touch the feet you haven't been able to reach in months.

"I think Marcus is going to ask Mama to marry him."

"I think so, too. How do you feel about that?"

She's thoughtful for a moment and curls her feet up under her on the couch. "He seems like a good man, a bit young, but they make each other happy. Who am I to judge?"

We spend the rest of the night talking about the wedding and work. Then she fills me in on hearing Wyatt talking to Anna about having a baby and how, from his responses, it seems like Anna is completely on board. Sawyer better be careful; he's going to catch baby fever soon, too.

When the guys return from their show, I notice something different. Maybe it's my melancholy mood tonight, or my hormones, but they all look spent. They had this amazing post-performance high about them the first night we met them, but I'm not seeing any of that right now. I almost don't blame them; it's been ten years.

"You guys seem mellow tonight," I tell Noah when he bends down to kiss me.

"We're just tired. We've had eight shows in a row, we're looking forward to the night off tomorrow." Adding Utah to the back end of the schedule forced them to give up a couple of days off. I sometimes take for granted this is still a job to them.

Sawyer bundles up Cadence and Darren kisses Belle goodnight before grabbing Cadence's things. "We're off, ladies and gent. If Mel goes into labor, call me, and we'll get the buses heading to the nearest hospital." Sawyer lifts Cadence's little arm up in a wave as they exit the bus.

"Get some sleep, babe, we'll see you in the morning." With one last kiss, Darren goes back to his bus and a few minutes later we're on the road.

"Alright, you two, I've got work to do. I'm trying to get a few posts pre-written and ready to go. Noah, go push our girl into active labor." Belle effectively waves us away, and Noah eagerly follows me into the bedroom.

Suddenly, he's more alert. We haven't been having a lot of sex lately because I've been so uncomfortable. Once we're both naked in bed, Noah spoons me from behind and pulls my leg back over his hip.

With his mouth pressed to my neck, he kisses me in my favorite place as his fingers glide through the wetness between my legs. When Noah slides into me from behind, I gasp. He feels incredible.

"I love you, Mel," his heartfelt words a passionate plea, "and there's nowhere in the world I'd rather be right now. Your body is my home."

"Oh, Noah!" All it takes are his beautiful words for me to fall over the ledge. As my walls contract around him, he thrusts harder and deeper. "I love you, Noah." As I say the words, his body trembles behind mine, throbbing inside me as he lets his love fill me.

"Damn, Mel, that was so hot. Quick, but hot." We lay together, coming down from our post-sexual high as the baby swims around in my belly without a care in the world.

"I've got to pee," I whine, and Noah laughs, helping me up.

"I have to say that might be the one thing I won't miss hearing when you have the baby."

We both quickly throw on some clothes and I waddle to the bathroom while Noah gets us some water.

"Did your water break yet?" Belle asks when I come out.

"Somehow I don't think it works that fast, smartass."

"Dammit!" she says. "I'm still keeping the faith. I've just got this feeling he's going to come today. After all, it's his due date."

It's about one in the morning and my body feels it. "We'll see. I'm off to bed. Don't stay up too late, Belle. The point is for you to get some sleep tonight."

She rolls her eyes at me. "Yes, Mom, but I'm on a roll. I just need about fifteen more minutes and I'll be done. Goodnight, you two."

As Noah and I walk back into our room, his phone rings. "It's Sawyer," he says, smiling, putting him on speaker phone as I use my handy metal bar to help me get comfortable in bed. I swear Sawyer makes him happier than I do most of the time.

The stuffed Winnie the Pooh Sawyer bought for Nate has become my sleeping companion. He's propped between me and the wall and eases the pressure off my back. I don't think the baby will mind at all, considering he's technically using it, too.

"What's up, Sawyer?" Noah asks, still standing in the doorway.

"Hey, we wanted to give you a heads up. We're pulling off the freeway in about five miles for the night. Have you noticed the fog out there it's insa—"

Everything after that moment is a mixed blur of sounds and images I'll never be able to clear from my mind. It all happened at once, and yet it was like we were caught in this endless warp in time.

This massive bright light exploded in front of us, and all the power in the bus flickered until it finally went out. I grabbed on to the metal bar with both hands as I watched the phone fly from Noah's hand as he flew backward through the bus with a look of sheer terror across his face.

But the screams were the worst. I couldn't see Belle, but I could hear her screaming, until she wasn't and everything was silent. An intense pain shot through my body as it slammed against the wall with such force I thought for sure I was dying. The ringing in my ears from my head cracking into the wall was so loud, but the wetness between my legs sent me into shock. I felt the blackness coming for me as I drowned in the warmth between my legs. Soon, there was nothing but darkness.

Slammed Emergency Post

Dearest Slammed Family,

My name is Sam Stevenson, I'm the owner of SOS Publishing, who is the parent company of *Slammed*, Inc. This morning, at approximately 1:30 A.M., pacific standard time, Bus One of the Bastards and Dangerous caravan was involved in a multiple fatality accident.

The accident scene is still under investigation, and many details are being withheld at this time. The following details have been approved by local authorities and families, to share with you all.

Bus One was the only bus from the tour affected.

The occupants of Bus One at the time of the accident were as follows:

Noah Weston
Amelia Weston
Belle Dixson
Harold Scott (their bus driver)

It is with an extremely heavy heart I give you the following information.

Noah Weston and Amelia Weston were air lifted to the closest trauma center with critical injuries. There is no word on the status of their unborn child at this time.

Belle Dixson and Harold Scott were pronounced dead at the scene of the accident. The entire SOS, *Slammed*, and Bastards and Dangerous family are devastated and in shock. Please, use your light to lift them all up in prayer today, and in the coming weeks, as we keep vigil over Noah and Amelia, as well as the rest of their family as they struggle to move forward.

Harold Scott was a valued member of the Bastards and Dangerous crew and had been with the band for eight years. Please pray for his family in their time of need.

Belle Dixson was a close, personal friend and her light is going to be missed in my life and the lives of her loved ones. I know you all loved her, too, which is why you follow her blog. The only slight comfort is that her daughter Cadence was on Bus Two at the time of the accident with her father, Darren Miller. Belle would have moved heaven and earth to keep her baby girl safe, and she was. Please pray for Belle's family today, and in the days to come, in their time of need.

Hug your loved ones, keep them safe, and let them know they are loved, today and every day. I will personally update this blog as more information is released.

My condolences to us all,

Sam Owen Stevenson

acknowledgements

First and foremost, if you are still here and reading after that ending, I want to thank you. I know series are hard to read, especially when they leave you hanging on a cliffy, but I promise I'll try to do you proud with the next book. This series has by far been my favorite and hardest to write. It was initially supposed to be a duo of books, but these characters have a story to tell and two books quickly turned to three, and if you're in the reader group, you're well aware of this already.

With each book, this section is the hardest to write because I don't want to leave anyone out. This time, I decided to keep it simple.

My readers, friends, family, bloggers, and anyone I work with in the book industry: I am thankful for you all. My life would be dull without you brightening it up. I love logging on to social media each day and reading your messages and posts. It's one of my absolute favorite things, especially when you're battling it out in the reader groups and picking teams.

Lastly, I have to thank my family. My husband and kids inspire me and lift me up daily. They make my world go 'round; without them, I'd be a "Sad Song", too.

XoXo – until EP

Dee

Just an Illusion – EP
D. Kelly

Just an Illusion Series

Just an Illusion EP

Copyright © 2017 D. Kelly
Editing by – Beyond DEF
Cover design by – Regina Wamba – Mae I Design and Photography - http://www.maeidesign.com
Formatting by – Brenda Wright, Formatting Done Wright
Original lyrics written by Dee Kelly

Dee Kelly www.dkellyauthor.com

This book contains mature subject matter and is not appropriate for minors. Please note this novel contains profanity, sexual situations, and alcohol consumption.

EBOOK - 978-1-64007-444-6
Dee Kelly
P.O. Box 940123
Simi Valley, CA. 93094

dedication

For anyone who has ever been submerged in the darkness and found your way through to the light, this book is for you.

Warning – Per the request of *The Side B* reader group. Please have wine, tissues, and chocolate in hand. I'm pretty sure if you've read *The B Side* this is a given, but I'm doing my due diligence by extending the warning.

D. Kelly

"Every man's life ends the same way. It is only the details of how he lived
and how he died that distinguish one man from another."
– Ernest Hemingway

Amelia

Present Day – Two Years After The Tour

Last night, as I wrote about the crash, my hands trembled with such force Karen had to take my computer away. I spent the rest of the night crying, wrapped in her loving arms. Everything changed that night. One moment I was making love to Noah, and the next ... total chaos. There were only two things I knew instinctively that night: I'd lost Belle, and I was in labor.

What happened after the impact has never been clear to me— mostly flashes of memories, which are hazy at best. Not being able to piece together the particular order of events was driving me crazy. For months, I struggled with soul-stealing nightmares, until I read the first part of Sawyer's new journal. I'm not sure why he started with the accident, other than it was the coping mechanism he'd learned in therapy. But when he trusted me with his pages—all his innermost thoughts—it softened my heart. He let me read them because he wanted me to have a clear reference of what they saw, what they heard, and what *they* went through. He also wanted me to realize I wasn't alone in what I was going through. They needed to be able to lean on me as much as I was leaning on them.

When I read his words, my world spun on its axis. I tried pretending I was reading a story and it wasn't my life within those pages. But when I finished, pain shot through my chest as if I'd been stabbed in the heart with a dagger. Each breath more painful than the last, it felt as if it were being pulled out one millimeter at a time. Once I recovered from the shock, I was numb. I thought knowing would change something, make me feel better somehow. In a way it did, but in other ways, everything was worse.

That night irrevocably changed my life. It changed all our lives. Each of us lives with gaping holes in our hearts which will never be healed, no matter how much we try. And in the beginning, I didn't try. I gave up; all I wanted to do was die.

D. Kelly

I *now* see it wasn't fair of me to put my grief above theirs while each of them, in the midst of their own issues, willingly took on mine. They tried so hard to lift me up just the slightest bit each day. It wasn't much, but it was enough for me to not take a handful of pills and end it all. I thought everyone would have been better off without me, but in the deep recesses of my mind I knew I couldn't leave Nate without his mother. He was the shining star in my darkness, even if it took me a long time to admit it. Motherhood wasn't ever my dream, and Nate's entry into the world was unconventional, but my son is the spitting image of Noah. He owns my heart just like Noah has since the moment he first smiled at me. Last night, before I went to bed, I sent him the second part of my pages. It was late, and he was probably asleep, but I had to do it before I chickened out. Besides, I owe him those pages ... and so much more. I want to work my way through this for him, for us, for our family. I'm just not sure I'm strong enough.

This morning, I woke to the sun streaming through my window. The scent of freshly brewed coffee and cinnamon rolls leads me to the kitchen, where Karen sits with my Kindle.

"Good Morning, Amelia. How do you feel today?" With love in her eyes, she passes me a cup of coffee.

"I'm okay."

"Good, and you will continue to be okay," she says as she places a roll on a plate with a fork and a knife for me. "I finished the first part."

The moment of truth. "What did you think?"

"Well, I may be biased, but I think it's one of the best stories I've ever read. Even if you don't publish this as the story you owe them, I think you could still publish it and it would be a best seller." The way her eyes twinkle confirms she's not placating me.

"I'm not sure that's something I'd ever do. Mostly, I'm curious to see what he thinks about it all."

"You know he supports you in everything you do. He always has." That is also the truth. "I'd like to stay and read the second part while you write the ending."

"You're welcome to stay and read, but I'm not sure I'm going to be finishing." *Not after last night.*

"Amelia," she squeezes my fingers in hers, "what do we always say?"

"The only way out is through," I whisper.

"Yes, and sweetheart, you've already been out *and* through. Sometimes, you have to go back and shut the door that was left open in your rush to escape. Another *will* open, but you have to first close that door."

The tears begin to pour freely from my eyes. "But what if I can't?" My sobbing words fall on her shoulders as she pulls me close to her.

"You are one of the strongest people I've ever met. Not only *can* you do this, you *will* do this. I'm not saying it's not going to hurt, but losing him would hurt much, much worse."

"Why is he so stubborn? Why is he making me do this?"

Her eyes soften as she meets my gaze. "Because two years is a long time to watch the woman you love wither away in front of your eyes. I know you don't want to hear this, but he's right, Amelia. You're not living, you're existing. There's a difference."

"Living hurts."

"No, sweetheart. Pain hurts, tragedy hurts, loss hurts. But living makes the pain less. It moves the tragedies into the past. Loss should be a reminder to live each day to the fullest."

Live today like there's no tomorrow.

Sniffling, I ask, "How do you stay so positive?"

"I'm not sure being positive has anything to do with it. There's a cycle to life, Mel. Everyone is born with a death sentence. When we choose to live our days being sad and miserable, it's a slap in the face to those who would give anything for one more day. Especially when those people are the ones who would be moving heaven and earth to make you whole again. It's time for your light to shine again …for good this time. No more peeking out into the light only to retreat into the dark."

I hate that she makes sense. Even worse, she's absolutely right.

"Karen, can you call Anna? I'm going to take a shower. Tell her to bring her Kindle and tequila. If anyone else deserves to read this as it happens, it's her."

"Of course, but I also think we need to call Rory. Let's put all these demons to rest."

Rory. She's got every right to be here. This divisiveness is killing their family.

"Okay. Rory, too. But warn her about the sex and not to read it. I can't be responsible for traumatizing her. Not again."

"Consider it done."

I'm not sure there's enough tequila in the world to write this last part of the story, but I'll try for him. Fortunately, a couple of years ago, Sawyer wrote out what happened that night, hoping it would help with my memory. All I need to do now is hold on to the courage to retype his words before having to find my own again.

The Accident

Sawyer

Two years ago

With the exception of Cadence – we're having a boys' night. Noah declined the invitation to join us because he didn't want to leave Mel so close to her due date. I know I wouldn't have.

"Do you think Noah is going to knock Mel into labor?" Wyatt asks, and the rest of the guys snicker. But not me. I'm too excited.

"I fucking hope so. I can't wait to meet Noah's kid. My nephew is going to be the shit."

Noah and Mel are probably going to have the most perfect kid in the world. The two of them are so sweet and even-tempered. Mel's got a little bad girl tucked away deep inside; it's a riot when she releases her. Like the time she punched that girl at the hotel. That was one of the best things I'd ever seen. Or like the time I kissed her in my bathroom. *Damn* …I know I'm not supposed to think of her like that anymore, but that was still one of the hottest experiences of my life and I didn't even make it to second base. Noah is a lucky bastard.

"Sawyer, Luther wants to talk to you," Mac calls out, catching my attention. I love talking to Luther; we could shoot the shit for hours, but typically not at night. He likes to stay focused on the road when it's dark.

"Hey, Luther, what's up?" I ask, climbing up to the front.

"You see that?" he asks, gesturing in front of us. "My guess is it's still a few miles out."

About a quarter mile ahead of us, all I see is Noah's bus and fog. Lots and lots of dense fog.

"Where's the next exit?"

"About five miles ahead," he replies.

"Call it. Tell the drivers to get off for the night."

"You got it, boss."

We don't take chances with weather. I'm extra conservative that way, but I've seen people die before their time in tragic ways. I'm not going to be responsible for someone else's death because my tour takes precedence. Fuck no. *Life* takes precedence.

"Guys," I call out, "we're stopping for the night. Bad fog up ahead." My phone is already in my hand and I'm calling Noah. Suddenly grabbing onto the wall for support, a wave of nausea strikes me.

"What's up, Sawyer?" Noah sounds happy as can be.

"Hey, we wanted to give you a heads up. We're pulling off the freeway in about five miles for the night. Have you noticed the fog out there? It's insane so we're calling—"

My words are cut off when I see the explosion of light ahead of us. On the other end of the line, I'm met with blood-curdling screams before the call drops completely. The sound of metal against metal carries through the night. It's muted by our soundproofed bus but still audible. I'm not sure what the hell just happened, but I instinctively know it's about to change our lives.

My heart races as Luther slows the bus and talks to the other drivers, telling them to do the same. My mind is processing a million thoughts a minute as the guys yell, trying to understand what the fuck just happened.

"Call for help. Tell them we're going to need choppers." Luther is moving before I even get the words out of my mouth.

They hadn't even entered the fog yet, but something took out their bus. As soon as our bus stops, I'm off and running. I'm shaking like a leaf and have no idea how my feet are even moving beneath me. All I do know is I need to get to Noah fast. Something is wrong with him; I can feel it.

Please, God, protect my family.

"Holy shit, Sawyer! Holy shit!" Wyatt's screams travel through the night air behind me.

The ominous fog is still a bit in the distance, leaving the devastating scene in front of us clear and vivid. I'll never be able to erase this from my mind. The entire front quarter of the bus has been sheared off and is ten feet away with a massive delivery truck impaled in it. The road is littered with glass and debris, and jagged metal and sparking electrical wires make it difficult to determine how to get inside.

My thoughts continue to race as I cry out frantically for Noah, Mel, and Belle. My heart sinks in my chest knowing there's no possible way Harold survived the impact. Hell, I'm not sure any of them could have. The bus is askew on its side, blocking the entire roadway.

"Noah! Mel! Belle! Please answer me! Where are you?" My frantic cries are balanced on a sob as I fight back my tears. I can't lose my shit, not yet, they could still be okay. We have the safest buses in the industry. They have to be okay.

Mac and Ryan are right behind me, and the echoes of Warren and Darren arguing in the distance about who will take Cadence back to the bus catch up to my ears.

"Noah, please answer me!" I scream.

The electrical system is sparking like crazy, and someone is working on spraying it down with a fire extinguisher, but I'm just focused on getting into this bus any way I can.

Turning on the flashlight on my phone, I carefully make my way through. Everything is in disarray. The kitchen and living area items are comingled; everything seems to be piled on top of something else. The impact was so significant it eradicated all the safety options put in place to keep the furniture down. My gut is screaming no one could have survived this. But I won't believe it—can't believe it—until I know for sure.

The others are calling out, having made their way into the bus with me. Their pale, stricken faces take in the scene with wide, fear-filled eyes.

"Alright, you guys, let's move things carefully and see if we can find them," I instruct, tears streaming down my face. I've never been so fucking scared in all my life. My family is in this disaster zone somewhere, but I have to remain calm if I'm going to be any good for them.

"Shh … do you guys hear something?" Darren asks.

Someone is moaning. *Thank God. It means someone is alive.*

"Over there!" Wyatt screams.

Mac and Ryan jump into action, moving the couch and table off the victim. It's Noah. My tears begin to fall harder, but I don't care as long as he's alive.

Falling to my knees next to him, I check his pulse. It's strong, but he's not moving. "Noah, can you hear me? Noah! Answer me!" My wounded cries go unanswered, but he continues to moan.

"Do you guys see the girls anywhere?" I call out as they carefully work their way through the bus, moving furniture one piece at a time.

"Noah, please talk to me. Do you know where the girls are?"

"Sawyer," he gasps, as if breathing is the most painful thing in the world. "Mel … my room."

"What about Belle? Was she in my room?" I press, hoping to keep him talking until help arrives.

"Belle ... flew. She flew, Sawyer," he answers through gasping breaths.

What the fuck does that mean?

"Is she in my room, Noah? Belle ... did she go to my room?"

He gasps again, an awful, wheezy sound escaping him. *Fuck, where are the emergency crews?*

"She flew out ... outside."

No. He's just out of it. That can't be right.

Before I have a chance to say anything, Darren runs outside.

"Someone go with him!" I shout. Ryan runs after Darren and I hold Noah's hand tightly. "We got you, Noah. Everything is going to be okay. Keep breathing."

"Mel ... find Mel."

"Sawyer," Wyatt says, leaning down, "go to Mac. He found Mel. I'll stay with Noah." Wyatt is crying as he sits next to Noah and takes his hand from me. I don't want to leave him, but I need to check on her.

Carefully making my way into the bedroom, I see her right away. The dresser is lying across her lower legs and her head is bleeding, but she's awake. Before I can lean down and check her out, Darren's wails echo though the night. I heard that cry when my mom found out what had happened inside J's house that day. It's the sound of unnatural loss. The animalistic cry you hear when someone has been left behind in the worst imaginable way.

My heart can't take much more of this. We have to get them out of here before there's any more loss.

"Princess, please talk to me," I plead as I bend down.

Tears are streaming down her cheeks, but she looks at me stoically. "Sawyer, I'm in labor." Her words are calm—*too* calm. She's in shock.

Mac looks to me and down at the dresser. With a nod, I help him move it off of her.

What we find under the dresser is terrifying. Her pajama pants are soaked in blood. I've got no clue if she's injured somewhere or if it's from the baby. If they lose this baby it will kill them. It will kill us all.

"Oh God! Sawyer, it hurts!" she cries out.

I don't know what to do. She can't have this baby here. This is too much. Belle is gone. Noah and Mel ... Harold. *How do we tell their families? How do we come back from this?*

498

"Sawyer, I know it's a lot, man, but you've got to focus," Mac says firmly.

"Okay, Princess, tell me what hurts."

She hisses and blows through her mouth. "My back, my stomach, my wrist, my head, and my legs. Where is Noah?"

"Noah is in the front of the bus. He's hurt, but I think he's going to be okay."

"Belle … She's gone, isn't she, Sawyer?" Tears continue to stream down her cheeks, but she's trying so hard to be brave.

"I'm not sure, but I think so."

"She was screaming. It was the worst sound I've ever heard. God, Sawyer, she must have been so scared and in so much pain." Her breathing becomes rapid as she continues, "What am I going to do without her? And Cadence …" Mel's bravado fails as she begins to wail. "Oh God, what is going to happen to Cadence if she doesn't have her mom?"

"Shh, Princess, we don't know anything for sure. Right now you need to focus on *you*. We need to get you to the hospital and check on Nate. Cadence will have all of us, and we'll keep Belle alive the best we can. I need you to take a steady breath."

She blows breaths in and out and groans when the pain gets bad. "Sawyer, where is Noah? Why can't I hear him?"

"Wyatt, how's it going in there?" I call out so Mel can hear his reply.

"It's okay. His breathing sounds like shit but he's still talking to me. He wants to know how Mel is!"

Unsure of what to say, I look to Mac for help, but he only shrugs.

"Tell Noah he's going to be a dad tonight. Mel's in labor."

A few minutes later, Wyatt enters the room. "Noah wants to talk to you, Sawyer. It's okay, I'll stay with Mel."

"Sawyer, tell him I love him and I need him with me for this."

"Will do."

As I make my way back to Noah, I can hear his breathing getting worse. Thank fucking God I hear the choppers in the sky. Being out in the middle of nowhere really sucks sometimes.

"Mel says she loves you and needs you with her tonight. Are you ready to be a dad?"

Noah looks up at me with sad eyes. "I'm so fucking ready, but I'm pretty sure I'm going to miss it. Tell her I love her, and I'm sorry for everything." His voice is raspy, his breathing shallow. "I need you to promise me something, Sawyer."

"Anything you want, Noah, you know that." I squeeze his hand and choke down my tears. I know he's going to be okay, but he looks so fucking frail right now.

"When they get here, you need to go with Mel. She needs someone to hold her hand through this. I watched her with Belle and she was terrified. Don't let her do this alone. Make them bring me to her as soon as they can. I don't want to miss this for the world." He gasps loudly and releases a painful hiss.

"What else hurts, Noah?"

"My head, my ribs … I think they're cracked. That's it. If I could breathe better and stand up without feeling like I'm going to tear a lung, I'd be with her now. Promise me, Sawyer."

"I don't want to leave you, Noah." It's pointless trying to hold back my tears.

"I love you, Sawyer, and I know you love me. I *need* you to do this. Take care of my wife and my son until I can. I need my little brother's help. Please don't let me down. Wyatt will stay with me."

Mel's groans carry from the other room as the bus is flooded with light. The emergency crews' voices are getting louder as they come closer. I'm so fucking relieved they're here.

"I promise, Noah. You won't miss anything. I'll make sure of it."

"Is this the first victim?" one of the flight medics asks.

"Yes, this is my brother Noah Weston. His lungs are bad. His wife is pregnant and in the back of the bus. She's in labor."

"Show us where she is," the other medic says as the first one attends to Noah. Two more medics climb on the bus behind him as I stand to lead him to Mel.

Once we get in the room, I fill them in. "She was pinned under that dresser over there. I don't know if the blood is from an injury or the baby."

"Ma'am, when is your baby due?" he asks Mel.

Mel's only reply is a groan.

"She's due today." I bend down so she can squeeze my hand.

Wyatt goes back to Noah as another medic comes in and reaches for her free hand. Mel screams when he lifts her wrist.

"She's got a dislocated wrist. This is going to hurt, but I'm going to pop it back into place and splint it. You'll feel better once it's splinted."

"Shouldn't a doctor do that?" I ask, hoping they can wait.

"My name is Dr. Michaels. I'm a trauma physician at Harborside where we're transporting your brother and his wife. We've got the best medical team and equipment in the state. Trust me, this has to be done." He turns to the other medic. "Cut off her pants and assess her injuries."

Taking Mel's hand from mine, he quickly runs an I.V. and gives her hand back to me when he finishes. Within seconds, he pops her wrist back into place and Mel screams in pain.

Wyatt rushes into the room. "Noah wants to know why she's screaming."

"Dislocated wrist. How's he doing?" I hate not being able to be in two places at once. Even if he hadn't asked me, though, I'd never leave Princess alone.

"They're getting ready to put tubes in his chest. He's got a collapsed lung. The doctor said it couldn't wait."

Dr. Michaels looks at the other paramedic and tilts his head toward the front of the bus. "I need to get back to him. She goes first, get her on the board. She's dilated to eight centimeters and we need to know if we're dealing with any pelvic fractures. If she can hold out, no meds. The rapid scan is waiting and the second chopper is en route."

The paramedic agrees to the plan and the doctor heads back to Noah.

"She's got quite a few deep cuts on her legs, probably from the dresser," the medic tells us as another medic joins him to get Mel on the board. "It doesn't look like any blood is from the baby. How the hell is she so beat up but her abdomen untouched?"

"The bar, the soundproofing, and Winnie the Pooh," Mel replies through a groan. They pause to see if she continues, needing as much history as possible. "I held on to the metal bar by the bed when we were hit. That's how my wrist got fucked up. When I flew up, I slammed against the wall and my head hit the bar, but my belly was cushioned by all the soundproofing. Then, when the bus flipped on its side, my wrist snapped and I lost my grip and I fell. So did Pooh. My belly landed sideways on him."

Turning to the medics, I fill them in. "My brother had a bar attached to the wall at the head of the bed so she could get out of bed easily while pregnant. The walls in here are covered in soundproofing, and Pooh is a three-by-five-foot stuffed animal I bought for the baby. Mel slept with him to take pressure off her lower back."

Suddenly, the sound of a heartbeat echoes through the room. "Baby sounds good on the monitor. Heartbeat is a little fast, but I don't think it's anything to worry about. Call in and make sure OB is on standby in the trauma center," the first medic says to the second before they carry her out of the room on the board.

"Noah!" Mel calls out when she sees him on the floor. "I love you, Noah. Please fight, baby." She's crying, and after seeing the tube hanging out one side of his chest, so am I.

"I'm good, baby. You take care of Nate and I'll be there soon. I love you so much. Be strong, Amelia, you've got this."

"Noah—"

"You promised me, Sawyer. Take care of them. *Please.*"

"You got it, but only until you get there. Has anyone called my parents?" I ask.

Mac speaks up for the first time in a while, "Warren did, they're on their way with everyone. They'll arrive in a couple of hours." I've never heard Mac sound so solemn before.

When we exit the bus, I spot Darren about fifteen yards away. He's on the ground crying and rocking with Belle's limp body clutched in his arms. Ryan is trying to talk to him, as are the first responders, but he's ignoring them.

I turn away quickly and throw up in the roadway. My psyche can't handle this shit. My best friend is in agony and I can't do anything to help him right now. Mac's arm is on my shoulder and he turns me to face him.

"Go with Mel. Darren is in shock. We'll get him to the hospital, too. Just give him time to hold her one last time. It's the only goodbye he's going to get."

"Cadence ..."

"She's with Warren and she's fine. We got this, but Mel needs you and they're about to take off. Go, Sawyer, now." His firm tone brings me back to the here and now. Breaking into a run, I hop into the chopper just in time for takeoff. I'm able to stay with Mel while the medic keeps watch over her.

The trip to the hospital is the longest twenty minutes of my life. As soon as they unload Mel it's absolute chaos. I try to follow the conversation, but the only thing I know for sure is they are scanning her in some sixty second body scanner to make sure she can deliver.

Once she's out, I'm by her side and we're rushed into a huge trauma room which is already set up with what they need for the baby.

"Get her out of these clothes and wipe her down as much as possible," a doctor barks as he looks at his iPad.

"Multiple lacerations on her legs need debridement and sutures, her wrist needs to be cast, there's a five centimeter laceration on the back of her head, three centimeter laceration to her forehead, and multiple contusions." One of the many people is calling out all this information as the doctor keeps his eyes on the iPad.

What the fuck is he doing?

When he begins to speak, I understand. "She's got three non-displaced fractures in her lumbar spine L2-L4. They're going to make delivering this baby quite painful. No hip or pelvic fractures. All other scans are clear aside from the wrist."

Once Mel's clothes come off, someone immediately sticks an ultrasound onto her belly while a new doctor positions herself between Mel's legs. The nurses manage to wipe her down fast and get a gown on her. I can't imagine what Mel must be thinking right now because I'm dizzy with all of this and trying to remember every detail so I can fill Noah in.

"Baby looks good from what I can see on the scan and ultrasound. We'll have to do a full check upon delivery," the doctor says as she preps Mel for delivery.

"Sawyer, I'm scared." Mel's fragile voice reaches my ears and I'm about to lose my shit. My entire world is in this room and on that bus. *Fuck, I need Noah and so does she.*

"I know, Princess, but I'm right here. I won't go anywhere until Noah gets here. I promise." I pull her hand to my lips and kiss her softly, hoping I'm giving her as much support as I'm taking from her.

"Amelia, I'm sorry for what you're going through right now. I know you're in pain, but I need you coherent. After you deliver, I will give you medication. My name is Doctor Giles and I'm about to deliver your baby. Do you know what you're having?"

Dr. Giles is trying to be optimistic but I can tell she's worried.

"A boy … Nathaniel. It means gift of God," she whimpers as tears stream down her cheeks.

"Okay then … Nathaniel is ready to meet his mom. You're crowning. I'm so sorry because this is going to hurt like hell. On the next contraction, I need you to push, Amelia."

"Noah's not here, I can't do this without him," she wails.

My heart breaks for both of them. She's such a mess I can't even video this for her because I'm sure, other than Nate, she's going to want to erase this night from her memory completely.

"You *can* do this, Princess. I told Noah I'd get you through it. Do it for him and do it for Nate. And for fuck's sake, do it for yourself so you can get some pain relief. I got you, Princess, you just have to push."

On the tail end of my words, she has her next contraction and releases a painful scream. The staff in the room exchange sad looks and I know this is far from normal.

"Good job, Amelia. His head is out," Dr. Giles says.

I look down so I can describe this moment for Noah and I'm in absolute awe as the doctor suctions his mouth.

"Mel, he's got so much hair." When I meet her eyes, sadness is all I see. "I'm going to tell Noah every fucking detail, Princess. I promise."

Another contraction begins and the doctor tells her to push again. A few more pushes and a few more gut-wrenching screams and Nate's finally out and screaming himself.

"He's crying, Sawyer. Oh God, he's crying. Is that good or bad? I don't even know." Mel's working herself into a frenzy. They rush the baby to the side of the room and start checking him out.

"Amelia, I'm going to give you something to help you relax as well as some pain medicine. Not enough to knock you out because I still need you with me for a bit, but it's enough to knock the edge off."

"What about Nate?" she asks frantically as the nurse puts the meds in her I.V.

"Doctor, one minute Apgar is seven," the nurse calls out as Mel's eyes roll back a bit. At least she's getting some relief and the medicine is starting to work.

"Doctor, five minute is a ten, respirations and oxygen are both normal. Eight pounds and ten ounces, twenty-one and a half inches long. Can Mom have a peek before sending him for his scans?"

Dr. Giles smiles and nods emphatically while she tends to Mel. "Yes, bring the baby to Mom."

Noah is yelling out in the hall. Mel seems a bit loopy but she smiles. "Sawyer, get Noah. He needs to hold Nate first. He's waited so long for this."

"I want to wait with my wife! You can assess me in there." Noah's insistent voice carries into the room as I rush to open the sliding door. Wyatt is trying to calm him down but it's no use. I'm sure it hurts to yell, but Noah is nothing if not determined to see his wife and child.

"Please. His baby was just born, let him hold him for just a minute."

The doctors with Noah exchange concerned glances but relent. "For exactly as long as it takes for the results of your scan to load to my device and not a second longer," one of them replies firmly.

"I'll wait here," Wyatt says sadly, knowing they won't let him in.

Noah's bed is rolled in next to Mel's. He looks like hell but he's beaming. "Is he okay?"

"Yeah, Noah, he's pretty perfect," I tell him as the nurse brings Nate to meet his dad. I quickly pull out my phone so I can get a picture. The nurse carefully places Nate in Noah's arms. Even though it looks hella painful for him, he couldn't be happier. Noah tries to move him but can't, so I help him lift Nate so he can give him a kiss. With one hand balancing the baby, I use my free hand to snap a few photos of this moment.

"Amelia, baby, I love you. Look what we made. He's perfect, Mel, absolutely perfect." Noah is crying and Mel is super loopy, but with every ounce of energy she has, she leans over and kisses Noah.

"I love you, too, Noah, so much. Nate looks just like you. He's perfect." She places a tender kiss on top of Nate's head as tears stream down her cheeks. In the midst of everything, their joy is palpable. I allow myself a quick minute to be happy for them. Belle must be shining down on Mel right now.

"Amelia," the doctor says, trying to catch her attention again, "I'm going to need you to lie back, please. We're almost done. One more push to expel the placenta."

Noah's hands begin to tremble and his eyes begin to droop. I take Nate back and kiss the top of Noah's head. Noah's body slumps to the side as the doctors rush back in and the room once again turns into a frenzy.

"Noah, can you hear me?" one doctor asks. Noah mumbles, but he isn't giving them the response they're looking for. "Get him to the O.R. now!" the doctor calls out, and a team of people rush Noah from the room before I can even ask what is going on.

"Where are you taking him?" Mel cries out softly. She's completely drugged up and not coherent at all.

"Yes, where are you taking him?" I ask.

"Noah's scans show he has an epidural hematoma, which is bleeding in the brain. We need to get him to the operating room to stop the bleeding."

What? No ...

The doctor rushes out of the room behind the team pushing Noah's gurney. This can't be happening ... not now. I stumble backward against the wall as I cradle Nate in my arms. Noah will get through this, he has to ...

For Nate.
For Mel.
For me.

"Give her the medication I ordered so she can sleep. We need to get her cleaned up, suture her wounds, and get her to the floor. Mr. Weston, please give the baby to the nurse for his tests. We'll bring him back as soon as we're done."

I don't want to let him go. He needs someone with him; he's too little to fight by himself. Noah would go with him. "You're not taking him anywhere without me."

With an agreeable nod, the doctor relents. "That we can do. Follow the nurse to the scanner."

As we exit the room, Wyatt is leaning against the wall crying. He tries wiping his tears away and follows us. When the nurse tries to take Nate, I don't want to let him go. "Is it safe for him?"

"Safer than not doing anything. Because of the trauma, we need to get a clear picture." She smiles kindly at me. "You'll have him back in your arms in less than two minutes, unless there's an issue," she cautions softly as I hand him over.

Wyatt pulls me into a hug and we both dissolve into sobs. "Anna's already on a plane with Sam," he says, trying to catch his breath as he pulls back. "Everyone else is on their way. Mac said they finally got Darren away from Belle. That was the worst thing I've ever seen."

"It took us twenty minutes to fly. They won't be here for at least an hour," I reply.

"I'm so glad the baby made it. How's Mel?"

"Fucked up. Broken wrist, three broken bones in her back, so many cuts and bruises. And she still managed to push that baby out. I'm pretty sure she's got a hell of a concussion, too."

"Does she understand what happened to Noah?"

"I don't think so, she was kind of out of it. She freaked when they took him, but they knocked her out right away. I'm not sure what we do, Wyatt. I need to be with Nate and Mel, but I need to be with Noah."

"Noah is going to be fine. He didn't survive Sara's attack to give up now. He's a dad and a husband. Noah isn't going to give up."

He's right. Noah will be fine, we all will. *Except Belle and Harold.*

"When we were leaving, Mac was setting up all the security precautions for the hospital. Noah and Mel are supposed to be on some state-of-the-art VIP floor. Warren texted me and said he called

Harold's wife and it was the hardest thing he'd ever had to do. He also said your parents were going to wait to tell Veronica about Belle. They wanted her secluded on the private jet first."

"This wasn't supposed to happen, Wyatt. I should have been on that bus and Belle should have been on yours. It should have been me, not her."

"Fuck that, Sawyer, it shouldn't have happened at all. Cadence doesn't deserve to grow up without a mother. Mel didn't deserve to have what should have been the happiest day of her life turn into her biggest nightmare, and Noah ... Fuck, man, Noah is a goddamn saint. He deserves this least of all."

"Mr. Weston?" The nurse is smiling as she walks out of the room with Nate. "All his scans are clear. This little boy really is a gift from God. Most traumas don't end this happily for the infant. Someone has this blessed baby."

Belle ... she somehow saved him.

I clutch Nate closely when she hands him to me. She looks at me and Wyatt and shakes her head.

"Let's get the two of you into some clean scrubs while we bathe the baby. We're moving Amelia to the VIP floor and Noah will be there after his surgery. You two can wait for the doctors and your family in the private waiting area. After you're settled, I'll bring Nate to you and you can give him his first feeding. How does that sound?"

It sounds like a terrible idea. His parents should be feeding him, not me.

"His parents—"

Her sympathetic eyes meet mine. "Are incapacitated right now, but I'm pretty sure they'd rather his uncle feed him than Nurse Reynolds, although it would be my pleasure if you're not ready."

Take care of my wife and my son until I can. I need my little brother's help, don't let me down.

"It's fine. I'd be honored to take care of Nate until they can. In fact, I'd prefer it."

"Good. Let's go get you all settled in. It could be a few hours before Noah is out of surgery."

Waiting

Sawyer

For the last hour, Wyatt and I have been pacing around Mel's room. She's completely out of it, but it makes us feel better to be with her and Nate. I've felt sick to my stomach all night and I hate that Noah is still in surgery. All I could think of while I was feeding Nate was how Noah was missing his first bottle. One thing I knew for sure is Mel wasn't going to breastfeed, so at least I didn't have that guilt plaguing my subconscious.

There's a soft knock at the door and Nurse Reynolds peeks her head in. "The doctors will meet you in the waiting room in a few minutes. I'll take the baby to the nursery until you come back. Amelia will probably sleep through the night, so we can take care of him while you rest."

"No, I'll take care of Nate, but thank you for the offer. I'll come get him when we're done."

Wyatt and I exchange sad glances and walk to the waiting room. Within seconds, two doctors sit with us and I know right away it's not good news. They have shitty poker faces.

"It's bad, isn't it?" I manage to choke out.

"Yes, Mr. Weston, I'm afraid it is. Noah suffered severe blunt force trauma to his head."

Wyatt interrupts, "Yeah but he'll be okay … right?"

"No, I'm sorry, he won't be. There's no easy way to say this … Noah is on life support but he has no brain activity."

No …

No …

No … this isn't happening.

"Wait … what exactly are you saying? How is that possible? He was just talking to us and holding his son." Wyatt clutches my shoulder as tears begin streaming down my cheeks.

"Mr. Weston, Noah was alert and oriented at the scene. His pupils were equal and reactive, he was completely coherent and

Just an Illusion Series

responding properly. He complained of a minor headache but showed no signs of distress. His Glasgow Coma Scale was a fifteen, which is the best score you can get. His heart rate was elevated but nothing abnormal, considering the circumstances."

The doctor sighs and meets my eyes. "Noah's brain injury was what we call catastrophic. After impact, he went into what is called a lucid interval. Sometimes these intervals last only minutes, other times, hours. It's why we needed to get him scanned immediately upon arrival. With his extensive injuries he was fortunate to make it to the hospital, let alone talk to his wife and hold his child. Many would say it's a medical miracle."

He's not saying what I think he's saying. This isn't happening. Not to Noah. Please, God, not to Noah.

With a sympathetic gaze, he continues, "At this time, Noah is being kept alive by artificial respirations made by the life support. Once we remove those respirations, he will pass away. Noah developed an epidural hematoma when he struck his head. The bleeding inside his skull was severe enough to cause his brain to shift and herniate, which has left him with no neurological activity."

My body breaks out in a cold sweat. I hear his words, understand them, but they're not breaking through.

"He's brain dead? Noah is brain dead?!" Wyatt exclaims, clamping down tighter on my shoulders.

"Yes, I'm afraid he is. I'm sorry for your loss. I know this is difficult to hear, but we'll monitor him over the next twelve hours. We'll check his neurological functions in six-hour increments. While there is no hope for recovery, it's hospital protocol and required by law. Do you know if your brother has an advanced directive, or someone assigned to be his medical power of attorney? We need to know his wishes. Otherwise, his wife will have to make them for him. In her condition, I'd prefer to not put more stress on her if possible."

Brain dead.
Noah's brain dead.
My brother is dead.

The buzzing in my ears tries to swallow me alive but I push past it. Breaking down now isn't an option—I have to be strong. I'm the only one who can be.

"I'm not sure. Noah was a planner. Our attorney would have all that information, but … I know for sure Noah wants to be an organ donor." Those are words I never thought I'd have to say.

"If you could get hold of him in the morning, that would be best. In the meantime, you're welcome to spend as much time with your

509

brother as you and your family need. Mr. Weston, we're very sorry for your loss." The regret in his eyes is sincere, his tone nothing but compassionate. "As far as organ donation, we aren't technically supposed to bring it up until he's been officially declared brain dead, which will come after twelve hours. At that time, we'll have a representative from the Organ Procurement Network come and talk to you and your family about the process and how it works."

My resolve not to break goes out the window with his words. This is real and Noah isn't coming back to me ... ever. All his dreams and wishes ... gone. Four kids lost their parents tonight, three people lost their spouses, two sets of parents lost their children—we should have *never* done this final tour.

I barely realize the doctors are leaving as Wyatt and I hold one another, sobbing. Fucking hell. How am I going to tell Mel? My parents ... I don't think I can handle that feral cry from my mom twice in one lifetime.

"What happened?" Warren cries out as he walks into the room with everyone else behind him. Wyatt and I pull apart and take them in. The vacant look in Darren's eyes says more than words ever could. But that's not the worst part. They're barely five steps into the room when my entire family and Veronica rush in behind them.

"Sawyer, what's happened?" my mom asks, clutching my dad tightly. Jordan, Diane, Rob, and Rory are all lined up with them.

"Sit down, guys. We need to talk." My voice sounds foreign; I don't even know where the will to speak is coming from. I'm doing everything I can to not let what the doctor said permeate into my psyche because when it does sink in, the reality of losing Noah may actually kill me.

They stumble to their seats and Wyatt and I do our best to relay the events of the night and what the doctor said. If I thought my mom's grief at Jordan's house was bad, I was wrong. This is a million times worse. I just broke all their hearts in one fell swoop, and the collective sounds of their grief is almost as painful as knowing I have to say goodbye to Noah. Darren is sitting on the floor against the wall, knees curled up to his chest, sobbing.

I wish I were with him.

"Where's my baby girl?" Veronica manages to choke out.

"Didn't you guys—"

"Mel is my baby girl just as much as Belle is ... was ..." she trails off, crying. "I need to see my Mel and her son."

My mom stands up and clutches Veronica. "I'd like to see Mel and Nate as well, then someone needs to take me to see my son." She sobs in agony, but she and Veronica hold each other tight. While my family and friends grieve and try to console one another, Cadence sleeps the night away in her carrier. I've never been happier to see her safe and sound.

As I lead Mom and Veronica to Mel's room, I can't stop the tears from falling. Wiping them away is pointless because they're relentless. "She doesn't know," I say, pausing outside her door, "and I don't know how I'm going to tell her."

"The only way out is through, Sawyer. We'll tell her together as a family. She's going to need us all more than ever right now." My mom is walking through the depths of hell but her family is still her focus.

After we enter Mel's room, Nurse Reynolds brings Nate in. "I thought you might like him with you," she says softly as she passes him to me.

"Thank you," I reply, and she leaves us to grieve. Looking down at him now has a whole different meaning than it did an hour ago. My nephew is officially fatherless. I'm officially brotherless.

Twinless.

Noah and I have always been connected. I don't know who I am without him. We came in as a pair; I never imagined us going out any differently. I'm nothing without Noah.

Mom reaches over and takes Nate from me. "He's the spitting image of Noah," she says through a broken smile.

"Does she know about Belle?" Veronica asks as she sits by Mel's bedside.

"She suspected, but I'm not sure how much she'll remember. She's pretty banged up and was in an excessive amount of pain. I still don't know how she delivered him in that much agony."

"She had an angel looking out for her. My Belle." She turns her attention back to Mel. "Baby girl, I'm so glad you're still here with us. I don't know what I would have done if I'd lost you, too."

My mom leans over and kisses Mel on the cheek before passing Nate to Veronica. "I'm going to go see Noah."

She flees the room so quickly I don't know what to do, but I'm compelled to stay and listen when Veronica begins speaking.

"Tonight will always be remembered as one of the worst days of our lives. Someday, as our sadness lessens, we'll put the happiness ahead of the pain. Nathaniel, you are the bright light in our darkest day. You and your mama were saved for a reason. God knows what He's doing even if we don't understand. Happy birthday, little man. Welcome to the world."

It's through her words I'm reminded even more of Noah's belief in fate. As Veronica cries over her losses, she's also rejoicing over new life and the fact Mel was spared. If I know anything about Mel, she's going to wish she wasn't. We're more alike than we are different, especially now that we're the siblings left behind.

Exiting the room quietly, I give Veronica some privacy. As my body finds purchase against the wall, my legs give out and I sink to the ground. Burying my head in my hands, I'm sure my cries can be heard throughout the building, but I don't care—my pain is all-consuming and it's demanding to be set free.

Within minutes, Darren is sitting next to me, both of us lost in our grief. Eventually, Veronica comes out of Mel's room with Nate. Darren, seeing Nate for the first time, stands and reaches his arms out to hold him.

"He looks like Noah, look at all that hair. Belle would be so pissed she missed this. Life is so fucking unfair."

This baby is like a healing balm when you hold him. Your sadness lessens because you want everything to be okay for him. Pulling my phone from my pocket, I pull up the photos I got of Noah when he got to hold Nate.

"This is all he's ever going to have of his dad," I tell them sadly.

Veronica gasps and holds my wrist. "And it will be the most precious gift he will ever receive. You need to forward those photos to your email or back them up to the cloud so you'll always have them. I know Mel will be grateful for them. I'm going to the chapel. I need some time to try and get right with God."

After she leaves, Darren and I move back into Mel's room. No one else has been by yet. I'm sure they're all keeping vigil over Noah. As much as I want to see him, I can't when they're all in there.

"She looks peaceful. How bad are her injuries?" Darren asks wearily as he takes a seat next to her bedside.

"Nowhere near as bad as they could have been. They said Nate shouldn't have made it. You saw that bus ... no one should have made it out. She's got cuts, bruises, sprains and strains, a broken wrist, and three broken bones in her back. She'll need help and be in pain for a while, but she's alive."

"That's what Belle would have wanted. I just wish she'd made it out, too. Her *and* Noah. I don't know what I'm going to do without her, what Cadence is going to do without her mom. What any of us are going to do without Noah." He's trying to hold back his sobs since he's holding Nate, but it's useless.

"I'm so fucking sorry, Darren ... for everything."

His shattered gaze meets mine. "It wasn't your fault, Sawyer. I know this is how you compartmentalize shit, but knock it off. We all lost tonight. My losses don't outweigh yours or hers … it's all just fucked up. Cadence and Nate are the biggest losers in all of this.."

"Noah …" Mel calls out softly in her sleep. My heart can't handle breaking hers.

There's a soft rap at the door and Warren enters with a wide-awake Cadence. She's excited to see Darren, and he forces a smile for her. "Hey, baby girl," he says, standing and holding up Nate. "It's your new buddy. Say hi to Nate."

Warren brings Cadence close to Nate and she grabs his tiny hand in hers. It's almost like she's letting him know she's got him. She's very much like Belle in that respect already. I can't help but wonder if they'll be like Belle and Noah, even though they're not here to guide them. Nature versus nurture and all that shit.

Darren and Warren swap babies and Warren chokes on a muffled cry as he holds Nate. Darren clutches Cadence to him like a life preserver; it's the first time he's held her since losing Belle. Taking a seat next to Mel, Warren looks back and forth between her and her son.

"It's a miracle they made it out of the bus. The police said off the record it looks to be a high-speed collision, no surprise there. What they don't know is what caused it … drugs, alcohol, mechanical failure or something else. We have to wait until they complete the investigation for an official determination. Regardless, no one should have made it out of that bus alive."

Listening to Warren talk about the accident pisses me off. It should have never fucking happened. "I need to see Noah now." I tell them before storming out of the room. When I make it to Noah's room I pause outside the door. I don't want to be an ass to anyone, but I need a few minutes with him.

When I walk inside, I'm surprised to see only my dad. When his eyes meet mine, I recognize the brokenness in them—they look how I feel inside. Wordlessly, he comes to me and pulls me into his arms.

"I love you, Sawyer. I don't know if I say it often enough, but I hope you know it with all your heart." He's sobbing and clutching onto me as if his life depends on it.

"I love you, too, Dad. We've never wondered about your love for us. Neither of us, not once." He straightens a little in my arms as if those words lifted him up somehow. "Would you mind if I had a little time with him alone?"

With a kiss to the top of my head, he releases me. "Somehow we'll figure out a way to get you through this. I promise. You and Amelia both."

After my dad closes the door behind him, I take a deep breath. Seeing Noah like this hurts me in a way I've never felt. I'm shattering somewhere deep inside and I don't think whatever is breaking will ever recover.

His head is wrapped in a large bandage, and he has a tube breathing for him. He's pale...I've never seen Noah before without color in his cheeks, he's always been bigger than life. There are so many monitors—you'd think this was in an effort to save him, not to determine we need to let him go.

Pulling the chair as close to him as I can, I take Noah's hand in mine and lay my head against his thigh. His hand is warm but never once does he move. I wish I could pretend he's sleeping, but I know it's not the case.

"Fuck, Noah, I'm so fucking angry right now." My chest heaves as I gasp for air. "This isn't how our lives were supposed to end up. In the last six months, every happiness you ever wanted was handed to you on a silver fucking platter. You and Mel were supposed to make all these gorgeous babies and I was supposed to find a girl as good as her and make some of my own."

I'm hysterical and don't even bother wiping away my tears. "Warren says the truck driver was speeding. You, Harold, and Belle better be kicking his ass hard up there. Are you there, though? Wherever *there* is? Because you're still here with me right now and I'd give anything, Noah, *anything* at all to have you back.

"They said you were a medical miracle and you should have never made it off the bus. You had to have been in way more pain than you were letting on. Why didn't you say anything?" I wish he would answer me. My chest hurts from crying and my throat is raw, but I have to talk to him while there's still time. "I did what you asked and stayed with Mel, but we should have had more words, Noah. If I'd *known* it was the last time we'd ever talk, I would have said so much more. You're my best friend and the most amazing brother. I wish a brain was like a kidney and I could give you mine ... you deserve to be here so much more than I do. Mel deserves her husband and Nate deserves a father."

I'm trying to breathe through my sobs but it's no use; this will never be okay. I don't want to let him go.

"Sawyer ..." I hadn't heard Anna walk in. She leans over me and wraps her arms around me. "I'm so sorry, Sawyer." Wrapped in

Anna's arms, I allow myself a few moments to grieve. I'm not only crying for me, I'm crying for Noah, too. I don't care how much he believes in fate, he would have never been on board for this shit.

After a few moments, she crouches down next to me and turns my face toward hers. Anna has seen me at many stages of vulnerable before but she's never seen me shattered.

"What can I do for you, Sawyer?" she asks as her own tears stream down her cheeks. Her hand covers the back side of Noah's and her fingers grip mine, too, since I'm still holding him tight.

"Rewind time and have it be me."

Shock mars her beautiful features as her tears fall harder and faster. "Don't say that, Sawyer. We'd be just as lost without you as we're going to be without Noah."

"He's got a wife and a kid, Bethie. I'd give myself a million times over for him to be here with them."

She exhales softly as her determined eyes meet mine. "This is the most fucked-up situation we've ever been in, but this was fate."

She sees the anger flare in my eyes and holds up her free hand. "Hear me out. It doesn't matter what we think, Noah believes in fate. He's talked about it since we were kids. His belief was the core of who he was, and for us to discredit that now isn't fair to the way he lived his life. There's not a doubt in my mind Noah would have called it fate to justify losing Belle. There's nothing we can do but say goodbye, honor him and his legacy, and take care of Mel and Nate for as long as they need us."

Anna has always been a straight shooter; it's why we're such good friends. She's never been one to bullshit or sugar-coat anything. I might hate what she's saying, but I also know she's completely right. Noah would call this fate no matter how bad it sucks ass.

"You're right, Bethie, but I don't know how to let him go. I don't know who I am without him. I'll never be whole again."

She sighs and takes a seat on the edge of Noah's bed. I sit up and meet her gaze. "Gradually, Sawyer. We all take it gradually. First, we say goodbye, then we let him go because … he's already gone, Sawyer. Then we take a pause and say a prayer for all the people he's going to save. Noah's last heroic act is to save lives. As we move from one day to the next we make sure Mel and Darren do, too. One day at a time."

"Okay, Bethie, gradually. One minute, one hour, one day at a time."

She swallows and nods. "Good. Other people would like to come in before Mel wakes up. Do you think you can handle that?"

D. Kelly

If I had my choice I wouldn't leave this room until after Noah is gone, but I can't be that selfish.

"No, but I'll try."

There's a soft knock at the door and my sisters and Rob poke their heads in. Their sadness is overwhelming. Right now, *everything* is just so fucking overwhelming. I need air. Diane hugs me as Rory sits next to Noah and cries. "Has anyone called Eli?" I ask, knowing Mel could use her friend.

"He's on his way," Rory answers.

Anna and I leave the room. I take a deep breath as she rubs my back. "Have you seen Nate yet?" I ask, and she shakes her head. "Alright, let's go see him because he helps ease the pain."

Anna follows me down the hall to Mel's room and I'm surprised to see my mom at her bedside, clutching her hand. Nate is sleeping in the bassinette next to the bed and I scoop him out and into my arms. This little guy is the only reason I'm still standing right now. I'll never break my promise to Noah; I'll watch over him and Mel until my dying breath if they need me to.

"He's Noah's mini-me," Anna says softly.

"Isn't he?" my mom replies with a sad smile. "He's the only thing keeping me from losing my mind right now. Knowing Noah was able to leave part of himself with us …" She doesn't finish her thought, but we get it. I wonder if we all feel the same. I wonder if Mel will. She was so hesitant to have a child in the first place, I'm terrified for what is going to come next without Noah and Belle being here for her. I honestly don't know if Nate will be enough to keep her going, but I hope he is. For all our sakes.

"Has she woken up at all?" I ask, passing Nate to Anna.

"She's beginning to stir and has been calling out for Belle," Mom answers.

The oppressive sadness hanging in the air between us is ridiculous. As much as I don't ever want to leave this hospital, I can't wait to get out of here.

"I'm afraid for her, Mom."

She looks up at me with broken eyes. "Me too, Sawyer. But it's up to us to get her through this, no matter how hard it is for us. It's what Noah would want."

Leaning down, I kiss her head and wrap my arms around her shoulders. "I love you, Mom, so much. I'm sorry I couldn't save him."

When she hears my words, she stills and stands, nailing me with her angry mom gaze. "Sawyer Weston, this is not your fault. Don't

516

ever blame yourself for this. The doctor says he was beyond saving. I'm so thankful I didn't lose both of you tonight. I don't know why you weren't on your bus, but I'm so happy you weren't."

Perspective–it's an odd thing. I wish I had been on the bus, I wish Belle had been saved, but I never once thought what it would do to my parents and sisters if they'd lost us both. This is too much to deal with right now. I should find J and get one of his anxiety pills.

"Belle … Noah … please answer me." Mel is calling out in her sleep, and my heart takes a dive into my stomach. She's not dreaming, she's remembering. Taking the seat my mom just vacated, I grab her hand.

"Shh, Princess, it's okay. We're here and we've got you. You're safe now, I promise."

"Sawyer." Her eyes flutter open with my words and I'm regretting speaking. Things are only going to go downhill from here.

"Hey, Mel, we're here," I say as my mom pours her a cup of water.

"Here, sweetheart, take a drink." She holds the cup to Mel's lips.

"Can we please move the bed up a little bit?" Mel asks, her eyes becoming a little more focused with each passing second. Anna walks to her bedside with Nate in her arms and Mel smiles up at her.

"Anna, you look good with a baby."

"Maybe someday," she says as she lowers him to Mel. "Can you hold him?"

Mel releases my hand and nods. "I think so if you can prop him in my good arm. I don't want to whack him with my cast.."

Anna lowers the baby into her arms, and we watch as Mel coos at him for the first time and places a loving kiss against his head. "I can't believe how much he looks like Noah. Where is he?"

Reaching out for Nate, I hand him back to Anna as Mom and I exchange pained glances.

"I'm going to take Nate to meet Wyatt. I'll be back in a few minutes," Anna says. Mel doesn't say anything, but her eyes are focused on us.

"Mel, what's the last thing you remember?" I ask as my mom takes the seat next to me.

"Everything is foggy, Sawyer," she answers on a sigh as tears begin to stream down her cheeks. "It wasn't a dream, was it? Belle is gone, isn't she?" Her pained words break my heart, especially since this is only the beginning of her nightmare.

"Yeah, Mel, she is." Nodding, she closes her eyes. "Noah … I remember kissing Noah as he was holding Nate. Everything after that is fuzzy. Where is he?" Her tone is becoming frantic and my mom takes her hand again.

"Amelia, Noah was injured in the crash and needed surgery." Tears are streaming down Mom's cheeks.

"He's okay, right? Noah's okay?" She rips her hand away and tries to sit up further. The painful cries falling from her lips pierce me to my core. Her body is bent and broken but she's only now realizing that herself.

"No, sweetheart, I'm afraid Noah isn't okay."

Mel stops moving and the color immediately drains from her face. "You're lying!" she screams, and Mom pales at her accusation.

"Princess ... Noah is on life support."

"Wha- what do you mean? Life support?"

For the next few minutes, my mom and I explain everything the doctor told us, but Mel is in denial.

"No, I don't believe you. I want to see him." She pushes herself up and moves her legs over the side of the bed, crying out in pain. I rush to grab the wheelchair in the corner of the room.

"Mel, stop! Let me put you in the chair. You're injured and you shouldn't be moving around like this. Please let me help you ... I promised Noah ... please, Princess, let me keep my promise."

She relents, her body sagging like a ragdoll, the fight in her suddenly gone. I lift her up and carefully put her in the wheelchair as my mom rolls her I.V. stand next to her. After removing her blood pressure cuff, the three of us make our way to Noah's room in silence. Diane and Rob are with him when we walk in but exit wordlessly upon our arrival.

"Noah," Mel cries out softly before wailing, "Oh God no ... please no ... Noah!" Before I can blink, Mel bounds out of the chair and into the bed with Noah. She curls into his side and rests her head against his heart.

My mom clutches my hand for strength as we helplessly watch Mel fall apart in front of our eyes.

"You're wrong. I hear his heart beating. It's strong and steady. Come on, Noah, wake up. Tell them they're wrong. Tell them you're just napping because you need to be extra strong so you can be Nate's daddy. Please wake up and tell them, Noah ... please."

I'm not sure how long we watched as she cried, her head on his chest, listening to Noah's heart beating in her ears. Long enough for me to pray she was right and we were all idiots. Long enough to hope love could bring him back to her ... to us. Long enough to wish I'd left before she made her next request.

"Go get Nate for me."

She never looked up, but my mom immediately complied. Within minutes she was back with the baby.

"Can you lay him on Noah's chest please?" Mom again does as she's asked and Mel wraps one of Noah's arms around Nate, as well as her arm with the I.V. in it, and pulls them all into a family hug. It's the saddest thing I've ever seen. Mom flees the room sobbing, but I can't bring myself to leave, to give them privacy. Instead, I make my way to the corner of the room and try to distance myself as much as possible. She's only got one semi-good arm and I may need to grab Nate at any given time.

"This is our family, Noah. Me, you, and Nate. It's everything you ever wanted, all you have to do is reach for it. Don't leave us, Noah, not when we need you the most. Please, God, don't take him from me. They're all I have left."

She's wrong; she has all of us but she can't see it through her pain. And it's not my place to bring it up. Not now.

Hours passed as I sat in the corner and kept watch over them. Each of Mel's periodic pleas more heartbreaking than the last.

"Come on, Noah, time to wake up. Show me those gorgeous eyes and that panty-melting smile. Sing for us, please. Nate just got here and there are mud fights to be had, guitars to be played, lessons to teach, and you know he's going to need a brother or sister. He needs his daddy, Noah, and we haven't even had a year. We only got one Thanksgiving, one Christmas, one New Year, and you're supposed to give me fireworks."

She hiccups and sobs as Nate sleeps soundly, wrapped in their love. "Don't forget you promised me fifty years, Noah … at least. Baby, please wake up."

Tony walks in with his laptop bag hanging off his shoulder. When he sees the sight before him, he runs his hands through his hair and collapses into a chair next to the door. His eyes catch mine before he drops his head into his hands and cries.

Tony and Noah have always been close. They've been friends since high school and are both major planners. They geek out on plotting life's unexpected scenarios. And even if they had a plan for this, I'm sure they never expected to implement it.

Making my way over to him, I place my hand on his shoulder. "Who called you?" I ask in a low tone.

"Warren did, after you got the news. I brought … the paperwork. Can I talk to Mel?"

With a nod, I reply, "I'm not sure how receptive she'll be."

A light rap on the door is followed by two doctors entering the room. They're ones I haven't seen before. Another doctor trails in behind them; he's the one who gave us the news about Noah.

"Mr. Weston, we need to perform Noah's six-hour assessment. It would be best if you all waited outside and we'll let you back in when we're done."

"Go to hell!" Mel cries out from the bed. "I'm not leaving. Any tests you need to do you'll do in front of me. You're not killing him before his time. Noah's still in there and he's going to fight."

With the patience of a saint, the doctor replies, "Very well, Mrs. Weston, but you and the baby will need to move during the testing."

I take my cue and pry Nate out from under Noah and Mel's arms.

"Amelia," Tony says, "why don't you let the doctors do their tests and we can go over Noah's wishes?"

"I'm not leaving, Tony. You can come back in and talk to me when they're done." Her head still on Noah's chest, she doesn't even look up. With a resigned sigh, Tony and I leave the room.

"So he had a plan for all this, didn't he?" I ask once we're in the hall. Diane comes up to listen and takes the baby from me.

"Yes, in fact ... Noah updated everything a few days after the wedding. Advanced directive, medical power of attorney, will, you name it and it's been updated."

"Well ... that's good. I guess. At least Noah will get everything the way he wants it. I suppose that's important right now." Diane's words echo through the hall, but the emptiness in them carries most of all.

Everything except his wife, his kid, and his life.

"I'm going to get some coffee. I'll be back."

After taking a piss, and getting some coffee, I take a glance outside. There is a sea of people sitting vigil outside the hospital with signs and candles. Crying fans are everywhere, just waiting for some kind of update. I overheard Sam say he was posting one and needed approval.

I duck into an empty stairwell and close my eyes. We had a blast the past ten years, but none of this was worth the expense of losing Noah, Belle, and Harold. I'd give it all back in a heartbeat if I could.

I'm trying to think what Noah would do right now and, picturing the fans outside, I know.

As I make my way back to the waiting room, I'm determined to do something good. When I enter, my eyes take in my weary family and it firms my resolve even more.

"Look, this is shit, but who wants a project?"

Eli looks up from next to Rory. I didn't even realize he was here yet. "I'll help. What do you need?"

"We need food. Catered, something good. Any price, it doesn't matter. There are hundreds of people outside the hospital … get them food, too. Food for us, the staff, and the fans. It's what Noah would do and therefore, it's what we should be doing. If the staff can't get out and is stuck eating hospital food, that's an issue. And as much as we don't want to eat, we have to. Mel needs us, Nate needs us, and Noah needs us to be strong for them."

Warren smiles up at me and nods his head in approval. Even Veronica smiles at me as she kisses Cadence while she sleeps in her arms. "We're on it, Sawyer. Go back to Mel and take care of her," Eli says with tears in his eyes.

When I get back to the room, Tony is outside talking to the doctor and a woman. "It's time to talk to Mel about what's next. This is Mrs. Johnson, she's the hospital transplant coordinator," Tony informs me, and I give a slight nod.

"So … the testing?"

"Was what we expected, Mr. Weston. I'm sorry, but as I stated before, this is only a formality." My heart drops. Even though I knew what to expect, I was hoping Mel's impassioned pleas could make the impossible happen.

After entering the room, we pull four chairs to the bedside and Tony opens the dialogue.

"Amelia, can we have a conversation about Noah's wishes?"

With a loud sniffle, her broken eyes meet his. "I guess so."

"Two days after the wedding, Noah updated his documents. He has an advanced directive specifically prohibiting heroic measures to extend his life in an instance such as this. He's also expressed his wishes to be an organ donor. Amelia, are you following me so far?"

"Yes," she whispers.

"Okay, even though these are Noah's wishes, he's given you medical power of attorney, which means you have the choice of whether or not to honor these wishes. He's put his faith in you, to choose what is best for him since he can't. If you should choose to not be his medical power of attorney, he's requested Sawyer be appointed."

Fuck me.

Mel gingerly sits up and grips the rail for support as tears stream down her cheeks. "But why? I can't make this decision for him! Why would he do that to me? Why would he make me be the one to decide if he lives or dies?" Her emotional pleas are heartbreaking, but I understand her thoughts because I feel the same way.

"Because you're his wife and there's no one he trusted more than you to make sure his wishes and best interests are being looked after. Except for Sawyer, who has always been his designee until you became his wife."

"Mrs. Weston," the doctor intervenes, "I know this is an impossible situation and you should make an informed decision. Our hospital is one of the best neurological institutions in the country. We have technology other facilities would love to have at their disposal. That fact your husband made it for the birth of your son is a miracle. After twelve hours, and with two doctors' signatures, we can officially declare him brain dead. We're at the halfway point. If you would be comfortable bringing in specialists from other facilities to perform additional neurological checks, I'd encourage you to do so, but I don't expect any other outcome."

Mel's eyes flare with anger. "So my husband's life is only worth twelve hours? Is that what you're saying?"

"No, not at all. I'm sorry for what you've been through, but many hospitals would make this call at six hours with the injuries your husband sustained. If there were some hope, *any* hope at all, I'd give it to you. With injuries as catastrophic as his, there isn't any hope left."

Mel's eyes dart between us and Noah as tears stream down her cheeks. I feel like I'm swimming inside a fishbowl and I can see the world outside but nothing makes sense.

"Four specialists. Find them, Tony. Get whoever you have to, fly them from wherever you need to, I will pay *whatever* they ask."

Then she turns her fiery gaze back to the doctor. "No less than twenty-four hours and four specialists. After that, I'll give my consent *only* if all four specialists agree with the determination the other two already gave."

She then turns to the transplant coordinator. "And you want my husband's organs, right? I have to give consent for that?"

The coordinator meets her glare with a sympathetic look. "I'm here because the family said Noah wanted to be a donor. If that's something you'd like, too, I will call in The Organ Procurement Network to get things moving. One of their representatives will come out to speak with you all a bit more. Mrs. Weston, I understand how difficult this is, I—"

"You what?" Mel asks softly.

"I was in your place last year when I lost my husband."

"I'm sorry," Mel says. "Noah is the most selfless person I've ever known. He would want to donate. I will give consent if, and only if, all six of these doctors come back with the same answers and not sooner than twenty-four hours."

That's it. Mel just set a ticking clock and the countdown begins now.

Left Behind

Amelia

For twenty-four hours straight, I pray for a miracle I know deep down will never come. With my head resting on Noah's chest, I listen to his heart beat every second I can. I only move long enough for restroom breaks, doctors to check him, and for them to check me.

Everything in my body hurts. I've never felt pain like this before, but the pain in my heart, in my soul, trumps anything my body is going through. Most of the time Sawyer sits in a chair in the corner while I cry, weep, and plead with God not to take Noah. I wait anxiously for Noah's loving arms to suddenly wrap around me tightly and for him to kiss the top of my head like he's done so many times before. But it never happens; Noah never so much as flinches.

When the last specialist finishes, Tony, Sawyer and I talk over the results. They all show the same thing, Noah is gone. Each of the doctors went over their results with us but we wanted to look them over one last time as a whole. Six of the world's best neurological experts unanimously agree—nothing more can be done.

After we finish, the doctors step back inside and have me sign the necessary paperwork. I can barely scribble a line I'm so upset. The hopelessness in the air suffocates us all. Before leaving, the doctors agree to sedate me so I can say my goodbyes. When I wake up, it will be over; however, it will only be the beginning of my nightmare. I've got no idea how to live without Noah and Belle.

With their deepest sympathies ringing in my ears, I know my time is up. I have to find a way to say goodbye to the love of my life so the people who have loved him his whole life can say their goodbyes, too. I've been selfishly taking up almost all of what little time we had left with him, but they had so much of his past and I had so very little.

Tony and Sawyer follow the doctors out, but Sawyer returns a few moments later with Nate. My son, who is perfect in every way and who I'm terrified to even touch. But I will for Noah, so he can say goodbye. Bringing the baby close, I line his lips up to Noah's cheek and press them together. I know it's not exactly a kiss, but it's the best I can do, especially with the tube in the way. I pull Noah's arm around Nate and position us into a family hug the best I can.

My eyes catch Sawyer's—his are bloodshot and broken and my heart aches for him. I wish I could comfort him right now in his time of need, but I can't even see past my own grief to help him with his.

"Say goodbye to Daddy, Nate," I say on a sob as I pass the baby to Sawyer to take back to whoever has been keeping him while I've been here. When Sawyer leaves, I press the call button for the nurse so they can medicate me as I try to figure out how to say goodbye. The first thing I do is kiss his head, his cheek, and the corner of his lips before bringing my mouth to his ear.

"I don't know how to do this, Noah. How do I say goodbye to you when I just found you?" I pause and try to clear my throat. It's pointless; I want to be strong for him, but my crying supersedes my strength. "We were supposed to be a family and now I'm alone. I can't be the mother he needs. You should have been the one who lived, you are the better parent for him." My sobs are uncontrollable, but I have to find a way to push through. "I pray you and Belle are together right now. Take care of her, Noah, watch over her for me. I'm not sure how to live without you both, or if I even want to. She's my best friend and you're the love of my life, what am I supposed to do without you guys?"

The door opens and I nod as the nurse comes inside. There's never going to be a good time for this, and as much as I'd love to stay in Noah's arms forever, his family is waiting. I pull his arm around me and rest my head over his heart. After injecting the medicine into my I.V. port, the nurse leaves and I feel it taking me fast. "I'll love you forever, Noah. Thank you for loving me and showing me what love is. Please watch over Nate and me and if you can, keep me from messing this up. I'm so scared, Noah, but I love you, I love you … I love you …"

When I wake up, the sun is streaming through the window of my hospital room. I feel like Noah is in those rays of light somehow. Mama and Eli are at my bedside and Sawyer is sitting on the floor in the corner of the room. His head between his legs, his body is wracked with sobs, and Nate's bassinette is next to him.

"He's gone?" I whisper.

Eli squeezes my hand. "Yeah, Mel, about three hours ago. I'm so sorry."

Silent tears stream down my cheeks, but I'm numb. "How did I get back here?"

Mama looks to Eli and he shrugs. "Do you really want to know?" he asks, and I nod. "Sawyer carried you back and tucked you in before saying his goodbyes."

My eyes dart immediately to Sawyer, a whole other piece of my heart breaking for him. He's a good man, but he's going to be just as lost as I am without Noah.

"Can you give us a minute?" I ask, and they both exit the room. "Sawyer, can we talk?"

He looks up at me and shakes his head.

"Fair enough. Can you at least come closer so we can cry together?"

He complies, wheeling Nate over with him. My eyes take him in like a much-needed breath. My body relaxes slightly as I see his tiny body move as he inhales and exhales. All Belle and Noah would have wanted is for their children to be safe, and they are.

"Thank you for taking care of us."

Sawyer looks up at me and speaks through his pain. "I promised him I would, and I always will." His hand meets mine and he squeezes it lightly.

"I think you would have even if you didn't promise. But Sawyer … we're … we're not your obligation. You don't have to be there. I won't hold you to it. I don't want to be anyone's last promise or debt. You're off the hook, okay?"

Those words are painful to speak because I need Sawyer right now. He's all I have left.

"There's no hook, Mel … you're family. We look out for each other, always."

The two of us settle back into our own grief and I eventually drift off again, letting the medication take me under so I can forget, at least for a little while.

I wake up to Cadence babbling. When I look over, Eli and Darren are sitting next to me and Sawyer is sitting in the corner of the room. At least he's in a chair this time, and he's feeding Nate.

A pang of regret fills my heart that I'm not the one taking care of him right now, but I'm not ready. "Hey, baby girl," Eli says as he gently squeezes my thigh.

"Hey," I croak as Darren turns Cadence toward me. As soon as she sees me, she smiles, and I smile back at her through my tears. She's Belle to a T. Darren looks about as bad as I feel, but at least he's putting on a brave front for his daughter.

"The doctors say you can go home tomorrow and then we can all get out of here," Darren says as he sets Cadence at the edge of my bed. Her fingers wrap around mine, and when she pulls them to her mouth, I feel it right away.

"She got her first tooth."

"Yeah," he says remorsefully. "Belle knew it was coming and she was right. I hate that she's not here for this, for any of this." Darren's words split me open again and a steady stream of tears begin to flow.

"Me, too. What do you mean everyone can leave? Who's here?"

"You're joking, right, Mel?" From the look I give him he must be able to tell I'm not and he shakes his head in disbelief. "No one has left this hospital since you guys were brought in. Not one of us. We came in as a family and we go home as a family," Darren chokes out.

"They don't have to stay ..."

"Yes, they do. Family sticks together. You're one of us now, get used to it." Sawyer's tired-but-firm voice leaves no room for argument. "But just so you know, Diane and Rob left a little while ago to get back to the girls. They said to give you their love."

A doctor and a nurse enter the room so Eli and Darren move to step out. Darren bends Cadence toward me and I place a kiss against her sweet little cheek.

"Mrs. Weston, how are you feeling?" the doctor asks and quickly corrects himself. "Physically, how are you feeling?"

"About the same, I guess. Sore, achy, broken, sad."

The nurse moves to take my vitals and begins removing the tape from my I.V. when she's finished.

"We're moving you to oral medications. You'll be discharged with something for pain and anxiety, as well as an antibiotic for your wounds. We'll go over all your discharge instructions with you in the morning. Please be mindful that you are slightly concussed and will have to take it easy for the next three to six months."

"Why so long?" I ask in a panic.

"You have three fractured vertebrae. There's no treatment for them other than rest, restrictions, and time. We'll get you a brace to wear if it helps with the pain, but it's not necessary if you're careful."

"I didn't realize ..."

"I'm sure you didn't. It's been a rough few days and you're extremely lucky to be alive ... so is your son. I'd go as far to say you're both miracles. You'll need lots of help, but it seems like you have a good family support system."

"She does." Sawyer's statement, once again, is firm and commanding.

"Very well. Nurse Reynolds is going to help you through a shower and give you your first dose of oral medication. She'll assess your limitations as well as show you how to care for your wounds."

"Okay, thank you."

The nurse helps me up. Never once does Sawyer make a move to assist, but he watches cautiously from the chair just in case. In the restroom, she helps remove my gown, and I gasp when I get a look at myself in the mirror.

I'm black, blue, and purple pretty much everywhere. After removing the bandages from my head, she proceeds to remove the rest from my lower legs, where lines of staples fill my skin.

"We want to keep these covered while you heal a bit more, but you can remove the bandages for the shower. You'll want to avoid taking a bath until after your postpartum recheck."

I'd imagined all of this so differently. Noah hovering over me in the hospital tending to my every need, acting every bit the proud father he would have been. As sobs wrack my body, I grab onto the safety bar on the wall.

With a sympathetic gaze, Nurse Reynolds nods toward the shower. "It will make you feel better even if it hurts. Do you want the shower chair, or do you think you can stand?"

I appreciate her for not making me feel weak, for not acting like I shouldn't be grieving, for not making me feel any more vulnerable than I already do.

"I think I'll be okay."

She lines up some toiletries on a shelf in the shower and turns on the water, then puts a shower bag over my cast. "I'm going to stand here. If you need help with anything, I'll get in with you. My scrubs can be easily changed if wet."

"Okay." As I step into the shower, the warm water feels like it's pelting my skin in rapid fire. It's on the softest setting, but fuck it hurts.

Between my painful hisses and my curses for not being able to get the shampoo in my hair properly, Nurse Reynolds takes it upon herself to step inside and help me. I'm too sad to be embarrassed about it.

"I have a daughter your age," she says as she soaps up my hair. "You remind me of her." She pulls the showerhead down and rinses my hair before conditioning it. "I was on duty when you were brought in. What you went through wasn't easy, and what you're going to have to go through next will be hard. I witnessed you giving birth to that little miracle in there and I know you've got a tremendous amount of fight inside of you. When you feel like you're at the end of your rope, please remember that." She sounds like she's speaking from experience, but I don't have a reply to give her.

After she finishes my hair, she steps back out and dries off a bit while I finish. Never once does she worry about her own comfort as she waits for me. After helping me dry off, she helps me into what she calls after-delivery panties and a fresh gown. I'm not sure I feel any better, but I do feel clean. The last of any physical particles from that night have been officially washed down the drain.

Mama is sitting next to my bed when we come out of the bathroom; she looks so tired and worn. It makes me feel guilty I'm here when Belle isn't. "Hey, baby girl, let me help you brush your hair."

My heart floods with love for her. "Mama, can I have a hug first? Please?"

With tear-filled eyes, she gently wraps her arms around me. "That I most definitely can do."

This woman is my world. The only one aside from Belle and Eli who has seen me through darkness before.

After Mama brushes my hair and helps me get settled in bed, Nurse Reynolds brings me some medications and I thank her for all her help. When she leaves, Karen and Owen come inside, followed by a girl who's about my age. They step aside to let the girl do her business; she seems nervous.

"Mrs. Weston, my name is Debbie and I'm from the hospital records department. I know the timing isn't the best but I need a moment of your time."

Sawyer comes closer and stands next to me with Nate, practically waiting to go in for the kill if she missteps. I can see the determination in his steely gaze.

"We need to verify that Nathaniel is your son's given name. It is what we're currently using on his medical records. This document is

D. Kelly

his official birth record. I need you to confirm the information, make any necessary corrections, and fill in the blank spaces."

I hold up my broken wrist so she can see the cast.

"Oh, in that case, I can fill it out for you. We'll have you sign it the best you can with your other hand once you confirm the information. We've completed the parent information already so you can let me know if there are any changes needed when you review it before signing."

Swallowing over the lump in my throat, I answer, "Okay."

"Is Nathaniel his given name?"

"Yes."

"What is the middle name going to be? Or does he have one?"

The memory of Noah and I deciding his name hits me hard.

"It's perfect. Nathaniel, it is. What about a middle name?" I asked him.

"What if we wait to meet him for that? We can make a list and see if his personality or his looks match."

"That's perfect, Noah. Did we really just name our little boy?"

He chuckles at my excited squeal. "Yeah, Mel, we sure did. I love you."

"I love you, too. Always."

"Noah. That's his middle name. Nathaniel Noah Weston," I tell her without a doubt in my mind. He looks just like his daddy and should carry his name.

Everyone around me is crying, but Karen nods frantically, as if my choice is the best thing she's ever heard.

"Okay, please look this over and we'll get it filed."

After reviewing the document, I sign it the best I can and she leaves. I'm so tired. Between the shower, the medicine, and the stress, all I want to do is sleep.

"Amelia, we need to talk to you about something," Owen begins, and Sawyer maintains his protective stance next to me.

"Baby girl, we need to plan the services and would like your input," Veronica finishes.

Services.

Plural.

My input ...

"Do whatever you want, but as far as my input goes ... closed to the public and a joint service. I can't do this twice. If that's okay with you guys, the rest of it is details I don't need to be a part of."

"Mel ..." Karen begins, but I close my eyes and shake my head.

530

"No, my husband and sister are … gone. I'm sorry if it's selfish, but I can't wrap my head around it. I don't need a funeral to understand. If it were up to me, there wouldn't be one."

My body begins to tremble as I feel the impending breakdown coming. "I'm not trying to be a bitch. I know people need closure. Make the arrangements and I'll be there. I'm just not capable of anything else right now. I'm sorry."

My sobbing steals my breath and my words as my body shakes uncontrollably. I'm not sure how Noah thought I was strong enough to make these decisions. I'm not. My strength came from him and now he's gone.

"Alright, Amelia, we'll take care of it," Owen says, effectively ending the conversation. "Also, the nurse brought this for you." Owen hands me a small bag.

I'm barely able to get it open, but my heart drops when I look inside. It's the last of Noah's effects. It's pointless to try to stop crying at this point.

"There's another bag with his clothes and shoes, but they're probably not in a condition for keeping," Karen adds softly.

I dump the contents onto the table in front of me—his wallet, his wedding ring, his eyebrow ring, and the guitar pick from Nate's birth announcement. He carried it with him for luck. *Whole lot of fucking good it did him.*

"Karen, can you keep these for me until we get home?" I want to put Noah's ring somewhere safe so Nate can have it one day.

"Of course," she replies.

"Thank you. Now, can someone please get me a wheelchair? I need to go to the chapel."

Mama reaches out for Nate and Sawyer gets the chair for me. After helping me into it, he pulls out his phone and texts someone.

"Is everything okay?" I ask, wondering what could be so important right now.

"Yeah, the rest of the hospital isn't as private as where we are. They're doing their best to keep people out, but I want Mac to clear the chapel just in case."

Fucking fans and fucking paparazzi. My sobbing has barely subsided but I'm suddenly filled with rage.

Once we're inside the chapel, Sawyer pushes me to the front where the candles are.

"You might want to move me away from those. I'm likely to burn this place to the ground given the chance."

He pulls me back to the end of a pew. "Do you want to sit?"

D. Kelly

"No, but you might want to leave for this." If I didn't know better, I'd swear he almost smirks at me.

"I'm not going anywhere, Mel. You do what you gotta do." He sits on the opposite side of room and he hunches down, rubbing his face with his hands. He looks like hell and I wonder if he's even slept.

"Mama always told Belle and me in our darkest hour we still have to find a way to get right with God. Because as much as God takes away, He's also the one who gives. So I'm going to get real with You right now, God. You're a motherfucking son of a bitch."

Sawyer draws in a sharp breath, but I don't care. My blasphemous soul can go to hell because it's not any worse than where I am right now.

"Who the fuck do You think You are? Why am I here? You've taken away everything and everyone I've ever gotten close to!" My chest heaves and my body aches, but it feels damn good to get angry. "Every time I let love into my heart, You rip it away. You should have just taken me and put me out of my misery. Instead, You took two of the best people I've ever known. I don't understand it and I won't … not ever. What have You ever given me? A family who was ripped away one at a time? A husband to love but only for a short while? A best friend who was a sister in every way that mattered …"

My sobs are relentless; I can barely breathe. Everything in my body hurts as my anger succumbs to sadness once again. "That beautiful baby boy who looks just like his daddy but doesn't have one anymore? What am I going to do with him? He *needs* Noah, asshole! He needs Noah …"

There's no point in pleading and screaming anymore. I'm never going to be right with God after this. With my head in my hands, all my grief comes pouring out. Eventually, Sawyer picks me up and carries me back to my room, leaving the chair behind.

Karen is sitting next to the bed, with a bottle on the table beside her. She's holding Nate and eyes me with a concerned gaze. When Sawyer puts me down, I'm still trying to catch my breath from all the crying.

"Amelia, I think it would be good for you to feed your son," Karen says as she tries to hand me the bottle.

"I'm tired and sore. If you don't want to do it, let the nurse do it." I'm exhausted; the last thing I want to think about is Nate.

"I'll do it, Mom. Why don't you try and take a nap," Sawyer says as he takes the seat next to her. With a hesitant glance thrown my way, she relents and gives the baby to Sawyer. My eyes are heavy and flutter closed as Sawyer takes over his brother's job.

The next morning, after a breakfast I barely touched, I'm given extensive discharge and follow-up instructions along with quite a few prescriptions. Karen is sitting in the corner with Sawyer and Nate and everyone else is on their way to the airport.

"Sawyer, can you give me a few minutes to help get Mel dressed?"

Sawyer picks up the car seat Nate is already snuggled in, sleeping peacefully. "I'll be right outside if you need me."

I can't move. I'm not even trying. There's no point because there's nowhere to go from here. "Come on, Mel, if you stand up we can get this done quickly," Karen says, and I notice her exhaustion for the first time. She's aged a decade in only a few short days and it's all my fault. I try to stand for her, but it hurts everywhere.

"Why are you helping me?" I wail as I sit back on the bed, exhausted.

"Oh, sweetheart," she replies with nothing but a mother's pure love reflecting in her eyes. "Because you're our daughter, and we love you. Noah would want us to help you through this."

"But I'm not family anymore, am I? He's gone and you're not obligated to help me. It's okay."

"Amelia, you will always be our family. No matter what, that will never change. You are Noah's wife, you are Nate's mother, and you are *our* daughter." Her voice cracks as tears begin streaming down her cheeks. "I know you're hurting, we all are. But listen to me when I tell you this … The only way out is through. I know you can't see it now, but until you can find your own way out, we will guide you through."

"Karen," I cry, collapsing onto her shoulder, "I can't do this without him. I can't live without him. We should have gone together and Belle should have lived."

"Shh," she whispers as her fingers weave through my hair. "There's no rhyme or reason to life, things happened the way they were supposed to. I'm going to miss Noah, for the rest of my life but he would have wanted you to live. I won't pretend this is going to be easy. But I will be here to help you, Amelia, every step of the way." I'm amazed at the way she's been keeping herself together for her family, but seeing her cry makes me feel even closer to her in this moment.

She unties the hospital gown and helps me get dressed. Somehow, I will my body to move enough to put on the pajamas she brought for me and climb into the wheelchair. I'm ready to go home … the thought of which sends me into a panic.

The door opens as I look up at Karen with fear-filled eyes. "Where am I going? I don't even have a place to live anymore. And Nate … Oh God, I don't even know where I'm going." As I lower my head into my hands, Sawyer sends Karen outside.

The next thing I know, he's crouched down in front of me, pulling my hands away from my face with his own tears covering his cheeks.

"You listen to me, Amelia Weston, my house is your house. It's *our* house. No one is making you go anywhere. You were Noah's wife and what was his is now yours. Nate's nursery is ready and waiting for him. You're family, Princess, get used to it. We're not letting you go anywhere."

"Okay," I manage to choke out through snot-filled sniffles as Sawyer passes me a box of tissues.

"Hang onto that, you'll probably need it."

"Thank you."

"Sure," he says.

"No, Sawyer, thank you for giving me a place to go."

"You don't have to thank me for that. Friends help friends and I need you right now as much as you need me. Without Noah … He was my everything, Mel, and you're the only one who truly gets that."

After a few moments of silence between us, Karen and Nurse Reynolds come inside followed by Mac.

"Are you ready, Amelia?" Nurse Reynolds asks.

Am I ready to leave the last place I ever saw my husband alive? I have no words for her so I just give her a slight nod.

"Mel, you should know there are still a lot of people outside. They're here for you and Nate." Sawyer's confession doesn't exactly surprise me and yet it does. But when we finally make it to the doors of the hospital, I'm shocked at exactly how many people are here. They're stretched as far as the eye can see. There's a mass memorial with candles and photos, offerings of love and support.

"I want to see that," I tell Sawyer, pointing to the massive display of love for Noah.

"Mel, I don't think that's a good idea," he cautions.

"Fine. Mac, push me over there, please. Karen, can you put Nate in the car?"

Sawyer grumbles and pushes my wheelchair to the other side of the drive where the memorial is set up. When we reach the front, a hush falls over the crowd and no one moves.

As I gaze over this display of love, I'm crying before I realize it. There are photos of Noah everywhere, but not just him. Most of them are of the two of us or of our first family photo. This is their way of acknowledging our family. Because they're still here even when he's gone, it says so much.

Finally, I look up at Sawyer, who is also crying, and tug on his arm. "What's going to happen to all of this stuff?"

"I guess someone will come along and toss it eventually." That's what I thought.

"Can you get someone to take all the bears and stuffed things up to the children's floor? And maybe collect the flowers and send them to patients who don't have any family here? And the photos and signs … get someone to send those to me." He looks at me like I've lost my mind.

"It's what Noah would do, Sawyer. It's what he'd want." Next, I turn to Mac.

"Feel like yelling?" I ask, and a small smirk picks up on the corner of his mouth.

"For you, anytime."

"Tell them thank you, that Noah would have loved their kindness, and to honor that we're going to give the flowers and toys to people inside the hospital but that all their notes, photos, and signs will be sent to me. And tell them …"

I'm not sure about this next part, I'll do it but for Belle.

"Tell them I'll update the *Slammed* blog when I'm feeling up to it with a proper thank you of my own."

I'm continuously wiping my tears away as Sawyer turns us around to face the crowd. They listen to Mac's words with rapacious attention. Most of them are crying just like us, and for one of the first times ever, I feel for them. They're suffering Noah's loss in their own way. Just because they didn't know him doesn't mean they didn't love him.

I don't miss the few reporters in the crowd, or the flashing of their cameras, but there's really no story here anymore. We're just a family grieving; they'll go away eventually.

Once we're at the car, Sawyer and Mac help me into the back seat where Nate is positioned in the middle between Karen and me. He's sleeping contentedly as if nothing is amiss, and I guess, in a way, for him it isn't. This is the only reality he will ever know. That thought alone sends my emotions into overdrive once again.

"Are Noah and Belle back home already?" I ask to anyone who will give me an answer.

"Sweetheart, they're flying back with us. The funeral home is meeting us there." With her words, my grief again bubbles to the surface. I'm still crying thirty minutes later when we reach our destination. Mac carries me onto the plane. I don't argue because I'm not sure I could have even made it up the steps. As Mac carries me to the far end of the plane, I'm overcome by the sadness shrouding all of their faces. Sawyer boards with Nate and straps him in between Karen and Owen. I'm glad; he's probably a comfort to them and right now he's an extra burden for me to deal with. Sawyer straps in next to me and then helps me with my seatbelt. As the plane takes off, my one good hand grips the arm rest and Sawyer peels my fingers off and holds my hand. He knows how scared I am to fly, but he doesn't release me when we level off in the sky. His head falls back onto his seat and his eyes are closed. Within minutes, he's asleep. If him holding onto me allows him some rest, I'll give it to him because I'm going to need his help over the next few weeks.

Everything Has Changed

As we all walk into the house, I don't know what to do. I feel Noah everywhere and just stand in the foyer like a lost puppy.

"Come on, Mel, why don't I help you get settled in bed. You need your rest." Eli's kind words wash over me as I follow behind him. When we reach my room, it's just as we left it after the Fourth of July, and it's suddenly too much.

Noah's shirt is tossed haphazardly onto the bed. Without thinking, I lift it to my face and inhale his scent. As I collapse onto the bed, I burst into tears once again.

Eli pulls me into his embrace. "Let it all out, baby girl. I'm here for you for as long as you need."

My eyes dart around the room, taking in all our memories. Noah had so many of our photos framed and put on the wall, the dressers, and the bedside table. Everything about this room screams "us." But "us" is no longer a thing.

"I don't want to be here, Eli. Why didn't I die, too?" I sob, clutching onto his shirt.

"It wasn't your time, Mel. If you had died, Nate would have, too. He's the reward of your love. Someday, when you've gotten past your grief, you're going to be thankful beyond words to have him with you."

"I love him, but I'll ruin him. I don't know how to be his mom."

Eli brushes my tears away. "The same way you loved Noah … with your whole heart. You'll learn the rest as you go, and I'm here as long as you need me."

"Thanks, Eli, but I think I need some time alone. Can you make sure someone is taking care of the baby, please?"

"Sure thing. I'll check back in a little bit. Try and rest."

He closes the door behind him and I walk to the dresser and pick up a framed wedding photo. Noah's eyes were dancing with happiness and mine were filled with love. We were blinded by it and I'd never been happier. There's a package next to it, and my stomach plummets as soon as I see the return address.

Taking the box with trembling hands, I sit on the edge of the bed. When I finally manage to get it open and pull out the album inside, my body slides to the floor. Noah and I were so excited about our maternity photo shoot. We haven't seen these yet, not even online proofs—the photographer was old school and preferred the element of surprise. I've only turned one page in the album, but the guttural wails falling from my lips are far louder than my previous sobs.

Within seconds, Sawyer is at my side. When he sees what I'm looking at, he drops to the floor next to me.

"Noah would have loved these."

His words hit straight to my heart. "Why is this happening, Sawyer? Why did we lose them? I'm so lost over Noah I haven't even begun to process losing Belle. And these pictures are everything we dreamed of but now they're literally just memories."

He rubs his eyes with his hands like I've seen him do so many times over the past few days. "I don't know, Mel. I don't have any answers for you. I thought after what I went through as a kid I'd been through a lifetime of heartache. But this ... it hurts so much more."

The two of us sit, drowning in our tears and grief as I numbly thumb through the pages of this album. They're everything Noah and I wished for when we had them taken. More than anything, I wish we could go back to that day. I want to be in the moment again where Noah is kneeling in front of me, kissing my belly, while he looks up at me adoringly. Nate's name was carved in the sand in front of us. It took Noah over an hour before he considered it photo-worthy. I just want to hear Noah tell us how much he loves us, one more time ...

"Sawyer," I say through my sniffles, "I know this is the worst timing, but was anything recovered from the bus?"

"You're worried about *things*?" he snaps.

His reaction makes me feel awful. "No, well ... not exactly. Our wedding album was on the bus. It's irreplaceable. And Noah's guitar, and my camera and laptop with all the pictures I'd yet to upload. They're my last memories, Sawyer. *Our* last memories."

I'd gotten so many more brother shots the last few days we were on the road and I can't remember if I uploaded them to my computer and backed them up to the cloud or not. But my wedding photos ... I can't lose those, too.

"I'm sorry, Mel, I honestly don't know. I'll find out for you, though. I promise."

J peeks his head inside the room, and my heart sinks. He's got huge black bags under his eyes and is incredibly pale. Noah was so excited for me to get to know Jordan better and I feel terrible we didn't get the chance before.

"How are you feeling, Mel?" he asks timidly, still lingering in the doorway.

"Probably no better than you but with some physical pain thrown in. How are you doing?"

With a shrug, he walks in and sits on the edge of the bed above us and looks down at the album in my hand. "I'm fucking numb. This kind of shit shouldn't happen to people more than once in a lifetime, especially to people like Noah."

"Amen to that, brother," Sawyer says as J looks over our shoulders at the photos.

"I'm going to miss his happiness so much. I hope Nate gets that from Noah most of all. No offense, Mel."

"None taken, J. I hope everything Nate becomes all comes from Noah." My answer quiets them, but it's the truth.

"Mom sent me in here because Diane and Rob just got here with the girls and some food. She's insistent both of you come to the table. Mel, Mom said you have to eat at least a few bites to take your meds and keep up your strength."

"Let's get this over with," Sawyer says as he stands and helps me off the floor.

"Go ahead without me. I'll be there soon. I need to use the restroom first."

I never realized how many muscles sitting, standing, and wiping involve just to take a fucking piss. When I'm done in the restroom, I take a look in the mirror. Aside from the cuts and bruises, Karen isn't the only one who looks like she's aged. I have, too.

As I step out in the hall, I'm pulled to the nursery. This room was supposed to be the happiest place in the house. What I didn't expect to see was Nate fast asleep in his crib. I cover my mouth to hold back my cries and watch him, wishing I could hold him and knowing I can't.

"You won't break him, I promise." Diane's tender words meet my ears as the tears escape my eyes.

"I'm pretty sure you're wrong about that," I whisper.

"Oh, Mel, I felt the same way with Saylor, but I promise it will get better. You'll see. You just need some snuggle time." She takes in my horrified expression and frowns. "You're the best thing for him," she states firmly.

"I got his dad and his aunt killed. I'm cursed, Diane, and the farther Nate stays away from me the better."

Within seconds, her arms are wrapped around me, her own tears falling against my cheeks. "There is no one in this world who could have loved my brother more than you did. Or Belle. Amelia, trust me ... this baby will be the best part of your life, but you can't shut him out. If not for you, and if not for him, do it for Noah."

"He'll suffer for it in the long run."

She places a kiss on the side of my head "No, Mel, *you* will. The only way Nate will suffer is without his mother's love."

I want to believe what she's saying. "I love him enough not to hurt him like that. I'm bad luck, Diane."

"Then so are we. Look at our tragic history. If you consider this bad luck, you have to account for ours as well. It's not luck at all, Mel, it's fate. And yours is to be the best mother you can be to Noah's son. For whatever reason, this is the way things are supposed to be. Don't waste a second being fearful because time waits for no one."

She releases me and walks toward the door. With a reluctant glance over her shoulder, she leaves me alone. As I look down upon Nate, I wish with all my heart things were different. His life was supposed to be so much better than this. Leaving him to sleep, I notice the baby monitor is on. At least someone is taking good care of him.

Feeling lost, I wander back into my room, forgetting why I got up in the first place. I sit down on the bed as Saylor appears at the door, the sadness on her face plain as day.

"Auntie Mel?" she asks cautiously. My appearance probably scares her.

"Hey, Ladybug."

She walks over to me and looks me over with her sad eyes, running her fingers across my cast.

"You're one big ouchie. Can I kiss you and make you better?"

The goodness in her reminds me so much of Noah. "You can try, but I've got a lot of owies and they might take a while to heal, even with all the kisses in the world."

She climbs up next to me on the bed, leans over, and kisses my cheek. "My mommy says Uncle Noah and Belle are in heaven now. I'm going to miss them, but I'm glad they're not there alone."

She's such a precocious child, but it's nice to talk to someone who isn't hovering over me.

"I'm going to miss them, too, sweetie."

She looks up at me with sad eyes, and I'm overwhelmed with the urge to hug her, so I do. Briefly. "Auntie Mel, Uncle Noah was the only one who called me Ladybug. Can you … still call me that? I don't want to ever forget him."

"We won't let you forget him, Saylor, I promise. But if you want me to keep calling you Ladybug, I will."

"Thank you. Grandma says you're supposed to come with me to eat dinner." With the determination of a grownup, she holds my good hand and tugs until I stand, leading me into the kitchen, never once letting me go.

Standing in this room, in the middle of everyone who was so near and dear to Noah and me, I'm at a loss. I feel their sadness, but I'm convinced the only ones who understand what I'm feeling are Sawyer and Darren. It makes me a judgy bitch because I know their loss is equally profound, but I can't find it inside of me to accept their pain is as large as mine.

Karen leads me to the table and sets a plate in front of me. "Karen, I …"

"Even a few bites, Mel. Just enough so you can take your medicine," she says, already knowing what I'm going to say. That's a mother's job, though, right? Belle would have been an amazing one. She would have helped me find my way and would be giving me so much shit right now for not hugging Nate and keeping him close. I just … can't.

Everyone is here. Eli is sitting with Rory, but his eyes are locked on mine. He was there when my mom died—he knows how bad it got—and he's worried because this is so much worse. Mama pulls up the chair next to me and lightly squeezes my thigh under the table. Marcus is right behind her with his hand on her shoulder. He's her rock; I'm comforted knowing she has someone who can take care of her when I can't.

Wyatt, Anna, Sawyer, Darren, J, Warren and Sam are all around the bar, and right next to Sawyer is Nate's baby monitor. Knowing Sawyer is so willingly stepping in when I can't–when Noah can't— reminds me of a conversation Noah and I had a few days after the wedding.

"Hey, Mel," Noah said as he stroked my arm while spooning me from behind. We'd just finished making love and I was beyond relaxed in his arms.

"Hmm …" I murmured, and he chuckled.

"Look, I know it's not the best time for this talk, but I think it's important after the Sara stuff. If something were to happen to us, who would you want to raise Nate?"

The seriousness of his tone made the hair stand up on my arms. I turned to face him. "I know you're a planner, but don't you think this is a bit much, Noah?"

His expression was pained just for a second before he flashed me a brilliant smile. "Humor me. I like to be prepared, and this is one of the most important preparations we can make."

"Alright, I guess if it were up to me I'd say Belle. She's the only person I know who would automatically fight for him if something went wrong. What about you?"

His green eyes met mine and his expression softened "Sawyer. There's not a soul on earth I would trust more."

Sawyer with a baby? I could understand his choice but still thought Belle would be more ... responsible. "Maybe they could share? I think Belle would be more structured, especially with Cadence."

"Yeah, maybe they could. Although, I think some responsibility would be just what Sawyer needs to put his head on straight."

Wrapping my hand behind Noah's head, I pulled his lips to mine. "It's a good thing we won't ever have to find out. You promised me a minimum of fifty years, Mr. Weston, and I expect to cash in each one of them."

"Good, because I don't ever make a promise I don't intend to keep and my vows are the most important promise I've ever made. I love you, Mel."

As I blink back my tears, my attention goes back to the baby monitor. Noah was spot on; I hate the fact I'm here to know that.

After eating a few tasteless bites, I push my plate away. Karen places my pills in front of me, which I take eagerly. All I want to do is go to sleep and dream of happier times. Mama helps me get ready for bed and after she hugs me goodnight, I reach out for her.

"I'm so sorry I couldn't save her." Unable to hold back the floodgate of tears that opens once again, she pulls me back into her embrace while she cries tears of her own.

"Oh, baby girl, it wasn't up to you to save her. That was up to God. Belle was my world and I'm struggling to accept this. The only consolation I have is the rest of you survived. Those babies were meant to carry on their parents' legacies. God gave us a part of them in these children, and I'm going to cherish every moment I have with them. Belle wouldn't want you blaming yourself. Hell, that girl would want you to throw a party honoring her life, not mourn her."

"Yeah, well, Belle didn't always have the most realistic expectations. I'm going to miss her, miss *them*, for the rest of my life." My sadness is overshadowed by my sleepiness as I release a yawn.

"Get some rest, Mel. I'll close the door behind me. We'll get each other through this, I promise."

After she leaves, I turn on the baby monitor next to my bed. Noah had to have the best of the best so he picked a monitor where there's basically a miniature video on each handheld portion. I think there are three, if I remember correctly. I have one, Sawyer has one, and Karen probably has the other. My eyes flutter closed as I watch Nate sleeping peacefully on the monitor.

"Mel, you have to wake up!" Hands are on my shoulders and my eyes snap open.

"Jesus, Eli, you scared me!" My heart is racing, my body drenched in sweat. "What are you doing here?"

"It's my night to take care of you." He points to the big cushy chair in the corner, where his pillow and blanket lie.

"I'm okay. I don't need a babysitter," I grumble.

"From that nightmare you were having, I'd beg to differ." He takes a seat next to me and hands me a cup of water from the nightstand.

"I was dreaming about the accident."

"Yeah, I could tell. Are you still seeing your therapist?" he asks hesitantly.

"No, it's been years."

"If things don't get better soon, you might want to start again. Look, I can't pretend to even understand what you're going through. But I do know what you went through when Iris died. This is … it's worse than that."

"I'll be fine, eventually … but I appreciate your concern," I reply as I hand him the cup.

"Will you, though? Be fine? Because I'd be a fucking mess. Hell, I *am* a fucking mess and this doesn't affect me nearly as much as it affects you. There's no shame in needing or asking for help, Mel."

"I'm not helpless, Eli! I'm lost, sad, terrified, broken, angry, and so fucking alone." I collapse onto my pillow and let the tears come again.

He leans down and kisses the top of my head before standing. "The last thing you are is alone, and I never said you were helpless.

543

You're one of the strongest people I've ever known, which is probably why you and Nate are still here with us. But even the strong need help. When we're broken and weary and the fight goes away from us, that's when our friends and families pick us up and carry us until we're ready to pave our own way again. Let us carry you, Mel, until you're strong enough to do it yourself. Let us be your family."

Eli takes his place in the chair again and curls up with the blanket. I do need their strength to carry me through. But without Noah's love, it all seems pointless. What could possibly be better on the other side of this grief without Noah and Belle?

Goodbye

It's been ten days since we left the hospital. Ten days with a house filled with people. Ten days of hovering and tears. Ten days of pain and frustration. And two full weeks without Noah and Belle.

I've spent two weeks in a medication-induced haze, watching my son from afar. I haven't held him, haven't fed him, haven't even changed a diaper, and no one has tried to make me. They know as well as I do that I'm detrimental to him. Hell, I'm pretty sure I'm detrimental to myself.

I spend most of my time in bed, ensconced in Noah's scent still lingering on the sheets and pillows. But for how much longer? How long will I hear his voice in my head? How long will I smell him as if he's right next to me? If I die today, I'll still hear him, still smell him, still picture him in my mind. But then there's Nate. I can't touch him, but I can't bear the thought of leaving him, either. Noah would hate me for these thoughts, so I try to push forward, one day at a time.

Each night, I watch the monitor as someone takes a rotation with my son. Even Darren spent a night juggling Cadence and Nate. He's hurting as much as I am but he finds solace in our kids where I only find pain. Everyone cries when they hold him. Poor Nate probably thinks excessive tears are a normal part of life.

Today is the day I've been dreading most—the one where we have to say goodbye to Noah and Belle. It's going to be a large service with only friends and family, but people have lots of "friends" in this industry. It's going to be hell, but it would have been anyway.

All the kids are staying with Rob's sister here at the house and her friend is coming to help her. They're both teachers by trade; I've been assured they will be fine with the kids. I'm a horrible mother because I never even asked otherwise and only nodded when I was told. I know Darren and Sawyer wouldn't leave these kids if they weren't going to be safe. Plus, there's so much security all over the place I don't think anyone could easily get in.

I've been so drugged up I haven't paid attention to the media, but even in my haze I see the stress Sawyer is carrying on his shoulders. Tony and Warren have been meeting with Mac and Ryan daily in the office, and whenever I walk into a room, the TV is quickly snapped off. It's not like I will be searching this up on the internet when my phone and laptop are replaced; I have no desire to do so. Any emails with press-related inquires will be deleted, just like they were when my parents died.

"Ready, Mel?" Sawyer asks, stepping up behind me. I stand up slowly, the bruises may be healing some but my body still feels like it was hit by a freight train.

Mama helped me get dressed earlier and I've been staring out the window ever since. It's been raining today, which is odd in the middle of summer, but it sure does make Veronica happy. She says only the best of the best get God's tears at their homegoings. Out of all of this, even as angry as I am, that somehow gives me comfort. Belle and Noah *are* the best of the best.

"I'll never be ready for this," I say, turning toward Sawyer. He's dressed nice but looks like hell.

"Yeah, I know the feeling. Look, I wanted you to know all the non-essentials are going home tonight. It's time we have some space and figure out what to do with Nate or how it's going to work when everyone isn't around. He needs some kind of normal, Mel. It's time." His words are soft and I know he's just trying to find his way, too.

"Whatever you think is best, Sawyer. This is your home."

"Don't do that. This is *our* home. What was Noah's is now yours, of that I'm sure. I … Fuck, this is hard. I need you here, Mel, okay? If you guys aren't here I can't be, either. Not alone without Noah. I meant it when I said we're in this together for as long as it takes."

"Yeah, okay."

Taking my hand, he leads me out to the limos waiting in the drive. There are two of them, and we're the last to get inside. I can't bring myself to look at anyone even though I feel like they're all staring at me. I close my eyes and rest my head against the seat and don't open them again until we arrive at the church.

At my request, we got here last so everyone is already settled inside. We're to enter through the back, which has been blocked off by police and private security. With my parents, I learned when you arrive first you have to listen to everyone's condolences twice—once when they arrive and again when they leave. This is better. I don't need to hear how sorry or sad everyone else is. I can barely handle my own grief.

We're ushered into the first two rows and I promptly lose my shit when my eyes catch sight of Noah and Belle's caskets side by side, with their larger-than-life photos next to them. Which in turn seems to cause a domino effect because everyone around me is now crying.

As I look at their photos staring back at me, it's almost like I'm separated from my body. Before I can stop myself, I'm standing.

Painstakingly slow, I make my way up to their caskets. Pausing, I lean my head against Belle's casket first and kiss it. I whisper so only she can hear me—at least that's my hope. "You will always be my sister, and I will love you forever, but never in a million years will I say goodbye to you."

As the tears stream down my cheeks, I make my way to Noah's darker casket. I lean across it with my entire body and put my ear to the wood and listen. I'm not sure how long I've been up here in front of everyone, but the hushed whispers grow louder. Eventually, Sawyer comes up and tries to comfort me, to see where my head is.

"Princess, let me take you back to your seat."

"No, Sawyer. I'm trying to listen. I can't hear it, but if I listen really hard I might be able to."

"What are you listening for?"

"His heartbeat, Sawyer. Why can't I hear it anymore?" I can hear Karen's sobs and a few others over my tearful plea, but if they'd just be quiet and let me listen maybe I could stop their pain, maybe … he's not really gone.

The next thing I know, I'm being lifted off Noah's casket and carried out of the room by Sawyer. Tears are streaming down his cheeks and mine, and I keep asking him why the entire time. As he sets me down on the couch in the visitors' room, he drops to his knees in front of me and takes my hand in his.

"Why, Sawyer?"

"I don't know, Mel, but he's gone, and he's never coming back."

Then Sawyer drops his head into my lap and sobs. I fold myself over him and cry with him because it's all we can do. We're two lost souls trudging through this miserable earth while the keeper of our hearts is on an entirely different plane of existence. At least I hope he is because if there's no heaven I won't ever see Noah or Belle again; I can never accept that.

There's a knock at the door and Mac steps quickly inside closing it behind him. "They're starting. Do you two want to come back out or …" Even Mac is at a loss. I've never seen him at a loss for anything.

"What do you want to do, Mel?"

"I don't know. What do you want to do?" I ask Sawyer, turning his words back around on him. Considering my current mental state, I probably shouldn't make the decisions.

"I'm not sure I want to go back out there, but I'm pretty sure Noah would do it for me. I can't go alone, Mel, so I'll stay here with you if you're not okay."

"I'm not okay, I'll likely never be okay again." The pouring rain outside catches my attention.

"Does she need a doctor?" Mac asks, and when I turn my attention back to them I see real fear in Sawyer's eyes. This day is hard enough; the least I can do is not make it any worse than I already have.

"No, I don't. I'll try not to let my crazy show anymore today. You're right. Noah would do it for you and he'd do it for me, too. So we'll do this for him."

"You're not crazy, Princess, you're just left behind. I understand," Sawyer says as he stands and helps me to my feet.

Mac ushers us back to our seats while everyone stares at us. They must all think I'm losing my mind after that. Who knows, maybe I am.

For the next hour and a half, we sit and listen and cry. The words spoken about Belle and Noah by friends and loved ones ripped me to shreds. There was so much I wish I could get up there and say because that's what best friends do, but I'm too lost inside my own head to even think coherently, let alone speak that way.

After the service, we drive straight to the graveside, where I stay in the car and watch from the window. No one fought me too hard after claiming pain and exhaustion; it wasn't a lie but it wasn't exactly the whole truth. I just don't have the fight left in me to see them bury the two people I love most in the world.

About halfway through the service, Eli joins me in the limo and knows exactly what I need. Wordlessly, he pulls me into a hug and lets me cry. We stay in this position long after the service is over— until the limo pulls up in front of the house. When he finally releases me, I feel alone instantly, but I better get used to it because this is my life now.

Everyone except Sawyer exits the car. When my eyes meet his it's like looking in a funhouse mirror. We're the same but different. Same grief, same vacant stares, same feeling of isolation, but I know he's the only one who hurts like me. No one else can understand this feeling but him and Darren.

"You ready for this?" he asks.

"Making small talk with people about my tragic loss and how happy I should be that our children survived? Yup. I've never been more ready for something in my life."

Sawyer snorts at my words and I actually laugh—so does he. Soon, we're both laughing so hard we're crying. It hurts like hell, but neither of our tears are from my words, just the oppressive sadness surrounding each of us.

He helps me from the car and the house is teeming with people. I turn to him and whisper in his ear, "I know I'm not supposed to drink with my pills, but if you want me to play nice someone needs to get me a shot of whiskey."

"I got you covered, Mel. One shot won't kill you, just wait an hour to take your pills. Deal?" Considering I'm not supposed to take them for at least that long, anyway, it's a no brainer.

"Deal."

He leads me to the sofa and has me sit next to Anna. Across the room, Darren already has Cadence in his arms like a shield and Mama has Nate. Sawyer brings me my drink and hands Anna one, too. Whiskey and Coke has never tasted this good.

"Karen would shit if she knew what was in your cup," Anna says with a light laugh.

"She probably would, but I'm sure she can understand my need," I say, nodding my head toward Karen, who looks miserable in the middle of a crowd of people offering their condolences. As I continue glancing around, I notice a girl hugging Sawyer. She's pretty, *too* pretty, and extremely handsy. Even after he released her, she's still touching his arm.

Anna follows my stare and groans. "What the hell is she doing here?"

"Who is she?"

"That's Lola. She briefly dated Noah in high school. It didn't take him long to figure out she wanted the twin experience, if you know what I mean."

"Together?"

"That's what *she* wanted, but neither of them were up for that kind of thing. So she thought she'd try and get them one at a time. After Noah dumped her, Sawyer didn't give her the time of day. She's always been an attention whore, so it doesn't surprise me she's here. She must have come with her brother. He was good friends with the guys back in the day."

"Guess she didn't get the hint back then." My eyes narrow as she loops her arm through Sawyer's elbow.

"Lola is bad news, Mel, and Sawyer is in a bad place right now. Let's just hope he remembers how much trouble she is."

"The last thing I need right now is some stupid trick trying to trap Sawyer at his most vulnerable time. Noah would never forgive me for letting that happen."

Anna's eyes soften with my words. "I never realized you were so protective of Sawyer."

"I'm protective of anyone Noah loved. But I love him, too. He's family and one of the very few people holding me together right now."

Anna's hand rests softly on my thigh. "Look, Mel, I'm here for you. I can't begin to replace Belle … and I wouldn't ever try, but if you need a friend I can be that for you. Besides," she pauses and looks around before continuing, "we haven't told anyone except for Wyatt and Warren, but Sam is bringing us back to the L.A. office. With everything that happened he feels we're needed here more so he found replacements for us in San Diego."

"Thank you, Anna. I appreciate that more than you know." I try to blink back my tears. "I'm sorry you have to come back. I know how important opening that office was for you."

"I'm not. I love San Diego, but this is my home. Actually, Sam is giving me the promotion anyway. We only had a year left, so this is a good move for me. It's just hard to be happy about it when my heart is broken. Noah was and will always be one of my favorite people."

"Mine, too," I whisper, leaning my head on her shoulder.

Darren walks over to us and stops in front of me. "Mel, can you hold Cadence for a few minutes, please? I have to take a piss and I don't want any of these people passing her around."

I want to say no but, between the pleading look in his eyes and the smile on Cadence's face, I can't. "Yeah, of course. Prop her against my cast so I can hold her steady with my good arm."

With a look of relief, he passes her to me with her binky and her bear. "Hey, baby girl," I say, and she keeps on smiling and cooing back. I haven't been around many babies, but she's always been such a happy girl.

"She's adorable," Anna remarks.

I nod. "She's Belle through and through. This isn't fair, Anna. None of this is fair."

Out of the corner of my eye, I see Darren talking to Sawyer with Lola hanging out in the background just waiting to pounce.

"No, it's not fair, but we can do our damnedest to make sure both these kids have the best life possible in spite of their rough start in life," Anna says as she squeezes Cadence's foot.

"Yeah, I hope so." Wyatt is heading toward us with Nate in his arms. Anna stands and points for him to take her spot next to me.

"I've got to go to the restroom. I'll be back." She places a kiss on his cheek before she leaves.

Wyatt and I have hardly spoken since the accident, and I'm suddenly overwhelmed with guilt. Watching as he holds Nate makes it worse. He's Noah's best friend and I haven't even thought about his pain. When I turn to look at them, Nate is smiling in his sleep. It's the first time I've ever seen him do it and trying to hold back my tears is pointless.

"My God, he looks even more like Noah when he smiles." My heart is racing; I'm doing everything I can to keep from losing my grip on Cadence.

"He does," Wyatt concurs and then looks me in the eye. "Mel, I'm sorry I haven't been around much for you. I wanted to be, but …"

"You're lost in your grief. I get it, Wyatt. I feel the same way. No apologies are needed."

"Thanks. Do you think I can … I'd like to stay in Nate's life and yours. I don't think I could handle losing you guys, too."

"Wyatt, you're family. Noah loved you and I love you. I expect you to be in our lives. Noah would want you around Nate for as long as you're willing. These kids are going to have a lot of people looking out for them and they're going to need it."

"So how are you recovering?"

"Slowly, but the physical pain is nothing compared to the hole in my heart. I'd take on this kind of pain for the rest of my life for just a few more minutes with Belle and Noah."

Wyatt looks back down at Nate and tucks his blanket around his arm. "Yeah, I don't even know how you're standing. I'm barely hanging on without Noah. I can't imagine if I'd lost Anna, too."

"It sucks."

"You can say that again. If you need anything, call me. Even just to talk. Besides, I'm pretty sure you're going to want to collect on that favor I owe you."

His words make me chuckle a bit. "I'm sure you're right. I'll hold you to that someday."

"Eventually, we'll all be okay. Noah would want that. He'd want it more than anything."

"I know, Wyatt. I just don't know how to move forward right now."

"Me either, Mel."

We sit together in mutual silence, holding onto these kids for dear life. As much as I try to block it out, voices carry in this big house and I'm reminded how thoughtless people are when they don't think you're listening.

"She should sell her story to the media. There are enough of them outside, she could make a mint."

"Who do you think got his organs? Will there be some kind of tell-all about the celebrity transference?"

"Why isn't she holding her own baby?"

"Did you see the way she lost it in the church? Someone should really have her committed."

This is why I don't talk to people I don't know … because they're assholes.

Hours later, almost everyone has left. Lola finally took her cue to go after slipping Sawyer her number. I hope to God he has the good sense to throw it away. Tony has requested to talk to the band and family before he leaves, so we're all gathered around the kitchen table and he's pulling a stack of envelopes out of his briefcase.

"Normally, I'd do this in my office, but Noah was specific in his requests of how he wanted things handled."

I can't breathe. We just buried him and we're already talking assets? I fumble my way into a chair and take a seat, clutching onto the arms of the chair for support.

"In each of these envelopes there is a video from Noah on a USB stick. He made these two days after the wedding. In your own time, when you're ready, watch your video. He's left each of you something in his will and there's a letter inside breaking down your inheritance. When you're ready, come talk to me and we'll put things in motion."

My tears are falling in rapid waves as Sawyer's hand clutches my shoulder. He needs comfort, too, but I can't give it to him right now.

"Why so soon?" I manage to choke out.

Tony shrugs. "It's what Noah wanted. He didn't want things to linger and wanted everyone to be able to move on quickly."

"Excuse me," I say, scrambling to my feet and moving as fast as I can to the backyard. Taking a seat on the edge of the grass, I stare out at the ocean. I can't do this; I can't go on without him. The thought of even trying has my stomach churning so hard and fast I barely have time to stand and lean over the wall before throwing up on the bluff below.

"Here," Tony's voice comes from behind me. He's handing me a handkerchief to wipe my mouth.

"Thanks."

He's got one large envelope in his hand with my name on it—in Noah's handwriting.

"I'm sorry, Mel. I thought it was too soon, too. But Noah had a mind of his own. There's no time limit on this … watch it whenever you're ready. If you need money or anything before you're ready to watch, let me know. The bulk of Noah's estate is now yours and Nate's."

"What if I'm never ready?"

His eyes soften as he nods in understanding. "Then I'm happy to talk over the estate with you whenever you might be ready for at least that. Also, there's a video for Belle. I gave it to Darren, with explicit instructions to let you watch it if and when you want to."

"Okay."

"I thought he was crazy, you know? I thought he was just being prepared like we always were, but he insisted something was going to happen, almost like he knew it was coming."

"What? He thought he was going to die?" My stomach lurches again and I grip the wall for support.

"He didn't tell you." Remorse flashes over his face. "Shit, I'm sorry, Mel. I assumed you knew. After Sara, Noah had this doomsday feeling. He saw his doctor and they thought it would get better, just some sort of PTSD from the shooting. Noah couldn't shake the feeling, so he was hoping for the best and preparing for the worst. He told me he was going to talk to you about it, but with the baby and everything … he was probably waiting for the right time."

"He must have been so scared."

He shakes his head. "I don't think so. Noah had never been happier than the last year after he met you. He told me he had everything he ever wanted in the palm of his hand and was holding onto it forever."

Forever.

"Well, our forever didn't last very long, but I'll cherish every second we did have for the rest of my life."

"Let me know if you need anything, Mel. I'm only a phone call away." Tony pulls me into a quick hug and releases me before handing me my envelope and heading inside.

I grab a bottle of water from the table and rinse my mouth a few times before sitting back down in the chair. The sun is setting; it's a beautiful sight. Noah and I thought we would have infinite sunsets together out here like this. Instead, this is the first of many without him.

Long after the sun goes down, I finally go back inside. Sawyer is sitting at the kitchen table next to Darren and both of them are staring down at their envelopes. I toss mine next to theirs, grab the bottle of whiskey between them, and pour myself a shot. After tossing it back, I take a seat across from Sawyer.

"Is everyone gone?"

He looks up at me with bloodshot eyes. I'm not sure if it's from the alcohol or his sadness, but my guess is the latter. "Yeah. The family is gone. Wyatt, Anna, and J are in their rooms."

"Hey, since you're both here, I'd like to talk to you about something," Darren says, pulling our attention to him. "I know it's a bad time, and you're going to have to adjust to a new normal, but I was wondering if you care if me and Cadence stay here indefinitely. If it's not cool, I get it—"

"Darren, you are welcome to stay here forever, if need be," Sawyer replies without a second thought, and Darren turns his attention to me.

"Belle was my sister and that makes you my brother. You don't have to go anywhere, Darren. You and Cadence always have a home wherever me and Nate are. Besides, it will be nice having them grow up together. They can share the nursery."

He shakes his head. "No, that's okay. I like having Cadence with me. I'll just put a crib in my room."

"Speaking of ... Mel, I don't want this to be uncomfortable for you, but Diane told me what you said about being unlucky." The softness of Sawyer's words surprises me. I figured he'd be angry. "You're not cursed, Princess."

"No, you're not," Darren adds.

"Thanks, guys, but I'm not sure I'll ever agree with that."

"Maybe not, but you're going to have to get over it. Nate has one parent, Mel. Fucking *one*. And it's you. I'll help you for as long as you need, especially while you're healing and on medication. But we're going to have to wean you into Nate's life a little at a time here.

It's not fair to make him suffer because you're afraid. You have to get over yourself."

"Get over myself? I'm trying to protect him!" I scream and pour myself another shot, knocking it back before continuing my rant. "If I had never agreed to go on tour, if I had never let Belle convince me to go to your show, Noah would be alive! Belle would be alive! And none of us would be feeling this soul-crushing grief!"

"I know you need to get it out, Mel, but you're not the only one with regrets. I wish I'd never convinced Noah to do one last tour. If I hadn't been so selfish and wanted closure, this would have never happened."

"If I hadn't been a selfish prick and wanted Belle and Cadence with me every second, they wouldn't have been there, either. This is no one's fault, except for the asshole who took out your bus."

"If the three of us have this much bad juju combined, this house is going to slide right off this bluff and into the ocean," I reply dryly, attempting a joke.

"At least we'll all go together. Until then, we're going to figure this out, okay?" I can tell by Sawyer's tone he's hanging on by a thread.

"Okay," I answer with a resigned sigh.

"Okay," Darren replies. "We do this together, all of us."

D. Kelly

Empty Spaces

Over the next four weeks, we develop a routine of sorts. Someone is always at the house during the day to help with me and the babies. Usually, it's Karen. About a week after the funeral, she and Owen retired. Not because Noah left them financially solvent, but because they want to live the rest of their days with no regrets. Eventually, they plan to travel, but right now they're hovering over all their kids and grandkids–the kind of love-filled hovering everyone needs right now.

I've weaned myself off all my medications except the anti-anxiety drugs. My back still hurts but unless it's a really bad day, ibuprofen is all I will allow myself. I want to feel the pain and not be lost in a fog. I'm still having nightmares about the accident. Whoever is on night duty with the kids is usually on night duty with me, too. I feel helpless, but in a way, it's a good thing because I can withdraw and not deal with things and no one gets upset with me.

At night, when I'm not sleeping, I watch the monitor and listen to Sawyer talk to Nate. Darren refuses to give up night duty with Cadence, but she's also sleeping for longer stretches now that she's eating some solid foods. He still gets up with Nate every other night so Sawyer can get some rest. I've been able to skate most of my duties and still haven't held my son, but my cast comes off later today and I'm sure that's going to change really soon. I'm terrified.

Right now, it's three in the morning and Sawyer is singing to Nate. I relish finally hearing Sawyer sing solo and uninhibited and I love watching the tenderness between the two of them. Nate has no idea Sawyer isn't his dad–his protector. But it breaks my heart at the same time because this should be Noah's time with his son. The bonding he always craved. His chance to tell his son all the things he wanted. Instead, Sawyer tells Nate a story. It's a slightly different variation each night, but I love listening to it. Once Sawyer finishes singing and feeding Nate his bottle, he changes his diaper and sits down with him and story time commences.

"Once upon a time, there was a famous rock prince named Noah. One day, Noah met his match in a true-life, rock-royalty princess named Amelia. The first time Noah saw Amelia, he knew he wanted her to be his queen, but Princess Amelia wasn't so sure. Sometimes, princesses come from lands filled with ogres and not even the most handsome prince can break down their walls. But Prince Noah won her over with his friendship and, eventually, his love. When Princess Amelia finally gave in to the prince, they had a magical love affair. Their love created a new tiny prince. That's you, Prince Nate. Prince Noah and Princess Amelia were never happier. Then, one of those nasty, mean ogres came and took Prince Noah and his friend Belle away. This made everyone in the rock kingdom very sad, especially Princess Amelia. To ease her sadness, all of Princess Amelia's friends and family helped pick up the slack until she started to feel like herself again. One day soon, Nate, your mommy is going to realize her little prince is her whole world. Until that day comes, we're going to keep loving you enough for both the prince and the princess."

Every time Sawyer tells Nate the story, he falls sound asleep in Sawyer's arms by the time the story is over. The sight of them together fills me with love. Knowing Nate is loved by so many, when I can't even bring myself to show him how much I love him, makes the pain a bit better. After Nate is asleep in his crib, Sawyer comes to see me. Some nights we talk, and some nights I pretend to be asleep. Tonight, I pretend to be asleep.

The bed sinks down next to me and Sawyer lies down. With a soft sigh, he begins to speak. "He's getting so big now. I mean, I know he's only six weeks old, but his eyes are already green and bursting with the same happiness Noah's had. It's like being with him gives Noah back to me in a small way. Princess, I wish you'd let yourself love him. He needs you."

Sawyer pauses and turns over, facing me. Even though I'm facing the wall I can still feel him at my back as his fingers brush against the bottom edges of my hair.

"I'm not sure at what point you need an intervention, Mel. I don't know if this is grief, if it's post-partum depression, if it's really your fear of being jinxed. Whatever it is, I'm failing Noah. He wanted me to take care of you two and I'm trying so hard. It kills me to see you doing this to yourself, but I get it, too. I miss the fuck out of Noah. You and Nate make it a little easier for me, and I wish we could make it easier for you. Instead of sitting around all day listening to that sad playlist of death songs you made and watching videos of you guys, you need to focus that energy into your son, Mel.

"I'm lost here and I need a fucking sign. Something to show me what I can do to help you because I don't think enabling you to ignore Nate is the way to go. But when anyone mentions how withdrawn you are, I lose my shit on them because I understand that, too. You lost your husband, your best friend, and your fresh start. I lost my brother, my best friend, the other half of my soul. I want you to go at your own pace, Princess, but I'm not sure how much longer I can carry us both."

With those last words, Sawyer kisses the top of my head and leaves. When he does, I allow myself to fall apart.

Getting my cast off was surreal. It was the last visual reminder of the accident. My pain is still real, but my staples and stitches came out weeks ago. My bruises are gone, and the only re-check I need is for my back. Sure, the physical scars will always be there, but the mental scars will never go away, either.

When I walk inside the house, I find Rory and Eli visiting with Karen. Sawyer and Darren are on the floor with the kids, and I say a quick hello before going to my room. A few days after the funeral, a new computer and phone showed up, along with a copy of my wedding album. Sawyer ordered them for me in the midst of all the hell we were going through, just like Noah would have.

We're supposed to get all the stuff back from the bus as soon as the investigation is officially closed, which Tony swears should be any day. Thankfully, Noah's guitar wasn't on our bus like I had thought. It was on Darren's bus since they practiced there before napping that day. One day, Nate is going to be able to have his dad's prized guitar; it gives me a bit of peace I didn't have before.

Back when my mom died, my dad was consumed with his grief. We both were, but in different ways. I found more solace in my friends, and Dad found solace in watching interviews, movies, videos, anything he could watch where he could see her, hear her, and enjoy her presence one more time.

I gave him a lot of hell for it—called it unhealthy, begged him to move forward for all of us—but it was futile. His drug and alcohol use became excessive, a way to escape the pain when he couldn't be with her. I never understood why he tortured himself. I wanted to be enough to get him through because I was still here. And he loved me, I know he did, but not in the way I needed to be loved back then. I needed my dad but he was already lost.

Now, I understand. I can't *not* listen to Noah sing, can't stop watching videos and interviews. Snippets of the two of us together are fleeting, but they exist. We have more photos than anything. But our wedding video is my favorite; I can watch it in a twenty-four-hour cycle and not tire of it. Sometimes, I curl up in one of his shirts and spray it with his cologne while listening to the EP he made me for Christmas. I just need to feel Noah, and since Nate has family taking care of him, he doesn't need me, especially not now. I'm too hurt, too sad, too lost inside of myself, living in memories. Functional people should be with him, not me. I know the day is going to come when I have to stop watching, stop wallowing, and start being a mother. But for now, I'm just happy Nate is too young to understand, to know what I went through when I lost my parents. Even if he's missing my love now, he won't remember it. I hope.

There's a knock on my door and Rory sticks her head inside. "Can I come in?"

"Sure," I reply, sitting up on the edge of the bed. Rory sits next to me and takes a look at my computer screen before shaking her head. "What, Rory?" I ask in an exhausted tone. I'm positive she's going to jump my shit.

"Mel … I know it hurts. I miss Noah, too. But what you're doing isn't okay. You have to live for him."

"Don't tell me how to feel, Rory, or how to live. He was my entire world." My seething words don't even make Rory flinch.

"Noah believed in fate above all else. I have to believe in that, too … for him. He'd want us to focus on the positive things."

"What positive things could there possibly be?!" I'm yelling now, but fuck her for trying to tell me to focus on the positive.

"Come on, Mel. I know it hurts, but be fair here. Even if it wasn't good for us, good *did* come from this tragedy. A father of three got his heart and is able to raise his kids. Two teens with congenital defects got his kidneys, two visually impaired women each got a cornea, and a young mother got a liver. Six people, Mel. Six lives enhanced and spared because of Noah, even more if you count their families."

I never wanted to know about the people Noah saved. Not yet, anyway, because I knew it wouldn't sink in the way it should. Instead of finding some solace in those facts I'm filled with a furious rage I'm all too happy to unleash on her.

"What about my son, Rory? What about him? Doesn't he deserve for his father to have been spared? What did he do wrong that he's going to have to grow up without the only person who wanted

D. Kelly

him before he was conceived? Does Belle's daughter deserve to grow up without a mother? It should have been me. I lost my husband and my best friend. My God, it should have been me, too. Why couldn't we have gone together?"

In a flash, Rory jumps up. I see it coming, but I'm stunned. Rory fucking slapped me. "Stop being a selfish bitch! Get your ass up and out of bed. My brother didn't stay with you so you could waste away. Noah begged Sawyer to stay with you and Nate. Live for *them*. Live for Belle, for Noah, put some good back into the ether. Acknowledge the fact there's a whole family … hell, a whole goddamn *world* who lost him. You're not in this alone. We can't lose you, too, so wake the fuck up and let us help you. Live with us, cry with us, laugh with us, build his legacy with us, so people will never forget!"

"You slapped me," I say numbly.

"Fuck, Mel, did you even feel it?" she asks as she shakes her hand out.

"Not really," I answer, and she starts crying.

"That's the problem. You're lost inside somewhere. We're *all* hurting, but we're checking in. You're completely checked out. If you can't let us help you, you're going to have to get professional help."

My mind flashes back to Sawyer's words last night. They're right. Karen and Sawyer are standing at the door and Sawyer's eyes are flaring with anger.

"Did you really just slap her?!" he screams at Rory.

She nods. "I'm sorry, I just didn't know what else to do. She's lost! Noah would kill us if we let her continue down this path."

"I'm sorry, I didn't mean to be a burden to you all … I'm going to go for a drive and clear my head. I'm not mad, Rory. I just need some time." Pushing past Sawyer and Karen, I grab Noah's keys and my purse and leave.

My hands tremble as I get behind the wheel of his car. I've never driven it, haven't even been inside of it since we were home for Fourth of July. It smells like Noah, like home. I've got a plan, even if I'm not sure how to execute it. The first thing I do is go to Target and buy a sleeping bag, a flashlight, and some water. Next, I go to the bank and get cash. Lots of cash.

When I pull up to the cemetery, they're closing the gates. As the guard goes to lock the side entrance, I catch his attention.

"If you forget to lock this gate tonight I'll give you a thousand dollars."

He takes in my appearance, the sleeping bag, and my bottle of water. It's probably my sunken eyes that sell him on it, though.

"If you're not out by five a.m. I'll be in trouble."

"I'll be gone by then, I promise."

He holds out his hand and I pass him the money. "I'm sorry for your loss. I've been a fan of Bastards and Dangerous for a long time." The gate closes behind me with his words.

"Thank you," I whisper before walking toward where Belle and Noah are buried. My phone continues to go off with message after message and I pull it out to silence it before putting it back in my pocket.

This is the first time I've been here since the funeral. Pushing aside the flowers covering their graves, I lay out the sleeping bag between them. I'm half on Belle and half on Noah, but I face her first.

"Hey, Belle. You have no idea how much I miss you. I must talk to you a million times a day, but it's not the same when you don't answer." I reach my arm out and lay it over the grass as if she can somehow feel me. Wishing I could feel her.

"Do you remember the night Sara shot me? You rushed into the hospital screaming for your sister and told me if I died it would have sucked. Well, it fucking sucks big, hairy balls. I miss you so much. Your laugh, your jokes, your never-ending positive attitude."

Pausing, I pull some tissues out of my pocket and take a sip of water.

"I've tried to find some comfort in knowing you're not alone. That you and Noah went together, and for as long as your family looked after me, my family can now look after you. But then I see Cadence smile or crawl … because she's doing that now … and I become angry you're not here for it." My voice cracks as I try to choke back my sobs. "I hear your screams in my head, and in my nightmares, and I know your death wasn't easy. You didn't deserve to go out like that, Belle. You were such a good mom, a great partner, and the best sister and friend I could have ever asked for.

"You'd be so ashamed of me now. Both of you would. I'm worse than a horrible mother, I'm a completely absent one. I haven't held Nate since before Noah died. I haven't sung him a lullaby, or told him any stories, haven't even tried to make him smile. But Belle … his smile is all Noah. His eyes are Noah's eyes, his personality is Noah. He's everything I could have wished for, and all I want to do is hold him and love him, but I'm so scared.

"Without me, he'll have a chance at a normal life. Don't worry, I'm doing my best to keep my distance from Cadence, too. I don't want the black cloud of death that follows me hovering over our babies."

D. Kelly

Sighing, I run my hand over her headstone. "I'm trying to protect them, Belle. Maybe it's wrong, but it's all I know how to do. I love them so much, and I love and miss you more than I ever thought possible. Darren has a handle on it all, though. You'd be so proud of him, he's a great dad. Please give my family hugs from me, especially Noah. I'd ask you to take care of him, but I have a feeling he's taking care of you all."

It's dark outside now, the moon is full, and the stars are bright. I haven't felt this peaceful in a long time. Too bad I didn't bring my pills. I could have taken them all right here and died at peace under the stars with my two best people. Noah would say it was fate that I didn't bring them. I'm going to call it a missed opportunity.

I sit up for a bit and lean against Noah's headstone.

"I'm not sure why I'm here, Noah, other than I got my cast off and can finally drive. Rory and I got into a fight today, but I'm sure you already know that. I know she's right, and deep down in my heart I know you'd be so disappointed in me. Nate is this perfect little innocent human, but I don't think he's hurting any without me. You'd be so proud of Sawyer, though. You were right, too. He would have been the perfect guardian for Nate should something have happened to the two of us. You don't know how much I wish that were true. I'm lost, Noah, somewhere deep inside myself. I move through the days, I eat tasteless food, I shower, and then I drown in our memories. I don't know how to be thankful for life anymore. I'm too bitter, angry, and sad to even try. Your mom keeps telling me 'the only way out is through,' and maybe she's right. But I don't want to go through. I want to drown in the darkness and stay in your arms for eternity."

There's a light breeze and I swear I smell Noah, but it's probably just the lingering scent from his car on my clothes. Even so, it makes me feel like maybe his spirit is here with me somehow. I've been here a long time; I'm sure Sawyer is worried, but I need this. Being here reminds me of a conversation Noah and I had in Vegas on our first trip.

"What's your dream now?" I asked him. "I mean, you've accomplished more in twenty-eight years than most people do in a lifetime."

"I want a life. A domesticated one. My sister Diane and her husband Rob are happily married. My nieces are the light of their lives. I want that. I want a legacy, kids to love and carry on my life cycle. I want to grow old with someone and take care of them during all the shit life throws our way, knowing she'll take care of me, too. I know it sounds morbid, but it's easy to love someone through the

good times, but the ultimate test of love is making it through the bad and coming out on the other side stronger than ever."

"It's not morbid. That's as real as it gets. Too many people give up, they don't fight, and they let go of the best part of their lives so easily. In the heat of the moment, everything seems so black and white, but life isn't black and white at all. It's in those shades of gray where we all get lost, question our morality, make the bad choices that affect the rest of our lives. Those make-or-break decisions are the crux of our being, and having the right person by your side is everything."

He kissed me with such passion after that. My heart was beating so fast I thought it was going to explode. Now, I feel like my whole life is just one huge blob of gray. I'm haunted by the past, by our memories, but were they all just an illusion to begin with? Noah believed in fate, but how could anyone be so evil to give us everything and then tear it away so quickly? What plans could fate possibly have for me that would make that okay?

Another memory slams into me so hard I lose my breath. One night on the bus we were all drinking and playing a game. It was only a few weeks into the tour. I don't think Wyatt could have ever known how prophetic his question would be.

We slammed down what had to be our fifth shot and I knew if I had more I'd pass out or throw up. Maybe both.

"Alright, my turn to ask a question!" Wyatt yelled out.

"Shh. Dude, not so loud, that was my ear you just yelled into," Sawyer replied, rubbing his ear.

"Yeah, yeah, suck it up, buttercup. If you had the choice of having every happiness handed to you for a limited time, or never knowing happiness at all, which would you choose?"

Sawyer whacked Wyatt on the back of the head. "What a stupid fucking question. Why would I want something only to have it taken away? I'd rather never have it at all."

"I'm with Sawyer," I told them with a slight slur to my words. "Don't give me something and take it away. It's only going to piss me the fuck off."

"Depends on what it is," Darren said. "I mean, if it's some really good pussy, I'm cool with having that for a limited time. But if it's, like, really good pussy, who is also a cool-ass chick and someone I could spend my life with and not get sick of ... yeah, fuck that. Don't give me that and then take it away."

D. Kelly

"You guys are dumb. I'd be sad as fuck if someone took Anna from me, but I wouldn't give up our time together for anything. She's my every happiness."

"Aww, Wyatt, you're so fucking sweet. I want that someday. Some guy who talks about me to his friends the way you do about Anna even when she's not here." As I leaned my head against Darren's shoulder Noah looked over at me and grinned. *"You didn't answer."* I said, pointing at him.

"You should know my answer. Fate gives and she takes away, but I'm going along for the ride as long as it lasts. If I were lucky enough for someone to give me every happiness, I'd enjoy it while it lasted, cherish every second, and worship her every day. Some people don't ever get that."

"Sometimes, I wonder how the two of you came from the same womb. You're night and day," Darren said, laughing.

"We're alike in all the ways that matter," Noah replied, and Sawyer agreed with a slight nod.

"Damn, Noah, did we jinx ourselves with that conversation? I miss you so much. It's only been six weeks and the pain gets worse with each passing day. I can't handle much more of it. I want to be with you and Belle. But whenever I consider it, leaving and joining you two, something stops me. Or should I say someone?

"Your legacy, Noah. I wish you were here to see him. He's the absolute best of you, and even though I'm afraid to fuck him up, he's still mine. He's my link to you and … I don't think he'd ever forgive me if I left him. I don't think I'd ever forgive myself, either, no matter how much I want to be with you."

My tears are flowing freely as I pull my phone from my pocket and set the alarm for four in the morning. It's already after eleven. I didn't realize I'd been here thinking for so long. It's nice being somewhere peaceful where no one is constantly hovering over me. Ignoring all the missed calls and messages, I tuck myself into the sleeping bag and lie down.

"This isn't the kind of sleepover I ever expected to have with the two of you, but I guess I'll take what I can get right now. Maybe I've officially lost my mind because sleeping in a cemetery alone, with my best friend and husband buried beneath me, is probably proof I've lost all my marbles. How would you handle this, Noah?"

Noah would do exactly what Darren is doing, what any other normal human being would do—he'd be cherishing his time with Nate. As I curl up into a ball, the torrents of tears and sobs come harder and faster. Breathing hurts, everything hurts, but it feels good

564

to get it out. Letting the grief rip out of me and soak into the soil beneath me feels almost like Noah is helping me through.

I've been out here a long time. I should probably feel guilty for worrying them, but I haven't had this much uninterrupted time to myself since the accident. It's cathartic, but I feel like this is going to be my life from now on. Shrouded in an endless pit of grief. Is that a life worth living? I'm not so sure it is.

"Fucking hell, Princess!" Sawyer's voice travels through the night, but I'm convinced I'm imagining it until he lifts me into his arms. I thought I was dreaming him and I wonder how long he was yelling before I woke up. "Are you okay, Mel?" he asks, his tone much softer now as he clutches me to his chest, sleeping bag and all.

"I'm lost, Sawyer. I'm just so fucking lost." My words are muffled between sobs.

"Me, too, Mel, I got you, okay?" Sawyer takes me to his SUV and sets me inside, pulling off the sleeping bag so he can strap me in. The clock on the dash says it's two in the morning.

Once Sawyer pulls away from the cemetery, he turns his attention to the road. "You can't disappear like that, Mel. Do you have any idea how scared I was?"

"I'm sorry. I just had to escape … Rory and just everything … I needed to breathe, Sawyer. Noah's video taunts me from where it sits unopened on the dresser, Nate weighs so heavily on my conscience. I don't know how to live anymore, Sawyer, but I don't know how to die, either!"

Sawyer whips the truck to the side of the road, slams on the brakes, and turns to face me. "You don't get to die, Princess. Not now, not on my watch. We will figure out a new way to live and it starts tomorrow for both of us. If you don't want therapy yet, I can respect that, but I'm done giving you the easy way out. Tomorrow, you are going to start being the mother you're supposed to be. You'll do it for you, for Nate, for Noah, and for me because I can't do it all by myself anymore, Mel. I can't be alone."

Sawyer drops his head to the wheel of the car and his chest heaves as he sobs. Reaching over, I pull his hand away from the wheel with mine. When he turns to me, I unbuckle my seatbelt and throw my arms around him. We stay like this, hugging, for a long time. Long after both of us have stopped crying. Eventually, he releases me and I put my seatbelt back on. Once we're both strapped back in, he pulls out onto the road heading home.

"How did you find me?"

"Tracked Noah's car. I knew where you were for hours, but I thought you needed time. Once it hit midnight, though, I started to worry something had happened to you."

"Something did. I think I officially lost my mind tonight."

Sawyer looks at me and shakes his head. "Maybe you're finally getting it back. The last few months have been hell, Mel. We're all bound to break at some point, but it's what we do *after* the break that defines us."

"I'm going to need you, Sawyer."

"I'm not going anywhere, Princess."

We spend the rest of the ride lost in our thoughts, but every so often I catch him looking at me with a worried expression on his face. It reminds me of the time Noah disappeared to see Sara's parents; and it makes me feel like shit. The last thing I want to do is worry Sawyer.

When we walk inside, Darren is pacing. He turns and pulls me into a huge hug. "Are you okay?"

"Yeah, I guess I am."

"You should have hit her back," Darren says angrily.

"She didn't deserve to be hit, she was doing what she thought was right. We're all just doing what we can. I get it."

Sawyer crosses his arms. "I told Rory to stay away for a while, Mel. No matter what she was trying to accomplish, she didn't have the right to hit you. Not now, not ever."

"I'm going to lie down. Goodnight, guys."

As I walk down the hall, I pass my room and stand in the doorway of the nursery. The nightlights are on and I can see Nate sleeping soundly in his bed.

"Get some sleep, Mel. Tomorrow, we're going to tackle motherhood," Sawyer says, squeezing my hand before going to his room.

After I'm showered and in my pajamas, I stare at the photo of Noah and me on the bedside table. The one Belle took when we announced our relationship at the meet and greet. Neither of us had a care in the world. We lived each day of our relationship like the happy couple we were. I couldn't imagine it any other way. From the second Noah and I met we were instant friends. Anyone with half a brain cell would want to fall in love with their best friend the way I did. But now I'm alone and I'm supposed to find a way to move on. Fuck that.

Turning on my phone, I scroll through the messages. A few from Karen and Darren, more than a few from Eli, and all the rest are from Sawyer. The last one he sent before he picked me up was a video link to "Hemorrhage" by Fuel—his way of letting me know he understood where I was and what I was going through. But it was also his way of letting me know I'm not alone.

Two months ago, I thought Noah and I were in this lifetime together. Now, the only thing I know for sure is Sawyer is walking this hell with me to the bitter end. I'd give anything for things to go back to the way they were, but if I can't have that I'll happily take Sawyer's friendship. It's the only thing I have to hold on to right now.

As if he's reading my mind, my phone buzzes with an incoming message. It's the link to "The Great Escape" by Pink. I don't think there's anything else he could have sent to make me understand exactly how he's feeling right now. If there's one thing I do know, it's how grateful I am for Sawyer Weston.

D. Kelly

Amelia – Present Day

When I look up from my computer to stretch a bit, Anna, Rory, and Karen are all engrossed in their Kindles. It's bittersweet having them here, reading these pages. I'm not even sure why I'm letting them, but I know Noah would be proud of me. Writing all of this down has been one of the hardest things I've had to do yet. I've cried more tears the past few days than I have in the last few months. I'll never get over losing Noah, never get past this lingering sadness that fills my heart when I think of him, and neither will Sawyer. Losing Noah pushed us together in ways I would've never thought possible, but as I typed out the words of my story, I was also able to finally admit to myself how much underlying chemistry there has been between us all along.

My computer dings with an incoming message and I instinctively know it's from him. He's had more than enough time to read the pages I sent him last night. Butterflies take flight in my stomach as my nerves kick into overdrive. My mouse cursor hovers over his message while I bite my lip in hesitation. My biggest fear isn't his response, it's opening all these old wounds again for him as well. I don't think I could have done this with him here, or if he hadn't finally given me an ultimatum, but I wish he were here with me reading it so I could gauge his reactions. The last thing I want to do is hurt him any more than I already have. Sawyer deserves all the happiness in the world, and I know Noah would want that for him. Taking a deep breath, I click on his message.

Hey Princess,

Wow. You've literally left me breathless. Your writing has always been good, that's why we hired you after all, but this ... it's intense. While reading your pages, I realized a lot of things, the biggest of all being, I owe you an apology. I thought by giving you an ultimatum it would make you realize all the things I already know. What I've realized, instead, is we all go at our own pace and I'm a world-class asshole for making you try to move faster than what you're ready for. You didn't fall out of love, it was ripped away from you, and I know that better than anyone. I'm sorry for putting my dreams ahead of your fears. That's not to say I don't still wish you could make a decision because I do–and I think it's what is best for us–but I'd never leave you for not being ready. Love isn't about being on the same page, it's about compromise and understanding. I'm sorry you're going through this alone and that I pushed you into it. If you can't do this now, if you're not ready, then stop. We'll talk when I

568

*get home, but my love isn't going anywhere and neither am I. I
promise. Sometimes, I forget this isn't just about us falling in love and
the consequences of that, it's also about you being okay with loving
someone else. Especially when that person is me.*

My hands begin trembling again as I try to type back a reply.

Hey yourself,

*Sawyer, please don't doubt my love for you. My hesitation has
less to do with you and more to do with my own fears and
insecurities. But I don't need to explain them to you; you know them
better than anyone and recognize them before I do. Your words mean
the world to me but so do your actions. You've been a great friend, a
wonderful partner, and the best father figure to Nate. No one, other
than Noah, could love him as much as you do. It's time for me to
catch up to life. To know if I can truly give myself to you as freely as I
gave myself to Noah. I want that more than anything, which is why
I'm trying to claw my way through the last of the darkness so I can
live in the light with you. Don't worry about me, either. I'm not alone.
Karen, Anna, and Rory are here. Yes, even Rory. It's time to bridge
this gap between us all. Sawyer, I'm a mess, but thank you for loving
me in spite of it all. I want you to read this as I go, so I'm attaching
what I have so far of the last part of the book. This part hurts most of
all so you might want a drink. I have a feeling the next bits will be
better, though. Have faith in me just a little bit longer —I hope it will
be worth it.*

After sending the message, I head into the kitchen and knock
back a shot. Anna meets me there and pushes her glass toward me and
I fill it up for her.

"I'm proud of you, Amelia," she says after tossing hers back.

"Why?"

"Maybe because most people would work something like this
out with their therapist. I know you've already had your fair share of
time on the couch, but still. Life hasn't always been kind to you and
you're fighting. For a while I wondered what would happen when you
and Sawyer started hooking up. I knew the first day we met that
Sawyer had it bad for you and it nearly destroyed him when you
married Noah."

"Yeah."

"Hey, don't do that. Don't be sad. You and Noah were given a
brief infinity of bliss most people don't find in a lifetime. You've
found it twice, Mel. Noah would want this and Sawyer finally came
to terms with that. It's your turn to fully embrace the idea that it's
okay to love him with your whole heart. It doesn't negate what you

had with Noah. If anything, it shows how much of a gift Noah's love was to you for you to want that again with someone else."

After we knock back another shot, she smiles at me. "People think it's wrong, Anna. They're disgusted by us."

Anna shoots daggers over to Rory. "She's protecting her brother's legacy by lashing out. The fans don't know you and Sawyer. They're just being keyboard warriors right now. Mel, you're my best friend, so I'm going to tell you the truth. You and Sawyer are two of the most broken people I've ever met. You were broken before Noah, and you were positively shattered after him. But the beauty in that is you're flawed in the same places. Noah knew that. We even talked about it once."

"You did?"

"Christmas Eve, the day you got your tattoo. Noah and I were sitting in his office wrapping presents we didn't want Wyatt and Sawyer to see. We were talking about how he was going to propose to you on New Year's Eve. He asked me if I thought Sawyer still had feelings for you. I lied and said no."

"Why did you lie?"

She shrugs. "Noah knew I was lying, but Sawyer was trying really hard to let you go at that point. I knew he would do it for Noah. Anyway, Noah said some things I'll never forget."

"What did he say?"

With an easy smile, she leans back against the counter. "He said he and Sawyer were destined to fall in love with the same women and even though they were blessed with many things, this one thing was their curse."

"Our families and their fucking curses," I grumble, but she keeps smiling.

"He told me how well you guys had gotten to know each other and then he sort of offhandedly mentioned how you and Sawyer would have an epic love story. He thought it was ironic how scared of love the two of you are and was pretty sure you picked him because you were terrified you'd repeat your parents' mistakes with Sawyer."

"That's not true!"

"I know, and so did Noah. I think he was just venting because he said the two of you would have an epic love story as well. Then he bragged about how smart and brave you were and said you'd never let yourself repeat your parents' mistakes. He just wished you realized that. But then, with a huge smile, he said if you didn't love him just a bit more than you loved Sawyer you wouldn't agree to marry him when he asked you."

"Oh God." My hand flies to my mouth as the tequila begins to churn in my stomach.

"Relax, Mel. Let me finish," Anna says, diving back into the rest of her story. "So I asked him, 'What if she says no?' and he flashed me his panty-dropping smile and said one day you'd say yes to Sawyer and he'd be just as happy for the two of you as Sawyer would be for him if you agreed to marry Noah."

"What in the ever-loving fuck? Was he drunk?"

She laughs. "On love, maybe. I then pointed out how much closer you'd gotten since Sara and how much you loved him."

"I loved him so much.".

She nods at the wistfulness in my tone "He knew. I'm going to try to pull this as close to word for word as my eidetic memory will allow. He said he knew you loved him, and he wouldn't be proposing if you didn't, but that love wasn't quantitative and he believed you could love someone with your whole heart and soul and still be in love with someone else. That one didn't negate the other and he thought that described you and Sawyer. You were in love with Noah but you still loved Sawyer."

"Jesus …"

"Noah was a class act and he loved you both unconditionally. He felt like Sawyer was suffering silently because he was in love with you but didn't want to hurt Noah, and he wasn't wrong. But Noah, being the amazing man he was, wrapped up the conversation saying if you changed your mind and wanted Sawyer instead he'd be hurt but he'd also be happy for you both."

Anna smiles at the memory. "And that's the thing, Mel, he would have been. Noah didn't say it with an ounce of sadness or jealousy, only love for his twin and for you."

Tears fill my eyes and I knock back another shot. "That breaks my heart, Anna. I wish Noah would have talked to me about these things. It sucks knowing he and Sawyer had these painful conversations behind my back."

"Noah and Sawyer always had painful conversations, but that's a perk of being a twin. They could have those discussions and still be okay."

"I loved Noah with every ounce of my being. Back then, I didn't think of Sawyer the way I think of him now, not with this kind of love. That's what's so hard. He feels like he's second choice. I don't feel that way, but if Noah were still here I would have never opened my heart to Sawyer like this. How do I show Sawyer I love him just as much as Noah but on a … I don't know, a parallel plane? The love

I have for both of them doesn't intersect and it never has. I don't love Sawyer more than I loved Noah and vice versa. I don't compare them or even try to. They're both amazing men in their own right. I hate how Sawyer feels like this is some kind of contest and he placed last."

Anna wraps her arm around my shoulder and pulls me in for a hug. "These pages you're writing today are the saddest but they're also the most important to Sawyer because these pages tell the story of the two of you. Let your words show him how much you care for him. Let him *feel* your love for Noah could never negate your love for him. You know what else I'm proud of you for?"

With a groan, I look to her and shake my head. "I can only imagine."

"You always think before you speak and you've never fully admitted your feelings for him as openly as you just did. Rory kind of hates you right now and you don't give a flying fuck she's within earshot. Writing this story has been good for you, Mel. It's not a matter of do you or don't you, can you or can't you. It's a matter of you getting past the point where you care what other people think about *your* life. Even though there have been ups and downs, you guys have been together since Nate's first birthday. That's longer than you were even with Noah. There are only two people in your relationship ... you and Sawyer. Aside from you, there's not a soul on earth who could love Nate as much as Sawyer does. Biology aside, he's Nate's dad in all the ways that count. It's time to embrace your family and fuck anyone who has an issue with it."

"It's just so much to handle."

She squeezes my shoulder. "Yes, but you're almost there, Mel, and then you can breathe."

"I hope so. I should get back to writing. Veronica is going to be here with Cadence soon because she has to work tomorrow."

"I'll stay and watch Cadence. You need to finish this book, Mel. I'm about halfway through the first part and can't wait to dive into the second. I've heard stories, but since I was never really on tour more than a few days at a time, this is nice to read and see some of what I wasn't around for."

"Thanks for offering to stay. I could definitely use the help. Although, I can't wait to see Cadence right now. All this writing about Belle and Noah is really bringing that sadness back to the surface. I need some baby hugs."

Anna laughs. "You mean toddler hugs, right?"

"Ugh. Don't remind me. They're both getting so big so fast."

Anna bounces her shoulder against mine. "Maybe you should think about giving Nate a sibling."

"Jesus, Anna! Let me try to come to grips with my love life first."

"I'm just saying … time waits for no one, and …" She looks up at me and her eyes soften. "I'm just going to be blunt. People say it's too soon for you to be moving on and that's one of your struggles. In the past, I'd have agreed with them, but I don't feel the same way after seeing how Noah and Belle were ripped away from us. Every second with someone is a precious gift. Don't let some arbitrary time or lack thereof set your course, Mel."

My heart feels like it's freefalling into my stomach, but at the same time Anna's words make the most sense of all. Time is a precious gift and you never know when it's going to be up.

"Thanks for the pep talk, Anna. You always know how to set me straight."

InstaLove

"Good Morning, Mel. Are you ready to do this?" Sawyer is standing next to my bed with a cup of coffee for me.

Grumbling, I sit up and take the coffee from him. "I'm terrified, Sawyer," I confess quietly.

"I know you are, Princess, but trust me on this, okay? You need this just as much as he does, you just don't know it yet."

"Sawyer, I've never in my life wanted anything more than I do that little boy in the next room. Half of the tears I cry are for him. There's an ache in my heart where he should be, but I'm bad luck, Sawyer. This black cloud that follows my family took Belle and Noah. I can't let it take him, too. Maybe I should go away—"

Sawyer takes the coffee away from me and pulls me into a hug. "I promise, Mel, holding him will heal you in ways you can't begin to imagine. And for the last time, you're not cursed. Belle and Noah would be so fucking pissed at you right now for pushing your son away and blaming yourself for something caused by the actions of a stranger. They'd be pissed as hell at me for letting it happen, too."

"I'm scared."

"I'll be there every step of the way, I promise. Go get ready and meet me in the nursery."

Sawyer releases me and leaves, closing the door behind him. I look over at our framed wedding photo and lose myself in Noah's bliss for a minute before forcing myself to try to do this.

A knock at my door delays the inevitable a few minutes.

"Come in," I call out, and Eli comes inside.

"Shit, Mel, your face is bruised," he says, coming closer and running his fingers over my cheek.

"Tends to happen when someone hits you," I answer with a shrug.

"She should have never fucking touched you," he spits out.

"Maybe not, but I get it, Eli."

"Well, I don't. I broke up with her." His words stop me in my tracks.

"Not because of me?"

"Partly. Her hitting you was the last straw. Rory is a cool chick, but there's no chemistry there. I was going to break up with her the day after your accident. When I got the call you'd been hurt I knew I couldn't do it then. Getting to you was my only priority."

"I'm sorry, Eli." I'm not surprised, but I was hopeful it would work for them.

"I'm not. Rory's a little young for me and she's got her eyes on someone else, anyway. It's a pipe dream, but who knows. We're going to stay friends if she can leave you alone and let you grieve at your own pace."

He takes a seat in my chair and I sit on the bed. "Is that why you're here? To tell me?"

"If only. I'm here for a few reasons. Sawyer called me last night and told me you were sleeping in the cemetery. Mel … I can't even believe I'm about to ask you this. Are you suicidal?"

Eli's baby blues bore deep into my soul. I want to tell him no, but I can't. "Possibly."

"Fuck," he says as he swipes a tear away from his cheek. "Baby girl, we need to get you back into therapy."

"I know," I answer, letting my own tears fall freely.

"Alright, so you know I can't let you out of my sight until we figure this out, right? I want you to understand something. If you were to do that, it would destroy what is left of Veronica, of the Westons, not to mention what it would do to me. You'd make Cadence and Nate miss out on learning about their parents from the person who knew them best. You'd willingly be making Nate an orphan, Mel."

Eli rises and comes to sit next to me, placing his arm around me. "We're going to get you through this. I'm making you an appointment for today."

"I'm sorry I'm so weak, Eli." My words are choked on a sob.

He pulls me into his embrace and kisses the top of my head repeatedly. "You're the strongest person I've ever met, Mel. But even the strong can't handle it all."

After a few minutes, I pull away. "Why else are you here?"

"Moral support. Sawyer told me about his plan to make you sink or swim with Nate today. If you swim, we're actually going to work on some music."

"You and Sawyer?" The shock in my tone makes him laugh.

"Crazy, isn't it? He was working on some lyrics last week but wasn't coming up with the right melody. I got Joey's guitar out and

D. Kelly

we worked through it. He's wants to work on it some more. Sawyer needs an outlet right now and he's got to need it really bad to want to work with me. So do your best not to sink today because Nate isn't the only one who needs you," Eli says before leaving my room.

Music is in Sawyer's blood, but I wonder if working with Eli has more to do with him trying to avoid reminders of Noah. If that's the case, it won't work. Noah is going to be in everything we do for the rest of our lives.

I take my time showering and getting ready. Once I'm finished, I walk over to the nursery. Sawyer is inside holding a bottle.

"Perfect timing. I just changed him, but he's hungry. It's show time, Mel." Sawyer walks to the doorway, leaving me standing just inside the room. I can't see Nate from here, but I can hear sucking noises coming from his crib.

I inch closer until I'm finally pressed against the rail. My fingers grasp the edges as I look down at him. His green eyes find mine while he sucks on his hand. He's wearing a pair of blue jammies that say "Daddy's little slugger" on them, and my tears begin to fall.

Nate fusses, but I'm paralyzed. When his fussing turns to full-blown crying, I don't know what to do. I look to Sawyer for help, but he doesn't move.

"You can do this, Mel. Pick him up."

That's easy for him to say.

Instead of moving, my fingers grip the crib harder. My heart aches with incredible pain. Listening to him cry is *killing* me, but so is my fear. In my peripheral vision, Sawyer's pushing buttons on his phone and that's when the music begins piping through the surround sound in the house. Every room is linked to it, including this one. "Inner Demons" by Julia Brennan begins playing and a sob escapes me.

Sawyer comes closer and places a hand on my shoulder. "Pick him up, Mel. It will be okay, I promise." As the second verse starts, my fingers release the rail of the crib. By the third verse, I've picked Nate up and am clutching him to me. The second he's wrapped in my arms his cries magically cease. I breathe him in as my tears continue to fall. He smells like perfection, like Noah. I don't even understand how that's possible, but I inhale him like he's the last bit of oxygen I'll ever get.

"Oh God, Sawyer, oh my God."

Sawyer guides me to the glider while I keep clutching Nate and kissing the top of his head. As his heartbeat syncs with mine and he lays across my chest, I cry it all out. Nate isn't even fussing for his bottle anymore. Deep inside I know it's because he needed this just as much as I did.

"This is the closest to Noah I'm ever going to be again. Why didn't I do this before? I'm a horrible person, Sawyer."

"No, Princess, you're not. You're the best kind of mom there is. You were protecting him from perceived danger the only way you knew how. But you're not a danger to him, Mel, you're his lifeline."

"No, I'm not. He's mine."

Relief floods Sawyer's features. "You'll be okay to feed him?"

"Yeah, I think so," I tell him, looking back down at my beautiful boy.

"Alright, I'm going to work on some music with Eli, but if you need me we'll be right out in the living room."

When Sawyer leaves, I turn Nate in my arms and look down at him. A huge smile breaks out on his face followed by a yawn. My heart melts as I allow myself these precious moments to enjoy him and feed him.

Nate falls asleep while eating and milk dribbles down his chin. I wipe it off and put him over my shoulder to burp him, wondering if I should while he's sleeping. As he lays against me and I rub circles over his back, I hear Sawyer singing. The words are sad, but his voice is even more so.

Adrenaline courses through my blood
But I'm not high
You're my only drug
Darkness closes in all around
Grips my heart and slams it down
Blood oozes
People scream
Smoke rises
Where's my queen?
Hollow voices
Bright lights flash
Death surrounds me
My whole life
Is shredding fast

It's the same few lines over and over, but they tweak the music as they go. It's haunting but beautiful. Acoustic, but the way he sings it is like he's screaming low. It's obviously not done yet, but it could be a hit.

That's insane to even think about. The band would never continue without Noah. But will Sawyer? He doesn't seem to want a solo career, but Noah wanted that for him so much. Not wanting to lay Nate down but knowing I should to build up some sort of routine with him, I put him back in his crib.

Something has been bothering me since yesterday, and since Eli and Sawyer are both here, I can ask them. When I walk into the living room, they stop what they're doing and look up at me.

"Everything okay?" Sawyer asks cautiously.

"Yeah, he's sleeping and he ate, he even burped." Both of them smile, and Eli motions for me to sit next to them. "Um, I have a question you guys might know the answer to. Yesterday, when Rory was yelling at me, she said I needed to help you guys build his legacy. Do you know what she meant by that?"

They exchange hesitant looks and I sigh. "Look, whatever it is I'm not going to break. If I'm still standing here after last night, and after holding Nate for the first time in weeks, I'm okay, I promise."

"Have you watched your video yet?" Eli asks, and I shake my head.

"Then you're not ready, Mel," Sawyer states simply.

"Have you watched yours yet?" I ask Sawyer, and he nods.

"I think I watched it too soon, so don't go there if you're not ready, Princess."

"I just want to know what Rory meant. She shouldn't have said anything if I can't know, but she did, so would you please fucking tell me?"

"I'll tell you, Mel," Eli says, and Sawyer shoots daggers at him. "A condensed version."

I lean back against the cushion and pull a pillow over my lap. "Noah left you a lot of money. He knew you struggle as it is with your parents' money, so I guess it was mentioned somewhere that maybe the family getting together and starting a foundation in his memory could be a good way to help you."

"Oh. Is this what you guys want, Sawyer?"

"We want you to be okay, Mel. Rory is struggling, too, because she's focusing on the wrong things. Instead of grieving, she's thinking about what she can do in Noah's honor. If and when you decide you want to do something for Noah, we can talk about that and help you. If that's what *you* want."

"What I want is for things to go back the way they were before Utah. I guess I should be thankful Noah was a planner, right? But it's almost too much. Videos and wills, advance directives and medical powers of attorney. His mind was constantly moving, but I was just basking in newly-wedded bliss. How come he didn't trust me enough to talk to me about any of this? Why didn't I have any warning?"

Eli pulls me close and I lay my head on his shoulder. I used to feel so safe in his arms, but now … I just wish he were Noah.

Sawyer releases a sigh. "He didn't want you to worry. Seriously, Mel, Noah thrived on this kind of thing. I know he was stressed about that feeling he couldn't shake, but Noah geeked out on being prepared. Besides, as soon as you delivered Nate, Noah would have made you go see Tony and put all that together anyway. He was just giving you a little time, not hiding things. Noah would have never hurt you like that, not in a million years."

The doorbell rings and Sawyer gets up to answer it.

"That would be your therapist for the day. Are you ready for this?" Eli asks.

"You got my therapist to come to the house?"

"No, your therapist can't get you in until next week because she's out of town. This one was willing to make a house call."

"Hello, Mel. How are you doing today?" Diane is standing next to Sawyer, looking at me with kind eyes.

"We're going to let you guys talk," Eli says as he stands and grabs his guitar while Sawyer gathers his music. I'm in shock; I didn't even know Diane was a therapist.

"I'm not sure what to say," I stammer as she sits across from me.

"Well, how about I go first?" she asks, and I nod in agreement.

"I'm probably not the best person for this. In fact, I know I'm not. I'm on leave from my practice because I'm still grieving. But because I know what you're going through in some aspect, I couldn't just sit by and let everyone worry about you without seeing how you're doing for myself."

"I held Nate today for the first time since the hospital," I spit out.

"That's good, Mel. How did it make you feel?"

"Like the worst person in the world because I hadn't done it sooner." She raises a brow at me and I continue. "Also, like I had a part of Noah back in my arms. It hurt so much, but it was the best kind of pain."

With tears in her eyes, she smiles. "Last night, you slept in a cemetery. Can you talk to me about that?"

For the next hour, I open myself up to Diane. I'm not sure why. Maybe because I feel like it would make Noah happy. Or maybe because I know she was a huge part of Sawyer's recovery when he was a kid.

"Did you become a therapist because of Sawyer?" I ask, needing to satiate my curiosity.

"In part. I knew I wanted to help people because I saw how much Sawyer and Jordan were affected by what happened to our family. It wasn't until Sawyer was in high school and grew so much from his journaling that I decided I wanted to be a grief counselor."

I didn't realize she was a grief counselor. That makes all the sense in the world now.

"Mel, I've seen people so consumed by grief that it ate at them until they took their own lives. Thinking about suicide and actually taking steps toward it can be a fine line. But I don't get the impression it's one you're walking."

"I'm lost, Diane."

"The best of us often are. Going back to therapy will be good for you. I'm willing to stay here all week until you can see your own therapist if you want me to."

"I think I'll be okay, but could I call you if I need to?"

"Absolutely. In fact, maybe we can go to lunch with the girls when you feel up to it. They love you, Mel, and I think you could help fill a void for them, too."

I'm not sure what it is about that idea but it makes my heart a little lighter.

"I'd like that a lot."

Later that night, Sawyer shows me how to give Nate a bath. "Who would have thought I'd be learning how to do this from you?"

"Hey now, I'm a pretty awesome uncle if you haven't noticed already."

"You're a pretty awesome friend and brother, too, Sawyer. Thank you."

"You're welcome. So are you ready for your first night on baby duty?" he asks, effectively changing the subject.

"I think so. And if this goes well, I should probably step up and do it every night."

Sawyer pauses and turns toward me. "Actually, I'd really like to keep helping you every other night. Being with Nate helps me feel close to Noah."

"You're not just saying that because you don't want me to do this alone?"

"You're never going to have to do this alone, Princess, but no. I'd do it by myself every night, but it was time for me to share him with you. Being with Nate makes me feel good and nothing else really does right now."

Sawyer holds out a towel and I lift Nate from the baby tub so Sawyer can wrap it around him. "Yeah, Sawyer, I'd love the help. God, why does he smell so good? I just want to eat him."

Sawyer laughs. "I don't know, but I understand the feeling. Some nights I want to hug him so hard just so he's close, but I know he's too tiny for all that just yet."

Sawyer sits with me as I get Nate dressed and feed him his bedtime bottle. After I put him to bed, we go to the kitchen and sit at the table.

"Do you remember everything from that night?" I ask.

"Unfortunately. How much do you remember, Mel?"

He looks eager for my answer, and I wonder if he's wanted to ask me this for a while.

"Noah talking to you on the phone, and then everything is in slow motion until my body hit the floor and I blacked out. After that, I don't remember much. Flashes of people, things, lights. I remember talking to Noah on the way out of the bus and that they were working on him. I remember the fear and the pain."

He's listening to me with rapt attention, so I continue.

"I don't really remember the flight, but I remember your voice keeping me calm. The way you held my hand ... I knew I was safe with you. I remember how scared I was when they started hooking me up to all that equipment and cutting off my clothes and just how bad everything hurt. I didn't know anything could hurt that much."

"What about now, Mel? You don't take your pills anymore, and you never mention the pain, but even with the cast off and all your stitches and staples out your back must still hurt."

The concern on his face is touching. This is a whole other layer to Sawyer. I wonder if he's changed from the accident, or if he's always been like this deep down but kept that part of himself hidden. I have a feeling it's the latter.

"There's no pain unless I'm moving around. When I sit I'm good. It can get uncomfortable at night, and I'm sure I'll still need a lot more help with Nate because of my lifting restrictions but I don't like drugs, Sawyer. Especially after my dad. The ibuprofen helps knock the edge off. If I have a bad day I'll take them, I promise."

"Okay, you know what's best for you. I have a question for you now. When you have your nightmares, what are you dreaming about if you don't remember much?"

"Mostly Belle's screams and the fearful feeling something is wrong with Noah. How scared I was when I felt the fluid rush between my legs. It's weird, Sawyer. That's why I wish I knew what happened because it's all just these random flashes of things but the order doesn't make any sense to me."

He folds his hands together as if in prayer and shakes his head. "I'm sorry, Mel. I wish I could help you."

"Me, too. I do remember being pissed you were watching me give birth. I was mad and scared about so many other things. But you were doing it for Noah and it made me happy at the same time that you were there doing that for him, for us, so you could give him those memories."

Sawyer looks up at me with a smile so wide his dimple is showing. "I didn't want Noah to miss a detail, but that was one of the greatest things I've ever seen. Don't get me wrong, it killed me that you were in so much pain on top of the normal labor stuff, but I don't know … watching a baby being born on a video and seeing it in person is so much different. Seeing that head of hair come out and then his little face, hearing him cry and watching his little hands curl up to his mouth … It was breathtaking, Mel. I know you didn't really have a choice, but thank you for letting me be there."

"I didn't have much of a train of thought to kick you out, but I don't think I would have. There's no way I could have done it alone."

"I'm glad." He reaches over and squeezes my fingers. "Because seeing my nephew come into the world was one of the highlights of my life."

Sawyer stands and yawns. "Goodnight, Mel."

"Goodnight, Sawyer."

Long after Sawyer goes to bed, I sit at the table and think about his words. That man has seen just about everything there is in the world and he called Nate's birth one of the highlights of his life. I'm not sure what I'm feeling but *I'm feeling* and I have Sawyer to thank for it.

One early morning, about five weeks later, there's a light knock at my door. I'm up and watching the dolphins play in the ocean.

"Come in," I call out, and Sawyer enters with one hand behind his back.

"Happy birthday, Princess." He pulls a small plate with a cupcake from behind his back and hands it to me. "I know you said you didn't want to make a big deal out of your birthday this year, but thirty is a big one and you at least deserve a cupcake."

"Sawyer, thank you."

"That's not all," he says, flashing me his dimple smile, and walks out to the hall before returning with a gift. "Don't be mad, but there's no way you would have sat back and let one of our birthdays pass without doing the same."

I'm not much in the mood to celebrate this year, but I understand where he's coming from.

"Open it," he says, handing me his gift.

"Sawyer," I gasp after tearing off the paper. My eyes fill with tears as I look down at the framed photo.

"It's a reminder and a gift. Do you remember how mad you were when Warren told us it was your birthday? And how mad Noah was you didn't tell us yourself?"

I laugh at the memory. "He called me a stubborn Scorpio."

"And he was right. I know the last thing any of us want to do right now is party. But Noah would want us to celebrate you on your big day. *I* want to celebrate you, but I understand it's hard. Next year, watch out. I'm going to make up for it big time."

He leans down and kisses the top of my head.

"Thank you, Sawyer. I love it."

"Happy birthday, Princess," he says again, and leaves me alone with my memories.

The photo is of the five of us on the bus. The birthday cake had just been cut and we're all laughing because it was filled with pineapple instead of strawberries—definitely not what they had ordered. It was kind of gross so we all ate around it, except for Darren. He loved it so much he scooped up all of ours and ate that, too. It was a great day.

D. Kelly

Slammed Blog Post

Merry Christmas *Slammed* Family,
My name is Amelia Weston and I'm Belle's sister. I'm sure most of you are also aware I am Noah's wife. I'm sorry it took me so long to update this blog for you all. Grief is a powerful emotion and I haven't been myself lately. Who am I kidding? I'll probably never be myself again.

Sawyer, Wyatt, Darren, and I would like to thank you for the outpouring of love and support you showered us with during our time of need. We know how much you all loved Noah and Belle and that you are going to miss them just as much as we will.

I'm sure you understand the guys will not be finishing out the remainder of the tour without Noah. For those of you who didn't get to see the show, we are deeply sorry for that.

Since the accident, I've spent most of my time healing, grieving, and learning how to be a mom. This isn't the vision I had for my life, and every day without Noah and Belle hurts more than I could ever begin to explain. But with the love and support from our families, I'm moving forward one day at a time.

With Darren's permission, I'm sharing a photo of Cadence and Nate taken this morning, on their first Christmas. Belle and Noah would have been proudly posting this picture to every social media outlet they could find, so we thought it was appropriate to share it with you.

In honor of Noah and Belle, *Slammed* has given me permission to post periodic updates to this blog. Don't get too excited, I'm not a blogger–that was Belle all the way. But I am a proud mom and aunt and the least I can do is share some important milestones their children achieve. Besides, if I constantly post pictures they become worthless to the paparazzi. Our kids may be a bit safer out of their line of sight.

Enjoy your holiday, Slammers, and thanks for reading.
With love,
Amelia, Sawyer, Darren, Wyatt, Cadence, and Nate

Five Months And A Day

Five months and a day—that's how long it's been since the accident. I've been going to therapy for the last fourteen weeks. Even though it's a constant struggle, the thoughts of joining Noah and Belle are pretty much nonexistent at this point. I've come to understand I was never really a danger to myself, but it's more about how I don't know how to cope with this massive amount of guilt.

I've started writing Belle letters. I'm still not sure how to grieve for her, so I write down everything I want to tell her or talk to her about each week and seal it on Sunday. They're just for me, and when I'm ready I'll have to burn them, but it helps me feel closer to her.

The holidays were rough and the New Year was even worse. Sawyer kept me blissfully liquored up and took on more Nate duties for me through the harder days. Nate started crawling on Christmas day; I swear it was Noah somehow making his presence known. Cadence is walking now and with every single milestone these two hit, my tears flow in abundance. Mama comes over as much as she can to spend time with us, so does Karen.

Rory and I still haven't talked much, but one of my promises to myself for the New Year is to finally sit down and watch Noah's video. Maybe once I hear what he has to say I can listen to Rory with an open heart. It would hurt Noah, knowing Rory and I are at odds, so I want to make things right. Eli and Sawyer are still spending a good amount of time together. Unfortunately, up until Thanksgiving, Darren, Wyatt, and Sawyer were not.

I was convinced they all needed group therapy to learn how to stay friends without Noah, but something amazing happened. On Thanksgiving, Anna and Wyatt announced they're having a baby. Anna is due in May and she's having a boy. Something clicked into place after their announcement and they've been thick as thieves ever since, even bringing Eli into the fold. He's getting ready to go on tour soon. I don't know who is going to miss him more, me or Sawyer.

After Noah died, there was a part of me that was hesitant to let Eli comfort me. I didn't want him to think we could try again. That was me being an idiot because Eli has so much more respect for me and Noah than to try anything like that. In fact, Eli has spent many nights in my big, comfy chair so he could be there to pull me from the nightmares plaguing me.

Tonight was one of those nights. The nightmare was so bad I tweaked my back and flared up my injury. Sawyer had just put Nate back to sleep when it happened. My nightmares scare him just as much as his scared me last year. After he coaxed me from the terror, he brought me a pain pill and a muscle relaxer. The doctor says I'm almost fully healed but these flare-ups could happen every so often.

As I lie here waiting for the pills to kick in, my mind races with all these errant thoughts. A lot of things have happened in the last few months. The most important being we found out the cause of the accident. It was truly that—an accident. The other driver had been coming down an incline when his brakes failed. No one knows why. He was forty-five with a wife and three young kids.

I feel like I should do something for them—Noah would have— but I'm just not sure what I can do. Anything seems like an empty gesture. The same thing goes for Harold's family. The band took care of them, but there's this nagging feeling that Noah would want me to do more. Which is another reason why I need to watch his video; I need to know what he expects from me. I spend my days still listening to the EP he made for me and a sad playlist I made that reminds me of him. Ray LaMontagne's "A Falling Through" is setting the tone for my melancholy mood right now.

Every day, I show Nate and Cadence pictures of Belle and Noah. Cadence already says Mama and Dada and it's the sweetest and most gut-wrenching thing. I know when Nate finally starts saying Dada I'm going to lose it. Even so, one of the things I've come to realize the past few months is Nate saved me. From the second I held him in the nursery that day, something clicked. I never imagined I could love someone the way I love him. It's all-encompassing and I often hope Noah felt what I feel in that brief moment he was able to hold Nate in the hospital.

"Hey, Mel?" Sawyer calls from the doorway.

I blink back my tears and turn to him. "Come on in, Sawyer." He's holding his journal. He's been writing in his spare time lately. I haven't seen him without a notebook in his hands for months. He sits down on the bed and props himself against the headboard, so I follow suit.

"Even with therapy your nightmares are getting worse."

"I'm sorry. You can just let me get through them … you don't have to keep waking me up."

He turns his green eyes to mine and they're filled with pain. "I know what that's like, Mel, and it fucking sucks. I've been working on a project for myself the past few months, but I realized tonight maybe it could help you."

"What kind of project?"

He exhales and runs his hand through his already messy hair. "I guess you could say I'm chronicling my life with Noah. I started with the tour because it's the freshest in my mind. Noah was more than my brother and twin, he was my best friend. I remember everything now, but someday I won't."

A single tear slips down his cheek and he brushes it away quickly. "The more I started writing, the more I realized I'm not only doing it for me. I'm doing it for Nate so he can really know his dad."

"Oh, Sawyer … that's … honestly the best gift you could give him."

He laughs lightly. "I'm no writer, Mel. These are just recollections of what happened. The only people I'm comfortable sharing this with are Nate and you."

"Me?"

"Yeah. There's something I can share with you that might help. I started this journal the day after the funeral and I began with the night of the accident. Maybe if you read this, it will help jog your memory and eventually put your mind at ease enough to stop the nightmares."

Holy shit. Do I want to read this?

"How bad is it, Sawyer?" I whisper.

"Pretty much every detail from when I got on the bus until after you woke up. You don't have to read it now, or ever, Mel. It was just an idea."

Reaching for his hand, I squeeze his fingers. "Thank you, Sawyer. I'd really like to read it. It's scary, but it might help."

"Can I ask you something, Mel?"

"You can ask me anything you want, Sawyer. I'm always an open book to you." The two of us talk a lot now. I've learned about their childhood and he's learned about mine. We've bonded over a lot of Pop-Tarts these past few months.

"This playlist of sad songs you have going all the time is depressing. But how did the song playing right now end up in the mix?" He's referring to "Meet Me Halfway" by Kenny Loggins."

His question makes me blush. "It's kind of embarrassing, but it's sort of like my death anthem? My dad played it constantly when my mom died. When he died, I played it all the time to remind me of them. I did the same when my grandma died, so it was just a natural instinct to put it on this playlist. And because it's kind of a song about fate and destiny, it reminds me of Noah."

"That makes sense. I was just curious. We all have our musical likes and dislikes. Noah loved eighties music, so I was wondering if it was something he used to play for you."

"No, I didn't even know he had a soft spot for the eighties, but I do, too. It's kind of bittersweet, you know? Learning things about him now. I want to know everything, but it makes me angry I didn't have the chance to learn it from him myself."

"We sure got fucking gypped, didn't we, Princess? You know what kills me? Knowing my kids will never get to know their Uncle Noah. He's always been the most important and influential person in my life and my wife and kids will never know him."

I squeeze his hand again and catch his eyes with mine. "It would bother him, too, Sawyer. He was so proud of you. We often talked about what he wanted to do after the tour and do you know what he wanted most?"

"To be a dad, have sex, and make lots of brothers and sisters for Nate?" he says with a chuckle.

"Well, yeah," I say with a smile, recalling Noah's excitement for all of that, "but he wanted to manage you. Noah said you are the most talented person he'd ever known and he hoped you'd keep working in some capacity. Personally, I think he really wanted you to go solo."

"He wanted to manage me?"

"More than anything."

Sawyer leans back against the headboard and blows out a breath. "I'm not sure what I want to do, Mel. Right now, I know the first year isn't for doing anything but being with you and Nate. I hope you don't think I'm overstepping, and I know I can't replace Noah, but I love the fuck out of Nate. I want to give him everything Noah would have, my time, my love, just everything."

This vulnerable part of Sawyer is what drew me to him in the beginning. It's the part of him that used to make me weak in the knees. This is the real Sawyer. Ever since the accident, Sawyer has been more of his true self than I've ever seen.

"Noah wanted you to be Nate's guardian if something would have happened to us. We had agreed you and Belle could split custody. No matter what happens in the future, this is what Noah would want. You're not overstepping, Sawyer. You're the only person I trust to guide Nate in the same way Noah would have."

Sawyer clears his throat. "Do you think you'll get remarried someday?"

I'm still wearing my wedding rings. I can't imagine ever wanting to take them off.

"Right now, I can't picture it. I don't want to be sad for the rest of my life, and I know there can be a lot of good step-parents out there, but ... I don't want someone stepping into my world and trying to guide my son. And I don't see how a relationship could even work if I weren't willing to bend on that a bit. Especially if there were other kids ... eventually. In Noah's absence, Nate is mine and yours to guide. I don't expect you to be my co-parent. You've got your whole life ahead of you, but I hope you two will be close enough that he'll see you often and not hesitate to pick up the phone when he needs you."

"I'm not going anywhere, Mel. We're in this together. We'll figure out logistics and stuff when and if it comes to that."

After yawning, I turn the question around on him. "What about you? Are you putting more thought into marriage and kids now? I know you mentioned in your wedding speech you'd been thinking about it."

"I've always wanted kids. With the limited time I spent with Saylor and Emme, it cemented what I knew a long time ago. Now, with all the time I've spent with Nate and Cadence, I know it even more. The relationship part, though ... I'm not sure. I don't like letting people into my world. Maybe I'll just hire surrogates or something and be the cool single dad."

Sawyer would make an amazing husband, but I'm not sure I'm the right person to convince him of that. Selfishly, I don't want to encourage him right now. The sooner he starts dating, the sooner Nate and I stand to lose him. I can't imagine any sane girl out there will have much compassion for his relationship with his brother's widow and her kid.

Sawyer stands when Nate starts crying. "Do you want me to take over tonight? I know he's teething and uncomfortable."

"Nah, I got it, Mel. You need to rest. If you can't sleep, read the journal. Maybe it can help."

An hour later, I've finished reading Sawyer's journal and my heart is shattered into a million pieces. I haven't cried this hard in a while. There are so many things I never knew, like Darren holding

D. Kelly

Belle's body in the middle of the road. I can't even begin to imagine what that must have been like for him. Even after all that, he's still managed to push through for Cadence. It makes me feel like such a coward.

What hurts most is reading how selfish I've been. Not that Sawyer said so. On the contrary, his words perfectly explained my pain and grief. But this amazing family put my needs before theirs when we were all hurting so much. I understand Rory's fury on a whole other level now. Everything they've done since the accident they've done because they don't want to let Noah down. And also because they love me and my son.

There's one other thing I have to know for sure. I have to see it for myself, so I head to Sawyer's room. Even though it's three in the morning, he's sitting in bed strumming his guitar.

"Is it true?" I ask as he looks up at me.

"Is what true?" he replies, confused.

"You have pictures of Noah and Nate?" As I walk closer to the bed, he pulls his phone from the bedside table.

"I'm sorry I didn't show them to you sooner. I wanted to, but with your injuries, I was waiting until you were better. Then there was the incident at the cemetery and the therapy. I wasn't sure when a good time would be."

"Now, Sawyer. A good time is right now. Please," I plead as I climb up next to him.

Sawyer hands me his phone and I'm breathless as I look down at it. Noah's eyes are filled with a happiness I've never seen, a peaceful glow radiates from him. His smile is everything. In the subsequent shot he's kissing Nate; my heart fills and shatters at the same time. I'm not sure I could have handled seeing these before—I'm barely hanging on now–but they're the best gift anyone could have given me.

"Thank you, Sawyer," I tell him through my sobs. Sawyer sets his phone aside and pulls me into his arms.

"They're backed up on my computer and the cloud, and I'm pretty sure everyone in the family already has them, too. I didn't want to take any chances losing them. You can thank Veronica for that, it was her idea."

Words begin flowing from my mouth as tears continue to fall from my eyes. I ramble about Sawyer's journal, how painful it was for me to read it, and how it filled in so many missing pieces. I apologize again and again for being selfish. My medication has fully kicked in by now and I don't hold anything back. Sawyer continues to hold me, comfort me, and reassure me in my time of need.

The next thing I know it's morning and I wake up alone in Sawyer's bed. Freaked out, I'm wondering how and why I'm here, then it all comes back to me. After using the restroom and washing my face, I make my way to the kitchen for some coffee.

Sawyer is lying on the couch with a pillow and a blanket and Nate is lying on top of him. My heart aches at the sight. My mind easily flips Sawyer's face for Noah's as I imagine them together. At the same time, there's a huge part of me that is in awe of the love between Nate and Sawyer; I'd never want to see that disappear.

As quietly as I can, I make Sawyer and myself a cup of coffee. I know as soon as Sawyer smells the coffee he'll wake up. Even though he's conditioned himself for late nights on the road, he's still a morning person. When I set our cups on the table, Nate lifts his head and looks around. My little monkey is a morning person, too—the one trait he didn't get from his daddy.

When Nate sees me walking toward him, he blesses me with a huge smile. His two bottom teeth have finally poked through. Again, it's another beautiful moment laced with lingering sadness; Noah is missing another milestone. I've got to try and get past this because Nate and Cadence's lives are going to be filled with milestones Noah and Belle aren't here for. My therapist says I'm always going to be reminded of Noah and Belle in the happiest times and finding balance is key. I need to find a way to turn that sadness into happiness, be thankful I'm here to see these blessings, and celebrate with enough joy for all of us.

"Nate! Look at your new teeth!" I exclaim as I scoop him out of Sawyer's arms. Darren and Cadence make their way out and Nate smiles when he sees Cadence toddling toward him. He thinks Cadence walking is the funniest thing and it makes him laugh big, deep, belly laughs that have us all in stitches.

"Dude! You're going to be eating cookies with Cadence in no time," Darren calls out as Sawyer sits up.

"Sorry, Sawyer, I didn't mean to kick you out of your bed last night. I made you some coffee."

Sawyer heads straight for the coffee and takes a few sips before talking. "It's all good, Mel. Nate had a rough night, but he went right to sleep after those teeth popped through. I figured he'd be less likely to wake up if he were sleeping with me. Besides, you needed your rest after last night."

"Yeah, speaking of … do either of you have plans today?"

"I'm free all day," Darren says.

"Actually, uh, I have plans with Lola," Sawyer replies, and Darren and I whip around in surprise. I'm not sure what I was expecting him to say, but it wasn't that.

"What do you need, Mel? I can help you," Darren asks, avoiding Sawyer's comment like the plague. He doesn't like Lola, either, from what Anna has told me.

"I'm going to watch Noah's video today and I need someone to take care of Nate because … well …"

"Say no more," Darren says, holding up his hand. "I'll take care of him."

"Are you really going to do it?" Sawyer asks with a concerned expression.

"After reading your journal last night, yeah. I have an appointment with my therapist tomorrow afternoon, so the timing couldn't be better."

"I'll cancel on Lola."

"No, you don't have to. I don't want to mess up your date."

Sawyer laughs loudly. "It's not a date, Mel. She's been calling since the funeral and wants to catch up over lunch. I'm not going to get her off my back until I meet up with her."

"You give us enough of your time. You should go. Darren will help today. I have to start doing more things myself. I've been selfish too long."

"Hey, where is that coming from? You're one of the least selfish people I've ever met." Darren nails me with a what-the-fuck look and I respond with a shrug as I take Nate to change his diaper. He and Sawyer continue talking about it when I walk away.

"You know, Nate, Mommy has been a mess since Daddy and Auntie Belle went to heaven. Sometimes I wonder if I'll ever get my life back on track, or if there will ever be a day when I'm not sad. You make everything better, baby boy. Mommy has to do something really hard today, so you're going to spend the day with Uncle Darren." Nate smiles and kicks his feet at my words.

"If you want my opinion, you're not doing any worse than anyone else in your situation would have. It takes time and patience, Mel. Fortunately, we've got that in spades."

Sawyer's words caress my soul, but I don't turn around. I won't be able to keep myself from crying if I do. I'm not sure why he feels the need to follow me when it's obvious I need a minute.

"I canceled on Lola. Noah's video wrecked me, Mel. Even if Darren can help with Nate, someone needs to be here for you."

After picking up Nate, I spin around. "I don't want to be your burden, Sawyer, and I don't want to get in the way of you living your life. *Even if* it is with Lola."

"Whoa ... take three steps back and breathe, Princess. Number one ... you're not a burden, you are my friend. Number two ... I get to choose how to live my life and family never gets in the way, family is *always* priority. And number three ... what's your beef with Lola?"

My eyes roll back and I take a deep breath. I could kick myself for saying anything about her. "Nothing. I just heard she was bad news back in the day and don't want to see you wrapped up with someone like her. Noah wouldn't, either."

He leans back against the wall and smirks at me. "You know she used to date Noah, right?"

"Yeah, and I heard she showed her inner tramp and he dumped her ass."

"She did, and he did, and I'm sure you also heard I turned her down, too. I'm not interested in Lola, Mel."

With a sigh, I catch his gaze with mine. "It's not my business if you are."

"The hell it's not."

His vehement tone stops me in my tracks. "I don't know what you want me to say, Sawyer."

"I want you to say you're going to hold me to a higher standard, Mel. I want you to say you're going to call me on my shit. I want you to say you're going to do anything and everything in your power to keep me in line like Noah would have! I'm doing everything Noah would have wanted and expected of me and I expect for you to do the same."

"Sawyer, you're a grown man and it's not up to me to keep you in line. But I have called you out on your shit since day one and I will continue to do so. If you want me to tell you when I think Noah would agree or disagree, I can easily do that. Stay the fuck away from Lola. I don't know if she's crazy or just a whore, but one usually follows closely behind the other."

With a smile too sinful for his own good, Sawyer begins clapping. "There she is. I was beginning to wonder if the snarky bitch inside you was still there. I'm glad to see she was just taking a breather." Sawyer grabs Nate from me and kisses me on the cheek. "I love you, Mel. Thanks for showing me you still care."

Sawyer takes Nate out of the room and leaves me standing behind in awe. He's never told me he loves me before. I know he doesn't mean it like *that*, but this whole incident is surreal nonetheless.

Final Goodbye

A few hours later, I've taken three shots of tequila, written an entire extra page to Belle about how fucked up this is, and am now curled up with my laptop, tissues, and a rescue shot of tequila. The video is queued up and my finger has hovered over the play button for about a half hour now. I haven't read the paperwork inside the envelope, but I know it breaks down my inheritance. *Like I need another fucking inheritance.*

Tossing back the last shot, I hit the play button and reach for the tissues. As soon as Noah's smiling face appears, my heart feels like it's rupturing.

"Hey, Mel! Damn, you're beautiful. And yes, I fully realize I can't see you right now, but in my mind I can, and I'm picturing you on our wedding night. When you finally watch this video, I hope you're about ninety-five years old and creaming in your granny panties thinking about what a hot, young stud your husband used to be."

Noah always knew what to say to make me laugh; it feels good to laugh with him one more time.

"These videos are hard to make, and I'm not sure I could update them again if I even wanted to. I'm sure I've told you by now that I've had an ominous feeling I just can't shake, so this is me trying to be proactive by being able to say some important things to the people I love."

No, Noah, you didn't tell me anything. I've been completely blindsided by this and I'm angry at you for that. But I love you so much for trying to protect me.

"I'm so in love with you, Amelia Weston. Fate brought you into my life for a reason, and I've never been happier. I know letting your defenses down and allowing love in was hard for you, but I hope it was worth it, Mel, because I can't imagine my life any other way."

Nothing has ever been more worth it.

"It's funny, you and Sawyer are so much alike in that aspect. I thought for sure you were going to pick him. Never in a million years did I think I'd be able to wear you down and show you how worthy you are of love. But each day that passed you showed me how amazing you are and how strong you are by pushing past your fears and demons and letting me inside. Thank you for that. Your love is the greatest gift I could have ever received. It's amazing to think our love multiplied into a beautiful baby boy. He's going to be perfect, Mel, just like you. And you're going to be an amazing mother to him, I have no doubt."

I'm bawling my eyes out. Noah was always so happy and so passionate about everything, especially love. He gave me so much in our limited time together, taught me so much, made me *feel* so much. I'm not sure I'll ever be able to let him go.

"There are a few reasons I'm making this video. I know how hard it's going to be for you to watch it, especially if something bad happened to me. I've had an amazing life, Amelia. I've been abundantly blessed with family, wealth, happiness, the love of a wonderful woman, and a child of my own. I've experienced love and loss. I was blessed not only with siblings but with a twin. My parents were the absolute best and my friends have always been an extended version of my family. I've never lacked for anything, and it's important you know this.

"I think people are put on this earth for specific reasons. After the Sara incident, I felt like my reason was up. Like maybe fate intervened that night but it was only a temporary delay. I get how stupid that probably sounds, but I feel it in my gut. That's why I'm making these videos, Mel. People need to know my hopes and wishes for them. They need to know how much they were loved by me and how much I know I was loved by them in return."

I hit pause because my tears are falling too rapidly for me to even see the screen clearly. Noah has to be one of the strongest, most faith-filled people I've been fortunate enough to know. Belle was the second, and the fact I've lost them eats away at my heart. But seeing him on the screen talking to me fills my heart with the joy I've been missing for the last five months. Even though I don't want to keep listening, I also can't stop, so I press play.

"We've talked briefly about some of this, but I'm going to whip through it again. My parents and family are well taken care of now. Please don't cut any of them out of your life or Nate's. They'll be your lifeline, I promise, you just have to let them in. I've left Jordan enough to pay off the bar and then some. Don't let him give it back. He'll eventually approach you ... *don't* give in. Make sure Nate grows up with his cousins, they'll be important to him. He needs to grow up with the stability of a good family.

"I know it's asking a lot, but please take care of Sawyer, Mel. I can't even begin to imagine how losing him would affect me. But Sawyer is much more jaded than I am. He's been through so much pain and loss and this could push him to the point of no return. We've never really been apart. Twins have a special bond and ours is going to be severed forever. You and Sawyer are more alike than different, and I've watched your friendship blossom. Sawyer doesn't trust anyone, Mel, and he trusts you. Be his friend, be there for him in my absence. Let him love you, and in turn love him back. You're going to need each other.

"I've left my portion of the house to you. I'd like you to stay there with Sawyer for now. I understand if it's hard, but it's Nate's home, *our* home, and it's a place where you and Sawyer can be safe and heal together. I know none of this is going to be easy and I know you think you're cursed. Baby, you are not cursed. Shit happens for a reason. Even if it doesn't make sense to us, there's still a reason. I know it's asking a lot, especially now, but trust in that."

Pausing the video, I yell out my frustrations. "Fuck you, Noah. Fuck you and your fate, and your reasoning, and your death. You should be here with us, and I'm so angry you're not. Now I'm just supposed to have faith and believe it's all for a reason? Hell no!" *I hate this feeling, I hate being so angry, and I hate most of all that he's not here anymore.*

Unpause.

"You done yelling at me now?" He chuckles, and I love and hate how he knows me so well. "Yeah, I know you're not going to change overnight and that right now you're probably pretty fucking pissed off. Truthfully, I'm not happy thinking I may not be around either. I'm going to miss out on a lot of truly epic shit, but that means you have to pick up the slack and enjoy everything twice as much. I mean it, Mel. You better enjoy the hell out of life if for no other reason than for the fact I'm not there to do it myself.

"I'd never trade it, though. If I had to choose a brief infinity with you, or never having you at all, I'd pick the brief infinity every time. My life has never made as much sense as it does when we're together. I've never loved anyone the way I love you. And God knows I've never been happier or had better sex."

Oh God, how I miss sex with Noah. That feeling of being loved while in his arms was like nothing I'd ever had before. Not even with Eli.

"Do you remember that day on the beach when we talked about there being more than one true love out there for people? I want that for you, Mel. If you're not getting those fifty years with me, I want you to get them with someone who loves you more than his passion in life. Someone who will make you his passion like I did. And if you can find someone like that, I know he'll be a good father figure to Nate because he'd never want to hurt you by disrespecting me. You deserve to have a family and Nate deserves to have those brothers and sisters we talked about."

Who does he think he is? Encouraging me to find someone in his final goodbye?

"Now, I know you're not going to be ready for any of that for a long time but when you are, just remember what my thoughts are. I never want you to feel guilty for loving again, Mel. Life is too short for regrets, and I'm sure Belle will be reminding you to live today like there's no tomorrow more often than you'll want to hear it, but she'll also be right."

If only he had known how much harder this would be because I lost them both. How much I miss her hugs, her guidance, and her sunshiny disposition. Damn, I'm really not drunk enough for this.

"Until you're ready, maybe you could do something for me. I'm leaving you a lot of money, Mel. Even after taking care of everyone and leaving a very sizeable trust for Nate, it's still a lot of money. I don't want to tell you what to do with it, but I know how much you already struggle with your parent's fortune. I've laid out a financial plan with Tony on how much money I'd like to see put aside for your future and Nate's future, as well as any future kids you may have. You don't like to think that far ahead, I know, but if you could do this for me it would make me happy because I'll know you're taken care of.

"As for the rest of the money, do something good with it. Maybe a scholarship fund or something to benefit people in some way. Find something you know I would have loved to do and do it for me. Build a legacy in my absence, and maybe my family can help. Especially Rory. I know she's going to be lost and lashing out, so if she could be a part of whatever you set up, it can help both of you heal. If you wouldn't mind keeping up the holiday dinners for Dr. Martin and his staff, you'd make me happier than I can even say."

Sawyer and Warren did that for Thanksgiving and Christmas; maybe I can take it over from now on. Easter is coming up in a few months.

"Amelia Weston, you are the love of my life and always will be. I could sit here forever and talk to this camera but to be honest, you're sleeping naked down the hall and we're two days into our honeymoon. There's nothing I want more right now than to go curl up with you and make love until I'm cross-eyed. All these videos have been a necessary evil, but they're sad and emotionally taxing. I can't begin to explain how much I hope you're old and gray as you watch this and laughing about how paranoid I was for nothing. That would be my ultimate wish. Thank you for loving me, for being my wife, and for giving me my firstborn son."

He blows me a kiss and the video cuts off.

After closing my computer, I curl into a ball and turn into an inconsolable mess. Within minutes, Sawyer is pulling me into his arms to comfort me.

"Why, Sawyer?" My question is nothing new, but his answer is.

"I don't know, Mel, but be thankful you got to hear him say he loved you one last time. I know I am."

How many people get that in a tragedy? Not many, I'm sure. "I just miss him so fucking much."

"Me, too."

Sawyer lays with me for hours while I cry and never once lets me go. Eventually, I cry myself to sleep with the images of Noah's smiling face in the forefront of my mind.

When I wake up it's after midnight. I slept the entire day away. The baby monitor is on next to the bed and Sawyer is in with Nate. After using the restroom, I make my way out to go get something to drink but pause at the sound of Sawyer's voice.

"Your mom had a rough day today, Nate. She's going to be okay, though, she's a fighter. I don't know if I've ever met anyone tougher than her. Your dad was such a romantic, in love with even the idea of love, and his whole world centered around your mom. I think Noah needed closure more than the rest of us, Nate. I love him, always will, but listening to him talk to me after he was gone was so hard, and what he said ... well, that's an even harder discussion."

I wonder what was on Sawyer's video. I could never ask; they're meant to be private, I'm sure.

"Today was your mom's turn to watch her video, so she's probably going to have a few rough days ahead of her. Don't worry,

D. Kelly

little prince, we won't let her drift away from you like last time. I promise."

Blinking back my tears, I tiptoe away so he doesn't know I was listening and grab a bottle of water and a few grapes. Noah's video left me with a lot to think about. Most importantly, I need to go see Tony. Not only to discuss Noah's estate but because I want to honor his preparedness and do some of my own. The way Belle and Noah were ripped away from me, I want to make sure there are safeguards in place for Nate should something happen to me. It's time I start honoring my husband and this can be the first step.

"Hey, Princess, how are you doing?"

Sawyer grabs himself a water and some Pop-Tarts and sits at the table. Like so many late nights over the past few months, he passes me one.

"I think it's time, Sawyer. I need to figure out how to honor Noah. I'm going to make an appointment with Tony."

"Alright, it's time I talk to you about something," he says hesitantly.

"What's wrong?"

"Nothing, I just don't want to make you angry or upset you. And please believe me when I say this is completely up to you."

"You're making me nervous, Sawyer. Just spit it out."

His eyes meet mine as he laces his fingers together. "The label has been starting to hound us about releasing an album. We've got some tracks we laid down that were never released and they know it. They're our tracks, we did them here and we don't owe the record company anything. They're just trying to capitalize on Noah's death."

I'm not sure how that makes me feel, but my dad's label did the same thing after he died. Industry standard, I suppose. "How does this affect me, Sawyer?"

"It doesn't, really. We're not doing it. And if we did, it wouldn't be for the label. We would do it to fundraise for whatever foundation you set up or cause you decide to donate to, but … you do realize you own all of Noah's music, rights, and royalties now, right?"

An overwhelming sadness settles over me at the thought. "No, I didn't. It doesn't surprise me, but I haven't looked at any of the paperwork yet."

"Don't be mad, but the guys and I have been talking about how best to help you when you're ready. We think you could make a huge amount of money to kick off whatever foundation you start by releasing Noah's EP to you."

Those words are like an arrow through my heart and I release an audible gasp.

"How could you even suggest that? You know how private Noah was! That EP is special to me, Sawyer. You want me to just sell Noah out like that?"

Sawyer is taken aback. "Fuck no, Mel. We'll release whatever music you want from the backlist as a fundraiser. We just thought if you wanted to have the most financial impact, it might be something you'd like to consider. There's a lot that would have to go into it, anyway. We'd need rights and permissions from each songwriter on the EP to even move forward. It's a longshot at best. But what I know for a fact is Noah let down his defenses and sang to you in a worldwide televised feed. If he thought his music would help a good cause, I think he'd be on board."

"But it's my music, Sawyer! It was my gift. I don't want to be selfish, but how could I take something so special and commercialize it to the masses?"

He scoots closer to me and squeezes my hand. "You can be selfish all you want. This is your music, Mel. It was just an idea, one of many. I'm sorry I brought it up. Let me know when you need help. The family is ready to sit down with you at any time if you'd like their help as well. You're not alone in this, Mel."

"Is this what everyone wants?" I ask softly. Why does everything have to be so hard? Why can't Belle and Noah just be here with us?

"Wyatt, Darren, and I are the only ones who have discussed this. We want what you want. The only thing I want is to help you move forward. Each day you seem slightly better, each day I feel slightly better. I miss the fuck out of him, Mel, so if I can do something to help honor him and keep his memory alive, I'm all for it. When you're ready."

"I'll think about it, Sawyer, all of it. I'm going to lie back down." When I stand, I kiss his cheek and leave him alone at the table. Some days, life is just too hard.

It's been a long day. I met with my therapist this morning and Tony this afternoon. The meeting with Tony was completely overwhelming. I don't know what I was expecting, but finding out how large Noah's fortune actually is was a big shock. I know I have to do something because all that money can't just sit in accounts

D. Kelly

when it could be doing so much good. But what kind of good is the question.

I also filled out paperwork to make Sawyer Nate's legal guardian should something happen to me. Darren is the backup if something happens to Sawyer. I can't imagine separating Nate and Cadence; they're already so bonded to each other. But if something were to happen to Darren, Nate would go to Diane.

I'm currently sitting on the beach watching the sunset while letting the day sink in. Wyatt should be here soon. I want to talk to each of them about what they think Noah would want. They're his brothers and know him better than anyone.

It's hard not to sit down here and remember being here with Noah. This house is one constant reminder of him. I've thought about moving out, to see if it would help, but the idea of not being here is even more painful than staying. I hate that I'm so confused by everything.

"Hey, Mel," Wyatt says, plopping down in the sand next to me.

"Hey, Wyatt. How are you doing?"

"Ah, you know … same old same, I guess. Anna is over her morning sickness now, so that's something good."

"That's really good. I'm happy to hear that. Thanks for meeting me. I was hoping we could talk about Noah and his wishes."

Wyatt draws through the sand with his fingers, but his eyes are hidden behind his sunglasses. So are mine, for that matter.

"Sawyer said he talked to you last night about the EP."

"Do you think Noah would want that? His EP out there for the world? You were his best friend, Wyatt. If anyone would know his thoughts on this, I should hope it's you."

"Shit, Mel, I don't know. I think pre-Mel Noah would have never made that EP to begin with. Noah was gifted, but he was sort of shy. With you he wasn't, with you, he was willing to share his talents because he knew it would make you happy."

"He made me so happy, Wyatt. With or without his talents." I remove my glasses to wipe away my tears.

"Honestly, I think Noah would shy away from the whole idea. But if someone came up to him and said 'Hey, if you release this EP you could save some homeless teens, or fund some college scholarships, or pay for organ transplants for underinsured people' … Whatever it may be, I don't think Noah would have hesitated. Being altruistic was Noah's second nature. The guy loved to spread happiness."

"Yeah, I guess he did," I reply with a sigh.

"How are you doing, Mel? Watching Noah's video must have been hard. I know it was for me."

"Each day is a struggle, but I'm pushing through. You guys help. Just your texts and being around really does help me want to push forward each day. Of course, Nate is my driving force behind it all. It's hard to stay sad around him because his happiness is contagious, just like Noah's was."

Wyatt leans back in the sand and blows out a breath. "I know we'll all be okay at some point, but Noah was my best friend for over half my life. I spent more years with him than I did without him."

"That was me and Belle."

"Shit, Mel, I'm sorry. Sometimes I forget you got a double whammy in all of this. Well, not forget, but you know what I mean."

"Yeah, I do."

"I just never thought I'd have a kid Noah wouldn't be an uncle to. That he'd have a kid and never be here to make that kid as awesome as he was."

With a sardonic laugh, I turn and face him. "We're in the same boat, Wyatt. Cadence's first birthday is coming up. I want to give her the world's best party but nothing will make up for the fact Belle isn't here for it. And in a few months it will be Nate's turn. Veronica and Karen spend so much time with them and I'm thankful. Diane and Rory and the girls are always over spending time with them. They have family. But the pieces I wish they had the most are gone."

We fall silent for a bit and enjoy the early evening and the company of someone who understands.

"When Anna has the baby you guys should spend more time with us. All the kids should be raised together just like you all were. Sawyer … he's a great father figure for Nate. Sometimes, I wish Nate had been twins."

"Really?" Wyatt asks, sitting back up.

"Yeah, I wish he had someone to have that bond with, like Noah and Sawyer had. But then other times I'm so glad he's not. Not only would it have been harder but God forbid something ever happen. I see how hard this is for Sawyer and how much he's hurting. I wish I could help him somehow, but I think letting Sawyer help us is helping him. I wish that weren't the case because I feel like we're holding him back, but I guess he's like Noah in more ways than I imagined."

"Sawyer loves you guys. He's always been focused on his family, more than Noah ever was. I think it's because of what went down with J when they were kids."

"Probably."

Wyatt stands and dusts himself off. "Come on," he says, reaching his hand down to me. "I need to meet Anna for dinner, but let me walk you back to the house."

He pulls me into a hug. "Mel, do what feels right to you because I think whatever makes you happy would make Noah happy."

Family Meeting

It's been two months since I watched Noah's video. Two more months of thinking, watching videos, and listening to his music and the death playlist. Darren and I spent Belle's birthday getting shit-faced while Sawyer watched the kids. It was the first birthday in twenty-one years I didn't spend with her.

Tomorrow is Noah and Sawyer's thirtieth birthday. Sawyer said to keep the day free–as if I ever go anywhere. He's been absolute in his plans, so the family is coming over tonight to celebrate. I'm also going to talk to them tonight about a foundation for Noah. It's time; maybe moving on with something positive to do will help alleviate all this lingering sadness I carry. It's been seven months since the accident and the only thing I know for sure is life without Noah and Belle is the saddest place in the world.

"Amelia! Sweetheart, give me a hug. How are you doing?" Karen pulls me into her embrace and asks me the same question she always does. I love her so much. We've become so close these last few months; I'd be lost without her.

"I'm okay, Karen. How are you?" There's been a shift in Karen. She's laser-focused on the family but not in a hovering way. She looks tired and worn out, but she's never without a smile. The more time I spend with her makes me realize how much Noah was like his mom. Losing Noah has certainly taken its toll on her; I can't imagine how it must feel. As much as I miss Noah, if something were to happen to Nate, I'm not sure I could go on.

"I'm happy to be here celebrating Sawyer's birthday, but I'm struggling a bit knowing it's our first one without Noah."

"I'm sorry, Karen. I know my own pain, but I can't imagine yours."

Sawyer just finished changing Nate and brings him to me.

"He helps, Mel. Having Nate with us helps immensely." She holds out her arms for him and I pass him off to her.

"Ma, Ma, Ma," Nate says when Karen kisses him, and he holds his arms out for me.

"Mel! When did he start that?" Karen squeals in delight, and Sawyer smiles from across the bar.

"He just started it yesterday. It makes my heart flutter every time." What I don't say is that I'm dreading the day he says any form of dad because it's going to rip me to shreds.

"You're such a big boy, Nate!" she praises him and takes him in the other room to tell everyone.

Sawyer has a strange look on his face so I move closer to him. "Are you okay?"

He shakes it off and smiles. "Yeah, just thinking."

"About what?" I ask, bumping my hip against his.

He leans back against the counter and meets my eyes. "Do you really want to know?"

"Of course, Sawyer. You're my best friend these days. I want to know everything." His cheeks turn slightly pink with my words. In Belle and Noah's absence, and with Eli on tour, Sawyer and I are the best of friends these days.

"Maybe I just have the blues. I'm fucking thirty now. Everyone around me is having kids, starting a family, and I'm not even dating. By the time I find someone and settle down, Nate will probably be in high school."

What he says makes me feel sort of shitty. Maybe Sawyer would be further along if we weren't holding him back.

"You'll find someone when you're ready, Sawyer, and I hope she'll be worth the wait. You deserve the best. This has been a hard year for us all. If Nate and I are holding you back from ..."

"Stop, Mel."

"No, Sawyer, I'm serious. If you're not going to the bar with J or dating more because of us, it's okay. We'll be fine. I'll miss Noah forever, but I'm doing better now. And tonight, after we talk about the foundation, I'll have something else to focus on."

"Amelia, I promise you aren't holding me back. It's been a rough year and I'm not ready. You know I self-sabotage. I guess I feel guilty even thinking about moving on when Noah isn't here to do that, too."

I pour us both a Jack and Coke and take a sip while looking over at everyone chatting and laughing in the family room. If you were an outsider looking in you'd never know the kind of hell this family has been through the past year.

"Noah would want you to be happy, Sawyer. More than anything. I'm pretty sure his birthday wish for you would be to move on, fall in love, and be creative again."

"Those are a lot of wishes," he answers with a smirk.

"Well, Noah was nothing if not a positive thinker. I'm sure they all fall in line with his thinking."

I know this isn't the thirtieth birthday Sawyer was imagining. It's been a hard day for us all; this would have been a huge Weston family celebration for the twins. Sawyer is good at talking to me about things, but he still holds back where Noah is concerned. I wish he'd open up more because maybe I could open up to him more, too.

After cake has been served, the babies are asleep, and Saylor and Emme are settled in with a Disney movie, I gather everyone around the kitchen table. Wyatt pulls out the chair for Anna and helps her sit. She's due in two more months and is getting more uncomfortable by the day.

"Amelia, what did you want to talk to us about?" Owen asks the question they all have been dying to.

"I'm ready to start a foundation for Noah. I want to call it The Noah Weston Foundation for Kind Acts. And I want to fund different things. This is where I need your help. I'd like each of you to email me a list of things you think Noah was passionate about."

"Oh, Amelia," Karen cries out as she covers her mouth.

"There's more. I've been sitting on my parents' inheritance for years, so I want different divisions within the foundation. I want to have The Belle Dixson Scholarship for the Arts. I want to do something that honors both of my parents as well. I've followed Noah's request and set up financial security for me, Nate, and any future children I may have."

A wave of pride flows through me as they all nod and smile at me. I'm going to make Noah proud of me.

"Other than the funds already set aside, I'm going to use the remainder of both of my inheritances to fund this foundation and really make it something wonderful."

Rory is crying and raises her hand. Things with us have been strained but she doesn't need to act like she's in school.

"Question, Rory?"

"Can I help please?"

"I'm hoping you all will. This is going to be a family effort. I have no clue what I'm doing, and the people who loved Noah most should be on the board of directors. Sam, I was hoping you could help me with figuring some of this out or pointing me in the right direction. Tony, if you don't mind, I'd like your help, too."

"I'd be honored, Amelia," Sam says.

"Me, too. Count me in," Tony replies. "Pro-bono," he adds with a smirk.

Sawyer is beaming at me. I talked about my next announcement with him, Darren, and Wyatt a few weeks ago.

"Also, I decided if Sawyer and the guys can get the necessary permissions, I'm going to release Noah's EP as the first official fundraiser once everything is up and running."

"Mel, are you sure?" Anna's shocked tone matches her expression.

"Yeah, I talked to Wyatt about it at length and he reminded me of something. No matter how much Noah would have hated the spotlight, if he knew it was going to help people he would have been all in. I just hope we can create something he would be proud of."

Suddenly, everyone is talking at once and I'm being pulled into hugs from all directions. It still amazes me how easily I've fallen into this family and accepted their love and affection. It's such a stark contrast from that first Thanksgiving.

As they all head back into the living room, I grab Sam's arm. "Can we talk for a minute? Alone?"

With a nod, he opens the sliding glass door and steps out onto the patio. "Is everything okay?"

"I owe you an apology. It's been seven months since the tour and we haven't talked about the book. Sam, I'm sorry, but I need to pay you whatever I owe you for breach of contract. I know I still have a few months left but there's no way I can write this book now. I'm not sure if I'll ever be able to."

His expression turns serious and his eyes lock on mine. "Amelia, you almost died. You lost your husband and your best friend. You could have filed any number of lawsuits but you didn't. We're even. No one expects you to write this book. Not now, and if someday you get the motivation to try your hand at it, then you know we will publish it. I hope you haven't been worried about this along with everything else."

Relief surges through my body with his kind words. "Not until lately. I really thought maybe I'd be able to do it, but each time I try … I just can't. The computer expert Sawyer hired sent us everything he was able to recover from my laptop. It was all there, Sam. I did upload my camera that day, so I have all those pictures of Noah and

Sawyer now. It was such a relief. But that's when I realized I can't do the book. I'm so sorry."

Sam wraps his arms around me and kisses the top of my head. "We love you, Amelia, and we're happy you made it through and stayed with us. Nate should be your priority now. Everything else is a moot point."

Hours later, when everyone is leaving, Saylor looks up at me while yawning. "Auntie Mel, can I come over and play with Nate this weekend?"

"Ladybug, you can come over and play anytime you want to."

"Me, too?" Emme asks sweetly, and I drop down to their level.

"You, too."

They both kiss me goodbye and then wrap their arms around Sawyer. "Happy birthday, Uncle Sawyer. We love you," they call out in a singsong tone as their parents usher them out the front door.

They were the last to leave, so we head back into the kitchen for some cleanup.

"I've got it, Sawyer. Why don't you have a beer and tell me what the surprise is for tomorrow."

"On that note, I'm off to bed. I'll see you in the morning," Darren says before heading to his room.

"We're getting memorial tattoos in honor of Noah. My friend Ben is coming over tomorrow and doing them here. Do you want in on the action? Ink up that virgin skin of yours, Princess?"

He's so smug, but he has no idea. "My skin isn't virgin, Sawyer. I've got a tattoo."

His eyes widen in surprise as he finishes taking a draw of his beer. "No shit?"

"No shit."

"What is it? Where is it?" He's suddenly intrigued and it makes me laugh. I can't believe Noah never told him.

"You really don't know?"

He's shaking his head, his eyes never breaking contact with mine. "It's right here," I say, motioning to where the tattoo is under my clothes, "and it says Weston."

"Shut the fuck up. When did you get it?"

Taking a seat next to him, I grab his beer and take a sip. "Christmas Eve, not too long after everything went down with Sara."

"Before Noah even proposed," he muses.

"Yeah." I look up at the clock and see it's after midnight. When we sang "Happy Birthday" tonight, everyone sang to him *and* Noah. While I know it was instinct and they will always share a birthday, it also feels like Sawyer should be celebrated as well.

"Happy birthday, Sawyer," I say, leaning in to kiss him on the cheek. He was in the process of putting his beer down, though, and when he turned I caught his lips instead. My heart races.

This is all sorts of wrong.

"Oh shit. I'm sorry, Sawyer. I didn't mean ..."

Sawyer flashes me that sinful smirk of his. "It's okay, Mel. I know you were aiming for my cheek."

"So uh ... what do you want for your birthday?" Stammering, I change the subject.

"Just for the four of us to get our tattoos and toast to Noah."

The sadness in his voice makes me feel bad. "Can we at least toast to both of you? I know you guys are twins, and it's harder for you than everyone, but Noah would want you to be happy on your birthday."

"Sure, but doing this will make me happy and so will getting started on the foundation. I'm going to be your right hand through it all."

"I'd love that, Sawyer."

Nate's crying and I'm on duty tonight. "His Majesty awaits. Goodnight, Sawyer."

"Goodnight, Princess."

"Are you sure you're ready for this, Mel?" Wyatt asks, concern lacing his voice.

"I'm sure. There's nothing more I'd rather do than get this tattoo."

Before last night I hadn't even given it any thought, but the idea of a memorial tattoo for Noah makes me happy. They've all already done theirs and they look great. It looks like a sheet of music paper with three lines. The first line contains the first line of musical notes from their very first song. The second line is where Noah's name is. The third line is the last line of notes from their final song "Just an Illusion". It's surreal how everything has come full circle like this, but I think Noah would love it.

Since the guys have a lot of tattoos already, they put theirs where it made sense on their existing canvases. For me, I chose to put mine on my back on the left side of my shoulder.

The doorbell rings and Darren goes to grab it. "You ready to start, Mel?" Ben asks.

"Yeah, I'm ready."

Mac and Ryan walk in carrying a couple of bottles of alcohol with bows on them and pull Sawyer into a hug.

"Someone let it slip you were getting memorial tattoos for Noah. Any chance we can get in on that action?" Mac asks.

"You'd want to?" Sawyer asks, surprised, as my eyes fill with tears.

"Hell yeah. We spent the last nine years with you guys. We loved him, too," Ryan adds.

"Shit, guys, you're right. Of course you can join us. Maybe we should call Warren, too," Darren replies as he looks around.

"That's probably a good idea. Anna was pretty mad she couldn't do it because she's pregnant, but she says she's getting hers as soon as she can," Wyatt tells them.

"Alright, Mel, this may sting a bit, but you've had one before in a more sensitive spot. It won't be any worse than that was," Ben tells me as he turns on the gun.

Sawyer is texting on his phone and looks up at me with admiration when he finishes. "Who would have ever thought I'd be getting a tattoo with a princess?"

"Please, you're lucky this princess deems you worthy of her time. Let alone, decided she likes you enough to be best friends with you."

The guys laugh at my words and Sawyer takes a shot and smiles sinfully at me. "I completely underestimated you the first night we met."

"Did you guys hear that? Sawyer just admitted he was wrong!" Wyatt calls out, and they all give Sawyer some shit.

"Hey, I'm secure enough in my manhood to admit my mistakes. In any case, Princess was a compliment … she turned out to be more of an evil queen."

"Evil, my ass. You just don't like being told things the way they are. I think it burns that rock star ego of yours just a bit."

"Damn, Sawyer, every time I do a tattoo for you there's usually some groupie drooling all over you. This is a nice change of scenery. You remind me of my wife, Mel. She's pretty as can be on the outside, but it's something special when her inner bitch comes out to play," Ben says, chuckling.

Sawyer throws a look Ben's way. "Hey, Ben, you know you're tattooing rock royalty, right?"

Oh shit. It's no secret, but Sawyer must have a reason for being a dick. Whatever it is, it better not fuck up my tattoo.

"I thought *you* were the rock royalty," Ben tosses back good-naturedly.

The guys are gathered around with similar smirks on their faces.

"No, for real. You don't know who she is?"

"Aside from Noah's wife? No, man, you know I don't keep up with that kind of shit." Ben pauses what he's doing and looks at Sawyer.

"She's Joey Triton's daughter."

"The fuck?" Ben says, and pushes back from behind me for a minute. They all laugh as Ben stares at me in awe.

"Why did you guys do that?" I grumble, irritated they chose now to fuck with their friend.

"Aw, don't be mad, Mel. Ben is a huge Joey fan. He's got a picture in the shop of him, his dad, and Joey at a concert. Sawyer just wanted to make him cream his pants a bit," Darren says, still snickering.

"Alright," Ben says, composing himself a bit and throwing a murderous glare their way. "Let's finish this up and we'll make yours look even better than theirs. It's what they get for being assholes."

Ben does make mine better by putting a small red heart next to Noah's name. After he finishes, I go to my room and grab a few things I got for Sawyer.

When I come back in the room with his presents in hand, his eyes light up. "You got me gifts?"

"Mmhm. Even though you're an asshole, I got you gifts."

He passes me a shot of tequila, which I knock back immediately. The first present is a coffee mug with a picture of him and Nate on it. It says "World's Best Uncle." It's super cheesy, but with his coffee habit I couldn't resist.

"This is so cool!" he exclaims when he opens it.

The next present is a big box filled with Pop-Tarts. I figured it was time to contribute to the fund. I've eaten my fair share of them lately, that's for sure.

"Jesus, Mel, there's enough in here to last us months. Good call."

When he moves to open the last gift, my heart flutters. I wanted this birthday to be about him but I couldn't let it go by without Noah being a part of it in some way. I took one of the brother pictures recovered from my computer and put it in a wooden frame with "Brothers Forever" engraved on it.

As he rips the paper off, his eyes lock onto the photo and fill with tears. It's the two of them standing next to each other with their guitars at their sides and they each have an arm around each other.

"Thanks, Mel. I needed this today most of all," he whispers as he blinks back the tears. Suddenly, he's pouring everyone a round of shots and lifts his glass. "To Noah. Happy birthday, big brother, wherever you are."

The doorbell rings and Wyatt lets Warren inside.

"Tattoos all around but no one called the gay guy. I see how you all are." His eyes twinkle mischievously as he pulls Sawyer in for a birthday hug.

"Sorry, Warren, I've just had a one-track mind lately and thought it would just be like a brother thing. But then we included Mel, and when Mac and Ryan came and gave me shit I realized I was wrong not asking you all. We've all been like brothers these past ten years or so. My bad."

Warren picks up the photo and looks at it fondly. "You know I'm just giving you hell. But I've definitely got room for a new tattoo. Looks like we'll be keeping you busy a bit longer, Ben."

"I came prepared. I know how you guys get once I open my case."

"Should we call Veronica?" I ask Darren. She took both kids for the night, but it's the first time either of them have spent the night away from us.

"I already did. She says they're fine and we should enjoy ourselves. She'll let us know if something changes."

"In other words, 'Don't call me again. I raised Belle and Amelia and I know what I'm doing.'"

He laughs. "That's pretty much the vibe I got."

"It feels strange not having them here. I feel like I should be doing something."

"It does, and we *should* be doing something. Enjoying ourselves for once," he says as he puts an arm around my waist.

"Do you ever feel like they're going to walk in the door any minute?"

"All the time. They were both so full of life it's like that happy energy still lingers. Do you ever think about moving?" he asks in a low tone so no one else can hear.

With a nod, I reply, "More often than I'd like to admit. It's hard living where we have so many memories, but I can't imagine living without them, either."

"Same here."

"Don't you two look cozy. Want to share what you're whispering about?" Sawyer asks as he saunters up to us. He's buzzed; it's nice seeing him seem like his normal self.

"Just missing our babies," I reply, not wanting him to know the whole truth.

"When did we get old? I fucking miss them, too. Remember when birthdays were for partying hard?"

"Some birthdays were spent partying *too* hard," Wyatt answers, and Darren nods his agreement.

"Well, speaking of partying hard, are we still throwing a big bash for Cadence?" Sawyer asks, changing the topic.

Darren shrugs, but I nod enthusiastically. "Yes. All the family, two cakes, lots of pizza, and goodie bags for Saylor and Emme. The perfect party for a one-year-old."

"Two cakes?" Darren questions.

"Oh yeah. Belle was big on babies having their faces smashed into a cake. So one for Cadence and one for the rest of us."

"That seems like such a Belle thing to be into," Darren says, rolling his eyes.

"Belle used to send me video links whenever she saw a really good one. I don't know why she thought it was so funny. I always thought it was mean, but I know Belle would do it if she were here, so Cadence is going to partake. I'm sure Veronica will do it for us. I don't have the heart."

"Nate won't get the same treatment?" Sawyer asks.

"Nope. He can have his own and eat it with his hands, but I'm not shoving his face in."

"Come on, guys, enough kid talk. It's a party ... let's get shitfaced," Wyatt calls out as he pours another round of shots.

After everyone retired to their respective rooms, Sawyer walked me to mine. I've had more tequila shots than I have in ... I don't even remember how long ... and everything is swimming.

"Goodnight, Princess. Thank you for my presents."

I lean against the wall for support and laugh when I almost fall.

"You're welcome, Sawyer. Goodnight." As I turn to go inside, I trip over my foot and start falling fast toward the floor. Sawyer reaches around my waist and pulls me flush against him.

"Careful, Princess. Let me help you." He leads me to the bed and turns off the light next to it. I don't even care that I'm still in my clothes. I just want to sleep. "Goodnight," he says, leaning down. I expect him to kiss my cheek, but his lips float briefly across the top of mine before he turns and walks away. It was only the whisper of a kiss, but my whole body tingles.

It didn't mean anything, though. We're just drunk and it was a bit more friendly of a kiss than I'm used to. It's not a big deal. At least that's what I try and tell myself because, as I curl up under the covers, my heart feels like it's a very big deal and not in a good way.

Unsteady

Today marks ten months to the day of the accident. Each time we hit one of these markers we're all a bit on edge. Something feels different today, though. Things haven't been this tense since Cadence's birthday. That was a rough day for us all, including Veronica, but we did our best and made it through. I think we're doing okay because Cadence is one happy little girl. Her favorite word is daddy and she uses it often. She calls Nate "NaNa" and it's adorable.

Rory was here most of the day going over some things for the foundation. The two of us are back to being friends again, which is good because I missed her. Sawyer thinks he's close to getting some permissions from the artists who own the songs on EP, so that's positive news.

Both of us were hungover the day after his birthday, and we've never mentioned the near-miss, not-a-near-miss kiss we had. It was fine by me because it was a mistake no matter what it was. Lately, he's been spending more time in the garage working on music. I'm not sure what kind, or what he's planning on doing with it, but I'm afraid to even ask.

As I work on clearing up the paperwork from our meeting today, Sawyer comes out of his room freshly showered and looking good. *Too good.*

"Going somewhere?" I ask.

"Yeah, I'm taking Lola out tonight."

My heart races a million miles a minute with his words.

"I thought you didn't like her?" I snap.

"She's been there for me, Mel. I feel like I owe it to her, and maybe to myself, to try to see where this goes."

"Oh, well … um … okay. Have fun."

"Sure thing."

"Hey, Sawyer?" I call out as he walks toward the door.

"Yeah, Mel?"

"Just be safe tonight, okay?"

His expression softens slightly. "Of course."

When Sawyer leaves, I sit at the table and stare out at the ocean. Veronica has Nate and Cadence tonight, so I'm flying solo. Between her and Karen, they've been taking the kids at least once a month. It's supposed to give me and Darren time to go out and do things, but neither of us ever do. It makes them feel closer to Belle and Noah to have them spend time with them, and for that reason alone I'd never deny them. It's just lonely when they're not here.

I spin my wedding rings around on my fingers and miss my husband more than ever. My nightmares have all but vanished with just a few rogue dreams here and there. After I read Sawyer's journal, they started coming more frequently but in the right order, at least the order according to the journal. Then they slowed after a few weeks. Last night, I had the first one since this time last month. I know it's the anxiety of what day it is that must be bringing them on.

I reach for my phone to text Anna and hesitate for a split second. Now that she and Wyatt are new parents, I hate to bother her. They had their baby last month; he's the cutest little thing. Jacob Miles Smith made his appearance on May eleventh at three in the morning. He was a big boy at almost ten pounds, and he's absolutely perfect.

Fuck it. She would want to know this.

Sawyer just took Lola out on a date.

Within minutes, my phone is ringing. "Hey, Anna."

"Are you kidding me?!" she squeals.

"Nope."

"Jesus, Mel, did he give you any notice or anything?"

"No, but it's not like he needs to. I'm not his mother."

She blows out a frustrated sigh. "You're one of his best friends and you live with him. Did she just show up there?"

"Hell no. I would have lost my shit. He knows better than that. What am I supposed to do, Anna?"

"Noah would *hate* this." She says and I hear her filling in Wyatt.

"Maybe she's changed. Sawyer is a grown man and he wants more, Anna. Maybe Lola will be it for him." The words taste foreign on my tongue. She's bad news, I just know it.

"I'll talk to him, Mel. Maybe if he hears it from me it will make a difference somehow. I'm not saying people can't change, but I don't think she's one who ever will."

"Maybe. I'm sorry to bother you with this I know you're busy with Jacob. How is he, by the way? I miss him already."

She laughs. "He's good. You just saw him yesterday, but you're welcome to come by anytime."

"And you're still feeling okay?" I don't know when I suddenly became this mother hen to everyone, but it's definitely become a new part of my personality.

"I'm great. Wyatt is a doting father and husband."

"Good. Make sure you tell him I said to keep his O game away from you until the doctor says it's okay."

She cracks up and yells it out to him. I can hear him saying "yeah, yeah" in the background.

"What are you and Darren up to tonight?"

"He's having dinner with his parents, the kids are with Veronica, and I'm sitting here spinning my wedding rings in circles and getting ready to drown myself in a bottle of tequila."

Anna is silent for a minute. "Be careful, Mel. Remember what happened last time."

I told Anna about how Sawyer kissed me. She hugged me and told me it would be okay and that it probably didn't mean anything. I felt so guilty. I love my husband with my whole heart and I'd never want to do anything to hurt him. But Anna being her typical, blunt self, reminded me I can be married in my heart forever but I don't have a physical husband anymore, and I technically didn't do anything wrong. It felt wrong, though, even if a tiny part of it felt right.

"Yeah, I know, Anna. I won't get too drunk. If I do, I'll do it in my room."

"You could come over if you want to."

"No, you three enjoy your bonding time. I'll be okay. I'll talk to you later."

A few hours and a half bottle of tequila later, I'm listening to music and filling some photo albums with pictures. Building memories for Nate always makes me feel better. I'm building them for Cadence, too. I've got matching albums for them because they're together in almost all their pictures.

I wonder if Belle was right and they'll grow up and get married. How adorable would it be to have all these childhood memories of them at their wedding one day? But then I think realistically and think it's more likely they will grow up like brother and sister and never cross that line.

"Unsteady" by X Ambassadors plays through the house and I stand up to get some water. Hearing shuffling by the front door, I check out what's going on. Ryan is on guard tonight because the guys don't leave me alone without someone guarding the door.

Sawyer and Lola are standing at the door and she hands him something. He sees me and shoves it in his pocket and pulls her in for a hug. Whatever it was fell, but he doesn't realize it.

"Let me walk you out," he says to her and pulls her outside quickly.

Walking over to the door, I pick up what he dropped and my blood runs cold.

I'm so furious as I walk back into the kitchen, I can barely put one foot in front of the other. Is this why he's been acting strange lately? Because he's using again? Fuck!

It takes every ounce of willpower I have to not go beat that bitch down so she can never give him or anyone else drugs again. I won't live like this, and I won't subject my son to this kind of environment. I wonder if Darren knows. Hell, I wonder if Darren is using with him.

"Dammit, Noah, what do I do now?" I scream, releasing a desperate sob.

"Princess, what's wrong?" Sawyer asks, turning me toward him.

"Don't fucking touch me!"

"Seriously, Mel, you're freaking me out. What's wrong?"

The concern on his face is evident, or maybe he's an even better liar than I knew. "You have the audacity to ask me that?"

"Is this about Lola? It was dinner, Mel. I didn't even kiss her."

I bring my hands together in a slow clap. "Well, fucking bravo for you. Were you too high to get it up, or were you just using her to score?"

Immediately, he reaches into his pocket and his face pales when his hand comes back empty.

"Looking for this?" I ask, waving the baggie in front of my face.

"It's not what you think, Mel. I can explain."

"Tell it to someone who cares, Sawyer. I'm done! I will put up with a lot of shit, but this isn't part of it. How long have you been using?"

Fury masks his features as he leans back against the counter and crosses his arms. "Is that what you think of me now? That I'm a druggie addict liar? Do you know me at all?"

Tears begin falling from my eyes as I toss the baggie to the table behind me. "I thought I did, Sawyer, but I'm not sure anyone has ever surprised me more."

I turn and go to my room, locking the door behind me. Once I have my pajamas on, I turn off the lights and cry myself to sleep. Just like I have on the anniversary of this day for the past nine months. But tonight, the pain is worse because I feel like Sawyer is slipping through my fingers and I can't imagine my life or Nate's life without him.

When I woke up this morning, I pulled out my suitcases and opened them up on my bed. Now, I'm sitting here looking at the whales playing in the ocean, sipping my coffee, and debating my next step.

I'm freaking out on the inside but trying to stay rational. I can't live here if Sawyer is using. I can't have him around my son. But should I call the family and have an intervention? Karen and Owen can't lose another child, and I can't wrap my mind around why Sawyer would start using again. I know the anniversary days are hard, and we all cope the best we can, but why didn't he talk to me if he was feeling this desperate? Why couldn't he say something?

"Mel, can we talk?" Sawyer calls through the door.

"Come in."

He gasps as he walks inside. "You're leaving?"

With a sigh, I turn to where he just took a seat on the bed. "I'm not sure what I'm doing, Sawyer. I want to help you but I don't know how. I thought we were friends." Tears begin streaming down my cheeks again. He reaches out to wipe them away but I smack his hand. "I've never been as vulnerable with anyone as I have been with you since the accident. It breaks my heart you were hurting so much you couldn't talk to me *and* went back to drugs."

"Mel," he runs his hands through his hair frantically, "you don't understand."

"Please enlighten me because I'm at a complete loss, Sawyer. Before last night, I never thought my heart could be broken any further. I was wrong. You shattered whatever was left. But I can't raise my son in a house with an addict. I won't."

"I'm sorry. I was angry last night and let this go on too long. You were right, Mel. Lola was bad news."

Releasing a combination of a snort and a laugh, my eyes lock on his. "Tell me something I don't know."

"Look, this is kind of embarrassing, okay? I took her to dinner at Duke's and when we got in the car afterward, she did a line right in front of me."

What the hell?

"She just busted it out right there?"

"Yeah. I was shocked, too. I was texting Wyatt back because *someone* told him and Anna I was making a bad life choice by going out with Lola."

His tone makes me chuckle. "Well, it seems like that someone was right."

"Yeah, you were. The whole way home she was telling me about her dealer boyfriend and how he's the best in the business. That baggie was basically her calling card. My sample to test the goods for myself. She was hoping I could spread the word to my industry friends. I felt like I was being punked."

I feel like a ten-pound weight has been lifted from my chest. "So you aren't—"

"No, Mel, I'm not using again. I wouldn't do that. Losing Noah was hard, and the urge was strong when it first happened, but do you know what was stronger? My love for you and Nate. He needed me, Mel, and that was more important than any high."

"I'm sorry, Sawyer. I was drunk and it was a bad night. When I saw that, I freaked out. I don't do well around drugs after my dad, and I felt like I'd somehow failed you." I'm crying again, but this time he pulls me from the chair and into his arms.

"Don't leave, Princess. I don't have a clue what I'm doing with my life, but I do know you and Nate are the only things I've got that make it worth living right now."

"What about the drugs?"

"I ran them down the drain last night. That's not my life anymore. I feel sorry for Lola that this is her future. She's an addict who plays people to get her boyfriend business. I mean, he's basically pimping her. She didn't even mention him until after dinner. She was all flirty and touchy feely. I know I could have fucked her if I wanted to but all I could think about was coming home … to you."

"Because me and my scrapbooking are such high excitement for a Friday night."

He leans his head against mine. "Because you're my best friend, Mel, and I missed you."

"You better not let Anna hear you say that."

He laughs lightly. "People can have more than one best friend. Both of us are blessed with many of them. You're the one I spend the most time with, though, so you're the one I miss most."

The underlying tone to this conversation is heavier than I'm willing to admit to myself. Right now, I'm just relieved it was all a misunderstanding.

"Can we agree Lola comes nowhere near this house anymore? I can't have that around my son or Cadence."

"For sure. I told her I wasn't interested and put her in the car so Ryan could take her home. I didn't even want to be associated with her in case anyone was taking photos or something."

"Okay."

He kisses me on the head and stands us both up. "What time are the kids coming home?"

"Around five, I think."

"Good. Get dressed and let me take you to breakfast."

"You want to buy me breakfast?"

"I want to do a lot of things, Mel. I was sad yesterday, ten months is a long time to be sad. I know things will never be the same, but after last night I realized we need to start living a little more outside of this house and our bubble."

He's ready to move on. I knew it would come but it stings a bit.

"Sawyer ..."

"Nope, no arguments. We've walked this road together thus far and we're going to keep walking it together. If I'm getting out of my bubble, so are you. Breakfast and the farmer's market, okay?"

"You don't play fair, Weston."

"Neither do you, Weston. Get dressed."

The waitress brings our food and places a hand on Sawyer's shoulder. "I'm sorry about your brother, sweetie, and your husband," she says, turning to me. "He was one of the good ones."

"Thanks," he replies, and I nod. She's an older woman, probably mid-fifties, with a kind smile.

"Let me know if you need anything else."

As she walks away, he looks at me. "Sorry, I forgot I haven't been in here since before the accident."

"It's alright. Do you know her well?"

"I guess ... we used to come here a lot. Especially after pulling an all-nighter in the studio. The food is good, greasy, and fresh. This is Darren's favorite breakfast spot."

The diner is small and filled with mostly elderly people. No one blinked twice at us when we came in.

"Makes sense. It's pretty low-key."

He chuckles. "That's why I like it. Darren has a love affair with their banana pancakes."

Taking a bite of my banana waffles, I groan with pleasure. "I can see why."

Sawyer pulls his lip ring into his mouth and bites down on his lip. He's holding something back, I only wish he'd tell me what.

"Tell me one thing about you no one knows," I say, trying to get him talking again.

He thinks about it for a minute and then flashes me an adorably shy smile. "When I was a kid, I wanted to be a doctor. Blood always made me queasy, but it was even worse after everything went down with J."

"That explains why you always took such good care of me. You're the only one who jumped at the chance to change my bandages."

A slight blush creeps into his cheeks. "It might not have been for completely altruistic reasons. It was an easy way to somehow be able to touch you. Even so, you needed help, and Noah couldn't do it after the Sara thing. Then, after the accident, you needed help and I didn't want Eli putting his hands near you."

Putting my fork on my plate, my gaze meets his. "You like to help people. There's nothing wrong with admitting that. I never felt needy asking your for help. You would have made a good doctor, Sawyer. You still could if you wanted to. You're young enough to go back to school."

He laughs and shakes his head. "Nah, it's not for me anymore. How about you? Tell me one thing no one knows about you."

"The day I found my dad, the police were the ones to give me my birthday present and card after they cleared the scene. I've never opened them. They're in my bottom dresser drawer."

"How come?"

"I don't know. Maybe because it's the last gift I'll ever get from him, or maybe I want to save it for when I really need to feel close to him."

"And Belle didn't know?"

An ache fills my heart because I lied to her and can never make it right. "No. I told her I opened it and it was just some jewelry. She would have never let me get away with not opening it."

"Maybe you should think about why that is. Enough of this sad talk, let's go to the farmer's market and have some fun."

D. Kelly

We had a fun afternoon and came home with lots of fruits and vegetables. We even stopped at the toy store and got Nate some presents for his first birthday. The house is already overflowing with baby toys, especially since Cadence's first birthday, but you only turn one once and I can always donate them when they're done with them.

Our fun day took a nosedive after Veronica brought the kids home. I'm sitting on the floor changing Cadence as Nate crawls right up to Sawyer's legs and says the word I've been dreading.

"Dada."

I know it's a natural progression in language, and he hears Cadence say it all the time so I'm surprised he hasn't said it sooner, but still … it steals my breath away.

Sawyer's eyes meet mine because Nate is reaching up for him, so I nod for him to pick him up. I don't know what to do, but Sawyer seems to hold his own.

"Hey, little man. Uncle Sawyer," he says, pointing to himself.

"Dada."

"Uncle Sawyer," he says patiently, but now Nate thinks it's a joke and laughs.

"Dada."

"I'm sorry, Mel. I don't know what to do but to keep saying it."

"It's okay, Sawyer. It's natural, right? He sees Cadence call Darren that all the time and to him you're his Darren. It only makes sense."

Sawyer sighs with tear-filled eyes and hugs Nate close. My heart aches for all of us. This is an impossible situation, but I'm not sure I'll ever be okay with Nate calling anyone else Dad.

"You've got the best dad in the world, Nate, he's just not here to do his job. You've got Uncle Sawyer, though, and I may not be the best but I make a pretty good substitute."

"You are the best substitute, Sawyer. Thank you," I whisper as I pull Cadence in for a hug.

"Ahmel," Cadence says, placing a big, open-mouth, slobbery kiss on me. It makes me laugh, which makes her laugh and do it again. She's such a little copycat. We think "Ahmel" is short for Auntie Mel.

The rest of the night I found myself sort of hoping Nate would call Darren Dada, too, but he never did. My son is a smart cookie and he knows what it means.

After the kids are in bed, Sawyer and I are sitting on his bed talking about some upcoming meetings he has this week with one of the songwriters. Both of us are in a little bit of a funk tonight.

"Mel, I'm sorry about earlier."

"There's nothing to be sorry for. I hate that Noah isn't here for this, but it does sort of make me proud that Nate is smart enough to realize that's what you are to him."

"No, I'm not." His tone is adamant while mine is resigned.

"I know, Sawyer, but you are in all the ways that matter. He's too little to understand it now, but he knows who protects him and keeps him safe. Biology doesn't make a parent, Sawyer."

He turns to me with wide eyes. "No, it doesn't, but love does. Noah loved the fuck out of him."

"He did, and it's what makes this all the more tragic. We can show Nate videos and photos and tell him until we're blue in the face how much Noah loved him."

"And we will," he snaps.

"Yes, of course we will. But at the end of the day, it's *your* love he has. It's *your* hugs that make him feel safe, it's *your* voice that sings him to sleep. I know you want to be a part of his life, Sawyer, but I think over the next year or so you're going to have to decide how big of a role you want because he's already attached."

"There's no deciding. I want it all, Mel."

Nodding, I turn back to him. "But your future wife might not, and your future kids may not understand. You really need to think long and hard about this."

"There's nothing to think about. Any woman who doesn't understand this isn't the kind of woman I'd want to spend my life with."

"Fair enough."

Part of me is relieved to know Sawyer is adamant about being in this for the long haul with Nate. The other part of me is worried Sawyer may sacrifice something good and end up resenting us. There's nothing I can do, though, because this is our life now and Sawyer is an integral part. I wouldn't be able to function without him.

Happy Birthday

Today is Nate's first birthday. The family has been here all day and things are finally winding down. We're putting our love for my little guy in front of our pain, but that pain is just below the surface for us all.

Mama went to the cemetery and put down flowers. I haven't been back since the night I almost slept there. I can't; it's too hard and honestly, it's pointless. Noah and Belle's spirits are long gone. I do feel like they're looking down on us today but maybe that's just wishful thinking.

Instead of going with her, I did the next best thing: wrote Belle a new letter and updated the *Slammed* blog.

Slammed Blog Post

Hey *Slammed* Family,

It's Mel again. This week marks a year since we lost Belle and Noah. It's bittersweet, to say the least, because this week also marks a year since I gave birth to Nate. He's the light of my life. Every day I spend with him is one I will cherish forever.

Today is Nate's actual birthday and I'm trying not to focus on the sadness of it. Instead, I'm putting my blessings in front of the tragedy. Nate and I could have easily died in that crash, and while some days I wished I could have gone with Noah, I'm glad to be here now as the mother of a happy one-year-old.

Noah believed in fate, and one thing I *do* know is it was fate my son survived that horrendous crash.

This upcoming year is going to be filled with amazing things. We are officially launching The Noah Weston Foundation for Kind Acts. Noah was known for his generous spirit; we would like to continue that legacy in his honor. We're working on releasing some previously unreleased music as our first fundraiser. I'll keep you up to date once I have more information. Updating this blog is my way of trying to keep Belle close to my heart. You guys gave her life, and she loved being able to share all the good things with you.

The last post I did was for Cadence's first birthday. Today, you're getting Nathaniel Noah Weston's first birthday photo. Next to his picture you'll notice another first birthday image from years past. When you put them together, other than the age of the photograph itself, you can't tell them apart, can you? Nate and Noah are twins twenty-nine years apart.

This past year has been hard, but it's also given me the biggest blessing of my life. Today, and moving forward, I'm going to put my complete focus into my blessings.

Until next time, *Slammed* family.

With love,

Amelia

"Damn, Mel, I can't believe he's a year old already," Eli says as he wraps his arms around me and pulls me into a hug.

"Me, either. Thank you for coming back for this, I'm so glad you were here. I needed an Eli fix just as much as Nate did."

Those baby blues of his meet mine. "I'm only a call away. If you ever need me, I'll hop the first flight. The tour will be over in a few months and I'll be back here annoying you before you know it."

"Not possible. Well, maybe a little possible, but I'll take annoying Eli over missing Eli any day. Be safe out there, okay?"

He hugs me tighter and whispers in my ear, "It was a freak accident, Mel. I'll be fine. You have to try to get past this fear that as soon as someone leaves something is going to happen to them. But on the off chance it does, you know I love you always."

"Me, too. I'm trying to get past it, but I've had to try to move past a lot of things this year. Being fearful is a work in progress."

"Sawyer said he's been trying to get you out of the house more."

Of course he did.

"Yeah, we've been taking the kids to the park now that the paparazzi has backed off a bit. He reminds me often they need the chance to be kids."

"And you, my dear friend, need the chance to enjoy life again. Stop living in the past and putting your sole focus on the kids and the foundation. Live your life because tomorrow isn't promised to any of us."

I pull back from him and shoot him a nasty glare. "It's only been a year, Eli."

"Exactly. You and Noah had less than that. I'm not trying to say your pain isn't valid, but don't let the best year of your life keep you from enjoying the eighty or so you have left."

"Eighty?"

With a lopsided smile, he replies, "I'm bad at math, sue me. But fuck it, maybe you will get eighty more years and outlive us all. The keyword being 'live'. Come on, Mel, it's time. Take some baby steps to   happiness."

"You're a pain in my ass, Eli, but I love the fuck out of you. I'll try, okay?"

"That's all I can ask for," he says, kissing me on the forehead. "My plane leaves in a few hours for Nashville. Let me know if you want to fly in for a show. I'll hook you up."

"Thanks, Eli. Travel safe."

As I'm standing in the foyer after Eli leaves, Saylor flies into my legs. Sawyer is chasing her and she's laughing uncontrollably. "Save me, Auntie Mel! Uncle Sawyer says he's going to feed me to the fish!"

Sawyer is laughing just as hard as she is. "He wouldn't do that, Ladybug. He'd miss you too much."

"Hm, I didn't think about that. I *would* miss my little namesake. Alright, I won't make you fish food. But you have to give me some love before I let you go." He swoops her into his arms.

Saylor throws her arms around his neck and kisses him loudly. "I love you, Uncle Sawyer."

Her words melt my heart almost as much as the smile on his face does. He's in full-blown dimple mode, making my heart flutter in a way it shouldn't.

"I love you, too, Saylor."

"Are you ready for your first cousin sleepover next weekend, Ladybug?" I ask, and she nods excitedly.

"Yes! Me and Emme made room in the playroom so Cadence and Nate can sleep in their travel beds with us. Mommy and Daddy said they have to sleep with us, too, so the babies don't get into trouble if they wake up. It's going to be so much fun!"

Saylor runs off and Sawyer grins at me. "It's going to be okay, Mel. They'll have a blast. It's good for them to do this, and it's what Noah would want."

"I know, but they're only one. Sleepovers at Grandma's are one thing, but at their cousins … it's just a sign of how fast time is going by."

"We should do something."

"Like what?" He's got an evil look on his face and I'm not sure I like it.

"Let's go to a club. We can go dancing."

"Uh, I don't think so."

"Why not? I know you love to dance, Mel."

"It wouldn't … it wouldn't be right," I stammer.

"The fuck it wouldn't. Your best friend lived by the motto 'Live today like there's no tomorrow.' You're existing, Mel, but you're not living. One night of fun won't kill you, and I won't take no for an answer."

Sawyer saunters off, effectively ending our conversation, but there's no way I'm in the mood to go clubbing with him. I can only imagine the siege of women who will descend upon us if we're out in public. Just the thought makes me shudder.

"Hey, Mel, we're going to get out of here. Call or text me if you need me later. I can come back or you can come over." Anna pulls me into a hug. When she releases me, Wyatt hands me Jacob to kiss goodbye.

D. Kelly

"You guys, he's so perfect. I can't believe he's three months old already."

They exchange a glance and Wyatt clears his throat. "We were wondering if you'd be interested in being Jake's godmother. You can say no because I know you're not in a good place with God right now, but we'd love it if you'd consider it."

"Really? You want me?"

Anna smiles brightly. "Absolutely. Sawyer and Darren have already agreed to be co-godfathers. You're our best girl, Mel. There's no one we'd rather have than you."

Placing a kiss on top of little Jake's head, I nod. "I'd love to. Thank you."

Wyatt takes him back and heads out to the car while Anna stays behind. "Mel, I know the next few days are going to be rough. I meant what I said. If you need anything, even to vent or just cry, call me."

"I will, thank you."

After they leave, I head into the kitchen and Nate toddles right to me. I scoop him into my arms and smother him with kisses. He started walking last month and now he's pretty much running most days.

He rubs his eyes and yawns, and when I look up at the clock I see it's already after eight. "Even birthday boys need their bedtime. Let's give everyone kisses night night and get you in the bath."

We make the rounds and Karen takes the longest with him. Her eyes are filled with tears as she wishes him a final happy birthday and sweet dreams. Then she hugs me hard and whispers into my ear, "We love you, Mel, and we're so proud of how far you've come this year. Each day is a new chance to take another step. I know these next few will be hard for us all, but call if you need me."

"You, too. Thank you, Karen."

Nate is so sleepy he barely makes it through his bath. Once his jammies are on, I sit with him as he drinks his bottle. Cadence is completely off her bottle and binky now; that's my next goal with Nate.

"Happy birthday, Nate. A year ago, your daddy and I were eagerly trying to get you to make an appearance into this world. He loved you so much. Do you remember how he used to sing to you when you were in my belly? Probably not, but he did it all the time. You loved hearing his voice, and he loved how you would kick when you heard him. I never thought anyone could love you as much as he did. Not even me.

"But you know what? I was wrong. I love you at least that much, if not more, and so does Uncle Sawyer. He loves you to the moon and back. You're so lucky to have him since you don't have your daddy. It's hard to believe it's been a year since you came into this world and your daddy and Auntie Belle left it. She would have loved you to pieces, just like she did Cadence."

I look down and Nate is fast asleep. When I stand up to put him in the crib, Sawyer is standing in the doorway watching us. He was probably there the whole time.

"Ready to get drunk?" he whispers as I lay Nate down. I grab the monitor, even though he's been mostly sleeping through the night the past few weeks, and close the door behind us.

"So completely ready to get drunk. Who is still here?"

"Just us and Darren, but he said he wanted to be alone with Cadence tonight and went to his room already."

Sadness fills my heart. "Do you think we should get him anyway?"

"No, I think he needs time with his little girl to remember Belle. Go sit down, you've been going all day. I'll get the stuff and bring it to the couch."

A few minutes later, Sawyer appears with a tray filled with tequila, shot glasses, salt, limes, a couple of bottles of water, and cake. He's thought of it all.

"Aren't you thoughtful bringing cake, too?"

"Well, I know you have to eat so you don't puke when you drink. Want Pop-Tarts instead?"

"Maybe. Depends on how drunk we get."

He pours the first shots and cuts up the limes. "As drunk as possible tonight. Lick your hand, Princess."

I do as he asks and he does the same before sprinkling salt on each of us. After licking it off, we take our shots and suck the lime. We repeat this three more times before we lean back to talk.

"Remember that night at Sully's? You made fun of me for wanting food and now you're supplying my need."

He looks at me and laughs. "I was going through some shit and I was being a dick. I needed to get laid and took it out on you."

"Ugh, don't remind me. I'll never forget the look in that skank's eyes when she asked if we wanted to join in."

Sawyer's eyes widen. "She asked you that?"

"Oh yeah," I reply, laughing. "Pissed Noah right off. She said something like she wasn't into chicks but we could totally swap."

He grabs his head and shakes it as he laughs hysterically. "No wonder Noah was so pissed. He was super sensitive about anyone asking us to swap or for a threesome."

"Did that happen a lot?" I ask, pouring us more shots but forgoing the salt and lime this time.

"More than I'd like to admit. There are some freaky people out there. I mean, I've had my share of threesomes, for sure, but never with my own brother."

This discussion could be interesting and I'm all for interesting right now since I'm floating on a drunken cloud. "Two girls and a guy, or two guys and a girl?"

With a wicked smirk, he knocks back his shot. "Both."

"With Darren?"

"A few times."

"With two guys, do you … do stuff with the guys?" He blushes and pours another shot. "Oh my God, you did! With Darren?"

"Fuck no. Why are we talking about this?" He's still blushing; I think I've hit a sensitive spot with him. This is fun.

"Because I'm seriously intrigued. How far have you gone with another guy, Sawyer?"

"Intrigued in a good way?"

"Hell yeah. I mean, I don't know about most women, but I know Belle and I both thought the idea of a threesome with two bisexual men is seriously hot."

His eyes roam over me as if he's seeing me in a whole new light. "Don't get too excited, Princess. I've only kissed another guy once and it wasn't for me. I'm a pussy connoisseur, not a dick enthusiast. But, uh …"

"What? Tell me. I won't tell anyone, I promise."

"Let's just say it was kind of a fantasy fulfillment night so I let him go down on me with her."

"Was it hot?"

"Yeah, but I closed my eyes. It was more of the two mouths at once that was hot. They were a couple and it was like a holy grail fuck for them because of who I am. I get the appeal, but at the end of the day I just want to sink into a tight, hot, wet pussy."

"Jesus, Sawyer!"

"You asked, Princess," he says with a chuckle and pours our next shots.

"Were you high?"

"As a fucking kite."

"Can I ask you something?"

"Sure," he says as we toss them back.

"How long has it been since you've had sex?"

"Fourth of July weekend last year, when I spent the rest of our downtime with J."

"Wow, that's a long time."

He leans back on the couch and I lay my head on his shoulder, fully feeling the effects of these shots.

"There hasn't really been an opportunity, I guess, and it just hasn't been a priority. I've had my hands full lately."

"Mmhm. With your cock, I'm guessing."

Oh shit. Did I really just say that?

Laughter comes barreling out of him. "You're so fucking drunk, Mel, but I like it. You let your guard down. I'll tell you all about my hand if you tell me how many times you've gotten yourself off lately."

"I haven't."

"What? Like not at all?"

"Nope. BOB got lost in the crash, I guess. If he didn't, I don't want to know what item number he is from the crash investigation inventory."

Sawyer is laughing again. I forgot how much he laughs when he's drunk. "You could have bought a new one or ordered one online. And what about your hand?"

"I don't like using my hand for everything. It just doesn't work the same. You need one for your clit, one to slide inside, but then your boobs are neglected. Enough about me, we were talking about your hand."

"Princess, I use my hand almost every fucking day, sometimes more than once." I'm blushing but I'm not sure why; his answer doesn't surprise me. "Now that you're drunk I want you to make me a promise."

"Drunk promises aren't very responsible, Sawyer."

"Even so, I'm going to hold you to it. Promise me you'll go to the club with me next weekend when the kids are gone."

With a groan, I turn and face him. "I don't want to be under siege from fans or paps. I don't want you to take off with some chick and forget I'm even there so you can get laid. A club seems like a really bad idea, Sawyer."

Sincerity shines in his eyes. "None of that will happen, I promise. I know a place with private VIP rooms. Just you, me, Darren if we can get him to come, and a good time. Come on, Mel, say yes."

There's nothing more I want in this moment than to make Sawyer happy even though I don't understand why. "Okay, as long as you promise you won't ditch me."

"I'd never ditch you, Princess."

"What do you miss most?"

Sawyer wraps his arm around me, pulls me closer, and sighs. "Everything. I miss his laugh and his happiness, talking to him about things no one else would get, I miss my brother, my friend. I miss his love most of all."

"Me, too. Like everything you just said. Noah had a way of making it seem like everything was right in the world even when things were fucked up. He knew just what I needed to hear and when I needed to hear it. You're good at that, too, Sawyer. You guys share that trait, among others."

"What others?" he asks sleepily.

"I don't know … you're good at making me feel safe and getting me to talk. You make me laugh and you push me outside of my comfort zone. You made me be a mom and Noah would have been so thankful to you for that."

"You didn't need me, you would have been a great mom on your own. All you needed was the time to realize it."

I can't keep my eyes open anymore. "Thanks for making Nate's first year a good one," I mumble, wondering if he even understood what I just said.

"Thanks for letting me be a part of his life. It's the best thing that's ever happened to me."

In the middle of the night, I wake up bleary-eyed. I'm still drunk, and I miss Noah. I'm so lonely. It doesn't ever seem like anything is going to fill this gaping void in my heart where Noah used to be. Feeling Sawyer's arm around me, knowing his firm body is here, fills me with need. I know it's wrong, but it's been so long since I've allowed myself to feel anything and right now I'm feeling everything, *with him*.

His hand trails down my arm softly, and I don't think he knows I'm awake. He's so careful—probably hoping he doesn't wake me up—but I allow myself this moment to enjoy these sensations. After a year of misery, I deserve something, don't I? When a soft moan falls from my lips, he whispers, "Princess?" and fuck if that doesn't make me even needier for his attention.

As I lean my head up toward his, I use my arm to pull his face to mine. Pulling his bottom lip into my mouth, I tug on his lip ring the way I've imagined too many times. I'm a horrible person, but I never claimed to be a saint. As he tightens his arm around me, his tongue tentatively seeks mine. This isn't uncontrolled passion like our other kisses—this is soft, seductive, and exactly what I need from him. As his tongue caresses mine, my body floods with need. Maybe it's the tequila, maybe it's the loneliness, or maybe it's just him.

"Sawyer, please ..." My anguished words are filled with desperation.

"Please what, Princess? You've got to tell me what you need."

Why is he making this harder?

"Fuck me, Sawyer. Fuck my pain away. I need to you make it stop."

He squeezes me tighter in his embrace and kisses the top of my head. "I can't do that, Princess. The only way to ease your pain is to let it bleed out onto the floor while you drown in it." With those words, he releases me and walks away. A minute later, the sound of his bedroom door closing echoes through the hall.

Not even Sawyer wants me now. Who can blame him? I'm a sad, pathetic mess. And he's my husband's brother. God, what is wrong with me?

As I stand up, the room begins to spin but I manage to grab my water and the monitor and head to my room. Hopefully, in the morning, I'll realize this whole thing was one big nightmare.

D. Kelly

Amelia – Present Day

Karen took a break from reading and made us all lunch. As we sit around the table, it's quiet at first; that is, until Rory decides to finally speak up.

"Why didn't anyone tell me you and Sawyer kissed first?"

"Because it wasn't relevant to what is going on now, Rory. That night was a fluke, but it's also the night Noah laid the groundwork to steal my heart," I tell her.

"Everyone knew Sawyer had feelings for you but me." Her words sound like a petulant child but I'm trying to have patience with her.

"Look, Rory, I don't know what you want me to say. Sawyer had feelings but he was trying not to. Maybe everyone knew, but they didn't matter to me at the time. My heart belonged to Noah one hundred percent."

Anna looks up from her pasta and turns to me. "Do you really think that's true?"

"Of course I do. I've always had a bond with Sawyer, there's no denying that. But never once did I question my decision to be with Noah. I felt terrible because I saw how badly Sawyer was hurting."

Pausing, I take a drink of my mimosa. "As I write these pages now, the one thing I do realize is even though I wasn't in love with him back then, it's probably why I was able to fall for him so easily now."

Rory's eyes flash with anger. "And you love him now, right? You think it's okay to just step on your marriage and put us all in the middle of your sordid affair?"

"Rory, that's enough!" Karen shouts. "Listen here, young lady, I've had enough of you judging Sawyer and Mel for making the best of an awful situation. There are things you still don't know, but you'll find out soon enough if Amelia continues telling the truth in this book. I strongly suggest you reserve your judgment for when you finish reading and know the whole truth. There's a lot more than a black and white story here. Love is messy, Rory, and someday you'll understand just how messy it can be. We'll be there for you when that day comes, but please try to keep reading with an open mind."

"It makes me sick, Mom, and it makes me miss Noah," she sobs.

"I know, sweetie. Trust me, Noah would want you to know the whole story and he wouldn't want you angry with Sawyer and Mel."

"I'm going to go get some air." I push away from the table and head out the back door. It's cold out but it's no longer raining. I don't

636

go down to the beach as much as I used to; it's too hard. Noah and I had some of our best times down on that beach.

I lean over the wall and look out at the waves crashing against the shore. The sound calms me more than anything—it centers me when I'm off kilter. My phone buzzes in my pocket and when I pull it out there's a video clip from Sawyer. I open it up to find "On the Road Again" by Willie Nelson.

Fuck.

That means the roads are clear and they're coming home earlier than what I was prepared for when they thought they were snowed in. I should have figured this would happen; snow rarely sticks in California if it's not winter. It doesn't matter now. They'll be here in a few hours and there's no way I'll be finished with this book by then. He'll just have to sit and read it with everyone else. I don't know how this turned into me working my way toward a decision to the whole family sitting around reading something I never wanted to share in the first place.

I send a text back to him with a link to "Lego House" by Ed Sheeran and go back inside. It's time to finish our story.

Second Chances

When I wake up, regret washes over me like a cold shower. But so does the realization Sawyer and I have been playing a dangerous game for months and it's finally come to a head. I've got feelings for him. I don't know when it happened, but it did. It's wrong, and it's dirty and sinful, but I'm starting to feel whole again. Sawyer makes me feel alive; it's a heady sensation after the hell I've lived this past year.

Our kiss last night was everything I needed from him. If only I hadn't fucked it up by asking him to take away my pain. That had to have hurt him. I'm so used to being able to say anything to Sawyer, but I crossed the line last night. I've got to figure out a way to make it right.

It's still early and Nate is asleep. Sawyer is standing at the coffeemaker when I enter the kitchen. I look like death warmed over, but he doesn't even flinch.

"Good morning," he says as he sips his coffee and leans against the counter.

"Sawyer, about last night … I'm sorry."

The heaviness I feel every morning when I wake up was still there this morning, but it was accompanied by embarrassment, regret, and longing.

"Why are you sorry? Because you wanted me, or because I wouldn't fuck you?" His facial expression is stoic. I don't know what answer I'm supposed to give him that would make this better either way. "Because I'll tell you why *I'm* sorry, Princess. There's only one thing in this world I want more than I want you and it's never going to happen. We're self-destructive people, Mel, and fucking our pain and anger away isn't going to get us anywhere."

"Sawyer—"

"No, let me finish. I'm tired of dancing around the obvious. Noah is gone, and we're left picking up the pieces. Don't you think I know it's wrong to be in love with my dead brother's wife? I've loved you from afar for long enough. If you want me, you'll have to come

638

to me. You need to want me for who I am, Mel, not because I remind you of something you've lost."

It's as if he's slashed a dagger through my heart. I've never wanted Sawyer because he reminds me of Noah—just the opposite. Their looks are similar—not identical—but it's hard to get past those eyes sometimes. Noah's eyes were always full of love and life. Sawyer's are filled with depth, sorrow, knowledge, and desire. I try to blink back the tears; it's futile. Ever since Nate was born, my emotions have had a mind of their own.

"I've never wanted you for anything other than who you are, Sawyer. I know you're not Noah, that you never will be Noah, and I don't ever want you to be him, either. I'm sorry I didn't realize you were in love with me. I love you, too, Sawyer, but I'm not sure how."

"I don't need you to reciprocate my feelings, I'm just telling you they exist. I know better than anyone that you're still in love with Noah."

His sadness echoes through the room and my guilt is eating away at me. "Tell me, Sawyer, what's the one thing you want more than me? Maybe I can at least help you get that."

Sadness clouds his features as he shakes his head. "Noah, Mel. I want my best friend and my brother back. I need him. I need his advice, his friendship, and his heart and love for life. It should have been me, and I regret being where he should be every fucking day."

The rawness of his words steals my breath as I crumple to the floor. The pain he told me to feel last night is working itself out of me in a god-awful way. Through my sobs, I begin screaming at him.

"Do you think that would make this better? How broken do you think we'd be without you? If it were reversed and you were gone, Noah wouldn't be Noah anymore. He'd be a shell of himself and he'd feel exactly like you do now. And what about me? And Nate? What the hell would we do without you, Sawyer? You're our everything!"

My words stun even me. Have I moved so far away from Noah that I wish for Sawyer instead?

"You'd have Noah, your husband, and you'd get through."

"Yeah, just like we're getting through now. I don't want to live in a world without Noah, but dammit, Sawyer, I don't want to live in a world without you, either. None of this is fair, *life* isn't fair. Every day, a part of me wishes I'd died with them."

"No, Mel, don't say that." His whispered words are filled with pain as he drops to the floor next to me and squeezes my hand.

Through stuttering breaths, I try to speak over my sobs. "Why? It's the truth. You're not the only one who lives with survivor's guilt.

D. Kelly

But there's this other part of me that knows I need to be here for Nate. If there's one thing I can give Noah it's to be a mother to his son. Something I never really wanted, and wasn't good at in the beginning, but I loved him, Sawyer. I just couldn't imagine living up to the kind of parent Noah would have been."

He wraps his arm around my shoulders, letting me sob into him. "Nate needs you, Sawyer, and so do I. But I loved my husband and I don't know how, if ever, I'll be ready to move on or give you that part of my heart where Noah lives."

"I don't want Noah's place, Princess, I want my own." He practically chokes on his heartfelt words, and I feel awful.

"I know, Sawyer, and you have one. But I'm not sure the love and friendship I have with you can evolve into the same kind of love I had for him. I'm sorry, I know that's brutal, but it's true. I'm still numb a lot of the time. I'm tired, Sawyer. I'm sad, and I want a physical connection with someone. I want to be brought back to life. Sex and intimacy with someone may do that. And last night I felt it with you. Those beginning sparks of something incredible. I know it's selfish that I want it to be you, but I can't imagine wanting it to be anyone else. I've lost everyone who has ever meant anything to me. I can't lose you, too."

I've bared my heart to him. I'm literally crying and bleeding out on the floor like he asked. He hugs me tightly and releases me. "I need to think, Mel. I'm going to the beach."

Mel. I'm always Mel when he tries to separate his feelings and Princess when he lets his defenses down. As much as I used to hate Princess, it feels like a kick to the heart every time he calls me by my name.

When Sawyer closes the sliding glass door behind him, I curl up into the fetal position and let the dam of tears burst. What kind of person wants her husband's brother? Have I just been burying my feelings for Sawyer under my love for Noah this whole time? Or has Sawyer already secured his place in my heart without me even realizing it? That's the part that scares me most of all.

I'm not sure how much time has passed when Darren finds me on the floor crying my eyes out. "Shit, Mel! Are you okay?" he calls out and sets Cadence down with her toys.

He gets on the floor and pulls me into his arms, trying to check me over. "I'm fine," I cry out through another sob, but the concern on his face lingers. Nate starts crying, which makes me cry even harder.

"I'm going to help you to the couch and then I'm going to go take care of Nate."

With a nod, I let him lead me there and I curl up with a pillow and watch Cadence play. She's starting to look so much more like Belle; it makes me happy and sad at the same time. When Darren comes back, he puts both kids in their highchairs and gives them some breakfast. While they happily munch on some Cheerios, he comes back to me.

"Talk to me, Mel. What is wrong?"

"Sawyer loves me," I manage to spit out.

"Shit."

Darren walks away and comes back a few minutes later with coffee and a banana. "Eat this and then we'll talk."

As I sit up and sip my coffee, I watch Darren as he multitasks with both kids. He's such an amazing dad and a great person. Belle chose right when she picked him. Mac strolls into the kitchen and the kids smile at him. They love Mac, and he loves them. I would have never guessed this big, burly bodyguard would be a baby magnet.

"Go do what you have to do, Darren. I've got the kids."

Darren must have called or texted him. Great, everyone knows what a basket case I am today.

"Come on, Mel. Let's go talk." We walk to my room and sit on the bed. "What happened?"

"We got drunk last night and talked. Nothing new, but the talk took a more … sexual turn, I guess. I don't know, Darren. I was drinking and I'm so lonely, and he's Sawyer. Nothing happened and we passed out."

"Okay, then, what's wrong?"

"I woke up in Sawyer's arms and felt … at home? I don't know, but it felt right so I pulled his mouth to mine and kissed him."

"This is obviously going to get worse," he says, leaning up against the headboard.

"I'm so embarrassed. I asked him to fuck my pain away."

"Shit, Mel. Talk about bruising a guy's ego."

My tears start falling again. "I didn't mean it like that, though. Maybe I did. I wanted him in that moment. Him. Sawyer. Not Noah. But having sex with anyone the first time after losing someone is going to be hard, right? I didn't mean it to be offensive, I was just being truthful."

"Last time I went to my parents' when the kids were gone, I left early. I went to the bar and fucked some random chick in the bathroom. She couldn't have been more different than Belle. Blonde, voluptuous, legs for days on end. The old me would have brought her home and gone at it for days. It was the worst sexual experience of my life. It hurt so much that she wasn't Belle."

He looks at me with his own tear-filled eyes. "I had to get it out of the way. I'd hoped if I just did it … maybe the pain would lessen. It didn't, it only made it worse. I wasn't ready and I shouldn't have pushed myself."

"I'm so sorry."

"Me too," he replies with a sarcastic laugh. "I wasn't trying to keep it from you, but you're Belle's best friend … and I was ashamed." The raw pain exuding from him is like a mirror of mine. We're some pair.

"You have the right to move on if you're ready, Darren."

When he smiles at me, I know I'm in trouble. "And so do you, Amelia. I'm sorry Sawyer told you he still loves you, but now that you know, you should also know he never stopped. At least I don't think he did. He respected your choice and would have never gone after you once you and Noah were married. But love is love, Mel. You're lucky enough to have someone who cares for you as deeply as your husband did. If you're going to fall in bed with someone, I would imagine that could make all the difference in how hard it is to accept you're fucking someone new."

I knew today was going to be bad, but now it's depressing on a whole other level.

"I can't be with Sawyer, Darren. You know that."

"Why not?" he asks.

"I'm pretty sure hooking up with my husband's brother is frowned upon."

"Who the fuck cares? Look Mel, I can't tell you what to do or not do, but I *can* tell you we don't get to pick who we love. I can also say if the kind of love I had with Belle were to find me again I'd grab onto it with both hands because I know how fast it can disappear."

They were the perfect soul mates. At least Belle had that—she'd found her one true love. So did Noah. I guess there is some comfort in that–they died knowing they were deeply loved.

"What else happened to make you lose it on the kitchen floor?" he asks, pulling me from my thoughts.

I take a deep breath and fill Darren in on everything else up until he found me.

"You two have horrible timing. Today was the worst day for either of you to decide to let your feelings out. You guys will work this out, but will you do me a favor?"

"Sure, name it."

"It's been 365 days since Noah died and you've spent every one of those days with Sawyer. You didn't even know Noah as long as you've known Sawyer now. Don't discount being able to love him because I think you already do. Think of the qualities you'd want in a long-term partner and think of the qualities he's shown you this year. I'm not saying this as his friend, either. I'm saying it as yours. You deserve to be happy, Mel, and that growth we all wanted to see in Sawyer, we've seen it this year. He's so in love with you he hasn't even fucked anyone else. That says more than I ever could."

"I hear you, Darren, I just don't know right now. I'm so confused."

He leans his head against mine and squeezes my leg. "Today is going to suck. But remember, you decided this year was going to be better. Give yourself today but get back on the happy trail tomorrow. The last thing Noah and Belle would have wanted was our misery. I'm slowly realizing that more and more with each passing day. Besides, it's hard to be sad all the time when we have the cutest kids in the world."

"We really do, don't we? At least if they had to leave, we got to keep a piece of them with us."

"Get some sleep, Mel. I'll keep an eye on Nate for a while. I could use time with him today anyway." He kisses me on the head and leaves. I reach over and pick up a photo of Noah and me from the bedside table. We had so much happiness in such a small window of time. Imagine if we'd actually gotten our lifetime's worth.

"Back away from the door, Sawyer." I hear Darren's voice but keep my eyes closed.

"I just wanted to check on her."

"She's fine, no thanks to you," Darren snaps at him.

"What's that supposed to mean?"

"Do you have any idea what condition she was in this morning? I found her curled up in the fetal position crying so hard she left snot on the floor!" Darren is whisper-shouting, but I can hear every word.

"I told her."

"Yeah, I know."

"She doesn't love me," he says dejectedly.

"She doesn't know what she feels. She's hurt and confused and she feels guilty."

"You don't think *I* feel guilty?" Sawyer pleads.

D. Kelly

"I know you do. I don't think this is a bad idea, but I'm not the one in the middle of your love triangle."

"Well, I wish I wasn't, either. Being in a triangle with your dead brother's wife doesn't exactly make me brother of the year, does it?"

"Wyatt told you he said it was okay."

"That doesn't make it right, Darren," Sawyer adds with a sigh.

I'm so confused. Who said what was okay?

"Look, today was the worst day for all of this to happen. Give it time, Sawyer. It's hard to jump back into sex and dating after what we went through."

"How much time? I'd wait for as long as it takes, but what's the point if it's not going to be a positive outcome?"

"Being able to put someone else's needs above our own is the true sign of love. You did it when you backed away from her in the first place. She did it when she kept Nate because she knew it would make Noah happy, and he did it by showing both of you love exists in the first place."

Sawyer sighs and I can imagine him running his hand through his hair. "She said she'd go out with me this weekend to the club. Are you going to come?"

"Nah, after that girl in the bathroom I think I'm going to stay away from clubs and bars for a bit."

"I'm getting a private room," Sawyer tries coaxing him.

"It's alright, you two should go and have fun. I'll probably hang out with Wyatt. After this week, it will be good for you to both get out. I've been going out of the house more and more. You two are still the ones being hermits."

"I'm working on it."

"I know. Let her sleep and come have a drink with me."

Their footsteps echo down the hall and I turn over, releasing a breath.

Noah, I don't know how to do this. I want my love to be for you, I want my heart to belong to you, but you're not here and he is. Every day it gets harder to say no, to deny myself the touch of someone else. But why does it have to be him I crave? Why does it have to be all kinds of wrong?

Later in the evening, I spend some time pulling out the photo albums and showing Nate pictures of Noah and Belle. It's mostly just me pointing and saying "Daddy" and "Auntie Belle." But it's like he suddenly gets it, and as I'm pointing to Noah he says, "Dada." The dam of tears bursts like never before.

"Yeah, baby, that's your daddy."

But as I go through the motions of putting him to bed, my heart aches. I don't want Nate calling anyone else daddy, but I feel like I've just taken something monumental away from Sawyer. I'm so emotional today, I just don't know what to think anymore.

Sawyer is walking up the hall as I'm coming out of the nursery. He takes one look at my face and pulls me into his arms.

"Why are you crying?"

"I don't know," I say, sobbing into his shoulder.

"Come with me, we should talk." Sawyer releases me from his hug but holds my hand as he pulls me to his room. We take our usual seats on his bed against the headboard and he turns to me with the saddest look in his eyes.

"I'm so sorry about earlier and about last night. Especially this morning. It wasn't fair to dump my feelings on you like that."

"It's okay. What I said was mean and I didn't want it to come off like that. The truth is I don't know how to move on with someone else. And the fact I want it to be you is so fucking hard to wrap my head around." Sawyer is inching closer to me as I'm speaking, and my heart feels like it's going to pound out of my chest.

"I'm worried, too, but I can't help how I feel about you, Princess."

I bite down on my lip as his are now just a mere breath away from them. He's going to kiss me, and so help me God, I want him to.

"Me, either."

"Do you really want to try something with me? For me to be your first after Noah?" His lips press softly against mine and my arms are immediately around his neck, pulling him closer.

"Yes." My breathless word is captured by his mouth. His tongue traces the seam of my lips and I relish the feeling. I open to him and our tongues meet, not tentatively like new lovers, but as if they're old friends being reunited. A soft moan escapes me as he clutches me tighter, releasing one of his own.

"God, Sawyer, I want you."

"You've got me, Princess, you always have," he replies, pulling me on top of him so I'm now straddling him. As I suck his lip ring into my mouth and tug on it, he laces his fingers into my hair. His hardness presses up against me as I grind against him, needing to feel what this is doing to him.

D. Kelly

Sawyer and I have never lacked chemistry, but this is different than before. It's a deeper connection, not hurried or frenzied like our first kiss. We take our time kissing and getting to know what turns each other on.

Sawyer releases my hair and glides his hands under my shirt, caressing my ribs until they find my breasts. I sigh into his neck and bite down, easing the sting with a swipe of my tongue. His hips push up against me as he hisses his approval. When he licks a trail from my collarbone to my ear, I practically combust.

"You're so fucking hot, Princess, and I bet you'll be even hotter coming when I'm buried balls deep inside of you." His sinful words push me to the point of no return.

Leaning back, I pull off my shirt and unhook my bra. "You talk a good game, Weston, now back it up." When I slide out of my bra, Sawyer flips us over as his lust-filled eyes trail down my body.

He pulls his shirt up over his head and throws it to the ground. I tug his lip ring between my teeth and he groans with appreciation. As soon as I let go, his tongue darts into my mouth, stealing my breath and my sanity.

"Sawyer ..." I hiss as his mouth leaves mine. His teeth clamp down on my hardened nipple and my body bucks into his, yearning for more. When his tongue circles my nipple to ease the pain, I practically melt into the bed. He repeats the bite on my other breast and my body thrashes under his, but in the best kind of way.

"You're so fucking feisty," he says with a devious glare as he slides one of his hands into my yoga pants. He cups my pussy hard as he rotates his attention between my breasts. I'm walking a tightrope between pleasure and pain; it's euphoric. "You're fucking drenched, Princess, and I haven't even gotten to the best part."

With those words, he slides a finger inside me and my eyes roll back in my head. "God, yes ..."

A second finger works its way in and Sawyer groans. "So fucking tight." He pulls my pants and my panties off. The wicked look in his eyes is about to set me off. He takes in every inch of my body and then drops his pants. I've always admired Sawyer's body, but when he drops his boxers I have a whole new appreciation for what's been hiding underneath.

His cock is hard and just the sight of it makes my mouth water. He walks to the bedside and opens his top drawer for a condom and I take the opportunity to flip over and pull him to me. As I lower my mouth onto his cock, I'm not sure I've ever been so blinded by need and lust before. With one hand around his base, the other lightly cupping his balls, I suck him in deep. When he hits the back of my throat, I choke back my gag and open wider, wanting to fit all of him inside.

"Jesus, Princess," he gasps, gripping my hair and guiding my mouth up and down. "You're so fucking good at this." He hisses, and I swirl my tongue around the pre-cum beading at the head of his dick. Tasting him on my tongue floods me with need, so I release him and pull his mouth to mine. The carnal need for Sawyer to taste himself on my tongue is strong. He fucks my mouth with his tongue, seeming to enjoy the taste of himself, turning me on even more.

Lowering my mouth to his nipples, I tug his piercing into my mouth, and he smacks my ass. "Oh fuck," I moan with delight, and his eyes light up.

"Fuck is right, Princess. It's time to get dirty."

He pushes me back against the pillow and crawls between my legs, spreading them wide open. His eyes meet mine as he swipes a finger through my wetness. When he sucks that finger into his mouth and licks it clean, I almost come.

Sawyer spares me no mercy; his mouth immediately suckles my clit and he lightly nips it between his teeth. My body arches from the bed, but he drops one hand over my waist and holds me down. "You're not going anywhere until your pussy is drenching my mouth with your cum, Princess."

With a combination of his tongue and a few well-placed fingers, I'm right on the edge. He slides his tongue inside of me and fucks me relentlessly with it. I'm drowning in pleasure, barely holding myself back from the most epic of all orgasms, when he pinches my clit between his fingers and sends me soaring on the biggest high as he licks up every drop of my release.

Sawyer looks up at me and languidly licks his lips. It's so fucking sinful I can't stand it. Then he rips the condom package open and sheathes himself before crawling up my body. Pulling my leg around his hip, he positions himself at my entrance but doesn't push in.

"Are you ready for this?" he asks softly.

"Please, Sawyer, I need you."

With my words, he drops his mouth to mine and kisses me relentlessly. I taste myself on his lips and it's incredibly sensual. As his tongue plunges into my mouth, his cock plunges into me.

"Damn, Princess," he says with a hiss, "you're so damn tight."

Sawyer drops his mouth back to my breasts and rotates between them. There's pain, but there's even more pleasure, and I feel myself building up again. I wrap my legs tighter around him and pull him closer to me so he's as deep as he can possibly be.

"Jesus, Sawyer, what are you doing to me?" I cry out, meeting him thrust for thrust.

"Making your body a slave to mine." My body trembles with his words. "Come for me, Princess. Let me feel that sweet fucking pussy choke my cock." His mouth covers mine, his tongue matching his fucking, and with my legs wrapped around his waist and my arms around his neck, we're fused together as one. Every part of me is rubbing against him and I can't hold on anymore. I blissfully give everything I am to Sawyer.

"Sawyer … Oh, Sawyer! Yes!" My body shatters around him as he comes inside me with a ferocious roar. I've never heard anything so damn sexy and feral in all my life.

"Holy shit, Princess … that was …"

"Incredible," I fill in as he wraps his arms around me and rolls us over so we're still connected.

"Fucking life-altering," he replies as his eyes shine with happiness. I wonder if mine do, too. I refuse to be sad right now because there was nothing about sex with Sawyer that I could ever regret.

We lay together in silence–the good kind, where we're both letting the amazingness that just happened sink in. I love that he's still inside me and still has his arms wrapped around me like he doesn't want this to end. But when he finally pulls out to get rid of the condom, I feel empty.

He goes into the bathroom and comes back with a warm cloth. When he spreads my legs and starts wiping me off, I'm stunned. "What are you doing?" I ask in a teasing tone.

"Taking care of my Princess. Besides, you don't want to sleep in all that wetness, do you?" he asks with a raised brow. Suddenly, my mind isn't on the sex anymore; I'm thinking about sleeping in Sawyer's bed. Can I do that? I mean, it's not like we haven't before, but it was innocent then and this is far from innocent now.

"Uh, no, definitely not," I reply as my mind races. I will not feel guilty for this, but even as I think the words, my hand begins to feel heavy under the weight of my wedding rings. Is now the time I'm supposed to take them off?

Sawyer finishes drying me off and climbs back into bed with me, naked. "I've lost you already," he says sadly.

"No, you haven't. I just … It doesn't matter. We can talk about it another time. I don't want to wreck this. That was incredible and I don't regret it. Do you?"

His hand caresses my cheek and he kisses my lips tenderly. "Not in a million years. Mel, I know we're going to have some ups and downs, but if we don't talk about them we'll never get through them. What's wrong? I promise I won't be mad."

"I don't know how to explain it. It was like I suddenly felt the weight of my wedding rings on my hand. I don't think I'm ready to take them off, Sawyer, but what kind of person does it make me that I'm not?"

"It makes you an honest person. This isn't going to happen overnight. I want to be in this with you for the duration, Mel. I've never met a woman who affects me the way you do. I've known since that first night you were different. But you didn't feel the same way, and I can't blame you. I know what I seemed like back then, but I've changed." His words plead for understanding, but he doesn't have to explain himself to me.

"Stop, you don't need to tell me that. I know you've changed. I see it every day. I have so much love and respect for you, Sawyer, I can't even begin to describe how much. This morning, when you said you wish it had been you, it killed me to hear you say that. You've become my everything, but that doesn't change that what we're doing isn't right. If anyone finds out …"

Sawyer crashes his lips to mine and kisses me relentlessly until I'm struggling to catch my breath. "No, Mel, I don't care if anyone knows. What we're doing isn't wrong. Unconventional, maybe. But wrong, never. I know you're not there yet, and that's okay I'll wait as long as it takes. I love you. I've never had sex with someone I've had feelings for before and you're not going to take that away from me. From us."

His heartfelt words weigh heavily on my soul, but I think we need to test the waters first. "Can we navigate through this a little while, just the two of us, before letting people know what's going on? I'm barely finding myself again and I need time to … acclimate to the idea of me and you being an us."

The sadness in his eyes slays me, but he nods his agreement. "Okay, under one condition."

"What's that?"

"You have to give this a fair shot, and it starts with you sleeping naked in my arms tonight."

"Okay, but I have one more rule."

"Shoot," he says, snuggling closer to me and covering us with a blanket.

"My room is off limits for anything other than talking, okay?"

"That goes without saying."

I curl up in Sawyer's arms and fall asleep feeling safer and calmer than I have since Noah. I'm not sure what the hell I'm getting myself into, but at least I'm not in it alone.

Adjustment Period

The next few days were sweeter. Sawyer and I were stealing kisses when we could but still managed to keep things light. I think we both needed a bit of space after the night we spent in his bed. I was looking forward to our night out, but Saylor and Emme got sick and we had to postpone. The following week was more of the same. It was kind of nice doing the flirting thing with Sawyer and sneaking kisses.

That weekend, the guys met up with Rob, J, and even Eli flew in for his weekend off. They all went on their first male bonding trip to a cabin in Big Bear. It was supposed to be a fun trip to honor Noah and his promise to Sawyer that they would all still get together once a year to bond. It was especially important to Sawyer since he postponed the family Disney World vacation until October, in hopes we'd all be in a better place by then. I've already decided I can't, but I'm hoping the rest of the group can make it work.

Unfortunately, what was supposed to be three days of fishing and fun for them turned into one night of drunken tears and a bunch of men letting their emotions get the best of them. They turned around and came home the very next day. For the most part, Darren and Sawyer hid in their rooms all weekend, but I was able to push my own issues aside long enough to spend some time catching up with Eli.

Spending time with Eli was a great distraction because while they were all up in Big Bear, Diane, Anna, Rory, and I had our own pity party here. It mostly consisted of reminiscing about Noah, crying, drinking tequila, and eating way too much junk food. All the kids had a sleepover with Karen and Owen, so we were free to drink as much as we wanted.

When Sawyer got home the next day and didn't talk to me, I was irritated and tried chalking it up to him not feeling well and being upset about his shortened weekend. As the weekend went on, I realized he must have been having second thoughts, which was a relief because so was I. By the following week, I'd decided being with Sawyer was definitely a mistake. What kind of woman sleeps with brothers anyway, and twins at that? My moral compass is so far gone I don't know my head from my ass anymore.

It's been six weeks since we slept together. After the first week, Sawyer went from avoiding me to spending almost all of his free time in the garage working on music or whatever. He even blew off a foundation meeting. And while I was pissed, I was glad because no one would pick up on our tension and suspect something. I think both of us must have realized we moved too quickly and are now walking, talking, emotional disasters, doing our best to keep our distance from each other. Either that or Sawyer realized what he thought was love was only lust and he doesn't know how to tell me he made a mistake. While he spends his days avoiding me in the garage, I've been sitting in my room trying to decide what to do about Noah's things.

Diane brought it up the night she was over. When she walked into my room and saw his wallet and keys sitting on the dresser like they were just waiting for him to come in and grab them, she started crying immediately. Then she looked in the closet and saw everything just as he'd left them. She thinks I can't truly have closure until I do something with his clothes and personal effects. As I lay back on the bed, I think about her advice.

"It's been over a year, Mel, you have to move on. You have the biggest memory of Noah walking around this house every day. Nate will give you more pleasure than hanging onto things, I promise you."

Her sympathetic gaze met mine, but I wasn't sold on the idea at all. "This is his house, Diane, and these are his things. It's not right to mess with that."

"No, what's not right is you living in a museum as if you're waiting for him to walk back in that door. Noah is gone, Mel. There's nothing that can bring him back to us. You need to think about sorting his things. Some stuff to keep for you or Nate, offer some things up to the family, and then donate the rest. Noah would love the idea of someone less fortunate walking around in his clothes."

I opened the drawer and pulled out my anxiety medication. It's something I was hardly taking at all, but ever since that night with Sawyer I'd been taking them consistently again. My therapist said it was normal, but at that point I didn't even know what normal was anymore.

"I'm not there yet, Diane."

She leaned against the dresser and looked me over thoroughly as I popped a pill. "You seem different lately and I can't put my finger on why. If you need to talk, I'm happy to be a sounding board for you. I'm also happy to help you with all this," she added, gesturing around the room. "When you're ready, of course."

"Will I ever be ready? Because I feel like I started moving forward only to be thrown backward. Do you know this whole year I've missed Belle like crazy but I'm not sure how much I've actually grieved for her because I've been so busy being angry at Noah for leaving me and grieving for him? What kind of friend does that make me? What kind of sister?"

"I don't think you're giving yourself enough credit, Mel. I saw you at the funeral, I heard what happened at the cemetery, and I know you've been grieving for both of them. That's why this has been so hard. I know this is going to sound clinical, but I'm going to say it anyway."

I looked at her, hoping whatever she was going to say would put some kind of spin on this to make me feel better because I'm tired of being off kilter.

"Losing a friend is easier than losing a spouse. Not the loss itself but coping afterward. You're doing all the things for Belle you know she would want. You're taking care of Darren, of Cadence, and filling the void she left. You can rationalize that in your mind as still being a good friend. But losing your husband, your partner, your co-parent ... it's different. You lose intimacy, your sounding board, your true north. You're grasping at straws to be okay with moving on without them, to figure out if and when it's okay to love again someday, questioning everything you do and wondering if they would agree and want it, too. It's never going to be an easy path to walk, but remember we're here and you never have to walk it alone."

"I miss him more than I ever knew it was possible to miss someone."

"Sawyer is right there with you, Mel. You guys need to keep leaning on each other and you'll find your way through."

If she only knew. We've gotten ourselves into such a mess. I cross the room and open Noah's closet and am overwhelmed by his scent. It wraps around my senses and pulls me into a false sense of security. Turning off the light, I close the door behind me and lie down on the floor. I'm not ready, not when I can come in here and imagine lying in the dark with him, sharing stories and our bodies.

"Mel, where are you?" Sawyer. Of all the times he wants to talk to me, he comes in here now.

"In the closet," I call out, and he opens the door.

"What are you doing?"

"Going crazy. What did you need?" Short answers and to the point. This has been our routine for weeks now.

"Actually, I thought maybe I could convince you to come out with me to get some coffee and take a drive. I think it's time we talk."

"I'm perfectly comfortable sitting here drowning in the scent of my husband. Thanks, but no thanks."

He sighs loudly and walks inside. Then he reaches down and pulls me up by the arms. "This isn't a suggestion, Mel. And what you're doing right now isn't healthy. You're regressing and that's the last thing you need. Come on. Darren said he'll watch Nate."

"Fine," I mutter and put on my flip-flops. "But it better be a big-ass coffee and some pastries."

"Anything for you, Princess," he says with a laugh.

We climb into Sawyer's SUV and take off. It's strange going out with just him and no bodyguards. Maybe things will continue to die down now that the band isn't putting out any more music and the tour has been done for over a year. The interview requests have slowed; I guess you can only hear no so many times before you give up.

He pulls off at his favorite coffee place and throws on a hat. "I'll be right back."

It's a beautiful day and there are tons of people at the beach. It will calm down a little bit once school starts again but not much. California sunshine keeps people at the beach year-round. Sawyer gets back in the SUV with a bag of pastries and a tray of drinks—two waters and two coffees. One of the cups says "Princess" on it and I take it from the tray. He hands me the bag and I dig through until I find a vanilla scone. At least he knows what I like; that earns him some brownie points.

"So where are we going?"

"J called when I was in the coffee shop and said he needs to talk. Do you mind if we pop by there first? It will save him a trip later."

"Sure, but where are we going afterward?"

"I just want to drive, clear my head, and talk. We need to talk, Mel."

"Okay." I'm dreading our talk. I'm not sure it can go anywhere positive. Hopefully, we can find a way to get back to normal, whatever that is. For someone who says he's in love with me, he sure doesn't act like it. And that's okay because I'm sticking with my decision that letting Sawyer get me off was a really bad idea. Even if it was fucking phenomenal.

"Thanks for the coffee," I say, hoping to break this awkward silence.

"It's the least I owe you after the way I've been treating you." His candid confession catches me off guard, sending us back into silence.

He pulls up in front of a cute little house. "I thought J lived in an apartment?"

"He moved a few months ago. I guess the bar is doing really well."

We get out of the car and J opens the door before we even get to it. "Hey, guys. Welcome to my humble abode."

The inside of the house is nice. It feels comfortable and well lived in. Our house is cold in contrast and definitely isn't homey. Maybe that's just Sawyer's style because other than the kids' toys, there's nothing friendly about it.

Jordan has black leather furniture, wooden accent tables, and a huge TV. There are rugs throughout the house, covering the hardwood floors.

"Oh, look at your kitty!" I cry out, inching toward the orange and black cat sitting on the chair. He's big and roly poly and I just want to squeeze him. The second I get close, he rears up and hisses, swiping his paw at me like he's possessed by the devil. "Holy shit, what's wrong with him?"

Jordan and Sawyer laugh. "Fuck if I know. He was a stray and I took him in. He's an ornery son of a bitch so I named him Fat Bastard. I'm hardly ever here, so I don't get in his way and he doesn't get in mine."

"Remind me to keep Nate away from here," I grumble and sit down on the couch opposite of the crazy fucking cat.

"He's not like that with everyone. He cuddles with me sometimes and I'm pretty sure Allie gives him a cat boner or something. Whenever she's around, he curls up in her lap and purrs the whole time. He even licks her sometimes."

"So what's going on, J?" Sawyer asks as he sits next to me, which is a little too close for my comfort. I scoot farther down the couch, but Sawyer smirks at me and scoots closer. *Asshole.*

Jordan reaches for some envelopes on the table, handing one to me and one to Sawyer. "You can open them. Yours is just this month's rent, Sawyer. Nothing big."

I know exactly what is in this envelope and when I open it and see the check I close it and give it back to him. "Sorry, J, that's yours."

A confused look passes over his face as he tries to hand it back. "This isn't a joke, Mel. You need to take this shit off my conscience."

"I'm not joking, J. Noah made it a specific point in his video to me that I was in no uncertain terms allowed to take money from you. Not rent, not your inheritance."

"That bastard. I don't want his fucking money. I don't need it." He's pissed, and Sawyer is watching our interaction carefully.

"Expand," I say with a shrug of my shoulders.

They both whip their heads toward me and say, "What?" at the same time.

"Noah wanted you to use that money for something important to you. He was so mad at you that you wouldn't let him buy you the bar outright in the first place. He told me early on he'd taken care of his family in his will. But later, the more we got to know each other the more I learned. He said he hoped you would fulfill your dreams one day and open more locations. This is your chance."

"You're seriously not going to take this money back?" he asks, his frustration growing.

"I can't. In fact, it was a codicil of the will. If I take it back, I lose my inheritance. So if you don't keep that money there will be no Noah Weston Foundation for Kind Acts." I'm doing the best I can to say it with a straight face. Noah would have never put a stipulation on my inheritance and if J knows him at all, he'll know that.

Sawyer flashes me a look that tells me he knows I'm fucking with J and it makes me want to smile, but I don't. I keep my expression stoic.

"Noah wouldn't do that. Why are you lying to me?"

With a smile, I reply, "Because Noah wanted you to have it. He didn't put it in his will, but he really did put it in his video. Don't make me go against his wishes, Jordan. My psyche can't handle any more shit."

"Well, what if *my* psyche can't take it?"

Sawyer jumps in and takes the reigns, "J, you are his brother and he wanted you to have it. You're the only one who has an issue with it, and I know you're proud, but fuck … Noah was so fucking proud of you. Don't do this for you, do it for him. Have you watched your video yet?"

"I can't," he answers, looking down at the floor.

"Do you want me to watch it with you?" Sawyer offers, and it makes me melt. That's the last thing he wants to do, but he'll do it for his brother.

"Yeah, but not tonight, okay? I've got a huge private party at the club to get ready for and I'm pretty sure I need to be drunk before or after or both."

"Tomorrow?"

J looks Sawyer in the eye with determination. "Tomorrow. Any time after two. You know I need to sleep and you wake up way too fucking early for me."

"Alright, I'll see you tomorrow. We're going to get out of here before Fat Bastard eats us."

Jordan laughs and scoops the reluctant cat into his lap. "His bark is bigger than his bite."

"Keep telling yourself that. He needs an exorcism." I bend down and kiss J on the cheek. "Come over for dinner soon and play with Nate. He misses his uncle."

"I don't think he's old enough to miss me, but let me know when and I'm there. Can I bring Allie?"

With a raised brow, I take a step back. "Are you going to finally admit there's a you and Allie?"

His sheepish smile confirms it before his words. "Yeah, at least I think so."

"Then yes, bring her. She's sweet, J, you should hang on to her."

Sawyer squeezes my hand to get me to stop talking but I pull it away quickly. J shakes his head and nails Sawyer with a glare. "Looks like I'm not the only one with shit to work out. Go take care of business, dear brother of mine."

My heart takes a swan dive into the depths of my stomach. Jordan knows. Fuck, who else did Sawyer tell? Storming out of the house, I wait by the side of the truck until Sawyer hits the alarm to unlock it. We ride in silence for a while. I'm so frustrated with him and pissed off that people seem to know about what we did. Finally, Sawyer speaks.

"He's my brother, Princess."

"And so was Noah, Sawyer!"

Sawyer clutches the wheel so tightly I'm surprised he can still turn the wheel when he needs to. After about twenty minutes, Sawyer punches in a code at a gate and pulls the SUV down a long, winding driveway. The house is beautiful and almost looks like an old plantation house. He continues driving behind the house and pulls up under a large oak tree. The yard is filled with them.

"Where are we?"

"My grandparents' house. Well, I guess it's my house now. I bought it when they died." His confession shocks me. This place is beautiful. "I wanted to bring you somewhere to talk where we could be comfortable and speak freely."

D. Kelly

"There's no point, Sawyer, we're a mess. Everything is a mess." I'm so emotional I just want to go home, but he brought us here and I know this place has to be special to him.

"Indulge me, Mel, please?" He gets out of the car and comes around and opens my door. Taking my hand in his, he leads me down a flagstone path to a cute little gazebo. We take a seat on a floral outdoor couch and I back up against the arm with my arms around my knees, facing him head-on, like I used to do when Belle and I were going to get deep.

"Alright, Sawyer, I'm here and I'm listening. Why don't you start by telling me who knows about the two of us?"

Sawyer blows out a breath and scoots closer, wrapping his hands around my ankles. "J and Diane," he confesses. My head spins.

"Why?" The anguished word falls from my lips and he squeezes me tighter.

"Fuck, and Rob and Darren, too," he adds quickly. My heart is racing; I really wish I had my anxiety meds with me right now. "When we were in Big Bear, Darren and I thought we were alone. He told me he heard the two of us that night and was wondering if it meant anything significant."

I close my eyes and put my head on my knees; I can't look at him right now. "We weren't as alone as we thought. J and Rob had come back because they were out of beer. Rob and I have history. He's not a fan of my past behavior with women. We got into a fight. He accused me of using you and being a disgrace to my family. He sucker-punched me and I punched him back. J and Darren broke us up and took us to separate corners. While he was in his, he called Diane."

"Was that before or after she came to the house that day?"

"Before." His answer is so low it's almost inaudible. It makes sense now, what she said about falling in love again. I feel like such an idiot.

"I was ashamed, Mel. I didn't mean to betray you."

"They must think I'm a whore."

"Don't you dare say that," he says angrily. "You are the farthest thing from a whore. I fucking love you, Princess, and you're making it out to be some sordid affair when you say things like that."

"Isn't it, though?" I ask through my tears. "He was your brother, Sawyer! What do Diane and J think about it, huh? You tell me how disgusting they think we are!"

"Diane was pissed at Rob. That's the real reason she got so shitfaced with you that night. She's happy for us, Mel. She's on our side. It's not surprising because she's the only one in my family who has known all along how I've felt about you. She's my sister and she's a shrink, she's always been my sounding board. She hears the shit that was too fucked up to tell Noah, at least right away. I never kept any secrets from him."

"Except when it came to me." He averts his gaze from mine. "Sawyer, except when it came to me … right?"

He shakes his head. "No, I'm sorry, Mel, but he knew how I felt about you."

I pull away from him and rush to stand, but the world spins around me and the dizziness pulls me toward the ground like a centrifugal force. As usual, Sawyer is there to catch me when I fall. He gently lays me down on the couch. "Don't move," he cautions sternly and runs off. Like I could move if I wanted to.

He's back quickly with the water out of the truck and he leans me forward and sits behind me, positioning my body against his chest. "Drink this," he says as he tilts the bottle to my lips. After taking a few sips, I push it away.

"Did Noah think there was something going on with us?" I'm terrified of his answer. My heart can't take knowing Noah thought I was cheating.

"Hell no. I admitted my feelings for you in a drunken stupor and after that, I denied them. Noah didn't believe me, but he let it go for the most part. Every once in a while, he'd say something and I'd deny it. If Noah thought there was something going on with us he would have never married you, he wasn't that kind of guy."

"What about J?" I'm trying to wrap my head around all of this but it's too much, too soon.

"J's torn. He was the first person to confront me about my feelings for you that first Thanksgiving. He doesn't judge us, he's just not sure how to feel about it. But he also said it's not really his place to have an opinion on our lives and if we're happy we should go with it."

With my eyes closed, I release a deep breath. "Sawyer, this is a lot to take in."

His arm wraps around me tightly, like he's afraid I'm going to run away. "I know. It's why I've been avoiding you. I've never done this before, Mel. Relationships, love, this isn't me. I don't know how to do this and I'm not good at it, but I want to try with you."

The passion in his words is fierce. "Sawyer, when you were gone, I lost my shit over Noah again. You weren't the only one

D. Kelly

avoiding talking. Maybe we moved too fast, or took a direction we never should have in the first place, I don't know, but I—"

His finger moves against my mouth, effectively keeping me from speaking. "Don't say another word. Don't say it was a mistake, don't say you want to give up. Give me another chance, Mel, please. Let me take you out tonight, to the club, on a proper date. Don't end this because I'm an idiot."

"It's been six weeks, Sawyer. It's okay, I'm not mad. We can try to go back to the way things were before." It hurts me to say the words. I've never been this torn up over a man.

"I know it's been six weeks. Six long weeks that my hand hasn't been able to keep up with the needs of my cock because nothing can imitate the feel of your sweet pussy wrapped around me. Six agonizing weeks without tasting your essence on my tongue. Six weeks without hearing you sigh as you sleep. Four weeks without feeling your body against mine. Four weeks without tasting your tongue in my mouth, without feeling your arms wrapped around me, without seeing you smile. I know I fucked up, Princess, and I won't ever do it again if you give me another chance."

Damn him and his dirty mouth. Those words shoot my libido into orbit. I don't care about the pain when all I want is for him to make me feel good. "Alright, we'll go out tonight if we can find someone to watch Nate." Everything in my body tells me this is a bad idea, that this can only end in more heartache.

"Darren already agreed to watch him."

"You talked to him before me?" My frosty words only make him pull me closer to him.

"Actually, he told me to pull my head out of my ass and take notice that I'm not the only one who was miserable. He thought it would do us good to make up. You've been within my grasp for weeks and yet, you've never been so far away."

With careful ease, I sit up, not wanting to get dizzy again. "Why did you bring me here?"

He flashes that dimpled smile and I melt under its shine. "I've always loved this house. When I bought it, my family thought I was insane. I guess that's my fault. They thought I couldn't let go of the childhood memories of my time spent here. The truth is, I've always thought this would be the perfect place to raise a family someday."

"How long have you owned it?" I ask as he laces his fingers through mine.

"About eight years now. Like you, I have someone come out and maintain the pool and the yard. If you follow that path over there

660

you'll come across a treehouse where we had many sleepovers. And if you keep following it, there's a creek down there, too. I haven't done anything with the inside of the house. It's dated, the wallpaper is probably older than me, but the house is huge and I figured one day I could gut it and redesign it with my wife."

Noah never mentioned anything about this house or spending time in a treehouse. It's just another reminder of how little time I actually had to get to know him. But in a way, I don't mind the not knowing. I like being able to learn things about Sawyer I don't have to hear secondhand.

"This place must have meant a lot to you."

"Yeah, it did. There's nothing but good memories here."

"Well then, give me the grand tour."

Sawyer spends the next hour showing me around his home. I'm blown away by the amount of land and privacy here. Even more so, how happy and relaxed he seems. Sawyer isn't an uptight person by any means, but he seems to be in his element here.

"Why have you been living at the beach this whole time? You seem so at ease here."

He pulls me close and plants a chaste kiss against my lips. "I love the beach house. For a guy in a band in his early twenties, it's the place to be. The band as a whole has incredible creativity there. There's something about the ocean that brings it out in us, I guess. This house has always been special to me, but I don't want to live here without a family to go in it."

"Why did you bring me here, Sawyer?" I'm dying to know the answer and absolutely petrified at the same time.

"I think you already know the answer to that, Princess. Someday, I want this to be our home. I want Nate to grow up catching crawfish in the creek and spending nights in the magical treehouse with his cousins or maybe, if I'm lucky, his brothers and sisters."

Needing a minute, I turn away from him, step over to the side of the porch, and look out onto the backyard. Hummingbird feeders hang all around and the pretty little birds flit from one to the next, sampling the sweet nectar. His arms wrap around my waist from behind as he rests his chin on my shoulder.

"I'm not talking about our immediate future, Mel. After the last few weeks, I wanted you to understand where my head is. I'm in this for the long haul and will do whatever it takes to get there. You need time and space? I'll give it to you, to an extent. You still want to keep things secret for a while? I'm willing to deal with that. The only thing I refuse to do anymore is hide my feelings from you."

Turning around in his arms with tears in my eyes, I lean my head against his chest. He moves his hands to my back and rubs soothing circles. "I've spent the last four weeks convincing myself this is a mistake. Missing my husband more than I ever have and kicking myself for betraying his memory. The fact remains he's gone and we're here. As much as I know this is a bad idea, I still want to see where it goes. One day at a time. That's all I can give you right now."

"I'll take that, Princess. One day at a time." He tilts my chin up with his finger and his mouth descends upon mine. The taste of his lips is enough to make me want to wrap my legs around him and fuck him right here and now, but we really should take it slow. There's something about Sawyer's kisses. It's as if each stroke of his tongue against mine steals a piece of my anxiety and replaces it with calm. Being in his arms is relaxing and there's no place I'd rather be.

A New Beginning

My hands tremble as I look down at my wedding rings. I'm going on a date with another man. Isn't this the point where I should be taking them off? I pull a silver chain from my jewelry box and slide my rings off. Bringing them to my lips, I kiss them tearfully and slide them onto the chain. *I'm not taking them off completely, just moving them closer to my heart.*

After I dry my eyes and finish applying my makeup, I step back and look at myself in the mirror. I haven't put on a dress since their funeral. The first thing I notice is the shape of my hips and the fullness of my breasts. After having Nate, my body changed. Losing the baby weight wasn't an issue because I barely ate for months. Things have definitely toned up since I started working out again, but I can't believe I never paid attention to the more womanly shape my body has taken on.

My brown hair cascades over my shoulders, and my tight, red dress doesn't leave much to the imagination. After tucking my ID, credit card, and anxiety medication into my black clutch I'm ready to go. My four-inch black Jimmy Choo's will bring me closer to Sawyer in height and to his lips.

"Ready, Princess?" he calls out as he knocks on my door.

"Yeah, come in," I answer as I psych myself up to have a good time.

He whistles. "Holy fuck, Mel."

After catching a glimpse of him, I'd rather push him down the hall and straight to his bed. One look at him in his dark denim jeans, black boots, and charcoal-gray button-down has my pussy aching for him. My tongue darts across my glossy lips as he stalks toward me with a determined, predatory gaze.

His mouth crushes mine as he pulls me to him with one hand. I sigh into his kiss and let him elevate me to a higher place. As quickly as he starts, he backs us into the hall and pushes me against the wall. "Sorry, I didn't mean to do that in there. You just look so fucking hot, I couldn't help myself."

D. Kelly

I blush at his words and he brushes his thumb across his lips, checking for lipstick. "Smudge proof, don't worry."

A wicked smile flickers across his lips. "Maybe I should make it my mission to prove there's no such thing."

"Maybe you should."

Suddenly, his eyes are wide and he grabs my left hand. His gaze darts between my hand and my necklace. "Shit, Mel, you didn't have to—"

This time, I press my finger against his lips. "If this is truly a new beginning, yes I did. They're still close to my heart, I couldn't bear to lose them completely. But it's okay, this is right somehow. It's the next step." I wish I knew what he was thinking right now, but considering the way he laces his hand in mine and squeezes it, I have an inkling.

Darren comes barreling down the hall as Nate and Cadence come running after him. "Damn, you two look sexy as fuck."

I crouch down and hold my arms open wide. "Come give me hugs and kisses, you two." Cadence reaches me first and kisses me smack on the lips. She's just about a year and a half now and owns so much of my heart she might as well be mine. There's nothing I wouldn't do for this little girl. Nothing.

Nate is only thirteen months, but he's picked up a lot from her and is pretty advanced for his age. He climbs up onto my knee, practically throwing me off balance, and places a hand on each of my cheeks as he kisses me with a wide-open mouth. It's adorable and kind of gross all at the same time; I'd never change it for the world.

Sawyer holds on to my arm to keep me steady and once I've had my fill of them, he helps me stand. "Have fun tonight. Don't worry about us, we'll be fine," Darren says before swooping the kids up and running with them into the nursery.

We hurry to the door to avoid any crying. It's usually fine, but Nate's separation anxiety kicks in every once in a while and I won't leave when it does. I feel like it's his own form of PTSD kicking in since I didn't have anything to do with him for so long.

As we step out into the driveway, there's a Town Car waiting for us. With a raised brow, I look to Sawyer and he smirks as he opens the door. "I'm not going to apologize. I wanted a car with a divider so I could talk to you, or do things to you, that we don't need Mac or Ryan seeing or hearing."

"Hm, I wonder what those things could be," I reply, and with my teasing tone he takes my hand and places it over his hard cock and groans.

"I should have worn slacks," he grumbles, and I laugh. Then he pulls my hand to his mouth and kisses it. "I actually wanted to share something with you. Remember that song I was working on with Eli?"

"Yeah, it was really good. At least what I heard of it."

"Well, I was limited in what I could let Eli hear because of the lyrics. But when I was spending time in the garage the last month, I laid down tracks for it and finally finished it."

"Sawyer, that's amazing. I'm so proud of you. What are you going to do with it?"

His shy smile greets me and he pulls out his phone. "Aside from play it for you? Nothing. It's personal and private."

"You mean I finally get to hear you sing solo?"

"That you do. I should warn you not to freak out or anything. A lot of times when I write lyrics, it's another way of journaling. A way to purge those demons. But there's always truth in them, so I want you to understand where my head was."

"I understand that more than you think. We've talked about this before. It's the same way with writing. There's always truth buried somewhere inside my fiction. Does the song have a title?"

He scoots closer and wraps his arm around my shoulder. I could drown in his masculine scent. "Amphetamines."

"Seriously?"

With a shrug, he replies, "I know, but it fits, Mel. You'll see, listen."

He presses play on his phone and a melody as haunting as the lyrics I heard previously begins to play. When his voice fills the car, I'm sucked in completely.

Adrenaline courses through my blood
But I'm not high
You're my only drug
Darkness closes in all around
Grips my heart and slams it down
Blood oozes
People scream
Smoke rises
Where's my queen?
Hollow voices
Bright lights flash
Death surrounds me
My whole life
Is shredding fast

D. Kelly

Can you hear me?
I scream your name
All while knowing
Nothing will ever be the same
Blood oozes
People scream
Smoke rises
Where's my queen?
Darkness closes in
Fates collide
They are welcomed
To the other side.
But not you
Not my queen
Even if ...
You wear his ring.

Holy shit. He's staring straight ahead as if he's afraid to look me in the eyes. I can only imagine how hard that was for him.

I reach over and stroke his jaw, waiting for him to turn toward me, but he doesn't. Instead, I turn his head and look him in the eyes. "Sawyer, that was stunning. You are so incredibly talented."

"You're not mad?" His fearful words are matched by an equally fearful expression and my heart fills with love for him.

I hike up my skirt and throw my legs over him so I'm straddling him. Cupping his face in my hands, I lean in close so my words whisper over his lips. "No, baby, I'm not mad. I'm in awe of your talent and I'm so fucking proud of you."

As soon as the word baby slips off my tongue, my heart races. Not with regret but with the knowledge I'm falling in love with him. Before I have time to think about it further, he kisses me. Sawyer draws out this kiss—it's slow, passionate, and his hands are locked onto my ass while each stroke of his tongue sets my body on fire.

We stay like this for the entire trip to the club. As the car begins to slow, we break away breathlessly. My lips feel swollen, and my face is flushed, but the blissful expression on Sawyer's face is worth it. He moves his thumb to his lips again and I laugh. "This lipstick was worth every penny. You're still nice and clean."

"I wouldn't mind being marked by you, Princess, that way everyone knows I'm yours."

Christ, I'm pretty sure I just dripped a little down my thigh with his heated words. I wouldn't mind marking him, either. I move off of him when the car stops and he helps me out. A guard is waiting at the back door of whatever club this is and ushers us inside.

Upon entering, it's obvious by the lush lobby we're in this is their VIP entrance. A busty brunette in a dress so low-cut her nipples are practically on display smiles flirtatiously at Sawyer. "Mr. Weston, welcome back. We're excited to have you with us tonight." She rakes her nails down his arm and I want to claw her eyes out. Instead, I exhale slowly and catch the slight smirk on Sawyer's face with my reaction.

"Down, Princess, I'm all yours," he whispers into my ear, nipping it when he moves away.

Busty Barbie leads us down a hallway illuminated with red lighting from sconces placed intermittently on the walls. She takes us into an elevator that lets us out on the third floor and then down another hall. She slides a key card into a door and passes the card to Sawyer, along with a business card.

"Everything is here as you requested. If you need anything, pick up the phone and dial the extension on the card and you'll be sent directly to my personal line. Should you need anything else tonight, or … whenever, my personal cell is on the back. Feel free to use it *anytime*." This breathy, obvious bitch is getting on my last nerve.

Sawyer looks down at the card and back at her. "Thank you, Dawn. I'm sure we'll be fine, but I'll call should we need anything."

I turn around and roll my eyes so I don't have to watch her fake ass anymore. The room is large and dimly lit, with windows overlooking the dance floor. Leather couches and a table topped with snacks and water on ice fill the room. A bottle of Patron and two shot glasses are in the center of the table. Looks like Sawyer thought of everything. I hear the door close, but my attention is captured by a bowl of condoms next to the couch.

Sawyer's arms wrap around me from behind and his lips move to my neck. "Don't be mad, Mel. She's got no chance in hell with me."

"Sawyer, what kind of club is this?" I manage to squeak out. He turns me to him, the sinful gleam in his eyes telling me all I need to know. "You brought me to a sex club?"

"Not exactly …" I flash him a dirty look and he laughs. "It *is* a sex club, but it's also a regular club. Their members can pay for VIP perks, hotel rooms, and private rooms, and they also get special nights that aren't open to the public. They actually have a sex night where it's a little more risqué, but tonight isn't that night."

Pulling away from him, I cross my arms. "Did you rent a room?"

He throws his arms up in surrender. "No, Princess."

D. Kelly

"But you're a member?"

"Well, yeah," he says, smiling sheepishly. "But not for the reasons you think. Everyone here has to sign a non-disclosure agreement. No one who isn't a paying member can get in on member nights. Tonight is a member night, so if anyone sees us in the hall or whatever they can't say shit to anyone. I wanted to protect you because I know you're not ready for anyone to know about us yet."

"Oh … so what is the name of this club?"

He motions for me to take a seat and then sits next to me. "It's called The Scene. It's owned by a friend of Ben's."

Sawyer pours a shot of tequila and knocks it back. Then he pours another for me, licks his hand, and shakes salt on it. "Lick it, Princess," he says, and although I'd rather be licking his cock, I do as he says and knock back the shot. He leans in with a lime between his teeth and I suck it before he spits it to the floor and pulls my mouth to his.

Sawyer kisses me with a desperation some women only dream of, and I return it with the same amount of reckless abandon. When he pulls away, it takes a moment for me to catch my breath. Once I do, I've got questions I'm dying to know the answers to.

"Have you ever used the rooms here?"

He leans back and angles his body toward mine. "No, the only rooms I've ever used here are like the ones we're in now. And before you even ask, I've never been here on a date. Just with the guys. It's a chill place to hang out and stay low key."

"Do you know how many women you've slept with?" I blurt out.

He doubles over in laughter. "Where did that question come from?"

Now I'm laughing at my ridiculousness. "I don't know. I guess you're just really good at … being sexual? I figured it took a lot of practice?"

"Sorry, Mel, I couldn't tell you how many girls I've been with. I'm not even sure I could give you a ballpark estimate. I know that's probably a huge turnoff. Do you know your number?"

"Of course, but I'm not really proud of mine, either. I was kind of a whore in my teen years. Do you really want to know?" I'm hoping he says no because the only person who knows my number besides me is Belle, although it's grown by one since she left me.

"No, I don't. Thinking of you with other guys will only piss me off. I get you've been with Eli and Noah. I can handle that, sort of. It's easier to deal with if I keep the mindset Eli had a small dick and you were doing him a favor."

Just an Illusion Series

I practically choke on my water. "You believe that if it makes you feel better," I tell him with a wink, and he groans.

"You know, Princess," he says, moving closer to me, "I don't think it has to do with practice so much as chemistry. I've never felt so connected to anyone. I'm drawn to you. Even when I should have been letting you go I was never able to keep you out of my thoughts."

I want to admit I feel the same way about our chemistry, but if I do it's like soiling Noah's memory somehow. Noah and I were off-the-charts compatible, but no matter how much I don't want to admit it, Sawyer and I are electrifying. I knew it all the way back from that first kiss we shared in his bathroom.

"Good, because I only want you to have eyes for me," I reply, and he slides his hand up the skirt of my dress. "Sawyer, what are you doing?" The words fall from my lips as his finger slips inside of me. He pulls it out, brings it to his mouth, and sucks it in. When he's finished, he drops to his knees between my legs.

"Tasting what's mine," he growls before swiping his tongue across my panties and inhaling loudly. "Fuck, Princess, the smell of your pussy makes my cock ache for you."

"Sawyer," I cry out as his fingers move my panties to the side and his tongue laps up my wetness, "the windows, we need to stop." He chuckles against my pussy and the vibration lights me on fire. He pulls his head back and lowers my skirt.

"No one can see in, they're one-way mirrors." He pulls my mouth to his and shares the flavor of me on his tongue. I love how everything about him is so sexually charged, but it raises concerns about his capability of commitment.

"I need another drink," I say as we separate.

"Your wish is my command," He says, pouring us each a shot.

"Can I ask you something?"

"You always ask me that, Princess, but there's never going to be a time you can't ask me anything. I love it when you say or ask what's on your mind. I don't ever want you to worry about anything."

There he is, the sweet man who lives right under Sawyer's rough exterior.

"Do you think with your sexual history you'd have a problem remaining faithful in a relationship?"

"I'm not a sex addict, Mel. I enjoy sex. I enjoy women. I especially enjoy *you* - much more than anyone who has ever come before you. The answer is no, I don't think I'd have a problem being faithful. Especially being faithful to you. For me it was never really about having X-amount of women. It was about the release. Freeing

669

my mind and relieving stress and anxiety. And sure, maybe some of it was kind of a high because so many women wanted to fuck me just because of who I am. But that's the part that got old the fastest."

"Really?"

"Oh yeah. I mean, it's one thing to see someone and think 'Damn, they're hot, I'd like to hit that.' It's another thing to plot landing a rock star and hope to keep him tethered to you by getting knocked up. Or by hoping your pussy is the one to cast a magical spell and get him to want to be with you and buy you things. Groupies are the worst. It's all about bragging rights."

"So why did you do it for so long?"

"Because it was my only option. Blowing off steam with a quick fuck was better than any release I could get from exercise. I need sex, Mel. But something changed when I met you. Even the quick random fucks weren't enough. You have no idea how guilty I feel for the amount of times I got myself off thinking of you."

As he pours us both another shot, I let his words sink in and down my shot. I can't even be mad at him, there's no point. He's allowed to get off to whomever or whatever he wants; in a way, it's flattering he chose me.

"That day on the bus, the day I was supposed to be interviewing you and you were late. Were you really watching porn and jerking off?"

"Drink this," he says, handing me another shot. After knocking it back, I grab a couple of crackers because I'm starting to get lightheaded. "I wasn't watching porn, but I was jacking off to mental images of you riding my cock. For the record, it's so much better than I could have imagined."

"Shit, Sawyer," I hiss.

"What? I'm being honest."

"You sound borderline obsessed." I'm only half-joking with him.

"Maybe I was, am, I don't know. You're the first woman who has ever made me feel, Mel. Our kiss in my bathroom was the hottest kiss of my life up to that point. But as I got to know you, I started to fall for you. Your smartass mouth, the way you didn't put up with my shit but still wanted to get to know me. *Me*, not Sawyer Weston from Bastards and Dangerous. The way you loved my brother and my family. How you acted with Saylor and Emme. All of it, Mel. You fucking took my breath away. You *still* take my breath away. Dance with me."

"There's no music," I say, relieved to lighten things up a bit. Sawyer grabs a remote from the table and presses a button. The room fills with the beats of the music I've been feeling beneath my feet all night.

He pulls me to my feet as the beginning notes of "Chandelier" by Sia pipe into the room. We move over to the window and look out at the people dancing below. Sawyer moves behind me and pulls my back to his front. His mouth moves to my neck as he blazes a trail of kisses along my collarbone. I'm completely buzzed and not even paying attention to the music anymore, just him and the incredible things he's doing to my body.

Song after song plays while Sawyer plays my body like his own personal instrument. His erection presses into me and his mouth drops to my lips. His mouth never leaves mine as he pushes me back against the window.

"Open your legs wide, Mel," his husky voice murmurs against my skin as he drops to his knees in front of me. He hikes my skirt all the way up and peels my panties off. We're right in front of the window and I hesitate. "Remember, they can't see anything," he reassures me as his tongue greets my clit. He lifts one leg over his shoulder and groans. "I want these heels wrapped around my neck tonight when we get home."

The thought of fucking him again makes me even wetter, and from the way he's relentlessly working his tongue against me, he's appreciating that fact. When his tongue hits my clit again, and his fingers slide inside of me, tingles flood my body as I grip his hair.

"I'm going to come, Sawyer!" He hooks his finger just right and as his teeth graze my clit, I'm off like a rocket.

As I ride wave after wave of endless bliss, he swaps his fingers for his tongue, making my body hum. The way he insists on drinking down every drop of my release makes me drunk with lust. With careful ease, he places my leg back on the floor and turns me around to face the window. "Lean forward, Princess, and keep your legs spread. I'm going to fuck you now."

With my head against the glass, I hear the sound of his zipper and the tear of the condom wrapper. "Arms up," he commands, pulling my dress over my head when I comply. I'm not wearing a bra with this dress because it's got built-in support. His hands cup my breasts and he pinches my nipples. His whispered words flutter against my ear. "Imagine they could look up here and see us, Princess." He takes one hand and thrusts his cock into me, making me cry out with pleasure.

"Do you know how fucking hot that would be for them to look up and see us fucking? For them to see your eyes roll back into your

D. Kelly

head as I thrust into your body? See that guy down there in the blue shirt by the D.J. stage? He's looking up this way." Sawyer moves a hand down to my clit and circles it while he pinches my nipple. "Do you think he can see us? He'd be so fucking jealous that I'm balls deep inside *my* Princess."

"Fuck, Sawyer!" My orgasm comes without warning. My pussy clenches around his cock as he slams into me harder and harder.

"That's it, Princess, ride my cock like you fucking own it because you do." His teeth come down on my shoulder and he bites me again and again. The pain is exquisite. I know I'm going to bruise, but the thought of him marking my skin excites me.

"Make me yours, Sawyer, please!" My walls convulse around him again as he slams into me one final time.

"You're so fucking amazing, Mel," he says huskily into my neck after screaming his release. As my heartbeat comes back down to normal levels, I relish the feeling of his body clinging to mine. I know this is only the second time we've done this, but I love how he likes to hang on to me after sex.

"You're sure they can't see anything, right? Because that guy is still looking up this way." He laughs against my bare skin and turns me in his arms.

"As much as I'd love for the world to know you're mine, I'd never let anyone watch the way you fall apart under my touch. That is for my eyes only."

Sawyer hands me some napkins to wipe off with while he disposes of the condom. Then he picks up my dress and helps me back into it. He even adjusts my boobs to make sure they're situated right. That is such a man thing to do and it makes me laugh.

"What? You need to make sure the girls are looking good. I'm just helping you out."

"Thanks, I'd hate to walk out of here lopsided."

"Well, your freshly-fucked hair is a dead giveaway to what was going on in here." His devious smile is met with one of my own.

"Yours isn't much better than mine."

"I'm sure it's not, but men can use the just-fucked look as a style. Women, on the other hand, don't typically opt for that look. It's okay, though, I'm happy to give you that freshly-fucked look anytime."

"Gee, thanks."

Laughing, he pulls me into a hug and I melt into him. I still don't know what it is about Sawyer but he just makes me feel so damn safe.

"Do you want to stay and do some more drinking and dancing?" he asks as he releases me.

"No, I want to go home and wrap these heels around your head instead."

He pulls my hand to his cock, which is already hard again, and groans. "This is what you do to me. Let's get home."

The two of us walk hand and hand back to the elevator and out to the main desk. Dawn is standing watch and looks like she ate something sour when she sees the two of us appear. She quickly schools her features and flashes a fake smile at us. *Yeah, bitch, who gets the last laugh now?*

"I hope you enjoyed your evening, Mr. Weston. We look forward to seeing you again." I'm pretty sure I can taste her bitterness on my tongue.

"Thanks, we had a blast," he replies without even looking her way. This is a much different man than the one who talked to her when we first arrived.

After helping me into the car, he turns to me. "There's a time to be pleasant and a time to show people you know what assholes they really are. Don't ever doubt my ability to be faithful to you when I'm being nice to someone to get something I want." His eyes lock on mine; they're radiating with such sincerity it leaves me breathless. "I'm in this for the long haul, Mel. Whatever it takes to end up in the house by the creek with you."

When he lowers his mouth to mine, I lose myself in his kiss. I don't think about Noah, or how messed up people are going to be over this situation. All I think about is Sawyer and how he's brought me back to life.

D. Kelly

Amelia – Present Day

Anna and Rory are both finishing up the second part of the story while Karen is already done with the first part of the third and anxiously awaiting more. She's in the kitchen making cookies since she knows the guys are on their way back now.

The doorbell rings and I call out, "I'll get it." I need to get up and stretch anyway. When I open the door, Cadence barrels into my arms.

"Auntie Mel!" she cries out, and I hug her close. Veronica looks down at me with all-knowing eyes as I stand up with Belle's mini-me wrapped in my arms.

"Mmhm, I heard you've been writing and you didn't fill me in."

"Hey, Mama," I say, putting an arm around her. "It wasn't intentional, I just had to meet this ultimatum head-on. Before I knew it, I'd somehow thrown myself under the bus and let people read it."

"You already know your heart, baby girl. And you know my thoughts on all this BS. Tell anyone who doesn't like your choice to suck it up or get out. Life is too short and too precious to worry about other people's feelings at the expense of your happiness. I don't need to read your story to know you love him and would lay down your life for him. I got you, baby girl, even if the others don't."

Reason one billion and ten why I love this woman. "Thank you. So how was your weekend?"

"We had a blast, didn't we, Mel?" Veronica calls Cadence Mel. Short for her middle name, Melody. She didn't like the fact Belle named her something that couldn't be shortened into something she deemed cute.

"I had fun with Grandma and we ate chocolate chip pancakes!" she says with a smile—Belle's smile—and every time I see it, I feel like Belle is with me.

"Daddy!" Cadence screams, and I see Darren walking up the drive. They're back. I release Cadence and she runs like a bat out of hell into Darren's arms. She is the light of his life and vice versa.

Veronica places a kiss on my cheek and squeezes me tight. "Think about what I said. I'm going to go talk to Darren for a few minutes before my husband starts thinking he's off the hook making dinner because I'm catching up over here."

"I will, Mama. Drive safe." She and Marcus got married a few weeks ago and they're enjoying their newlywed bliss. Belle would have been incredibly happy for her.

Wyatt comes inside with a sleeping Jake and kisses me on the cheek. "I hear you've been working hard. I'm proud of you, and Noah would be, too, Mel."

"Thanks, Wyatt," I whisper.

Eli, J, and Sawyer are standing at the edge of the lawn. Sawyer has Nate in his arms but when Nate locks eyes on me, he points frantically and Sawyer releases him. He runs excitedly to the door and throws himself into my arms. "Mommy! I caughted a fish!"

"You did? That's so cool!" I kiss the top of his head and inhale him deeply. He's been gone for three days and I missed him like crazy.

"Daddy Sawyer did, too," he says with a bright smile. Noah's smile. Noah's eyes. Noah's floppy brown hair, and Noah's love for everything. He's even got Noah's stubbornness. Uncle Sawyer never stuck. He still calls Noah "Daddy" when he sees him in pictures. And whenever we talk about Noah we call him "Daddy" because I will *never* take that away from him. But from the time he could say the words, Sawyer has been Daddy Sawyer.

Rory is still pissed about that, too, but everyone else is used to it. As much as Noah loved Nate, biology doesn't completely make a parent. Sawyer's love, time, and dedication make him just as much a father to Nate as Noah is. I think it was hardest for Sawyer to accept, but Nate is a stubborn two-year-old and there's not much to do except go with what he wants in this case.

"Are you and Daddy Sawyer stinky like the fishes?" I ask while tickling him.

"No," he replies through a mouthful of giggles. "Mommy, Cady!" he yells, pointing to Cadence. It was hard to decide to keep them apart this weekend, but they wanted to make a real go of the guys weekend again and it seems like this time it worked out better. Unfortunately, the timing didn't work out for Rob to go. Diane is pregnant, with a girl again, and due any day.

"Go ahead, get Cadence, I know you probably missed her more than me." As I release him from my arms, I hear his voice.

"It's okay, Princess, I missed you enough for both of us." As I rise, my eyes meet his and they're filled with nothing but love. He pulls me into his arms and clutches me tight. "I'm so fucking sorry, Mel. I should have never done that to you."

Through tear-filled eyes, I look up at him. "It's okay. In a way, I'm glad you did. You're right, Sawyer. You've all been right. I'm not living, not the way I should be. I'm still not done, but I'm going to finish and I'm going to give you an answer. One you deserve, I hope."

He lowers his mouth to mine and kisses me eagerly. It's been a long three days without him, but the clearing of a throat nips our welcome kiss in the bud.

"Eh-hem."

"Back off, Watts, she's mine now."

"You wound me, Weston, now get the fuck out of my way and let me greet my best friend properly. I haven't seen her in months."

Sawyer releases me and Eli scoops me into his arms. "Hey, baby girl, I've missed you."

"I missed you, too, Eli." My muffled words vibrate against his shirt and he laughs.

"Sorry, I just needed to squeeze you. I hear you've been doing some novel-worthy writing this weekend."

"Is that so?"

"Yup, your future husband, baby daddy, partner for life, or whatever the fuck you guys are going for told me it's some damn good reading. Then he also said I couldn't read it because it was for his eyes only."

I roll my eyes at them. "The two of you are ridiculous sometimes. You can read it whenever you want, Eli. You already know all my drama. You should go say hi to Rory, she's reading it now."

"Yeah, maybe I'll just go home and catch up with her another time. Give me a call when you make your decision, baby girl. Your heart will never lead you wrong." Eli kisses me on the cheek and ducks out the door in a flash.

Sawyer chuckles. "Well, on the plus side, you know he's got our back."

"Rory asked earlier why no one ever told her you and I kissed first. I think she's struggling reading this just as much as I struggled to write it."

He releases a sigh and hugs me again. "I'll deal with her later, but you're my main concern right now. Want to go in the bedroom with me and write while I catch up on what you've written?"

"That would be really nice."

"I missed you, Mel, and I can't apologize enough for what I put you through."

His heartfelt words wrap around me tighter than his hug.

"I missed you, too."

Thanksgiving Trouble

After our night at the club, Sawyer and I fell into an easy relationship. We let our friends in on our secret but kept the family out of it. At times, it was hard because they're over often and aside from Rory, Owen, and Karen, pretty much everyone else knows. With as pissed off as Rob was, I couldn't imagine letting the rest of them find out our shameful secret, so we spent months walking a precarious line between friendship and love in their presence.

The Disney World trip came and went, but we didn't go. Only Diane and Rob, Rory, Karen and Owen and the girls went. For the rest of us, it was still too close to the good memories we shared in Florida with Noah. Especially for Sawyer and Mac.

I'm still wearing Noah's rings around my neck so they're close to my heart. I'll never forget Karen's reaction when she noticed.

"You took off your rings," she said with tear-filled eyes.

"Yeah, but I can't take them off for good. I need them close to my heart for now," I answered, clutching them between my fingers.

"It's a step, and with each one you take you'll start to move through the darkness and into the light."

"Are you angry with me?" I asked, fearing she'd be disappointed.

"Amelia, why would you think that? You're beautiful and you're young. I loved Noah dearly, but I don't want you to pine away for him forever. I want you to be loved, to give love again." I pulled her into a hug and we cried together.

I feel like that was a missed opportunity. Right then I should have sat her down and told her about me and Sawyer. Oh well, we'll come clean when the time is right.

Today is my birthday, and Sawyer says we're celebrating hitting the other side of thirty in style. I'm not sure what that means but there was no arguing with him. I'm trying to figure out what to wear when he knocks and then opens my door.

"I could have been naked."

"Then it would have been like it was *my* birthday. I can walk out if you want to strip, or better yet, I can stand right here and watch." He licks his lips as if already imagining it.

"Perve."

"Damn straight, but only when it comes to you."

"Good, now what should I wear?"

His heated gaze has me flustered and he pulls my body to his and bites down on my neck. "Nothing."

"Sawyer—"

His mouth crushes against mine and our tongues meet eagerly, stealing my breath and my sanity. When he pulls away, he rests his head against mine.

"Wear whatever you'd like, we're going to the house by the creek. I've got a surprise for you. If I asked you for a favor, would you do it for me? No questions?"

Giving Sawyer a no-questions-asked favor could get me into a lot of trouble but it could also be a lot of fun. "Sure."

"Bring your dad's present and card with you."

My heart races in my chest; I want to take back my answer. He sees the fear in my eyes and tilts my chin up. "Princess, I promise we won't do anything you don't want to. Just bring them, okay?"

"Okay."

Two hours later, we're sitting in his gazebo as the crickets and frogs chirp and croak the night away. Sawyer has some blues playing subtly in the background and we're eating dinner under twinkly lights.

"Are you okay?

"Yeah, why?" he replies with a furrowed brow.

"You seem nervous."

"I've never done this before, maybe I am."

"Done what?" I ask.

"You know … the whole romance thing."

"This is beautiful, Sawyer, and it means more to me than you know. Thank you."

A sigh of relief escapes him and he smiles brightly. "You're welcome."

After we finish our lasagna, we take our wine and sit on the couch. My dad's present sits between us like a ticking bomb. Sawyer turns to me and nervously clears his throat.

"There were a lot of things I wanted to give you for your birthday. The more I thought about it, the more I realized they're just things and you can buy your own things. Then, I realized maybe there is something I can give you that's better than something bought." He picks up the card and the gift. "The last thing I want is for you to cry on your birthday, but I think in this case tears would come regardless. You are the best person I know, Amelia Weston, but you have a hard time letting go of the past and moving forward."

"Sawyer…" I'm choked up and don't even know what to say, but when he flashes me his nervous smile again I know saying anything is useless. He's out of his comfort zone, too.

"My gift to you, if you'll let me give it to you, is freedom from your past. I'll be here to hold your hand, wipe away your tears, and be your shoulder to cry on. This present is fifteen years past due, and I want to be able to help you eradicate at least one demon lingering in your closet. This is the one."

My eyes fill with tears and my heart feels like it's going to burst in a million pieces. This is the sweetest, scariest, most romantic thing. And for Sawyer to open his heart like this says more than I could ever convey.

With trembling hands, I take the card first and open it. I barely skim the words and dive right into the handwritten message inside.

My Mellie Sunshine,

Happy Birthday. You're almost all grown up now and soon you'll be leaving me to live a life of your own. I know the past couple of years have been rough and I'm not the dad you deserve. Losing your Mom wrecked me, but my vow to you this year is to get my shit together and be the man you deserve to guide you. Come Monday morning I'm going off to rehab, and when I get out we'll start a brand-new adventure, just the two of us. You are my world, Amelia, and I love you endlessly.

Dad

Tears are streaming down my cheeks as Sawyer is doing his best to wipe them away. Setting the card down, I clutch his shirt and sob into his chest as he rubs my back and whispers comforting words into my ears. This hurts a lot, but my heart feels like a burden has been lifted from it.

When I'm all cried out, I look up at him and he wipes away the remainder of my tears. "For so long I wondered if it was really a suicide or an accidental overdose. I'm still not sure, but based on this I can believe he wanted help and I know he loved me." I kiss him briefly while he hugs me tight. "Thank you, Sawyer, for always knowing what I need before I can admit it to myself."

"You're welcome, Princess, but we've still got one more to go. Are you up for it? Or do we need to save it until next year?"

His words make me smile; he's just as persistent as Belle used to be but in his own way. I reach for the present and pull off the old, frayed ribbon and then the paper. Inside the box is a photo of my parents when they were young and in love. I've never seen it before and it leaves me speechless.

"You're the perfect combination of them. You have his hair color and your mom's eyes. His smile and her nose. I don't know how I didn't see it when we first met you."

"You weren't looking for it."

"True. There's something else in the box, Mel."

Pulling my attention off the photo long enough to pull the last thing out of the box, I open the drawstring bag and gasp. "It's my Mom's locket. She wore this everywhere." I pop it open and inside is a photo of me as a baby and my dad. I clutch it in my hand and hold it close to my heart.

"Thank you, Sawyer. This is one of the best birthdays I've ever had."

There's cake to be had and dancing to do, but as Sawyer puts his arm around my shoulder and pulls me close, I'm feeling a peace I haven't felt in years. We don't need words as we sit and look out at the stars, we just need each other.

Things have been perfect the last couple weeks, maybe too perfect. Thanksgiving is right around the corner, and with Thanksgiving comes family.

"Mel!" Sawyer calls out from the office.

"I'm in the kitchen!" I just got back from the store with all the things I need to make sweet potatoes. I didn't make them last year, so this time Darren made sure to ask since I'm in better spirits. I'm glad I went to the store alone, though, because I was flooded with the memories of when Noah and I went shopping for that first Thanksgiving. It's hard to believe that was two years ago.

Sawyer flies into the kitchen and scoops me into his arms, spinning me around. "We did it, Princess, we fucking did it!" His excitement is contagious, but I have no idea what we're celebrating.

"What did we do, babe?"

With dimples on full display, he backs me up to the counter and lifts me up. "We got the final artist to sign off on the EP. It's time to move full speed ahead, Mel. Noah is going to be blowing up the airwaves."

"Oh my God, Sawyer, that's amazing." My tears begin to fall–a combination of happy and sad tears. I'm still not sure this is the right thing, but I know with my whole heart Noah would want the exposure for the foundation most of all so we can help even more people.

Sawyer swipes away my tears with his fingers and kisses along the trails they left on my cheeks. Soon, his mouth is against mine and I tug his lip ring with my teeth. The action elicits a sexy hiss from him as he pushes himself against me.

"Damn, Sawyer, the way my body reacts to yours should be illegal."

"It probably is in some states," he answers before his tongue greets mine. My fingers slide through his hair and I open wider to him, wanting to taste every inch of his mouth.

"Oh my God!" The shocked scream comes from behind us, and I realize I must have forgotten to close the door when I brought the groceries in.

Sawyer pulls back slightly with his head against mine. "It's going to be okay, Princess," he says before looking up at Rory's furious glare. Panic floods through me. I've never seen her this angry, not even when she hit me.

"Rory, let me explain, this isn't as bad as it looks," Sawyer begins, and I hop down off the countertop.

"Really? It looks like you're about to fuck your twin brother's wife. Am I wrong?" She inches closer and Sawyer steps between us.

I move away from his protection; I don't want it and don't need it. Whatever Rory has to say, I deserve.

"It's not like that, Ror. I'm in love with her and I have been for years."

Her furious gaze flits between us before it narrows in on me. "You are a fucking whore!" she screams, and I flinch. "Not just any whore, either. It wasn't good enough to fuck one half of the BAD twins, you had to fuck the other one after the first one died. How dare you betray my brother like this, Mel? How fucking dare you?!"

"Rory, that's enough! You have no idea what she's been through, what *we've* been through, and how much we've agonized over this decision."

"Oh, fuck you, Sawyer! I'm sure you agonized just as hard over fucking Mel as you did Marilyn, right? You going to blame this on drugs this time, too?" She's in his face, and I've never seen Sawyer as angry as he is right now.

"You two, stop, please. She's right, Sawyer. I fucked up."

D. Kelly

"Damn straight you fucked up! Were you this much of a whore when Noah was alive, too? Were the two of you fucking behind his back?"

My head begins to spin and I have to hold on to the counter to keep my balance. That's exactly what people are going to think.

"Enough!" Sawyer roars, and I'm so thankful the kids are with Mama today. "Rory, you don't get to come into our home and accuse us of doing something hurtful to Noah. No one, not even you, could have loved him as much as me or Mel. There was never anything between us before he died. Grief does things to people and it bonds you in unimaginable ways." He's so angry his hands are shaking.

"I'm pretty sure the only one who loved Noah in this room is me. You're fucking his slut, and since she's fucking you that makes her worse than a whore. I mean, come on, what kind of person fucks a set of brothers, anyway? Aside from a floozy, a tramp, a hussy, a whore, a harlot, a tart … should I continue?" Rory says through her tears.

"Get out of my house and don't you even think about coming back until you're ready to apologize and accept our relationship."

"Sawyer, no, you don't mean that. I'm sorry, Rory, it's my fault."

"Tears aren't going to get you out of this, bitch. Wait until I tell the family."

Sawyer sneers. "Most of them already know. Now, get out and don't come back."

"Does Mom know?" she demands, not backing down an inch. When Sawyer doesn't reply, she snorts. "Yeah, that's what I thought, so that's where I'll start." The door slams shut behind her and I slide to the floor, my body shaking like a leaf, the tears falling harder than they have in ages. Everything about us is wrong. Nobody is going to understand.

"It's okay, Mel. Everything is going to be okay." Sawyer sits next to me, trying to reassure me, but he doesn't sound so positive himself.

"No, it's not. She's right. Everything she said is right. I *am* a whore, and what kind of person bounces between brothers? Everyone is going to think we're sick and disgusting."

"It doesn't matter what they think, the only thing that matters is us." He reaches for my hand but I pull it away.

"Don't you see? I'm bad for you and for your family. I won't be the cause of your family splitting apart. I can't, Sawyer. You've all been nothing but kind and welcoming to me and look what I've done."

682

My chest heaves with every sob. Sawyer sits with me for ages trying to comfort me, but I'm too far gone. At some point, I hear Darren talking to Sawyer but their words are muffled. Shortly afterward, Sawyer carries me to my room and lays me on the bed. He pulls the anxiety medication from the nightstand that I haven't taken in months and hands me one with a cup of water.

"I'm going to let you get some rest, but don't give up on us, Princess. We're just getting started." With a kiss to my forehead, he leaves, closing the door behind him. The photo of Noah kissing me at their signing, our official coming out photo, mocks me from the nightstand. "Oh, Noah, where did I go so wrong? How did I get so utterly and completely lost?"

Is it even possible to make things right after this? I'm not even sure.

I feel like my eyes have barely closed but it's nearly dusk when I open them. My phone blinks at me from the nightstand and when I reach for it, I see there are missed calls from both Karen and Diane. A lot of them.

Before I can even give myself a moment to think about what to do next, her voice travels through the house and I jump out of bed. I'm sure she's the first in a succession of Westons who are going to come unleash their fury on me. Who could blame them? Rory was right in calling it like she's sees it—I'm nothing but a whore. Maybe I should just take Nate and go. They'd probably all be better off.

"Mom, now isn't a good time," Sawyer says, his voice becoming louder the closer he gets to my door.

"I'll decide what is and isn't the right time, Sawyer," she replies. She doesn't sound angry, just firm.

"I'm serious, Mom, you need to go home." Sawyer is pissed. He's in protective mode and has been since Rory unleashed havoc on us.

"Sawyer Joshua Weston! Get out of my way. I'm still your mother, and I don't care if you're a grown man or not, I'm not leaving until I see Mel."

Wearily, I swing open my door. "It's okay, Sawyer, let her have her say."

With an apprehensive look between us, he steps back and allows her inside, but he doesn't move. Karen turns and closes the door behind her, effectively locking him out. I'm sure he's still listening at the door, though.

"Is it true?" she asks with tear-filled eyes.

"That I'm a whore who betrayed her husband with his brother? Yeah, I guess it is. Are you here to fit me with my scarlet letter?"

Just when I think Karen is going to unleash holy hell on me, she pulls me into her warm embrace. "Rory was wrong, Amelia. It wasn't her place to judge you. You are not a whore, you did not betray your husband, and you don't need to defend yourself to any of us. Least of all Rory."

"What ... why ..." With an exaggerated sigh, I take a seat on the edge of the bed. "I'm not sure I understand."

"No, I don't suppose you do." She takes a seat next to me. "Love and loss go hand in hand. You loved Noah and he loved you immensely, there's no denying that. If Noah were still here, I have no doubt the two of you would still be as happy as you were on your wedding day."

She pauses and walks to the window, turning her gaze to the sun setting over the ocean.

"Sawyer has loved you from the moment he set eyes on you. He's never said so in as many words, but a mother knows. The two of them always fell for the same girls. I used to think it was a curse, but now ... maybe it's a blessing. I know you love him, Amelia. You've always loved him in your own way. And I'd like to think Noah is pushing the two of you together somehow."

My jaw drops with her words and she turns to me with a smile. "Maybe I'm being selfish, it wouldn't be the first time. You're our daughter, and with Sawyer you still will be. No one will love Nate like Sawyer does, and no one will be able to keep Noah alive for him the way Sawyer can. He'll be Nate's father in every way but never diminish that Noah is his dad. Seems like the best of both worlds to me."

"Karen, I'm not there yet, and I don't know if I ever will be. It's been over a year and Noah is still this huge, gaping hole in my heart. My soul aches every day without him. Sawyer deserves more. He deserves better than I can give him, especially in my current state. Maybe even ever. He wants my love and I wasn't sure I could give it to him. I didn't know how to take that from Noah and give it to Sawyer. I tried, I really did, but seeing how Rory sees us, how everyone is going to see us, it makes me realize how wrong I was to try. How wrong the two of us are for even doing what we're doing in the first place."

She sits next to me and holds my hand. "It's not wrong. Unconventional, maybe. Noah wanted you happy. He would want this for you two and this isn't speculation, it's a fact. You need to have Sawyer show you his video from Noah. Maybe it will help you understand. I've said too much and I should go now. No one else will be coming by to bother you two. Just think about what I've said and don't be so quick to push him away."

With a kiss to my cheek, she heads to the door.

"Karen, you're his mom, why would you encourage this?"

She pauses and turns back around. "They're both my sons and I know them better than anyone. The sadness of losing Noah is with me every moment. But it's like I told you when we first met, you're a good friend to Sawyer and he cares about you deeply. I'm ecstatic to see Sawyer in love and letting happiness in again. Losing you to Noah hurt him immensely, getting you back this way is tearing him apart, too. His guilt is just as great as yours, I can see it in his eyes." She sighs softly. "I've suspected there was something going on with you for a while now. You make each other happy, and you deserve it after the year you've both had. There's no greater gift than loving someone who has been through the depths of hell with you and understands exactly how you feel. Together, the both of you can rise from the ashes and have happiness. Let his love in, Mel, and love him in return. I promise Noah will always be there, but you deserve to be happy."

When she opens the door, Sawyer is propped up against the opposite wall with stormy eyes. Karen kisses his cheek and looks between us. "Heal each other." Then, turning to Sawyer, her shoulders sag a bit. "Show her the video, Sawyer, it's time."

"Mom!"

"I know," she says, cutting him off, "it wasn't my place to tell her, but it's time, Sawyer. Be angry with me if you must, but you need to do this before it's too late."

Karen shows herself out and Sawyer moves to the bed, propping himself up against my headboard, and settles in for a talk.

"Why does she want me to watch Noah's video, Sawyer?"

He looks at me with sorrow-filled eyes. "After we got the videos, my parents asked each of us if they could see them after we watched them. I'm not sure if it's because they wanted to have just a little bit more Noah, or if they wanted to be sure we were all honoring his wishes. I agreed before I saw my video, but after I watched it, even though I didn't want them to see it, I felt like I couldn't take back my word."

D. Kelly

"So she's seen it, I get that. What is in there she wants me to see? I'm not sure I can go through another video, Sawyer. I haven't even gotten up the courage to empty his fucking closet."

He tilts his head back and looks at the ceiling. "It's complicated, Mel, and if you want my opinion, if you can't handle what Rory said today, you definitely can't handle watching Noah's video."

"Do I need to? Is it a necessity?"

"My mom thinks it is. I'm not so sure. What he says could make you feel better or it could push you further away. It all depends on your state of mind."

"Ha! I'd say my state of mind is pretty fucking fragile right about now."

He runs his hand along the side of my face and gives me a soft smile. "I'd give anything to take away your pain right now and for you to believe Rory is wrong. She's lashing out because she doesn't understand. Rory has always been stubborn like Noah and she doesn't like to see things from a broad perspective."

"Sawyer—"

"Stop. I'll give you whatever you need, Mel. Time, space, Noah's video, name it. Just don't end this. At least not before you know the whole story and for that, you need the video."

"The holidays. Give me the holidays. I need time to think and figure out where my head is. Do you think you can keep Nate for a few days?"

"Days? Where the fuck do you think you're going?"

"Eli isn't taking a holiday break this year. He's spending Thanksgiving in Arizona. I'll fly there, watch his show, have dinner with him, and come back the next day. I don't want to be here for Thanksgiving."

"Absolutely not. They can have Thanksgiving at my parents' house and we'll have our own here."

"I'm not breaking your family up at the holidays, and it's already supposed to be here like it is every year. Rory will be fine if I'm not around, and Nate should be with your family for the day."

"Nate should be with you on Thanksgiving, wherever that is."

"Please, Sawyer, I'll fly out on Wednesday and be home on Friday morning. Don't make me feel guiltier by making me stay."

He shakes his head but eventually agrees. "Alright, I don't like it but if this is what you need, I won't stand in your way."

Fun With Eli

"How was Thanksgiving?" I ask Sawyer as I'm getting ready for bed. From his extended sigh, I'm guessing not well.

"Miserable, and even more miserable without you."

"What happened?"

"Do you even care, Mel?" he snaps, and I flinch.

"Of course I do."

"Can I ask you something this time?"

"Sure, Sawyer, ask away," I answer as I slide into bed.

"Do you miss me?"

"More than you could probably imagine."

"I miss the fuck out of you, Mel. Come home."

I laugh and turn off the light next to the bed. "I'll be there in less than ten hours. Now, stop avoiding and tell me what happened."

"You first. How was your day?"

"It was good. Eli and I spent the morning and afternoon together, I hung out backstage at his show, and they had dinner catered in for us. Afterward, I got to watch while he did some interviews and everyone fangirled all over him. I can't tell you how much I don't miss that part of touring."

"That's it?" he asks, surprised.

"Well, yeah, it's a tour and a holiday, you know how busy things get. I mostly wondered what you all were up to today and Mama wasn't able to fill me in since she was at Marcus' house."

He laughs. "Like Anna wasn't texting you updates."

"Not like you think she was. It was more about the amount of drama and lack of alcohol, but not what kind of drama."

"Yeah, so Mom decided not to make her traditional egg nog. Since I prohibited anyone from spending the night, she used it as an excuse for people to not drink and drive. I'm pretty sure she did it because it's Rory's favorite and she's pissed that Rory drove you away."

"That's not exactly fair," I begin to protest.

"Fuck yeah it is. If Rory wouldn't have been such a bitch to us, you would have never left. Saylor and Darren were really happy you made the sweet potatoes and left them for us all. I've got a picture for you, too, hang on a sec."

My phone buzzes in my hand and I take a look. It's a photo of Nate and Cadence eating their first batch of sweet potatoes. "Sawyer, that's adorable! I should put that on Belle's blog tomorrow."

"I wish you would have been here for it. Families are supposed to be together on the holidays and there was enough drama with or without you. Rory sulked the whole time. My mom didn't even speak to her. Diane tried to play go-between but once Rory figured out she knew about us, that was the end of that. My dad was oddly quiet, and everyone else sat around uncomfortably, waiting for it all to be over."

Shit, that sounds miserable. "I'm sorry, I thought it would go better than that."

"Just promise you aren't going to duck out on Christmas, too."

"I promise. Christmas is for families and besides, Eli will be home for Christmas," I add with a light laugh.

"Not fucking funny, Mel. You're not running from me and back to him, are you?"

"Sawyer, no. You know that's in the past and if I can ever work it out in my head, my heart, and with your family, someday you will be my future. Okay?"

"We'll figure this out, Mel, because I'm not letting you go."

When we hang up, he sends me the video link for "Hold You in My Arms" by Ray LaMontagne, and my heart soars. Even when I'm lost, Sawyer is always trying to pull me from the abyss.

After I listen to his goodnight song, I send him one of my own, "Tangled Up In You" by Staind. No matter how fucked up I am, everything about me right now is exactly that. Tangled up in him.

When I arrive home the next morning, Sawyer meets me at the airport with a grim look on his face.

"What's wrong?"

"You'll see," he says, taking my hand and pulling his sunglasses back down. As soon as we exit the airport, we're under siege by paparazzi.

"Amelia, is it true you and Eli Watts have rekindled your romance?"

Between camera flashes, more questions are shouted out.

"Is it true you and Eli Watts were married last night in a secret ceremony?"

"Amelia, don't you think it's too soon to be dating after losing your husband?"

"Amelia, where are your wedding rings? Is that an indicator you have already moved on?"

Holy shit. My head is spinning by the time Sawyer shoves me into the SUV and Ryan takes off like a bat out of hell.

"What the hell happened to spark all of that?" I cry out, and Sawyer passes me the *L.A. Times*. There's a photo on the front page of the entertainment section of me and Eli hugging when he picked me up at the airport.

"This? Two friends hugging is what they're going off about? Unbelievable."

Sawyer pulls my hand to his mouth and kisses it. "I'm sorry, Princess. The house is under siege, too."

"Why is this even news? This makes me so angry. *You* don't think it's true, do you?" I ask, turning my attention to him.

"Come on, Mel, you know me better than that. I've seen Eli pull that same spinning hug on you every time he sees you for almost three years now. That hug is as innocent as can be."

I take a picture of the photo and send it to Eli.

Have you seen me on the news yet? Guess we're all the rage again.

His reply comes within minutes.

Eli: Not yet but I can remedy this real quick. Give me five minutes.

Shit.

Please don't do anything we're going to regret.

He doesn't respond for the next fifteen minutes and when my phone does finally ding, it's a link to one of the most popular gossip websites.

Who is this gorgeous redhead Eli Watts has been spotted with around town? Rumors about him and Amelia Weston are just that if this morning's lip-locked couple is any indication. Our reporters spotted her going into Eli's room last night and leaving there with a classic morning-after look just a few moments ago.

Time to fess up, Eli. Who's the hottie?

I show my phone to Sawyer and he cracks up and pulls out his own phone.

"What are you doing?"

"Sending Eli my thanks."

D. Kelly

"Shouldn't I be the one doing that?"

He flashes a killer smirk at me. "Well, you're the one with slow fingers. Get to typing, Princess."

He can be such a cocky bastard, but I'm dying to know who she is because I didn't see her when I was there.

Who is she?

Eli: Some fangirl who was hanging outside of the venue last night. She was hot and I got a heads up there could be some gossip about us so I figured I'd be able to have some fun and squash some rumors at the same time.

Did you get her number?

Eli: Nah, she was a one and done. Pretty sure she would have been a stage five clinger.

I love you, Eli. Thank you.

Eli: Anytime, baby girl. Tell Sawyer I got his back.

Eli's text gives me the feels. It's important to me Eli approves of who I'm with and based on our talks yesterday, he more than approves of me and Sawyer. Turning my attention back to Sawyer, I ask, "When did you win Eli over to the dark side?"

"I'm the dark side, am I? I guess I can see where you came up with that. Good thing for me, you *like* walking on the dark side."

"Stop being a cocky bastard and fill me in. I'm curious. I thought you guys hated each other."

"It turns me on when you call me names, Princess," he murmurs against my ear, and I look down to the obvious bulge in his pants.

"You're so fucking dirty," I retort in a hushed tone.

He laughs. "You fucking love that about me." Crossing my arms, I sit back and glare at him. "To answer your question, I don't know. After the Sara shit, we buried the hatchet, and he was always helping me taking care of you after the accident. We became friends. If I did something special, other than that, I'm seriously not aware of it."

When we get home, the paparazzi are no longer lingering. Eli definitely worked his magic in my favor. When we get into the kitchen, there's a tin on the table with my name on it.

"Cookies?"

Sawyer turns a frosty glare on me. "Yes, Mom said I had to leave those for you. She even put a note inside."

As I pop off the lid and pull out the note, he never takes his eyes off me.

Amelia,

We missed you at Thanksgiving. I understand why you left but if you ever do it again, especially at a holiday, you'll have to deal with my wrath. Sawyer was miserable without you. Remember what I said, you are loved, and no one but you believes the crap Rory said. She's hurting and taking it out on you. I'll see you before, but it goes without saying, I'll see you at Christmas as well. Enjoy your cookies. There are twelve, and if there are any missing, you let me know.

Love,

Karen

"Haha! You're mad because she left me a cookie count in her note."

"Can I have one?" he asks, flashing me puppy dog eyes. "Come on, Mel, you know her cookies are my favorite."

I put the lid back on the tin and hop up on the counter. He steps between my legs and I put my hands on his waist. "You can have as many as you want if you make me a promise."

"What kind of promise?"

"I did some thinking while I was gone. I'm struggling a lot with what Rory said. Even more, I'm struggling with why I can't seem to pack up Noah's things and what that means for us. I want to enjoy the holidays with you and Nate."

"Me, too," he says sweetly.

"We need to take a few steps back, okay? I'm going to start sleeping in my room again. And I want to stop having sex."

"Are you serious?" he asks with wide eyes.

"Yes. We keep doing this hot, super-hot, cold thing. We jump into explosive, mind-numbing sex, but don't you think it's weird we've never made love?"

His hand cups the side of my face. "It's not that I haven't wanted to, but I didn't think you were ready for that."

Nodding, I agree. "I haven't been. But I need to be if this is ever going to work. So, from now until the new year, no sex. We go slow. I need to dial back the whore a bit so I can make myself believe I'm not one."

"I'm going to fucking kill Rory." His venomous words make me sad.

"She's entitled to her opinion and I need to figure out how to deal with that. After the new year I'm going to watch Noah's video to you. By then, after a month of taking things slow and dealing with my internal conflicts, maybe I'll be in a better place to move forward."

"Whatever you need, Princess. But does no sex mean I can't fuck you with my mouth?"

Damn, he's got such a talented mouth that is good for so much more than singing. "For now, yes. But maybe we can gift each other oral for Christmas. After all, it would be rude to refuse a gift."

"Well, if that's the case, I'm going to gift you a specific amount of orgasms from my tongue that you have to claim on Christmas Eve and Christmas Day."

"Thanks for the heads up. I'll make sure to gift you some sixty-nine coupons. You know how much I like sucking you off while you're going down on me."

He laughs and pops a kiss on my lips. "And you say I'm dirty. You're just as freaky as I am, Princess, but I fucking love it. You can have all the time and space you need because we're going to get through this together."

"Thank you," I whisper against his lips.

"You're welcome. Now, take what cookies you want because these bad boys are all mine."

Slammed Blog Post

Hey, Slammers!

Happy Thanksgiving Weekend!

This year, I missed Thanksgiving with my family and instead spent it with a dear friend of mine. Most of you are well aware Eli Watts and I were childhood sweethearts, but what you may not know is he's one of my very best friends and was spending the holiday alone. Friends don't let friends spend holidays alone, so I took a couple of days and caught up with my oldest and dearest pal.

On the way home, the paparazzi were in full vulture mode. I understand it's their job, but this is my life. So I thought I would take this opportunity to clear things up. I'm not dating Eli, or seeing him in any form other than friendship. It's true that I've taken off my wedding rings and keep them close to my heart around a chain. It was a hard thing to do but a necessary step in my healing. Noah and Belle have been gone for well over a year now. Each passing day is a painful reminder they're gone but also a reminder I'm still here. I've debated about talking to you all about this, but I feel it's important. I loved Noah Weston more than I've ever loved anyone. He was the light of my life until *his* light was extinguished. There is someone special in my life who has helped me through this past year and we're tiptoeing into the waters to see if dating is something I'm capable of right now.

I know many of you are already judging me and thinking it's too soon. I'm not necessarily sure I disagree with you, but then I'm reminded of my best friend and her zest for life. Belle didn't just close her blog with "Live today like there's no tomorrow." It was her motto for how she lived her life and how she wanted me to live mine. Deep in my heart, I know Belle would be disappointed in me if I didn't at least try to see there's a brighter future out there for me somewhere. So, for her and these beautiful kids of ours, I'm dipping my toes into the shallow end of life. Enjoy this picture of Nate and Cadence eating sweet potatoes on their first Thanksgiving with real food.

Happy Holidays, Slammers!

Amelia

House of Cards

"That was painful."

Sawyer brings a bottle of wine and two wine glasses and joins me on the floor. We're leaning against the couch in front of the fire.

"It wasn't as bad as Thanksgiving was," he says as he uncorks the bottle.

"Really? I'm sorry I made you go through that alone."

Today is Christmas and everyone just left to go home. I feel bad they're not doing their normal family sleepovers, but I'm also relieved Sawyer and I get some time to ourselves.

Sawyer kisses me on the cheek and passes me a glass. "It's alright. I'm glad you got to keep Eli company over Thanksgiving. Even though I wasn't happy about it then, you needed time to think. Besides, I had Nate keeping me company and that's almost as good as having you."

"Speaking of Nate, how do you think he and Cadence are going to do as co-sleepers?"

For Christmas, we got rid of the cribs and put toddler beds in the nursery for Nate and Cadence. Tonight is their first night trying it out.

"I think they'll be fine. The first few nights could be an adjustment, but they were so excited. I think it was the right call. It's time Darren separates from her a bit." Sawyer's tone makes me think Darren may start bringing people home. I can't picture it; I don't think he'd ever bring some random chick to the house where our kids live.

"Whenever I think of how close he keeps her, I think about your journal and how you described him with Belle at the accident. It hurts my heart, and I completely get why he keeps her close. I hate Belle went through that, and thinking about her fear in those moments kills me, but I'm so glad you guys took Cadence to your bus that night."

Sawyer runs his hand up my thigh and gives it a reassuring squeeze. "I've thought a lot about that night and the things that led up to it. It pains me to admit it, but I'm starting to believe in fate more than ever. Noah might have been on to something."

"How can you even say that?" I ask, my eyes filling with tears.

"Because Cadence was teething for a reason. We switched up our sleeping arrangements for a reason. That bar … Winnie the Pooh … They saved you, Mel. They're the only reason you're still with me. What are the odds? Noah knew something bad was coming, and it sucks Belle was in the middle of it, but Mom said something at the hospital I'll never forget."

"What did she say?"

"She could have lost us both that night, Mel. What if Noah and I had both died? I don't know why I was saved, but I can't help but feel like it's because I was supposed to be here for you and Nate."

"Well, I think fate is a crueler bitch than karma."

"I don't disagree with you, Princess, but as hard as it is to accept I'm still here, and I'm glad we're together."

We hear the slide of footed pajama feet against the floor before we see which kid is coming out of their room. Nate shuffles in clutching his new Build-A-Bear he got from Saylor and Emme for Christmas and immediately climbs into Sawyer's lap. I grab our wine and put it on the table so it doesn't get knocked over.

"What's the matter, Nate? Want to come here?" I ask, holding out my hands, but he clutches Sawyer while shaking his head.

"No, Daddy Sawyer," he says firmly, and my heart plummets and bursts with happiness at the same time. *Holy shit.*

With wide eyes, Sawyer corrects him. "Uncle Sawyer, buddy, say Uncle Sawyer."

"Daddy Sawyer," he says again, turning into Sawyer's chest, hugging him fiercely.

"Mel, I'm sorry … I didn't …" Sawyer stammers. My eyes are fixed on them. The family resemblance is strong. Any outsider looking in would assume Sawyer is his father. Nate's eyes flutter closed as Sawyer's hands rub continuous circles against his back.

Sawyer shakes his head and tears begin to fall. I'm not sure if he feels bad, or if he's happy, but for some reason I feel like this is another sign from Noah. Just like last year when Nate crawled on Christmas for the first time.

"It's okay, Sawyer."

"How can you say that?" he hisses.

"Because to Nate you're his dad. There's no denying that anymore. We'll still tell him about Noah and call him Daddy but it's time we face the truth. No matter what happens with us, you're Nate's dad now."

Without a word, Sawyer stands up and carries Nate back to his room. He comes back a few minutes later with tears streaming down his cheeks.

"This isn't right, Mel. It's not fucking right."

He sits back down and grabs his wine, gulping it down. "I'm not so sure about that anymore. When Nate sees Noah in photos, he calls him Daddy. He knows Noah is his dad. But he called you Daddy Sawyer, he knows the difference." My tears are falling as freely as his.

"We'll keep correcting him until he stops saying it."

Tracing my thumb across his lips, I press my head to his. "You can try if you want to because this is about your comfort level most of all. But I'm pretty sure my son knows what he feels. He feels you're his father and he loves you so much he's honoring you with that title, too."

"Fuck, Mel, this hurts so much."

"I know, but doesn't it feel good somewhere inside to see how much you mean to him?"

Sawyer is quiet for a long time but eventually nods and hugs me as he sobs. "It's a double-edged sword. Nothing has ever felt this good and hurt this much at the same time."

"Seems to be the story of us right there."

"We're moving past that, Mel. We're in a good place." The pleading in his voice would bring me to my knees if I weren't already sitting.

"I know, baby, and you'll move past this, too. It's sad, Sawyer, but it also makes me so proud. Proud of you for being everything Nate needs. Proud of him because he knows better than either of us what he wants from his relationship with you. You've been a better parent to him than I have. You caught us when the world was ripped out from beneath us."

"I didn't have a choice."

"Oh, but you did. Out of anyone, you had the most right to fall into your grief and drown. When Noah died, you lost part of your soul and that's something none of us can understand. You are so strong, Sawyer. Noble, loving, fierce, and still a fucking cocky bastard, but you're my cocky bastard. I love you."

His tongue meets mine with an easy grace. He cups my cheeks with his hands as he kisses me slowly and thoroughly. Our emotional state is raw but the love flowing between us is real. This is the kiss I'm going to remember until my dying day. The night Sawyer and I let down all the barriers between us and truly became one by the fireside. The night our son taught us the real meaning of love.

"I love you, too, Princess," he says as he wraps his arm around me and we lean against each other in front of the fire. It's me and him against the world and I'm more than okay with that.

A week later, Sawyer approaches me with a USB stick in hand. I've put off watching Noah's video. Sawyer has been patient, but he misses our intimacy and knows in order to get it back I have to watch this video.

"It's time, Mel," he says, handing it to me.

Clutching it in the palm of my hand, I bring my eyes to his. "Are you going to watch it with me?"

He swallows hard. "I will if you need me to, but I think you should watch it alone."

I'm stronger now, but I'm still going to need some liquid courage to get through this. "Time for tequila shots."

He follows me into the kitchen and takes out the tequila and shot glasses. Sawyer shoots one, and I toss back three. "Come here," he says softly.

Sawyer brushes my hair from my face and cups my cheeks. "Remember, Mel, I loved you before the accident. Please, don't forget that." His mouth crashes onto mine and I moan as he steals my breath. He kisses me as if this is the last time and the thought petrifies me.

Once he releases me, he walks me to my room. "I'll be in my room if you need me."

After he leaves, I settle myself on my bed with my laptop. I understand why Sawyer wouldn't want to watch this again. My video wrecked me; I can imagine his did the same to him. I lean back and press play, once again watching as Noah's larger-than-life smile fills the screen.

"Hey, Sawyer," Noah says sadly, running his hands through his hair. My poor Noah. I wish I could reach through the screen and hug him.

"I can't imagine how fucked up this is for you right now. I'm sorry, man. Just know I would have tried like hell to stop whatever took me out, I'm sure. Fuck … this blows. Hopefully, this is all for nothing, but you know I had a bad feeling after that shit went down with Sara. Nothing has felt *right* since. Don't get me wrong, I've had

D. Kelly

every wish fulfilled and I'm having a baby with the love of my life. But Sawyer, that feeling … it won't go away. The doctor still thinks it's posttraumatic stress, and I fucking hope he's right. In case he's not, I've got a few things to say."

The floodgates have already opened and tears are flowing endlessly down my cheeks. Seeing him again, hearing him talk to someone like they're in the room with him, is breaking my heart. Why couldn't he have told me? I wish I could have been his rock like he was mine.

"I love you and I hope you know that, that you'll *always* know that. This past year for us was different. I don't think I've ever felt closer to you and further apart at the same time. I know Mel was a huge part of that and … I owe you an apology. It was obvious you were attracted to her from the beginning, but at the time I was swept up in my own desire. Although you felt the need to tell me on many occasions you would never try to take her from me, you didn't have to. I know you'd never hurt me on purpose. Marilyn fucked us up but we were better for it. You grew from that experience, we both did. When Mel came into the picture, I could see both sides of her and us. That probably doesn't make any sense, does it?

"Mel has this wicked streak in her. She's blunt and to the point, making her the perfect woman for you. And yet … she's sweet and vulnerable, and even though she didn't want to, she opened herself up to the possibility of love, making her the perfect girl for me. I've never loved anyone the way I love her, and neither have you. It's okay, Sawyer. Don't ever feel guilty for falling in love with a good woman. Especially one who could complete you and make you a better man. Even if she is my wife."

Noah swallows and grabs a glass of water, taking a gulp. He chuckles to himself and shakes his head. *Where the hell is he going with this?*

"For a hypothetical situation, this is still hard as fuck. Literal last words are a bitch. So I'm just going to spit them out. I expect you to take care of her and Nate if I'm not around. I know this will sound demented to most people, but you're my twin and you'll understand this. If Mel falls in love again and gets married, I hope to God it's with you."

Pause.

Hold the fuck up. Please tell me this is not what I think it is. Noah, please tell me you didn't do what I know you did.

Unpause.

"There's no one else on this planet who will take care of them and love them like you will. They deserve that, Sawyer, and so do you, because the fact remains that right now … Amelia Weston is the only woman I can picture you making a life with. How fucked up is that? I'm not saying you won't meet someone and fall in love and make a family. You can, and you should. But I know you, Sawyer, and I've watched the way you've let Mel inside your barricaded heart so easily. Even while you pushed me away, you let her deeper into your world. It hurt, but I understand it better than anyone. She has that effect on me, too."

Pause.

I'm going to be sick. "Noah, how could you do this? How could you put this kind of guilt and pressure on your own brother?" Bracing myself for more of this madness, I hit play.

"My wife loves me, and I know she always will, but I want her happy, Sawyer, and I want you happy. If the two of you can find that together, it's fate. Even if I died tomorrow, I'd do it all over again to have this brief period of bliss with Mel. There's no one I'd want to spend ''til death do us part' with other than with her.

"Don't close yourself off and don't shut down. Keep Mel from doing that, too. She thinks she's cursed and this tour was supposed to cure that for her. Damn, for her sake, I hope it did. If not, one of us is going to have a hell of a time convincing her she's not. The only other person I've ever met who is as broken as Mel is you. Heal each other, Sawyer, make each other whole in my absence. I'm going to leave Belle a video, too, telling her to make you guys see the light. If anyone can, it's her.

"I'm not really sure what else to say. This already sounds like some backwoods redneck shit, doesn't it? Take care of my kid and marry my wife, brother."

Noah pauses and cracks up. His laugh wraps around me like a hug; I wish I could feel his arms again in the flesh.

"For real, Sawyer, it's okay. If I could handpick anyone for Mel it would be you and vice-versa. Take care of Mom and Dad, Rory, Diane, and J for me. But especially Rory. She's always been my sister and Diane has been yours, but Rory is going to need you now. Kiss the girls for me and remind them often how much Uncle Noah loves them, how much I love you all, because even though I'm not there my love always will be.

"And Sawyer, even if it's not with you, make Mel have some more kids. Nate can't be an only child and Mel is going to be the best mom, I just know it. With all of you in his life, I have no doubt Nate

699

will grow up knowing how much I loved and adored him. Just promise me you'll be happy, Sawyer. It's all I've ever wanted for you.

"One last thing, I left all my rights and royalties for the music to Mel. My intention was for you, Wyatt, and Darren to split everything into thirds and have equal say, but the more I thought about it the more I realized it's another way to keep Mel in the family. Other than the three of you, there's no one I trust more to look out for my interests in my absence than her. She's the best thing to ever come into our lives, Sawyer. Don't ever forget that. I love you, bro, with all my heart. Until we meet again."

The camera fades to black and once again, I can't contain the guttural cries working their way out of me. This was a game changer. My house of cards has just come falling down around me.

Unlike last time when I watched Noah's video to me, Sawyer doesn't come to check on me. He knows as well as I do this changed everything. It's why his last kiss to me was more of a goodbye than anything.

I could throttle Noah, I'm so angry with him. How could he put that on Sawyer? Make him think he has to fall in love with me to fulfill Noah's last wishes. Why would Noah put that on him? It's a horrible thing to do to anyone, let alone your vulnerable brother in the midst of his grief.

I'll never be able to trust Sawyer's feelings for me are real after that. I have to get out of here, I need to drive. When I open the door, I can hear Sawyer splashing Nate in the bathtub. Good, easier to make a run for it.

Once I'm down the street, I pull over and send him a text letting him know I'm going to Anna's for a while. He'll leave me alone there. The whole way over there I can't stop crying, can't stop thinking about the video and about me and Sawyer.

No wonder he backed away from me after we had sex; he was having second thoughts. It probably wasn't good for him, he just felt like he owed it to Noah to be with me. This whole time I've been keeping him from what he really wants—other women.

As I throw my car in park, their front door swings open and Anna and Wyatt are waiting for me.

"Jesus, Mel, you look like shit. Sawyer just called and said you were on your way over. What happened?" Anna asks.

"What happened is I found out I'm the biggest fool on the planet. My husband pimped me out to his own brother. Guilted Sawyer into wanting to be with me. This whole thing is one big illusion."

Anna looks at Wyatt and he shakes his head. "That's not true, Mel. Nothing could be further from the truth."

"Have you seen Noah's video to Sawyer?"

"No, I haven't but I know–"

"No, you don't know. I thought I knew, too. Until I saw the video. God, I'm such a fool. I fell for his game, hook, line, and sinker. How gullible could I be?"

Anna guides me into the house and Wyatt grabs his keys and kisses us both on the cheek. "I'm going for a drive."

"Tell Sawyer he's a bastard!"

"Come on, Mel, let's get you something to drink and calm your nerves so you can explain all of this to me."

Over the next two hours, Anna gets me shitfaced. Sawyer has been sending me text after text, but I'm avoiding him. And I tell Anna everything.

"You're in love with him, aren't you?" she asks softly.

"Yes, no, I think so. Shit, Anna, I'm still such a mess. I don't know. But I have to be, right? Or this wouldn't hurt so damn much," I wail.

She hugs me. "It's okay, Mel. I know you're hurting and you believe what you're feeling, but I'm going to give it to you straight. You're wrong. Sawyer would never pretend to care for you if he didn't."

"No, you don't get it," I say, wrenching myself out of her grasp. "He doesn't even know he was brainwashed into it. Noah played him like a fiddle and took advantage of his grief."

She's looking at me like I've lost my ever-loving mind. At this point, maybe I have.

"How about we get you settled in the guestroom for the night and we talk about this in the morning over a cup of coffee? It's late, and Sawyer said he's got Nate covered."

I'm drunk as hell so it's not like I have a choice. She gives me a pair of pajamas to borrow, along with a bottle of water and some ibuprofen, and leaves me to sleep. I pull out my phone and scroll through Sawyer's messages, only stopping when I see he's sent me a song. When I click on the link, it's "Right Here Waiting" by Staind. In my alcohol-fueled haze, I send him back one of my own, "Gravity" by Sara Bareilles.

Then, as I've become so accustomed to doing over the past year, I pray for the pain to stop as I cry myself to sleep.

In the morning, I wake up feeling like shit and do my best to piece myself together before I beg Wyatt and Anna's forgiveness for crashing in on them last night.

"Good morning," Wyatt says, looking up from the kitchen table. "Can I get you some coffee?"

"Yes, please. I'm so sorry for last night, Wyatt, I just didn't know where to go."

He brings me the coffee and takes a seat. "It's okay, Mel. You're welcome here anytime. Anna had to go into work for a little bit, but she said she'd check in on you later."

"Where's Jake?" I ask, looking around for my adorable godson.

"He's with my mom, she took him to the park. I'd like to talk to you about Sawyer if you can handle it."

"I'm not sure what there is to say."

As he sets his coffee down, his shoulders sag. "I've got thoughts and opinions on all of this. I'm not sure if you're ready to hear them or take my words to heart. Sawyer is a mess, you need to talk to him. The video aside, he loves you, Mel. Sawyer has never loved anyone and he loves you. Don't take that lightly."

"Wyatt, it's not that easy."

"Nothing worth having ever is. After you've talked to Sawyer, if you want to talk to me as your friend, as Noah's best friend, you let me know. I'll pay off that favor I owe you in spades, but you have to be ready to hear what I'm going to say with an open heart. Deal?"

"Deal. Thanks for the coffee, but I should probably get home. No matter how upset I was, leaving like that was a dick move."

Wyatt laughs. "Well, if anyone can understand being a dick, it's Sawyer. Remind him of that if he gives you shit."

On the way home, I stop off for pastries and coffee at Sawyer's favorite place. I figure if we're going to have a painful discussion we can at least do it with comfort foods.

He's sitting at the table with bloodshot eyes when I come in. He doesn't look like he slept a wink last night.

"Where's Nate?"

"Darren took the kids to his parents for the day. Do you hate me, Mel?" His sorrowful eyes meet mine and my eyes fill with tears again.

I put the coffee and pastries down and sit across from him. "I could never hate you, Sawyer. I'm angry, so fucking angry, at Noah and at you."

"Do you remember how I asked you yesterday to remember I loved you before the accident? Why do you think I did that? I knew you were going to be pissed and assume shit that wasn't true."

"Yeah, and do you remember how you kissed me goodbye right after that?"

"I didn't kiss you goodbye!"

"Then what was it?" I demand.

"A kiss, Mel! It was a kiss. An I love you, I'm worried about you, and I wish I could watch that video with you but it would fucking steal my soul for a second time kind of kiss!"

"Don't you see it, Sawyer? He brainwashed you. He took away your ability to think rationally and planted the seed that you had to be with me and take over for him as my man, as Nate's dad. It's fucked up! You had buried those feelings for me after the wedding and he played on that. It's not your fault, I understand."

The look of abject horror on his face silences me. "Do you want the absolute truth?"

"The truth is all I ever want, Sawyer."

He slumps down in his chair and blows out a breath. "The truth is I never stopped thinking about you. I tried to stop your wedding a thousand times in my mind. I didn't care if Noah got hurt, I wanted you. I was willing to throw my relationship with Noah away if it meant getting the girl. If I'm guilty of anything it's being a horrible brother, not being brainwashed by Noah."

Wow.

"That may be true, but I still feel like there are other elements at play. This shouldn't be so hard, Sawyer. Every time something good happens to us, something else shatters our bubble. Maybe this isn't meant to be."

"Don't say that, Princess. You bring me to life. We'll figure this out."

"I think you should date other people." I practically choke on the words as they come out.

"What in the world are you talking about?" He's looking at me like I've lost my mind.

"Noah tricked you into thinking this is how your life should be. I don't want to be your obligation, Sawyer, I want to be your *life*!"

Within seconds, he's on his knees in front of me. "Don't you know you're my Princess but someday I want you to be my Queen? There's no one else for me, Mel, it's you or no one."

"I'm sorry," I say, leaning over and kissing the top of his head. "You deserve someone who isn't tainted."

Pushing my chair back, I stand up and leave him on the floor. Walking away from him is one of the hardest things I've ever done, but I can't cope with the thought that he's with me out of guilt.

Amelia – Present Day

"How many times did you think I was insane over the last two years?" I muse.

Sawyer smiles as he looks up from his computer where he's reading. "Not more than once or twice, why?"

"You're a jerk."

"Maybe, but I'm your jerk, whether you like it or not."

I lean over and kiss his cheek. "Is everyone still out there catching up?"

Sawyer came back in here a few minutes ago with cookies and milk for both of us.

"They are. Everyone is on the most recent section, so they'll probably catch up to you soon."

"No pressure or anything. How did this turn into something I was doing to help me give you an answer to something everyone we know is reading?"

Sawyer flashes me his dimple smile. "You're a good writer, Mel, and an even better person. Our family wants to see us happy and when I left, neither of us were in a good place. As far as Rory goes, I think deep down she wants to understand and she's tired of the fighting and the anger. Thank you for inviting her."

"I'd do anything for your family, Sawyer. You all have saved me more times than I can count."

He pulls my hand to his mouth and kisses it tenderly. "Where are you in the story?"

"I'm just about to talk about your night with Dawn."

He groans. "Just remember you love me and breathe through your anger."

"I'll keep that in mind."

Date Night

It's been a few weeks since I told Sawyer to date other people. Every day he finds a way to tell me he loves me and that I'm an idiot for pushing him away when we're just going to end up together.

Tomorrow is Valentine's Day and all day today I've been kicking myself for keeping him at a distance. After putting Nate to sleep, I finally work up the nerve to apologize to him, but what I see when he opens his door takes my breath away.

"Hey, Mel, what do you need?" he asks as he puts on his watch. Sawyer is dressed to kill and my plan to talk to him crashes and burns.

"Never mind, it can wait. Are you going out?"

His eyes rake me over and I feel like a slob. I'm in jeans and a t-shirt, but fuck, he could be heading to the Grammy's with how mouthwatering he looks right now.

"Yeah, I have a date."

"You what? I mean … good for you." I'm stammering over my words as my heart breaks into a million pieces but it's my fault this time. Maybe I wasn't wrong after all.

"I've got a few minutes if you want to talk … about *anything*." He's giving me an opening, and I want desperately to take it, but I can't.

"Who's the lucky girl?" Like I even want to know.

"Dawn," he says, like I'm supposed to know who that is. Then it comes to me in a flash.

"The hostess from the club?" I shriek.

The corner of his mouth kicks up in a grin. "The one and only."

"So I guess you're going to sleep with her." *Fuck, Mel, use your filter!*

"Any reason why I shouldn't?" he asks with a malicious grin.

Yes, because you're fucking mine.

"Uh, no, I guess not. Have a nice night, Sawyer."

Twenty minutes after he leaves, I text Anna.

Sawyer went out on a date with a tramp from that sex club.

Anna: Seriously?

That's what he said.

Anna: I'm sure you don't have anything to worry about, he's just letting off some steam. I guess you didn't talk to him?

No. Once I saw how good he looked I didn't want to get in his way.

Anna: Text him!

I can't. Maybe this is for the best.

Anna: That's bullshit and you know it. You need to tell him you love him. Don't risk losing him to save face. Not now when you've both come so far.

I send Sawyer the link for "Girl Crush" by Little Big Town and wait to see if he sends anything back.

Anna: Did you text him?

A song, I haven't heard back yet.

Anna: Can the two of you ever grow the fuck up and use your words?

It's our thing.

Anna: I know and if you weren't fighting it would be adorable, but you are.

sigh I know, but let me see if he texts back.

A few minutes later, I get a link for "Over It" by Katharine McPhee. If I weren't so sad at his song choice, it would make me laugh.

Quickly, I fire off the link for "Between the Lines" by Sara Bareilles, and when I don't hear anything back from him or Anna for a bit, I decide to text Wyatt.

I know it's late, but are you busy? I think I'm ready for that favor.

Wyatt: I'll be there in twenty minutes. You better have your heart open for this, Mel.

I do.

Wyatt: See you soon.

Then I shoot off an apology text to Anna.

Sorry, I hope you two weren't in the middle of anything.

Anna: Nope, gives me the perfect chance to wrap his Valentine's Day gift. Besides, you need to hear what he has to say. It's time all these secrets come out of their fucking closets once and for all.

I shoot another song to Sawyer, this time "Run Run Run" by Kelly Clarkson and John Legend. I get the tequila out and take a shot of courage before Wyatt gets here and then leave the bottle out in case he wants one, too. As Wyatt enters the kitchen, my phone goes off again.

"Hang on a sec, it's Sawyer," I tell him as I pull up the link. It's for "Don't Let Me Let You Go" by Jamie Lawson and my heart floods with hope.

Fuck it. I send him the one song that reminds me of both him and Noah, hoping he interprets the meaning right. After sending him the link for "Breathe Again" by Sara Bareilles, I turn my attention to Wyatt.

"Do you want a drink?"

"Maybe just some water, thanks." After handing him a bottle of water, we sit down on the couch.

"The two of you are a mess, you know that, right?" he asks.

"For sure. I've never met anyone who drives me as crazy as he does, but he also makes me feel so incredibly loved in spite of all my flaws."

"You're both flawed, it's why you work. Alright, Mel, after our talk you can consider us even. No favors owed. Noah was my best friend and there are some things I think I should keep to myself, but you and Sawyer are here and it's more important to me that you both are happy."

"Why do I feel like this is going to sting?"

He pats my hand. "Because it will, for a few reasons."

"Okay, hit me."

"I'm not sure the best place to start so I'll go with my video. That was a motherfucker to watch, but I'm glad I have it. Noah asked me to look out for Sawyer. He wasn't sure how Sawyer would take his video and losing his twin and thought maybe he would self-destruct.

"Anyway, he wanted me to encourage Sawyer to be with you. I'm sorry, Mel, because I didn't do what he asked of me. Truth is, I'm not sure how I feel about you and Sawyer. There are days I'm still struggling with not having Noah around. We're all family, but to encourage you or Sawyer didn't sit right with me. So I didn't really do anything. If you love him, if he loves you, that's something I think you should figure out yourselves and not because Noah or anyone else thought it was right or meant to be."

His words fill my heart with joy. "Thank you, Wyatt. Sounds like you understand why I took Noah's video to him the way I did."

"For sure, but don't thank me yet because I'm not completely innocent in this. The night of the accident, Noah begged me to tell Sawyer it was okay."

That's what Darren said to Sawyer outside of my room that day.
"What was okay, Wyatt?"

"For him to love you. For the two of you to be together. It's the first and only secret I ever kept from Anna. I didn't tell anyone for about six months. It was something I needed to work out in my head and not be influenced by anything except my conscience and Noah's wishes. It wasn't until after Sawyer watched Noah's video that I told him. In the beginning, I thought about telling him but we weren't all in the best place, and then we were all trying to keep one foot in front of the other, you know?"

I pull my feet up under me on the couch and lean back. "I completely understand. You shouldn't feel bad. You did what Noah asked in the end, you passed along his message."

Wyatt shakes his head. "That's where you're wrong. I passed on his message to Sawyer, but I didn't pass on his message to you. Part of me still doesn't want to but I owe it to all of you. But first, I need to tell you what happened the day you were sick when we were in New York."

"That started off as a bad day." I reply, and he nods.

"We were at breakfast and Warren was pissed that Sawyer and Darren were late. Noah and I volunteered to go get them and, par for the course, fans were staking out the elevator so we ducked into the stairwell. When we reached the second-floor landing, we heard a man crying.

"Noah held me back, recognizing it was Sawyer before I did. That's when Sawyer confessed to Darren he was in love with you."

"No …" Gasping, I cover my mouth.

"I'm afraid so. Noah already knew, but Sawyer was good at playing it off. I wanted to let them know we were there before things got bad, but Noah held me in my place. The more Sawyer cried, the more Noah's body trembled. He was feeling every bit of Sawyer's pain as he confessed to Darren how much your rejection hurt him."

"Oh my God."
Poor Noah.
Poor Sawyer.

"Sawyer and Darren were hashing out Sawyer's feelings. He was gutted by your kiss and rejection and was trying to find a way to balance his pain and his happiness for you and Noah. He wanted to tell Noah about the kiss, he didn't want either of you carrying that burden around. Then Sawyer mentioned why you wanted to keep it secret, how you were protecting their relationship and family at the risk of your own, and Noah's eyes lit up."

"Why?"

Wyatt chuckles. "Patience, young Padawan, I'm getting to that. Sawyer started being self-deprecating, comparing all of Noah's good to his bad. It was fucking brutal to listen to and even worse to see how much pain Noah was in listening and not being able to reassure his twin. At the end of it all, Sawyer pledged to do good things and never fuck up his relationship with Noah again."

"That's it?"

"No, but that's all we stayed for. I thought Noah was going to lose it but instead he pulled me into an empty conference room and we texted Darren and Sawyer to get their asses to breakfast. Finally, I asked Noah what he was going to do. I thought it was going to be a Marilyn-level fuck up but as usual, Noah surprised the fuck out of me.

"He begged me to never repeat what we'd overheard and confessed how awful he felt that he couldn't help Sawyer through this no matter how much he wanted to. When I asked if he was pissed, do you have any idea what he said?"

"That he hated me? I can't imagine him not being upset with me." This conversation is painful as fuck.

"Nope, he said his main takeaway was that he'd officially broken down all of your walls. He kept saying, 'She loves me, Wyatt, and she's going to marry me. Maybe one day she'll even have my babies.' He was relieved, Mel. Instead of being angry he was blown away that you were protecting his family because of your love for *him*."

"I was dumbfounded. Noah found what he considered the biggest silver lining in what should have been the biggest betrayal. I understood why you were protecting Sawyer, I would have done the same thing, but Noah was forever surprising me and this moment was no different.

"When you announced your pregnancy that night, I was so relieved. The timing couldn't have been better. I knew it would be what finally got Sawyer to let you go. The genuine happiness Sawyer had for both of you was the icing on the cake. There were a few times after that when Noah said he sort of led you into a conversation where you could have told him what happened but you didn't."

"Oh no. He had to have been so angry with me," I sob, wiping away my tears as I struggle to wrap my head around the fact Noah knew.

Wyatt laughs. "Noah was a saint, Mel. Any normal person would have been mad. He was so fucking proud of you for fighting to keep your family together. For not rolling over and throwing Sawyer under the bus. At some point, I started wondering if we should get him checked for some sort of chemical imbalance. No normal person could be as inherently good as Noah was."

"He was the best person I'd ever met, and I don't think I'll ever meet someone again with a heart like his."

"I think you're wrong about that. I'm pretty sure you're raising him already."

His words make me smile. My little Nathaniel is Noah to a T.

"Wyatt, why are you telling me all this? Why now?"

He leans back and exhales. "Because you watched Sawyer's video and I've seen how destructive it's been. Noah didn't plant that seed. Mel. He didn't convince Sawyer to fall for you and make a family with you. Sawyer has been on that road almost as long as Noah was. Right or wrong, first choice or second, Sawyer loves you. I wouldn't be a true friend to you, Sawyer, or Noah if I didn't let you know the backstory."

As his words sink in, my phone buzzes. "You going to check that?"

"It can wait a minute. Tell me the rest. What have you been keeping from me, Wyatt?"

The pained expression on his face is heartbreaking. "Nobody knows this, except for Anna, but she was sworn to secrecy. I hope you'll be able to forgive me but I had to tell someone. When we were in the helicopter on the way to the hospital, Noah was so content, almost euphoric. He was in this weird state of bliss out of nowhere, the medic even checked his med log to see if someone had given him something he wasn't aware of.

"He turned to me with a classic Noah smile and said, 'Wyatt, at Mel and Sawyer's wedding, tell them not to worry, it's in the bag.'

"I remember laughing and thinking he must have gotten some really good drugs and they just forgot to mark it down. I mean, you guys had just been married and you were having his baby. Then, he said, 'Tell Mel she's still going to cash in those fifty years as Mrs. Weston, Mrs. Sawyer Weston.'"

I'm stunned and still crying.

"I'm sure that's how my face looked, too. I was in shock and then he dozed off. Like no big deal, whatever. When he woke up again, it was like nothing had ever happened. He was anxious and demanding to get to you and his baby. When he died, you were destroyed, rightfully so. There was no time for me to squeeze in a conversation about what he said. I felt torn. I didn't want to say something and have it lead you to a path you would have never taken, and I didn't want to keep something so important from you once you were on that path. So yeah, I understood exactly how you felt about his video because it's how I felt about the secret I was keeping."

I've wiped away my tears and am trying to catch my breath. "So why tell me now? After all this time?"

"Have you seen yourself lately? You're a mess, Mel. It's obvious to everyone but you how head-over-heels you are with Sawyer. And if you haven't noticed, he's a fucking disaster himself. Secrets have a way of coming out, and now they're all on the table. I'm officially declaring my support for the both of you, not like you need it."

I throw my arms around him and hug him hard. "Thank you for telling me. I'm glad I know everything now."

"Well, there's one more secret I can't tell you. It's Sawyer's to tell, and he's promised me he'll tell you before tomorrow."

"Great," I grumble.

He chuckles as he stands. "I'm pretty sure this secret will make you happy. Have some faith, Mel, I think it's about time we all did. I'll see you later."

"Thank you, Wyatt. For everything. We're totally even now. In fact, at this point, I probably owe you another favor."

"I might take you up on that in babysitting hours. I think Jake needs a brother or sister."

With a laugh, I pat him on the shoulder. "When you get Anna on board with that one, you let me know."

After Wyatt leaves, I put away the tequila and open a bottle of wine. Turning on the music, I play the song I sent Sawyer earlier. I've listened to this song a lot lately. It describes my love for Sawyer and Noah perfectly. How my love for Noah still holds me back, but all I want is to breathe Sawyer in.

Earlier this evening, I took off my necklace with my wedding rings and put it away with Noah's ring. It was an especially bittersweet moment—one I never thought I'd be faced with when Noah slid those rings on my fingers. I know it's the right call; I can't hang on to the past, not when Sawyer is my future. I was hoping he'd notice the subtle change but he was so focused on his date, he didn't.

It's after midnight and I should probably go lie down, but I know I won't sleep. If he comes home smelling like her, I don't know what I'll do. God, what if he doesn't come home at all? What if his head is between her legs right now?

"You must be in a reflective mood." His voice startles me and I jump out of my seat, nearly spilling my wine.

"You just scared the shit out of me. What are you doing here? And why would you say that?"

He's got flowers in his hands—a big bouquet of red and white roses filled with baby's breath. He'd better not be bringing her back here or we're going to have words.

"I'm sorry I scared you, that wasn't my intention. I'm here because I live here and this is our home. And I say that because you shoot tequila when you want to forget or have fun, and you drink wine when you want to think or relax."

"You think you know me so well."

Sawyer moves closer and my breath catches. He really does look sexy tonight. He pulls his lip into his mouth and tugs on his lip ring. That move gets me wet every time and he knows it.

"I'd like to think I know you intimately."

I move back into the living room, trying to put some distance between us. "Where's your date?"

"She's right here."

"In our house?" My panicked tone brings his cocky smirk front and center.

"Did you read your texts, Mel?"

Shit, my phone. I reach down and grab it off the coffee table.

Sawyer: I'm on my way home. We need to talk.

P.S. I lied, I never had a date.

"You never had plans with her?"

"Nope, I threw away her card in the room at the club. Why would I need it when I have you?"

My frustration with him takes over. "Why would you do that to me?"

He stalks toward me and places the flowers on the table before pulling me to him. I haven't been this close to him in weeks but my body instinctively curves to his.

"Because, Princess, it's Valentine's Day and I want to do something. But in order to do it, you needed to talk to me. I figured if you thought I had a date it would at least get you mad enough to open up."

"I was ready to open up before you left, but … Fuck, Sawyer. You hurt me! I thought you were off fucking Busty Barbie."

He's laughing. "I'm sorry I hurt you, but I didn't know any other way to break through to you. You hurt me, too, Mel. I don't know how many ways I can say it. I was in love with you before the accident and I'm going to love you for the rest of my life. Why would

D. Kelly

I downgrade to Busty Barbie when I've got a real live Princess right here?"

He brings his lips to mine and kisses me tenderly. Resting our heads together, his eyes meet mine. "Are we good now?"

"I think so."

"Mel, I noticed it earlier and didn't want to read into it, but …" His eyes drop to my chest, the hopeful lilt in his voice trailing off like he's scared to even speak the words in case it's not true.

"I'm taking another step, Sawyer. I don't need the protection of those rings anymore. Not when I've got you to keep me safe."

He closes his eyes briefly and they're shining with love when he opens them. "Are we still taking things slow?"

"If slow involves sex then yes, we're taking things slow."

"Good," he answers, leading me to his bedroom. "Slow is exactly how I want to take you tonight. I want to make love to you, Mel. Do you think we can manage that?"

My heart flutters like crazy and I pull his hand to my chest. "Can you feel that?"

A sinful smile spreads across his mouth "That's from me?"

"That's all you, baby. Make love to me."

As I pull my shirt over my head, he works the button on my jeans. While kicking off his shoes, he manages to slide my pants and panties down. Lifting my legs out one by one, he slides his hands up the backs of my legs, pausing at the apex of my thighs and inhaling deeply.

"Fuck, I've missed the way you smell."

He pulls my legs apart and his tongue dives in and flicks my clit. I fully expect him to work me to orgasm with his mouth but he surprises me and pulls back, continuing his journey up my body. Pausing long enough to unclasp my bra, I let it fall off my arms as he stands back, perusing my body from head to toe.

"You're wearing far too many clothes, Sawyer. If I'm going to be your eye candy, you need to be mine." I walk toward him as he slowly and methodically takes his time with each and every button on his shirt.

My hands move to his pants and unbutton them. As his slacks slide down his legs, I run my hand over his exquisite package. The wetness from his cock seeps through the cotton of his boxer briefs and I drop to my knees so I can pull them down and give him a proper hello.

Using both hands, I stroke him until he throws back his head and hisses his frustration. Then I drop my mouth over him and suck him in. My tongue swirls around the tip of his cock while my hand works his length. I'm enjoying the taste of his pre-cum too much to give him the blowjob he deserves.

"Stop being a cock tease, Princess, and lie down." He pops out of my mouth when I laugh, but he's laughing, too, as he guides me to the bed.

Standing at the foot of the bed, his eyes rake over my body. As he lowers himself to the mattress, he reaches for my foot. He massages one, then the next, and it's heavenly. I can't hold back my cries of pleasure as he continues his massage all the way up my legs.

Sliding his fingers through my wetness, he teases me but doesn't linger long. As if he can't resist, he brings his finger to his mouth and sucks the wetness from it and his eyes roll back in his head.

Paving a blazing trail of kisses from my abdomen to my breasts, he takes his time licking and sucking me thoroughly, until his mouth finally catches mine in a slow, delectable kiss. When he pulls away, he moves his mouth to my neck, his lips caressing me in just the spot to make me buck beneath him. "Flip over, Princess," he murmurs against my skin.

When I turn onto my belly, he reaches for something on the table. I can't see it but I feel wetness trickle down my back. He pushes my hair off to the side and works the oil into my skin. I'm so relaxed I could almost fall asleep. After rubbing it in, he begins to suck and lick it off. Leaning over my shoulder, he captures my lips with his. He tastes like vanilla and I deepen the kiss, wanting more of everything he's giving me.

His erection presses against my backside and he groans against my skin. "Someday, Princess, I want you here, too."

"Anything you want, as long as you're careful."

Groaning, he slides off of me and rolls us over, then reaches for a condom. When he's fully sheathed, he settles himself between my legs and lowers his mouth to my breasts.

Paying equal attention to each one, he slides inside of me.

"Sawyer ..." His name falls from my lips as I relish the sensation of him entering me after so long. I've missed this connection with him so much.

He laces his fingers through mine, and our bodies sync with each other. His thrusts are slow and deliberate, and so incredibly deep. Every time he pushes into me, I feel myself drowning in his love. He lowers his mouth to mine and steals my breath with his kiss. My orgasm builds but I don't want to come yet. He pushes deeper and deeper, sensing my hesitation.

D. Kelly

"Come with me, Amelia," he says, and it's not his words but the sound of my name on his lips that sets me off. It's rare when he uses it and when he does, it's everything. Clenching his hands tighter in mine, I let myself crash into him with everything I am. I'm never holding back from him again.

"I love you, Sawyer." My words are whispered against his lips and with them he finds his own release. His body trembles and shakes against mine, as if he's feeling it in every cell of his body.

"I love you, too, Amelia. For now, and for always."

A little while later, we're cleaned up and curled up together. I haven't had a good night's sleep in weeks but being in his arms feels like home.

Just as I'm beginning to fall asleep, he brushes his finger over my cheek. "Hey, Mel?"

"Hm?"

"Will you move in here with me? I want you in my bed each night, I want your things mixed in with mine, I want you to make my bathroom messy, even though it will drive me fucking crazy."

His words are passionate, but there's an underlying hesitancy and I wonder how long he's wanted this. "I'd love to drive you crazy, Sawyer. Name the time and place."

"Tomorrow morning, your stuff to my room, I'll even help you pack."

"As long as you bring the coffee and Pop-Tarts, I'm in. I want to be wherever you are."

Sawyer kisses me sweetly and we fall asleep, bodies entwined, and I know I want this with him for the rest of my life.

Unfinished Business

Cadence turned two this week and I can't believe so much time has passed. I have loved watching every second of her growth and consider myself beyond blessed to be here for it when Belle can't be. Last month, Noah would have been thirty-one—another milestone he wasn't here for. It was a hard pill for all of us to swallow. We did our best to make it through and make it special for Sawyer. I'm not sure he'll ever get to a place where his birthdays are actually happy again, but I hope he can.

We have a foundation meeting next week so I can announce my final choice of causes to launch with. It's been hard trying to narrow them down; I feel like something important is missing but I can't put my finger on it.

Noah's EP releases in June and the hype around it is staggering. Sawyer and I have a ton of interviews lined up over the next few months. Neither of us wanted to do them, to subject ourselves to the spotlight that way, but we're doing this for Noah and we agreed to do it together.

I've also made a decision and I need to act on it today before I chicken out. It's something Noah was supposed to help me with, which makes it a bit more difficult. Even so, I've made the calls and things are set up and waiting for me, I just need Sawyer to hold my hand. I'm hoping if I can get through this, I can get closer to being able to pack up Noah's things. To get some final closure so I can stop holding back any piece of myself from Sawyer. Ever since Valentine's Day, we've been closer than ever and I don't want to lose any of the momentum we've gained. I'm tired of getting close to him only to have to take three steps back.

His arms wrap around me from behind and I fall into them with ease. "You're up even earlier than normal."

I spin around in his arms and hug him fiercely. "I need to do something today. Will you help me?"

"Of course, what is it?"

"I'd rather show you. Mama is keeping the kids until tomorrow, so now is the perfect time."

"It must be important, you didn't even wait for me to shower with you."

"It is. Besides, last time we showered together we almost forgot to use a condom. We have to be more careful."

His expression softens. "Would it be so bad if we forgot? Or stopped using them altogether?"

Whoa, where did this come from?

"Sawyer, this is a big conversation to try to have first thing in the morning before coffee. Can we table this for now and come back to it later?"

"I'll agree because you have something on your mind. But I do want to come back to it soon, Mel. We need to start thinking long-term and it would be nice to give Nate some siblings that would be close in age."

After he hops in the shower, I find my anxiety medication and take one. I'm not taking them so much anymore, but talking about certain topics really flares me up for some reason. Living in the now with Sawyer is all I want but whenever we begin to discuss anything future-related, I freak out. I wonder if it's because I'm not over Noah yet and I haven't fully accepted the loss of our future together.

That's silly, though, right? Sawyer makes me just as happy as Noah did, some days it seems even more so. But I chalk that up to the short amount of time Noah and I had together. Whatever it is, it's all the more reason why today is so important.

Once Sawyer is dressed, Mac picks us up. I've already given him the address and he stopped for coffee and pastries on the way over.

Sawyer looks inside the pastry bag and pulls out a butterfly donut. "You must be buttering me up," he says before taking a huge bite.

"Maybe a little bit, but I also know what makes you happy and cinnamon tucked into the center of some dough seems to be your favorite."

"You're my favorite, but this is a close second." While he groans his appreciation and continues eating, I sip my coffee and think about the day ahead of us.

We ride in silence, Sawyer giving me much-needed space. That might be one of my favorite things about him; he's an excellent judge of my moods and adjusts accordingly. He can also be a bit moody himself and I pride myself on being able to pick up on them and give him what he needs as well.

When Mac pulls up to the gates of the estate, he punches in the code I gave him earlier and Sawyer lets out a low whistle. "Is this what I think it is?" he asks, looking out the window.

"If you think it's my parent's house, then yes." Outside the front door is a pallet full of cardboard boxes, rolls and rolls of bubble wrap, and there should be quite a few tape guns and markers out there somewhere.

"What's going on, Princess? It looks like a packing party."

The car comes to a stop and we all get out. "Mac, you're welcome to take a tour, hang out by the pool, make yourself at home inside, or we can call you when we're done."

"I've got my shorts and I'm ready for a dip. Thanks for the heads up, Mel. Let me know if you need help. I'll come do the heavy lifting."

"Hey! You trying to say I can't do some heavy lifting?" Sawyer asks. Mac laughs while I try to hold back my own laughter.

"I think what Mac meant is we've got a lot to do and all hands on deck would be nice."

"Or that I've got a hundred and fifty pounds on you, give or take, and it's all muscle." Mac's still laughing.

"Yeah, yeah, Popeye. Go to the pool and eat your spinach."

Mac heads off to explore, and I pull Sawyer down to my lips for a kiss. "Your body is hot, Sawyer, and your muscles are nothing to laugh at. But you pay Mac to be as big as he is for a reason. He keeps you safe, so you can keep coming home to me."

"You always know just what to say, Princess. Now, tell me why we're here. What's really going on?"

Lacing my fingers through his, I look up at him. "I'm not good with closure, obviously. My dad has been gone for over fifteen years and this house is the same as it was when my mom died. I'm pretty sure I got my avoidance from him."

"You're babbling, Mel."

"I know, but this is hard. Don't get mad. The other day, I was sitting in Noah's closet again."

Sawyer exhales softly and squeezes my fingers tighter. "Why do you keep doing that to yourself?"

"Because I don't know how to let him go, not completely. And I know it's holding us back. Last night, I realized if I can't even let my parents go and pack up their things, there's no way I'll ever be able to pack up Noah's. This is me trying, Sawyer. The only way out is through, right? That's what your mom tells me all the time."

"I'm on board, Mel, with whatever you need from me, but I just wish ..." He pauses, his eyes reflecting his pain.

"What do you wish, Sawyer?"

"It's selfish, and I know things worked out this way for a reason and I wouldn't change them for so many reasons, but I wish I wasn't second best ... that I would have been your first choice all along."

His words make me gasp for air. "Sawyer, please don't think that. I don't know how to explain it. Honestly, the fact you feel that way makes me extremely sad. There is *nothing* second best about you. I don't want to diminish the way you feel because if you are feeling this way this is something we have to rectify. Can we talk about this later? When we have all the time in the world to focus on how I can get you to understand there is nothing second place about you in my heart?"

"Yeah, I'm sorry I brought it up. Today is going to be a good day. Come on, show me Joey Triton's house."

Sawyer's words have really affected me. He must be rationalizing those thoughts in his head because he's seen how difficult it's been for me to try to move on from Noah. But I have to make this right somehow. Sawyer is too incredible of a person to ever consider himself second best of anything.

"Wow, this place is amazing." The awe in his tone makes me smile. I think Sawyer is fangirling a bit right now.

"Come here, let me show you something I know you'll love." I lead him down the main hall into my dad's office, which is really two adjoining rooms filled with awards, guitars, and a desk.

"Holy shit, Mel!" Sawyer releases my hand and walks around the room slowly. He takes everything in as if it were a museum.

"Fuck, Princess, you can't get rid of this stuff. Name your price, I'll buy the house and everything in it, as is. We'll turn it into a smaller version of Graceland or something."

"If I thought you were serious, I'd give it to you," I say with a smile.

"You'd just give me a multi-million-dollar estate? No questions asked?"

"Of course I would. *Are* you serious?"

"It's tempting, but no. All I want is for you to get whatever closure you need. And maybe that Martin over there, that's a fucking classic."

He's looking at that guitar like he looks at me when he's about to devour my body. "It's yours. Whatever you want, you can have. I'm thinking we can auction some of the leftovers off to raise money for the foundation."

"You're not keeping anything?"

"As we go through it all, I'll figure out what is actually sentimental and put it aside. I've lived without anything in this house for most of my life, and I never spent much time here anyway."

He spins around the room and shakes his head. "Okay, here's what I think. We call Darren, Wyatt, Warren, and Ryan, and get them over here. Take an hour or so and walk down memory lane. Then pick a room and start there. After you've cleared a room of what you want, we can go through behind you and decide what any of us want or what to auction off. Anything left gets donated. They'll get a kick out of being here and you get a clear conscience."

"You're sexy when you take charge," I tell him, hopping up on the desk.

With a groan, he stalks toward me. "And you'd make my every fantasy come true if I could spread you out and fuck you over Joey's desk. But since he's your dad, and that has to be crossing some sort of invisible creepy line, we'll forget I ever said anything."

Taking his hand in mine, I lead him down the hall to my childhood bedroom and close the door. "Not over his desk, but how about in my childhood bedroom? That has to be all sorts of wrong on some level."

He pushes me against the wall and holds my hands above my head. "So wrong, but so fucking right."

Three hours and three orgasms later, we've all found our groove. The guys have all busted a nut over the Triton legacy. It hasn't been nearly as hard as I thought it would be to do this, either. Maybe after losing Belle and Noah, dealing with the loss of my parents seems further away and less painful.

"How are you doing, Amelia?" Warren asks as he enters my parents' bedroom.

"I'm doing better than I thought I would be. I think I built this up in my head to be harder than it actually is."

"Oh, I don't know," he says, looking at a photo of my mom and dad hanging on the wall, "I think this would have been very difficult for the woman who sat down in my office almost three years ago. But for the Amelia standing in front of me, who has ridden the flames of hell and managed to extinguish them, it's a piece of cake."

"I haven't extinguished anything. Noah's closet taunts me daily, as does his office."

His expression softens. "Give yourself time, it hasn't been all that long."

"Mama packed up Belle's apartment in less than a month."

"That was a different situation and you know it. She didn't have the luxury of letting it sit. And from what I understand, you haven't gone through any of those boxes she has waiting for you, either."

"Well, maybe if I can do this, I can face those."

Warren gives me a sad smile. "Even if it takes you another ten years, the world won't stop turning. There's no rush."

"There is, though. I need to stop hurting Sawyer."

"Is that what you think? That you're hurting him by not erasing all traces of Noah? Come on, Mel, please tell me you don't really believe that?" The astonished look he shoots my way slays me.

"I love him, Warren. But something is holding me back. If I can do this, I can move forward, right?"

Warren pulls me into a fatherly hug and lets me sob onto his chest. "You will always love Noah. Loving Sawyer won't change that. It won't put Noah on the back burner, and it won't change what you had. And it shouldn't. Every love is different and all the great loves of our lives should be unique. But Sawyer brings you to life in a different way."

"How do you mean?"

"Noah coaxed you out of your shell. He made you his world and that made him happy. You two explored love and relished each new fun and happy thing. But you two were safe. There's nothing wrong with that. You would have had a timeless marriage, and it would have been a privilege to be a part of your journey."

He pauses and looks me over. "With Sawyer, you've blossomed. You're happy and playful. You've thrived in your role as mother and aunt. It's like your whole aura has opened another dimension. You give as good as you get and you're living outside of the box. The two of you suffered one of the worst losses anyone could imagine and you rose out of the ashes drenched in love for each other. With Sawyer, your Triton shows, Amelia, and it's pretty fucking incredible to witness."

"Are you saying you think I picked Noah because he was safe?" The panicked words fly from my lips as I try to catch up with my emotions.

"Absolutely not. You picked Noah because he was the perfect man for you at the right time. The tides have shifted, Mel. Now

Sawyer is the perfect man for you at the right time. You're not any happier now than you were then, it's just a different kind of happiness that radiates from you. And from him, he's not that cocky bastard you put in his place that night."

I nail him with a raised brow and he laughs, lifting his arms in surrender. "Okay, maybe he is, but he's a lot more than that now. You challenge each other in all the best ways."

Taking a seat on the edge of the bed, I make a confession. "I'm in love with him, Warren, head over heels, but I'm terrified of the future and I can't talk to him about it. He mentions kids and I need anxiety pills."

He takes a seat next to me and sighs. "I'm an old guy who has spent most of my years with rock stars. Most of them, commitment-phobes. That's not you, Mel. It could simply be that you're terrified to plan because you're afraid it will be ripped away from you. Like your parents, like Belle, like Noah."

He's right.

"I'm all for living in the moment. I did it for years before Sam. But there's something to be said for living in the moment and still planning for the future."

"Thanks for the pep talk, Warren. What do you say we finish up here and go back to the house and drink?"

"I say that's a hell of a plan. Did I ever tell you about the time Joey and I threw your mom in the pool …"

Later that night, Sawyer and I are lying in bed and I'm tucked into his arm. My fingers trail over his chest and I'm overwhelmed with emotions. Maybe it's the tequila shots we did, or maybe I'm coming down from an endorphin high from earlier today.

"Sawyer," I whisper softly.

"What's up, Princess?"

"Someday, I want to have lots of babies with you." His arms tighten around me with my confession.

"Define lots."

"Two, maybe three …"

He chuckles against the top of my head. "I consider lots five or six, but I'll take two or three for now. Besides, since twins run in the family, it could be five or six kids in the long run."

"If we have kids, do you think—"

"When, Princess, there is no 'if' allowed in that sentence."

"Okay, when. Do you think you'll love them differently than Nate?" The thought makes me sad, and he's quiet for a long while.

With a sigh, he responds, "I might." My heart shatters. "I'm not sure I could love any child more than I love Nate. He'll always be my favorite kid, but you can't tell anyone that, it's like a parent handbook law or something." Relief rushes through me, temporarily. "Do you think you'll love our kids as much as you love Nate?"

The question throws me because my automatic answer I want to give makes me sound like a horrible human. But I don't want to hold anything back from Sawyer anymore, no matter how bad it makes me sound.

"Mel? Did I lose you?"

"I'm afraid I'll love them more because they're a part of you."

He stills with my confession. "That will never happen, Nate is too awesome. If anything, you'll just be like all the moms and claim you love them the same."

"Can I ask you something?"

He laughs again. "I thought we already decided you could ask me anything, anytime."

"You said you loved me before the accident. Do you know when you realized you knew?"

"It was the night at Sully's. When you saved me from my sleep demons. That night, you treated me with love and compassion, and I knew I was already a goner."

That was so early. Noah and I hadn't even had sex at that point.

"The night you kissed me in your bathroom, I knew there was something special about you. Scary special. Belle and I even talked about it afterward."

"You talked to Belle about me? How did that conversation go?"

"You know how Belle was, she had so many questions."

Sawyer smiles. "She was a force to be reckoned with, for sure. What did she want to know?"

"She was blown away that you nicknamed me. She said she'd never heard of you doing that before. And she wanted to know what it was like to kiss you."

He groans against my neck. "And what was it like, Mel? Tell me and maybe I'll do it again."

I whimper as he flicks his tongue against my heated skin. "I told her kissing you made me believe in the devil because nothing could feel that good without being completely damning to my soul. Our chemistry scared me."

Just an Illusion Series

His mouth moves across mine, his tongue swiping over my lips and slowly dipping inside to meet mine. This feeling is everything it was back then and more. Before I can lose myself completely in his kiss, he pulls away, leaving me breathless.

"What did she say?"

"She said I shouldn't push you away because if it felt that good you must have been sent by God himself."

Sawyer chuckles against my lips. "Sounds like she might have been onto something."

"Hm, maybe she was," I answer, lost in the memory. That was a great day. It was the first day I joined the tour.

"Is that actually how you felt?" he asks softly.

"Yeah, it really is. It scared me, a lot. All I could think about was my parents and what a disaster their marriage turned into with all that chemistry."

Sawyer props himself up on his elbow and trails his fingers down my arm. "We're not them, Mel, and we never will be."

"I know that now, but I was scared back then. Getting back on a bus, heading out on tour, it was all frightening but in the best possible way. My favorite thing about waking up in the morning was talking to you. Getting to know all the little things you deemed it okay for me to know. Becoming your friend was one of the best feelings in the world. But then ..."

"Then what?" he prompts.

"We ended up in the same elevator the day I was drunk and you were with that groupie."

He groans. "Don't remind me. I was a complete ass."

"You were, and I was so jealous. I wouldn't admit it to myself then, but I was fuming. I wanted to scratch her eyes out."

He brings his lips to mine and his tongue dips inside my mouth, taking a quick taste. "She was a horrible lay if that helps."

"Jesus, Sawyer. No, it doesn't." But I can't hold back my laughter.

"Why are you telling me all of this?" he asks.

"I'm not sure. I think I want you to realize my feelings back then weren't so cut and dry. If I hadn't been ruled by my fear, the decision between you and Noah may not have been so black and white. I hate that you feel like you're in second place. It hurts my heart, Sawyer. A lot."

Sawyer wraps his arms around me and kisses me again, deeper and slower. With each stroke of his tongue against mine I don't just feel that spark of chemistry, I feel his undying love. When he releases me, I run my thumb across his lips.

"What about Noah? Did he know?"

"No, I never told him, there was no point. Whatever feelings I had for you were separate from him. Even though I played it safe, I don't feel like Noah was the safe choice. At the time, he was the only choice I was comfortable with, and I will always cherish our time together and our son. But that says more about me than anything. I wasn't ready for the overwhelming sensations that come from loving you back then, but I am now. The two of you cast some kind of spell on me. And I will never, ever, regret my time with him. I consider our love and marriage one of the biggest blessings of my life. I will always miss him."

"Me, too."

"Sawyer, you make me whole. You bring me to life, and you are also one of my biggest blessings. Someday, I'm going to figure out a way to write this down, to show you my feelings in a broad sense so you can understand it was never first or second, win or lose. It was … fate." He groans, and I laugh. "I know, but I guess Noah rubbed off on me after all. Fate gave me to him to make his last days the best of his life. And fate gave me to you so the rest of our days can be the best days of our lives."

"Sometimes, it gets to me that Noah had you. I was already second out of the womb so I've got issues in that department. If I get down in the dumps about it, I promise it will pass. Even if I was a little bit of a sore loser, I was happy for you and Noah. Without the two of you we wouldn't have Nate and our son is the light of my life. He is all the best parts of you and Noah in one perfect little package. The way his eyes light up when he calls me Daddy Sawyer is the best high I've ever had. The point is, I know we're where we should be right now and there's no point dredging over the past again and again because we're already living our future."

It's times like these I completely understand how I fell in love with Sawyer Weston.

"Sawyer?"

"Yeah?"

"Make love to me."

He bites my bottom lip and flashes me that sexy-ass dimple. "It would be my absolute pleasure. And Princess, just so you know … you're the only woman I've ever nicknamed."

I'm not sure why that makes my heart soar, but it does.

Something's Missing

Today, we're at the building we secured for running the foundation. We've been doing everything behind the scenes out of the house up until now, but Sawyer and I decided to hold a lunch for the core group and give a few speeches as to why we're doing this and what it means to us.

We're all gathered in the conference room and Sawyer defers to me to begin.

As I look around at all of them, they seem so happy to be here. I hate to put a damper on their mood, but this is going to be sad before it becomes happy.

"Thank you for coming today. We have all been working tirelessly to get things organized to launch this foundation in Noah's memory. It may be called The Noah Weston Foundation for Kind Acts, but Belle, my parents, Harold, and even Sara, will all be well-represented here."

Taking a deep breath, I continue. "When we lost Noah and Belle, I lost a huge part of who I am. They were the two best pieces of me and I didn't know how to process their loss. All of you helped me find a way to the other side of my grief. What you probably don't know is that I spent so much time grieving Noah, that I've avoided fully accepting losing Belle. I write her letters, one a week, and put them in a sealed envelope."

Karen gasps and Darren's eyes grow wide.

"In the beginning, this was the only way I could cope. I've only written her two letters the past couple of months. Today, I wrote what I hope will be my final one. You see, losing Noah was devastating, but losing Belle … I think that's what threw me over the edge. It was a snowball effect. I put all my energy into missing Noah and avoiding the reality that Belle is truly gone. She was my best friend and my sister for over twenty years. Each day I see her living through Cadence. She has Belle's laugh, her smile, her personality. And each day it's become a little easier to accept Belle is gone."

My tears are streaming down my cheeks now, but they're cathartic.

"Our children have been blessed with the best parts of Belle and Noah. We're the luckiest people in the world to have pieces of them still with us. This foundation has given me hope, and by doing something in their honor, I've been able to feel a bit more at peace with moving forward without them.

"Noah's love was one of the most incredible gifts I'd ever been given. I want that same love to radiate through this foundation and everyone who works here. This will be a happy place that helps make dreams come true. This foundation should encompass everything Noah and Belle were, what they believed in, and what they were passionate about. Which means our focus will be love, happiness, people, and the arts. Before we toast, I'm going to turn this over to Sawyer to say a few words."

I take my seat and Sawyer stands, flashing everyone that dimpled smile of his I love so much.

"It's kind of hard to follow Mel's lead, she's good with words by trade," he jokes, and everyone laughs. It's not really true anymore, but he wishes it were.

"This foundation is something Noah would have loved. Given time, I'm sure he would have started one on his own. Noah was retiring from touring, but he would have never retired from making people happy, including himself."

Sawyer's a bit choked up and takes a drink of water before continuing.

"These past two years have been hard for us all. We lost the heart of our family, but the Westons are strong and Noah would hate seeing how long we've mourned him. Starting this foundation is good for each of us because we were all touched by Noah and lucky enough to be loved by him immensely.

"There are still days when I wake up excited to talk to Noah. Those days are harder than the rest. Having Nate around really helps. I may have lost my twin, but a piece of him lives on through his son and that is a priceless gift. I'd give everything I have to bring Noah back to us but since that's not an option, I'm pouring everything I am into the success of his foundation."

Rory glares at him from her seat but at least she's keeping her mouth shut.

"Over the next few years, we plan to release an album a year. Some music from the Tritons, some of ours, and some we'll solicit from other artists. The industry is already buzzing about the upcoming release of EP, and I've got some meetings set up with artists to appear on future albums. I miss Noah every day and will do whatever I can to keep his legacy alive as long as possible. I know we all will. Everyone, please raise your glasses."

As everyone raises their champagne, there's not a dry eye.

"To Noah. May your love and spirit always be with us."

Sawyer's toast is perfect and I can't help but think I feel Noah's warmth in this room.

It's been a about a month since our soft launch at the foundation. It's now up and running, and even though I wanted to be a bigger part of it, Sawyer and I decided to hire a larger staff. Rory is the only one in the family working full-time. In spite of how she feels toward me and Sawyer, she's doing a phenomenal job. In fact, she's already set up a fundraiser for the holidays to auction off donations Sawyer and the guys have been able to secure from their famous friends, as well as the stuff we got from my parents' house which sold a few weeks ago.

I'm so proud of everything we've accomplished and all the good things we're doing in Noah's memory. But recently, I started noticing a level of sadness taking over my life when I spent too much time focusing on it. I'm hoping I'll be able to find a better balance someday, but I'm happy taking a step back and being a mom right now. And I think that's where Noah would want my focus most of all.

His EP released a few weeks ago and has already gone multi-platinum. There's already a lot of buzz about Grammy nominations and it makes my heart happy. Noah's voice was a gift to the world; releasing this EP was the right choice.

Now, I'm sitting at the kitchen table going over the list of funds we've agreed upon so far. There are twenty on the list, which is a lot, so they won't all roll out at once. I'm looking at the top six we're starting with but it still feels inadequate.

The Noah Weston Fate Grant – for those who believe all things are possible

The Belle Dixson Scholarship for the Arts

The Triton Family Musical Scholarship for Underprivileged Youth

The Harold Scott Scholarship for International Studies

The Sara Stone Fund for Mental Health Awareness and Treatment

The Bastards and Dangerous Musical Equipment Grant for Up and Coming Musicians

"Mommy!" Nate calls out as he and Sawyer come in with the groceries. "I got popsicles!" he says, clutching the box to his chest.

"I see that. Is Daddy Sawyer going to clean you up after you make a mess?"

"Of course," Sawyer says as he places a kiss on top of my head.

"Where's Cady?" Nate asks sweetly.

"She went to see her grandma, she'll be back soon."

"Okay, popsicle?"

Sawyer laughs at his one-track mind and puts him in his high chair. He's pretty much outgrown it but sticky messes require containment.

"Why are you scrunching your face like that? It's too pretty to be scrunched."

"Something's missing, Sawyer," I reply with a frustrated sigh.

"Are you still going over that list? We've been around and around with this, Mel."

"I know, but it's eating away at me. It's like Noah is telling me there's something vital we're missing and I have to figure it out."

Sawyer's shoulders slump and he abandons the groceries and takes a seat. "Do you remember when I asked you if I should start being more philanthropic after your run-in with Sara?"

"The day you were drunk?" I ask, remembering the conversation well.

"Yup, that was the day. A few days later, I read an article on the rate of homelessness among California's college students. The numbers are staggering, Mel. It's not just California, either. We're just at the top of a long list."

"That's horrible. I had no idea."

"Right? Me, either. So I started thinking about what our lives would have been like if we hadn't gotten our big break, and I felt guilty."

"Why?"

"Because I have a lot. Not as much as Noah did, but I'm not far behind him. I've made some good investments of my own over the years. For someone with so much, I sure didn't pay it forward very well. Not like Noah always did."

"Sawyer, you have a wonderful heart and you are extremely generous with your friends, family, and employees. You take care of people in your own way."

D. Kelly

"Yeah, I know, but after reading that I felt like shit, so I decided to do something about it."

Sawyer exhales and his gorgeous green eyes meet mine. "What did you do?"

"I sat down one day and started calling universities in California. Some of them keep rosters of their homeless students, others have 'unofficial' rosters that faculty or students report. I told them an anonymous benefactor would like to donate housing or funds for housing for some of their students."

Who is this man? I've always known Sawyer was good, but why hide this?

"And what did they say?"

"Daddy Sawyer, I sticky," Nate calls out. The popsicle is gone but his hands and face are a mess. Sawyer grabs a wet cloth and makes a game of it while wiping him down. Then he opens the high chair and scoops Nate out. Nate hugs him and gives him a big, loud kiss. "I love you, Daddy Sawyer."

My heart melts every time, and lately ... well, my ovaries are screaming they want more of that soon.

"I love you, too, Nate. Go play with your toys so I can talk to Mommy."

"Okay!" he says as he runs toward the stockpile of toys in the living room.

"They said yes. But then I struggled with how to do it. There were so many kids and I could never pay for as many as I wanted to ... I'd be broke. The day I was really agonizing over it, I was working on my laptop down in the garage. It was the first day Noah decided to record your EP and he walked in on me with all my shit spread out on the desk."

"Noah knew?"

"Noah was my partner, Mel. I'm sorry we didn't tell you. We didn't tell anyone, at first. A lot of the time he was working on your music he was also working on this with me."

This is it. This is what Noah was trying to show me. I know he's been trying to get me to figure this out. I just know it.

"Can you explain all of this to me? Please," I beg, and he tugs my hand until I rise from my chair and leads us to the couch. As we sit where we can watch Nate play, Sawyer throws his arm around my shoulder.

"Are you mad, Princess?"

"Never. I told Noah a thousand times and I'll tell you now. Your money isn't my business or my concern. I love *you*, Sawyer. Not your bank account, not your altruism, not your Bastards and Dangerous persona, just you—the man behind it all."

"That might be the sexiest thing anyone has ever said to me," he says huskily against my lips.

"Well, maybe I need to step up my game." His tongue meets mine, and I let myself fall into his kiss. As he pulls back, he sighs. "Explain, please."

With the sincerest of looks on his face, he begins.

"You should know this wasn't something we were keeping from you forever. Noah never wanted to keep it from you at all. The day he found me, we laid out a plan, contacted Tony, set it all up, and went from there. It was the first time in a year we had something bonding the two of us. I needed that so much, you have no idea. In a way, it reminded me of us being kids again and having super-secret twin stuff no one else knew about or understood."

"It made you happy."

He smiles at me. "So fucking happy. And for the first time, I understood the high Noah got from helping others like he did. Once me, Noah, and Tony realized this was so much bigger than us, we started recruiting angel investors. Tony took care of most of it, but Noah and I brought in some close friends we knew would want to contribute and still remain anonymous."

"But not me?"

"Not you, not yet. This sounds so lame now, but I didn't want you to know and think I was doing it just because I wanted to be like Noah. You're the one who inspired me to do it. After our talk in the kitchen that day, I wanted you to see me for more than what other people saw me."

"You're not being fair to yourself, Sawyer. You're one of the most incredible people I know. You have the biggest heart and no matter what your reputation was, by now you have to know I know your heart."

"Yeah, I do."

"I'm so proud of you guys, tell me the rest. Don't leave anything out."

My eyes tear up as I imagine how excited Noah was for this. I've never been sure about the afterlife, ghosts, souls, or whatever, but ever since Noah died I swear he's been giving me signals and signs. This was one of them.

"We started with California universities and they posted signs and sent out email alerts to their students. We had ten thousand applications in twenty-four hours. That's when we realized we couldn't do it alone. We tried for the first couple of months, but with our schedules and the sheer demand, it wasn't conducive to helping people quickly. Instead, we set up a lottery system, those who were chosen were vetted, and they were housed after that."

He squeezes me closer and continues. "By May, we were able to house a thousand kids. It didn't seem like a lot, but it was something. It helped that the schools worked with us to get a lot of them in dorms and on meal plans with a discounted rate. Noah reminded me about an abandoned apartment building I bought a few years ago that was within twenty miles of one of the schools. I was going to dump it to a developer, but after talking it over with Noah and Tony we came up with a better plan. We worked with some businesses who donated time and supplies and got it ready to use in three months. Then, the accident happened."

"Noah never got to see it?"

"He saw photos and loved it. It's a large complex and can fit a thousand students. After the accident, I delayed the opening by four months. It killed me, but I wasn't in the right frame of mind to move forward and I knew Noah would want me putting my own personal touch on everything."

"Does anyone else know?"

"Only Tony and the other investors."

"How are things now?"

"So far so good. It's still a California-based project, but word has spread and donations continue to flood in. We're up to three thousand kids now. What's really cool is some of the kids who graduated last year are now working and have started sending in donations to help pay it forward." Sawyer looks down at Nate and shakes his head. "I think about Nate and it slays me. I'd die if that happened to him. Some of these kids come from incredible homes, but bad shit happens and they're left grasping at straws. When I think about my own kid being in that situation it makes me work harder to help these kids now."

"Hey," I say, turning my body toward him "That will never be our kids, Sawyer. We've already made sure of that."

A slight blush creeps into his cheeks and then he smiles. "You said *our* kids."

With a quick glance at Nate, who is busy pushing cars around, I flip myself onto Sawyer's lap. "Yes, I did. We will have kids, Sawyer, we just need to figure out when."

"Now, Princess, I want them now."

"Patience is a virtue."

"Says no one, ever," he replies with a pout.

"I need a little more time, but I promise it's been on my mind a lot lately. I love watching you with Nate, it brings out so many emotions in me I can't even begin to describe them. It also turns me on."

His eyes glaze over with need as he hardens beneath me. "Thinking about turning you on turns me on."

"Mommy, can I hug, too?" Nate pulls on the back of my shirt, and Sawyer's excitement fades away beneath me.

He chuckles against my neck. "Kids always have the best timing."

"Come on, Nate, climb up." Within seconds, we're all wrapped in a big family hug. This is my family. A bit different than I'd imagined in the beginning, but our love is real and so is our happiness.

After Nate is tired of us, he hops down and a lightbulb sparks in my mind.

"Sawyer, is Eli one of your investors?"

He pulls his lip ring into his mouth and tugs at it. Sawyer does this when he's trying to find a way out of something.

"They're private investors for a reason, Mel. I can't confirm or deny that."

"Mmhm, and did you guys ever think I might want to invest? Noah knew I was trying to figure out what the hell to do with my inheritance."

This time, his tone is laced with sadness. "He was going to ask you when he took you on a tour of the apartment building. He wanted you to see what we'd been working on. By then it was more the element of surprise. You guys were married and you and I had been through a lot. I was excited for you to know, but ever since the accident … I've been enjoying it being my last secret endeavor with Noah and wasn't ready to give that up, I guess."

"That makes complete sense. Can you at least tell me the name now?"

With a wide smile, he responds, "The Sunshine Project."

"Are you serious?"

He laughs. "We both thought it was appropriate. Joey called you Mellie Sunshine and we both agreed you'd brought more than your share of it into our lives. It seemed right, and Noah thought by doing something to honor your dad it would help you figure out where or how to invest your money."

I'm rapidly blinking back my tears. "Is this apartment building close?"

"About an hour away. Do you want to go see it?"

I nod, and he stands, taking me with him and then setting me down. "Nate, you want to go for a ride in the car?"

Nate jumps up with his cars in his hands "Yes, Daddy Sawyer!"

After Nate is buckled into his car seat, the perfect idea hits me. "Sawyer, this is it!"

With a perplexed look on his face, he answers, "I'll bite, what is it?"

"What you should use the vaulted music for! Yours and my parents."

"For The Sunshine Project?" he asks, and I nod excitedly.

"Even if you split the proceeds three ways, to Sunshine, to the foundation, and to yourselves, I bet it would be a massive amount of money."

"Noah also left a yearly endowment to the project that will continue to grow with interest. That's part of his will that was only disclosed to me. Fucking hell, Princess, you're brilliant and this is a perfect idea!"

As we drive down PCH, with the ocean glittering under the sun and Nate singing his own singalong in the back of the car, I can't help but think this is all a sign from Noah. A bit of fate is shining down on us today.

Suddenly, Nate belts out a lyric louder than the speakers and Sawyer and I exchange knowing glances. This little boy is going to take after both his daddies and his grandparents. God help us all.

When we got back from the student dorms, I was still struggling to wrap my mind around it all. I'm so fucking proud of all the guys. In my heart, I know all the men near and dear to me are part of this project. While Sawyer bathes Nate, I add a few more causes to my list and feel like I can breathe a bit easier.

The Noah Weston Grant benefiting The Sunshine Project

The Joey and Iris Triton Grant benefiting The Sunshine Project

The Harold Scott Grant benefiting The Sunshine Project

The Bastards and Dangerous Grant benefiting The Sunshine Project

The Andy Reynolds Grant benefiting The Sunshine Project

The last one is the driver who hit our bus. It finally seems right to do something in his honor. I hope everyone else agrees.

"You ready for bed, Princess?" Sawyer asks, placing a kiss on top of my head and looking over my shoulder. "Andy, huh?" he asks softly.

I look up at his glassy eyes. "Do you mind? I feel like Noah would want this one most of all."

"You've got an amazing heart, Amelia. I'm so proud to have a piece of it. I don't mind. I think you're right, Noah would want this."

"Make me a promise, Sawyer." I stand and wrap my arms around his waist.

"Anything, Mel."

"Let's not keep secrets from each other. Even though there were reasons, I'm finding out Noah had some small secrets from me and I don't like it. Can we agree to be like Anna and Wyatt and no matter what it is we agree to vault, we tell each other as the exception?"

Suddenly, he's hugging me tighter. "Hell yeah we can. There's no one I want to keep secrets with more than you."

Wedding Blues

It's been a week since Sawyer took me to the apartment building, and I've learned all about their group and the real estate Sawyer still has that he'd like to convert for more students. They're even talking about a few buildings farther away and hiring a couple of full-time drivers to bus them back and forth to classes. Luther is at the top of our list to be in charge of the drivers.

"Damn, you look hot!" Sawyer exclaims as he walks in the room looking damn fine himself. Today is Mama's wedding; it's been such a bittersweet morning for me. I'm the matron of honor, and Mama gave me Belle's favorite necklace, bracelet, and earrings to wear in honor of her. She said it's a way to have both her girls with her on her special day.

"You don't look too shabby yourself," I reply, fidgeting with the bracelet.

"Breathe, Mel. It's going to be okay." He steps closer and stops me from tugging on the bracelet.

"I know, I'm missing her more than ever today, Sawyer. It will be two years next month since we lost them. How is it even possible?"

"Come here," he says, pulling me into his comforting arms. "Today is supposed to be a happy day. Let's focus on that. I know Belle and Noah got cheated, but they lived every day to the fullest while they were here. How many people can say that? It sure beats what we've been doing the last two years."

I pull away, my anger flaring. "Yeah, well, maybe they wouldn't be living each day to the fullest if they'd lost us!"

"That's not what I meant, Mel, and you know it. Please don't pick a fight with me today. I want to go to the wedding and dance with my beautiful date and come home and make love to you. Today is about love, Mel, be a lover, not a fighter."

He's so fucking cheesy sometimes, my anger immediately dissipates and I bust up laughing.

"That's my girl. I knew my Princess was in there somewhere."

"Mommy!"

"Auntie Mel!"

Cadence and Nate fly into the room with Darren hot on their tails. I'm dying with their cuteness and pull out my phone to take a photo. Nate is the ring bearer and wearing a tux, and Cadence is the flower girl and wearing a dress similar to mine.

"Sorry, guys, they got ahead of me. What did I say about running?" Darren chastises them.

"No running until after Grandma gets married. Sorry, Daddy," Cadence replies with a sweet smile that is all Belle. It gets Darren every time, and I'm pretty sure she knows it.

"It's okay, monkey, just don't do it again. We don't want to make Grandma sad on her wedding day."

"Okay, Daddy."

"Okay, Uncle Darren."

"I'm going to take them over there now and you guys can meet us there," Darren says, ushering the kids out of the room.

"It still cracks me up that the notorious men of Bastards and Dangerous all have cars with multiple car seats in them."

Sawyer flashes me a devious grin and paces toward me like a predator. I back up slowly against the wall; I would be all for this game if we weren't on a schedule. "Princess, I'll rock a mini-van like a motherfucker if you give me enough kids and car seats to fill it."

His husky voice washes over me like the finest whiskey and as much as I want to tell him yes, I'll have a thousand of his babies, I can't. Not yet.

"Soon, Sawyer, I promise. I need a little more time."

"I don't want to be an old man before I'm a dad again, Mel."

Again. Just the use of that word makes me melt. He could have easily left it out. I throw my arms around his neck and pull his mouth to mine. "I promise, Sawyer, it won't be that long."

Sawyer's mouth meets mine and he slides his hand up my dress, maneuvering his finger through the side of my panties and inside me, where I want him most. Groaning into his mouth, he kisses me harder and deeper before pulling back and removing his finger at the same time.

His lust-filled eyes lock onto mine as he sucks his finger into his mouth. I watch as he swirls his tongue around it and bite my lip as lust flows through me. "God, I want you."

He kisses me again, this time soft and slow, and I taste myself on him. "I'm going to work you up every chance I get tonight. By the time we get back here you're going to be begging for my cock."

"What if we skip all that and I beg for it now?"

Sawyer throws his head back and laughs. "I'd love to hear you beg for it now, but we'll be late for the wedding if we don't leave in about two minutes."

"Fine, but if you tease me like that all night you'd better be ready to keep it up all night because I'm going to fuck you 'til morning."

He leans down and bites my neck and I inhale deeply, wishing for more. As his tongue licks over the bite, his husky voice greets my ear. "Stamina has never been my issue and you know it, Princess. Threaten me with a good time all you want, you'll be the one begging for mercy in the end. Maybe tonight you'll finally let me have that ass. My cock has been dying for a new place to play on your body."

"Fuck, Sawyer, let's go before you make me come with your words."

He pulls back and his gaze locks on mine. "That's what I thought."

A few hours and many emotions later, Sawyer and I are dancing under the stars. I'm trying to be a good sport and have fun, but I haven't been to a wedding since mine and Noah's; this one is triggering so many memories.

Mama looks incredibly happy, even though we both shed a few tears before the ceremony. As I watch her and Marcus dancing, I want what they have. I had it once with Noah, and I want it again with Sawyer, but something is holding me back.

"You look a million miles away," he says solemnly.

"I'm sorry, it's been a long day." With a sigh, I lean my head on his shoulder as the lyrics from I "Just Wanna Love You" by The Shires wash over us. I can't help but feel the part in the song about the storm is where we are right now. We're at an invisible impasse. As much as I thought I'd let Noah go, today has proved I haven't—not completely—and it bothers me immensely. Sawyer deserves so much more than what he's getting from me.

This wedding is starting to send me spiraling downward. My emotions are getting the best of me and I find myself clinging to Sawyer, wishing for relief.

"Do you want to go home, Mel?"

"Would you mind? I think I'm just … tired."

"No," he says sadly, "I don't mind, but I'm pretty sure the word you were looking for there was overwhelmed. You're lost in your memories of him, and there's nothing I can do to change it or help you."

Darren left with the kids about an hour ago, so Sawyer and I wish the happy couple a good honeymoon and make our way to the car.

We're quiet on the drive home; I'm pretty sure Sawyer is upset. That makes two of us. I'm frustrated I'm having so many emotions tonight, and I'm even more frustrated he's not being more sympathetic to me.

When he pulls into the driveway, he turns to me, his sadness slaying me. "I'm going to work on some music in the garage for a while. I'll be in later."

Just like that, all his promises from earlier are gone, but I'm not really in the mood at this point. "Alright, I'll see you later."

Inside, I kick off my heels and carry them to my room. The sound of giggling kids carries into the hall. At least they're having a good night.

After putting on my pajamas, I go into the kitchen and open a bottle of wine.

"I thought I heard someone come in. You're home early, what happened?"

"Want some?" I ask, holding up the wine.

"Nah, I'll just grab a beer, thanks."

"Will things ever get easier, Darren? God knows I'm trying, but then something happens and *bam* ... back three steps again."

"I'm not sure, Mel. You've made it further than I have. I'm back to randomly fucking people, but it's not messy when emotions aren't involved. Belle's the only person who has ever evoked those kinds of feelings in me."

"Am I a horrible person? I love Sawyer, so much, but tonight brought back all the memories of my own wedding. Noah and I were so happy that night."

Darren takes a long draw of his beer. "I don't know, Mel. I don't think you're a bad person at all. Maybe if you were involved with someone outside the family it wouldn't be as difficult. But you can't help who you love, and you and Sawyer are pretty fucking perfect if you guys can get past all your shit. Besides, it was your first wedding since, maybe it won't happen again."

"Yeah, maybe not."

As he picks at the label on his bottle, he looks at me. "Don't think you were the only one affected tonight. Sawyer is being sensitive right now because he was reminded of your wedding, too.

You're not the only one who has lingering feelings and guilt about Noah. Sawyer is in this with you, Mel."

"I know he is, but I don't feel like he's sympathetic to it anymore."

"Shit, today was miserable for me, too. The last wedding I attended was yours, and Belle was my date. Her mom got married and she wasn't there but I was. Do you realize how much that fucks with someone's head?" He chuckles. "Well, yeah, of course you do. You're not alone, Mel, we're all here. But do you really need Sawyer's sympathy? If it were me, I'd rather have his support."

"Sawyer said he's working on music. Do you know if he's been working on anything new?"

Darren's eyes widen in surprise. "No, but I wish he would. Sawyer needs that creative outlet. Hell, we all do. We could never tour again without Noah but fuck, I wish we could just jam and let out some stress without feeling guilty for doing it without him."

"I think Noah would want that. To use your music as an outlet and a way to relieve some stress. He'd want you guys to be happy."

Darren smiles and tips his beer bottle toward me. "And he'd want you and Sawyer to be happy, too. Today was rough, but for all his roughness, Sawyer is one of the most sensitive people I've ever met. Don't be too hard on him, Mel. He loves you more than he's ever loved anyone, except Noah."

"Thanks, Darren."

"Yeah, no problem. Can you watch Cadence tonight? I need a release of my own, if you know what I mean."

"Sure, have fun, and double bag that shit."

"You know it, Mel. Go talk to him, I'll be here a little bit longer."

I decide to take Darren's advice and go downstairs to the garage. "Heathens" by Twenty One Pilots is blasting down here. Sawyer is sitting on the couch, crying, looking at a photo of him, Noah, and me. I back up against the wall and out of sight, feeling like I'm intruding on a private moment. Belle took that picture of us and I framed it for Sawyer that first Christmas we were all together.

Instead of bothering Sawyer, I head back upstairs, deciding it's time to make another post on Belle's blog.

Slammed Blog Post

Hey, *Slammed* Family!

This late-night post is more for me than you. However, you are all my lifeline to Belle right now so there is no one I wanted to share it with more.

Today, our mama got married and Belle wasn't here for it. Yeah, it's been one of those days. Time is a strange thing, an infinite loop of happiness and sadness. Today was one of those strange times. Watching someone get married is one of the best feelings in the world, especially when it is someone you've hoped would find their happy ending for a long time.

Our mama deserves to be happy, especially after these past few difficult years. Next month will mark two years since we lost them. Can you believe that? In some ways it seems like yesterday, and in others it seems like a lifetime ago.

Tonight, I missed Noah more than I have in a while. His loss hits me at random times but at the wedding—my first wedding since ours—it hit me hard. It hit Darren and Sawyer hard, too, but for different reasons.

Darren went to his mother-in-law's wedding without his bride. Even though he and Belle never officially tied the knot, Darren is family in every way. The last wedding he went to was mine, with Belle by his side.

And Sawyer, well … this is a bit more complicated and I hope you all will bear with me because I have some explaining to do. Today was also Sawyer's first wedding since my wedding to Noah. The memories and guilt plagued us both just below our happiness. You see, it's time to come clean with you, *Slammed* Family. Sawyer and I are a couple now.

This may surprise some of you, probably most of you, because we keep our relationship extremely close to the belt. For those of you who think it's wrong and we're assholes, join the club. There are a few family members who are right there with you. And at times, Sawyer and I are with you, too.

The rest of the time we are happy. We're in love, and no matter how wrong it may seem, I would have never made it through the past two years without him. Sawyer is an amazing father to Nate and loves him purely, in a way no one other than Noah or I could. Nate has the love of a father, an uncle, and someone who keeps the memory of his own father alive daily all wrapped in one incredible package.

Why tell you this now in a midnight confession after a half a bottle of wine? Because I just saw something that broke my heart and I don't know how to fix it. I thought maybe, by telling the world my secret, it could somehow help ease the hurt both Sawyer and I carry around.

If any of you have ever walked in total darkness and had to find your way to the light, you'll understand my post. Losing Noah and Belle was the darkest time in my life. Having Sawyer with me to not only walk me through but understand my pain makes getting to the light almost bearable. I'm still not out of the dark completely but I'm working my way through as best as I can.

On a lighter note, I want to personally thank all of you for your support with the launch of The Noah Weston Foundation for Kind Acts. Your donations continue to pour in, as do your notes of love and support. You made the release of his EP beyond amazing. I used to struggle with releasing his album to me—to the world—but now, every time I hear one of those songs, it makes me happy to know his fans are experiencing the joy that was Noah Weston. He had the purest heart of anyone I've ever known.

I'm pretty sure his son will be a close second, followed by Sawyer. These Weston men are a caliber of their own. I consider myself blessed to be a part of their world. In closing tonight, I leave you with a picture of the ring bearer and the flower girl. Could these kids of ours be any cuter?

Much love to you all.

Mel

Amelia – Present Day

With a sigh, I stretch my arms above my head.

"Where are you now?" Sawyer asks for about the umpteenth time.

I hit save and send him what I just finished. He's only a chapter behind me and catching up fast. I'm making everyone else wait for the second half of this third part. I want Sawyer to finish it first.

"I'm about to write the last chapter. Well, the ending is still to be determined, but at least I'll be caught up to the here and now."

"Have I mentioned how fucking proud I am of you for doing this?"

"You might have, but can I ask you something?"

He laughs hysterically. "You're never going to stop asking me that, are you? I'm yours, Mel, ask away."

"What do you think about the book so far? Are you learning anything you didn't already know? Does it make you feel any different about everything, or anything?"

"Put our computers on the floor for a second," he says, passing his computer to me after I put mine down. "Come here." He lies on the bed and pulls me into his arms. Using his hand to brush my hair away from my face, he kisses me tenderly.

"I'm not sure I can express everything I've felt while reading this book. You brought back some of the best times of my life and some of the worst. This story is real and it's us. It's everything, Mel, and then some."

A sigh of relief escapes my lips and he brushes his over mine briefly.

"You know how you doubted my love for you was real until Wyatt told you his story?"

"I wouldn't say doubted, more worried it was a subliminal love."

"Uh huh, anyway, I guess there's always been this part of me that has kind of wondered the same thing. Was I just a substitution for Noah, someone you fell for because I helped you and maybe it was more of a … I don't know … owed … kind of love? Do you know what I mean?"

"Yes, I understand what you mean, but you could have asked me."

He sighs and brushes his lips against mine. "I was terrified of your answer. Through your words, I understand your love is as real as mine. Reading your emotions from our first kiss, and all of our interactions, proved that to me without a doubt."

"What about the Noah scenes?"

"Amelia, I'm so happy my brother had someone who loved him as much as you did. His life was cut short but he experienced it all because of you. What I understand now, that I'm not sure I could have ever understood before this book, is we *did* have a spark but it wasn't our time. The timing was yours and Noah's and you lived it to the fullest. But Mel, the story is ours. Mine and yours, do you see that? From the first kiss in my bathroom, until whenever fate decides it's over, this is our story."

Tears are streaming down my cheeks. *He gets it.*

"So you understand now that you never were and never could be second best?"

"I do, Princess, I totally fucking do."

"Can you also understand that it's going to be natural for both of us to have days where something reminds us of Noah, and those days will be harder than others, but it doesn't diminish our love? I need this most of all, Sawyer. I need to know you have my back even if my mind is temporarily lost."

His hands caress my back in soft circles and his eyes are bright with love. "As long as you understand I'm here with you and can help you through it. No pulling away, no hiding out in Noah's closet, no listening to your death playlist. In fact, I think your next order of business after the closet should be replacing that fucking playlist with something happier. Or something sexier we can listen to while we fuck our blues away."

"I like that idea, and I have a surprise for you but I want to write the last chapter before I show you. Then, while everyone else is catching up, maybe I can relax for a bit."

Sawyer bites his bottom lip and grins. "Actually, I was hoping you'd let me take you somewhere while they are all reading. I have something to talk to you about. Something I realized was long overdue when we were up at the cabin."

Popping a quick kiss on his lips, I hop up and get our computers. "It's a date, Weston. One more chapter and I'm all yours."

The Beginning of the End

Sawyer never came to bed that night, and my emotional state after that took a nosedive. Sawyer started spending more time in the garage over the next two weeks and I started spending more time in Noah's closet.

The thing is, I was sad, but my time in the closet wasn't all about Noah this time. For some reason, I feel close to him in here and I've been talking to him about Sawyer. I know it sounds crazy, but it helps me since Sawyer and I aren't exactly talking.

Ever since the wedding, Sawyer has been pulling away from me and it hurts so much. After I saw him crying I'm hesitant to even try talking to him. He's hurting; I don't want to make it worse and I don't know how to fix it. They're leaving tomorrow to go to the cabin in Big Bear for their second try at an annual trip. More than anything, I want things to be okay with us before he goes.

Call it separation anxiety or PTSD, but I worry every time someone leaves the house. It's subtle most of the time, but he'll be gone for three days; a lot can happen in that amount of time. If something were to happen, I don't want any anger between us.

I'm in the kitchen making coffee, trying to psych myself up to talk to him today and fix this, when he comes in fully dressed.

"I made you coffee," I say, trying to open up a dialog.

"Thanks, but I'm meeting someone for coffee. A meeting with a new angel investor."

"Oh, okay. Have a good day, I guess. Will I see you later? I'd really like to talk today."

Leaning against the counter, he crosses his arms and stares me down. I hate when he does this; it's intimidating and I don't want to feel intimidated by the man who owns my heart. "Yeah, sure. I've got some errands to run and stuff to put together for tomorrow. I left you a list of stuff to pack for Nate if you have time, it would really help me out."

Nate. He's taking my baby away for three days. What am I going to do without them? I've never been alone in this house for more than a few hours, let alone three fucking days.

"Of course. Whatever you need." I'm emotional, and I wish he'd just leave so I could fucking cry in peace.

"Thanks, Mel, I'll see you later."

Grabbing his keys, he leaves. No kiss goodbye, not even a second look back. I'm pretty sure Sawyer has finally decided he's done with me. I thought after reading the blog post he'd be happy. I didn't get a reaction out of him one way or the other. The readers, on the other hand, had plenty to say and a lot of it wasn't kind.

Maybe that's part of it for him. Not the readers but the family. Rory, Rob, and Owen are still causing issues. Well … that's not fair. Rob has come around; he was even going to go with them until Diane's due date interfered. I get a personal vibe from him that he's not okay with us, but maybe it's just me looking for something that isn't there. Same with Owen. He hasn't said anything one way or the other, but his lack of opinion makes me think it's not favorable. And we all know where Rory stands; she becomes angrier and more bitter each time I see her. At least she maintains a professional manner in the office, albeit a cool one.

"Good morning, Mel," Karen says, coming into the kitchen. She spent the night here last night because she was up late working on foundation business with me. Last week, she came over and found me in the middle of a closet meltdown. She's been hovering ever since. It might have to do with me breaking down and crying about Noah and Sawyer and babbling about the things I kept from Noah and how they feel like lies even though I thought I was protecting him. She was quick to remind me some things Noah knew, and some he didn't, but there were also things he kept from me.

Karen also reminded me that just because you're in a relationship doesn't mean you have to know every single thing the other person does. Sometimes, secrets aren't a bad thing. But I don't want secrets anymore and maybe I'm living in a bubble hoping for the impossible.

"Good morning, Karen. Did you sleep well?"

"Yes, but I always do when I'm here. The sound of the ocean is the best sleep medicine there is. Where is everyone? It's awfully quiet in here."

I pass her a cup of coffee and we both take a seat at the table. "Sawyer had a meeting. Darren took the kids to get breakfast before your big outing at the zoo today. They're going to have a blast."

"You're welcome to come. It might do you some good to get out of the house."

"Thanks, but Sawyer said we could talk when he gets home and I really need to see where we're at. I think he's going to break up with me."

Karen's mouth drops open but she recovers quickly. "Surely, things aren't that bad?"

"I'd like to say no, but I think they are."

"Amelia, Sawyer loves you and I know you love him. Whatever happens when he comes home, I think the two of you should take the weekend to reassess your feelings and reflect on how different your lives would be without each other."

She squeezes my hand and I squeeze hers back. "I know how my life would be without him, I'd be miserable. I don't need the weekend to know that, but maybe he does."

"It will be okay. I'm going to get ready so I can get out of here and give you two a chance to talk."

I'm sitting in Noah's closet listening to "My Immortal" by Evanescence, thinking about how I'm finally going to try to pack up this closet while they're gone this weekend, when the door flings open with a bang.

Rage fills Sawyer's features when he sees me sitting here. This is not what we need right now at all.

"Unfuckingbelieveable! Jesus, Mel, what the fuck are you doing to yourself?"

I scramble to my feet and come out of the closet. He's already left the room. "It's not what you think," I call out behind him.

"Really? Then tell me what it is. Because it looks to me like you're mourning your husband with your death playlist again and I'm getting really fucking sick of always being in second goddamn place with you!"

I wasn't listening to my death playlist at all, just my awesome female singer playlist, but I'm sure now isn't the time to bring up that minor detail. Although, to him, it's probably not a minor detail.

"You're not in second place with me, Sawyer. I wish you could understand that." I hate this and I wish I could go back in time to Mama's wedding and change that night.

Sawyer is pacing, practically ripping his hair out with his hands. "I've tried to let it go, but I can't. I'm angry, and you're regressing into this sad wife again. I can't do this anymore, Mel. I thought I could wait forever for you, but I can't."

"Are you breaking up with me?" Panic rises in my voice.

"Maybe I am because there are some things I can't get past."

"Like what?"

"Let's see, for starters, I'm tired of second-guessing everything I do with you because I'm wondering if Noah did it first. Or because I know he did and I don't want to trigger any memories for you."

"Sawyer—"

"No, let me get this out. Do you know how many times I've wanted to kiss your tattoo because it's *my* name on your skin? But it's also his and it was his gift, so putting my lips on that part of your body is pretty much off limits forever. Do you know how much that kills me? To know there is a part of you that will forever be off limits to my lips? Or how many times I've thought about putting rings on your fingers but never actually went there because he did it first and you only recently felt okay enough to take them off?"

His face is getting redder and his eyes have never been filled with this much fury before.

"What about kids, Mel? We can't have them because you did that with him, right?"

"Sawyer! You're not being fair!"

"No, maybe I'm not, but fuck it, Mel. I'm tired. I want more. A thousand ways and a thousand times I've let you know how much I want you and backed off because you need time and space. I'm sick of everything! I want to make us a home, Mel. A real home, not a house we exist in. Not this shrine to everything Noah!"

Ouch, that fucking hurts, but he's not wrong; this house isn't a home and it never really has been.

"I love my brother, but I'm so tired of living in his shadow when it comes to you. If you can't even empty his closet, you'll never make a home with me."

"It was one bad night, Sawyer. That's what I wanted to talk to you about."

With a resigned sigh, he sits next to me. "That's the thing, Mel, it wasn't one bad night. It was the final straw for me in a series of reminders. The first thing you did after one setback was start regressing into the closet. I'm just a way for you to pass the time until things get real."

My pulse races. He can't end this. "You're being unfair and you don't know the whole story! Yes, I've been in the closet, not because I'm regressing but because I feel close to Noah in there for some reason. It's like my confessional where I talk to him about *you*. I came to the garage to talk to you that night but I saw you holding that picture and crying and I didn't know what to do. I wrote the blog post hoping you'd understand how much you mean to me. You've been shutting me out and I take that very personally. I'm not the only one who goes back and forth from hot to cold! What else should I be doing? What else can I do? I've been trying to give you space because you're going through something right now but fuck, Sawyer, I've missed you."

"Nothing, Mel, I don't know. While I was down there looking at that photo, I realized what a complete fool I've been. Noah would want us happy and right now, I'm not fucking happy. So I've decided to do something that is either going to make me happy or lead me to eventual happiness because that's what Noah would ultimately want for me. He wouldn't want me to be miserable or hanging by a thread, waiting to see if today is the day I'm going to finally hit one of your triggers."

"What are you going to do?" I ask fearfully.

"I'm giving you an ultimatum and whatever you decide, I'll go with, but I need your decision by the time I get home on Sunday."

Nothing in the world pisses me off more than an ultimatum but with Sawyer, it terrifies me. He's serious this time.

"What is it?" I manage to choke out.

"You need to make a home with me, Mel. A real home where we live, both physically and with a zest for life. Some days you radiate happiness and other days you're barely existing. I need you to radiate with me in a place that is warm and welcoming with drawings on the wall and even the occasional crayon scribble the kids leave when they shouldn't. And yes, I said kids because I want them with you, in our home. We're a family, Mel. At least, that's what I hope for every fucking day. I want pictures of us on the walls. Me and you and our love."

"What if I can't?"

"Then I will always love you but I can't be with you anymore. I can't live in Noah's shadow or his shrine. I know he was your past, he was mine, too. But I hope to be your future. It's your call. I'd even be willing to stay here if you can get rid of Noah's things and turn your old room into something productive. Maybe another nursery or an office for you. You're lost, Mel. You need to get back to writing. If not the story you owe SOS about BAD, something else. One of your romances, a tell-all about Eli, whatever … just do something to get those creative juices flowing again. You need to live, Mel. Above anything else, that's what Noah would want and it's what I want, too."

"So that's it? Three days to decide?"

With a sadness so profound it steals my breath, he replies, "Yes, and I guess you could technically say three and a half. Nate, Darren, and I are staying at J's tonight. It's closer to the mountains and keeps him from having to come all the way out here. It's why I asked you to pack him up earlier."

"You're taking him tonight?"

"He'll be fine, I promise. You need this time … correction, *we* need this time." I can't wrap my head around any of this right now. "Come say bye to him. My mom dropped him off when I got here and she took Cadence to Veronica's for Darren."

Numb, I follow him out and smile at my son, who is excitedly holding the handle of his suitcase while Darren shows him how to roll it back and forth. It's hard to believe he's going to be two in just a few days.

"Nate, give Mommy a hug. We're going to spend the night with Uncle J."

"Mommy, I going fishing."

As I pull him into my arms, my emotions take over and tears begin to fall. "I know you are, baby. You're going to catch all the fish in the lake, I just know it. I'll miss you."

"I'll miss you, too. I love you," he says before he releases me and runs back to his suitcase.

Turning my gaze to Sawyer, my anger flares. "Keep Fat Bastard away from my kid."

"He's my kid, too, Mel. I'd never let anything hurt him."

"See you when we get back, Mel. I'm going to take Nate to the car so you guys can talk." Darren gives me a quick hug and darts out the door. He'd better run. He knew about this shit and gave me no warning.

"Well, I guess I'll see you later," I say, turning toward the bedroom.

"Mel, please get past your anger and understand where I'm coming from with this. I want to make a home with you. But I need *all* of you in order to do it. I won't settle for less, and you shouldn't, either."

A few minutes after they leave, my phone dings. It's a clip for "Sometimes Love Just Ain't Enough" by Patty Smyth and Don Henley. It takes everything in me not to throw my phone. Instead, I lie down on our bed, mine and Sawyer's, and cry.

I won't let him do this to us, though. I'm back up in a flash and send him a link to "Always Take You Back" by The Night Terrors of 1927. I'm tired of crying, I've spent the bulk of the last two years crying for things that will never get better. Tonight, I'm making a few changes. For the first two, I need to take a drive. For the last one, tequila. Tomorrow, I'll do what I should have been doing all along and sit down and write. It won't be the story I owe them, but it will be a story all the same.

My phone goes off again before I leave the house. I dread looking at it, but I'm relieved when I see it's a text from Darren.

Darren: I'm sorry I didn't give you a heads up, but I think you both need this. Sawyer is having second thoughts, he's hesitant to leave you alone. Then I started having second thoughts, too. He's afraid you'll start writing and drown in your sorrow all over again.

Why are you telling me this?

Darren: Because I was an asshole and didn't try and get you to work things out sooner. Are you okay?

No, but I will be. You guys enjoy your trip. I'll be here when you get back.

Darren: Promise?

Yeah, I am going to write. I have to in order to work this out. Wish me luck.

Darren: You don't need luck, your words are gold – what you need is tequila.

I've got that covered … Is he still angry?

Darren: That wasn't anger, it was fear. He's worried what this means for you guys and he's worried about leaving you to work it out alone. I'll handle him, but you have to make this right. You guys belong together.

That remains to be seen, but I'm trying. Have fun this weekend. Gotta go.

The sun is starting to set and dark clouds are rolling in. This cold weather is unusual for August in Southern California, but it matches my mood. Although I haven't been here in almost two years, someone has because both Belle and Noah's graves have fresh flowers on them.

"Hey, guys," I say, taking a seat between them. "It's been a long time and I'm sorry for that. I'm not even sure I feel like you guys are here, but I needed to get out of the house to talk to you today."

A cool breeze begins to blow and I zip up my hoodie. "Anyway, I've kind of made a huge mess of things. If you've been watching, you already know this. I definitely have not been living like there's no tomorrow. But I have been living, at least I thought I had until Sawyer pointed out all my flaws today."

With a sigh, I lie back on the grass and look to the sky. Staring at their headstones hurts too much.

"Noah, I'm not even sure what to say to you. I love you, I will always love you, and letting you go has been the hardest thing I've ever had to do. It's been two years without your smiles, laughter, advice, and love. In some ways it seems like yesterday and in other's like it's been forever.

"Our kids are the cutest, most amazing little humans to walk the planet. You guys would be so fucking proud of them. It's like God knew the two of you were leaving and gave us mini replicas of you. They make our days better and a little bit easier, but they're still no replacement for you."

A car passes by on their way out, reminding me to hurry because it's getting late.

"I'm sure you already know Sawyer and I are together now. I've talked to you about this every day for the last two weeks in your closet, Noah, but in case you're not there I figured I could talk to you here today. You were right, I love him. It's more than that, I'm head-over-heels in love with this man. He makes the pain of losing you hurt less with each passing day. He makes me laugh, and he's such a wonderful father to our son. You'd be so proud of him, Noah, he's a different man. But I may have blown it all to hell because I still don't know how to say a final goodbye to you and pack up your things."

I swipe at my tears but eventually give up; they're going to keep flowing at this point.

"It's not just you. I haven't gone through your things, either, Belle. You know how I am with closure and goodbyes ... they're not my thing. Denial is an emotion I thrive on, I suppose. I did finally pack up my parent's house and sell it, though. That's some progress, right? You guys were taken from us so soon and so horrifically, I feel like at least your things should get some more time on earth when you couldn't. Is that bad? And what's really wrong with leaving a room filled with your things? I'm not even sleeping in there anymore."

It's as if I can hear them telling me, "You know why it's wrong, Mel. You have to move on."

And I know it's all in my mind, my subconscious is telling me what I want to hear, but I wish it were them because at least they would be here.

"You know what's funny? All this time I've been grieving and wishing for you to be back with us. The past few months when I have those thoughts, they make me sad, because if you were here I wouldn't be in love with Sawyer. I guess that's when I finally knew I'd really moved on. I hope that's okay. Your video seems to indicate it's what you wanted, but I didn't know that when I started falling for him. Sawyer gets me, Noah, in all the ways you used to and even in some ways you didn't."

I stand up, dust my pants off, and turn back around toward the headstones. "I will always love you, Mr. Weston, and I know if you'd never been taken from us we'd have had an amazing life. I'm trying to honor your wishes and collect those fifty years with Sawyer. I love you with all my heart, Noah. Rest in peace, my sweet husband."

I place a kiss to my palm and rest it against the top of his headstone and repeat the process with Belle's. "I love you, Belle, and I miss you constantly. Thank you for leaving me with Cadence. With her here I at least have a piece of you with me all the time. She's going to grow up to be an amazing woman, exactly like her mother was. I love you both, always."

I'm still crying when I reach the car but my heart feels a little bit lighter. Now, off to my next order of business.

It's almost two in the morning when I climb into bed. I've taken care of everything I needed to and even got through it with a minimal amount of tequila. Going to the cemetery again was difficult, but once it was over I felt like a huge weight had been lifted from me. Talking to Noah and Belle was something I've needed to do for a while now.

When I left the cemetery, I went straight to my next item on my to-do list. It was easy and something I should have done a long time ago that maybe would have helped avoid this entire mess.

The last task was extremely hard but the right thing to do and hopefully done in the right way. Time will tell on that one, I suppose. Either way, I did what I set out to do today. The flashing light on my phone catches my attention and I realize I haven't checked it since I sent Sawyer that link earlier. So help me God, if Fat Bastard got my kid I'm going to go ballistic.

As I open the message, there's a photo of Nate with that cat curled up next to him like a sweet little pussycat and the caption **"Our son is a cat whisperer. Fat Bastard never stood a chance."**

A few minutes later, he sent me another link to "It's Been Awhile" by Staind.

We may never have an easy love but we will never lack passion. Sawyer has more passion in his pinky than most men have in their whole bodies. I dig through my email and find an advanced copy of a song that was submitted for our next fundraising album last week; it fits perfectly. After sending him the file for "Now or Never" by Halsey, I turn off the light and try to get some sleep. Tomorrow is going to be the beginning of a rough three days.

When I wake up, the first thing I do is check my phone. There is absolutely nothing from Sawyer, which surprises me. Determined to get through these next three days, I send him one more song and hope it means something to him.

A few seconds later, he replies.

Sawyer: "I Have Nothing" by Whitney Houston, huh? That one could actually go both ways. You have 72 hours, Princess, make them count.

His words sting and I don't bother texting him back. Instead, I spend the bulk of the afternoon doing something I should have done a long time ago—going through Belle's things. I want everything in these boxes. Mama knew exactly what I would want, and I'm overcome with so many memories of Belle and me. I've stacked some pictures of the two of us on my old dresser in Noah's room and then set my favorite one of her and me on the coffee table for inspiration.

I've got her notes and articles, as well as Sawyer's journal, set up on the table. The sun is setting by the time I settle down to write with a glass of my favorite wine. I'm not ready for this whatsoever but for him, I'll do it.

Amelia – Present Day

"I'm finished." Well, caught up to real time anyway. Even so, I can't believe I just wrote a book about our lives in three days. I'm not sure I'll ever do anything with it; this book was for me and Sawyer. After all, we're all that matters in this relationship. It's sad it took me writing it all out to realize that, but I do realize it and I hope that's enough.

"I'm proud of you, Princess. Send me the last chapter so I can read it and then I want to take you for that drive."

"Actually, can you come with me for a minute? I want to show you something first."

Sawyer stands and holds his hand out to me to help me up. Before I take it, I fire off the chapters to everyone else who is out there waiting for them with baited breath. "I need to pee. Can you tell them I sent them the rest and meet me back here?"

He kisses me on the cheek. "I'll be right back."

After using the restroom, I splash my face with cold water and look in the mirror. I've aged the past few years, not in a bad way, but I'm no longer the girl who climbed on their bus that day with high hopes for breaking a curse and keeping her demons at bay.

"Ready?" he asks with an easy smile, and I grab my keys. "Where are we going?" I shake my head at him and lead the way to my old room. Noah's room.

"Impatient much? We're going right here."

"You locked the door?" he asks incredulously.

"I wanted to be sure you stayed out." When I swing the door open, Sawyer gasps behind me. He walks around the room in circles before turning back to me.

"Why?"

"Because I'm head-over-heels in love with you, Sawyer Weston, and because it was time." Boxes are stacked and labeled neatly in the corner, and all our pictures and photo albums are stacked up on the dresser.

"What are you doing with it all?" he asks hesitantly.

"Well, that was my biggest struggle of all. I know his things could benefit a lot of people and make decent money for the foundation, but I think the person who should decide what happens to them is Nate. When he's old enough, he can go through all of it and decide what to keep and what to get rid of. I packed the office, too. We just need to move all the boxes to storage with the rest of my parents' things."

"I can't believe you did this all by yourself. What about these?" he asks, gesturing to the photos on the desk.

"Yeah, that's the hardest part, so I thought we could figure it out together. No matter how much you wish you were first, I can't erase Noah from my past, and I don't want to. And I think Nate should grow up in a house where there is a representation of the love between his parents as well. I can take everything out of the frames and put them in photo albums if hanging any of them on the wall will hurt you."

I turn to him and brush my hand across his cheek. "Believe me when I say, hurting you is the last thing I ever want to do."

Sawyer's fingers trail over the photo of Noah and me on our wedding day. "Will there be photos of the two of us on said walls?"

Wrapping my arms around him, I pull him close to me. "There will be an overabundance of photos of us. I want our love to shine everywhere it possibly can. Two years in the dark is a long time, Sawyer. You've led me into the light and I'd like to stay here with you, if that's okay."

He crushes his lips to mine and I open for him immediately. I've desperately missed his touch these past few weeks. When we part, his eyes are filled with love. "Does that mean you want to stay here at the beach?"

"For now, while we renovate our new home. I was thinking we could let Darren and Cadence stay here indefinitely. His house haunts him because of Belle and this house will still be ours, we have a lot of happy memories here. Besides, I don't want to erase my memories of Noah and there are great memories here. But you're right, it's time to make our own memories, in our own home, with our own family."

"I love you, Amelia Weston."

"I love you, too, now go read that last chapter so you can take me where you wanted to."

When Sawyer and I left, everyone was sucked into the book. They barely even looked up at us as we walked out. Now, we're pulling into the drive of his house which is lined with twinkly lights as far as the eye can see.

"What is all this for?" I ask, and he grins.

"You'll see. Let's go down to the gazebo."

As we walk hand in hand along the lit-up path, Sawyer smiles the whole way there. We take a seat and listen to the frogs and crickets chirping. I have to admit, it's peaceful.

"After we left the house and I gave you the ultimatum, I felt like shit. I knew I was in the wrong for a lot of reasons and Darren and Wyatt had no issue reminding me of it every five minutes. It wasn't until we were up at the cabin and I was by myself under the stars that I was smacked in the face with a fact I failed to see before."

Sawyer's eyes are shining with sincerity as they gaze into mine. "I'm a cocky bastard, and it's probably why I assume a lot of things without giving them much thought. That first night up there, thinking was all that I did. And then I implemented my plans."

"What plans?"

"You're about to find out, and I'm glad I did it this way or you'd have never believed me otherwise, especially after you beat me to the punch by showing me Noah's room and agreeing to move in with me."

"Sawyer, you're being awfully vague."

He pulls my hand to his mouth and kisses it. "I know, but maybe this will help." Soft instrumental music begins to play; it's so subtle it sounds like it's coming from the trees themselves. Wyatt walks out holding up a big poster board.

"We're going to play a dating game of sorts to see how well I know the two of us."

"Are you serious right now?"

"As a heart attack."

I'm in shock but I'll go along with it. This is so un-Sawyer-like. "Alright, let's play."

"Good evening, I'm Wyatt and I'll be one of many hosts this evening. Our first question of the night is to Amelia. Well, they're all to Amelia, so let's get that out of the way. Mel, if someone asked you if Sawyer loves you what would you say?"

"I'd say yes."

"Ding, ding, ding," Wyatt says, flipping over the card, "Sawyer's answer was yes."

Wyatt walks off to where I can't see him, and Eli appears holding a new card.

"I'm Eli, one of your sexier hosts tonight. The next question is, if someone asked Sawyer if Amelia loves him, what would he say?"

"He'd say yes," I answer without hesitation.

"You're correct!" he says, flipping the card. "Amelia is two for two." Eli walks off and J replaces him.

759

"I'm J, your next host, and the best thing about me being here tonight is I don't have to watch your man mope anymore. Seriously, Mel, it was borderline pathetic. Good luck on your question. Before Sawyer left, he gave you a ridiculous ultimatum ... do you think he would actually leave you if you didn't comply?"

This one is harder because Sawyer was serious when he left. But Sawyer is so much like me, passionate and heated in the moment. "No, he loves me too much, and I love him too much to give up."

J flips the card and flashes his own sexy grin "The card says, 'No, and I was a dick for doing it.'"

Darren struts out this time waving the card above his head, and it makes me laugh. "Darren here, studliest host of all. Your man sure does know how to pout, Mel, but you know what else he knows how to do? Brag about his woman. You should have seen how fucking proud of you he was when he started reading your book. Jesus, woman, he wanted to come straight home and wreck our weekend of drunken debauchery. Luckily, the fates and the weather colluded against him."

"Fuck, Darren, your card," Sawyer growls at him, and Darren flips him off.

"See? He's an impatient fuck, but he's *your* impatient fuck, so I guess that's something. The question to you, my dear Amelia, is the following. Even if you two face adversity for the rest of your lives, and if Rory never gives you the time of day again, would you still remain faithfully in love with Sawyer? He was also asked this question, so I want both answers."

"My answer is absolutely, his was probably something like 'fuck yeah.'"

He flips his card over and jumps up and down. "That's my girl! She nailed both answers on the card, word for word."

Darren walks away and Eli comes up carrying two cards and gives them to Sawyer. He pats his shoulder, wishes him luck, then turns to me and kisses me on the cheek. "Love you, baby girl. Can I read your book now?"

"Of course, Eli, I'll send it to you when I get home."

As he walks down the steps, he turns around. "Hey, Mel? Am I in it?"

"You know it, Eli. You're a part of my life, right?"

"Always and forever. Later, gators, we out."

Sawyer and I laugh as the guys walk off into the darkness.

"What's all this about, Sawyer?"

"I'm getting there, Princess. Like I said, I had a bit of an epiphany that night. I realized everything I'd been saying to you was just words. All of my demands ... get rid of Noah's things, move into my house, we need to fuck, have my babies ... none of my demands were backed up by any promises."

"Sawyer, you're not being fair to yourself."

"No, Mel, I wasn't being fair to you. Why should you give into everything I wanted when I wasn't offering you anything in return? Sure, you had my love, and I hope you know it's forever, but that's just another empty promise, or it could be. I spent so much time worrying about stepping on Noah's trail I didn't realize I was missing opportunities to blaze one of my own."

"We've both made mistakes, Sawyer, and I think tonight has proved we're trying to fix them."

"That's what I want, Mel, more than anything. Close your eyes for a minute."

Honoring his request, I close my eyes and my heart begins beating rapidly. I love when he gets like this and can't wait to see what he has in store next.

"Open your eyes."

After opening them, I blink a few times, but the image in front of me isn't changing. Sawyer is on the ground, on one knee, holding a card that says "Will you marry me?" in one hand and a ring box in the other.

"Are you serious?" I ask, blinking back my tears.

"I've never been more serious about anything in my life. I've asked you for all the things I'd ask of my wife but didn't have the forethought to actually ask you to *be* my wife. I just thought it was a given, and that was my biggest fucking mistake. Marry me, Mel. Make a home with me, make a family with me, and let's build our legacy together and fuck all the damn time."

The last line makes me laugh so hard I lose the grip on my tears and they flow down my cheeks. "Yes, I will marry you, and make babies with you, and a home with you, and definitely continue building a legacy with you."

"No fucking?" he asks with a pout.

"Isn't that a given?" I ask with a smile. "But there needs to be some love making in there, too. How else will we make all those babies?"

Sawyer drops the card and holds up the next one. It says "She'll say yes."

"Were you that sure of yourself?"

"Hell no, but I hoped your love for me was just as strong as mine for you."

He stands, pulls me to him, and opens the ring box. When he hears my gasp, he grins in the sexiest way. "You've done the traditional ring, but I wanted something that represents us."

In the box are two rings—a black gold band for a man and a black and rose gold ring for me. The center is a princess cut pink sapphire flanked with diamonds, with diamonds around the band, and the wedding band is all diamonds and pink sapphires in an alternating pattern. It's breathtaking.

"Sawyer, I love it. Where did you find something like this?"

After he slides the engagement ring on my finger, he closes the box and tucks it in his pocket for safe keeping and then pulls me into his embrace.

"Remember when I said I'd been wanting to put rings on your finger for a while now?"

I nod, and he continues. "I had them custom made. I guess that was the beginning of me blazing my own path, even though I didn't realize it at the time."

"I love them and I love you. Take me home, Sawyer, kick everyone out and make love to me."

"It will be my pleasure."

When we arrive home, everyone is waiting for us in the living room. We might have taken an extra-long detour to make out a bit before we got here, but who can blame us? It's been weeks since Sawyer has touched me properly.

We walk in hand-in-hand and immediately notice all their Kindles are closed. Karen is crying and Rory is sitting cross-legged on the couch. Anna and Wyatt are whispering and laughing.

"Do you want to tell them?" I ask Sawyer, and he pulls me close.

"Before you all talk to Mel about the book and the last few days in general, we have news."

Darren, Eli, Wyatt, and J all wear the same smug looks on their faces. Even if they didn't stay to listen from the sidelines, they know my heart.

"We're getting married," Sawyer tells them excitedly.

Karen is the first to jump up and congratulate us.

"Amelia, you made it through. I'm so proud of you, sweetheart," she says, pulling me into another one of her epic squeezy hugs.

"I wouldn't have been able to without your love, Karen, thank you," I whisper into her ear, and she holds me a little tighter.

After everyone makes the rounds and fusses over my unique ring, Rory finally approaches us.

She sighs and looks at us with apologetic eyes. "I owe you both an apology, a big one. Mom and Diane tried to tell me it wasn't my place to judge you, but no one was sticking up for Noah, you know? It hurt so much to think you both forgot about him so easily. I realize none of this was even close to easy for you, either of you. Can you forgive me?"

Sawyer pulls her into a massive hug. "You're my sister, Rory, there's nothing to be forgiven for. If anything, I'm the jerk. We've never been as close as we should be, but I'd like to work on changing that. Noah would have been proud of you for sticking up for him. I know I was, even though I was pretty pissed, too."

"I'd like that." Tears stream down her cheeks as she turns her gaze to me. "What about you, Mel? I was awful to you."

"You were protecting my husband, Rory. I didn't like your words, but I understood your passion behind them and was thankful you were still looking out for Noah. I really did love him and I always will in my own way. We all will. Noah may not be here in the flesh, but he'll always be here in our hearts."

I pull Rory into a hug so she realizes all is forgiven. Family is more important than any grudges and from here on out, I hope there won't be any more anger.

"They're gone," Sawyer says as he closes the door to our bedroom behind him.

"Indeed, they are. What are we going to do with our time?"

"Actually, I have a question for you. Something you didn't explain in your book. Or maybe I missed it. What was the errand you ran after leaving the cemetery?"

With a smile, I point him toward the bed. "You caught that, did you? Go sit down and I'll show you."

Sawyer kicks off his shoes and takes a seat. I'm already in my pajama bottoms but didn't want to put on my camisole just yet. Once he sits, I climb on top of him and straddle him. Reaching into the bedside drawer, I pull out a blindfold we've been having some fun with lately.

"Put this on."

He bites his bottom lip as he slides it over his head. "We're getting kinky tonight? Does this mean I get to spank that luscious ass of yours?"

"You're getting ahead of yourself, Weston, but maybe."

After taking off my shirt and bra, I hop off and remove my pants and panties, too. He sits perfectly still and bites his lip again. I straddle him and pull his lip ring into my mouth.

"You know what it does to me when you tease me with your lip ring."

He grins. "I know."

I pull his hand between my legs so he can feel exactly how turned on I am. His hardness grows beneath me and he groans. He pulls his hand away and I hate feeling the loss.

"Keep the blindfold on, take off your clothes, and let me ride you, Sawyer."

"Do I get to fuck that dirty mouth of yours, too, Princess?"

"If you're lucky," I reply, watching as he carefully maneuvers out of his shirt without knocking the blindfold off. I scoot off of him while he lies down and tugs his pants and boxers down, but I'm impatient and pull them off the rest of the way.

"I want your back against the headboard."

"You're sexy when you're bossy," he says as he quickly complies.

I lower my mouth to his cock and he hisses as he laces his fingers into my hair and pushes me down onto his length. Once I've lubricated him with my mouth, I release him.

"You're being a tease."

"Trust me, you're going to love the reason why." I climb on top of him and slide down his length. The guttural moan that comes next is everything I was hoping for and then some.

"Condom, Mel … no fucking condom …" His words are strained, as are the muscles in his jaw. I love how fucking tense he is, how his hands are gripping my hips as if he's afraid he's going to do something he shouldn't.

"No more condoms, Sawyer. We're going to start working on some siblings for our son. Condoms would be counterproductive, don't you think?"

"Shit, Mel, it feels so good. I'm going to come."

"Take off the blindfold, Sawyer … now." I know he's probably going to come fast once he takes it off, but Sawyer recovers quickly and I've got no problem helping him rise to the occasion again.

"Holy shit, Mel!" he exclaims as I slam myself down on his cock. I want him to feel every sensation right now as he looks at me. His eyes are locked on my chest, but I'm clenching his cock hard as he's moving my hips into a rhythm that's about to set me off.

"Fuck, Sawyer!" I cry out as I come around him. He doesn't hold back, his release spills inside me and the sensation is beyond comparison. Sawyer's hands are still locked onto my hips as we both come down from the incredible high we just experienced.

"Don't you dare fucking move." His eyes have never left my chest. "Princess, that was the best thing I've ever felt in my entire life. Who knew sex without condoms would be like that?"

Leaning forward, I kiss him and he opens to me, his hands finally leaving my hips and weaving through my hair as he funnels his love into our kiss. I feel him begin to harden inside me. I knew it wouldn't take long for him to be ready to go again. When he pulls away, he pushes me back so he can look at me. His fingers move up to the tattoo over my heart, the one proudly displaying his name.

"Why did you do this? Especially when everything was so up in the air."

Covering his hand with mine, I hold it over my heart. "Come on, Sawyer, as much as I was worried you'd leave, I still knew deep down you could never do it. We're connected too deeply for you to abandon our love. As for the why … there are a few reasons."

"Such as?"

"Most importantly, you own my heart so you should have a place there. The three most important men in my life have a place on my body now."

He looks confused. "I don't get it."

"I know, baby, but I'm about to explain it to you. When I got the Weston tattoo it was for Noah, but it was also for me and our kids. It was my way of showing him I was accepting the love of his family into my life, his *whole* family, and that includes you. I loved the idea of the placement of the tattoo being where I would grow future Westons in my body. Each one of my kids will grow above that name, they pass under it as they come out of the womb, and it was also me declaring myself a Weston. Your family is my family."

"Noah never said anything," he replies thoughtfully.

"I know, it was a private discussion. There's something important you need to realize. Something I didn't realize you were doing until you said so. Look me in the eyes, Sawyer Weston, because this is important."

His green eyes meet mine and I smile. Taking his hand, I trail his fingers down to the Weston tattoo. "There isn't an inch of my body I don't want your hands or lips to touch. My body is my own and my tattoos are for me, just as yours have significance to you. I'm not going to let a piece of art on your body that may make me think of another woman keep me from enjoying every bit of you, Sawyer, and you shouldn't, either. Even if ... he's your brother."

"Yeah, but—"

"Nope, no arguing. What we do together is between us. How we enjoy each other is our business. The last time I looked you were still a Weston, and I'm about to be one twice over. Don't give power to the tattoo, it's just a thing. I belong to you, Sawyer, and my body is yours to do with whatever you please."

"Anything?" he asks with a lascivious smile.

"Any fucking thing you want. I'm done holding back, Sawyer. I'm yours for the taking."

"Well, Princess, let's get started on the next fifty years," he says as his mouth closes over mine.

Three months later, Sawyer and I have finalized the plans for our new house and the construction begins today. We're excited for this next chapter in our lives, and Darren was completely stoked when we said he could live here with Cadence. We did offer to let him come with us because our home is their home, but he wants to start his own new beginning with his daughter. I don't blame him but I'm going to miss them, especially Cadence; she's like my own child at this point. I'm not sure how she and Nate will deal with being apart but I'm pretty sure we will be one big rotating sleepover.

I got up early this morning and made Sawyer and me some coffee. I've got a surprise for him and have debated long and hard over how to give it to him. I think I nailed it, though. Karen came by last night and dropped off freshly-baked cinnamon rolls which will go perfect with our coffee.

"Morning, Princess," Sawyer says with a yawn as he enters the room in his boxers.

He's so damn good-looking. I'd be tempted to walk him right back into the bedroom if it wouldn't wreck the surprise.

"Morning, I made you coffee and heated up your mom's rolls for us. Come sit with me."

Sawyer takes his usual seat across from me and I can't help smiling when I look at him. A few days after he learned about my tattoo, he got one of his own. Same script, same place, but his says "Amelia" over the top of a Princess crown.

"Thanks, Mel. I don't know why I'm so tired this morning," he says, yawning again.

"I'm pretty sure I do. I think I have phantom cock syndrome." Sawyer busts out laughing. "What? It's got to be a real thing. You can't fuck for that long and not have phantom sensations," I say with a shrug.

"You should send that to Rhymin' Rieanne. Can you imagine the kind of song she could make out of that one?"

"I'm terrified to imagine and yet completely intrigued by the thought."

"Hey, what the fuck is up with my coffee cup?" he asks, sloshing it side to side.

"What do you mean?"

"This is my favorite cup, Mel, and someone wrote inside of it. What in the world is going on?"

I was so curious to see how he'd react to this. Part of me thought he wouldn't notice until the cup was empty, the other part thought he'd pour it out. Since he's at the sink now, it was definitely the latter.

After he pours it down the drain, he looks inside of the cup and then rapidly turns around, practically running to me with the cup in hand.

"Is this real?" he asks as he shoves the cup in my face. Written on the inside of the cup is "We're having a baby."

I take the cup from him and bring his hand to my belly. "It's real, Sawyer, you're going to be a daddy again."

He crushes his lips to mine, kissing me frantically, and then suddenly slows it down as if enjoying every second our tongues meet in harmony.

"Mommy! Is it our turn yet?" Nate calls out, and I break away from Sawyer laughing. I forgot about them. Oops.

"Yes, baby, come on out."

Darren, Nate, and Cadence come down the hall wearing the following shirts respectively: Uncle, Big Brother, Cousin. "Daddy Sawyer, Mommy says there's a baby in her belly!" Nate squeals.

Sawyer scoops him up and kisses him all over his face until Nate is laughing hysterically. "There *is* a baby in Mommy's belly. We're going to have to take really good care of her now so the baby gets here safe and sound, just like you did."

"Can my daddy see the baby, too?" he asks.

"Yeah, and my mommy? Can she see?" Cadence adds, and Sawyer scoops her up as well.

"I think your mommy and your daddy can see everything going on down here from heaven because they are the angels who watch over us.

Listening to Sawyer talk to the kids about Noah and Belle always gives me chills. Now that they're getting older he talks about them a lot more. We all agreed to be as open as possible with them about everything; so far, it seems to be a good plan. These two love their parents in heaven as much as they love the ones here on Earth.

"Alright," Darren says, kissing me on the cheek, "I'm taking these two to Wyatt's to show off our nifty new shirts and to drop off theirs."

"Theirs?" Sawyer asks.

"Yeah, I thought we should start this pregnancy off right. We're going to do a maternity photo shoot with everyone wearing a shirt with their title and relationship to the baby. We've got a huge family so it will be a nice big portrait we can put on our new photo wall in the house."

Sawyer looks at me with his jaw hanging open. "You made shirts for everyone in our entire family and extended family?"

I pull a bag from the chair and hand it to him. His is black and says "Daddy" in white letters across the front. "I did, but we need to wait until I have a belly because this one is mine." I hold up a pink shirt that says "Mommy" over the breast area and "Baby" on the belly area.

"God, I fucking love you."

"And on that note, we're out. Come on, munchkins, let's go see Jake!" The kids run off ahead of Darren and he gives us a wave as he takes off behind them.

"We're having a baby, Sawyer," I say, unable to contain my excitement any longer.

"One of many, I hope," he adds wistfully.

Unlike my first pregnancy, I have no doubts this is everything I've ever wanted. Nate has proven to me that motherhood is nothing like I was afraid of. It's filled with kisses and hugs and an abundance of love. Noah was the perfect man, and we had an amazing life, but the fears I used to carry with me never had time to be completely eradicated by Noah's love. Especially since he was taken so suddenly.

After Noah left us, Sawyer stepped in and took over. I've grown into the person I should have always been with him. The woman I wish I could have been for Noah. The woman Noah deserved to meet and to love. I know he's watching us and he's proud of me. I am who I am because he gave me the best gift of all: the ability to love and be loved in return.

"I hope so, too. I'm ready to fill that massive house with love."

"Our *home*, Amelia," he corrects.

"Our forever home, Sawyer."

Amelia
Fifteen Months Later

Dear Belle,

I thought I had written my final letter to you, and then today I realized I'm not done talking to you yet. I feel you and Noah looking down on us and blessing us with your love every day. I'll never understand why the two of you were taken away, but I think you both would be happy with how things turned out. At least, I hope so because nothing has been harder than living life without the two of you.

Today, Sawyer and I are getting married. Never in a million years would I have pictured myself saying those words, but I'm so incredibly happy. He's the most amazing man, and I can't believe I was lucky enough to be the one he fell in love with. We have two beautiful babies and a home filled with laughter and love. They say time heals all wounds, but that is a crock of BS. The place where you and Noah live in my heart will always be empty, but your children fill that void in a way that makes it hurt less.

Cadence and Nate are the best of friends and Darren is getting by. Out of all of us, he's been affected the most. He's trying to move on, but he's having a hard time finding someone as special as you were. And since I'm talking to you, I can admit I think he got the shit end of the stick. Even though I lost Noah, we still had our wedding and our 'til death do us part. It came faster than we could have ever imagined, but we still had it. I think Darren feels like he had everything he ever wanted within his grasp and let it get away. He's become a brother to me and I love him dearly. Someday, I hope he's lucky enough to find someone almost as amazing as you. I will always treat Cadence like my own, but it would be nice to have a mom who could fill in for you like Sawyer has done for Noah. I know that's what you'd want for them more than anything.

In any case, I'm rambling. I just wanted you to know that even though you're not here today, you are my honorary maid of honor. Not even Anna could fill that void, although she's become a wonderful friend in your absence. Today, more than ever, I'm missing my sister and that is why I had to write. After having Noelle, and watching the bond Cadence and Nate have with her, it started flaring up my memories of us. We had the best of times, Belle, and I cherish every memory. I promise our kids will have those kinds of memories, too.

I'd like to think you're proud of me because I'm finally living today like there's no tomorrow. I hope you'll continue watching over us and that we're making you proud. Maybe I'll write you again someday—perhaps on Nate and Cadence's wedding day.

All my love,
Mel

Sawyer and I are getting married at our new home. The wedding is at eight tonight and we'll be standing in the gazebo surrounded by friends and family. The property is draped with thousands upon thousands of twinkly lights; it's beautiful.

The construction was finished about three months ago, one day before we welcomed Noelle into the world. It was the closest girl name we could find to honor Noah and Belle. Sawyer and I wanted to honor them in our daughter. She's got my hair and Sawyer's green eyes. Nate is in love with his little sister; Cadence can't get enough of her, either.

I don't remember a lot from Nate's delivery, but I do remember the look in Sawyer's eyes when he was born. He had the very same look when Noelle was delivered—his eyes were filled with love for our daughter. Once we were left alone to bond with the baby, I'll never forget our discussion.

"Mel, I was wrong about something," he said, watching our daughter nurse for the first time. It was something I never planned with Nate, but I wanted to do it with Noelle and I loved it.

"About what?" I asked, wondering what could possibly be bothering him.

"I know I said I'd love Nate more but I'm pretty sure I love them the same. They're both amazing." His wondrous tone made me smile.

"I have a confession as well. I thought I'd love her more but I love her the same." Sawyer chuckled at our ridiculousness and bent over, kissing us both.

"We're still bottle feeding, too, right? You're going to pump as soon as you can?" That is mostly why I didn't want to breastfeed Nate. Trying to balance pumping and milk storage on the bus would have been a nightmare and I wanted Noah to be able to feed him whenever he could.

"Absolutely, I'd never take this experience away from you. Even though I didn't touch Nate, and I was in my own personal hell at the time, I loved watching you bond with him. I knew even then how much you loved him."

"You look beautiful, baby girl," Mama says as she zips up the back of my dress, pulling me from my thoughts.

"You do, Mel. Sawyer isn't going to know what hit him," Diane agrees while she feeds one-year-old Daisey. Diane is pregnant again, her bulging six-month belly supporting most of Daisey's weight. This time, they are finally getting their boy and Rob is getting a vasectomy. They both agree four is more than enough to call their family complete.

"Auntie Mel!" Saylor calls out. It's hard to believe she's almost nine now and Emme is six.

"Yes, Ladybug, what's wrong?"

"Can you tell Emme and Cadence I get to go first since I'm the oldest?"

"You know what, Saylor? I think I got it wrong. I'm looking at your beautiful face right now and I forgot how grown up you are. Instead of being a flower girl, how would you like to be one of my bridesmaids? You can walk down the aisle after Aunt Rory and right before me. I bet Uncle Warren would be thrilled to walk out with you on his arm. What do you say?"

Diane shoots me a beaming smile, and Saylor shrieks as she throws her arms around me. "Yes! Thank you, Auntie Mel, I promise I won't let you down."

"You could never let me down, Saylor, no matter what. Don't ever worry about that, okay?"

"Okay," she replies, still beaming.

"It's time, you guys," Anna says, waddling in, looking adorable as can be. She's eight months along and having another boy. Wyatt was completely bummed, he wanted a girl, but Anna is ecstatic. She said girls aren't her thing and although she will love any child in her life, she's happy to be a boy mom all the way.

"Places, everyone," Eli calls out, and they all line up at the door. "Here we are again, baby girl. How do I always end up giving my favorite girl to someone else?"

"Because you're the best friend a girl could ever have and we're much better as friends than we ever were as more."

"Right as usual, Mel. Are you ready for this?"

"I'm so ready for this. He makes me a better human, Eli."

Eli laces his arm through mine "You make him one, too. Oh, and I'm supposed to tell you there's been a last-minute change with the wedding march. There isn't one. Keep pace with me and you'll be fine."

"What do you mean?"

"Trust me, Mel, this is much better."

I try to calm my nerves as I watch my handsome three-year-old lead the way down the aisle. He's an adorable ring bearer and proudly takes his place next to Sawyer. Cadence goes next, followed by Emme, Anna, Rory, Saylor, and now ... it's my turn.

A beautiful guitar melody begins to play. Sawyer's prerecorded voice carries through the night, and I follow Eli's lead as I listen to the words.

It's our time
Take your place
I can't wait to see
Your beautiful face
White dress
Flower blooms
Pretty shoes
Walk to your groom
There's no time for fears
Only happy tears
You are so loved, my dear
There's no second-guessing
No will we or won't we
Just me loving you
With you loving me, too.
So much love
Fills this place
While our kids
Watch and wait
Our vows freely spoken
The rings are exchanged
We kiss through our tears
We take our places
As Mr. and Mrs.

What a blessed day
Always remember,
Our love is timeless
Our fears were for nothing
This time we will bloom
You're my Mrs.
I'm your groom
My true love
This song is for you

Holy hell. I'm a crying mess, along with most of the crowd. Even Sawyer is wiping away a tear. I can't believe he wrote and sang a sappy, anti-rock, wedding song for me. Eli places my hand in Sawyer's before taking his seat. Sawyer squeezes it tight before reaching up with his free hand to wipe away my tears.

"Will you sing that to me when we're alone tonight?" I whisper, still in awe.

"Anything for you, Princess."

Nate is standing next to Sawyer beaming proudly as he holds his ring bearer pillow. As the minister begins to speak, I notice there is a ring missing from the pillow. We weren't going to let Nate have the actual rings but Sawyer insisted we have some faith he could handle it.

"I'm sorry, can you give us a moment?" I say to the minister and then whisper the problem into Sawyer's ear.

His eyes flick to the pillow and back to me and he shakes his head. Then he turns to our guests. "If everyone can stay seated for a moment we're missing a ring and need to do a little backtracking to see if we can find it."

Sawyer walks back up the aisle and shrugs when he gets there and comes back down. "What do you want to do, Mel?"

Wyatt, Darren, J, and Anna have come closer to see if they can help. I turn toward the crowd and something catches my eye. The odds are impossible. Wyatt notices it when I do and we both practically race off the gazebo, stopping in front of Mama at the same time. She's holding Noelle and the diaper bag is at her feet.

My trembling hands clutch Wyatt's arm. "What are the odds, Wyatt? We're being crazy!"

He lifts the bag into his arms and starts digging through it. "No, crazy would be if we actually find the ring in this bag. *That* would be crazy."

After emptying everything into my arms and not finding the ring, we put everything back. When he turns the bag sideways, I'm reminded of Nate's favorite pocket. "Wait, Wyatt, check that side pocket. Nate is always tucking his cars and juice in there. It's his secret spot."

Wyatt puts his hand inside and pulls out Sawyer's ring. "I'll be a son of a bitch," he whispers as I clutch his arm with trembling hands. The memory washes over me, and I'm certain he's remembering, too.

"Wyatt, at Mel and Sawyer's wedding, tell them not to worry, it's in the bag."

A sob escapes me as Wyatt pulls me close and hugs me through my temporary lapse of mental faculties. We never told anyone about our talk, but Anna knew, and the way she's covering her mouth next to Sawyer, she's remembering right now, too.

"Come on, Mel, if this isn't a sign I don't know what is. Get married first and then tell Sawyer." He leads me back up the steps as I wipe away my tears.

"Are you okay?" Sawyer's concerned tone washes over me, filling me with love.

"I'm fine. In shock, but completely fine. Marry me now, I'll explain later."

"Deal."

The minister begins again and Sawyer keeps my hands in his as he speaks. We decided to make this wedding as different as could be from my last one, so we're exchanging our own vows.

"Sawyer, you may begin your vows," the minister says, and Sawyer's eyes meet mine.

"Amelia, it's taken us a long time to get where we are today. You are the only woman I've ever met who has challenged me, and you continue to do so each day. It's one of my favorite things about you. The past four years have been full of ups and downs but through it all, getting to know you and love you has been one of the greatest blessings of my life. We are blessed with two beautiful children, a wonderful home, an amazing family, and two guardian angels who watch over us and keep us safe. You've always been my Princess but today you become my Queen. I'm going to love, honor, cherish, and worship you, all the rest of my days. Will you do me the honor of becoming my wife?"

"I will," I say as he slides my rings onto my trembling finger.

"Amelia, you may now begin your vows to Sawyer," the minister says, and I keep my eyes locked on Sawyer's.

D. Kelly

"Sawyer, you fell in love with a paranoid mess." He grins at me, giving me the courage to keep going.

"You say I challenge you, but you are the one who continuously challenges me. You're constantly encouraging me to step outside my comfort zone to find the woman inside I'm meant to be. You taught me how to be a mother and how to love with reckless abandon. You gave me the strength to move on after the darkest days of my life. You covered me in a love so strong and secure I found my way out of the darkness and into the light once again. Every time I think I have you figured out, you surprise me in all the best ways. Life with you is never boring and never predictable. Even greater than your love for me is your love for our children. Your love and patience for them has no bounds. You are the best father, partner, and friend I could imagine. There's no one I'd rather be secret-keepers with than you. I promise I will love and honor you all the rest of my days. But I will also continue to challenge you to the best of my ability, be your best friend, your favorite secret-keeper, and no matter what you call me, I will forever be your Princess. Would you do me the absolute honor of becoming my husband?"

"I will," he says solemnly as I slide his ring onto his finger.

The sight of a wedding ring on Sawyer Weston's finger does something to me. He was always the beast who could never be tamed. That's what Belle used to say. It's not true at all. He's a man who wanted someone to love him in spite of his reputation, and I'm the lucky one who gets that honor.

As the minister speaks, I allow myself to get lost in Sawyer's eyes. I completely tuned out the rest of the ceremony but as Sawyer's mouth closes over mine, I don't worry about it. This is the best part anyway.

Once we receive hugs and congratulations, Sawyer pulls me into the house. Oddly enough, he parks us right in front of our photo wall. I let Sawyer choose which photos to put here and he surprised me by putting up quite a few of me and Noah. He said I was right and Nate needed to feel his parents' love. *All* of his parents. He also hung up that photo of the three of us right in the center of the wall.

"What happened out there, Mel? Before the ceremony?"

How do I even explain this to him?

"Come on, Sawyer, there's something you need to know," I say, pulling him into our living room and sitting next to him on the couch.

I fill him in on the night Wyatt came over and all that he told me. I never wanted to tell Sawyer this because I felt like this secret should be kept. I should know better, though. Secrets have a way of coming out and I can't expect him to share secrets with me if I don't with him.

"Are you telling me Noah predicted our future?"

"I don't know, babe, all I know is he was right. Maybe it was a fluke, or maybe it was fate and Noah got a flash forward before he died."

Sawyer leans back against the sofa and exhales. "Wow."

"I'm sorry I freaked out back there. I wasn't sure how to process something like that and since I hadn't told you about it, I felt even worse."

"It's okay, Mel. Technically, this was Wyatt's secret. God knows me and Darren kept a ton of them from him and Noah. I'm not angry with you, but I do feel like somehow Noah just gave us his blessing … for real."

"Me, too."

"Here you two are. I wanted to give you something and was hoping to catch you in private," Sam says as he walks in carrying a wedding present.

"Hey, Sam. Sorry, we had something to talk about but we're all set now. You want us to open your present now?" I ask.

"If you wouldn't mind."

Sawyer looks at me and motions for me to do the honors. I open the box and fold back the paper to a hardback book—my new book that's supposed to be coming out next month. *Bastards and Dangerous, The Story of Us*, by Amelia Weston.

I flip open to the first page and run my fingers over it as I read it... In my mind, this is the most important page in the book.

For Noah,
As promised, this book is for you.
Thank you for teaching me to breathe.
Thank you for showing me how to love.
Thank you for making me to believe in fate.
Thank you for leaving me with a piece of you. He reminds me daily all the ways in which loving you, and being loved by you, have blessed my life.
Most of all, thank you for saying it was okay.
We're trying to be okay together each day, because of you.

You're the angel who showed two beautifully flawed people that it's necessary to love and accept love in return.
You are our heart and soul and we miss you every day.

I can't stop the tears from streaming down my cheeks. "Maybe we shouldn't publish this. Maybe it's just supposed to be our story," I sob, and Sawyer wraps his arms around me.

"It's your call, Mel, I'll do whatever you want. How about I leave you two to talk it over?" Sam says, kissing the top of my head as I continue to cry into Sawyer.

"Is that what you want, Princess? I'm with you all the way. We've gone around and around. It's our story as much as it is yours. I thought you decided it was worth it since the proceeds are going to charity."

Everything is right with the world when I'm wrapped in Sawyer's arms. "It is. God, I'm being so ridiculous today. I feel them here with us, is that crazy?"

"No, I feel them, too, and I'm glad for it. They *should* be here, Mel. This is a happy day and they would be happy for us."

"You're right, and the book looks beautiful, doesn't it?"

"It does," he says, standing and helping me to my feet. "Come dance with me, Mrs. Weston. Let's eat cake and spend the night under the stars with our family. What do you say?"

"Lead the way, Mr. Weston. The sooner we say goodnight, the sooner you can whisk me off for our honeymoon, where we can work on baby number three."

He pulls me against him and slides my hand down to his cock. "You always know the right things to say to get me excited."

"Well, I *am* your wife, it only makes sense I know best."

"Fuck," he groans as his erection becomes even harder. "Say it again, Mel."

"I'm your wife … Mrs. Sawyer Weston."

"Come on," he says, pulling me quickly toward the door. "We need to wrap up this party so I can have my way with you again, and again, for the rest of my life."

"Who is teasing who with a good time now?"

He pulls me close and brings his lips to mine. "I am. Always and forever, Amelia."

Slammed Blog Post

Hey *Slammed* Family,

It is with a heavy heart I announce this will be my last post to this blog. I've held it hostage long enough and it's time to pass the torch to someone who will run it the way Belle intended all along. *Slammed Magazine* has an amazing blogger ready and anxious to take over this space and she'll keep you updated on all things entertainment. Trust me when I say Belle would approve.

As for me, this past year has been a crazy ride. Cadence and Nate are both four years old now and growing like weeds. Noelle recently turned a year old and she's a Daddy's girl through and through. Sawyer, Darren, and Wyatt are working on music again, both for fun and in an official capacity. Weston Brothers Records is now officially open and looking for new indie bands who need a little help getting noticed. Noah, Sawyer, Darren, and Wyatt have always been brothers in every sense of the word, and now they're in business together once again.

It's my personal hope that one day they let us all hear their voices in new music. They're all much too talented to stay away from the spotlight forever.

Since Sawyer and I got married nine months ago, a lot has changed. As you know, I released our story and it was an instant best seller. We received so many supportive messages after the release and Sawyer and I were both incredibly happy that you seem to understand our relationship a bit more now.

I'm enjoying life as a mom and an aunt immensely; that's partially why I'm giving up this blog. Talking with you all got me through some dark times, and I'm thankful you stayed around to follow Belle and Noah's legacy. I think this is the last step in healing, finally letting this blog go. A lot of you follow me on Instagram. If you want to keep seeing pictures of the kids, you can follow me or any of the guys there.

Before I go, I wanted to give you one last update. Sawyer and I are expanding our family from a family of four to a family of six. You heard me right. I'm six months pregnant and the twins are due at Thanksgiving. Talk about a blessing. My little Noelle is going to steal the official title as Daddy's girl because she'll be officially outnumbered when her twin brothers arrive.

Thank you, *Slammed* Family, from the bottom of my heart. Your comments over the past four years have helped get me through some tough times. In my last official signoff, I'm going to take this blog back to the spirit in which Belle intended all along.

Don't forget – Live today, like there's no tomorrow.

Xs and Os

Amelia

Just an Illusion Series

Please join us in the Just an Illusion – EP reader group! - https://www.facebook.com/groups/1916016678629629/

Want to know what Sawyer was thinking and feeling? Just an Illusion – Unplugged will hopefully answer all those questions for you. Click here to see where you can buy your copy - http://www.dkellyauthor.com/just-an-illusion-unplugged

Can't get enough of your Illusion Series crew? Be sure to sign up for my mailing list for your shot at exclusive content, giveaways, and more! http://www.dkellyauthor.com/mailing-list/

Keep reading for the exclusive Bastards and Dangerous interviews by Amelia Greyson.

D. Kelly

acknowledgements

For those of you who stuck with this series, especially after the first few chapters of this book, I'd like to thank you most of all. This story was personal to me in a lot of ways and difficult to write. These books are by far my personal favorites out of all my books to date.

Releasing a book takes a village. Readers, bloggers, designers, editors, photographers, formatters, PAs, friends, PR teams, and anyone I may have forgotten, all contribute to a book's release. The indie book world is an incredible village and I'm utterly blessed to be a part of it. Thank you for the pieces of yourself you give to me with every release. I appreciate you all so very much.

I can't even begin to thank everyone, but I'd love to thank my PA, Ashley Griffieth. She's been with me since before my first book ever came out and I'm thankful every day that she was brought into my life.

To my reader group, Dee's Dirty Divas, you guys are the best. Thank you for being a part of my group and chatting away with me.

To the original Diva's, D's Divine Divas, I love you ladies with all my heart.

To the *Side A* and *The B Side* reader groups, you guys have been absolutely incredible. I love hearing all your thoughts and seeing your posts. I'll be honest, I'm a bit scared to see what you say about *EP*, but I hope if there's one thing you can take away from this book it's that love still prevailed—even if, it wasn't what you wanted or expected. Of course, you already know I've been filling the *EP* group with posts and I'm ready and waiting to talk to you all about it.

To my family, thank you for supporting me and loving me through yet another release. I love you more than you know.

To my husband, I know this isn't the easiest career to support, but you love me in spite of it all. Thank you for constantly encouraging me and loving me.

For those of you who are waiting for more of *The Illusion Series*, the plan right now is for at least three more books. The first, *Just an Illusion – Unplugged*, is tentatively scheduled for January 2018. If you're dying to see Sawyer's side and inside his mind, this is your chance. It will be mostly—if not all—new material. If you've read *Catching Kate* you know I don't like to rehash material in the alternate POV if I can help it.

The other two books will be Jordan's and Darren's. For those of you who aren't in the group, a little-known fact is Jordan's book was actually supposed to release first but I decided the story was better told this way. Hopefully, you all agree.

Thank you all for reading, for your reviews, and for the many emails and messages you've sent me about this series. Based on your messages, these books made you feel. As an author, my ultimate goal is to write a story that pulls you in so deeply you feel it all.

Until next time.

All my love,

Dee

D. Kelly

Just an Illusion – Unplugged

Sawyer Weston is cocky and arrogant. With his sinful smile and sexy dimples, he's gotten his way most of his life. Infamous for his one-night stands and moves between the sheets, the lead singer for Bastards and Dangerous has never considered relationships—until he meets *her*.

With her curvy body, sarcastic mouth, and uncanny ability to put Sawyer in his place, Amelia Greyson has captured his heart. She can see into his soul and knows what he truly wants from life. Sawyer has a problem, though—she's dating his twin brother Noah.

Although he wants her with every breath he takes, Sawyer and Noah's complicated history prevents him from making a move on her. *Just an Illusion—Unplugged* tells Sawyer's story. Every thought, every feeling, are yours for the taking. Are you ready?

Just an Illusion – Encore

Coming October 2018

Sawyer Weston has done the unthinkable—he's fallen for his brother's girl. He'd never purposefully hurt Noah, but that's exactly what's going to happen if he can't get Amelia out of his system.

A stolen kiss between them finally brings Sawyer to his senses. No matter how much he wants her, Amelia has made her choice.

When tragedy strikes, Sawyer finds himself taking on more responsibility than he ever imagined. Can Sawyer remain the rock his family needs in their time of crisis? Or will he succumb to his deepest desires and fall in love with Amelia all over again?

Just an Illusion – Encore is the conclusion to Sawyer Weston's story. Every thought, every feeling, are yours for the taking. Are you ready?

For pre-order information click here - http://www.dkellyauthor.com/the-illusion-series/

Interlude – An Illusion Series Novel

Coming January 2019

Jordan Weston is good-looking, mysterious, and sexually uninhibited, but his life is more like the name of his bar—Just an Illusion. His cousins are the bad boys of Bastards and Dangerous, but their fame hasn't made everything rainbows and sunshine for him. He's haunted, flawed, and the sole survivor of a homicide that wiped out his immediate family.

Allie Baker, the most recent hire at the bar, can see through Jordan's façade. She knows he's everything she doesn't need, but she's beginning to crave his cocky attitude and the way he looks at her. The more she tries to stay away from him, the more she wants to get to know him.

Jordan knows falling for an employee is a bad idea, but Allie pushes buttons he never realized he had. Even though Allie desperately needs her job, she soon decides being with Jordan is more important. Will they be able to compromise, or will she let her chance at love pass her by for the sake of a paycheck?

For pre- order information click here –

http://www.dkellyauthor.com/the-illusion-series/

Keep reading for Bastards and Dangerous Interviews

Noah

Bastards and Dangerous Q&A by Amelia Greyson

Hey, Noah! Thank you so much for sitting with me today for this interview. I've compiled a list of questions from your fans, as well as some of my own. Are you ready to get up close and personal with me?

Noah: I'm always ready to get up close and personal with you, Mel, you know that.

Great, now that I'm blushing like crazy, I'll jump right in. This first question comes from Kim T. What's your favorite guilty pleasure?

Noah: That's easy ... indulging in you.

Come on, Noah! That's not what your fans want to hear.

Noah: Hmm ... maybe not, but it's the truth, and they asked for an in-depth personal interview. That's about as personal as it gets. I hope.

Alright, this next question comes from Lisa A. Would you ever pose for Playgirl?

Noah: <Insert panty-dropping smile> Nah ...some things need to be left to the imagination. The only one who gets to see my goods is the woman I'm intimately involved with.

That's completely understandable. Our next question was asked by just about everyone. Boxers or briefs, Noah?

Noah: Why is everyone always obsessed with our underwear? Ladies, what we carry our package around in isn't nearly as important as how we *use* our package. But to answer your question, I prefer boxer briefs.

I wonder how many of your fans are hitting up Calvin Klein on social media right now begging for a Noah Weston exclusive.

Noah: Probably more now that you planted the seed. Thanks, Mel.

Anytime, Noah, happy to help.

Noah: I'm pretty sure you secretly want to see the goods yourself. You know, if you ask nicely I might just show them to you.

Have you always been such a flirt? That question is all mine.

Noah: I'm a friendly guy, and a lot of time it gets mistaken for flirting when it's not. But with you, I'm *definitely* flirting, Mel.

And on that note, let's go to a question from Gayle C. Do you believe in fate?

Noah: More than anything else, except for love. We may never know how and why things happen, but I believe with my whole heart everything happens for a reason.

Does that have anything to do with why you do so many random acts of kindness?

Noah: Maybe? If you put good into the world, it can only result in more good things. I've been blessed with more than I need so why not share the good fortune? If it doesn't have anything to do with fate at least it's good karma, and we can all use as much of that as we can get.

What are you looking forward to most after the tour?

Noah: Seeing what's next. Ideally, it would have to be love, wife, and kids.

If you could collaborate with any artist, who would it be?

Noah: Sawyer. My brother is, without a doubt, the most talented person I've ever known.

Favorite holiday?

Noah: Thanksgiving. Being surrounded by all the people I'm thankful for every day is the best feeling there is.

Last question. If you could tell your sixteen-year-old self one thing, what would it be?

Noah: I'd tell myself that one day I was going to meet an author who was going to change my life and she was worth the wait.

Thank you for answering my questions, Noah, *and* for all the flattery ... it will get you everywhere.

Noah: Anything, anytime, anywhere, Amelia, you know that.

Sawyer

Bastards and Dangerous Q&A by Amelia Greyson

Hey, Sawyer! Thank you so much for sitting with me today for this interview. I've compiled a list of questions from your fans, as well as some of my own. Are you ready to get up close and personal with me?

Sawyer: Careful what you ask for, Princess. I've been known to bite.

Sawyer...

Sawyer: Calm down, Princess, you know I'm only joking. Ask away but know I reserve the right to plead the Fifth.

Fair enough. This question is from Karie G. What is the hardest part of being famous?

Sawyer: The loss of privacy. Some days you just want to be able to take your family out to dinner but you can't without being interrupted a thousand times. Everyone wants a hug, an autograph, a selfie. Don't get me wrong, our fans are great and they're why we're where we are today. There's not much I would change, but being able to have uninterrupted family time if I could change that? I would in a heartbeat.

Alright, this question is from Meghana S. What is the first thing that catches your eye when you spot a woman?

Sawyer: Her ass. <insert cocky smirk> What? I'm an ass man, at least if I see her from behind first. If it's up close and personal, it's usually her smile.

Her smile? Really?

Sawyer: Don't be so surprised. There's this thing about women when they smile. You can tell by the ease of it, by the lines in the corner of their mouths, by the way they throw their head back or even kind of shake their head as they laugh. Those are typically the women who know how to have a good time, who are confident in themselves, who are *nice*. I don't get a lot of downtime with women, so when I do, I want to find one who isn't a bitch looking for a celebrity fuck. Or even worse, a celebrity baby daddy.

And speaking of celebrity baby daddies, how do you prevent that?

Sawyer: Well, there's no surefire way to prevent a baby, I guess, but making it a cardinal rule to use my own condoms is a good start. Pulling out, even with a condom on, is the next best way.

How did this interview get so sexual? Let's take it back a few notches, shall we? This next question is from Dana S. What is your worst habit?

Sawyer: Speaking before thinking. I'm forever doing things I regret because I act first and think later.

Cindy L would like to know … Batman or Superman?

Sawyer: Batman. Always Batman.

What is the best thing about being a twin? What is the worst? This question is all mine.

Sawyer: The worst is being attracted to the same women. It can make for some awkward situations. The best is everything else. Noah is my best friend, he's my favorite person, he knows me better than anyone and loves me anyway.

Favorite holiday?

Sawyer: Christmas. There's nothing better.

Is it better to give or receive?

Sawyer: Are we still talking about Christmas? Because, sexually, both are pretty fucking nice.

Yes, Sawyer, <insert exasperated sigh> we're still talking about Christmas.

Sawyer: Well, then … not to seem too much like Noah, but giving is definitely better. The looks on my nieces' faces are priceless.

This question is from Jacqui N. She's an avid reader. Team Michael or Team Daniel from *The Acceptance Series*?

Sawyer: Considering I don't read shit for romance, except for you, Princess …

Wait, you've read my book?

Sawyer: I'd read the fucking phone book if you wrote it. But like I was saying, I don't know jack shit about romance teams. Even so, I'm going to go with Team Michael because my sister dated a Daniel once and the guy was a total asshat.

Alright, there you have it, Jacqui N. Sawyer is Team Michael for the win. Last question. If you could give your sixteen-year-old self any advice or words of wisdom, what would it be?

Sawyer: There was a girl who got between myself and my brother, and the whole experience is my biggest regret. I'd tell myself to never let that happen.

Thank you for spending some time with me today and letting me interview you. I know you don't open yourself up for these things often.

Sawyer: I'm not sure what it is about you, Princess, but I don't have the heart to tell you no when you ask for something. I'm pretty sure you cast a spell on me while I was sleeping or some shit, but in any case, you're welcome.

Darren

Hey, Darren! Thank you so much for sitting with me today for this interview. I've compiled a list of questions from your fans as well as some of my own. Are you ready to get up close and personal with me?

Darren: Sure, Mel. Just don't go trying to bang my bongo or anything, that's reserved for the other half of your troublesome twosome.

I wouldn't dream of it! Let's jump right into a question from Ashley J. What are your top-five favorite albums of all time?

Darren: That's an impossibly hard question and so fucking awesome. I'll give you the first five I remember having a big influence on me. *Purple Rain* by Prince, *Thriller* by Michael Jackson, Metallica's *Black Album*, *Hotel California* by The Eagles, and *Night Train* by Joey and Iris Triton. Just to be clear, that last one isn't because they were your parents but because it's a fucking kickass album.

Thanks, Darren. I'm sure my parents would appreciate the shoutout. This question is from Misti S. What is the first thing you want to do when the tour is over?

Darren: I'm going to Disneyland! <insert laughter> Damn, I've always wanted to say that. For real, I'm going to spend some time with my parents. They're getting older, and family is important, you know?

Yeah, I sure do. I think that's sweet. This question has been asked by quite a few fans. Boxers, Briefs, Commando?

Darren: Commando, baby.

That was so much more than I needed to know.

Darren: Well, hey ... you asked. When you're touring, every second is important, so underwear of any kind wastes valuable seconds. I want to be able to unzip, cover up, and ... well, you know the rest.

Yup, sure do. Let the banging of the bongos commence.

Darren: Exactly! You know what's up, Mel. Even if Boy Band was the one to teach you the ropes.

And on that note, next question! This one is from Gayle C. Do you have a fantasy destination you'd like to go to?

Darren: We've traveled so much on tour but we honestly don't get much time to enjoy where we go. I'd love to grab my girl and show her the Seven Wonders of the World. I think that would be an amazing thing to experience together.

I love that answer! I'm sure your girl would love that, too. <wink wink> Okay, let's switch it up a bit. Tell me about the friendships between you and your band members. Are there any love/hate relationships going on? Or are you all actually good friends?

Darren: We're all best friends … brother's, really. Noah and Wyatt are the two serious ones, so they spend a lot of time together. Sawyer and I are more of the party guys, so we're always together. It's hard to explain. We're all best friends, but we usually pair off. Noah and Sawyer's relationship sort of supersedes all of that, though. Their twin connection is just … I can't even put it into words, but I've always been envious. I'd love to have that kind of unique bond with someone else.

Me, too. Here's an interesting question from Dana S. Do you have a favorite song you like to perform at karaoke?

Darren: Yes! The absolute best karaoke song is "Sweet Caroline" by Neil Diamond. Everyone knows it and ends up singing along.

Favorite Holiday?

Darren: Halloween, hands down. The combination of candy and scary shit is a guaranteed recipe for getting laid.

How do you guys always turn everything to sex?

Darren: You're the author of *The O Factor* and you're asking me that? You're lucky we don't talk to you about sex 24/7 because seriously, Mel, I have questions about your book and your inspiration for said book.

Moving on. This one from Kim T. should be safe enough. Do you have any pets?

Darren: Nah, pets and bands don't mix. We're far too busy to take care of an animal the way it deserves. Maybe once we're done touring I might get a dog. I've always loved English Bulldogs and regularly donate to a few different rescues.

That's so true but super sweet you give donations. Our next question is from Cindy L. If given the choice, would you pick cake or ice cream?

Darren: Both. I'm not a take it or leave it kind of guy … I want it all.

You remind me so much of this reporter I know. She likes to bang bongos in her spare time.

Darren: You'll have to introduce me someday. <laughs>

Alright, last question. If you could give any advice to your sixteen-year-old self what would it be?

Darren: Don't sweat the small stuff. Just live in the moment because things always have a way of working themselves out.

For some reason that's exactly the answer I expected from you.

Darren: At least I didn't disappoint.

I don't think you ever could. It's always a pleasure to spend time with you, Darren. Thank you for hanging out with me today and answering my questions.

Darren: Happy to do it, Mel, and I can't wait to read it.

Wyatt

Hey, Wyatt! Thank you so much for sitting with me today for this interview. I've compiled a list of questions from your fans as well as some of my own. Are you ready to get up close and personal with me?

Wyatt: I'm always ready to hang out with you, Mel.

I'm pretty sure that's the first non-sexual answer I've received.

Wyatt: That isn't surprising, but none of the other guys have a wife, either.

True. Let's talk about Anna. Tell me about how you two met and how long you've been together.

Wyatt: Anna and I met in junior high. She was actually friends with Sawyer first. The two of us just connected. We talked all the time, hung out whenever we could, ended up dating, and never stopped. We got married earlier this year, and I've never been happier. She's the love of my life.

Your story is so sweet and so is Anna. The two of you really do make the perfect couple. How about we move into some fan questions now? Are you up for that?

Wyatt: Ask away.

Ashley G. is up first. Who do you admire the most and why?

Wyatt: Noah … without a doubt. He's my best friend and the most selfless guy I've ever known. I've literally watched him take off his shirt in the middle of winter and give it to someone who didn't have one, along with his jacket and a wad of cash. That's the thing about Noah, there's nothing he wouldn't do for anyone even if he's never met you. He's got this unflappable belief in fate I wish I could share.

How does Anna handle your time on the road? Does she get jealous of all the women around you guys?

Wyatt: Anna and I have strict rules about communication. We tell each other everything. If we didn't, this wouldn't work. I know it's hard to believe a man can have women constantly throwing themselves at him and not cheat. Truthfully, like anything else, that gets old fast. I don't want a woman who would so casually look at my wedding band then look the other way to have one night with a rock star. Fame is fleeting, but love is forever, and Anna is my rock. I'm sure there are times when she may seem jealous, but that's when we make sure one of us visits. It's not so much actual jealousy as it is the distance eating at us.

That makes a lot of sense. You two have something special, and it's nice to hear how much you cherish it and how hard you work at keeping it.

How about we lighten things up? Kim T. has a question for you. What is your favorite guilty pleasure?

Wyatt: Eating Darren's Fruit Loops in the morning. It makes him so mad because it's his favorite cereal. I usually wake up first, so fucking with him is easy. I'm not a total asshole, though. I always have an extra box on hand so he can get his fill. He freaks out just as much as Sawyer does when Noah takes his brown sugar Pop-Tarts.

You're so bad, but that's funny.

Wyatt: Right? They're so sensitive about their food. They should realize if it's on the bus it's a free-for-all.

Yeah, I'm pretty sure they don't agree with that at all, but I see your point. You're family and what's yours is mine and vice versa.

Wyatt: Exactly!

Dana S. is up next. Do you follow any pre-show rituals?

Wyatt: I do. I call Anna and tell her I love her because her love keeps me centered. I also hug each of my brothers before we hit the stage. Those two things keep me grounded and keep reality in the forefront. It's easy to lose yourself in the fame with fifty thousand fans clamoring for your attention. I don't ever want to get lost in that fantasy world and forget who I am and where I came from.

While we're talking about the guys and staying grounded, Meghana S. has a question for you. Is there ever any jealousy between the four of you and if so, in what regards?

Wyatt: Nah … I mean, nothing big. The only thing I can even remember is being bummed I can't bunk with Noah. Sawyer and

Darren would be much better bus mates, but there are reasons why things are this way. The main one being Darren and Sawyer on the same bus would be trouble with a capital T. And the second being Noah and Sawyer need their brother time. Those two are connected on a whole other level and don't do well when they're apart for extended periods of time.

So no fights over who has more photoshoots? Or who has the most fan mail or things like that?

Wyatt: <insert laughter> Not in years. Maybe in the beginning when it was all new we might have had little tiffs over superficial stuff like that. That kind of stuff gets old fast. I know we have like this ridiculous reputation of being rough and tough but we're pretty laidback about everything.

Well, what you're saying isn't anything different than what I've seen so far. It's nice to know what you see is what you get with you guys.

I want to ask you something I've been wondering for a while now. With seventeen American Music Awards and twelve Grammy awards, Bastards and Dangerous has obviously been well-received within the music community, but you are notorious for not attending the ceremonies and have even turned down appearance offers. The only year you did both shows was with your breakout album *Lost*. Can you tell me why?

Wyatt: We appreciate the awards and nominations, they mean a lot to us. We have done some performances and acceptance speeches via satellite so we could be there in some manner. The first year it was insane and so flattering. We were in high demand and didn't have much downtime at all that year. We were able to take the people important to us to the shows that year, but after that tour was over we sat down as a group and made some tough decisions. You're not a stranger to this world, Mel. It's crazy at times. As much fun and honor came from the award shows, it wasn't worth the stress of squeezing them into our schedules and making them priorities. We had to decide what events to schedule our tours around, our lives around, and oftentimes it came down to a scenario like ... if you go to the AMAs you won't be able to be home for Anna's birthday, or the birth of your niece, or your parents' twenty-fifth anniversary party. We have moments in the spotlight every day. Life is made of moments, family moments we'll never get back, so we do what we can to be there. Unfortunately, that's meant missing ceremonies. That being said, we're all looking forward to going next year because we won't be touring and we won't have to make the choice anymore.

Thank you for explaining that. I know it's hard for the fans to wrap their heads around why their favorite band wouldn't go to such a prestigious event. Now, maybe they'll understand a bit more as to why.

What's your favorite holiday, Wyatt?

Wyatt: Christmas. I love the smell of fresh-cut trees, and our families get together, so it's one huge celebration of family and love.

If you had to pick one, would you pick red licorice or black?

Wyatt: Red Vines Super Ropes ... those are the shit! I used to get them at the baseball field. Red all the way. But not Twizzlers, that shit sucks.

Do you believe unicorns exist?

Wyatt: Sure, just because I haven't seen one doesn't mean they aren't out there. I haven't seen a lot of shit I know is real so why not believe in unicorns, too?

Does the same go for aliens?

Wyatt: You're fucking with me now, but it's okay. Yeah, same for aliens.

Yeah, I was messing with you, but we have to have some fun, right? Your interview was a little more serious than the others.

Wyatt: That happens. I'm a pretty serious guy most of the time. I think it's why Noah and I are such good friends.

Okay, last question. If you could go back and tell your sixteen-year-old self anything, what would it be?

Wyatt: Damn, that's hard. My mom has always been a single mom. She was the best, but I know it was hard for her. When I got to high school, I really worried about her. She worked two jobs a lot of the time just so I wouldn't miss out on anything. She wouldn't let me work to pitch in because she wanted me to be a kid and enjoy my childhood. As soon as I got my first check, I paid off our house and gave her some money. Aside from Anna, my mom is my world. I'd tell myself not to stress about her so much because things were going to work out for her real soon.

Thanks for sitting with me and answering these questions, Wyatt. I've really enjoyed getting to know all of you in our weekly meetings and can't wait to continue them. You're all amazing men, and I'm honored to be able to call you my friends.

Belle

Hey, Belle! Thanks for sitting with me today for a few quick questions. I think it's important to learn a bit more about our favorite entertainment blogger who is keeping everyone updated on BAD this year.

Belle: Hey, Mel! You know I'm always happy to sit with you and shoot the shit no matter what it's about.

Cool, my first question for you is a simple one. When did you first discover Bastards and Dangerous?

Belle: It was the summer before I started college. I'd gone to a club in Hollywood where they were playing. I was hooked right away. That was the summer they got signed, and I've followed their career ever since.

I'm pretty sure not many people know this next bit of information. The night at The Greek, where BAD announced *Slammed* had an exclusive about them in their upcoming issue, that was a surprise to you. How did you feel in that moment?

Belle: Oh my God, I was so freaking excited! I was always a huge BAD fan, and to end up with a job where I could follow their career and write about them was a dream come true. Then to be asked to write exclusively for them for a year, by the band themselves? I could die tomorrow and my bucket list would be complete. It was the most amazing thing ever. I'm still in shock.

Before taking this job you were one of the most influential entertainment bloggers/reporters around. Your Instagram followers were pretty steady at about three million last year. Could you tell us your current Instagram follower count and how it makes you feel?

Belle: The numbers are insane. Almost overnight, I went from three million to about fifty million. BAD has eighty million, so I'm pretty sure those numbers will continue to grow. It's awesome but also a bit daunting. People should just know that while I'm definitely posting more things about BAD, I'm still posting other bands, and my daily coffee, my shoes if they're cute, my nails when they're looking badass. I'm still me, just with a cooler job aspect.

It was recently announced you're going to spend the last three months of The Illusion Tour on the buses with the guys and me. What are you looking to accomplish in those three months?

Belle: Being up close and personal with BAD is going to bring a whole new level of depth to my articles. Flying in once a month and attending shows and doing some quick interviews is great, but fully immersing myself in the experience is every reporter's dream.

Are any of the members of Bastards and Dangerous on your celebrity cheat list?

Belle: Uh, yeah! Darren Miller has been on my celebrity cheat list since I saw him play in that club. I couldn't get him out of my mind. I kicked myself for a good year for not introducing myself to him back then. After having met him and getting to know him better, I see why I was so enamored with him. Thankfully, I'm not dating anyone, so I don't need a cheat list.

Are you trying to tell us something, Belle?

Belle: <insert laugh> No, but a girl can dream, can't she?

Hell yeah she can! What has been your favorite part of covering BAD exclusively so far?

Belle: When I come to the concerts and get to see how moved the fans are by the experience. Not just the fans in the audience, either. Smaller venues means less tickets, but the parking lots are always filled to the brim with tailgaters. Those people in the lots are so happy to even be in proximity of the band. It's a heady experience for sure. One people will talk about for decades.

If you could see Bastards and Dangerous collaborate with someone on this tour, who would it be?

Belle: Wow, that's hard! There are so many people I'd love to see them do something with but because of the acoustical nature of this tour I'd say Ed Sheeran would be a great mix with what they have going on right now.

So what is up next for you? Do you have any idea where your career will go after this tour?

Belle: You know me, I live by the seat of my pants. I'm sure whatever comes next will be a great experience. Life is such a mystery. I'm just along for the ride.

What's your favorite pastime?

Belle: I'm in the beginning stages of dating someone new. You know how that is ... kind of scary and awkward but also really fun. I guess you could say he's my favorite pastime at the moment.

Is it serious with this guy?

Belle: I don't really do serious. I'm all about having a good time. Of course, I'd never rule out serious someday with the right person.

Could this mystery man be Mr. Right?

Belle: You're not going to let this go, are you? I'll never say never, but what I will say is he's Mr. Right Now.

Okay ...We've been friends for twenty years, I know when to back off. Tell us your favorite must-have while writing.

Belle: A latte or wine and either fresh fruit or chocolate. The time of day determines which order I have them.

What do you prefer a man wear ... boxers or briefs?

Belle: Who has time for underwear? Commando all the way, baby.

And on that note, I think our time is up. Thank you so much for sitting and chatting with me, Belle.

Belle: Like I'd rather be doing anything else. *Someone* else ... maybe. But anything else, not on your life.

Amelia

Amelia Greyson! It's about time I get my hands on you for some interview questions. Our *Slammed* readers have questions they're dying to know the answers to.

Mel: I'll do my best to answer them, but some things fall under my NDA so I might not be able to answer them all.

Excuses, excuses. It's all good, girl, we'll make it work. My first question is what everyone is wondering. Are you involved with any of the band members?

Mel: No. I've only been on the buses for a few weeks, so we're just getting to know each other right now.

Alright, tell us what it's like to share a bus with Noah and Sawyer Weston. I mean, girl …you're in the middle of a double yum sandwich.

Mel: <insert laugh> Belle, sometimes you are too much! I love being on the buses and being able to take in the countryside as we drive along. Hmm, what can I tell you about the guys? Noah is a sound sleeper. He works late nights and sleeps in as late as possible. Sawyer is an early bird. It doesn't seem to matter how late he's up, he's still awake bright and early taking in the sunrise over a cup of coffee.

How about the girls? Is it out-of-control crazy with women traipsing on and off the buses?

Mel: I'm pretty sure this is something that would be prohibited by my NDA, but the truth is, these guys aren't like that. Wyatt is married and I've never seen him look twice at anyone who isn't his wife. The rest of them do their job and get on the bus for the next stop. There's no juicy gossip here, they're just normal people doing a job.

Are they messy? Who is the cleanest?

Mel: Sawyer is a neat freak, which is nice since I'm on his bus. Noah isn't messy but he's not perfectly clean, either. I've got no idea about the other guys since I'm not on their bus. Warren has mentioned Darren and Wyatt drive him crazy with their mess, though, but you'll have to take that secondhand.

What can you tell us about each of the guys that might surprise people?

Mel: There's not a whole lot I can say, but I'm going to group them together as a whole for this question. They all have a reputation for being out-of-control jerks. I don't think anything could be further from the truth. From what I've experienced, they're four nice guys with a deep love for family.

I'm going to give you four categories and I want you to assign one member of BAD to each. Best Overall Personality, Funniest, Most Surprising, and Most Intriguing.

Mel: Funniest is definitely Darren … he makes me laugh often. Best Overall Personality is Wyatt. He's just so easygoing with everything and I've never seen him down. Most Surprising … definitely Noah. That leaves Most Intriguing and it's a perfect title for Sawyer.

Tell us about the book you've been hired to write. What makes this book different than most other band stories?

Mel: BAD hired me to write their story, but they don't want a fluff piece. This book is going to be an insight into their lives, their families, and fans. The perks of fame and the pitfalls as well. I think the best part of it is they will proofread every word, so not only do you know it's truly their story but it's got their stamp of approval as well.

Most people may not realize you're not a BAD fan. In fact, it caused quite a commotion when they found out you weren't a fan of their music. Now that you're immersed in it every day, have you changed your mind?

Mel: Way to put me on the spot, Belle. I'm not a fan of hard rock in general. But I'm fortunate enough to get to sit in on practice each day, and I have to admit I love their acoustic album. My favorite part of the day is getting to listen to them sing on the bus. It's different than watching them on stage. They're more relaxed and have fun with it. I take great joy in being able to witness them in that element.

D. Kelly

One question I keep getting asked is if you've seen them naked. Have you had any accidental bathroom encounters? Middle of the night snack attacks?

Mel: Nope. Sorry to disappoint, but there have been zero naked encounters. They're very respectful of my space and I am of theirs. We're in close quarters so I have seen them in boxers and an occasional towel as they leave the bathroom, but nothing to get excited about.

Oh, Mel, if that doesn't excite you there's something wrong with you. Most people would cream their panties at the sight of Noah or Sawyer in boxers or a towel.

Do you find yourself inspired enough to start other books? Your first book, *The O Factor*, is a nationwide bestseller. Do you think BAD will give you the inspiration you need for your next book?

Mel: Well, their book *is* my next book. As for future projects, I'm not even on that wavelength. I can only write one book at a time and right now my head is in conceptualizing this book. I can't say they won't inspire me at some point because, as an artist, you never know when inspiration will come but so far it hasn't happened. Sorry, ladies, no BAD themed romances in my foreseeable future.

Last question. Do you see yourself staying in touch with the members of BAD after the tour is over? Or is this strictly a work assignment for you?

Mel: We've all become pretty close in a short amount of time. We have so much more in common than I think any of us could have imagined. I'm pretty sure we're forging lifelong friendships here and I'm really excited about that. I feel very blessed to be in the presence of these amazing men every day. I can't wait to see where this journey takes us.

Well, there you have it, Slammers! My girl Mel gave us all the answers she could, and I'm sure we'll get even more over the next few months. Thanks for talking to me, Mel!

Until next time – Live today, like there's no tomorrow!

Xs and Os

Belle

dear readers...

The most important thing you can do for the authors you love is leave a review and tell your friends how much you enjoyed their book. If you wouldn't mind taking a few moments to rate and review this book, I would greatly appreciate it.

Sincerely,

Dee Kelly

D. Kelly

D. Kelly, author of The Acceptance Series, The Illusion Series, and standalone companion novels Chasing Cassidy and Sharing Rylee, was born and raised in Southern California. She's a wife, mom, dog lover, taxi, problem fixer, and extreme multi-tasker. She married her high school sweetheart and is her kids' biggest fan.

Kelly has been writing since she was young and took joy in spinning stories to her childhood friends. Margaritas and sarcasm make her smile, she loves the beach but hates the sand, and she believes Starbucks makes any day better.

A contemporary romance writer, D. Kelly's stories revolve around friendship and the bond it creates, strengthening the love of the people who share it. For all things D. Kelly, you can visit her website:
http://www.dkellyauthor.com

The Acceptance Series –
Breaking Kate – Book One
Catching Kate – Book 1.5
Releasing Kate- Book Two
Loving Kate – Book Three
Christmas with the Houstons – Book Four

Stand Alone Novels
Chasing Cassidy
Sharing Rylee
The Evolution of Us
The Last Resort Motel – Room 13

The Illusion Series
Just an Illusion – Side A
Just an Illusion – The B Side
Just an Illusion – EP
Just an Illusion – Unplugged
Just an Illusion – Encore (coming October 24th 2018)
Interlude – Jordan's Book (coming January 29th 2019)
(Untitled) Darren's Book (coming April 2019)
(Untitled) Eli's Book (coming July 2019)
http://www.dkellyauthor.com/all-books